I0819833

Christine Morgan's

ElfLore Trilogy

Published by:

Sabledrake Enterprises
PO Box 30751
Seattle, WA 98113
http://www.sabledrake.com
sabledrake@sabledrake.com

1st Printing – Summer, 2006

ISBN 0-9771005-1-0

Originally published by Rennaissance Alliance Publishing (now Regal Crest Press) as three seperate books:

Silversilk, published in August of 2001. 1-930928-66-1
Knight of the Basilisk, published in August of 2002. 1-930928-47-5
Truegold, published in March of 2003. 1-930928-92-0

Dedication

To the gamers . . . to all the gamers.
But mostly to the ones who've gamed with me.

Contents

INTRODUCTION

I suppose that under the circumstances, some word of explanation is in order as to why there's an all-new edition of ***ElfLore*** in print. If you're interested in nutsy-boltsy stuff and general ramblings, please read on. Otherwise, skip ahead a couple pages to where the action begins.

The book that you're holding is not an all-new novel. It is not even three all-new novels. It is three old novels that have been edited, polished, revamped, spiffed, tidied, tightened, tweaked, and collected here together for the first time as a new and improved hardcover omnibus.

Why? Well . . . to make a long story short . . . or to try, anyway . . .

Once upon a time, the three ***ElfLore*** books – *Silversilk*, *Knight of the Basilisk*, and *Truegold* – were published in trade paperback format by Renaissance Alliance Publishing, as part of their fantasy line. But for various reasons, RAP decided to mostly discontinue that line. My books were among those that got the axe. The rights were released back to me.

Now what? I wondered. I doubted that my chances of getting them picked up by some other fantasy publisher would be all that good. I was writing more horror than fantasy by then anyway. And we still had copies left to sell at conventions or over the internet or at local bookstores to the folks who wanted them.

Well, then, wouldn't you know, we went and ran out of copies. Couldn't get more, because the books had officially gone out of print. But there were still folks who wanted them! Something had to be done!

The decision to reissue the books as self-published under the Sabledrake Enterprises banner was an easy one. We've been doing Sabledrake Enterprises books for a while now (the ***Trinity Bay*** horror novels, the ***Silver Doorway*** children's books, and the RPG supplement *Naughty and Dice*, just to pop in a brief plug), and have been incredibly happy with the products and the experiences.

But I thought that, rather than do three separate books for three separate price tags, might it not be easier and more cost-effective to put the entire trilogy together into one volume? And while we were at it, how about hardcover? Just for chuckles. We could see about getting Christi to do the cover art, since somehow she is able to pluck my mental images of my characters directly from my head in a half-scary but altogether awesome kind of telepathy.

If we were going to do all that, though . . . well . . . I figured I should really go through the manuscripts and fix them up a little. The first of them, *Silversilk*, was written over eight years ago. Since then, I've written several more novels, reams more short stories, worked with some phenomenal editors and picked up tips and wisdom from many savvy and generous writer-types.

Storytelling may be an art, but actual writing is a craft. Like any craft, your skills can improve as you go along, as you grow and learn. I am a much better writer now than I was back then, and it shows. Boy, did it show. When I went back and took a good hard look at ***ElfLore,*** I was almost embarrassed.

No, I *was* embarrassed. In some places, I was damn near aghast. It was the literary equivalent of looking at old photo albums and seeing pictures of yourself wearing some fashion or hairstyle you sure thought was cool at the time, but you can later only look back on and laugh. Cringe, maybe . . . and blush . . . but laugh.

Needless to say, I couldn't live with myself if I reissued the ***ElfLore*** books without fixing up all those blunders. Some were continuity errors that I still cannot believe weren't caught the first time. Some were ordinary sins of the I-know-better-now variety, like a prevalence of adverbs and the painful overuse of other words than "said" in dialogue attribution (I found an "averred" in there, ouch).

And some of it that got cut was stuff that was fine in terms of writing, but unnecessary. Info dumps. Excessive description. I was supposed to be telling a story here, not doing an encyclopedia entry on the Emerin or a travelogue of the *Morvalan* lands. Good information, useful information . . . yes . . . to *me* as creator of that world. But not anything that the reader needed to know in so much detail. If people someday turn out to really want all that, hey, I would happily do an RPG sourcebook.

Anyway, as a result of this ruthless edit, the books as they ended up here changed quite a bit from the way they appeared in the trade paperback editions. *Silversilk* and *Knight of the Basilisk* most of all; I was more comfortable and experienced by the time I got around to *Truegold*, and so it escaped with the least intensive surgery and makeover.

Are they still the same basic stories? Yes. The main events are essentially the same, the characters are essentially the same. I don't think that anything too major was changed. But there were some smaller changes that had far-reaching effects.

How are they different? Dialogue, mostly. Characterization. More of a focus on people and interactions, less on world-building and history. More story, that's what it boils down to. The manuscripts came out shorter, but there's more story and less stuffing.

What about all the loose ends and unresolved issues? Ah . . . well . . . that is my blessing and my curse, right there in a nutshell. As someone who came to writing by way of gaming, I trained myself into the habit of automatically weaving plot hooks and leads and subplots into my stories, so that I would always have another adventure waiting in the wings. I can't seem to break that habit.

Not that I've really tried all that hard. It's nice, never being out of ideas. Maddening, sometimes, because there are still only so many hours in the day, but nice.

So, yeah, there are some loose ends and unresolved issues in the ***ElfLore*** books. I hope to someday go back and do something with them. This world, and the people who inhabit it, are very real and special to me. Heck, between writing in it and gaming in it, I've spent almost as much time there over the past (gulp) fifteen years as I have in the mundane world. I have titles and ideas in mind for many more trilogies – so sue me, I like trilogies in fantasy – and there's a lot of territory left to explore. A lot of those loose ends.

In the meantime, for those of you visiting this world of mine for the first time, welcome! This is really the *second* trilogy; the events in the ***MageLore*** books – *Curse of the Shadow Beasts*, *Dark of the Elvenwood* and *Archmage of the Universe* – take place some twenty years before. You don't need to have read the others to enjoy ***ElfLore,*** but if you come away from this experience wanting to know more, that's a good place to go next.

And, of course, there's the ***Silver Doorway*** books. I blame J.K. Rowling for those. Kids would drag Mom or Dad up to me at a signing or a con, pointing excitedly at the covers – which, being all elves and magic and monsters, pretty much screamed Fantasy-with-a-capital-F – and Mom or Dad would ask if my books were okay for kids like the Harry Potter books were. I had to say, "um . . . well . . ." and do the nervous cringing eyeroll thing that means: "they're kinda violent and there's some sex." Then Mom or Dad would say no, and the kids would leave all crestfallen, and finally it happened once too many times. I decided that I wanted to be able to at least say, "Not exactly, but how about *these?* Perfect for ages 7-12!"

Hence, the ***Silver Doorway*** books were born. They involve a trio of ordinary American kids, twins Katie and Kevin and their pesky little brother Sam, who discover that their aunt is a sorceress with a magical silver doorway in her basement. That doorway leads – you guessed it! – into the same fantasy world as the ***MageLore*** and ***ElfLore*** stories!

I've rambled a bit, as I tend to do. But I figure that since I wound up cutting at least 20,000 words out of the manuscripts before getting to this point, I could spare a few pages to let you know how this all came to be.

Writing itself may be solitary, but not all of it takes place in a vacuum. A lot of people have contributed in a lot of ways to this world, and to my lifelong loves of fiction and gaming. I'd probably forget someone and then kick myself for it later, so I won't try to list them all.

But to anyone who's ever gamed with me, beta-read for me, edited me, sent feedback, drawn art for me, accepted my stories, bought my books, inspired me, encouraged me, and just generally put up with me even when I was at my worst . . . none of this could have happened without you. Thanks, and I love you all.

Christine Morgan
Seattle, WA
May 31, 2006

The ElfLore Trilogy
Book I

Silversilk

PROLOGUE

The cool breeze rippling over Lake Jeline stirred his hair and blew gentle lover's breath in the curves of his ears. His keen gaze darted over the islands that dotted the blue expanse, then touched briefly on a distant cliff-town nestled on the far side.

He turned his back to the lake, and his attention to the stone rearing from the grassy earth. It rose chest-high on him. Its surface was flat, slanted, smoothed by dwarven masons. His fingers traced inlaid letters of truesilver that had been wrought by the magic of the elven people.

Three angled walls half-enclosed this boulder, known as Treaty Rock. He frowned as he studied the barrier. Any who stood before the stone, as he himself did now, would have the lake at his back and the walls blocking any view to the north.

The Duchy of Keyda. The wasted lands. Ruined and ravaged Keyda. No longer were her fields covered with green clover and flocks of sheep. Where villages and farms had once been, the husks of abandoned war machines now stood as silent monuments.

It seemed to him that the walls should have faced the other way. They should have opened toward the old battlefields instead of shutting them from sight.

But such was not the attitude held by his people. Honor the dead, yes, inscribe their names on these walls in truesilver and dwarf-wrought gold. The other events? Afford them as little further notice as possible. Forget the war, put it behind, mention it not. Best to move on, and not dwell on the violence and tragedy of the past.

"But the people should be *made* to remember," he said. "They should see the cost of their pride and foolishness. The wisest of the Elder Races . . . brought to war by a minotaur mage's cunning."

That, he knew, was truly why all concerned wished to pretend as if the war had never been. To have the author of their shame have been a minotaur, a race regarded as nothing more than beasts, a race *created* by, and once enslaved to, the elves – that was the worst of it all.

Such was Solarrin's legacy. Twenty years of war, thousands of lives lost, an entire duchy stripped barren, *aether*-drained and devastated.

And the Emerin . . . left without a king.

His mood grew even more somber as he instinctively shifted his gaze to the deeper green mass on the eastern horizon. The Emerin, his home.

To have lost their king was terrible but not wholly unexpected. Shaelan Perras had been well into his twelfth century when he insisted on leading his troops into battle. His people could feel nothing but pride that he had fallen defending the Emerin.

But . . . to have lost the king's only heir as well . . .

His frown deepened with the memories.

Too young, Prince Wyndrel had been far too young for war. Not even legally of the age of majority. Never mind that his bravery and skill had earned the respect of the generals and knights. The prince's youth had made him impetuous, stubborn, unwilling to listen to the guidance of his betters. That lattermost trait had, in the end, proved Wyndrel's undoing.

The Emerin was a land without a king. In the five years since the signing of the Treaty of Jeline, the Starleaf Council had come no closer to selecting a new ruler from among their ranks. The decision was long overdue. A choice had to be made.

And so, with grim purpose in his heart, he set his course toward the Emerin.

* * *

Part One:

Daughter of Dragon and Unicorn

Chapter One

Let not my heirs contest my passing.
– Elwyndas, The Feast of Winter's Eve, Act II

"The duke is dying," the Archmage of Gamelin said, his tone and gaze steady and calm.

Lady Evelyn clutched at her heart, wailing as if it were breaking within her breast. "Is there nothing that you can do?"

The Archmage noted that her eyes were dry, bright, and avaricious. No party to her playacting. "Magic, medicine, prayer . . . none can mend the Wasting Sickness."

"If he dies, what becomes of Gamelin?" her son George asked. "The war claimed my cousin, who was the duke's only child."

The Archmage did not reply, going to the window and looking down at the bustling wharves of Tradersport. He laced his fingers together behind his back, waiting. As expected, he did not have to wait overlong.

"Not his only child." The last man in the room spoke up from his spot near the doorway. "He is my father, too. The line continues in me."

"That's a lie," cried Lady Evelyn. "You have no proof."

"My blood is my proof. My mother's word is my proof."

George whirled, fists clenched. "Your mother is a lying whore! As for your blood, I'll see a river of it flow into the harbor before I'll give Gamelin over to a bastard."

"Enough." The Archmage's voice was cool, quiet, but effective in silencing them, though the exchange of heated glares continued. "Larind was invited by me to attend this meeting, and I'll not have him insulted in my Tower. He has a claim, else he would not be here."

"What a preposterous notion." Lady Evelyn said. "My dear brother would never –"

The Archmage's apprentice, who had been calmly watching the proceedings, now spoke up.

"Our spells confirm Larind's parentage. He *is* the duke's son."

Sputtering, red-faced, George could barely speak. "As . . . as if we're to take the word of *elves*."

"His Grace the duke," the Archmage went on, now with a hint of steel beneath his velvet tone, "knows it is his obligation to name his heir, while he is yet well enough to do so. It shall be his decision."

"When will we know?" George asked. "The duchy runs to disrepair while he rots and yet breathes."

"I believe you are mistaken as to the state of the duchy. Gamelin prospers. The loyal lords have all well in hand."

Evelyn huffed with disdain. "Oh, yes, well in hand indeed. That ruffian Sabledrake *ruined* this duchy. Thank the gods we don't have *him* to contend with anymore, but there are still those awful, awful Black Dragons of his –"

The Archmage's apprentice sat forward with flashing eyes. "Lord Windclyffe was a great man and one of the duke's most trusted friends –"

"As for the Dragons," the Archmage said, "they have many times proved their value, to myself and to the duke." He cautioned his apprentice toward peace and discretion with a single glance.

"By their spying and eavesdropping." George's lip curled in a sneer.

"Thus are the true opinions known," the Archmage said. "His Grace is very interested in the true opinions of his people. Not only the lords, but the commoners as well. He would know which man they would see succeed him."

Evelyn nearly choked, clenching her lace handkerchief into a tight little ball. "The *commoners*? He would take *their* wishes over what is right? George is his nephew, his own flesh and blood."

"Perhaps Gamelin would rather be ruled by an illegitimate son than a nephew who prefers the company of little boys."

Larind leaned against the wall and crossed his arms, his posture at once easy and insolent. The Archmage was fooled by it no more than he had been fooled by Evelyn's grief. A bowstring-taut tension held the duke's bastard at the ready, and woe to the man who failed to see such inherent warning.

George went white, then red again. He opened his mouth to retort, but words abandoned him. He settled for reaching for the dagger at his belt.

"Gentlemen," the Archmage said before George's hand could make the final irrevocable mistake of drawing the blade, "I will have no fighting in my Tower."

"Did you not hear what he said to my George? The insult –"

"Insults are not my concern," he said. He made a slight but definite gesture. Untouched by any hand, the door swung silently open. This display of his magic, a spell so minor it was among the first any child learned, quelled Lady Evelyn at once. "I have informed you of where we currently stand. The duke is dying but knows his duty, and will name his heir. Thus, for now, our business is concluded."

Lady Evelyn seized her son by the arm. "Come, George." As she led him toward the door, she regained enough of her haughty composure to shoot the Archmage a backward, scathing glare. In a meant-to-be-overheard voice, she added, "Won't it be *nice* when the new and rightful duke is able to review and amend the offices of his advisors?"

The Archmage smiled. His apprentice stirred as if about to speak, but at a stern glance from him, subsided back into the chair by the window.

Once the pair were gone and the door closed in their wake, Larind bowed. He did this not with a nobleman's schooled courtly courtesy, but with his own swordsman's economy of movement. "I am in your debt, Archmage. You, at least, are willing to give me a chance."

The Archmage inclined his head. "As you are the duke's true child, I would be remiss in acting otherwise. I'd suggest, however, that until this matter has been settled, you mind your back most diligently."

"Believe me, I'm well aware of that need. If George wanted a proper fight, my cousins and I would be too happy to oblige –" He socked a fist into a palm and grinned. "– but a draught of poison seems more his style. I'll be careful."

When Larind left, the Archmage turned to his apprentice. As one, they took deep breaths and relaxed, letting fall the aloof reserve that the folk of Gamelin seemed to expect of their race.

"Well, my daughter," Arien Mirida said. "What think you?"

As Ariana – for whom aloof reserve would ever be a hard-won battle – considered her response, he could not help looking on her with the admittedly biased eyes of a father's pride.

She was of a height with him, slender as a rapier and graceful as a swan, with a swan's elegant line of neck made more pronounced by the way her silver hair was caught up in an elaborate twist. Her skin was moon-pale, her ears a living poem of curve and point, and she had inherited the deep sapphire eyes of both her mother and grandmother.

"George," Ariana said, her voice a cultured and more dulcet version of Arien's own, "is a vile gutter-crawling snake and should be skinned and hung out to dry."

Dulcet even with such harsh words. Arien chuckled. "And here was I, just thinking that you were the very picture of a lady."

"A painting of a lake shows only the surface," she said, "as does a picture of a lady. Or did you not truly wish my heartfelt thoughts on the matter?"

"Wish them or not, I know I'll hear them. I know full well that Sabledrake women aren't in the habit of concealing their opinions."

"I can when needed. I know there's merit in cool silence as well as fiery speech, *Valanor*. You taught me that, though I confess, I do struggle. It was near all I could do to sit in this room and listen to Evelyn and George. If he becomes duke, it'll be the start of a dark age for Gamelin. Not that he'll be much in command. His mother will run him like a racing tagga dog, and as long as he's money enough to pursue his . . ." She shuddered. "His . . . entertainments, he'll let her do as she wills without a peep."

"Then you'd favor Larind?"

"Oh, assuredly. The nobles would squawk about the Bastard Duke, dreading that their own by-blows might start having expectations and making demands, but they've grown fat and complacent and could use a good shaking-up."

Arien nodded. "True indeed. The nobles prefer George, despite all of his faults. But the people share your view. The *commoners*," he mimicked.

"There is also a more personal and pertinent truth," Ariana said, "Larind as duke wouldn't see you stripped of your title, oust our family and put our feet to the road."

Arien waved it off. "Nor would George. It is not widely known, but when the duke invited me to take this post, he decreed it a lifetime appointment."

She laughed. "Had he any idea how long an elven lifetime might be?"

"Whether he did or not hardly matters. I have this lofty post for so long as I wish it."

"Unless George thinks to have you killed, and cut that elven lifespan short. Which would be a good trick, with the Black Dragons on your side."

"Said organization would swiftly be disbanded, did George have anything to say about it."

"You and Mother, both cast out of your places? Woe is us . . . we'd need go to Thanis and see if you could reclaim your spot at the Great Library. I doubt you could keep us on such a wage, so Mother'll be back to cutting purses in the Upper Rings just to make ends meet."

He regarded her with dry amusement. "I'd prefer to see neither of those things come to pass. Much as I loved the Library, I am far more content here."

"As Archmage. But tell me, *Valanor* . . . how often are you truly called upon to use your magic? In all these years, I've scarce seen you cast a single spell in the line of duty, barring minor ones such as truthsaying or the one you used to determine Larind's blood-claim. The rest is all for show."

"Astute, *Tashti*." The endearment was hardly fitting now that she was no longer a child, but she would always be his 'little loved one.' "Strange . . . had I remained in the Emerin, I would have one day held a seat on the Starleaf Council. I was groomed for that post, but when I left, thought I would never need use that training again. Now here I am, far from there and still embroiled in high government."

She rose and went to the window. Her slim hands rested on the sill, the sea air blowing a few wispy tendrils of silver that dangled to her collarbones. He knew by the set of her shoulders that something was troubling her, and was unsurprised when she spoke without turning to face him. "For what post am *I* being groomed?"

Arien's brows rose, and he reminded himself to step carefully here. "You are still quite young, *Tashti*. Your studies have progressed quite well despite your lack of formal schooling –"

"*You* taught me. How can you say I lack schooling?"

"I taught myself as well, from the grimoires in the Great Library. Neither of us have benefited from a proper, complete Emerinian education."

"Why didn't you study sorcery as a youth? Your talent is . . . *was* as strong as any in the Emerin, even before the Avantari influence."

"It was all a matter of politics. These jugglings and maneuverings here in Gamelin are nothing compared to the schemings of the Emerin. There, to become a truly master wizard, a Magelord or Archmage, one must forsake all rights to one's family lands, titles, positions, and inheritances. One is in effect, *removed* from the family and takes a new allegiance with the mages. I was the only heir to my father's lands of Taefallon *and* my foster father's lands of Karadan. Had I chosen a mage's path back then, I would not have been able to inherit either."

"If you went back now? Couldn't you petition to regain those lands?"

He sighed. "Had my name not been stricken from the Book of Lists once Count Elyvorrin learned of his daughter's sad fate, perhaps."

"Alinora," Ariana said, with the familiarity of one who had heard the tale many a time before.

"The count holds a strong place on the Council. I'm sure it was no difficult matter for him to have me denounced as a murderer and a deceiver."

"Couldn't you speak in your own defense? A simple truthsay, and they'd know that you did not murder Alinora. If you deceived, it was out of love."

"By the time I learned of the count's petition, the deed was done. Yes, it grieves me that I will never see the Emerin again. It angered me to have been unjustly condemned. But these things are not half so important to me as this new life that I've found."

"You've been wronged. Our family has been wronged."

"Would you have me go back, Ariana? To what end?"

"No, *Valanor* . . ." Now she turned to him, and her eyes were twin pools of midnight. "*I* wish to go."

He sat back and looked at her, a breathless and strengthless feeling hovering in the vicinity of his heart. His words came out in a bare whisper. "To the Emerin?"

"Years now, I've been wondering. What is my path? You've instructed me in magic, in diplomacy. Yet more and more, I feel that Gamelin's court is not where I belong. I yearn to *do* something with my life, to accomplish something more than being the most charming lady at the duke's ball. What better place to begin than the Emerin?"

"You are only twenty-seven . . ."

"Young by elven standards, I know, but I have not been *raised* by elven standards. We dwell in the human realms, live by their time. Brianna is no older than me and has five babes of her own now. I'm grown enough to face the Emerin."

"I grant you that point . . . but, *Tashti* . . . your mother is elfkin. Those few elves you've met here tend to turn a blind eye to it, whether out of deference to my title or whether they're more well-traveled and hence less hidebound than their counterparts. But to go to Perras Peliani, the great city, where there are elves whose families have never set a single toe beyond the boundaries of the woodlands for ten generations . . ."

She touched her ears, her cheekbones. "My elven blood runs true. Both you and Grandmother have said so many a time. They'll not know by looking at me or by use of spells."

"Even so, I have seen your quickness of temper. Could you truly ignore the insults you'd be likely to hear, should that truth become known?"

"I've heard many an insult here in Tradersport and still haven't littered the streets with dead dueling opponents. I can control myself in the Emerin, I know that I can."

"The Emerin is a saddened land now, and a dangerous one. Kingless, divided, even more fraught with political bickerings than ever. I have heard rumors that even the ruthless *Morvalan* have pushed their presence northward. It is not a good place now."

"*Valanor*, I am capable and clever. I may not be Mother's equal with a blade but I can defend myself. Oh, don't you see? My life has been a soft and easy one. I've never had to strive for anything. Yet I look on you, and Mother, and all that you've done. The differences you've made. I will never be able to save all the Northlands, as you did, but I should like to do more than lounge about court and turn away proposals."

The prospect of his daughter, his shining silver Ariana, in the Emerin . . . it filled his soul with a sinking leaden weight. She had no concept of how cruel elven society could be, how subtle and sharp, like a thin dagger-blade in the darkness.

And yet . . .

"I do admit, my life has been the richer for my struggles," Arien said. "You are elven, a child of the Emerin. You should at least once glimpse its wonders."

"Then you'll not refuse me?"

"Have I ever been able to refuse you anything?" He shrugged helplessly. To change the subject and hopefully lighten his mood, he asked, "But what are these proposals of which you speak?"

Ariana winced. "You made me too gracious a lady. I've both Gavin and Galen Chastain vying for my hand, not to mention other assorted hopefuls."

"Which explains why, not two days ago, I had the pleasure of Sir Gavin's company here in this very office," Arien said. "Looking back, I now see that he was trying to ascertain my stance on marriages 'twixt humans and elves."

"What *is* your stance?" she asked.

"Why? Just how hopeful is this young hopeful?"

"I asked you first."

He sank his chin onto the tips of his steepled fingers. "Your mother is the dark star that has eclipsed all others in my sight. I admired and came to love both of your grandparents. I have dear friends of many races. In detached reasoning, I have no moral objection . . ."

"But you'd not wish your daughter to marry one," she finished.

"Do you know why?"

"All I have to do is look at Grandmother, still with centuries before her, still fair and lovely as a summer's day, and think of Grandda. They loved so completely, and then he was gone. And he lived *long* for a human."

"She mourns him desperately," Arien said. "I would not ever wish to see you in such pain. In all love, there is that risk. Even to elves. Accidents and illness *may* leave one bereft. But with humans . . . their lives so short and fleeting . . ."

"That loss is a certainty," she said. "I know I could not bear to marry a man and see him aged and dying before I've even lived my first century. I could not bear to have him see me stay unchanging, have him know that he was just a brief part of my long life."

"Alas, the humans cannot seem to grasp it as we do. These very things, I said to Sir Gavin, and he replied that living for the moment was what mattered, and dwelling on the future only let those moments slip away unappreciated. But what matters most, I suppose . . . Ariana, do you love him?"

"As the friend of my childhood, and as a lover." She met his gaze with a mixture of defiance, frankness and apprehension. "Though I've kept that from Mother."

"Cat is ever still my innocent thief," Arien said. "Yes, I understand. She'd be at ease had you *slain* a man . . ."

"But not that I'd *lain* with one."

"Rest assured, I will keep that confidence. Though there are few secrets in Gamelin from the leader of the Black Dragons. She may know."

"Ah, but she still hasn't found my diary."

"I'd not be so certain of that."

"I am, else all of Tradersport would have gone aglow with red from her blushes." She tipped him a wink.

Arien raised a hand to quell her. "There are things that fathers would not wish to know in great detail as to the private lives of their daughters."

"Will Mother object to my leaving?"

"She would worry greatly, for she loves you dearly. But she was the one who told you to know your own mind and heart, and do what you deem best." He bent to retrieve a rind of candied fruit from beneath his desk.

"Still no luck teaching Darkfire to tidy up after himself, I see," Ariana said.

"Despite all my efforts." He flicked the rind into a wastebasket. "I should be thankful it is only fruit, and that Lady Evelyn did not behold it. She has dislike enough for me without my mannerless familiar adding to her rancor."

"He did learn some manners, or at least pretended to, when I would play tea parties."

"He endured those in good faith," Arien said. "Not many drakes would suffer wearing a bonnet for the sake of a few treats. Now let us go home, *Tashti*, and see what your mother will make of this request."

* * *

CHAPTER TWO

I have walked in the shadows, and they are my home.
– Elwyndas, Spirit of the Southern Lands

Terrible, Darkfire sent. *Teaching a child to steal. Just terrible.*

Cat shushed at him.

Why? He can't hear me. Only you and Arien share the mind-bond, thank the eldest dragons. I don't know what I'd do with your children clamoring in my head too.

"That's enough out of you," she said.

Tal looked up. "What, Mama?"

"Don't mind me. Darkfire fancies he's being witty. Careful. Don't let it slip."

He returned his attention to the lock, his tongue poking out of the corner of his mouth as he concentrated on his fingers.

The lock was one of a dozen set into a single large sheet of heavy oak. Cat had trained on it herself, under her father's watchful eye, and now as she taught Tal the same, she finally understood how pleased and proud Tahm had been as she mastered each new skill.

Tal squinted as he gave the pick the final turn. The click of the lock was very loud in the quiet room, making him twitch in surprise.

"Well done," Cat said. "That's your best time yet."

Most children have nice, normal apprenticeships. The black drake was lounging on the windowsill in the last of the day's sunlight, chewing on his talons. His tail dangled, twitching, a source of delight to three kittens that tumbled over each other trying to catch it.

"Which one now?" Tal asked, pushing too-long dark hair out of his face.

The human blood ran strong in her small son. His elven heritage showed only in his slight, tapered ears and the delicate look to his features that made children tease him and adults think him frail. But Cat saw better with her thief's vision, saw how Tal was quicker and more agile than some twice his age. Only ten, he could best his sister four times of five in swordplay, and climbed as if he'd been born in the treetops. Or, more likely, born to the rooftops.

"Try that one," she said, tapping the uppermost of all the locks. Elsewhere in the manor, she heard the front door close, heard old Bess quaver a greeting, heard the softly melodious voices of her husband and daughter in reply. "Quickly, now, Father and Ariana are home, which means I must be off soon."

"Ari's got a suitor," Tal said with an impish grin.

"Does she now?" Cat glanced toward the sitting room door, seeing that they were still alone. She eaned conspiratorially close to Tal. "And how do you know that?"

He's developed a habit for eavesdropping, Darkfire sent. *The boy is as quiet as a feather hitting the floor.*

"I heard her telling Brianna," Tal said. "Sir Gavin wants to marry her. She has him skipping in circles like a giddy goose."

"Shh, now, here they come." Cat rose and smoothed her grey tunic. Edged and trimmed in black, it bore two patches on the upper left side. One was the blue field and triple golden sun of Gamelin, the ducal crest. The other was a black dragon on a background of white.

Arien entered first, spotted Cat in uniform, and put on an expression of mock formality. "Good evening, Dragonleader."

"Greetings, Archmage," she said, equally formal. Then, with a laugh, she dashed to him and was drawn into the blissful circle of his arms.

"My love," Arien said. "Every day apart from you is like a year."

He met her lips in a lingering kiss, sending the familiar yet still enticing thrill of passion rushing in her veins.

It didn't seem that long ago to her that they'd first met, her stalking a band of rival thieves, him their unlucky victim. He had been shocked by her race and her ruthlessness. She had never believed any elf would speak kindly to her. That such a meeting could turn to so sweet and enduring a love still amazed her. Nothing had been able to prevent it. Not the curse that had haunted his family for generations, not his doomed love for a long-dead elfmaid, not even the bleak years they'd spent apart.

Their children, both so different yet each so clearly theirs, watched with nearly identical rolling of their eyes. Their evident embarrassment and bemusement at this show of affection was enough to make Cat try to step back, but Arien anticipated her and held her close. Darkfire's warm thoughts enveloped both their minds, bringing them even closer.

At last, they moved apart. Ariana greeted her with a soft kiss on the cheek – she had to bend down to do it, towering over Cat.

"How fare my wife and son?" Arien asked, unbuttoning his doublet.

"She wants me to open that lock," Tal said, sounding as morose as if he had just been given a dire punishment. "The hard one. I've *never* been able to open it."

Ariana perched on a low, padded stool and began the complicated work of unpinning her hair. "I always find it easier to use a key. Or a spell."

"A spell your father to this very day refuses to teach *me*." Cat looked pointedly at Arien, who merely did his best to put on an expression of innocence. "As for keys, well, when someone hides their best treasures, they don't leave the keys lying about."

"Ssometimes they even set traps," Arien said. "Enspelled traps. To, say . . . turn one to stone?"

"That was long ago. I do wish you'd quit mentioning it."

Tal clapped his hands, eyes bright. "And the bad wizard Solarrin had to magic you whole again."

"After everyone begged and Sybil asked oh-so-prettily," Ariana said. Her hair tumbled free, waves of silver to the small of her back.

"Not my finest moment, I grant you. But it's nice to know my children never weary of hearing those old stories."

"Perhaps those old stories will serve as guideposts to them as they create new stories of their own," Arien said. He and Ariana exchanged a glance that made Cat take notice.

"What are you two up to?"

Arien deferred to their daughter. Clasping Cat's hands in both of her own, Ariana said, "Mother . . ."

"She's getting married!" Tal sprang to his feet. "I told you so."

"Scamp!" Ariana cried. "You've been spying on me again?"

"*Are* you?" Cat asked. "Married? So soon?"

"Maybe she's with child." Tal dodged out of reach as Ariana let go of Cat's hands and tried to swat him.

"Tal!" Blushing hotly, Cat looked to Arien, but found no help there; her husband was trying not to laugh.

"*Niaschal.*" Ariana gestured and a shimmery globe of water appeared just above Tal's head. It splashed down, dousing the boy. "I am not getting married, and I am not with child and you talk far too much. How do you ever plan to be a Black Dragon if you can't keep your silence?"

Tal shook his head, flinging water all over Darkfire. The drake sent a wordless exclamation along the mental bond he shared with Cat and Arien, wings snap-fluttering as he flew in swift retreat to a high corner.

"Children, please," Arien said. "Look at the mess you've made. *Halnia.*" At his spell, the puddle on the floor vanished and Tal was instantly dry, though the result was to crackle his hair out about his head in a dark corona.

Arien, Cat said through the bond, *What is all this about?*

Let her tell it her own way, my love.

"I can too keep my silence," Tal protested, trying vainly to smooth his hair. "When it's important."

"And this isn't?" Ariana's voice was dangerous.

"Not like when someone says he'll *kill* me if I –" He slapped both hands across the lower half of his face. Above them, his silvery-grey eyes grew huge and round and dreadfully afraid. He burst into tears and tried to run from the room.

Ariana missed, Arien was too astonished to react, but Cat dropped to her knees and seized him by the shoulders before he got to the door. He wailed in misery.

"Tal . . . what is it? Someone threatened you? Who was it? You *must* tell me what happened."

He struggled and flailed at her, trying to pull away.

"Tal, stop!" Ariana threw Arien an imploring glance. "*Valanor*, do something."

Arien knelt beside Cat. "Son, hear me."

"I can't tell, I can't!" Tal sobbed. "He said he'd cut off my nose and . . . and my *ears*."

One of his wildly-waving fists clipped Cat just under the eye, but she would not let go. "No one will hurt you, Tal," she said. "I swear on your grandda's name. I will not let anyone hurt you."

He ceased his struggles but was still shaking, still looking at her in tearful panic.

Arien rested his fingertips on Tal's forehead. Cat felt a peculiar rushing in her mind, was briefly dizzied by the feel of a rainbow flowing past her at great speed. She and Darkfire both blinked and mentally recoiled.

"Tell us, and fear no more," Arien said in a low voice.

Tal relaxed at once. Cat glanced at Arien, knowing what he'd done. Many years ago, a near-fatal injury had left him unable to use his magic. The price of having it restored to him was to open himself to the mystical Avantari, which had infused him with a portion of their unearthly power. His mage's talent was now such that by mere thought and will alone he could accomplish things for which no spells had yet been written. Such as soothe their distraught child.

Tal's trembling ceased, and when he spoke, he did so steadily. "I was at the duke's castle yesterday to watch the knights at practice."

"Yes," Ariana said. "He followed me, but I caught him. I told him he could stay if he behaved, and I'd buy him a sweet on the way home."

"But I got bored with all the fighting. So I went exploring. I found a secret door in that round room with the pictures on the ceiling –"

"Between the green marble column and the suit of Perrifaulian armor?" Cat asked.

This is your influence, you know, Darkfire sent to Cat. *What next? Holding up coaches on the Northlands Road?*

"You went down the passage," Cat said, ignoring Darkfire. "Then what?"

Tal shivered again despite the soothing influence of Arien's magic. "There were two men in the corner . . . talking of killing someone. Killing Larind-the-Bastard."

Cat drew an infuriated breath. "Why am I not surprised? Was it Lord George?"

"They saw me before I could run, and the other one grabbed me." He raised his stricken gaze to Cat's. "I tried to fight him, Mama, tried to get away, but he was bigger than me and strong."

"It's all right, *Tashta*," she said, stroking his hair. "What happened next?"

"Lord George knew my name. The Mirida brat, he called me. He told the other man it was too bad there'd be trouble if I went missing, for he fancied the way I looked."

Ariana put into words the oaths Cat was thinking but couldn't bring herself to say out loud in front of her children. Then Ariana exceeded her, elaborating into a spate of curses spanning at least five languages. Darkfire's jaw unhinged as he gaped, though whether in response to Tal's words or Ari's was unclear.

Arien's face was pale and his lips tight. "What else, son?"

"Then he showed me a knife and said if I told anyone what I'd heard, he'd have my nose and ears off before he killed me. Please don't tell him I told. Please don't!"

"Don't you fret a moment longer about George, Tal," Cat said. "I'll have his head on a spike at the city gates before you go to sleep tonight."

"Cat –" Arien began.

They dared threaten our son! she sent, her thoughts a blistering fire.

"I know," he said. His voice carried a tone of icy promise that she'd only ever heard him to use once before, in a fortress in the south Emerin. That promise, he'd made and kept to an elf named Donnell. "We shall deal with this matter, you and I. Tal, henceforth you must not keep such things from us. No one shall harm you so long as your mother and I draw breath. Believe that, and trust in us."

Tal nodded. His tremors had eased, and he gazed up at them with a trust that ached right down to the core of Cat's soul.

In her mind's dungeon, Cat had already devised a thousand deaths for George and his minion, each more hideous than the last. She forced herself to sound calm despite the scenes of slow torture spinning through her imagination. "I think we've enough with the locks for tonight, haven't we?"

Ariana stood up. "Come, Tal, let's go and see if Bess has finished her baking."

I'll go with them. Darkfire swooped to the boy's shoulder. *To keep watch. I'll guard him as if he was my own hatchling. I just guard better on a full belly.*

The drake's levity failed to cheer Cat in the slightest. As they left, her fingers curled slowly around her dagger. "George."

"With cool heads and forethought, Cat. Cool heads and forethought."

"Yes," Cat said with a grudging sigh. "But we must get Tal out of Tradersport for his own safety. If Da were still alive –"

"Lift that pretty chin, my love. I know what to do. As it happens, the very thing that Ariana wished to tell you is the very answer to this thorny problem. She wishes to travel. She wishes to go to the Emerin."

She grappled with the idea, blinking up at him. "The Emerin? You've spoken to her about it? You agree?"

"Her explanations were valid, and her emotions sincere. How could I deny her?"

"You've never denied her, Arien, not one single thing since the moment you told her you were her own true father. But you always say she's still so young . . ."

"Like it or not, she is no child, not anymore. She is grown enough to take care of herself." His smile was rueful. "I understand that you were up to your pertly pointed ears in trouble when you were much younger than Ariana."

"Yet how could she take Tal with her to the Emerin? We both know what they'd make of him there. It is not Lenais. Ariana may be pure elvenblood, but Tal is as elfkin as I am. Perhaps we should keep him here after all. My mother, and Bess –"

"Miralina is still deep in mourning," Arien said, "and Bess far too aged for the responsibility. You were correct before. Best that we get Tal out of Tradersport and beyond George's reach. Not to the Emerin, no, of course. But with Keyda as it is, and the strife in the city of Unity, the best way for Ariana to travel eastward is by boat on the Maikha. And the best place to catch such a boat is, of course . . ."

"Thanis," Cat said, and a smile born of pure relief spread across her face. "Of course."

* * *

Edrold pushed open the door of the Island Lotus and inhaled with ravenous joy the mingled aromas of simmering oils.

"Well-a-day," the barkeep said. "Look who's come back. Your wrist healed yet?"

Several of the other patrons laughed.

Edrold joined in, with more heartiness than he felt. "If I can't pay this time, you can break the other one, Kerd, how's that suit you?" He swung his leg over a stool. "Palga oil."

"Oh-ho, the man must have the big marks." Kerd didn't budge from his spot, let alone reach to the shelves behind him where jars and vials glittered in the smoky light.

"This time I do. I've got good money."

"Then let's see it."

Edrold plucked a silver five-mark piece from his purse and spun it on the bartop. He jangled his purse that they might hear the clank of heavy coins, to prove he was as good as his word. And this was only a beginning, for the real reward would come when the deed was done.

"Who'd you rob?" Kerd, at the sight of the silver, wasted not a moment putting an empty bowl in front of Edrold. He took a wide-mouthed jar from the shelf and poured, filling the bowl halfway with a thick fluid.

The pungent smell of palga rose from it, better than any womanly perfume. Edrold chose a burning candle from the rack along the bar. He hunched over the bowl and touched the flame to the shiny surface, igniting a shimmer of blue-orange flames. More fumes wafted up into his face. He breathed them in, relishing the tingle as the potent drug went to work.

Two bowls later, he was pleasantly immersed. Accepted. The men at the bar, who had sat as silent witnesses to his wrist-breaking humiliation a few weeks back were now dearer than brothers. The women, from the sultry girls who worked the upstairs half of the Island Lotus to the little blue-eyed honeypot two stools down, were the most beautiful, charming creatures ever created by the generous gods.

"A round for the house!" Edrold spread his arms as if to embrace the lot of them. "To celebrate my new good fortune." Cheers greeted him, and when he added, "Make it Dragon Oil," the cheers rose into a thunderous roar of approval. All his friends, the best friends any man ever had, were clapping him on the back and telling him what a marvelous fellow he was, and could life get any more grand?

"Dragon Oil for the house!" Kerd dragged out a heavy brass urn decorated all around with images of dragons in flight, and tipped a bit into each of the bowls that were enthusiastically thrust toward him.

Edrold raised his in a toast. "To my benefactor. All hail Duke George!"

"Duke George!" they chorused, though normally this crowd would have as much use for any of Gamelin's nobility as they'd have for a silk stockings and a plumed hat.

Tapers were dipped into the Dragon Oil's gold and red swirls. The interior of the tavern took on a stranger illumination as the fluid ignited in slow-burning yellow and blood-colored flames. They wended its way around the swirls in hypnotic, dreamlike patterns. The fumes were strong enough to make even Edrold's seasoned head swim. He inhaled deeply, deeply, his lungs expanding as if they could go on forever.

Kerd appeared through the encroaching mist that clouded Edrold's vision. He was rubbing his hands together briskly. "I was wrong about you, seems."

"You are a prince, Kerd." He said it carefully, each word like navigating a particularly tricky step on a treacherous flight of stairs. "How much do I owe you for this bounty?"

"Two hundred fifty."

Edrold reached for his purse and found only his hip. Belt. Knife hilt. No purse. "My money!" He stood up, too fast, and the room whirled around him.

Kerd stared at him, bushy brows slowly bunching into a scowl. "This does not strike me funny, Edrold."

"I've been robbed, you numb ox!" Edrold seized his temples and bent over, hoping the rush of blood would clear his head. Instead, it only made him dizzier. The next thing he knew he was sprawled facedown on the grimy floor.

"You telling me you can't pay? You ordered Dragon Oil for the house and you can't *pay?* Oh, you misbegotten trollson, I'll break more than your wrist this time."

How quickly the jovial cheer in the Island Lotus changed. His former friends, brothers in all but name, surrounded him, lifted him, held him in place while Kerd laid into him with a length of wood wrapped in chain-cord.

A short but incredibly agonizing while later, Edrold suffered one final jarring crash and then realized the beating was over. Whimpering, he raised his head as far as it would go and saw what the dockworkers called Fishguts Alley, dismally lit by a single lamppost. If his nose hadn't been shattered, he would have known the place by the sheer stink of it.

Thrown out. Beaten within an inch of the grave and dumped in Fishguts Alley to die.

And die he would. His own blood clogged his throat. His breath felt like it whistled through the merest pinhole. With each convulsive heave of his chest, sharp splinters of rib jabbed at his innards.

Booted feet moved into view. He followed them up to the knee, where the black leather gave way to dark grey cloth. He saw a swordbelt, with a black-gloved hand resting on the hilt. Higher up, just as it was dawning on him that the slender body had feminine contours, he saw embroidered patches of the duke's crest and the black dragon. A familiar, battered, bulging purse was held in the other hand. The strings had been neatly cut.

Enormous deep-blue eyes looked down at him as he groveled in the filth, choking on his own blood. The face they belonged to was golden-skinned, a sharp, pitiless face framed in dark curls.

"Do you know," she said, "what is the most feared creature in all the world?"

Between the beating and the potent oils, Edrold could not have answered aloud even had he known what to say. He shook his head, as much to show his muddled confusion as to reply.

"A mother dragon, of course."

* * *

CHAPTER THREE

I left the best of me when we parted, and took the best of you along.
– Elwyndas, Memories, Chapter XII

"It wasn't so long ago that you could run through this marketplace faster than a rabbit before the hounds," Ariana said.

"That was ten years and five babes ago." Brianna lowered herself onto a bench. "I must rest a moment. Oh, my feet, my back. Care for a sweet, Ari?"

Ariana sat, tossing her hair back to let the warm light of the sun fall upon her face. She waved away the bag of candied berries that her friend held out. "Small wonder you've gained two stone."

"I'm feeding for two." She patted her swollen stomach. "It won't last, I'm sure. I'll have to run as fleet as a deer to keep up with him, judging by the way he kicks."

"Him?" Ari asked.

Brianna dimpled. "Roman won't accept anything less than a son this time, after all the girls. You'll see, once you've become a Chastain."

"Once I what?" Ari fixed Brianna with a stern look. "I say you again, I've no intention of marrying Gavin Chastain."

"Oughtn't you tell him so before he buys a ring? Goodness, Ari, what have you against marriage? You could do far worse. If Larind the Bastard, does become duke, the Chastains will be very well placed indeed. Besides, you're getting no younger."

"I am twenty-seven."

"My very point. You're of an age with me, and I've made something of my life."

"Forgive me, but I wish more than housework and husband and children to tend."

"Tosh. What do you think servants and nursemaids are for? Do you see me wearing myself away to nothing taking care of the manor?"

"Far from it." She touched Brianna's belly, which felt round and ripe as a plum. "No, such a life is not for me."

"Every man in Gamelin lusts after you, and most of the women would as soon see you in rags and ashes out of jealousy."

"Oh, surely now . . ."

"I speak true. They'd snatch those silver locks from your head, scratch that silken skin, and put out those sapphire lamps of your eyes if they could. I've heard them say as much."

"Unkind."

"Yet it's so. Elf-fair swordmaid, daughter of unicorn and dragon –"

"Daughter of *what*?"

Brianna pointed to the door of the Archmage's Tower, which bore the emblem of House Mirida, rearing unicorns bearing a star between them. "Haven't you heard the song?"

"There's a song?"

"Quite popular in the taverns, I'm told. I heard some of Roman's guardsmen singing it."

"A *song*." Ari groaned. "Praise Livana I'm leaving this mad place."

"Leaving? What's this?"

"My dearest Lady Falconhurst, I'll soon be bidding Gamelin farewell. Like my parents and grandparents before me, I mean to go out in the world and seek my fortune." She did not add that she was being made to take her baby brother in tow for the first part of the trip.

"Ari, this is too sudden, especially for you of all people. How is it that you've breathed not a word of it before now? Even to me? And Gavin . . . does Gavin know?"

Ariana shook her head. "In truth, best and most faithful of friends, I was hoping –"

"Oh, no you don't," Brianna said, shooting from the bench as if catapulted, and never mind the additional weight of her pregnancy. "You'd have me tell him for you? Once you'd already set Tradersport well behind you? Is that what you fancy?"

"Since you offer –"

"I offer no such thing. You'll tell him yourself, milady."

"If I do, he'll insist on accompanying me and I've already Tal to look after."

"This is the fault of your grandfather's stories," Brianna said, and sniffed. "Adventures and quests . . . pah! And here you are, too much a coward even to face Gavin yourself."

Ariana was stung. "I hadn't thought of it that way."

"Well, then." Brianna looked eminently satisfied, as if that settled that.

"I had best go and speak with Gavin at once."

At once proved to be an hour later, after she repeatedly assured Brianna of her genuine wish to do this. Ari was touched by her friend's concern, but dismayed by Brianna's lack of understanding. The plump, pampered life of a nobleman's lady was not for her. The desire to see the world, to live with risk and danger and excitement, these things were as foreign to Brianna Falconhurst as would have been the speech of the Perrifaulians.

She was finally able to extricate herself, and after a quick stop by the duke's stables, was astride her favorite horse and riding up the steep path that hugged the edge of the western bluff overlooking Tradersport. Chastain Hall stood at the very highest point of the bluff, defiant and commanding, as if daring the sea to come up and sweep it away. The hall was ivy-covered stone, four wings in a square around a central courtyard, and surrounded with stables and outbuildings. Orchards spread out behind it like a dark green cloud fallen to earth.

For many years, this had been as a second home to her. While her parents and grandfather had been busy establishing themselves, she and her grandmother had been frequent guests of the Chastains. Now, seeing their estate as if for the first time, she realized something that she had hitherto not contemplated.

Just as Gavin, the young and vital heir, would one day grow old and frail, so too was Chastain Hall itself far from eternal. Never mind its defiant stance. The bluff was made of chalk cliffs, soft and crumbling. Inch by inch, the inlet was widening, the cliffs falling away in pieces.

So, too, would the manor. Not this year or next, but within a few centuries it would be gone. Plunged into the sea.

The grooms rushed out to meet her as she approached the stable yard. She greeted them and inquired after their families as she removed her riding cape and hung it on a peg. A portcullis-guarded arched tunnel passed under the manor wall and surfaced again in the courtyard garden, where a pretty woman with white-streaked dark hair tended her flowers.

"Why, Ariana, how delightful to see you."

"Good afternoon, Lady Margaret."

"How is your grandmother? I've sent her message after message, begging her to come and visit, but she always declines. She's not ill, pray Galatine?"

"No, not ill. She's still mourning my grandfather. It would be disrespectful of her to resume her social calls so soon."

Lady Margaret made a tsking sound. "It's been, what, five years? She must get on with her life, being still such a young woman herself. Might some roses cheer her? I'll cut a bouquet for you to take."

"Ah . . . no, Lady. Thank you, but to us, the elvenkind, roses are the flowers of death."

"Oh, yes, I remember now. Poor Miralina. Then at least tell her that I do miss her, and hope to see her soon."

"I shall," Ariana said. "Lady . . . is Gavin about?"

A pleased, knowing little smile crossed the older woman's face. "Dame Cecily is instructing my boys in the dance. A proper knight must be well versed in the courtly arts as well as the art of war, you know."

"So I've heard." Ariana could only imagine how the lessons were progressing. In all the years she'd known them, Gavin and Galen Chastain had always far preferred swordplay, riding, hunting, and gambling to poetry, music, and dancing.

She followed harp music to the ballroom, where she paused just inside the door and watched with great amusement as two young men, complaining with every stiff and awkward step, danced with each other as partner. They were identical in their well-tanned, dusky handsomeness, but for a scar that split Galen's chin. He'd had it since he was Tal's age, and Ariana knew it well. In fact, she herself had given it to him while they were playing at war with sharp sticks.

"It's my turn to lead," he said.

"I'm the elder," Gavin said. "Thus, I should lead."

Dame Cecily, a pigeon-plump dowager with a puff of white hair and an overabundance of jewelry, left off her uninspired rendition of "The Princely Coronation" and raked her ring-encrusted fingers across the harpstrings indignantly.

"Gavin, for pity's sake, let your brother lead. Else one of you come and provide the music, and I'll do the dancing."

"Yes, Gavin, go on. See if you can snap the strings again."

"You play so much better, little brother, why don't you?" He spied Ariana, and pushed Galen away with such brusque force it would have sent a lesser man sprawling. "Ari!"

"Well, praise Helia," Dame Cecily said. "*She* can dance with you."

Ariana curtseyed. "My regrets, Dame Cecily, but I haven't time for dancing today. I must speak with Gavin."

Galen elbowed his brother and winked. Gavin replied by threatening him with a fist.

"Oh, very well . . . Galen could stand some practice with his poetry," Dame Cecily said. "Come along, young man. We'll walk in the garden, and I want to hear all of 'A Lily for Elara,' from memory."

"Delightful," Galen said, looking like he would rather be dancing with his twin after all. "*There is a lily so white and pure . . .*"

Gavin shut the door behind them, and turned to Ariana with a welcoming smile. "How I have missed you, Ariana. Come and sit with me?"

"I cannot stay long –"

"Just for a moment." He drew her out on the terrace, to a bench overlooking the orchards. "We'll have a splendid crop this year. Ever since your grandmother worked her plant magics on the trees, the harvests have been rich and fine and prosperous."

"I'm glad to hear it."

"Yes, the family fortunes are doing well. Once Cousin Larind is named duke, we'll be more influential than ever." He slid from the bench to one knee, and Ariana's heart sank through her body like a stone.

"Gavin, what are you doing?"

"I wasn't planning to ask you just yet, but when I saw you today, I knew I couldn't wait a day longer. Ariana, I want you to be my wife."

She brought her folded hands before her mouth. "I –"

"I can promise you a good life, Ariana. I'll be a loyal husband, a good provider. Say you will, and I will be yours forever."

"Oh, but you won't," she said, touching his face. He *was* handsome, and she had no doubt that he would do everything within his power to make her as happy as he could . . . for a time. "Don't you see, Gavin? I am elven. I will live long and long. You cannot promise me forever."

"No, I don't see," he said, seizing her hand and pressing kisses to it. "It doesn't matter. I love you."

"I care for you deeply, Gavin, but to take you as my husband would be unkind to us both."

"Is there someone else?" he asked. "Another elf? Is that why?"

"No."

He flinched, and she somehow understood it would have been easier for him if there had been. He could stand losing in fair competition, such was the way of knights. But to be deemed unworthy solely on his own merits . . .

"I've hurt you," she said, wishing for her father's diplomacy, now more than ever. "I never wished for that."

"Why can't we make the most of what little time we have? Love best we can with each passing day, each passing year?"

"Because I won't be here, Gavin. I'm going away. I leave tomorrow, and do not know when I will return."

His face went very still. "Going away . . . how long have you known this?"

"Not long. My father only gave his permission yesterday."

"I will come with you, then. You should not go alone. It's unsafe."

"I will not be alone. Tal rides with me, as far as Thanis."

"Tal!" His laugh was an incredulous outburst. "You're trusting your safety to your mouse-squeak little brother?"

"I'm trusting my safety to my own self," she said, more sharply than necessary. He knew full well she was adept with a sword, no shrinking, fainting maiden. Then she relented. "Gavin, your place is here. Larind will need every faithful knight at his side during the coming trials. This is your home."

"It's yours as well."

"Is it?" She shook her head. "I've lived here all my life, but I sense in my heart that my true home is elsewhere. My destiny is elsewhere. I must go to it."

* * *

The three horses reined in at the top of the rise. Ahead of them, the road dipped to a bridge across a white-rapids river, before climbing again into the foothills of the Bannerian Mountains. A square, squat fortress crouched on the far side of the bridge. A small village had sprung up around the fort, walled by tree trunks shaved into crude points.

"Border Outpost," Cat said.

Ariana stopped beside her and surveyed the scene, thinking that it did not at all resemble the wealthier districts in Tradersport. It did not even resemble the poorer districts. "It's not very pretty."

"They built it in a rush, during the early years of the war. It needn't be pretty. That catapult stop the fort could set a boulder atop *us* if they were of a mind."

"Is that the Stonedeep?" Tal pointed. White spray leaped as the tumultuous water churned around half-submerged boulders.

Cat nodded. "Every so often, some fool tries to raft from here to Fanrel Inlet."

"Over High Falls? Have any done it?" Ariana asked.

"Not and still been drawing breath when they washed ashore."

"Have you ever been tempted to try it, Mama?" Tal studied the water as if *he* might be.

"Nary once," Cat said. "You know I don't care for swimming, even in mild streams. And you'd best not be tempted either, son-of-my-blood. If I were to ever get word that you'd tried something so foolhardy, there'd be no telling what I'd do."

"Yes, Mama."

"I think," Ari said, smiling at her brother's doleful tone, "that I could have found my way here unassisted. The Northlands Road is nearly as straight in life as it looked on the map. Carters could point their oxen north and doze all the way to Verun."

"I know, but I wanted to see you off. Both of my children leaving me . . . I never thought it would come so soon. Besides, your father wanted me out from underfoot for a few days. It seems Lord George has some suspicions about the untimely demise of his hired thug."

"Did you kill him, Mother?" Ariana asked.

"He died by my doing, but not by my hands," Cat said. "I promised Arien long ago that he'd not have an assassin for a wife. It is a fine line, but I walk it carefully enough."

"What if I don't like Thanis?" Tal said. He had heard every word about killings and assassins, and it had not so much as made him blink.

Theirs was, Ariana reflected, the most peculiar family she knew.

"It won't be for long," Cat assured him. "Once your father and I have dealt with matters back home, we'll send for you. But until the succession in Gamelin has been settled, we daren't stray too far from home. Someone must look out for Larind. Come, there's an inn just beyond the gate."

The inn, for all that it was a shabby thing compared to the ones to which Ariana was accustomed, proved clean enough. The food, while plain, was plentiful and filling. But Ariana found the looks from many of the townspeople as sour as the ale.

"Why do they glare at us so?"

"The war," Cat said. "Many of these folk are Keydan by birth, escaped from their ruined homes and unable to go back. They've seen their families die, their sons sent off to battle. And who's to blame? The Elder Races. The humans of the Northlands suffered much because of the elves and dwarves. And we . . . or at least you, Ariana . . . are plainly elven."

"Why didn't the humans stay out of it? Hadn't the Northlands lost enough men during the Western Campaign against Hachland?"

"They couldn't," Tal said. "The war sucked them in, and then it was just fighting for its own sake. I've heard soldiers who were there talking of it."

Following their meal, they elected not to bed down in the common room on straw pallets, but paid extra to retire to a private room upstairs. Ariana was glad of that. Adventure, yes ... danger, yes. Sleeping on the floor next to smelly drunkards who brought their wenches with them? No.

The room was small and cramped, with a low, sloped ceiling. Like the rest of the inn, it was clean enough, but Ariana wouldn't have wanted to live in it or even stay there for any great length of time.

Their mother, being who she was, promptly began putting questions to them. "How would you escape this room, was there sudden need?"

"Must we do this?" Ariana said, without much hope. "I'm tired."

"Always, Ari, always. How would you escape this room?"

She sighed. "I'd go out the window."

"What's on the other side?"

"I don't know."

"Then look, daughter, look. It could be a dog kennel, could be a closed alley, could be anything."

Tal had already looked. "It's a mulch pile. Soft landing."

"And I'm ever so glad I know a spell of cleaning," Ariana said.

They laughed together, then Cat rummaged in her pack and came up with an oilcloth-wrapped bundle. "I brought this for you. Here, open it."

The first thing she saw upon unfolding the oilcloth was a shimmery silver fabric, and she immediately knew what it was. "Mother, it's your Silversilk! I cannot take this!" She lifted the mysterious cloth. Elf-woven of mist and magic and starlight, it was almost as strong as steel but light and flexible as silk. It would protect her as well as chainmail, and be able to mend itself should it be torn.

"Arien's, actually," Cat corrected. "You've grown so tall. But you can take it, and you will, and wear it besides."

"Does that mean that I'll have yours someday?" Tal asked.

Cat ruffled his hair. "Unless you become a giant like your sister."

Ariana draped the Silversilk over her arm and reached deeper into the bundle to find a large opal on a silver chain, made to be worn around the neck so that the gem was touching the skin.

"*Ilgilean*," she said, turning it this way and that, watching the candlelight chase itself in ripples over the smooth jewel. "A powerstone."

"And this," Cat said. "Take this."

"Your ring?" Ariana ran her thumb over the raised onyx dragon.

"Your grandfather gave me one just like it when I left Tradersport to stop Solarrin's plot. I gave that one to Greyquin, but want you to carry this one now. If ever you need me, send it and I'll come. Even to the Emerin."

"Thank you," Ari said, embracing her. As always, she was startled that a woman of such strength and vitality and presence, was so small. "I'll miss you so, but thank you for seeing why I want to do this."

"You're your father's daughter. Now and again, I see a bit of me in there . . . and there's a portion of adventuring spirit come to you from us both."

"I have something for Ariana too," Tal said. He handed it to her.

"Tal, you little scamp! This is Gavin's knife." She showed the Chastain coat of arms embedded in enamel at the crosspiece. "He thought he must have lost it, near went mad looking for it!"

Cat laughed. "As I was saying, you're Arien's daughter through and through, but Tal . . . Tal is *my* son."

* * *

Chapter Four

I like him not, though I love him well, for we are brothers.
– Elwyndas, Faemric and Dostrel, Act IV

Mischa Narrin regarded himself in the small mirror and combed his hair one last time, so that every rich brown strand was perfectly in place.

"Stop preening," his sister Jessa said from her perch on the windowseat. "You won't get any handsomer just from looking at yourself."

"I'm not preening. It's only that I can barely see myself in this miserable tiny ring of glass," he said.

"Your other will be back from the glazier's soon enough, you great peacock."

"Yes, and he's charging a fortune. I should make Rayle and Josef pay for it. They're the ones that broke it with their wrestling. I've better plans for my marks."

"Wine, women, and song," she said with a snort of disdain.

He laughed and tugged on her red-gold pigtail. "I don't care much for song, and if it came down to it, I could do without wine."

A voice from the doorway interrupted before Jessa could unleash one of her tart retorts. "Oh, is my Mischa still admiring himself?"

"I was," Mischa said, turning, "but I'll admire you instead. You look lovely, Sybil."

"And so do you, though I think those trousers are too tight," she replied, scanning him with her practiced eye.

"*You* think that?" He rolled his eyes at Jessa. "What's the world come to? When a priestess of Talopea, Goddess of a Thousand Pleasures, thinks anyone's trousers are too tight?"

"She's gone prudish with age." Jessa snickered.

"Me? Prudish? Nonsense." Sybil flapped a hand. "They show off your legs wondrous well, my boy. But faith, Mischa, how can you sit down without splitting them or binding the blood to your brain?"

"Just my legs? What of my rear?" he said, twisting to examine what he could see of it. "Mustn't forget that. It's one of my best features."

"The best of a fine lot. Are you to the Temple tonight?" Her voice took on a faint tone of worrisome pleading.

"Loathe as I am to disappoint you, I've an appointment with a young lady." He checked himself in the mirror again, baring his straight white teeth to make sure no flecks of food were caught in them. "Yolanda Martane."

"She's *my* age!" Jessa said.

"No, she's sixteen." He tossed a light cape over his shoulder, not because it was chilly out but because he liked the way the forest green cloth brought out the color in his hazel eyes.

"And you're thirty," Jessa said, clearly unimpressed. "Not that you act it. When are you going to grow up and get married or something?"

"Oh, dear, you're not thinking of that, are you?" Sybil asked.

Mischa chuckled. "Most mothers would be fretting if their eldest son had reached his third decade without finding a wife."

"Well, I'm hardly most mothers. I hate to see you limit yourself to one person." She brushed a speck of lint from his sleeve, adjusted his collar. "When I think that you could have been High Priest . . . and now you scarcely ever go . . ."

"Have I ever missed a festival or a holy day? Don't worry, Sybil. I'll not shirk my duties. It's just that I know I can have anyone at the Temple, man or woman. So there's no challenge."

"Challenge." Sybil shook her head. "He wants challenge. Sweet Talopea. Four children, only one follows my path, and then he decides he prefers coaxing virgins instead of enjoying full pleasures."

"Jessa's still young enough to change her ways," Mischa said, grinning at the girl.

She stuck out her tongue. "I'll keep my clothes on, thankee brother."

"I never should have named you after that woman," Sybil said. "I knew it was a bad idea, but Rayke insisted . . ."

"I'd best be going, or Yolanda might think I've given up my assault upon the ramparts of her virtue." Mischa cinched his swordbelt around his waist. It was finely-tooled leather, with a buckle designed to resemble Talopea's holy symbol.

Jessa snorted. "Thus girds himself for battle does the mighty warrior."

"Hush up, carrot-hair. I've found ladies like a man who looks as if he can defend them."

"*Looks* as if, indeed. You'd not hit the ground but for the pull of the earth."

"Be off with you, naughty child," Sybil said. "What kind of an example have I been to you?"

"The kind that made me grow into exactly the sort of son you would have wanted. Don't wait up." With that, he spun to let his cape flare behind him, and strode from his room.

A raised, covered walkway connected the house to the inn. It crossed over a large grassy courtyard, which was bordered on one side by stables and on the other by a garden. The yard was shaded by fruit trees and sturdy tables stood ready for patrons who might wish to do their drinking out in the cool evening air.

Near the back fence was a mound covered with grass and wildflowers. A wooden plaque was posted there, and Mischa did not need to read the words to know what they said. He'd been raised most of his life on the tragic story of the creature whose grave it was.

The inn was nearly twice the size of their private family home. Made of brick and stone, it stood three stories tall, with multiple chimneys protruding from the slate roof. In its shadow, two figures grunted and grappled and kicked up clouds of dirt.

"Unh."

"Ouch!"

"Baby."

"No, you trod on my foot . . ."

"Oh . . . baby."

An observer might have thought they were having a genuine fight, but Mischa knew that what his idiot brothers did, they did of their own choice. He paused to watch with a bemused grin.

Rayle, at twenty-two, was a near-perfect duplicate of his father. He had the height, the build, the blazing red hair and the crooked mercenary's smile. Stripped to the waist, glistening with sweat, he swung a heavy broadsword in arcs and swoops and lunges.

He would have been a fine figure of a man if not for the scars, in Mischa's learned opinion. Not that the two serving girls dawdling over their work in the garden seemed to mind . . . for all the good it did them. Mischa had never been able to understand how any son of Sybil's could prefer swordplay to loveplay.

Well, Josef had more reason than most, he supposed. Only a year removed in age from Rayle, the boys had been raised virtually as twins. But where Rayle caught the attention of girls, Josef made them turn away despite his formidable musculature.

Josef was more broadly built than Rayle, and taller. He had a barrellike chest and arms thick as tree trunks. His skin was a yellowish-olive hue, darkened to a rusty tan by the sun. His black eyes were small and set close together under brows that shadowed half his face. Short tusks jutted from his lower jaw, making it difficult for him to close his mouth all the way.

As the final cruelty, making the rest of him seem all the more hideous, orckin Josef was the only one of Sybil's children to inherit her thick golden hair.

"Still at it?" Mischa leaned over the walkway rail to give the girls a chance to admire his attire and show them that style and grooming were much more appealing than sweat and dust.

Rayle looked up and grinned broadly. "Watch this." He whirled the sword over his head and shoulders in a pattern that looked impressive but probably wasn't very effective.

"You didn't hit yourself this time," Mischa said. "Looks like you're getting better."

"I haven't hit myself in weeks," Rayle said, flushing.

"That's because you've been too slow healing from the last time to try it again." Josef, for all his fearsome looks, had a voice that was surprisingly even and pleasant to the ear. He occasionally slurred certain sounds thanks to his tusks, but that in Mischa's opinion only gave him an exotic almost-accent.

The girls tittered, and Rayle scowled. "I'm healed enough to whip your hide raw."

Josef immediately dropped into a wrestler's crouch. "Come on, then. I'll try to stay off your tender feet . . . baby."

"You two go on and beat the sauce out of each other," Mischa said. "I'm off for a true evening's entertainment."

The back door of the inn opened as they grabbed each other in strangleholds. Rayke stepped onto the porch.

"Boys!" he bellowed in a voice that could cut through the noisiest of barroom brawls.

The serving girls, the cook's nieces Sella and Naritta, quickly bent to their work again and tried to look busy. Rayle and Josef released each other and turned toward the large man, whose once-fiery hair was thickly streaked with white, and his beard was entirely grey except for a reddish blaze under his mouth.

"We were just practicing," Rayle said, wary, glancing at Josef as if to ask what they'd done this time and how much trouble they were in.

"And doing well, as usual," Rayke said. "But fetch your mother and sister down here. There's some visitors here you must meet. You, too, Mischa, come along."

"I'm going out," Mischa said. "Yolanda Martane."

"Your choice," Rayke shrugged. "I just hope you don't regret it for the rest of your life when you hear who you've missed."

His curiosity sparked – Rayke was not normally one to be coy – Mischa hastened across the walkway to a wide staircase that descended into the common room. A huge stone fireplace, big enough to roast an ox, dominated this space. At the far end was a raised stage where entertainers sometimes performed, and extending out from it was a newer addition, a partly-formed wall of glass blocks. Into this wall were set plaques of engraved steel, each bearing the name of a soldier who'd perished during the Keydan Campaign.

Sybil and Jessa caught up with him as he started down the stairs. "What's all the shouting about?" Sybil asked. "I could hear him even with the shutters closed."

"I don't know."

Josef and Rayle had come in from the courtyard, and both stood thunderstruck with expressions of amazement. The other patrons, few so early in the day, had left off their conversations and gambling to look at someone talking to Rayke.

Mischa moved closer to see who could draw such attention, and his own steps faltered to a standstill. He had to hold onto a table to keep his balance. Sybil stopped short with a soft sound of surprise.

"Blessed Talopea," Mischa and Sybil said together.

"You must be Sybil," the silver-haired enchantress said, her voice like rain on a waterfall and her welcoming smile like the rising sun. "You look just as I always pictured you."

Her face was stunning, her eyes were like sapphires of inestimable worth, her body was one made for long hours of worship on silken sheets, and Mischa could only stare.

Over a close-fitting suit of some fine, shining silver cloth, she wore a white doeskin riding outfit trimmed in sky blue. A thin swordbelt was slung low on her curved hips, supporting a saber on one side and a dagger on the other. A pale gem, shimmering with rainbows, nestled in the warm valley between her breasts. Mischa envied that stone its resting place.

"Well?" Rayke asked, a smug grin splitting his face. "Do I even have to introduce them?"

Them? Mischa noticed a scrawny little boy standing beside the woman, dismissed him in a heartbeat and went back to his admiring inspection of the woman.

"No, you don't," Sybil said, tears brimming. "Why, look at her, I know her as well as I know any of my own children. With that hair, and my Cat's pretty blue eyes, you must be Ariana."

"Ariana," Mischa echoed. He'd grown up on stories of his mother's friend Cat and her forbidden love with an exiled elven mage, and remembered them from Sybil and Rayke's marriage ceremony all those years ago. He'd known they had a daughter, but he'd never thought . . . never even *dreamed* that she would look like this.

"And this must be Tal," Sybil said, addressing the scrawny boy. "Are you as much of a trouble-maker as your mother always was?"

"More," Ariana said.

"They've come up from Tradersport on their own," Rayke said.

"Your parents aren't with you?" Sybil looked crestfallen. "It's been so long since we've seen them. How do they fare?"

"Fine and well," Ariana said. Her eyes met Mischa's, and he half-expected her to react with anger to his open appreciation. Instead, she glanced him over appraisingly, undaunted.

"I'm Mischa," he said, stepping forward and taking her hand. As he kissed it, he let his finger-tips brush the underside of her wrist and press suggestively into her palm.

"These are my other boys, Rayle and Josef," Sybil said. "If they can reel in their tongues long enough to say hello," she added, making the pair grin and fidget awkwardly.

Josef tried to hang back and make himself inconspicuous, as he always did when introduced to someone new. But Ariana would not have it. She went directly to him and threw her arms around him. His size and strength were rendered useless in the face of his shock as she kissed his cheek.

"I remember your father," she said. "Unca Alphonse, I called him when I was small. He was a great hero, and I loved him very much."

Josef went an even darker shade, now nearing the smoky iron red of a dwarf's furnace. "I never knew him." His deep, dulcet voice was a mutter. He put his big callused fingertips to his face. It was, Mischa suspected, the first time he'd been kissed by any female other than their mother and his former nursemaid, Zura.

"And this sprout is our little Jessa," Rayke said, swinging the girl up onto his shoulder.

"Da, quit it."

"Come and sit and tell me everything. How is my darling Cat?" Sybil asked, pulling Ariana toward the fireplace. "I've missed her so. What brings you to Thanis?"

"Give her a chance to breathe, Sybil," Mischa said. "And a glass of wine, I think."

"Ari's looking for adventure," Tal said as they all took seats around the big table.

"She's found it," Mischa sat close beside her. "Have you ever been to a Talopean Spring Festival?"

"Mischa." Rayle kicked him under the table. "She's our guest."

"I was only being friendly."

"No fighting at the big table," Rayke said. "You boys know that. Tal and Ariana are our guests for as long as they'd like to stay. Almond-stuffed goose and strawberry pie for dinner?"

"Strawberry pie . . . I adore strawberries." Ariana moaned, closing her eyes, and Mischa had to clench his fists to control himself. That was what she would look like in the very throes of pleasure . . . only moreso . . . and he could not wait to see it for himself.

As Rayke busied himself bringing platters to the table, there was inconsequential chatter that Mischa barely heard. He thought once of Yolanda Martane and then let her slip from his mind as easily as a scrap of silken undergarment might have slipped from his hand. He distantly heard the scrawny boy asking Rayke if he had been in the war, gazing with awe at Rayke's scars.

Rayke said something about how he had been, yes, for a while, but soldiering hadn't suited him. It had, he said, made a man of the Highlord though. And then they went on to talk about the

Highlord, his two sons Duncan and Geoffrey, his daughter Karina.

At that, Mischa felt compelled to contribute. "Well, perhaps they're all his . . . we only truly know that the High*lady* has three children."

"Let's not argue this again," Rayke said. "It's pure gossip and has nothing to do with us."

"It will if it becomes a matter of succession," Ariana said. "That's set Gamelin on end even now."

Then they had to talk about that for a while, boring matters of nobles and their governments. Mischa noticed that Ariana did seem quite well-versed in the way such matters worked, but what a waste of time that could have been spent on far more enjoyable subjects!

"You'll have to visit Talus Yor," Sybil said. "He and Arien were such good friends. And Pellander, that funny little librarian."

"There's so much to see and do here," Ariana said. "I'd like to visit Alphonse's grave . . . and even Alinora's. I feel I should do that before I go to the Emerin."

"The Emerin?" Rayke frowned. "I don't think that's a good idea, sweetheart. Why would you want to go there?"

She raised her chin and looked Rayke straight in the eye. Her voice was calm but sure. "I'm going to clear my father's name."

Sybil patted Ariana's hand and looked at Rayke. "She's on a quest. Just like those silly parents of hers."

"We shared in more than one of their quests," he said. "What if we –?"

"Oh, no you don't," Sybil said. "We're far too old and settled for that sort of thing."

Rayke flexed his arm, and the seams of his shirt strained. "Old, but not dead."

"I've better things to do with what heat remains in your blood, you randy bull."

Jessa made a disgusted noise.

"My brother cannot go with me to the Emerin," Ariana said. "Yet Tradersport has become dangerous for him –"

"Following in Cat's boot tracks, I'd wager." Rayke laughed. "Whose purse did you cut, boy?"

"It wasn't like that." Tal drew himself up and stuck out his narrow chest. "A man meant to have me killed."

"We hoped that perchance . . ." Ariana turned those heart-stopping eyes on Sybil.

"Oh, of course," Sybil said. "He can stay as long as he likes."

Josef stammered, cleared his throat, and said gruffly, "But you . . . uh . . . you shouldn't go alone."

"Yes!" Rayle sat straight up. "We'll go with you. Josef and I."

"Don't be fools," Mischa said. "Neither of you would survive a day in the Emerin. They live by their wits and manners there."

"Oh." Rayle glanced at Josef as if seeing his countenance for the first time. His thoughts might as well have been hung in letters of bright fire above him. "We'd not fit in."

"Which is why *I* will accompany Ariana on her journey."

Rayke coughed into his ale, spraying ale foam. "Mischa? You? Through war-ravaged Keyda? You?"

"Hah!" Rayle slammed a fist on the table. "We might not survive *in* the Emerin, but you'd never reach it, fancy-lad."

Sybil leaned forward and propped an elbow on the table. Though she was more ample now, especially in the hips and waist, her bosom remained as awe-inspiring as ever. She could still stop any argument with the right pose and a deep breath. "Calm yourselves, my menfolk. I think it would be a *wonderful* idea for Mischa to go with Ariana."

"I can manage on my own," Ariana said, drawing herself straight-spined and indignant. "I don't need a guardsman, or a nanny."

"I'd be neither, I swear."

"Mischa is a trained priest in the ways of Talopea," Sybil said.

"Is that meant to convince her or warn her?" Jessa asked.

"The goddess grants me the power of healing," Mischa clarified, prodding Jessa in the side where she was ticklish. She squealed and twisted away. "And I can use a sword."

"As a fashion accessory," Rayle said, nose wrinkling.

"You've always said you'd rather be dragged naked through a pit full of rats than leave Thanis," Rayke said.

"And you've always said I could use travel and experience and life-lessons," Mischa replied. "If Ari is to carry on in the family tradition, why not me as well?"

"He's only one thing in mind," Jessa said to Tal, in an aside that nobody missed.

"What say you, fair lady?" Mischa asked. "The decision is yours."

She surveyed him again, not without admiration but also with considerable dubiousness. "I admit, some company might be welcome, but . . ."

"Then it's settled. When do we leave?"

"He'll need to pack," Rayle said.

"He'll need armor," Rayke added.

Ariana laughed that silvery-waterfall laugh again, and Mischa's throat closed with the old familiar hunger. Yolanda Martane? *Here* was a real challenge.

* * *

CHAPTER FIVE

For all that I have heard, it is not as I expected
– Elwyndas, Nightfall in the Emerin, Verse 25

A stack of books propped the door open. The chamber beyond was cramped and cluttered, seeming small despite its generous size.

Ariana breathed deeply of the smells of ink, parchment, and the musty velvet that was the secret scent of silence. They were all familiar to her, as familiar as her family home. She would not have been surprised to see her father bent over the desk, deciphering some ancient tome in this office that had once been his.

But Arien Mirida was far away, and the man at the desk did not remotely resemble him. Though they might, she supposed, be near the same age . . . for surely she had never seen any human so ancient.

A pair of gnome-crafted spectacles had slipped so far down his round nose that they were in danger of falling off. The eyes behind the lenses were closed. His mouth was slightly open, toothless, and leaking fine threads of saliva. He was not fat, but there was a soft puffiness about him. Wisps of white hair floated around his pink skull, and his skin was as smooth and unwrinkled as that of a baby.

She heard a muffled clatter-rolling sound, and turned to behold a tall, twig-thin figure backing out of a closet-sized room. His scant hip held the door as he maneuvered a wheeled cart piled with books into the hall.

"Librarian Pellander?" she asked in a discreet Library whisper, not wanting to disturb the sleeping old man.

Pellander jumped. The door started to close, striking the cart and sending a stack of books to the carpeted floor. He tried to catch them, his bony hands moving like a flock of alarmed birds, and only succeeded in toppling another stack onto his feet. As he winced and hopped in pain, he lost his grip on the remaining books and they cascaded to join their brothers in a litter of open covers and exposed pages.

"I'm so sorry." Ariana hurried to his side, trying not to laugh.

"My fault," Pellander said, somehow managing to keep his voice low and soft, the hushed tones of all the Librarians. He stood on one foot and rubbed the other, long legs bent like those of a marsh-wading crane, robes hiked around gangly knees. "I didn't see you, milady."

She bent to pick up some books. "I shouldn't have startled you."

He drew his brows together over a nose like a letter-opener. "Do I know you? You look very familiar."

"I am Ariana Mirida. You once served my father."

"Arien's daughter!" Sudden dread swept over his face, eclipsing a delight that had not even had time to more than begin to form. "Of all times, why now? I was in the middle of reorganizing the archives. The place is all storm and chaos, I never wanted him to see his Library like this."

"My father is in Tradersport."

Pellander's entire body sagged in relief. "Oh, good. Not that I don't want to see him, you understand, but . . ."

"The Library is magnificent. I've never seen its like."

He puffed up with pride, and she wondered how he had ever been able to be involved in any plot against Solarrin when his every emotion was expressed by his entire body. "Do you really think so?" He offered his hand, realized it was streaked with ink and dust, withdrew it, wiped it on his robe, and offered it again.

She grasped it quickly, before he could pull it away for some other reason.

"So, what brings you to the Library?" he asked, bending to gather more books. "Visiting your father's old haunts?"

"And my mother's," she said. "I've just come from the Empty Mug."

He jumped again, looked around and hissed a shushing warning at her. Then, seeing that nobody was nearby, he motioned for her to continue. "Sorry. It's best if no one knows about my connection with the Nightsiders."

"Of course." Her lips kept wanting to smile.

"What did you think of my old friend, Calidar?"

"He's not . . . not as I expected," she said. "Not at all like my mother or grandda. He seems hard, cruel. And the others . . . there seemed to be an animosity among them that I hadn't expected, either."

Pellander nodded and finished replacing the spilled books on his little cart. He did not seem aware that Ariana was still holding several volumes. "The Nightsiders are divided. Half of them think Stryker should take command, but he won't while One-Eye lives."

"It's the Wasting Sickness, isn't it?"

"The Baroness Jolda was the first to fall ill with it, but most of the elder people in the city are showing the signs. Now One-Eye. He's a tough old soldier, though. He could linger for years yet. Look how long the Baroness has lasted. It's uncanny, I tell you. Odd, I thought I had more than this . . . oh, thank you." He relieved her of her burden, added the books to the cart, and almost caused another avalanche in the process.

"Do you know how to find One-Eye? Mother sent a letter with me. I didn't quite dare give it to Calidar, not once I'd met him. You say he's your friend?"

"He was. He still is. But Calidar's changed since the war. Captivity in Hachland didn't suit him. He snuck into Rappikan and kidnapped Princess Violet so Talus Yor could question her and learn the truth of what happened in Casteban. They caught him, after. Ever since, well, let's just say he's grown into ambitions of his own, and bitterness weighs heavy on his bones. Is Haleric – the Lord High Librarian – still sleeping?"

She peeked through the propped-open door. "Yes, like a baby. Will you succeed him when he retires?"

"Me?" He laughed. "I don't want the post. It's too much work, far too much."

Far too much work? More than he was already doing? She started to speak her mind on that matter, but gave it up. Pellander left the cart askew in the hallway and led her to a tiny room that was more closet than office. It had a window, blocked by a bookshelf. It had a desk, heaped with scrolls and sheets of parchment. Several empty kofa mugs made a precarious stack on a small round table, next to a plate holding a half-eaten pastry so old it was doubtless hard as a rock.

When Pellander wedged his angular form behind the desk, his head barely cleared the lowest of yet another set of book-crowded shelves. Ariana shifted a stack of unanswered Library correspondence to a table and sat down.

"The best one to see your letter to One-Eye would be Talus Yor," Pellander said. "He's been looking after him, though not even an Archmage's magic can cure the Wasting Sickness. Nor can the priests. Some say it's a punishment from the gods, for the war. Others claim it's a curse."

"What can you tell me of the elves? I mean to go to the Emerin, and I'd like to have some idea of what I'm walking into."

He reached up without looking and plucked a book from its place. She cringed, expecting the rest of the books to come with it and bury the gawky man in paper and binding, but they all remained steady.

"The Starleaf Council rules the Emerin now. High nobles. Counts, for the most part. Including . . . I'm afraid to say . . . Alinor Elyvorrin. You know who he is, of course."

"Yes. It bodes ill for my chances of getting my father's name restored."

"Now is not a good time to visit the Emerin," Pellander said. "You could ride into the middle of a civil war. Uncertainty breeds fear, even in the wise elves."

"I still must go there."

"I'd not try to stop you," Pellander said. "I knew your parents. They never gave up when all seemed impossible either."

* * *

Mischa picked up two shirts. "The royal blue or the pale blue?"

Josef grunted. "Silk. Pah. You won't last a week."

"Those dark-elves, the what-do-you-call-them, the *Morvalan*, they aren't going to care if your outfit matches," Rayle said. "They'll be more interested in trying to cut you open and string their bows with your gut."

"But the Emerinian maidens will care," Mischa said. "How am I to impress them if I look and smell like the two of you?" He folded both shirts and tucked them into the large backpack.

"Not a week," Josef repeated.

"Try this on." Rayle handed him a breastplate. "It should fit you."

"This is pointless."

"Weapons won't be." Josef went behind him and cinched the straps.

"Not so tight!"

"Quit whining," Rayle said, tossing Mischa a helmet.

He tucked it under his arm and went to look in the long mirror that had arrived from the glaziers just that morning. "Why, this isn't half bad," he said, surprised, as he turned back and forth. "Heavy, confining, but I look every inch a hero. And ladies, especially noble ladies, are very fond of heroes."

"Haarkon's bony buttocks, Mischa, you're the vainest thing I've ever seen." Rayle dropped onto the bed, disgusted.

"He'll never make it," Josef said. "Maybe we should go with him anyway."

"You heard Father," Rayle said. "He'd give us a wallop that would make Steel's own head ring."

"The last thing I need is my two brothers along and in the way, thank you. I'd much prefer to be alone with the fair Ariana."

"Try anything with her, and you'll need this armor." Josef knocked his rough knuckles against the metal. "It won't do much against magic, though."

Ignoring Josef's remarks, Mischa checked his reflection again. "She is without question one of the loveliest creatures I've ever seen. If even half the Emerinian maidens are her equal, I might never come home."

"You'll turn tail and run for the nearest inn before the week is out," Rayle said. "Loveliest creatures or no."

Mischa slammed the helmet onto his head. "You'll eat those words, brother mine. I'm off to enjoy the pleasures of the Emerin, while you two stay stuck here at home, doing chores. It's summertime soon, and you know what that means. Time to clean the loft."

They groaned in genuine dismay.

Mischa scanned his room for any forgotten items, then shouldered his backpack. He staggered, almost dropped it. "Oof. What's in here?"

"All the rubbish you put in there," Josef said. "The scented oils, the bottles of wine, the jars of strawberry jam . . ."

"She adores strawberries."

"When he dies," Rayle said to Josef, "I get his room."

* * *

Human by birth but raised by the magical god-servant Avantari, the Archmage Talus Yor had walked the world even longer than Ariana's own father. In her mind, somehow, that meant he should be venerable, wise and unearthly, radiating awesome power.

Surely his Tower, which rose in spiraling heights above the turrets of the Highlord's castle and was surrounded in a pearlescent mystical light, lent weight to her expectations. Matched dragon sculptures guarded the door and seemed to watch her as she passed. Man-sized clouds of pale mist took her cape and showed her to the waiting-room. Everything she saw gave off its own distinct magical aura.

He came in looking dashing and handsome and barely older than Ariana herself. Although her parents had told her all about him, this still came as a surprise. It shouldn't have, which left her chagrined at that surprise. As a result, she was knocked altogether off-kilter before he even said a word.

His hazel eyes were twinkling with delight, though there was an underlying glimmer of sorrow. In them, at least, she saw the age and hard experience she expected.

"Ariana Mirida. You are as beautiful as your father always boasted." He caught up her hand and kissed it in the elven style. Lingeringly, thrice, once on the back, once on the palm, and one last kiss on the tender flesh of her inner wrist.

"And you, sir, are as daring as my mother always warned me," she said when she could find her voice.

"Dear, pretty Cat finds me daring? Had I known that sooner, I might have tried harder to steal her away from Arien."

"Great as your powers may be, Archmage, there is no magic in the world capable of that. Govannisan curses could not keep them from falling in love, shadow beasts couldn't destroy them, and the gods themselves could not wrest them apart."

Yor released her and stepped back, grinning. "Then I shall have to set my will toward winning you, if your mother is to be forever denied me."

Ariana pressed her fingers to her temples. "I am plagued by suitors. Thank the gods for Mischa. He at least only wants to bed me."

"Suppose, then, I settle for asking you to dinner?"

* * *

The cool night air whipped tendrils of fog across the pale moon. It was half-full, as if Livana turned her face away like a shy maid. A few stray petals fluttered in the breeze, blown across the tended lawns of the Lord's Retreat.

"Now that you've dined and danced, how do the humble entertainments of Thanis measure up to colorful Tradersport?" Talus Yor asked as they walked a secluded path through the gardens.

"Even more opulent and splendid than my parents described." Ariana said. "I wonder, could that be the very rosebush where my mother hid to listen to the lords plot?"

"It may be. But that was many years ago. Even this place has changed much since then. It's owned by elves now, did you know that?"

"It's just as well that Tal didn't accompany us."

"My little namesake," Yor said, chuckling. "He's hit it off well with Sybil's brood?"

"With Jessa, at least. They have a flair for mischief. I hope Thanis will still be standing by the time our parents send for him."

"To withstand civil war and foreign invasion, only to be brought down by one boy . . . that would make for an embarrassment indeed. I'd hate to see all my hard work with Jarrell undone." He plucked a blue-violet bloom and tucked it into the regally braided coronet of her hair. "As you grace the garden with your loveliness, so let it return the favor."

"I see now why your legendary list of conquests is so long," she said. "You are sweet-spoken indeed, Archmage."

"Conquests. Such a word."

"What would you call it? Your many seductions?"

"I merely enjoy the company of fair and clever ladies. And, dare I say, they do not find it an ill-spent use of their time."

"Are you certain you're an Archmage and not a Talopean?"

"I've nothing against their faith, and certainly nothing against their Spring Festivals, but I assure you, I'd make a very poor priest." He laughed. "I've seen Sybil's son. Your mother would be horrified at the very idea of him as your traveling companion, if she's still as I remember."

"When it comes to what Mother calls *that*, she assuredly is. But I've no intention of becoming a notch on a Talopean's bedpost, not so easily."

They came to an area with a lovely marble fountain. Ari removed her glove and trailed her fingers in the water. "I could stay here forever," she sighed.

"You couldn't afford it and neither could I." He sat on the edge of the basin and stretched out his legs, gazing into sky. "Look."

She glanced up in time to see a blaze of white fire sketch its trail across the black canopy. "A falling star," she said, sitting beside him.

"Stars don't fall."

"No, I suppose they couldn't," she said, smiling. "They're just holes, after all. Holes in the skull of the great sky giant."

"What?"

"Alphonse once told me that the world rests inside the head of a great sky giant, who does battle with other giants. The stars are tiny holes knocked in his skull by the clubs of his enemies, and the sun is his ear. Light shines through from outside, you see."

"And how did he explain the sky being blue?"

"He told me all giants' skulls were blue on the inside. When I didn't believe him, he brought me a blue piece of bone to prove it. I believed him for the longest time, little knowing that it was some shard of orc skull he'd painted himself."

"Ah, to have lived such a childhood," the Archmage said. "Capable of such wonder and delight. The young outgrow it so quickly. It seems like yesterday that Duncan was a bowlegged babe toddling the palace halls. Before we know it, he'll have sons of his own. And Geoff . . ." His voice trailed off, and when he spoke again, it was quieter. "But that's just what children do, isn't it? They grow up."

"How do you do it? How do you keep sane, watching your friends grow old?"

He shook his head. "Despite my age, I'm not the one to ask. I lived most of those years in the Halls of the Avantari, where no one changes, no one dies. Duncan, Raneth, and Moriar were the first friends I had in the mortal world."

"I'm so very sorry about One-Eye. I know you are close."

He silenced her with a gentle gesture. "He'll be with his lady soon, and I hope that this time they find the happiness they couldn't while living."

"Was theirs a love like my parents have? One so deep as to make the world hold its breath?"

"You sound wistful."

"Do I?" She pondered it. "Mayhap I do, though I do not know if such a love is for me. I doubt I could give of myself so completely, love so consumingly."

"Nor I. So tell me, then, Ariana . . ." His voice dropped low and silky.

She looked up. Talus Yor leaned over and kissed her. His lips were warm, tasting of rich wine.

"What think you," he murmured against her mouth, "of being a notch on an Archmage's bedpost?"

* * *

"This boat will take you to Siram's Landfall," Rayke said. He elbowed Mischa. "Are you even awake, boy?"

"M'wake." He yawned and squinted at the eastern horizon.

"Have you never been up before dawn?" Ariana asked.

"I've stayed awake *until* dawn, does that count?"

"From there," Rayke went on, rattling the map he held, "you'll ride east along the river to Lambvale, and the road will lead you straight into the Emerin."

"Why not boat the entire way?" Mischa asked. "That sounds more pleasant."

"D'you see this section here, lazyshanks? A dwarven war machine went into the water and it's impassable by all but the smallest boats. Until someone comes up with a way to haul that thing out of there, it's the Lambvale Road or nothing. And as there's not been much traffic to and from the Emerin since the war, nobody is all that keen to get it done."

"Thank you, Rayke, for all that you've done," Ariana said. "I've had a wonderful visit. If Tal gets too troublesome –"

"I'll not," Tal said.

Ari knelt and embraced him. "Be good, and be careful."

"You be careful too." His silver-grey eyes met her blue ones solemnly. "Father says elves don't have to be swordsmen or wizards to be dangerous. He says the ones who aren't are the most dangerous of all."

"I know well enough what Father says." She kissed his cheek.

"And look after my brother," Jessa said. "Gods know *someone* has to."

* * *

CHAPTER SIX

Alas for the soldier, to fight, perchance to die, alone in a foreign land.
– Elwyndas, King Lamerryl, Act 1

"Mischa, behind you!"

He spun at Ariana's yell, raising his sword. A nail-studded club knocked the blade aside. The monster grinned at him, showing black teeth and exhaling a chortle of vile breath.

The ugliness of the thing was nigh enough to slay Mischa on the spot. He had never seen, nor imagined, anything so grotesque. It looked like the union of some liaison between wasp and man, with a hard shell of chitinous brown skin and eyes that were bulging, multi-faceted horrors. Yet it was man-shaped enough to walk upright, and wield weapons.

He was so engrossed in gawking that he forgot for a moment the threat of harm.

Suddenly Ariana was there, springing between them with the litheness of a deer and the savagery of a she-pantera. Her saber came down in a vicious arc and chopped into the top of the thing's head. A brownish fluid sprayed from the scalp, onto Mischa, sticky and steaming-hot and reeking like spoiled milk. His lunch of dried meat and fruit rose thickly in his throat.

Somehow, the creature – would it be a waspkin? as a child born of elf and human was elfkin, and of human and orc was orckin? – did not die. It whirled to swing its club at Ariana. Mischa was treated to a glimpse of a stinger dangling obscenely from its rump. Steel struck wood as Ariana turned the blow. Her face was a ghastly white shock of revulsion and horror, but she did not hesitate to press her counterattack.

Their horses, which they had been leading through this particularly dense clump of woodland, reared and stamped and rolled their eyes. The first waspkin had lunged out of the underbrush and panicked them, a choice it must have regretted for the final few fleeting instants of its life. Shod hooves came down again and again on the crushed body. It had been over so fast that Mischa hadn't been entirely sure of what he was seeing, and then it didn't matter anymore. Only a trampled pulp remained, all broken shell like shards of crockery glued together by a stringy yellow wetness. The smell from it was abominable.

Mischa wrestled down his rising gorge, knowing that he could not simply stand here and let Ariana save their skins. He was supposed to be her sword-companion, her protector. If he meant to win any pleasurable rewards from her, an aim thus far fruitless, he would have to impress her one way or another.

As he moved to her side, he spotted movement in the bushes beyond. A third of the waspkin beasts poked up a stealthy head. Its hands may have been pincerlike, but they had no difficulty holding a crossbow. The barbed bolt swung to aim at Ariana.

"Ari!" He charged, lifting his shield to cover his face and hoping his armor was as strong as his brothers claimed.

Ariana whirled and sidestepped, a graceful dodge that would have been more effective had it not taken her directly into Mischa's path. He could hardly see where he was going around the shield, but realized he was about to skewer himself on her sword. In his frantic effort to avoid such an embarrassing wound, he stumbled into her and knocked her back. She lost her balance and they collided with the club-wielding waspkin. All three of them fell in a thrashing pile.

Something struck Mischa's shield with a jolt he felt all the way up to his shoulder. The barbed bolt-head had plunged through, its point not a handspan from his nose. Streaks of something viscous-green and foul-smelling streaked it. Poison. He had never known that crossbows could fire with such strength. If that had struck him instead . . . even a scratch might have been the end of him.

The waspkin beneath them struggled and twisted. Mischa saw it try to bite Ari's ear. She rolled, and the jagged, dripping mandibles clacked on a lock of her hair, shearing through. Mischa scrambled off and tried to haul himself to his feet, the weight of his armor dragging at him.

The one in the bushes had ducked back down, out of sight. Mischa had no doubt it was reloading. He remembered Rayke's advice to Rayle and Josef about crossbows – shoot it once, drop it, and get a sword into your hand, boys. No point messing about, because anyone you didn't kill with your first bolt isn't going to give you time to load a second.

But the waspkin hadn't benefited from Rayke's wisdom and experience. Mischa, not killed by that first bolt, knew what he had to do. Insane though it was.

He flung aside the shield, not wanting to accidentally jab himself with that poisoned barb. Ari and the other waspkin, their own weapons lost in the scuffle, were punching and pummeling in the dust like common brawlers. Mischa hefted his sword and ran, shouting some senseless, wordless battle cry as he prepared to hurl himself over or through the bushes and –

The waspkin popped up. A crossbow in its hands. A loaded crossbow.

Mischa did not have time to ponder this contradiction of what Rayke had said. He did not even have time to stop his headlong charge.

As he swung, he offered the world's quickest prayer to Talopea to guide his aim, hoping She might be interested in preserving the life of one of Her young priests so that he could continue to serve.

He missed the waspkin but struck the crossbow just as it went off. The bolt that would otherwise have gone into his chest skimmed over his shoulder so close he could feel the breeze of its passage. The crossbow itself was cleaved into splintered junk.

At once, he understood. There had been two of them crouched in hiding, two, each with a loaded crossbow at the ready. When the first had fired and dropped to reload, the second had risen up to take a shot.

Now the first sprang up again and both of them attacked. He hacked wildly, shredding twigs and leaves from the bushes. The waspkin flung away their useless crossbows. One jabbed its stinger at Mischa and he heard it squeal-stutter against his breastplate without piercing the metal. The second waspkin slashed with pincers. He parried one, chopped through it with the blade's edge. Ichor spewed.

The other pincer snapped shut on his arm. Pain overtook the entire world. Mischa had never felt anything like it, never. His torn flesh seemed to shriek as much with offense as with injury. A flood of hot wetness doused him. Blood. His own crimson life's blood.

Then he was on the ground, writhing, gargling choked screams. He was dimly aware that the battle was still going on around him, that freezing darts of blue-white ice leaped from Ariana's hands and battered one of the waspkin like deadly hail, that Ariana's saber passed clean through the narrow waist of the other waspkin and sent its two halves falling in opposite directions. But none of that mattered. What mattered was the enormous sheeting agony that had replaced his left arm.

Did he even still *have* his left arm? He was afraid to look, lest it be lying on the ground some distance from him, the fingers still twitching and curling. He was more afraid to touch, because if he had to actually *feel* the gory, jetting stump, he would go mad. His right hand clawed at the earth instead, clinging to it, digging in, as if he could hold onto life by refusing to let go of this world.

"Mischa?" he heard, as if from very far away.

Not that he wouldn't welcome the next world . . . Talopea's eternal garden paradise. He just wasn't ready yet. There was still so much here he yearned to do, delights he wished to sample, indulgences he craved.

But if he was maimed? Mangled? Crippled?

He shuddered with new horror.

"Mischa!"

A cloudy darkness closed over him, suffocating and cold. Mischa no longer knew if he wanted to fight it or not.

"Ariana . . ." He barely breathed her name, but of course she heard. The darkness drew back as she leaned over him, some glorious silver specter.

"You're hurt," she said.

She was paler than ever. No tears yet glimmered in her sapphire eyes, but perhaps she had not let the full, terrible truth sink in yet. She would weep for him, lovely Ariana.

He feebly reached for her with his right hand. "The joys I could have shown you . . ."

She knelt at his side. Now she would caress his cheek, kiss him, express her regret at not having welcomed him into her bed even once in all the time they'd been traveling. He tried to tell her not to look at the savaged ruins of his arm, to spare herself such a sight that would no doubt haunt her for the rest of her days. But he could not speak. His strength was fading, and soon the darkness would return.

"It isn't so bad," Ariana said.

The dear girl hoped to comfort him, ease his passage with well-meant words. It was kind of her, but not necessary. He didn't even hurt as much anymore.

"Tell Rayke I died bravely," he said with effort. "And . . . tell my mother . . ."

Ariana sat back on her heels. "What are you on about, Mischa? You're not dying."

"It's too late, Ariana. Too late for me. You'll have to go on. You'll have to be strong."

"It only nipped you. Barely more than a scratch."

"My life's blood is pouring from me."

"Your life's blood is oozing out in a thin little line, you ninny. Quit acting like you've had your arm off."

"Haven't I?"

"Oh, for the gods' sake, look at it!"

Mischa risked a glance. He saw red, red everywhere, a vast spreading stain of it, soaking through his clothes. The sight sickened him as much as the warm, tacky feel of it. But his arm was not off. His arm was still attached. He could see his fingers, and they wiggled when he tried to move them.

"I'm not dying?"

"Of course not!"

Realizing she was right, that death wasn't yet upon him although surely it was imminent, Mischa sat up. He examined his arm. The chainmaily bit that dangled from the shoulder of his breastplate – he couldn't remember what Rayke called that part – was rent, and his shirt sleeve was ripped wide open. When he gingerly pushed the cloth out of the way, he revealed a jagged slash in his skin.

He moaned and tried not to faint.

"I thought you Talopeans were trained healers," Ariana said. "That your goddess grants you the power to mend wounds. How can you be skittish at the sight of a little blood?"

"It's never been *my* blood before."

"Are you honestly telling me, Mischa, that you've never been hurt a day in your life?"

"Bumps and bruises when I was small," he said. "And always someone nearby at the Temple to kiss it and make it better. Rayle and Josef, with their roughhousing, were always breaking each others' noses and splitting each others' lips, but I stayed out of their games."

Ariana's fine silver brows had climbed high on her forehead. "Even I've been injured a time or three."

"Why is it so hard to believe that I've been both cautious and fortunate? I am no coward, Ari."

"I never said you were. You *can* heal it, can you not?"

"I can." He cupped his palm over the bone-deep slash ... well, all right, perhaps it wasn't an actual slash . . . a cut . . . and a fairly shallow one at that . . . "Blessed Talopea, grant Your humble lover and servant the gift and the power. This I pray, that I might go on to further Your efforts and revel in all the bountiful and beautiful pleasures of life."

It flowed through him like sweet, mulled honey-wine. He could feel it spreading, a warm glow that abosorbed and consumed and washed away the pain. His flesh drew back together and merged, mending seamlessly, leaving no mark but a faint pinkish line that would fade without any scar. The full glory that was Talopea suffused him. He could almost see Her, a woman-shape of incomparable loveliness and desirability. Body and soul, he responded to Her presence, striving toward Her touch.

As he returned to himself, he realized that Ariana was watching him, still with those dubious brows arched high. She had taken a few steps back and looked poised to flee.

"Do you expect me to leap at you like some ravenous beast?" he asked, unable to keep from grinning.

"Is it always like that for you? A healing?"

"When we heal, we are in full communion with Talopea," he said. "It is the most intimate of all sensations, the greatest of pleasures."

"More than being with a lover?"

"More than being with ten lovers at once. But it does not make us into lust-maddened brutes, Ari, so you need not look at me like that. Although, if you were to suggest –"

"I think not," she said before he could finish. "Your arm is all right?"

"Good as new, though the same cannot be said for my shirt and this dangly chainmaily bit." He went to his horse, which had finally calmed. With washing-cloth and waterskin, he did the best he could to clean up, but he was covered with blood and ichor and other disgusting waspkin innards too vile to contemplate.

"Have you ever seen the like of them before?" Ariana asked, crouching to study with revolted fascination the one she had chopped in half.

"No, nor do I want to ever again. We should move on, before others come from their hive, or nest, or wherever it is that they dwell."

The idea that there might be more of them clearly startled her. She stood, looking around uneasily. "If there is a hive, I'd hate to see their queen."

Which was an idea that had not occurred to Mischa, and one he could have done without. He was more eager than ever to get their horses to someplace where the forest was more sparse and they could ride again. A saddle-weary rump seemed far less a concern now.

Ariana, however, appeared to be of another mind. Rather than rise from her kill, she had drawn a knife and poked curiously at the remains. Her other hand floated above the thing's carapace. Her fingers were fanned. She murmured something in the liquid language of the elves, too low and too fast for Mischa to interpret the words.

"What are you doing? It's dead, Ari, leave it. We should press on. I don't want to be anywhere near here come nightfall."

"I want to know what it is."

"Just a wasp-monster of some kind." Mischa had the reins of both horses, who tossed their heads and nickered, as ready as he was to put this place behind them.

"They used weapons, Mischa. They used cunning. They were not simple, mindless beasts."

"You're not suggesting these things are intelligent."

"No," she said, slowly rising and backing away from the waspkin with horror. "I'm suggesting they are men."

"I think I know men when I see them."

"Well, of course they don't look like men. But they . . . there is magic woven all around and through them. As if they were changed, somehow. Transformed."

"You mean by a spell? Is that possible? And if it is, shouldn't they have turned back into men when they died?"

"There are spells that can alter the appearance," Ariana said. "Beyond a mere cloaking of illusion. An elf might be made to resemble another elf, or even a human, or an orc."

"There is magic that can turn someone into an orc?"

"Mischa, you are not listening."

"I'm listening, Ari. I'm just not understanding."

She sighed and twisted her hair into a quick, sloppy braid, speaking as her hands flew. "I'm afraid I don't understand it much myself, at that. Shaper-magics are rare, and those who weild them often go mad from it. I have heard many different things, some nearly impossible to believe. Elves who take the forms of pantera or wolves or eagles . . . or merge two bodies into one – you need not say it, Mischa!"

"I wasn't about to," he said, which of course was untrue.

"Some say," Ariana continued, heading for her horse, "that the minotaurs were created by such shaper-magic, when beasts of burden were given a more manlike form. Legends of gryphons or centaurs or other such fanciful creatures might likewise be attributed."

"Have you any notion how abhorrent that is in the eyes of Talopea?" Mischa asked, shaking his head. "There are rumors in Thanis of some crazed mage who will, for a price, make an ugly man handsome or a slight woman buxom. If that is shunned by the Temple, I cannot guess what they would say to the likes of what you're telling me."

"I thought you Talopeans preferred handsome men and buxom women."

"We do! But to achieve it by false means?"

"You allow cosmetics, and corsets, and other false enhancements of beauty." She raised both hands and made a negating gesture. "Never mind. What I'm saying here, Mischa, is that these wasp-things . . . they may have once been men. They were intelligent, thinking beings. And we slew them."

"They would have done the same to us." He rubbed at his arm, which was no longer even sore, but the rip in his shirt sleeve rankled as much as any wound. "That one would have bitten your ear clean off."

Ariana shivered, and touched the ragged place where some of her hair had been unevenly snipped. "I know. We had to fight back. We had to. It's just that I've never killed before. I've hunted before, but never . . . killed. Not a person."

"Nor have I. Believe me, Ari, all this mess and violence is not anywhere near as exhilarating and romantic as Rayke and all his old soldier cronies make it sound. But you must have known what it would be like out here, away from civilization. Your parents must have told you."

"They did," she said. "And for that matter, I'm full aware that even the most civilized cities have their share of mess and violence. I've seen it in Tradersport, I saw it in Thanis. I've heard war stories and watched the combats in the Sand Pits."

"You're no swooning maiden, that is of a certain," he said as they began leading their horses away from the ghastly scene. It occurred to him that he had been injured while she had not, and that she had dispatched all of their foes while he'd scored but a single telling strike. He did not point that out to her. No sense making her feel worse. Or making him look worse.

"No," she said. "But it is a sobering thing, Mischa. My mother and my grandfather were both adept at dealing death. Even my father, when the need was great. Still, somehow, I never expected it to be something I'd have to get used to."

* * *

Celinar Elyvorrin threw down his riding gloves and kicked them across the floor.

It was his birthday, his own special day, and no one cared.

Adults hardly ever bothered with celebrating their birthdays, not unless it was for some landmark year like a coming-of-age, or a centennial. And thus, they forgot how important birthdays were to the young.

They were so unfair. Yes, he would miss Grandmother Donystria, but why had she gone and died right now? Everyone was thinking about *her*. All his mother did was weep, all his grandfather did was brood and build toward one of his fits of icy-cold rage from which only Grandmother had ever been able to dissuade him.

Now that she was gone, he and his mother were alone with Grandfather.

And everyone had forgotten his birthday.

He stalked across the room, which was still a child's room, the walls covered with murals of dancing animals and fairies. When would he get a proper room? Probably not until he was forty, of age, and that was still more than a score of years away. He deserved it now. So what if he was young? He was the heir, wasn't he? With Aunt Lionnen having forsaken her claim, there wasn't anybody else. The county would be his, Celinar's. Didn't that mean he should be treated as something more than a silly baby?

"Shadows take it!" He threw himself across the bed. "Shadows take it all!"

He kicked his feet against the velvet coverlet, never minding that his boots were still caked with mud and leaves. Bitter tears stung his eyes. He buried his face in a pillow and cried, drumming his fists and feet on the bed.

Someone tapped at the door.

"Go away," he said, muffled by the pillow.

"Very well."

That voice . . . ? Could it be . . . ?

Celinar was off the bed in a bound, wiping his eyes and sniffling. "Sir . . . Sir Tiercel? Is that you? Please, do come in."

The door opened to admit Tiercel Reyes. Straight and tall, the very image of an ideal knight of the realm. His white belt bore the golden buckle of the Order of the Lion. The sword Lionheart, awarded him by the Council for his great valor during the war, hung at his waist, gold-hilted, the sheath sparkling with gems. Even in ordinary clothes, he gave the impression of being arrayed in glittering mail.

His midnight hair was worn shorter than was fashionable, as the soldiers did to fit it better beneath a helm. It made Celinar acutely conscious of his own, which was shoulder-length, straight and smooth and silken-blond. His mother wouldn't let him cut it.

Celinar stood straighter. He admired all of the knights of the Emerin, but Tiercel . . . Tiercel shone like the Constant Star among the rest. Brighter, more dazzling, brilliant. His handsome face and piercing ice-blue eyes set ladies' hearts aflutter all over Perras Peliani, though he was yet to take a wife. Men, even aged warriors, were quick to obey him. And youths, like Celinar, lived in eternal awe and admiration.

"I apologize for disturbing you," Tiercel said. His impassive gaze swept the room, taking in the dancing animals on the walls and the litter of toys on the floor.

Though Tiercel showed not a hint of reaction, Celinar wanted to die with shame. He hastened ro explain. "This room would have been a nursery, had my parents had another child."

Tiercel nodded. "And, naturally. With the war, your father's death, and now your grandmother's passing, there has not been time to arrange another room befitting a young man."

"My mother's been in mourning. I thought it would be unkind to bring it up."

"Of course. I do not blame her for her grief. Your father was a brave man." His gaze went to the portrait over the dresser, and Celinar's followed.

"My father died because of human cruelty and dwarven greed." How different, that image captured in oils. His father, noble and never-aging, worlds away from the crushed *thing* that had been sent home to them. His mother, radiating calm joy instead of the sallow, melancholy creature she had become.

"Human cruelty and dwarven greed, yes, ever a threat to us." Tiercel closed the door behind him. "Might I sit down?"

"Please." Celinar said, hoping his giddy thrill of excitement did not show. He could not imagine why the noble Sir Tiercel should want to visit him, and was dreadfully afraid that as soon as he asked, the knight would conclude whatever errand had brought him here and then be on his way.

"Celinar, I come to you in confidence, on a matter of concern. May I speak freely?"

He could not contain a shiver as Tiercel addressed him by his given name for the first time. Addressed him as a man, almost an equal, though of course there were none in the elvenwood equal to Tiercel Reyes. "By all means." Curiosity was eating him alive. Why come to him and not his grandfather, if it was a matter of concern? What kind of concern?

"The day will come when it shall be you who rules this House. You will sit on the Starleaf Council, if it still exists."

"Yes, well, I . . . still exists?" Celinar frowned. "What mean you by that? There's always been a Council. Now that there's not a king, we need the Council more than ever."

"And now that we have no king," Tiercel said, "arguments among the men on the Council threaten to tear it, and our beloved Emerin, apart. We have just come from one war, Celinar, come from it sorely hurt and shamed. Now we face another. A war of the worst kind. A civil war amongst ourselves."

"We do?" His eyes felt like they might fall from his head, they had grown so wide. "Can no one talk sense to them? You're on the Council."

"And would mend these rifts if I could, rest assured. I should hate to see the Emerin and our people suffer more. However, I am but an advisory member, new and considered . . . well, inexperienced in government, and occasionally . . . brash. Some would say that my service to your family colors my view."

No one had ever spoken to him like this before. So frankly, so seriously. He was both flattered beyond belief, and frightened.

"You . . . you don't mean to leave our service, do you?"

"If I were to be released, what would become of me? I plan to remain as long as your grandfather permits it, and someday I would serve you as well. My only other course would be to accept an offer of a land holding, and I do not wish that. I love the Emerin too much to call only a part of it my own. By not being a lord, I can feel that it all belongs to me."

Celinar lowered his voice, smiling to show he was speaking in jest lest the knight think him treasonous. "Perhaps you should be king. Then all the lands truly would belong to you."

Tiercel threw back his head and laughed. "Who would have me be king? Each member of the Council has his own ambitions, each no doubt has a long, long list of friends, relations and political allies he'd see on the throne before me."

"I think you'd be a splendid king," Celinar said. "Everyone admires you."

"My young lord is too kind. Believe me, were I by some mischance to have the crown fall to me, I would serve the Emerin's interests with all my heart. But I have not come to you seeking support in some bid for the kingship."

"Then why did you come?" Celinar instantly wished he hadn't asked. Now Tiercel would complete his business and go, and there might never again be a chance for them to sit and talk as peers.

"I have known you all your life, Celinar. I fought alongside your father. Times such as these make boys grow swiftly into men, maturing them beyond their tender years. It seems odd to me that your family persists in treating you as a child."

"Yes!" Celinar sat forward, clasping his hands eagerly. "It seems odd to me, too! I've asked, begged to be allowed proper tutelage, but Grandfather will not hear of it. He watches me like a hawk. He barely lets me leave the estate, and only then guarded as if I were a baby."

"In part, I understand his worry. Your bloodline has seen much misfortune of late. Many have died . . . your aunt, your father . . . and well before they lived more than a fraction of their allotted spans."

"But that's not my fault. Why must I suffer for their poor fates?"

Tiercel sighed. "This war has had a greater effect than we know, a greater effect than some of our people are willing to acknowledge. We have seen more of our people into rosecloth in the past ten years than in the *century* before that. We are sorely outnumbered, and thus, sorely undone."

"Undone? How? I don't understand."

"The humans," Tiercel said. "The humans of the Northlands breed near as fast as orcs, and orcs themselves breed like untamed cats. We elvenfolk wait long to wed, longer still to sire children, and even longer *still* between them. We do not raise large families, and forge dynasties. The son of the Highlord, a scant year your junior, is already within a few years of being wed. Whereas you . . ."

"I won't even be betrothed until I'm forty." Not that he was in much of a hurry. There were some privileges of adulthood he looked forward to, and others he could do without. Maidens. Bothersome, fluttering nuisances.

"We have great gifts, yet they are improperly used." His ice-blue eyes burned. "Our wizards lock themselves away, devoting their time to study, when they could be out in the land causing things to grow or sharing their knowledge with others. A standard elven apprenticeship is thirty years, while a human could go from apprentice to master in half that time. Our courtships? Ten years or more. A human couple can wed and have a houseful of offspring in that same decade."

Celinar shrank back in his chair as he spoke, more than a little afraid of that cold, intense fire in Tiercel's eyes. "But it's the way things have always been done."

"So it is, and is it any wonder that the humans are such a threat to us? If we acted as swiftly as they, our people would be unstoppable. Think on it. A nation of elves, no longer letting the seasons pass like shadows on a wall, but living. Living faster, marrying sooner, having more children. The forest is vast, vast enough to support a hundred times our number. We have empty land standing idle while the Council sits and argues over trifles!"

He fell silent abruptly, uncurling his hands. Celinar saw that they'd been clenched so tightly that the signet on his ring had been impressed deeply into his flesh. He wanted to say something, but didn't know what, and didn't quite dare.

Tiercel took a slow, deep breath. "Forgive me, my young lord. I sometimes fear that I alone in all the Emerin see the terrible threat coming down upon us. It drives me to a frenzy, and I speak out of turn."

"Not at all," Celinar said. "No apology is necessary. You're right. Absolutely. There must be something we can do. Have you any ideas? Any suggestions?"

"We must take action," he said. "The humans not only thrive and grow, they covet what is ours by right as the eldest children of the gods. Their numbers increase and their territories cannot hold them for long. Where will they go? Where will they spread, to feed their thronging broods of children? We cannot pretend that nothing will happen. We cannot permit them to take over our world."

"Take a stand, you mean?" he dared ask.

"Yes." Tiercel's eyes flared anew. "The elves must take a stand. To do this, we need strong leaders and brave men. We need to find those who have not grown soft under decades of passivity or hidebound by centuries of tradition. I came to you, Celinar, because you are young enough to be free of these burdens yet man enough to speak for yourself. You see much. You know much. Far more than your grandfather credits you. Where can I find such people willing to take that stand with me?"

Celinar stood, feeling a fire spark in his heart. "Here! I am willing. I hate the humans, and I loath the dwarves, but most of all, I despise our people for letting this happen. Oh, let me stand with you."

Tiercel's hands fell on his shoulders. He leaned close. Those icy eyes bored into Celinar's own. His expression was pain and hope and wonder all combined. "Do you mean this, Celinar? Do you?"

"Yes! I do, Sir Tiercel, I do."

"My lord, you cannot know how my soul rejoices at this news!"

"Mine too," Celinar said. Tiercel was giving his shoulders such a squeeze that it hurt, and he wanted to yelp like a tagga-dog pup, but he gritted his teeth and told himself to be a man.

The steely grip softened as a sober shadow crossed Tiercel's face. "Yet it may be dangerous. Our people, in particular the older ones, the Council . . . they blind themselves to the truth and seek to silence those who express any other view. If you would escape their influence –"

"I would!" he said fervently. He was more than ready to escape all their influence. His mother, his grandfather of a certain, his tutors, the uppity domestics who for all they were only servants thought that they had a right to tell him what to wear . . . yes, he was ready.

"Then you must take swift action. Swifter, even, than our people are accustomed to do. You must not wait about while your youth passes. You must begin now to learn of the world and develop your talents. What path is it that you would pursue? Magic, as does your aunt?"

"Magic bores me," Celinar said, lip curling in disdain. "My heart yearns to be a knight, Sir Tiercel. Like you."

"Is it so?" He laughed warmly, and clasped Celinar's hands in his own. "My lord, my friend, once again you bring me near to tears of joy. Say the word, and I will take you as my own squire, and teach you all that you need know of the knighthood."

Celinar gasped. His thoughts whirled . . . himself, squire to Sir Tiercel? The famous, heroic, respected, beloved Sir Tiercel Reyes? Squire? Him? Celinar? A youth of only sixteen? He would be envied the length and breadth of the Emerin!

"Sir Tiercel," he said, hating how high and girlish his breathless voice sounded, "I would do anything to be your squire. But my grandfather would never agree."

"I will speak to him," Tiercel promised. "Count Elyvorrin is a wise man. I think perhaps he will, Celinar. I think perhaps he will."

* * *

CHAPTER SEVEN

Do you call yourself Kingmaker?
– Elwyndas, Veriandor, Act VI

Alinor Elyvorrin did not acknowledge the first knock. It was only when the sound came again that he left off staring at the slender ivory sculpture on the mantle and turned to the door.

"Who is it?" he called in so cold a tone that any self-respecting domestic should have withered in shame. "Valannin and Denethel preserve me, I have my wife to wrap in rosecloth on the morrow and when I say I do not wish to be disturbed, I *mean* it."

"Your pardon, milord. It is I, Sir Tiercel. If it is your will, I can return another time."

The one person, now that Donystria was dead, that he could not in good conscience send away. Loosing a heavy, fuming sigh, Alinor flicked his fingers at the door and swung it open. His look, with single raised eyebrow, implied his impatience while still being properly respectful to the knight.

Tiercel bowed, showing proper respect of his own. "I beg pardon for the disturbance, sir, but I must speak with you on a matter of urgency."

"Urgency? What is so urgent that it could not wait until after the funeral? Has the Crystal Throne cracked asunder? Has the king returned from the dead? What is it? Good news or ill? For if it is ill, sir knight, I charge you on pain of your own health to leave it for some other day. I cannot think of news good enough to allay my grief, unless you come to tell me you have at long last done away with the murderous wretch Arien Mirida."

"Nay, sir."

"Then away with you, for that is the only news that would please me. My son is dead, slain in the war. My wife is dead, taken from me by illness. My youngest, poor sweet Nystra, is dead, thrown by a horse that I forbade her to ride. My eldest daughter is dead, twice over if the tales are true, and her death alone can I avenge. The man who murdered her most foully, who revived her as his mistress instead of honorable wife, and who abandoned her to let her die as he cavorted instead with a creature of most perverse mixed blood . . . that man lives."

"Milord, you know I gladly would have slain him before on your behalf, but Ambassador Aethelyn's son bade me not, and I dared not defy him."

Alinor harrumphed. "Aethelyn's son. Since when do you, Sir Tiercel Reyes, give way to Idelhar Fistrel?"

"It was some years ago, sir," Tiercel said. "Before I was a knight of sufficient esteem and reputation to protect me from the Fistrels."

"And Idelhar, I have no doubts, made you spare Mirida only for his uncle the count to fling in my face. Bethelyn seeks to strengthen his position by weakening mine."

"Well do I know it," Tiercel said. "I assure you, they shall not triumph. You should lead the Council. And you shall. Unless you let yourself be ruled by your grief."

Alinor slumped in his chair, drumming his fingers on the carved and gilded wooden arm. "You are wise, Tiercel, wise despite your lack of years."

"I am pleased that you find it so, my lord. I wish only to serve you and the Emerin. That, in truth, is why I have come. I would serve you yet further. I speak of your grandson, my lord. Have you not considered tutelage for him?"

"Send him off to school?" Alinor shook his head. "He is the son of my son, my only heir now that Lionnen has sworn herself to Feyna Rel and forsaken us. I will not send Celinar away."

"I would never suggest such a thing. His place is here. But give him to me, my lord, as squire, and I will train him."

"You would take a boy of a mere fifteen winters as a squire?"

"Sixteen, I believe. Is not today his birthday?"

"Is it?" Alinor furrowed his brow. Fifteen, sixteen, what did it matter? Celinar was still barely out of swaddling clothes. Donystria would have remembered, though. "A squirehood . . . hmm, such would make a suitable gift."

They discussed the arrangements and specifics for a time, over a good dark wine that Tiercel favored. Alinor's spirits lifted as he planned for his grandson's future . . . until it occurred to him that such a conversation should have been held with Celin's presence as well.

"Would that my son had been more like you," he said without thinking. "Celin did not belong on a battlefield. He was a good man, but never sure enough, never decisive."

"For my part, would that my father had been more like you, milord," Tiercel said. "He, too, was a good man, but small-minded and not far-seeing."

"I shall do more than grant you my grandson as your squire." Alinor banged his fist on the arm of his chair, overcome with the perfection of his sudden plan. "I shall wed you to his mother!"

Tiercel froze, thunderstruck, his wine glass halfway to his mouth. "Milord?"

"You shall be Celinar's stepfather and guardian as well as his mentor. Thus, should misfortune befall me as it has my wife and children, I should at least rest easier knowing that you, Tiercel, will watch over my family, and my estate."

"But . . . I . . . I am not worthy . . . your daughter-in-law has not yet mourned the requisite time . . ."

"Be not so modest." Alinor waved the words aside. "I will inform Faessia of these matters. This winter will be soon enough for a wedding, with adequate time to arrange it and yet not so much that we must needs endure all that formal frippery. In the meanwhile, Celinar may begin his training as soon as you see fit."

"Thank you, sir," Tiercel said. He spoke slowly, looking rather like a man who'd taken a ringing blow to the helm. "I am undeserving of this, but I thank you."

* * *

"He agreed. The boy is to be my squire," Tiercel said. He could not contain a blackest scowl as he threw himself into a chair.

The room was windowless, dark and deep, secret or forgotten or never even known of at all by many in the household. It served Tiercel's hidden purpose well, and was a haven when his boot-licking servility to that venomous fool became too much to bear.

"And yet, angered thou art."

He could hear the smiling tone to the accented voice.

"Yes, angered I am. Why must you persist in speaking in that fashion?"

"Our way, it is and for long centuries has been. Thou wouldst do well our ways to respect, for all that thou mayst not entirely for thyself adopt them."

"I do not require a lecture from one who is scarcely more an adult than that whining pup Celinar."

"Why hast fury thy reason claimed? This thy intention was, the boy as thy squire to gain."

"That irksome Elyvorrin. Giving me the boy wasn't enough for him. He promised me his weeping hag of a daughter-in-law to wife."

A low, melodious laugh rang in the shadowed chamber. "And so, fallen hath the mighty Tiercel. Him who wouldst the advances of any maiden spurn, is to a widow betrothed."

"It is not funny!"

"Nay, 'tis. Just not to thee. A small price to pay it doth be, thy aims to achieve and the Cause to serve."

His mouth twisted. "If something happened to the boy, I might stand to inherit the lands and fortunes when the count died."

For a long time, there was no reply. He sensed disapproval, and it made him want to roll his eyes. Some people, for all their lofty speeches and highblown ideals, got skittish when matters came right down to the nit and the grit. Nothing came without a cost. A vow was fine and well, but a vow that stood in the way of one's goals? What was the use of that?

Finally, in a low and unreadable tone, the reply did come. "Thou art in nature most sinister, Tiercel Reyes."

Coming as it did from a *Morvalan*, he couldn't help but take it as a compliment.

* * *

"Celinar," his grandfather said, giving him a hearty and unexpected clap on the back as he strode into the family sitting room. "How good it is to see you looking so well. By Valannin, you have grown. Sixteen, is it? It seems only yesterday that the midwife brought me the news. And Faessia, you are as radiant as ever."

Celinar mumbled something senseless, taken aback. Beside him, her needlepoint a colorful heap on her lap, his mother looked equally stunned when the count bent to kiss her on the cheek. It was more affection than his normally reserved grandfather had shown to either of them in Celinar's living memory, and he did not know what to make of it.

"*Nantor*," Faessia said, her manners refined enough to let her incline her head in polite response, despite her wide-eyed astonishment.

"Here, put that embroidery away, Faessia." He gathered up the fabric and dropped it onto her sewing basket, then took her hands and drew her to her feet. "We must discuss the future of this family, and attend to the long-neglected matter of your son's education."

Celinar's heart leapt, but he cautioned himself not to become too excited, not to show that he had foreknowledge of it. But was Grandfather going to take his mother out of the room? They couldn't mean to go off and decide his fate while leaving him here, could they?

Instead, Grandfather led his mother to a chair by the window, a soft sunrise-colored chair draped with softer lace. Celinar could hardly believe it. That was Grandmother Donystria's favorite chair, and only she had ever been allowed to sit in it

"This . . . this was your wife's chair," she said in a meek little whisper. "None save her have ever –"

But Alinor pushed her gently into it and knelt at her side. "Dear daughter," he said, resting a hand on her arm. "You are the lady of the house. This chair is now yours by right."

She stared at him, open-mouthed. "Th . . . thank you?"

"Our family has been lost in despair for far too long. We have endured great losses, but we must not allow ourselves to dwell upon the past. You still mourn my son."

"Of course I do." She touched her braided widow's knot. "With every passing day."

Grandfather reached up, and Celinar thought he meant to touch the knot, too. Instead, he undid it, and tossed away the jeweled clip that had held it in place. Mother gasped as her russet hair fell free.

"No more mourning," Grandfather said. "Faessia, my daughter in name, you are alive. Yes, Celin is dead, but you are not. He would not want you to pass all your years grieving for him, and he would not want you to be alone. I have taken the liberty to arrange a second marriage for you."

Mother looked like she thought she might be dreaming. Or hoped she was. "What? But . . . I . . . you said you wished to discuss Celinar's future."

Alinor smiled. "Indeed I did." He snapped his fingers, and two domestics bustled in, laden with cloth-wrapped parcels. "Grandson, here is my birthday gift to you."

Celinar tore eagerly into the wrappings. If this was a dream, he did not want it to end. He cradled a helm in his hands. It was shining steel, inlaid with gold designs and the Elyvorrin crest, topped with a feather plume of purest white. "Look, Mother! A helm!" He opened into the others even more eagerly. "A sword! And a shield as well! Look, it has the Lion on it!"

"A squire's array?" His mother sounded baffled, and alarmed. "My lord, he is too young. We are not humans to send our children into adulthood before they are barely weaned."

"Your son is sixteen this day, and ready to begin training. I have given him as squire to Sir Tiercel Reyes, who shall be not only the boy's trainer, but stepfather as well."

"What?" She shrank back in the chair. "What? You cannot have said . . . I cannot have heard you correctly."

Celinar wasn't sure he'd heard correctly either. Could it be true? Sir Tiercel, his stepfather? That would be almost as good as having his own father back again . . . no, *better*!

"He has agreed to take you to wife, my dear."

"To wife? I am a widow but recently!" She wrung her hands, actually wrung them like some tragic lady in an Elwyndas play. "Does the memory of your son mean so little to you that you would send his widow to another man's bed before his blood is even cooled?"

"My son is seven years dead," Alinor said. "His blood is cooled and the flesh fallen from his bones long since. It would be a disservice to Celin's memory to fail to provide for you in all ways. You will wed Sir Tiercel this winter."

"So soon?"

She had gone stark white, as white as the plume on his shining new helm, and Celinar could not understand her reticence. This was Sir Tiercel they spoke of!

"You shall be the envy of women the Emerin throughout," Grandfather said.

With a wail, she threw herself to her knees and clutched at his tunic. "I beg you, *Nantor*, do not do this. My son will care for me."

"A woman needs a husband to look after her. The day will come when your son must devote himself to a wife of his own. Tiercel will care for you quite well."

"I do not love him," she said, and her voice broke in a sob.

Alinor detached her grasping hands from him. "As I do recall, you made such a similar undignified show of emotion when you were first informed of your betrothal to Celin, to your father's shame. Yet you grew to love him, did you not?"

"Please!"

"It is decided, Faessia. Our families have suffered enough pain. I have lost my wife, my daughters, my son. You have lost your own parents, and you have lost your husband. The fate of both our houses rests on the shoulders of that fine young man there. Now rise." He pulled her to her feet. "Rise and share your son's joy. It is his birthday. At tonight's feast we shall celebrate his new status."

* * *

"Elyvorrin worries me," Aethelyn Fistrel said.

"You speak my very thoughts." His brother spoke without turning from the window, which overlooked the wooded hills and lush vineyards of their ancestral estate.

"What of Sir Tiercel?" Idelhar asked. "'Tis him that worries me."

Now Bethelyn did turn, regarding his nephew with surprise. "Tiercel? Tiercel Reyes, bearer of Lionheart? Sir Tiercel the hero? What under the vast sky and lambent moon could possibly cause you concern?"

"Forgive my son," Aethelyn said, giving Idelhar a warning look. "Some years ago, he and Tiercel were friends, but a falling-out occurred between them."

That, father and son both knew, was putting it mildly. Some years ago, Aethelyn himself had been under the sway of the minotaur Solarrin's evil magics, and there was also that unfortunate business between Tiercel and Virine . . .

"A minor disagreement," Idelhar said. "No matter to concern you, dear uncle."

Bethelyn chuckled. "Your son practices your art well, brother mine. So like an ambassador. I am glad that 'twas you that chose to serve the kingdom in that fashion, and leave me the comfortable duties of home."

"For all we know," Aethelyn said, "you could be the eldest and the county yours by right after all. We have naught but the word of a midwife to say which of us first sprang from Mother's womb. In the excitement of such an unusual birth, it would have been no difficult matter to confuse us, identical as we were."

"Mother swore that you were the first, a smooth and diplomatic birthing. She labored hours more to bring me forth, given as I have ever been to stubbornness and tenacity."

"A trait that has served you well on the Council. We meet again in three days. Predictions?"

"Denryl will dredge up that ancient rumor about Shaelan's supposed brother, the founder of his line. Gariel may make some equally preposterous claim. We will argue into the dawning of the next day and settle nothing. False and empty claims all." Bethelyn muttered under his breath, something that might have been a curse. "Wyndrel should not have led the troops."

"We cannot change what was. Yes, Wyndrel would have been a fine king. But now it is left to us to decide the kingdom's future. Shall it be you to rule, my brother?"

"I have no wish to be king," Bethelyn said. "A county is more than enough for my ambition. I would do such a thing if there was no other way, and only to save our fair realm from those other bark-chewing fools on the Council."

"I see now why you were ill suited to become the ambassador," Aethelyn said.

* * *

High Steward Vangier stepped back, admiring his work in the meeting-chamber.

The long obsidian table was polished so that not so much as a fingerprint marred the glossy night-black surface. Six high-backed chairs were lined up along it, three to a side, and the section of table directly before each had been draped with a fine linen cloth bearing the colors and coats of arms of the six counts.

Upon each cloth rested a jade plate and matching bowl, a goblet rimmed with truesilver, eating utensils, a supply of creamy parchment in a white leather case, a gold inkpot, and a quill. All of the items were laid out in precisely the same pattern, all of the chairs were pulled back to exactly the same distance from the table. Even the feathers of the quills had been carefully chosen to be as identical as possible.

Three bowls of fruit were arranged on the table. Each held the same number of pears, apples, even grapes. Pitchers of chilled water had been filled to precisely the same level.

At one end of the table stood a seventh chair, larger and grander than the others. It was shrouded with maroon cloth, the color of mourning, with no place set before it.

Behind this concealed throne, the *valn* tree stretched its branches high toward the domed ceiling. Its leaves sparkled like stars, giving the council the name it had held for generations. Its roots sank deep beneath the marble floor.

The eighth chair had been removed to storage. In happier times, the queen or the firstborn prince would have filled that spot.

Vangier's smile was bittersweet as he ran his fingers over one of the table legs. It was wood, delicately carved, seemingly too fragile to support the weight of the obsidian slab. In the middle of the carvings were marks not intended by the artisan, marks made by an infant Prince Wyndrel's teeth.

The king had just laughed and ordered the marks left as they were. Someday, he'd said, Wyndrel would be a king, and those marks would serve to remind him that he had once been a child like any other man.

"Is all in readiness?" a woman's voice asked, shaking Vangier out of his memories. She curtsied. "My forgiveness, honored steward. I meant no intrusion."

"You merely startled me, Lishalla. I was thinking of other days."

"It is difficult not to." She sighed. "Never before has a time such as this been known."

"We need not worry over it," he said, patting her arm. "There will be a new king. The Council will choose well."

She sniffed with a worldly wisdom not befitting her station. "Laniar says the Council will just fall to fighting each other for it and we might be decades yet with no decision."

A leaf came loose from the tree and landed on the table. Vangier picked it up and ran his thumb over the sparkling surface.

"The fate of our land shall be decided in this room," he said. "It humbles one to think of it. These matters of are too grand for me. I am glad that I was common born."

"Not I! Would that I had been a princess!"

"That is the last thing you should wish. You, a serving maid, have more freedom than any princess would. They cannot marry where they wish, but for the good of the realm."

"Well, I can't marry where I wish now," she said pertly. "A noble knight would never think twice of taking a mere domestic to wife."

He chuckled. "Is it Sir Tiercel who has won your heart?"

She blushed. "I spoke merely as example."

"Ah, Lishalla, Lishalla. You give yourself away. There is no shame in having your dreams."

"There is no hope in it, either."

Vangier tucked the twinkling *valn* leaf into the ribbon of her little cap. "Perhaps not, but wishing harms no one."

* * *

"Prepared, art thou?"

"Yes." Tiercel reached for his cloak, then hesitated. His shoulders slumped. "No."

"Prayer, perhaps, thy troubles might ease."

He let himself be led to the back of the chamber, where a cleverly-made hidden door gave onto a low opening. As they passed through, into a much smaller and even more secretive space, Tiercel immediately began to feel better.

"You are right," he said, though sometimes he hated to admit it and the words tasted like ash in his mouth. "It has been too long since I've prayed. Too long."

The room was small, square, utterly plain. The walls, floor, and ceiling were dull, unadorned stone. In the center of the room was a rough chunk of rock, rising half Tiercel's height. A jagged crystal formation jutted from the top of the stone.

Tiercel drew Lionheart, looked at it, shook his head, and set it aside. "Give me Discordant."

"Here it doth be, the sword of thy true yet hidden self."

Its hilt was so much more *right* in his grasp. Discordant's humming power vibrated through him, sang in his blood.

He set the point of the blade on the floor before him, and went to one knee. The dark crystalline hilt winked dimly at him from above its grip wrapped in dragonskin, and the hum it emitted was faint but now audible as he pressed his brow to the crosspiece.

The other one stood silently behind him, impassive. Mocking him? Judging him? He, Tiercel, was as *Morvalan* as any, more than most. Was not his heritage there in the southland, a strong and glorious history? Yet he was the one that knelt, seeking, needing, while the other stood in firm and unshakable faith.

He raised a gloved hand and made a clutching, twisting gesture. "Kaledhol," he said, and just speaking the god's name made his tension drain away. "Lord of the unseen, protector, destroyer . . . guide me. Lead me to follow the Cause."

The crystal set into the stone began to glow, the colors swirling, spilling, spiraling across the blank walls. Forge-orange chased sea-green chased mushroom-white chased lynx's-eye-yellow, faster and faster. Tiercel closed his eyes and tilted back his head, letting the colors play across his face, seeing them through the blackness of his eyelids. Soon, his mind was at peace and his soul resting well within him.

"Well and swiftly done. A fine *Rhunvala* wouldst thou make, as thy uncle was."

"I dare not pursue such a path," he said without opening his eyes. "Not yet. When Elyvorrin's fortunes are under my control, and the kingdom relies most heavily upon me, when the Emerin is restored to its proper place and glory . . . then and only then shall I appeal to the *Odan Rhunvale*. Then and only then shall I take up and bear the sign of the basilisk."

*   *   *

CHAPTER EIGHT

Sing of the beauty of my people. Sing of their grace and peaceful wisdom.
– Elwyndas, The Song of Shannia, Part One, Verse Six

The advisory members were first to enter the Chamber of the Skies. Each bowed to the *valn* tree and the throne, then took their places in the half-circle of raised seats along the wall.

Hairic was first, Patriarch of the oldest and most respected family in the land. Then came Kysander Feyna, the Emerin's leading Archmage. Next was Doijyn, the King's Armsmaster, his once-handsome face still bearing the scars he'd earned in the war, the scars he'd refused to let the shaper-mages smooth away as if his flesh and skin were pliable clay.

Aethelyn, former ambassador to the human realms before retiring in favor of his daughter Virine, came next. He was followed by Quennar, head of the crafters. Bevain the Huntsmaster and Ostran the Dragonslayer entered together, the young archer supporting the aged, crippled hero. They were followed by Salwyndas, poet and playwright descended from the great Elwyndas himself. Lord Riachlain was close behind, having served on the council a mere thirty-five years, replacing Lord Karadan.

The last four members represented orders of elven knighthood: Sir Melarl for the Knights of the Hawk, archers; Sir Adrial for the Knights of the Eagle, warmages; Sir Danriel for the Knights of the Horse, lancers; and lastly Sir Tiercel for the Knights of the Lion, swordsmen.

Once the advisory members were seated, the counts entered in pairs. First were the two most powerful, the counts of Elyvorrin and Fistrel, followed by the counts Denryl Marrion and Gariel Aistrian. Lastly came Revandir Brindani and Kelnor Valnnatis.

The elves looked gravely at each other. The room was silent except for the soft rustling of the *valn*, and lit only by the light that sparkled from its leaves and reflected in the tabletop.

Alinor Elyvorrin and Bethelyn Fistrel locked gazes, each waiting for the other to speak first.

The tension was broken by Denryl clearing his throat.

"I, Denryl, have called this meeting. The Starleaf Council must resolve the matter of the Emerinian succession. The king has died with no heir, and it falls to those here assembled to select the man most worthy to assume the crown. The Crystal Throne must not remain empty."

"We hear and agree," murmured the seventeen other elves in unison.

* * *

"No," Mischa Narrin said, gripping his head. "This is all one city? It puts Thanis to shame."

Ariana nodded. "Perras Peliani."

"How many elves live here? Tens of thousands?"

"A million or more."

Beside her, poor stunned Mischa grappled with the very idea of so many people living in one place, while Ariana breathed deep of the sweetly fragrant air and looked in joy at the great city.

Towers rose in pearly spirals reminiscent of a unicorn's horn. Graceful bridges arched between them, seemingly too thin to support a mouse's weight but strong. There were no protective rails to offer handholds, but the elves that glided across did not so much as look down. Walls that sparkled like quartz curved seamlessly around ancient trunks. Buildings boasted rooftop gardens and orchards, and in places the trees themselves were shaped into artful, pleasing forms. The streets were divided by raised grassy lawns, all of it more parklike than citylike in a way Thanis could never hope to attain.

All around them, lampposts, doorhandles, even the hinges, were made into the images of woodland creatures or leafy patterns. Each building had at least one window of colored glass designs and scenes from elven mythology. A bowyer's window showed Denethel the Archer hunting a white stag, while the large windows of a music hall depicted a festival of Shannia, the goddess of beauty and song.

The elven men wore tight-fitting hose and tunics of rich fabric, with high collars and flowing sleeves, and light capes worn over one shoulder. They were beardless, as all elves were, and favored long hair. The women wore airy silken gowns with threads of silver or gold woven into the fabric. Their hair sometimes reached their knees, often elaborately styled. Jewelry was much in evidence for both men and women, even down to the clasps of their shoes . . . although no earrings, of course. That custom was distinctly human, unless the rumors of the *Morvalan* ways were true. Her mind shied away from that, which was no kind of thought for such a pleasant day.

"Yet for all the vast Emerin," she said, "which stretches to the distant eastern sea, this is the only city. There are a few other settlements, such as the mage's academy at Feyna Rel, or the Enclave to the north. Larenlan, the southernmost town, was destroyed during the war. All else is here."

"Talopea Herself would be awed at such beauty," he said.

Ariana glanced at him, and caught him gazing raptly at a trio of elfmaids. "You've passed from admiring the city to admiring its people, my friend."

"Not that the admiration seems much welcome." He did not quite pout, but she heard the pouty quality to his voice.

Could it be that he truly still not understand? "Mischa . . . you *do* know that elves generally find humans unappealing?"

"Don't even jest of such things. You may have spurned my offers night after night, but –"

"Oh, oh, Mischa!" She dissolved into helpless laughter. "You came all this way . . . oh, no! You are in for such disappointment."

"Unappealing how?" He flung out his arms and turned in a circle. "What's wrong with a human? Am I not tall, handsome, pleasantly formed?"

"Of course you are! But to elven eyes, you are rather heavy and thickly built, your features are on the coarse side, and you've hardly ears at all."

"But – but I even speak elven." He switched to that speech, butchering it with a strong Northlands accent. "The language of romance."

Ariana put a hand to her brow. "I'm afraid you have much to learn, Mischa."

"You could have told me all this before we left Thanis."

"I didn't realize then that your entire reason for making this journey was cached in your breeches. I thought you wanted adventure, *other* kinds of adventure."

"Splendid." He crossed his arms. "And you think this is funny."

"Well . . . yes."

He looked longingly at a woman in a short filmy skirt, walking a silky auburn tagga-dog along the tree-lined street. "There must be *some* who . . ." He trailed off wistfully.

"If there are, I trust you to find them."

* * *

In the chamber of the Starleaf Council, tempers were running high as flood-water and as barely controlled. Sir Tiercel, bolstered by his recent prayers, remained calm and even amused by the bickering.

"Your claim, Denryl, is ridiculous," Elyvorrin said. "Shaelan had no brother, legitimate or otherwise."

"You speak so easily enough, my lord." Denryl set aside his glass with care, as if he feared that he might snap it in his anger. "Yet I see you providing no proof."

"You are the one that must provide proof," Revandir Brindani said. "You are the one that makes the unfounded claim."

"Unfounded? I have letters, diaries –"

"Which could be falsely crafted," Elyvorrin said.

"Their veracity could be verified." Kysander Feyna flexed his fingers.

Tiercel knew this to be so. Spells at the Archmage's command could indeed back or disprove the validity of the objects.

"Unless you secretly support him, instead of remaining as neutral as you *claim*," Elyvorrin shot back.

"Gentlemen," Aethelyn Fistrel said as Feyna's eyes sharpened into dangerous points. "Let us remain with the matter of discussion."

"Thank you, Aethelyn," his brother said, rising from his chair and signaling to one of the domestics that waited inconspicuously on the far side of the *valn* tree. The domestic hastened to attend him, his face a mask of placidity.

Tiercel permitted himself a small smile. He had discovered as a page something that the rest of the Starleaf Council did not know. The place where the domestics gathered was supposedly beyond earshot, but by virtue of the construction of the room and the odd way sound was carried, there they would be able to hear with perfect clarity all that was discussed at the great table. There was another such spot located just outside, in a sheltered garden nook. These accidents of architecture had proved most valuable to an enterprising young fellow such as he had been, helping make him into the man he was today.

"And who appointed you officiator, Fistrel?" Gariel Aistrian asked. The youngest of the counts held and continually toyed with a braid of indigo hair, tied at both ends with a white ribbon. It was, or so he claimed, hair plucked from the tail of a blue unicorn that roamed his land.

"Bethelyn has officiated the council since before the king's death." Bevain the Huntsmaster spoke as one might correct a child.

"Let he who has wisdom show it by silence," Salwyndas said as Gariel bristled.

Tiercel hid his distaste for the poet by sipping from his glass of chilled water.

"We shall pause soon for midday meal," Bethelyn told the domestic. "Be certain that all is in readiness."

"How can you think of food at a time like this?" Elyvorrin said. "Must the fate of the Emerin wait for you to fill your greedy mouth?"

"If there is a mouth in need of filling, it is yours," Bethelyn said. "It is open overmuch of late."

Elyvorrin pinned his rival with a stare cold as an icicle. "We reach our decision today. It is your last chance to feast from the king's larders."

Before Bethelyn could reply, Doijin the Armsmaster aired his opinion. "Be still!" he bellowed in a voice that had tolled fear into the hearts of dwarven warriors, and slammed his fist on the table.

Several council members jumped, a scattering of leaves fluttered from the *valn*, and the group of domestics that had been straining their ears to overhear every detail winced in pain.

"Well said." Sir Melarl applauded. "I agree."

"As do I," Adrial of the Crown said. He looked to Tiercel. "Brother knight?"

Tiercel donned his most charismatic expression. "The differences between the most noble counts must be settled, but I see no reason why it cannot wait until after a meal." He smiled at Bethelyn with purposeful insolence. "I, too, am fond of the bounty of the royal kitchens."

Bethelyn's eyes narrowed as Elyvorrin chuckled.

Count Valnnatis cleared his throat. "Could we not dine here? It has been done before, and we could continue our discussion. I believe we are all agreed that the matter is one of utmost importance."

"I would suggest that we give ourselves a few moments, at least," Hairic said. "Let the servants bring our meal to table, and give those who would a chance to think."

"Yes," said Ostran. "I fancy a bit of a walk. My legs are too old for all this sitting about."

Salwyndas nodded. "Brighter burns the candle when the wick is trimmed."

Tiercel was glad to see that he wasn't the only one to look at the poet in confusion, but Salwyndas paid them no attention as he rose and followed some of the others to the door. As other conversations quietly began, Tiercel went to Elyvorrin's side.

"The meeting would seem to be off to an auspicious beginning, my lord," he said.

"So it would seem. Would you walk with me, Sir Tiercel? We can the better discuss our strategies away from prying ears."

"It would be my privilege."

* * *

Ariana caught her breath as she passed through the unguarded and trustingly open gates of the royal palace. A straight path of crushed semi-precious gemstones made a glittering river of mingled green and silver-grey. It was lined with hedges, which had been shaped by sorcery into fanciful designs of mythical creatures. She admired a centaur archer, a winged fairy, others.

Other paths branched off to the sides, one leading to a cluster of lacy willows, another to a raised dancing platform ringed with small tables.

Further on was a long stable with a fenced pasture where grooms exercised horses so light of step they could cross fresh-fallen snow without leaving tracks. There was a carriage of such silvered beauty that Livana herself might envy it, with domestics casting spells of cleaning and maintenance on its wheels.

To Ariana, the unseen essence of the place was even more fair than the building itself. The sensation of pure power, of strong *aether*, permeated the trees, the walls, the very earth. She raised her head and threw back her hair, gazing up at the dome that housed the Chamber of the Skies. Pride and a sense of rightness filled her.

"*Andralai*," she said softly. "I'm home. The heart of the elvenwood, the soul of my people, the fairest place upon the earth."

"Excuse me, milady?"

She turned, seeing a man in the violet and white uniform of the royal staff. Three guards ranged behind him at a discreet distance, their bows resting easy at their sides. Ariana had no doubt that, should there be need, those bows would be raised and fired, their arrows striking unerringly, in the blink of an eye. The undefended gates had not been a careless oversight after all. Some other means, some magical means, must have informed them of a stranger's presence. She was glad she'd managed to safely ensconce Mischa out of the way at a tavern across from the Northlands Embassy

"Honored Steward," she said, recognizing the insignia on his tunic and inclining her head. "I greet you. My name is Ariana Mirida, daughter of the Archmage of Gamelin."

He regarded her with speculative eyes. "The Archmage of Gamelin, you say?"

Ariana detected the insubstantial tingle of a spell being cast upon her. He was truthsaying her, she surmised. And perhaps reading the pattern of the *aether* that surrounded her, to determine if she were under magical control or harboring hostile intent.

"None other. I've come to speak with the Starleaf Council."

"The Council meets on matters of grave import to the entire Emerin –"

"I have no wish to interrupt, but can await their earliest convenience."

"High Steward Vaniger!" A youth in a white and violet banded tunic came loping across the grass toward them. "The Council wishes to take midday meal in the chamber."

"A moment, milady, I pray you?" When Ari nodded, Vangier went to the youth and gave him a stern little shake. "Kevan, why come you wailing over hill and valley for me? Cannot Lishalla see to it?"

"She sent me seeking you. There's some problem in the kitchens."

"And did she also tell you to shout so as to disturb all within these walls? You are no longer running errands for the knights. No helm muffles my ears."

"Yes, Vangier," the page said.

"I will be with Lishalla forthwith." He snapped his fingers to dismiss the guards. "But as you are here, Kevan, I've a new task for you. Show Lady Ariana to the Waterfall Terrace. She'll be our guest for the time being."

The boy looked at Ariana, and then went utterly still, eyes and mouth slowly widening.

"That is most gracious of you," Ariana said, surprised.

"It is customary to extend the hospitality of the palace to notable visitors such as yourself," Vangier said. "But I cry your pardon, if you'll excuse me. I must attend the Council."

Ari turned her attention to the boy as Vangier hurried off. "Kevan, was it?"

"My *lady*," he gasped. "I am Kevan Brindani, son of Count Brindani. It is the greatest joy of my scant years to be gifted by the sight of you."

"Your words are kind, Kevan, and I thank you," Ariana said, offering her hand.

He clasped it and looked like he would very much like to kiss it but couldn't quite muster the nerve. "Forgive my bluntness, lady, but are you wed?"

Another suitor for her collection? "Ask you for yourself, or some elder brother or kinsman?"

"Should any of my brothers dare profane you with their eyes, I will see them shorn bald and sent to wander the Wasted Lands."

"You have the manners of a courtier, I see. How many winters have you known?"

"Fourteen, lady. But I have lived a man's life in those years. I am already a trained seeker-mage, and will soon be a squire. Then a knight, then a landed lord, and eligible to wed. So, you see, lady, it is not too soon to begin courting."

Ariana looked him over with amusement. Copper-colored hair shorn into a page's bob, eyes of newleaf green, tall for his age. She smiled. "I am not yet prepared to promise my heart and my hand to any, Kevan . . . yet if I've not done so by the time you're of age, I'd gladly consider the suit of such a daring young man."

He beamed. "As a token of this pledge, then, would you grant me a scarf or glove, or a lock of your hair that shimmers like moonlight on the water?"

"How can I resist such an eloquent request?" She pulled Gavin's knife from her belt and carefully cut off a length of silvery curl. Given that she'd already had a lock snipped off by the waspkin thing, she was sure she could do no more damage by this small shearing. "Here you are."

"You have made me the envy of every other man in the palace, lady. Shall I show you to your rooms?"

* * *

"Tardiness, Vangier? How unlike you."

He knew the voice, which curled like smoke out of the shadows as he came back into the palace. Even had he not recognized it, he would have known who it was by the crimson flush that suffused the nearby Lishalla's cheeks.

"My apologies, Sir Tiercel," the High Steward said, turning to bow.

"The Council dispatched me to see what was the delay with their meal. You've kept them waiting, and there were no pages about to run messages."

And none too happy about it, either, Vangier could see. The hero of the realm should not be scurrying about like a common page.

"I was called away to greet a visitor, who wishes to have business with the Council . . . at their convenience, of course."

"Who might this visitor be? Who could be so important as to take you from your duties?"

Vangier told him, and recoiled from the sudden flare of interest in those winter-blue eyes. He did not know why that look should send such a qualm of misgiving roiling through his stomach, but it did.

"Is that so?" Tiercel said. "How very interesting indeed. Leave this to me, Vangier. I will make mention of it to the Council myself."

"As you will, Sir Tiercel."

* * *

CHAPTER NINE

What spirit listens at my keyhole? What secrets does it know?
– Elwyndas, The Haunting of Jacinth, Act XII

Kevan's feet seemed not to touch the ground as he left the Waterfall Terrace.

No maiden had *ever* left him in such a state. Not even an amethyst-eyed, sable-haired beauty he'd once glimpsed while secretly following the much-admired Sir Tiercel.

"Ariana." He breathed her name, her lovely name, and swayed with giddiness as the blood rushed to his ears.

"Kev? Is that you?"

He yelped, nearly leaping from his skin. "Jennic!"

Jennic dashed up. He was smaller than Kevan, thin and spindly, and similarly dressed in the outfit of a royal page. His strawberry blond hair was tucked beneath a feathered cap. "Have you heard? The Council might choose a king this very afternoon! Oh, Kevan, let us to the hiding-spot. I want to listen."

"Bother the Council . . ." Kevan trailed off. *She* had business with the Council. "Jen, that's a splendid idea."

"Truly? Truly, Kev?" Jen had to trot to keep up with Kev's longer strides.

They snuck out by way of the palace kitchens, where the cooks and domestics were so engrossed in busy gossip that two pages drew no attention. The subject of the gossip, naturally, was the Council and the various prospects who might step forth and claim the throne.

To have a king again was the fondest wish and desire of the entire Emerin, but nowhere stronger than here, in the very palace. For all its grandeur, it was a sorrowful and empty place after the loss of wise old King Shaelan and his son. Not thatr Kev remembered the king or the prince very well. He had not yet begun his service until a year after war's end.

It would be strange to have a new king. Any new king, any king at all.

On their way through the kitchens, he and Jen helped themselves to pastries from cooling racks, then juggled the still-piping-hot treats as they scurried out into the gardens. There was a spot, a secret spot that only the pages and some of the squires knew about, a spot where thanks to some trick of the gods, they could hide in complete privacy and still hear every word spoken within the Council chamber.

No one was watching. Kev lifted aside a drooping curtain of nellis vines and the boys slipped into a small alcove formed by a corner of meeting walls. Within, shade-thriving flowers bloomed in wild profusion. An old stone bench had grown a cushion of soft moss, and tiny violet-winged butterflies danced above the blooms.

"The Council went to dine," Kev said, when a few moments of intent listening brought only silence from within. "They must not be back yet. Here, Jen, look at this!"

His governess always made him carry a handkerchief, though he'd never had need of it until now. He drew it out and carefully unfolded the lace-trimmed cloth. Jennic leaned close, interested, and then puzzled when the wavy silver strands glimmered in the shadows.

"What is that? It looks like a lock of hair."

"It is," Kev said. "That of she whom I will one day wed, if the gods are kind."

Jen's eyes narrowed. At first he looked angry, and then he looked as though Kev might be playing some jest, and then he looked angry again. "What? Who?"

In whispers, trimmed with poems like his handkerchief was trimmed with lace, he told Jen all about Ariana. "While I showed her to her room, she asked me what I knew of the Council. And then asked me, did I hear any news, to be so good as to tell her. It was most fortunate you found me when you did. If they truly do settle the kingship this day, how pleased she will be with me for bringing her the tidings!"

"Have your brains melted and run out your ears?" Jennic whapped him on the upper arm in a stinging smack. "She could be a . . . a spy."

"A spy? Jen, don't be a fool. Since when are we at odds with Gamelin?" He heard a man's voice resonating in the empty air, seeming to come out of nowhere or through the very stones of the wall. "Shh, now. That's Beviar's father. They're done with their meal."

He could well imagine Bevain the Huntsman, with his forest-green tunic stretched across shoulders and chest made unfashionably broad. He had earned it by a lifetime of drawing the *tadis'rel*, the greatbow that few men had the strength to pull. Some said he could sink a truesteel war arrow through triple-layered dwarven plate at a hundred paces. Kev would have given anything to behold such a feat.

Well, almost anything. His hand closed on his cherished favor, the lock of Lady Ariana's hair, and he tucked it away again.

Bevain's words finally became clear as the Council must have resumed their places around the great table. "I speak not only for myself when I say that I am weary of this bickering. We have let the Crystal Throne sit empty long enough."

"Have you not listened, good hunter?" This was Quennar the Crafter. His quick hands were never still. Kevan knew that at the end of the meeting, Quennar's linen napkin would be twisted into a bird or a tree or some intricate shape, and the parchments he was supposed to use for notes would be covered with sketches. "For the past year, the counts have done nothing but attempt to make that very decision."

"Do not speak of us as if we are not here," snapped a third voice.

Gariel Aistrian. Kevan's father said the count was young enough to get away with temperamental outbursts that mightn't be tolerated from older and wiser heads. Kevan's father also said Gariel was sure to run his county into ruin on his mad dreams and pursuits.

"Do you think that I enjoy spending these days here?" he added. "You know that spring is the season when the blue unicorn is seen the most."

"Because spring is the season when the *gerni* mushrooms are at their highest potency," Bevain said.

A ripple of laughter followed his remark, and Kevan could imagine Gariel Aistrian's lips pressed tight and white with fury. The laughter was interrupted by Alinor Elyvorrin, his voice cutting through the mirth as cleanly and coldly as a well-honed knife.

"It is foolishness such as this that wastes our time. Now, shall we address the latest claim, or sit and chatter like domestics?"

"The latest claim is mine."

That quavering, anxious voice belonged to Denryl, count of Marrion. Kevan pictured the tall, thin man with his pale blond hair and eyes set in nests of worried creases. He had an astoundingly large family to support, a wife and daughters with expensive tastes in fashion, sons who went through wine and mistresses at the same voracious rate, and so many grandchildren that he needed a scribe to keep track of them all. Word was that Marrion was trembling on the edge of destitution. No wonder he had designs on the crown. He'd need the royal treasuries to keep himself afloat.

"Ah, yes," Alinor Elyvorrin said. "The claim that your line descends from a supposed Wyndrian Perras, brother to the late King Shaelan."

"It is not a supposition. It is truth. I will swear on the *valn* itself if I must."

"Do not," Bethelyn said. "The *valn* need not bear the stain of your falsehood."

"Falsehood?!" The word, which Denryl probably wanted to be a roar, came out in a strangled squeak not unlike the sound of a mouse with its tail trapped under a cat's paw.

"Said I falsehood?" Bethelyn asked mildly. "I meant rather . . . error."

"Let us at any rate hear of this claim, or error, or falsehood," Elyvorrin said, his tone bored and resigned. "So that we may dispense with it and move on."

"As you know," Denryl said, "my line is descended from our beloved late king's brother."

He got only that far before several of the Council members erupted in outbursts and arguments. King Shaelan had had no brother. Was Denryl prepared to offer proof of this? King Traehormic and Queen Vandinia had reigned ten centuries ago . . . but this was the Emerin, they kept diligent records, by Valannin, and surely something as momentous as a prince's birth would have been written down somewhere!

Bethelyn Fistrel called for silence, and finally got it. "As it happens, good gentlemen, in anticipation of just such an argument, a witness has been called. A witness able to confirm that Shaelan was in fact an only child."

"Preposterous!" Again, Denryl was probably trying to roar and bluster. "Shaelan Perras was in his twelfth century when he died! You cannot possibly have any such witness!"

"My nephew Idelhar will being him in," Bethelyn said, and there was a pause with much low and indiscernible buzzing from the Council. "Ah. Idelhar, thank you."

"Denethel's Bow!" That, of course, was Bevain. "Never have I seen a man so aged! Not even our dear, lost king."

"Will you speak your name for the Council?" The clear, young voice was that of Idelhar Fistrel, and it fleetingly passed through Kevan's mind that Idelhar had once himself been a page. Had Idelhar known of this spot? Did he know, or guess, that they were being overheard even now?

"Folistran, once the King's Physician. I served Traehormic until his death, when I laid aside my medicines." He even sounded ancient, as crackling and dry and brittle as yellowed parchment.

"I knew a physician called Folistar," Ostran Dragonslayer said. "He tended my burns after I faced Eandros."

"He was my son, good sir," the old man said.

"Hold a moment," Elyvorrin said. His words had a winter bite to them, one which Kevan suspected was caused by having his role as leader usurped by this surprise by his rivals, the Fistrels. "Am I the only one to see that they have brought a woman into our midst? The business of the Council is forbidden to women's ears, lest that woman be the queen herself."

"My wife is my eyes," Folistran said. "She guides me by her sight and her wisdom. Without her, I shall not speak here."

"It was my decision, Elyvorrin," Bethelyn said, "to overlook the rules this once. This man bears testimony vital to our discussion."

"The tradition *is* only tradition, not law." Kysander Feyna said. "In the Academy at Feyna Rel, we place no restrictions on the level of study a woman may attain."

"This is not your precious Academy, Feyna."

Kev shivered. He'd not want to be in the Archmage's spot. Everyone knew that Count Elyvorrin had harbored a fire of resentment toward Feyna ever since his only surviving daughter had spurned her familial ties and duties to pursue the study of magic.

"Nevertheless," Aethelyn said, "it *is* merely tradition, not law, that prohibits women from attending the Council. Or even, dare I say, holding a seat upon it."

"I agree with Elyvorrin," Doijin said, and it was easy to picture a scowl twisting his already scarred face. "The Council chamber, like the battlefield, is no place for a female."

"Yes. So too think I," Denryl said, obviously hoping that if they refused to admit the woman, the old healer would leave with his silence held, and there would be none to dispute his claim.

"Oh, for Shannia's sake." That was Sir Adrial of the Crown, a leading favorite among the women of court. "This good lady has not come to take a seat on the Council or interfere in our business. She has come as a loyal wife attending an infirm husband. This we must admire, gentlemen, for who among us will be fortunate to have our ladies by our sides for so long? Are we not noble lords? Are we not knights and wellborn? Where is our chivalry? Barring that, where is our simple courtesy? Tell me, mother of healers, your name."

The woman who replied did not sound old. She had a sweet voice, as high and clear as a bell. "Your words are kind, gentle sir knight, but I must correct you. I have been wed to my husband only ten years, and have no children of my blood. My name is Talian. Talian Maevarra "

"Will the Council hear the words of Folistran, King's Physician to Traehormic Perras?" Bethelyn asked. "Or will the Council not?"

* * *

Talian guided Folistran to a chair that one of the domestics had brought forth. He turned his sightless eyes to her and smiled. She laid her hand along the side of his face and pressed a soft kiss to his brow.

"Is there water?" she asked. "Old throats tire easily."

"Yes, my lady," the domestic said, bowing and then hurrying to fetch a glass and pitcher.

She knelt, her bones creaking slightly, to tuck Folistran's wrap around his feet. On the outer side, it showed the summer constellations in all their glory, while the inner side was lined with soft white cloth. She had made it herself, by hand instead of with the enchanted needles so much the rage among elegant ladies these days. He could never see the designs, but he could feel the love that had gone into every stitch.

The Starleaf Council was watching them, and she could tell that most of them were unnerved by the sight of her husband. They had one among them, called Dragonslayer, and he was aged. They had known their king, and he had been ancient. But Folistran was elder even than that.

"Thank you, Talian," he said, giving her the glass. She patted his hand and moved to stand behind him, her hands resting lightly on his shoulders so that he would know, even in his eternal darkness, that she was there.

"Tell us of the circumstances of Shaelan Perras' birth," Bethelyn said.

Denryl of Marrion looked distressed, looked almost as though he might cry.

"I knew his father well. We were young men together . . . oh, so many centuries ago. We schooled together, though he was a prince and I just a knight's son, and were closest of friends. I stood at Traehormic's side the day we were knighted. I stood at his side on his wedding day. I was upon the dais when he was crowned. There was even a tapestry of us, that once hung in the Queen's Parlor, though I know not if it is there still."

"There is an old tapestry there, encased in glass," Doijin said. "It shows two men, swords crossed as if in combat but laughing."

"Vandinia had it made as a jest, for by then I had laid aside weaponry to take up the mantle of my profession, and Traehormic detested swordplay above all else."

Many of them looked shocked by that, but Doijin nodded. "So it is written. The king was known for his skill, but known more so for his unwillingness to use it. This whim affected his rule not at all, for he had legions of men willing to fight in the king's stead."

"This proves nothing yet," Denryl said. His chin quivered and he firmed it. "Only that he has seen the tapestry."

"You question me?" Folistran's shoulders tensed. "You doubt my honor? I was King's Physician."

"Peace, my love," Talian murmured.

"*I* do not question, honored elder," Kysander Feyna said. "I need not even resort to a truthsaying, for I recognize the truth in your voice."

Mollified, Folistran sat back and groped for the water again. Talian refilled the glass and gave it to him. The hall was silent except for the rustling of the *valn* leaves above.

"Queen Vandinia was healthy and strong," Folistran said, "but the birth was difficult. Sixteen days it took for Shaelan to emerge from his mother's womb. I knew that another child would kill her, and this I told to my friend. He loved his wife too greatly to risk her for anything, even for more heirs. The human priests have great powers, and our magicians likewise, but there are some secrets we physicians have that are unknown even to them. At Traehormic's request, I took steps to ensure that Vandinia would never again conceive. Shaelan was her first, last, and only child."

"Valannin!" Hairic lurched forward. "Did she know what you had done?"

Folistran nodded. "I would never have attempted it without her permission. Far better, she agreed, to see the son she had born grow into a man rather than leave him motherless."

"Count Marrion," Bethelyn said. "You have heard this testimony. Do you yet wish to pursue your claim?"

Ostran Dragonslayer snorted. "Count Marrion might pursue this physician-magic 'ere his brood eat him out of house and home."

"His claim may still in part be true," said one of the other counts. "If the queen was unable to be a proper wife, he might have sired more on his mistresses."

"Treason!" Doijin shot to his feet. "You dare speak treason of our dead king?"

Kelnor recoiled so fast he rapped his head on the high back of his chair. "I mean no treason! A king is a man, like any other, with a man's appetites, and –"

Talian had to speak up. "My lords, the fact that a woman cannot bear children does not make her any less a woman. Folistran, have I ever been unable to be a proper wife to you?"

He smiled. "Nay. Such happiness I never thought to know again."

"She speaks sense," Feyna said before any of the others could protest. "Look back upon King Shaelan. All but one of his wives died childless. Ever, it seems, has House Perras been fated to have few children."

"Ah." Gariel Aistrian chuckled. "That, more than any other testimony, must disprove Denryl's claim. His bloodline certainly seems to suffer no similar affliction."

Several of them laughed aloud, while others hid smiles behind their hands.

"Very well. Very well!" Denryl rose, in his clumsy haste knocking a stack of parchment to the floor and spilling his glass. "I withdraw my claim. Are you well pleased by it?" He whirled on the two counts at the highest end of the table, closest to the tree trunk. "Fight between yourselves, jackals. But know this. My support you shall never have. Not until the day the Ring of Twilight gleams on your hand, or the Emerald of Karria itself sings at your touch."

"The Ring was lost with Shaelan," Bethelyn said coldly. "You know this as well as the rest of us."

Fresh arguments flared like scattered fires all around the table. Folistran's head turned this way and that, but the overlapping clamor was too much even for Talian to follow what was going on. All she knew was that these proud, stubborn, foolish men were never going to come to any agreement on their own.

"Blessed Livana!" she cried. "Listen to yourselves! It is nigh enough to make me glad I never had sons, to have to hear such bickering. Would that you did have this Ring! Or the Emerald, for that matter. If half of what I know of it is true, it would settle your differences and put an end to all this. Then, perhaps, you might accomplish something of use to this land."

Alinor Elyvorrin leveled his steady gaze at her. His green eyes had gone dark as a forest pool of dangerous unmeasured depths. If he knew who she was, if he even suspected . . .

"I believe your husband's testimony has been received," he said. "Thank you. The Council would not keep the Physician overlong, lest he tire."

Folistran paid no attention. "Yes, the Emerald of Karria. In my day, it was told that, of all men, only a destined king could lay hands upon it and call forth its powers."

"With all respect, your day was more than a thousand years ago, elder," Feyna said. "The time of Karria the Swordmaiden has long passed. We have grown beyond such barbarity."

"Still . . . the legend . . ." Aethelyn mused.

"Bright and piercing as the lightning, yet gentle as the glance of a doe," quoth Salwyndas. "Such was Karria herself described."

Elyvorrin flung up his hands in exasperation, ignoring the poet. "You will go to any lengths to avoid a rational solution to this, won't you, Fistrel? What do you propose? That we send a swordmaid to fetch the Emerald from its resting place, as the legends say? That by its touch, we should choose our king? I have heard some absurd suggestions put forth at this table, but that is by far the utmost."

"Indeed," Kelnor Valnnatis said, and laughed. "Even if we were to consider it, where in our land would you think to find such a woman? None of *my* sisters and daughters have been raised as swordmaidens. How ever would we marry them off?"

"It's all nonsense," Gariel Aistrian said. "Were the Emerald in fact here, we would of course abide by its choice as being the will of the gods. Why not? It is as good a method as any."

Kysander Feyna stirred, opened his mouth as if to retort, and then subsided into a mutter.

"But since that is as likely to happen as the sun rising at midnight," Gariel went on, "we must find another way to settle this matter of succession. Something reasonable and practical and realistic and fair."

"That is what we have been discussing since the ending of the war," said a man Talian recognized as the Emerin's leading craftsmaster. "And that, it seems, is what we are doomed to continue discussing until our bones turn to dust. Let us hear the claims clearly stated, and cast a vote. Let us have this over with."

Three or four of the others, of the counts, threw him sharp and irritated looks, as if to remind him that the advisory members did not vote anyway.

"What is your hurry, good Quennar?" Sir Tiercel asked. "This haste troubles me. It likens to the mood and manner of the *Morvalan*. I would sooner move we adjourn and take some time to let tempers cool."

He looked with deliberate significance at Count Elyvorrin as he said this, and Talian was sure some unspoken message passed between the two. What it was, she could not fathom, but she did not much like the faint chill it sent down her spine.

Elyvorrin stood, fastidiously adjusting the long snug sleeves of his tunic. "Sir Tiercel speaks with wisdom that belies his years. We should consider a while more, before rushing into any rash decisions."

"That would be well," Gariel said. "We all have other duties that need our attention. Could we not take at season or two to think on it?"

"This seems a strange suggestion from the honorable Elyvorrin all of a sudden," Ambvassador Aethelyn said. "After all, has it not been him urging us to make haste thus far?"

For a moment, grief showed through Elyvorrin's tight mask of control. "Other matters, family matters, have taken a greater place. I have only just seen my wife into rosecloth bindings, Fistrel. Have you forgotten? My concern now is more for my grandson and daughter-in-law than for politics."

"Sorrow carves the heart deeply, that it may hold the more joy," Salwyndas said.

Gariel Aistrian cleared his throat. "Noble count, forgive us. Your bereavement is fresh. Sir Tiercel has advised that we adjourn, and I hereby make it a formal motion. Let us leave this for another time."

* * *

Chapter Ten

And by this token, shall the true king be known.
– Elwyndas, Aelfwyn III, Act VIII

"What were you thinking, to call for a delay?" Elyvorrin whirled on Tiercel once they were alone and well away from the Council chambers. "Quennar had them on the verge of voting. It could have been finished this very day."

Tiercel stood his ground, but dropped his gaze. "My lord, hear me out. They would have voted, yes, but my heart tells me they would have chosen Fistrel."

"Fistrel!" Elyvorrin struck his fist against a curved section of wall. "He and his brother are twin thorns in my side, and that son of Aethelyn's is no better."

"Their introduction of the physician was a clever, masterful stroke," Tiercel said. "It unmanned Denryl Marrion with one clean slice, leaving only you as any real opposition. That bit of cleverness can only be courtesy of my cunning old friend Idelhar. But if cleverness is so admired, that is what we will provide."

He could see that his carefully chosen words intrigued the count, whose temper settled into a more speculative evaluation. At last, Elyvorrin nodded.

"Speak on, Tiercel. You have something in mind."

"Let us have closed doors between us and any others, first," he said, and glanced down the corridor to where a trio of domestics approached with their arms laden.

"So," Elyvorrin said, when the trio drew near. "How fares my grandson in his training thus far?"

"He is a most diligent and attentive pupil, my lord. Almost overeager to learn, dare I say."

"And what of Faessia? Did I not promise you that she was fair and quiet-natured?"

"Indeed, my lord."

Keeping up such nonsensical talk for the benefit of any others they passed in the halls, they soon reached the luxurious rooms that were Elyvorrin's quarters when he stayed at the palace.

"Now," he said as he closed and latched the door behind them, "tell me of this clever plan."

"I confess the words were first spoken by Count Aistrian."

"Gariel? That puppy? What does *he* know of this?"

"Nothing, sir. His unwitting remark was what stirred the thought in my mind. Do you recall how he spoke of the Emerald of Karria? He said that none could deny the Emerald's choice. That it was as good a method as any."

"And as I recall," Elyvorrin said with a frosty, forbidding look, "I said the entire matter was absurd, a waste of time and breath."

"Perhaps it is not so absurd after all. Give me your leave, my lord, and at the next meeting, you might be able to present the Emerald to them."

Elyvorrin stared at him, then laughed. "Tiercel, do you know so little of the legend? You are no woman, no swordmaid, else you deceive very well indeed."

"Verily, but I know of one. A swordmaid in every way. She could easily fetch the jewel from the Temple. Can you not see the looks upon their faces when you appear with it in hand? You would have proved, by a right undeniable, by the very will of the gods, that you, Alinor Elyvorrin, are meant to be the Emerin's own true king."

He watched Elyvorrin's eyes, watched emotions flicker through them like leaf-dappled sunlight and shadow. Greed and hope – could it work? The crown, his? The Crystal Throne, his? By the very will of the gods? And then came doubt. Suppose the Emerald could not be found? Suppose it did not in actuality possess such a power?

Suppose . . . suppose that it *did*, and it found Elyvorrin not worthy?

Tiercel saw him push that idea away as he might have pushed away a human beggar. Unthinkable. Of course he was worthy, was he not?

Lastly, suspicion took over.

"Why do this, Tiercel? What do you gain, should I become king?"

Tiercel arranged his features into an expression of shock and astonishment and hurt surprise that his liege could think so meanly of him. "My lord! I love and serve the Emerin. It would be gain enough for me to serve a noble king, and his successor."

"By all the gods . . . Celinar. If this were to succeed, he would be king after me."

"With your example and my guidance, he will grow to be worthy of any crown. For the Emerin, which I love with all my being, I would see a strong line of kings made."

Elyvorrin considered for long moments. Tiercel kept silent and let him, not wanting to overstate his case. At last, squeezing his shoulder in a firm grip, the count smiled.

"Your counsel is heartfelt and wise, Tiercel. A king could do much worse."

"You honor me, sir." He paused. "Or . . . dare I say . . . sire."

"Sire," Elyvorrin said. "Sire. Yes, I quite like that."

* * *

"You mean to *what?*" Mischa said, as if hoping that he'd misheard.

He had spent the afternoon at the embassy, bored and frustrated. Here he was in Perras Peliani, a city so grand it put even Thanis to shame, and Ariana had bade him sit, behave and stay put. As if he were no more than an impetuous child, certain to wander off and get in trouble. Finally, rather than returning for him herself, she had sent a messenger. Some besotted little elfboy in a terribly unflattering purple and white uniform, complete with tights and soft dainty slippers.

Now, here he was in the royal palace, fully and truly comfortable for the first time since leaving home. There were cushions galore, there was wine the likes of which he had never tasted outside the Lord's Retreat, there was a spectacular view of a magical waterfall outside their very window. And Ariana wanted to leave already.

"Retrieve the Emerald of Karria," she said again. "Kevan told me all before he fetched you here. If I bring it to the Council, they will have to grant me an audience. They'll have to hear my petition, and answer my request."

"Ari . . . we've only just come to a place where we can rest in civilized splendor. Look at this room. Have you *seen* the bedrooms? And the bath! Glorious! Are you *sure* elves know nothing of Talopea?"

"I'm sure, Mischa. We honor a goddess called Shannia, lady of beauty and art and music. But if you likened her to Talopea, I'm sure you'd be well slapped for your impertinence."

"So advanced in so many ways, yet so backward. At any rate, here we can wallow in comfort and luxury for the first time in weeks, but now you'd drag me off into the wilds again?"

"Only if you choose to go. It is a long way. I'd like the company, though, and an extra sword – even yours – might come in handy."

He made a sour face. "If the elves need this gem so, why haven't they already sent someone for it?"

"I don't know the whole legend, but it's said only a swordmaiden or a king can touch it without pain. They must think there's not a woman in the entire kingdom capable of doing it." She smiled. "They reckoned without me."

He clapped, hoisting one eyebrow sardonically. "Stirring speech."

"I can tell you're impressed."

"Impressed? I must be *mad.* Why else would I agree to go along?" Mischa polished off the last of his wine and tipped the empty glass toward her. "But not until I've had a hot bath, a full meal, and a good night's sleep."

"You pampered Talopean tagga-dog. Fine. Very well. A bath, a meal and a night's sleep."

"A partner for all three would be . . ."

It was her turn to give him the sardonic eyebrow. "Mischa."

"What *is* it with your stubborn family? My mother tried for years, and failed to ever sway either of your parents."

"My parents do well enough on their own, thank you. As do I."

"On your own, you say? That sort of thing is pleasant, I grant you, but no substitute for sharing."

"Not what I meant," she said. "I've other things on my mind."

He sighed with exaggerated woe. "Well, what do you know of this gem? Since it seems we won't be uncovering any other treasures just yet."

"Some say it's a weapon, others say it has the power of healing. The dwarves claim it was stolen from their vaults millennia ago. Don't look at me so, that was long before my grandda was alive."

He chuckled. "But how long has thievery run in the family? Might if you went back a few generations, you'd find a Sabledrake was involved."

She took a seat across from him, in a chair formed from a single piece of wood that was coiled at the base and rose to spread into a seat, and relaxed trustingly as the construction of the chair demanded. Any tension, any attempt to resist, would result in the sitter being dumped rudely onto the floor. This, Mischa had already discovered the hard way. Which was why he preferred the couch in which he now lounged, the couch that molded itself to his body almost as sweetly as a lover.

A book she claimed to have borrowed from that selfsame besotted elfboy was on a glass-topped round table beside her. She opened it on her lap.

"I'm not stealing it, anyway," Ariana said. "Unlike Mother and Tal, my impulses do not tend in that direction. Now, pay attention. The story has it that the Emerald was given to an Emerinian princess, Karria, by Denethel. My father was never much of a one for tales of the hunter-god. Our family mostly reverenced Valannin and Livana. This book Kevan brought me –"

"You have smitten that boy through the heart, and are taking merciless advantage of it," Mischa said.

"Do you mean to listen to this legend, or not?"

"I'll listen, I'll listen."

She began to read.

* * *

In a time when the Emerin was young, there lived a king of great wisdom and power. He had many sons and one daughter, Karria, fairest of all elfmaids. She was permitted every indulgence that a father's devotion could provide. Yet Karria yearned not for silk and lace, but for sword and arrow.

Out of love for her, the king allowed her to train side by side with her brothers, but out of love for her, when the minotaurs invaded the north reaches of the Emerin, he would not send her with them to war, denying her for the first time in all her life.

And so it was that Karria left the palace under night's concealment. Many days she searched the woods, until at last she began to find signs of combat. Ruined armor, broken arrows, scraps of cloth from the banner of her favorite brother . . . these things told a terrible tale. But Karria continued on.

Lost and alone, she heard the distant cry of a horn that called to her, pulled her, bade her to follow. Thinking it a battle call, she hastened to it.

She found not an army, but a hunter, tall and handsome and possessed of silent grace. Karria hid herself and watched as he lifted horn to lip again. This time the call was answered by many animals of the forest. She marveled at the sight, and then saw that the hunter's gaze had fallen upon her, and was instantly enrapt.

"And so the hunter has snared a better prize than any beast of the woods," he said, taking her in his arms.

When Karria awoke, she knew that what had passed had been no dream, for there beside her lay the horn.

As she passed through the wildwood, many times she felt the eyes of animals upon her and many times she was stalked by wolves or pantera, but none dared come close. At last she found the trail of her brothers and their legion, and followed it.

All too soon, her ears were greeted by the sounds of battle and came to a valley filled with the dust and smoke of war. Her brothers and their army were beset by a force of hundreds. Valiant and skilled though they were, their quivers had neared empty and their swordarms weakened, and their war-magics depleted unto uselessness.

Her sword flashing bright, she ran to them.

The sight of their princess among them, fighting as bravely as any man, rekindled the strength of the men. They fought with renewed purpose until the ground ran dark with minotaur blood. When the last foe had fallen, Karria's brothers held aloft its horned head on a spear and cried out in victory. They named their sister Swordmaiden, and made songs of her valor.

But her presence in battle had not gone unnoticed. In the night, the camp was again attacked. Karria was borne away by one in the garments of a priest of Dezra, brutal god of the minotaurs, known to have a savage appetite for maidens.

With reckless haste the princes gathered their men and marched, determined to save Karria, or, failing that, to avenge her.

They found her set upon a flat stone, her sword taken from her. The horn, which had seemed no weapon, was left at her waist. As the minotaurs chanted to their god, Karria freed herself enough to raise the horn to her lips. But before she could wind it, the sky was shattered by thunder and Dezra appeared.

A hundred feet tall,he stood, the minotaur god. Fearsome and mighty, with lightning striking from his horns and sulphurous smoke upon his breath.

Karria's arm fell limp as Dezra reached for her . . . then drew back his massive hand, roaring in anger. His voice, like a mountain shaking apart in gouts of flame, bellowed forth in fury that she was no maiden! She was an unfit sacrifice, an offense of an offering.

And then the sound of a horn, pure and clear, split the tumult of Dezra's fearsome wrath. Karria had sounded it.

The hunter answered the call at once. In one hand he held a bow of white aspen wood, and in the other an arrow fletched with the feathers of an eagle.

The arrow sped true, and grew as it flew, until the shaft might have been made from a single great tree.

The minotaur god's voice rang forth again, but in agony rather than anger as it pierced him. He vanished with a thunder that shook the earth. In his wake, the silence was deathly still. Elves and minotaurs alike stood unable to move.

The hunter came to where Karria lay, and loosed her bonds. As she looked up into his eyes, she saw a greater age than any she'd ever dreamed. A glow of power surrounded him and she finally knew him for who he was.

She held the horn out to him, and only then saw that it was broken in two.

Casting it aside, he gathered earth and grass and forest leaves into Karria's grasp and closed his fingers around hers. When he released her, she held an emerald as green as the heart of the woodland.

"I give you this Emerald as my token," he said. "To a right-born king, it shall be a great weapon for truth. To a swordmaid, a shield against sorcery. To all others, punishment and suffering. Build in this place a temple, tend it yourself, and in time I will come for you."

And so it was that Karria the Swordmaiden, princess and beloved of her people, became the first priestess of Denethel the Archer, god of the hunt.

* * *

Ariana finished reading and looked up, closing the book with one finger held in it to mark her place. Mischa lounged in deep cushions, regarding her with an expectant glint in his eye. She knew what he was thinking even before he spoke.

"Did you skip a page or two? Between the time he took her in his arms and the time she woke up? I think you did. Go back and read it again."

"I'm sure you can guess what happened."

"I'm sure I can. She was *loved* by the god. You don't really believe that, do you?"

"What an odd thing to hear from a priest. A priest of Talopea, no less."

"Oh, I believe both in gods and in lovers," Mischa said. "But that the gods take actual bodily form to visit amongst us, and deflower elven princesses? There's nothing like that in our Temple's teachings. More's the pity."

"Well, these are the elven gods we're talking about."

"Then how come you have no temples, no churches, no priests and priestesses and ceremonies? Only those little shrines?"

"I don't know. I told you, my father reverenced Livana, but no one in my family has ever been all that religious."

"Hmm," he said, refilling his wine glass. He tipped the bottle inquisitively in her direction.

"Yes, please."

As he poured, he said, "It does prove without a doubt the perils of virginity. I know a few girls back in Thanis who could benefit from hearing that story. Save yourself for marriage, and you might well end up sacrificed to the god of the minotaurs."

Ariana gave him a withering look. "To go on," she said in a firm voice, "A century to the day after the wounding of Dezra, her brothers returned to the site. They found the temple empty but for the Emerald. There was no sign of Karria. Denethel had returned for her as promised, and left the Emerald behind. At least thrice since then, Emerinian princes have made pilgrimages to test their destiny. There are rumors that one of them did indeed use it as a weapon, but that story isn't in this book."

"So how are *you* to get your hands upon it? Where is this place? How are we even to find it?"

She read again from the book. "*Thus did the Princes, Dalwyn and Aradal, agree that they should let the Emerald settle their differences, and choose who might be the next true King. From the Great City they rode northward, through the Towering Tree and across the River that is known as Fenne-dar, facing many Challenges and Trials along their way.*"

"That smacks of a classic heroic quest," Mischa said, with a marked lack of enthusiasm. "Long, grueling, wearying and hazardous. Challenges and Trials? I don't much like the sound of that. Like what?"

"I've heard that Prince Aradal was sorely wounded in battle with a greenlion, a giant pantera with a pelt of deep green fur."

"Pretty."

"And teeth long and sharp as daggers."

"Not pretty."

She grinned at him. "What do you say, Mischa? Coming with me?"

* * *

"The daughter of Mirida to the Emerin hath come?"

"The very one," Tiercel said. "I've not told Elyvorrin yet. Imagine his shock when she walks boldly into the Council chamber and announces herself. I'll be sorry to miss the look on his face, but I want to get that Emerald without delay."

"And so thou wouldst to Karria's Temple go."

"Though I am troubled," he admitted. "I mentioned the Emerald to Elyvorrin and he batted not so much as an eye. A temple, to most elves of the Emerin, is nothing but an oddity, a quaint old relic from days long past. The gods are distant and absent, remembered only in legends. Their names are invoked far more in casual oaths and cursing than in genuine prayer."

"A sadness and a shame to the *Alvalan* it is, that so far from their heritage they have fallen."

"And I was just like them. For too long, I was just like the rest."

"No longer, Tiercel. Opened have been thine eyes, restored hath been thy faith."

"I have seen the living proof Kaledhol's will. What of the others, then? Valannin, Shannia, Livana, and Denethel? What of them? They must be real, as well. And if they are, would not Denethel's only temple be sacred? Protected?"

"As absent ancestors to thy people are the gods, by only some few shrines honored. A death of the spirit do they suffer. Yet change that shall we."

"We have been wrong, so wrong, about so much!" Tiercel clenched a fist. "I see that now. The only path for the Emerin, the only path which allows it to survive and thrive instead of stagnate, is Kaledhol's path. The next king *shall* accept this message. I will tolerate nothing less. I'll not repeat my failure with Wyndrel. This time, they'll heed me, or die."

Gloved fingers wrapped slowly around a pendant and lifted it from a black-enameled breastplate. The jewel was held out toward him. It was a ruby, carved in the shape of a six-legged reptile with small vestigial, wings. "Behold, Tiercel. The basilisk. What means its gaze?"

"Destruction and death."

"To all save its own kind! Ever dost thou that part forget. Yet of it all, that part the most vital is."

"Spare me your soft-heartedness. We cannot bring change of this magnitude to the Emerin and leave every elf untouched and unharmed. Your vow is not mine. I have sworn to do what I must to save this land, and if that means taking elven lives, so be it."

* * *

Chapter Eleven

To see my child's child is to touch the immortal stars
– Elwyndas, Jerilaine, Act III

Ariana had just emerged from a deliciously warm bath and was brushing out her hair by the window's warm morning light when a flurry of soft raps came at the door.

"Who's there?" she called.

"Kevan, my lady."

"See? You've bewitched the boy," Mischa said, poking his head through the doorway of his bedroom. "He can't keep away."

"Remember, as far as he knows, as far as anyone knows, you're my servant. We mustn't let them know you're a priest. Let alone one of Talopea." Ariana opened the door. "Yes, Kevan, what is – oh! Hello?"

"Lady Ariana, I bring you a visitor. This is Lady Talian." Kevan was not struck speechless at the sight of Ariana in her long, clinging robe, though his eyes filled up his entire face. "She says she saw you last night in the gardens, and asked of me who you were. When I told her, she said she did have to meet you, most urgently."

"Please, come in," Ari said, stepping back to allow them to enter.

The ancient elf-woman accompanying Kevan had hair whiter than snow, reaching to the hem of her soft blue gown. She leaned on a cane of pale wood wrapped in gold wire. Her eyes, which locked in soft awe with Ari's own, were silver-grey and uncannily familiar.

Ariana stared, brows knit, then gasped. "Talian? Not … Talian Maevarra?"

Those silver-grey eyes glimmered with unshed tears as Talian touched Ariana's face. "Oh, child. You *are* your father's daughter." She held out her frail arms. "Come, dear one. Let me embrace the future I hardly dared hope to see."

Carefully, afraid that the brittle body might shatter at the slightest pressure, Ari put her arms around the old woman. Talian's head only reached to her shoulder, but the knowledge and wisdom in her bearing made her seem to tower tall. Ariana felt very young and very small, a child in every way.

Mischa came further into the room. Like her, he'd clearly just enjoyed a bath, but unlike her, his robe only reached to mid-thigh. "Ariana? Who is she?"

"Talian is my kinswoman! My father's great-aunt." The careful embrace broke, and Ariana made further introductions. She was aware from the corner of her eye that Kevan lingered in the doorway, beaming at having delivered such a joyful surprise to her, and also continuing to devour her with his gaze.

"An honor to meet you," Mischa said, touching Talian's palm in a flirtatious elven greeting. "I see that Ariana is not the only beauty in the family."

"Goodness me," said Talian, blinking as she looked him over.

Ariana was mortified at the realization that Mischa's Talopean pendant, rich gold and suggestively shaped, lay squarely in the midst of the expanse of nicely-muscled chest exposed by the open neckline of his almost indecently short robe. It was an unmistakable mark of his calling, and his presence here . . . hers in her robe as well . . . what must her kinswoman be thinking?

Hastily, before Kev happened to look away from Ariana's own less-blatantly displayed charms, she went to him. All she needed was for news that her traveling companion was a Talopean priest to get around the palace. Emerald or no Emerald, she could not imagine the Council being willing to take her petition seriously if they got wind of such a scandal.

"Kevan, you have my thanks. In so short a while, you've already proven yourself invaluable to me again and again." She was very conscious that her skin had still been damp from the bath, that the thin fabric draped her body as if made of gossamer.

"I am ever yours to command," he said.

"At the moment, however, I should very much like to speak with Lady Talian in private."

"What? Oh. Oh, yes, of course. I must be off anyway. All pages are to be schooled in the mornings. I pray to see you again, and soon." He bowed repeatedly as he backed out into the hall, unable to look away from her until the closing door came between them.

Ariana skimmed her fingers over her brow. "Mischa, would you mind awfully putting on something more demure? I thought we'd agreed that you would keep the badge of your office hidden away."

He looked much further down his torso than the pendant. "It is . . . ah, you mean this."

"Without delay, Mischa." She allowed a hint of steel to creep into her voice.

"Please pardon me, Lady Talian," Mischa said, offering his most winning smile. "I'll go make myself decent."

"Handsome young man," Talian said. There was a polite neutrality in her tone that made Ariana turn pink.

"It isn't how it seems, *Nantis*. Mischa and I are friends only."

"You needn't explain anything to me. It is none of my business. And even were it so, I would hardly forbid you. Why, I recall a night on a Thanis street, when I met your mother. I cast no stones of disapproval that night."

"She speaks of it," Ari said, more at ease now. "You gave her Father's journal."

"Yes. As I'd promised, I had been watching over him. But tell me, how did he come to break the curse? I know he must have, for here you are, but I thought I would have sensed the lightening of that terrible burden from my soul. I believed I was taking a most terrible risk when I married."

Ari told her the story. Mischa came back mid-way, dressed, and sat down to listen. He smirked several times, making her wonder if Sybil had related a much different version to *her* children than the one Cat and Arien had related to theirs.

"Your poor father . . . to suffer so needlessly," Talian said when Ariana had finished.

"You said you are married as well?" Ariana asked. "For how long?"

"A scant ten years now. Folistran is a good and gentle man. I dreaded to bring harm to him, but came to love him against my judgement all the same. When the curse never manifested, I told myself it must be because we were too old for the bright-burning flame of true love, that what we had was merely warm companionship and affection. Now, at last, I know better."

"Father will be overjoyed to know I've met you. He's believed you must be . . ."

"Dead? I was an old woman when I met him, so his concern is understandable. But there's life in these tired bones yet. And curiosity enough to wonder why you've come to Perras Peliani."

"To clear the Mirida name and win back my father's lands," she said. She raised her chin proudly, and hoped that Mischa had the sense not to laugh at such a dramatic proclamation.

"Arien means to return to the Emerin?" Talian asked, askance. "I never would have guessed that."

"Well, no . . . he's quite happy in Gamelin. He's Archmage there. And Mother would never be accepted here."

She sank back, feeling a little silly. What *was* she doing? Even with his name cleared and his lands restored, her father would never want to live in the Emerin again. Why had he not said as much to her?

Because she, stubborn creature that she was, wouldn't have listened. She was determined to have her adventure, and had seized upon the first plausible purpose.

"I confess," she said, "I hadn't planned quite *that* far ahead."

"So you hold the lands," Mischa said. "You'd make a fine noblewoman, and you've already captivated one devout admirer."

"I'm too young yet. Forty years is the legal age."

Not to mention, she wouldn't know the first thing about running a holding in the Emerin. If what her father had told her was true, she'd be under just as much – if not more! – obligation here to marry and settle down as she ever would have been back in Gamelin. She'd be in an even worse position, really. Gavin Chastain was not after her for a title or political connections.

"Forty years, yes, for now," Talian said. "Until and unless the *Morvalan* have their way and force even the most traditional among us to accept change and haste."

"*Morvalan*? Surely they have no foothold in the Emerin."

Talian sighed. "It is hard to say. Some call *Morvalan* any who desire changes more sudden than customary. But there are those in the south who are dark, as dark as the inside of a rotted tree. They worship a god whose name should never be said, when the rest of us have all but forgotten the gods."

"That is no way to be," Mischa said. "You elves are the longest-lived and best-looking of all the races. And you've magic. You should be thanking your gods every day for the many gifts they've granted you."

"The *Morvalan* have powers that cannot be explained by magic," Ariana said. "There are those among them who might be called priests. My father told me of a fell warrior who stole of the life force of his own men."

"What kind of a priest would do something like that?"

"*Rhunvala*," Talian said. "A blood knight, a warrior-priest of the Unnamed One. Their symbol is the basilisk, which destroys all within its sight."

Ariana fought a shiver. "All that aside, and back to what we were discussing, I hardly know anything about holding land. I wouldn't know where to begin if Taefallon were mine. There are so many things to think of. Taxes, guards, estates . . ."

"Why bother?" Mischa shrugged. "It sounds like too much work for too little pleasure."

"There's more to life than pleasure, though," she said.

He considered this, then said, "No there isn't. Everything in life comes down to pleasure, be it for shelter, food, loveplay . . . all is pleasure. Ask anyone why they do what they do, and those will be on their list."

"What of honor? Principle?"

"What of them? Honor doesn't please the senses. Principles never warmed a bed. Don't talk to me of intangibles, Ari. The world is too full of things that delight. Why trouble yourself for things that can't be touched or tasted?"

"Children," Talian interrupted. "Fascinating as this is, you've lost sight once more of the question. What, Ariana, would you do once the Mirida name is restored?"

"You could sell the lands," Mischa said.

Ari was aghast. "To one of those conniving counts? Alinora's father, perhaps? Never! And before you even suggest it, I will not consider marrying some stranger for a political alliance."

"Such arrangements are not –" Talian began.

"Not for me," Ariana said.

"Certainly not," Mischa said. "The very idea is appalling."

Talian looked at him. "Why is that? Marriages for land, alliances, and the like are quite common among nobility. Elven and human alike. It's the way of things."

"It's . . . *coinwenching*!" He nearly spat the word.

Ariana gaped at him. She had never seen such offended indignation in his face. "How is coinwenching any different from what you do?"

If she thought he had looked offended and indignant before, it was nothing compared to the livid outrage that turned him nearly brick-red and made him sputter. "Ariana! Why . . . I . . . I will pretend that I did *not* even hear that."

"But your Temple –"

"What goes on at our Temple is a glory to Talopea. To take *payment* for that gift? What a terrible thing!"

"All right, never mind, I'm most frightfully sorry," Ariana said. "Besides, if I'd planned to wed, I could have stayed home and married Gavin. This is all getting the cart quite a bit before the horse, anyway. I haven't got the lands yet, have I? Once I've found the Emerald, I can decide how to handle the rest of it."

"The Emerald? You don't mean the Emerald of *Karria*, do you?" Talian asked.

Trusting her ancestress for no other reason than the fact that her father would have done the same, Ariana told Talian how Kevan had overheard the discussions of the Council from the garden nook, and reported it all to her. Not word-for-word, but as much as he could remember.

"If they want that Emerald so much, they'll hear me out," she finished.

"I tried to talk her out of it," Mischa added.

Talian sat quietly for a while, clearly mulling over what Ariana had said. "And you *are* a swordmaid?"

"Not in my mother's league, but I can fight."

"She can. That much is true."

"Do you think I should do it?" Ariana leaned forward hopefully. "Do you, Talian?"

"I fear it is a great risk, and I fear for your safety. But . . . I cannot deny that if the Emerald were found, it would be to the ultimate good of the Emerin. It is a far better means to choose a king than by letting the crown be fought over like a toy among spoiled children."

"Crowns, kings . . . I care little for any of that," Ariana said. "The affairs of nations don't have much to do with me."

"So it's not for the sake of the Emerin," Mischa said, grinning. "Not to help choose the rightful king. Just to get the Council's attention."

"Whatever your reasons, I give you my blessing and I wish you well." Talian smiled. "Oh, child, you cannot know how good it is to see you and know that the Mirida line lives on. Someday, our name will be known once more."

"That's most likely true," Mischa said, and went to fetch more wine. "One way or another, I'm certain no one in the Emerin will forget *this*."

* * *

For this one night, this one special social occasion, Tavalara Ilhedrion had put aside her garb of mourning and forced everyone else to do likewise. This was Tavelorn's betrothal feast. It was a time of joy and merriment, and she meant to make sure they were joyful and married at all costs.

Tiercel wondered, sometimes, what his sister could have achieved had she turned her willful determination toward some greater goal than getting her son engaged to Liana Riachlain.

He should have been gone by now, bound into the northern reaches of the Emerin to the wilderness beyond the Enclave of the Shapers. But he had promised Tavalara he would be at the party, and would rather risk the downfall of the kingdom than the wrath of his sister.

It was the first time in a dozen years that the entire family had been gathered without anyone clad in maroon. His eldest brother's wife had died in childbirth, as so many elven women did, leaving only a daughter. His sister's husband had been slain during the war, and while they had a son, he was an Ilhedrion, not a Reyes.

The obligation to carry on the family name, therefore, rested now with Tiercel. It was with the air of one who was all-too-keenly aware of that fact that Tavalara pulled him aside during the dancing that followed the betrothal feast. Either that, or, having successfully found a match for her son, she was inspired to do the same for her younger brother.

"Vissania seems quite enamoured of you," she said. "Her father is a knight in your order, and on her mother's side, she has blood ties to two counties. She would be a good wife for you, Tiercel."

"Is not one wedding at a time enough to keep you busy?"

"You would not see the Reyes line come to an end, surely?"

"Trevorn may yet marry again." A glance at their brother's perpetually dour, pinched face made Tiercel amend his words. "Well . . . someday, perhaps . . . in a century or two . . ."

"Oh, Tiercel. When I look on Tavelorn and Liana and see how happy they are, I want that happiness for you. Once, I thought you and Virine Fistrel –"

He drew her further from the dancing and merriment before she could finish ripping the scabs off that old wound. "My dearest sister, there is something I must tell you."

"You have found someone?" she clasped her hands delightedly. "Tiercel! Who? Come, now . . . tell. You know you've never been able to keep secrets from me."

It was only with the greatest of efforts that he kept his expression composed.

Never able to keep secrets from her?

What, then, of how he'd become curious about the fates of his two uncles, never spoken of by his parents? What of how he'd traced one, Tanneivan, to Thanis? There, he'd found not a noble elflord but a thief and assassin of accomplished skill. Had he not kept from Tavalara the truth of how he had delved into the Reyes history and learned the truth of their ancestry, roots sunk deep in the forbidden southlands? He had even gone there, seeking to learn what had become of his other uncle, Terindor. And learned that not only had Terindor Reyes been *Morvalan* but *Rhunvala*. That the Reyes name was even more well-known and respected, almost revered, in the southern lands.

Thus had begun the course that brought him to this point.

No secrets from Tavalara? Oh, certainly not.

He was filled with the malicious temptation to *tell* her . . . tell her all of those secrets and more besides. Tell her exactly what he had done during the war, not just the deeds that had earned him heroic acclaim and the adoration of the Council, not just the deeds that had led to Lionheart being belted around his waist.

Oh, what would she say, what would his sweet sister say, if she knew of his involvement in King Shaelan's death? What would she say if she knew who had been the last one to see Prince Wyndrel?

Even now, she was going on about what a splendid example he was for her son Tavelorn. She continually held him up to his nephew as a shining pinnacle of what a proper man should be. Ambitious. Powerful. Admired. Well-connected. If Tavelorn had not already been committed to his chosen calling as a physician, Tavalara no doubt would have tried to see him become a knight as well.

In truth, if there were any of his kin who might one day be swayed to the Cause, it could be that his nephew was the one. He had the fire of youth, a keen blade of a curious mind, and no love at all for the humans. And, sometimes, Tiercel thought, a building resentment similar to the one that had long seethed within his own breast.

"So much better an influence than his father was," Tavalara said. "Ferannor was always content to be a lowly archer, to never seek an advance in rank. Not even an officer, certainly never a knight. He had no aspirations at all, Tiercel. You know I don't mean to speak ill of the dead, particularly my own dead husband, but gods help me, it is simple fact. If not for that horrid, pushy, overbearing mother of his, why, I doubt he would have married well at all."

He had to bite the inside of his lower lip to keep from grinning.

"Tavalara," he said. "There are two things I must tell you, both of some urgency and discretion."

She stopped her tirade against poor, hapless, dead Ferannor. "Yes, Tiercel?"

"Firstly, I must away tomorrow, on a mission that I cannot discuss with anyone. Know only this – the welfare of the Emerin is at stake."

"I am certain that you will conduct yourself in a manner that will make our ancestors proud," she said. Her mouth pursed, for she was clearly disappointed that his news was of so prosaic a nature.

He hid another grin, knowing full well that such a thing depended on which ancestors they were talking about. "Secondly, and on this matter I *must* rely on your absolute silence and discretion . . . Count Elyvorrin has promised me a wife. He wishes me to wed his daughter-in-law, Faessia, and become guardian to his grandson."

"Tiercel! A . . . a marriage into a count's family?"

"As the lady is still in mourning, I confess, her heart is not overflowing with joy at the moment and she is unable to muster much interest in the necessary proceedings. I've asked the count to come to you with whatever arrangements need be made. You are far better at such things than I could ever be."

He might have just handed her a king's ransom in truesilver and diamonds, judging by the way her eyes lit up.

"This is marvelous news! I assure you, I will do all that I can and more. When shall it be announced? When shall the betrothal feast take place? Has a date yet been set?"

He motioned for silence, and gave her the endearing smile that had so swayed his governesses when he was a boy. "In these things, dearest sister-mine, I trust you implicitly. As does the count. He has only recently lost his wife, *and* is caught up in this sad business that consumes the Council. He will need your assistance. Speak to him. Do as he bids. I know you will keep the best interests of our family at heart."

"You need not worry, Tiercel. I shall attend to every detail." She embraced him. "How happy you've made me. I've Tavelorn's wedding to look forward to, and now I've yours as well. These ten years will *fly* past."

"There is one more thing . . ."

"Anything that I can do or give, I shall with gladdened heart."

"I should present the lady with a token before I go . . . have you the ring that was our mother's, or has Tavelorn sealed his promise to Liana with it?"

"The ring he gave her was that which his father gave me, which came from his grandmother. The one you seek, I shall fetch for you straightaway."

Tiercel pretended a smile he did not truly feel, and kissed his sister's cheek. "My thanks, Tavalara."

As she flitted off to search for it, Tiercel returned to the festivities, responding to the greetings of the men and the flirtations of the ladies, heartily shaking his nephew's hand and effusively congratulating the blushing damsel.

And his soul burned with resentment at the time-wasting frivolousness of it all.

* * *

Part Two:

Forest Journey

CHAPTER TWELVE

There are wonders, my friend, for which no amount of learning can prepare you.
– *Elwyndas, The Tragedy of the Mages, Act XII*

"We'll stop here for the night," Ariana called over her shoulder, reining in her horse.

"Do you see an inn?"

The hope in Mischa's voice was something she truly hated to shatter, but . . . "No."

He heaved a long-suffering sigh and dismounted, massaging at his tailbone. "Tell me something, Ariana."

"I'll not rub that for you, if that's what you were wondering."

"After this long, I've about given up trying."

"Have you?" she asked, bemused. "*You*?"

He chuckled. "Well . . . no . . . we Talopeans never can. It's part of our charm. But what I wanted to ask was if you even know where we're going. Or have we spent all week riding in circles?"

"Of course I know where we're going."

"So we're not going to blunder into this shaper-mage place?"

"No, the Enclave of the Shaper-Mages should still be far to the west of –" She broke off and blinked at him. "You *did* listen when Kevan and I were looking at the maps. I confess, I thought otherwise."

"Fear not, I only listened to the parts that concerned me. I dozed off when that lovesick lad of yours was telling you more than any sane mind should need to know about the Council and their politics. It's a good thing for him you have . . . in a way . . . the Emerin's best interests at heart. Were you a spy or somesuch, he'd have doomed his kingdom for the sake of a kiss on the cheek."

"I almost asked him to accompany us. A seeker-mage could come in handy. But as he is so very young, I'd have had to broach the subject with the head of his Household."

"Seeker-mage, shaper-mage, what's that all about? I thought a mage was a mage." Mischa eased himself down on the grass and nearly purred as the last of the afternoon sun found him through the shifting leaves.

"Some of us are drawn toward different . . . *affinities* would be a good word . . . of the mage's talent. They learn some spells with far greater ease, while others remain beyond their grasp. Kev has a knack for finding, seeking, locating. His spells might tell him the direction of certain things. Fresh water, types of plants . . . precious metals or gemstones . . ."

Mischa rolled up on one elbow. "By the gods, you could make a fortune with a spell like that. The Montennor miners would pay a thane's ransom."

"Or chop such a mage in twain on sight. The war may be over, but the Elder Races are excellent grudge-holders. At any rate, I think we can make do without Kevan."

"And not have his poetry and spontaneous speeches of devotion to contend with. Such an effect you have on men, Ariana. Just how many hearts have you broken?"

"Honestly, Mischa, don't you think a heart is made of sterner stuff than could be broken by me?"

"Your heart, maybe. But I daresay the many suitors you've spurned might have something else to say about it."

She paused in gathering wood and brushed her hair out of her face. "Harsh words. After all, what matters it to you how many suitors I've had, let alone spurned? I thought you Talopeans generally opposed marriage?"

"Not true . . . my own mother is married. Dragged into it howling in protest, to be sure, but she's stayed wed for twenty years." He considered. "Which, now that I think of it, probably is something of a miracle . . . but you're no Talopean. Shouldn't a maid of your age be on the prowl for a husband?"

"I'd not have to prowl far, that's the trouble. It seems I can scare turn around without someone wanting me to wife on first sight."

"Well, you are one of the loveliest creatures I've ever beheld. And that's out of thousands, need I add?"

"You needn't. But tell me this, Mischa, do you never look for *other* qualities besides comeliness?"

"Passion," he replied. "Oh . . . is this the 'more than a pretty face' speech? You forget, Ari, I am as shallow as a lazy man's well."

"You said it, not I. Suffice to say that I have some of my mother's contrariness of nature. I wouldn't like being courted for appearance alone."

"So should you meet a man who can't abide the sight of you, he's the one you'll wed?" Mischa shook his head. "I feel I should point out that marriage is the furthest thing from *my* mind."

"How well I know it," she said, stacking sticks and twigs in a cleared circle.

"Then what could be the reason for your continued refusals? I know it's not because I'm human. You don't share that particular trait with your Emerinian counterparts. It must be something else."

"You're much too eager, my friend. I'm not in the habit of leaping into bed with a man on short acquaintance."

He studied his fingernails as if they were of the utmost fascination to him. "Talus Yor."

"What?! How do you . . . what makes you think I . . ."

"Ariana, please. I am a Talopean. We know these things. What has he that I haven't?" Mischa sat up and started counting off. "Dark hair . . . as do I. Warm hazel eyes . . . as do I. A well-turned leg, as the court ladies say . . . as do I. Really, Ari, he and I have so much in common, it's startling. You leapt into *his* bed quickly enough. Why not mine?"

"It's not as if he were a stranger to me. I've been raised all my life on tales of him." She cast a quick spell to kindle flame.

Mischa raised his eyebrows at her. "Tell me, are the tales true? Are the ladies and the gossip right about his prowess?"

"There is something to be said for centuries of experience," Ari admitted.

"What about years of dedicated training?"

"I'm sure there's much to be said for that, too." She smiled at him. "But we both know that the only reason you've undertaken this tiresome journey was to get me into your bed. Once you'd done that, you'd have no reason to stay, and I may yet need your aid."

"Do you take me for a knave that conquers and departs?"

"Yes."

"I'm deeply hurt by that, Ariana. Deeply, mortally wounded to the core."

"Mischa," she said in a tone of warning.

"And lucky that other ladies aren't so perceptive," he continued, unimpressed. "Because it's probably gods' own truth. But I'd hardly leave you to fend for yourself in the midst of the wilderness. For one thing, I've no idea how to get home from here. So, you've nothing to lose." He took her hand and brought it to his lips, doing his best to hold her captive with his gaze. "And everything to gain."

A warm and unexpected flutter went through Ariana. She snatched her hand away with a laugh. "Oh, you *are* good. I must credit you that."

"And you *are* contrary," he grumbled, sitting back.

"Get off your backside and help me ready camp, Mischa. I want to set the spells of warning before it gets dark."

The next morning dawned warm and clear, a fine morning for a ride through the green woods. As usual, the sun had climbed high before Ariana could get Mischa on the way. Certain aspects of this wayward adventuring life, as described to her by her mother and grandfather, just did not apply when traveling with a Talopean. She was fortunate in having her magic to make up for Mischa's indifference to posting a nightly watch, and his utter uselessness at anything resembling cooking. No magic, however, could compel him out of his bedroll until well past dawn.

The going was easy enough. A rudimentary path curved through undergrowth of low ferns and weaver's grass, so named because it was flexible and soft, woven easily into watertight baskets or cloth when shredded fine. This tidbit, which she had learned from her grandmother Miralina and now shared with Mischa, was greeted with no interest whatsoever on his part.

Colorful birds darted among the treetops, brightening the woodland with their song. Many of the pale-boughed trees were laden with ripening fruit. Though they'd only been a week gone from Perras Peliani, and the traveling food they'd bought there was far tastier than any similar Northlands fare of dried meat and hard cheese, the sweet fruit was a welcome addition to their day.

"Do you hunt?" she asked Mischa, after seeing a pair of rabbits flit across a glade.

He laughed. "Only for sport, and not the kind of game you're thinking of, I'd suspect. If left to my own woodslore, I'd starve. Why?"

"For fresh meat."

"That we'd have to skin, butcher and cook ourselves?"

"Have you ever left the city at all in your life before this?" And she had thought her own life sheltered.

"I've never even been to Arrowwood. All of this is new to me. That tree, for instance . . . I've never even *imagined* such a thing. Didn't you say something about a Towering Tree?"

She looked where he was pointing and her eyes widened.

It was of no species that she could name, so tall that it could have been growing since Kelvennor, or Valannin, or whomever, created the world. The branches high above were as thick as the boles of lesser trees. The bark was fissured with deep dark cracks, thick with layers upon layers of moss. The roots sinking into the earth were covered with platter-sized shelf mushrooms.

"Cut down, it could nearly span the Vale of Banneria," Mischa said.

She gave him a look. "Cut down? How human of you."

"Oh, not that I would. Besides, it would take a hundred foresters a hundred years to do the job."

"A dozen dwarves could do it in a matter of days." Ariana dismounted and approached, peering up and up until she was half-dizzied. "Towering Tree. This *must* be it, Mischa."

"It doesn't seem very healthy." He knocked his knuckles on a plated piece of bark as big as a war-shield. Something bright and small swooped out of the opening. Mischa recoiled and nearly fell out of his saddle.

"Only a bird," she said, lowering the hands she had raised in preparation for a defensive spell. "I thought –"

"That's no bird," Mischa cut in, gaping at the winged creature circling his head.

More of them emerged in a sudden colorful featherstorm. Ariana wheeled in their midst, trying to get a clear view of one. Unless her eyes were deceiving her, they were . . . people? Tiny people, no taller than the span of her hand, but with feathered wings, pale talons where their feet should have been, and plumelike crests standing up atop their heads instead of hair.

They trilled and chittered as they flew in complex orbits around her and Mischa, hovering close to them as if inspecting these large intruders. Their scrutiny gave Ariana ample time to return the favor. The males were brightly colored, red and gold and dazzling purple, while the females were dove-grey with brown and white markings. Their perfectly-formed humanoid bodies were covered in fluffy down. Their eyes were teardrop-shaped and overlarge, giving the creatures an endearing childish appearance.

After a bout of chirps and twitters that sounded like an urgent conference, the largest and brightest male darted away and paused, hovering with wings beating so fast they could barely be glimpsed. Ariana was put in mind of certain rare nectar-sipping birds brought home by sailors who'd visited the exotic southern isles. The male gave an imperious piping cry. He indicated a deep split in the bark, a split so tall and wide that it almost looked like a doorway.

"I think he means for us to go inside," Ari said in a whisper. "Recall, the book did say the princes went *through* the Towering Tree."

"In there? Into that dark, narrow space? There might be anything inside, Ari."

A bevy of the bird-creatures swarmed around her, grabbing strands of her hair with painful little tugs. "Ah! Ow! All right. Come along, Mischa, it's what they want."

"I see that," he said, waving away a group trying to coax him with similar hair-pulling. "How are we supposed to see where we're going? Or what we're stepping in? What if there are spiders?"

"*Tentalin,*" Ariana said, cupping her hand. A ball of heatless light, pale silver in color, manifested above her palm.

The light revealed a crooked crack winding toward the giant tree's heart. The earthen floor was uneven, crisscrossed with bulges that might have been part of the root system. A heavy smell of dust, woodshavings, and age hung in the air.

"I don't care for this.," Mischa crowded close to her out of more apprehension than arousal. "I've heard tell of flowers that lure and devour live prey."

"It looks harmless enough thus far, but this light won't do. We need something more lasting." She drew a silver mark from her purse. "*Karastalin.*" The coin came alive with a steady glow, clear and lantern-bright. "Now, onward."

"I'm sure the flowers I mentioned look harmless as well. Inviting, even."

Almost at once, the constricting passageway wending into the tree began to slope up in a spiral, like some strange stair in a castle tower. The bird-creatures flitted ahead, ducking low to avoid hanging streamers of black moss. Ari swept the moss aside, disliking the cobwebby touch on her skin. Further on, she began to see small blooms in it, like pale eyes, that contracted into tight buds as the light fell upon them.

Mischa trailed her, continuing to stay close and continuing to mind his manners. His tread was not so soft and sure as hers, and he occasionally grumbled under his breath when he stumbled or bumped against some wooden protrusion.

The passage dwindled so narrowly in places that she had to turn sideways. In those spots, she could hear the wood squeaking as Mischa's armor scraped through. The substance beneath their feet was spongy and strange, soft wood that gave slightly with each step. They seemed to keep moving in a spiral that climbed around and around, higher and further into the great tree.

Finally, ahead, Ariana glimpsed a faint splash of brightness. She closed her fist around the coin to darken it and saw that the new light had a greenish hue and the unmatchable clarity of a summer's day.

"We must have come through," she said. "Entirely through the tree. But how can that be? I thought we were moving inward and up."

"What difference does it make?" Mischa gave her a nudge. "I'm liking this musty coffin less and less with each passing moment."

Ariana moved forward, smelling fresher air and hearing the sigh of the wind. But instead of the welcome sight of the ordinary forest, the passage emptied into a vast circular chamber in the hollow heart of the tree. Sunlight filtered in through knotholes and cracks in the bark, making dust motes dance golden in the upper reaches.

More draperies of moss, some hundreds of feet long, dangled from above. The floor was covered with drifts of fallen leaves, each leaf seeming large enough to roof a peasant's hovel on its own. Waxy-smooth mushrooms, some growing as big as a man, dotted the floor and lower slopes of the wooden walls.

Their chittering birdlike guides described fanciful aerobatics in the open space. Ariana saw nests wedged in every available nook, some with even tinier bird-person faces peeping over the edges.

"Tell me I've gone mad," Mischa said, "for that looks like a staircase."

"If you're mad, I am as well, for I see it too."

The steps hugged the inner wall, this time a genuine spiral stair rising up into the leafy heights of this strange open tower. High above, they ended at a thick curtain of moss, blocking an archway formed by thick trunklike twists of wood. It was all too even to be a happenstance of formation, too natural to have been built or hewn. Shaper-magic.

The big male swooped to the bottom of the steps and uttered another of his piercing commands.

"Climb that?" Mischa looked up, and up. "With no handrail? Nothing but a wall on one side and a drop on the other? A long drop?"

"We've come this far."

"Yes, why quit while we're still alive?"

Still, he followed as she began the ascent. Ariana could hardly believe they could possibly be going any higher, for it already felt as though they'd come up an impossible distance from the forest floor. Yet up they went, Mischa squeezed over against the wall despite her assurances that if he *did* fall, she knew a spell that would prevent him from plunging to his doom.

At the top, she parted the moss. Golden-white sunshine fell upon her face. She squinted and gasped, then blinked to clear her dazzled vision … and gasped again. This time, it was in wonder. A meadow spread out before her. Starflowers, daisies, and dandelions lent yellow and white to a carpet of jewel-green grass. At the edges of the meadow rose what she at first thought were a ring of tree trunks, but then realized were the uppermost branches of the great tree itself. The meadow was cradled amid them.

Mischa stepped up beside her, rubbing his eyes and looking around again as if to convince himself he was seeing what he thought he was seeing. "You know, Ari –"

A new voice interrupted whatever Mischa had been about to say. A woman's voice, loud and merry. "Welcome, friends! Welcome!"

They whirled as one, and Ari had time to notice that Mischa, despite his dismal skills as a warrior, did have keen reflexes as he grabbed for his sword. She also had time to wonder if it was a knack honed by years of fleeing jealous husbands.

"Blessed Talopea," he said now. His hand slipped away from the sword hilt and dangled slack at his side.

The voice came from an immense chair, a throne, shaped from a living bough so that a canopy of swaying leaves shaded the woman sitting upon it. She was as short as Ariana's mother, but more than twice as heavy. She was, in fact, the roundest elf Ariana had ever seen. Abundantly buxom, widely hipped, and plump from her cherubically smiling face to her bare pink toes. Her hair was a shock of bright auburn, rising from her head in imitation of the crests of the bird folk, leaving her ears brazenly exposed, naked from lobe to tip. She wore a summery frock of leaf green that concealed very little.

"I am Drea," she said. "Welcome, to the first of the Tests."

* * *

CHAPTER THIRTEEN

Meet not a challenge only as an enemy to be slain.
– Elwyndas, March to the Eastern Sea (ballad)

"Tests?" Ariana echoed, thinking again of the legends she'd read in the book. "Do you mean Challenges?"

Drea did not laugh as did any other being Ari had ever met. This strange elfwoman shrieked her mirth with such volume that the bird folk perched on nearby branches scattered into startled flight before settling down again. She flung her head and kicked her bare pink feet. Everything bounced and jiggled. Mischa did not even try to keep the appreciative grin from his face.

"Did you think that the way to the Temple would be unguarded? Three Tests stand between you and your goal."

"How did you know –?" Ari began.

"The moment you came into my part of the woods, under the watchful eyes of my little friends, I knew your every word and every deed."

"How embarrassing," Mischa said.

"Nothing happened," Ariana muttered sidelong at him.

"That's what's so embarrassing."

"Would you mind being serious for once, Mischa?"

"Oh, why?" Drea waved her hands. "There is no danger for you here. So be merry. Woodglen! Come and play for us."

At her summons, a manlike being trotted toward them. From the waist up, he had the body of a human male, lean but muscular, with dark skin like a Perrifaulian and a cap of black hair twisted into corkscrews. But his legs were those of a goat, covered in shaggy fur and ending in cloven hooves. Looking closer, Ariana could see that two of the corkscrews on his head were not locks of hair but coiled horns with rounded tips.

"A faun?" Ariana asked in astonishment. "But they're creatures of legend."

Woodglen grinned at her, a saucy, flirtatious grin that could have been the rival of Mischa's. "Such a compliment, pretty maid, and we've only just met!"

He held a flat paddle-shaped piece of smooth wood and a small mallet. Bowing to Drea, he planted the narrow end of the wood in the ground between his hooves. By striking it with the mallet in various places, he produced an array of melodious tones. It was fascinating, but Ariana could not give it her full attention and enjoyment. The bird folk, and now a faun . . . this incredible, impossible tree . . .

"Where are we?" Ariana asked when the music ended.

Drea frowned. "We haven't yet begun the Tests, and besides, that would hardly be a proper riddle anyway. That's only a question."

"Riddles?" Mischa asked, peeling his gaze from her cleavage with what must have been a heroic effort on his part. "What are you talking about?"

"Three Tests await you." Woodglen spoke in a rolling, ominous voice, and accompanied this portentous intonation with a low gong on the wooden instrument. "Of Wit, Strength, and Will."

"Three Guardians," Drea said. "Three dire beasts that hearken back to a time when we shaper-mages thought ourselves the rivals of the gods. They guard the Temple from intruders."

We shaper-mages, she had said. But the Enclave was far from here, and what little Ariana had heard of it made it sound nothing like this. For that matter, what little she'd heard of the abilities of shaper-mages had prepared her for nothing like this.

"What kind of beasts are they?" Mischa asked, not looking very happy at the prospect.

Woodglen tolled that grim note on his instrument again. "Monstrosities, fearsome and deadly."

"Dragons?" Ariana touched the hilt of her sword, though not with any real conviction. Her parents might have slain wyverns before, but one dragon had nearly made a midday meal of Cat, Arien, Alphonse and Greyquin on their sole run-in with such a beast.

"Dragons?" Drea leaned forward, propping her elbows on her dimpled knees. This drew Mischa's gaze again, and probably pushed any thought of beasts from his mind. "No, not dragons. Worse than dragons, child. Terrible, and unnatural. The shedra's bite is mortal poison. The mind-leech leaves only an empty, breathing shell with the very soul sucked away. And the dreadhound . . . I don't even like to think about what it can do."

Ariana had never heard any of those. Nor seen their names in any of her father's books.

"Are you reconsidering yet, Ari?" Mischa asked. "I'm reconsidering."

She shushed him, looking at Drea with a slight frown. "But if these things you describe are so terrible and unnatural, why would Denethel, god of the woodlands, choose them to guard his Temple?"

A scowl like a swift cloud over the sun crossed Drea's face. "I have said too much already. Now it is the time for the riddling."

"You," Woodglen said, pointing his mallet at Ariana, "and our Lady each ask three riddles. Whoso correctly answers the most, wins. If that is you, then you may proceed to the next Test. If correct replies are tied, it is generously ceded as a win to you."

"And if I lose?"

"Then our gracious lady Drea is the winner."

"And you remain here as my subjects," Drea said, cheerily gesturing to the bird creatures.

"What?" Mischa cried, evidently coming to the same inescapable conclusion. "Turned into those? You mean those are people? I don't want to be a bird."

"But you'd make such a handsome specimen," Drea cooed at him.

"Of course I would. That does not change my mind."

"You said we were in no danger," Ariana said. All around her, tiny glittering teardrop eyes were returning her horror-struck stare with keen intelligence.

"It is a harmless shapeshifting," Drea said. "My little darlings are well and happy here."

"What if we refuse these Tests?" Ariana asked.

Drea only laughed. "Then you will never find the Temple, hot-headed one. You riddle with me, or your quest ends here, in failure."

Mischa touched Ariana's shoulder. "We'll just go. After all, this is hardly some fate-of-the-world matter. We don't *have* to do this. We can find some other way to make the Council listen to you."

"Did you come all this way to go home empty-handed?"

He quirked his lips. "Apparently, I did."

"I don't think you quite understand the terms," Drea said, before Ariana had to think of a reply. "If you do not best me in the riddling, you do not leave this place. You are mine forever, and you need not be anything as pleasant and beautiful as my little winged ones, either."

Ariana pressed her fingertips to her brow. She should have known. "All right, then. It seems we riddle."

"I know a few good ones, Ari." By the glint in Mischa's eye, she had a pretty good guess as to their content.

Woodglen struck a resounding note. "Only *one* may be Tested. The other must stay silent."

"This is my quest, so I shall do it," Ariana said. "But if I fail, Mischa goes free."

"It cannot be so," Drea said. "He would know this place and your fate."

"It's all right, Ari," Mischa said. "I trust you. And it isn't as if I'd survive the return journey on my own. You know that. I'd be better off a bird-man. Like the lady says, I'd make a handsome specimen."

"I'll begin," Drea said, clapping briskly as if that settled everything. "There is a mill with seven corners. In each corner lay seven bags. On each bag sits seven cats. Every cat has seven kits. The miller and his wife bring them seven mice apiece. How many feet walk in the mill?"

Ariana's jaw dropped. She wasn't sure what she'd been expecting, but it hadn't been this. She stared at Drea. Her mind whirled.

"That isn't a riddle!" Mischa protested.

"The other must stay silent," Woodglen said again.

Seven corners, seven bags, seven cats, seven kits . . . her father could have done this in the blink of an eye . . . four times seven times seven times seven times seven plus two plus two . . .

Ariana drummed her fingers rapidly on the grass, wishing she had a slate and chalk. Oh! Seven *mice* per cat . . .

Drea's smile became more and more of a smirk with each passing heartbeat. Woodglen and the birdfolk were watching with interest, Mischa with justifiable concern.

She thought of her home, her family. Darkfire letting the kittens play with his dangling, enticingly twitching tail. The way they leaped and gamboled, batting at it with their cunning little paws . . .

Her head came up defiantly, proudly. "Four."

"What?" Mischa smacked himself in the forehead. "Ari, can't you do sums? "

"The other must stay silent!" Woodglen raised his mallet. "I'll not warn you again, human."

"It's a trick question," Ariana said. "Cats and mice have *paws*. Only the feet of the miller and his wife count. Two apiece. That makes four. The answer is four."

"Well done." Drea applauded, beaming. "I was afraid this might be over too soon. Now it is your turn to ask me one."

Ari's flush of victory vanished. Three to ask and still two more to answer? She pondered. Tal was the best riddler of the family, seeing them as another type of lock to be picked or knot to be undone. Only their father, with his long memory that retained all he'd ever heard or read, could best him at it.

"So long as I eat, I live. As soon as I drink, I die. What am I?" she asked.

Drea gave her a chiding look. "An excellent first try, but the answer is fire."

Ariana nodded, her spirits sinking; she'd always thought that one was quite clever.

"What lives in the winter, dies in the summer, and grows with roots up?" Drea chanted in a sing-song voice.

Relieved, Ari smiled. That one, she knew . . . Arien liked to use it to confound those who'd been born and raised in balmy Tradersport. "An icicle."

Drea sniffed. "Very well, then, swordmaid, your turn."

One that she'd heard at last Harvestfest popped into her mind and she recited it. "Four stiff standers, four down hangers, two lookers, two crookers, and one switchabout."

"A cow," Drea said. "Is that the best you can do?"

Ariana sighed. She looked at the bird folk, tried to imagine herself spending the rest of her life as one of them – unthinkable. One more riddle each. If she got the next one wrong, and Drea guessed her final riddle as easily as she'd gotten the previous two, it was over. She and Mischa would.

"This one, I always save for last. None have ever guessed it. Are you ready to make your try?"

"I hope so," Ari said.

"Fire without heat. Beauty without life. Overhead and under feet. Bloodied without strife. What am I?"

Possibilities raced through Ariana's mind. She considered and discarded each almost as soon as they came to light.

A mage's illusions could create fire's image without its heat. And could be beautiful without being alive. But overhead and under feet? Bloodied? What else was fire without heat? Passion? No. Sunset? Maybe, and certainly beautiful, and bloodied, or at least with the appearance of blood. Overhead, yes, but under feet?

Drea was openly smirking now.

It was the best answer she could think of. "Sunset?" Even as she said it aloud, even before Drea's victorious trill of mirth and Mischa's groan, she knew it was wrong. "What is it, then?"

"The riddle game and its laws are older than old," Woodglen said. "She does not have to tell unless she wishes to."

"And I do not wish to." Drea hugged herself – it was quite a reach – and squealed and kicked her feet some more. "You have one left to ask. If I guess it, you stay here forever. If I cannot, you go free with my good will and a token to lead you on your way."

Ari pressed fingertips to her brow again, focusing her mind.

Advise me, Valanor, she silently entreated, thinking of her father. Ever cool and unruffled. She thought of him so vividly that at once it seemed she heard his voice in her head . . . yes, posing Tal the one riddle that the boy had been unable to answer.

Of course . . . that was her mistake. Playing at *rustic* riddles against one such as Drea . . . she needed to take a page from her father's book, so to speak, and try something more literary.

She looked up. "Girls have it, boys do not. It is in life, but not in death."

Mischa at once started to snicker, then stopped with a puzzled expression. Ari reminded herself to ask him just what answer had instantly gone through his gutter-mind, sometime later, when and if they were safe and not about to be turned into birds.

Drea also started to snicker, also stopped. "Oh, my," she said, in what sounded like earnest surprise. She swung her feet, played with her hair, chewed her lip and the ball of her thumb. Finally, hesitantly, she said, "A . . . a bosom? It is a bosom, isn't it?"

"No," Ari said. "It isn't."

"What, then?" Drea popped to her feet. "Tell me!"

"The riddle game and its laws are older than old," Mischa said, with a wide grin as he understood that they had won. "She does not have to tell, unless she wishes to."

"That is not fair! Ooh, rot and mulch, you *must* tell!"

Ari performed her most graceful curtsey. "Thank you for the amusement, lady Drea, but we must be going. We've passed your Test."

* * *

"There was something peculiar about yesterday," Ariana said the next morning.

Without stopping for much discussion, they'd only sought to put as many miles between themselves and Drea's realm as possible while the daylight held. But her mind had been troubling her all the night, and now she gave voice to it.

"No! Something peculiar? Bird-people, a man who was half goat? Riddle contests with the threat of transformation at stake? What could you possibly find peculiar about any of that?"

"The book said that the princes passed through the Towering Tree. We did not pass *through* that tree, Mischa. We came back out from the selfsame opening by which we entered." She looked down at Drea's parting token, an intricately braided and beaded length of green cord she had tied around her wrist like a bracelet. A quick spell later, she shook her head. "And this has no magic. It's pretty enough, but it's worthless. She said it would lead us on our way, but it does nothing whatsoever."

"Then what was the point of all that we went through?"

"I don't know," she said. "If Drea was tricking us, misleading us, I can't imagine for what purpose. I'll say you this, though . . . she's like no elf I've ever seen before."

"I'll say." Mischa winked.

"That, too, although it isn't what I meant."

"Well, didn't your youthful admirer tell you that those shaper-mages were madmen one and all? Or madwomen, as the case may be?"

"Kev did say that, and if Drea's an example of the breed, she certainly lends credence to it

"Then what shall we do?"

"What we would have done anyway, continue on. If that *was* the Towering Tree, then soon we should find a river. *Fenne-dar.* That's Lenaisian for *otter's paw.*"

"Why doesn't it have an Emerinan name?"

"Because, according to my grandmother who hailed from Lenais, the Emerinians can't be bothered with such things as exploring their own land," Ariana said. "They pay their visiting kinsmen to do it for them. Every map of the Emerin was first charted by a Lenaisian."

"The more I learn about this place, the more I wonder about its people," Mischa said. "A city millions strong, no poor, no hungry . . . plant mages instead of farmers, spell-wielding domestic servants . . . no temples or priests . . . money of paper and wax instead of good silver and gold . . . it all seems so . . . odd."

"The most advanced and enlightened civilization on this entire world? Odd?" She relented with a laugh. "In truth, I find it odd too. Not at all like Tradersport. Nothing like anyplace I've ever seen. But it fascinates me, Mischa."

"It would fascinate me much more if –"

"Yes, yes, I know what would fascinate you more."

They rode all day, and by dusk had come to a part of the forest where the trees were more sparse, the undergrowth more dense, and the ground beneath increasingly moist and boggy. Their horses did not care for it, picking their way fussily with many nickering complaints. Mischa did not care for it either, least of all the clouds of gnats that found him irresistible.

"We'd best walk them," Ariana said, sliding down. Her boots squelched into a mucky puddle, the bottom slick with sodden and half-rotted leaves.

"Was this in the book?"

"No, but a lot can change in two centuries."

He stopped, standing on a hummock with the reins dangling from his hands and black motes swarming around his head, and stared at her. "We're following directions two hundred years old? *A lot can change in two centuries*?" he mimicked. "Talopea's thighs, Ariana! Two hundred years ago, Thanis itself was little more than a boat dock and an inn."

Sudden movement and an angry buzzing from behind him made Ariana cry out, "Mischa, down!"

He spun instead of dropping. The flying thing struck him full in the chest. Mischa was knocked off-balance, took a large step backward to compensate, and fell off the hummock to land flat on his back in a splash of scummy green water.

Ariana's sword was in her hand, even as her eyes tried to deny what they were seeing. It was an insect as long as a man's arm, like some cross of dragonfly and scorpion grown to the size of a healthy dog. A segmented, dark tail curled under instead of over, flexing with hideous eagerness. Iridescent wings buzz-hummed as it sped straight for her. Like the waspkin, yet unlike them, it had sharp pincers and glittering yellow eyes.

No time for sorcery. She met the pincers with her sword, chipping one. It fles over Mischa as he thrashed and sputtered in the shallow water, and veered around to attack again.

The marshy terrain was treacherous underfoot. A misstep sank Ariana to the knee in spongy wetness. Her strike went wild, slicing off a row of thick stalks that wept smelly whitish fluid.

The insect landed on her chest, bristly legs groping for purchase. Two of its pincers closed on her arms in painful vise-clamps. She felt a blunt poke just below her ribs, like a finger jabbing at her. The stinger on that under-curled tail . . . and was it poisonous? Could a creature that looked like this *not* be poisonous?

Crying out, she dropped her sword and seized at the dragonfly-scorpion. It clung with the tenacity of a prickle-burr. New, sharp pain erupted in her left arm as the sleeve of her Silversilk gave way beneath sharp serrations. The insect's face was only inches from hers. She could see its mandibles working, and a multitude of Arianas reflected in its eyes.

She tried again to tear it away, fell, and landed on her side. Her hip struck a moss-coated rock, but the impact jarred the insect loose and she was able to shove it from her.

It righted itself at once, and its wings went into a blurring shimmer, preparing to launch.

"Hah!" Mischa reared up on his knees. He thrust his sword down, holding it in both hands. The point pierced the insect's carapace and passed through it, nailing it to the soft earth but not killing it.

"Crush it," Ariana said, trying to clear her mind enough to summon a spell.

Mischa brought his fashionable – though much the worse for wear by now – riding boot down hard. There was a sound like a nutshell cracking, and then the head burst apart. Its frenzied struggles ceased. It lay there, wracked with diminishing convulsions, leaking ichor from its head and middle.

"That," Mischa said in a thick, faltering voice, "was most unpleasant." Whether he meant the dragonfly-creature, or the faceful of swampwater that had doused him, she wasn't sure.

Ariana touched her torso where the stinger had jabbed, afraid of what she'd find. "Thank Livana," she breathed when she discovered only undamaged Silversilk. "It couldn't get through."

Her left arm, however, hadn't fared quite so well. The magical fabric had parted beneath the sharp pincer edges. A long slash trickled blood to her elbow. Only now did it begin to hurt, with a deep cutting throb.

"Uck, horrendous," Mischa said. "Look at us. Muddy and beslimed from head to toe."

She nodded, wincing as she pressed a handkerchief to her arm. "I must clean this wound. Let's go, before its mate turns up."

"Or its mother," Mischa added, nudging the still-twitching carcass with his toe. "Here I thought the Emerin was just as the songs would have you believe. Perfectly serene, a place of uncanny beauty. Now, I've not read *all* of Elwyndas, but I don't recall much talk of swamps in any of his plays or poetry."

"Elwyndas was a true Emerinian," Ariana said. "Which means, in all likelihood, he never left Perras Peliani."

They retreated to a comparatively dry and large knoll, where they tidied themselves as best they could. Ariana almost declined Mischa's offer to call upon Talopea to mend her wound, then decided she was being foolish. He could heal her without it going any further than that. After all, his mother had done the same for hers many a time. And it did hurt, and she wouldn't want to have an injured arm if there proved to be more dangers in their path.

"Trust me," Mischa said as he skimmed his fingers over her skin. "Let Her presence flow into you . . . feel Her touch . . . feel Her caress . . ."

Ariana shivered. "Behave yourself, Mischa."

"Shh. I'm not skilled at much in this world. Let me do what I can."

"It's only . . . only my arm that was wounded," she said, her breath a little more rapid than it should have been, her cheeks flushed pink. "Mind your hands."

"I promise, I'm paying close attention to where my hands are."

"Be quick about it or I'll tie on a bandage and call it good."

"And here I thought you elves liked to take your time, and make it last."

"Heal me, already, Mischa, or I'll give you a wound even your goddess might not be able to mend."

He chuckled. She could feel his breath on her neck, against her ear. A languid, sensuous warmth like molten honey was rushing through her body. Her arm no longer hurt. She barely noticed, barely cared.

"There," he said. "All better."

Hastily checking to make sure she still had her clothes on, Ariana shook her head to shake some sense and control back into it. "Oh," she said. "That puts what little spells of healing we elves know to absolute shame . . . not to even mention the medicines that the followers of Steel brew."

"And did I take liberties? No. Well . . . not many."

She checked her clothes again. "Thank you, Mischa."

"Not me. Thank Talopea. If you aren't certain how, I'd be happy to suggest –"

"Wait," she said, looking around. "Where is my horse?"

The other horse, Mischa's, was nearby, placidly grazing on some tall marsh grass. Of hers, there was no sign. She remembered letting go the reins when the dragonfly-scorpion had come buzzing out of the gloom, and had then been so occupied that she hadn't noticed the horse running off. Yet it was gone, with her bedroll and belongings still strapped to the saddle.

Mischa glanced at the ground. "Not much chance of tracking it, I suppose."

"Not that way."

"Perhaps we should have brought your suitor along after all."

"I may not be a seeker-mage," Ariana said, "but I do know a spell that might help." She concentrated, closed her eyes, and bent her fingers. "*Arala.*"

She felt herself slowly turn, as if manipulated by an unseen hand. When she opened her eyes, she knew which way and how far. And of course, that invisible tugging compass wanted to lead her right into the deepest part of the swamp.

* * *

CHAPTER FOURTEEN

Oh, most low and vile of villains, to do such a loathsome deed!
– Elwyndas, The Four Knights, Act III Scene V

"Do you think this is part of a Test?" Mischa slapped at gnats, with increasing wildness and futility, each slap only seeming to roil the cloud around him before it came back thicker than before. His horse kept up a steady swishing of its tail and flicking of its ears, likewise beset. "What were they supposedly? Wit, Will, and Strength? Which would this be?"

"It does test the will," Ariana said. "But I cannot believe that Denethel set that flying horror on us, or made my mount run off."

An expanse of sticky mud, interlinked brown pools and sluggish connecting waterways, slimy-looking hummocks opened out in front of them. They stood on the bank, looking at it with a doleful lack of surprise. Here and there, eddies in the murky water told of snakes or worse. Frogs called back and forth, sometimes interrupted by glottal honking cries of unknown origin.

"Care for a swim?" Ariana said at last.

Mischa sighed. "Must we?"

"The spell that leads me points through the middle of this mess."

"Wouldn't that mean it can't be very deep? If this is the way the horse went and all?"

She permitted herself a small, tight smile. "A nice hope, but I'm afraid the seeker-spell only takes me on a straight path to where the horse is now. It doesn't show me the path it took to get here."

"Suppose we go around?"

"We could . . ." She broke off a branch as long as she was tall, and used it to probe the depth. "But that could take a long time. I'm going across. I'd rather not be here when night falls."

"Oh, fine," he said in resignation. "After all, it's not as if we could get much filthier."

"That's the spirit." She moved carefully into the water, feeling her way with the stick. Her passage stirred up darker kofa-colored whorls from the bottom. She could feel the gluey mud sucking at her boots as if it wanted to suck them right off her feet.

He watched her wade out until she was knee-deep, his nose wrinkled in distaste. "On further thought, Ari, suppose I wait here, and you come back to meet me once you've found your horse?"

"If you wish. But I wouldn't, were I you." She pointed at a stout dark-colored tree that leaned precariously out from the bank. At head height from the ground, its bark was scored in parallel gashes, raw and starkly pale against the wood. "Those are fresh. I doubt you'd like to meet whatever is strong enough to leave claw marks in solid ironwood."

Mischa stared, his throat moving in gulps. As he turned back toward her with his brows climbed high and a question on his lips, a low, bestial and hungry grunt from somewhere off to their right decided him.

"What was that?" he asked, splashing quickly into the water and dragging his suddenly-cooperative horse behind him.

"Let's not find out."

Knee-deep, then up to their thighs, then hips. Skater-bugs indented the surface, skimming easily past them as if mocking their slow progress. Once, something slithery and coiling moved past Ariana's leg. She froze, but it passed on by without investigating, to her great relief.

"Being a bird-man wouldn't have been so bad," Mischa said. "Some of those females were actually quite pretty, now that I think of it."

"Next time, then, you can play the riddle game."

"Speaking of which, what *do* girls have that boys don't?"

"I don't have to tell you. Remember what Woodglen said?"

"What if I know the answer to Drea's riddle?"

"You do not!"

"I do so. Autumn leaves."

An aggravated cry burst from her throat.

"Now tell me yours."

"Girls have it, boys do not," Ari recited, slogging onward. "It is in life, but not in death."

"Yes, yes, what's the answer?"

"The letter I," she said, heaving herself onto a large island of a hummock for a rest.

"Clever." He led his horse out, and it promptly shook itself to throw off the mud and water, splattering them both.

They were both thoroughly soaked and weary and miserable by the time they reached what seemed to be the far edge of the worst of it. So much so that not even Mischa could muster more than a feeble grin as Ariana shed her clothes and summoned clean water over her head. It sluiced down, but the dousing couldn't pluck out the bits of twig, sodden leaves and dead bugs that had gotten tangled in her hair. She provided water for Mischa as well, and by dusk when the unnerving noises started up in earnest from the depths of the swamp, they were as clean and dry as they could be under the circumstances.

Ari made a small fire and they huddled near it, neither of them overjoyed at the idea of spending the night here but not having much other choice. The surroundings didn't encourage much of an appetite, either, so dinner was simple.

As she was making herself finish the last few bites of dried beef, Ariana sat up straight. She had heard something, or thought she had . . . it had almost sounded like a voice. A plaintive voice, calling from somewhere off in the distance.

"Did you hear that?" she asked Mischa.

"What? Is it whatever made those claw marks?"

"Help . . . help me." It was in Emerinian, the cry weak, despairing and full of pain.

"That!"

She jumped up and headed that way, carrying the branch she had been using all day. She had grown unexpectedly fond of it, since it had not once led her into quicksand or a nest of venomous snakes. If she had to, it would make a decent weapon. Not that she was any master of the quarterstaff. She'd really only tried it once in her life. True, that once had been enough to break Galen Chastain's arm, but that had been an accident.

In the direction from which the voice had come, the ground sloped up and was less damp, more solid and reliable underfoot. Ferns brushed at Ari's shins. Several of them were crushed and broken, as if something large had passed this way recently.

"Please . . . I saw a fire . . . is someone there?"

Ariana was about to answer when Mischa's hand closed on her wrist.

"Ari . . ." he said in a choke.

He was not looking ahead toward the source of that feeble cry, but staring off to the side. The plants there had been uprooted and mauled. Great dark stains had dried on the treetrunks. To Mischa, those stains probably looked inky black in the fading daylight, but to Ariana, they were the rusty maroon of crusted blood.

A few steps later, the breeze brought her the stink of death. She saw a heap of torn meat and entrails, and could not immediately discern what it was. Another step let her recognize it as her horse.

Or . . . most of her horse.

She sucked in an alarmed breath and instantly wished she hadn't as the stench overpowered her senses. Stumbling back, pulling free of Mischa, she turned and ran blindly away from the ghastly scene.

Her feet struck something warm and soft. She heard a pained grunt even as she tripped and went sprawling.

Something clutched her ankle. She yanked her foot free and raised the staff, ready to pummel . . . then saw a slender elven hand grasping toward her.

"Please," the same voice whispered. "Help . . . me."

"Mischa!" she shouted. "Here! I found someone. An elf. He's hurt!"

By the time Mischa came plunging over to them, she had gotten on her knees and eased the injured man onto his back. He had pale blond hair matted with blood, and his face was so badly bruised and swollen that she could not say for certain whether he was a youth or an elder. More blood oozed from between his fingers, where he held his other hand against his chest.

"Murder . . ." the elf said.

"It's all right," she said. "You'll be fine. Mischa, what happened to him? Was it whatever killed my horse?"

"If it had been, he'd be in pieces. This looks more like a beating, and here, a knife wound."

"My . . . baby . . ." the man said, and began to weep.

"Baby?" Mischa and Ariana said together, appalled.

"Killed . . . my . . . *baby*!" Torturous sobs wracked him.

"What baby? Where? Who are you?" Ariana leaned over him. "What's your name?"

Before he could answer, the man slumped into unconsciousness.

"Can you heal him?" she asked.

"If Talopea is willing."

As Mischa began to pray to his goddess, Ariana examined the man. His clothes were plain, even drab by elven standards. Nondescript grey and brown, unadorned by trim or embroidery. But he had a large, ornate truesilver ring on his forefinger. She lifted his hand to get a closer look, ruefully thinking that her mother would have by now had it off and tucked away in a pouch.

"Mischa, this ring . . . he's a Magelord. These are only given to mages who've mastered their chosen craft. My father told me –"

"Shh," Mischa said. His eyelids had drifted half-closed, his lips moving in soundless prayer.

Ariana fidgeted, trying to keep watch over them and also the forest, ears strained for the slightest noise. A spell to sense danger warned her of no imminent threat, but did not overly reassure her. Someone or something had butchered her horse, and someone or something else had most likely beaten this elf to a handspan from death.

A cool glimmer caught her eye from several paces away. She went to it, and found a fancy walking-stick, black oak chased with silver, topped with a smooth knob of opaque green-banded stone. Again, a piece of considerable worth and status. A wizard's tool.

Nearby, as if dropped, was a leather satchel similar to the one her own father sometimes carried. A book lay open beside it, fluttering in the gloom as the breeze tried to turn the pages.

Braced for the prospect of finding other victims – his agonized words, *killed my baby*, floated hauntingly through her memory – she went to investigate.

No bodies. Nobody. No sign of any others. Let alone a wife, and child.

The satchel was laced shut in what she recognized as a magical knotwork lock that would certainly foil Tal and might even be more than a match for their mother. The book looked to be filled with scribbled notes, advanced magical formulas far beyond her ability to comprehend, and bizarre sketches of plants and animals and monstrous figures the likes of which she had only ever seen in nightmares.

Mischa's horse whinnied. Ari spun and saw it back on the bank where they had made their little camp. It was prancing in fear, tossing its head, tugging at the branch where Mischa had looped the reins. Beyond it, in the water, there was a sloshing turbulence as if something large was moving beneath the surface. The horse reared and the branch snapped. Suddenly free, driven further into panic by the branch tangled in its reins, Mischa's horse bolted.

As it crashed off through the underbrush, the thing that had been in the water lunged up. Had the horse still been there, it would have met the fate of Ariana's unlucky steed.

Ariana, already running that way, skidded to a halt with her eyes trying to bulge from their sockets. She screamed without realizing or caring that she had.

Her first mad thought was that a giant serpent and an alligator were fighting over the same meal of womanflesh. But no serpent had such a hunched back, no alligator had such long trunklike forearms, no woman had such coarse and scaled skin.

It surged from the pond, muddy water coursing down its body, making the same glottal grunt that they'd heard before. The powerful coils that formed its lower body propelled it toward land, the thick yellow claws at the ends of its forearms already reaching eagerly to gouge the meat from

Ariana's bones.

The only thing that kept her from following the horse's blind course through the forest was the thought of her fearless mother, who had once ridden a wyvern and faced down the shadow beasts.

And of Mischa, lost in his healing trance, defenseless. Mischa and his patient.

Instead of fleeing, she sprang in front of the monster.

Only then, she realized that instead of her own sword or even her trusty swamp-probing branch, she had seized up the walking-stick with its banded green gemstone knob. She had it in one hand and whipped out her sword in the other, and wished in vain for her mother's knack of using both hands with equal skill.

The creature stretched its jaws wide, far wider than should have been possible, unhinged like those of a reptile. A chaotic snarl of fangs filled the cavern of its mouth. Blue-tinged foam dripped from them and from the plated, forked tongue.

Its murky brown gaze flicked to the walking-stick, and the creature screeched with such vehemence that Ariana was thrown a step back by a cold gust of reeking breath. Blue foam sprayed across her. Where it struck her skin, it first stung and then numbed spots flowered.

Aghast, she lunged and thrust. The tip of her sword skidded across scales, leaving only the mildest of scratches.

"No!" Someone struck her forcefully aside.

It was the wounded elf, tottering on unsteady legs but upright. He snatched the stick from Ari's grasp, a simple task as her fingers on that hand had gone numb and lifeless.

At the sight of him, the creature screeched again in purest fury. It lashed its tail, roiling the pond into storm-waves.

"Stay back," Ari said. "Its venom –"

"Idiot woman. Don't you think I know that?" He held out his hands toward the creature in a gesture of command. "Shedra! Shedra, hear me."

The creature subsided, uttering a growl that chilled the blood nearly as much as had its enraged screeches. Claws flexed at the air.

Shedra. One of the beasts about which Drea had warned them. She'd even said that it had a toxic bite. Ariana staggered. She felt arms around her, a body supporting her. Mischa.

"Ari, you're hurt!"

"Venom," she said thickly. "Paralytic . . . spreading."

Ignoring them, concentrating on the creature, the mage moved closer to the tail-lashing monstrosity. He crooned. "Yes, that's it, that's right. Obey Quisfahr. You know who I am."

The Shedra's lips curled back from its teeth. Foam frothed in runnels down its chin. It reached out, slowly, slowly, toward Quisfahr's extended hand.

"No," Ariana tried to say, but mostly mumbled. "It'll kill him."

"Come on, my pet, yes, come to me . . . come to your master."

A blistering fury lit the Shedra's eyes, turning them to pools of sullen orange fire. Its claws struck to disembowel.

Quisfahr jumped back and interposed the stick between them. The force of the blow splintered it. He landed on his back and the Shedra was upon him, looming over him. It stopped with claws poised, raising its head as if looking around toward some noise that none of the rest of them had heard. In that brief pose of alertness, Ariana saw that the Shedra's ears were long and tapered, a grotesque mockery of elven ears.

She wanted to do something, wanted to help, to save Quisfahr before he was gutted, but her limbs would not respond. Mischa held her, staring openmouthed.

The Shedra scented the air, tongue flicking out. A keen expression of anguish crossed its face. Then it threw itself back into the swamp, sending up a colossal splash and a bulging wake as it swam away at tremendous speed.

Quisfahr scrabbled after it to the water's edge. He flung his arms out in an imploring gesture. "Come back. Oh, come back!"

"Be glad it's gone," Mischa said, his voice shaking. "That beast nearly had you for supper."

"Shedra would never hurt me," Quisfahr protested. "I am her master."

"Pardon me if it didn't seem so from here." Mischa tightened his grip on Ariana as she sagged, deadweight, against him. "I have no quick healing that can rid you of poison, Ari."

"Out of here," Ariana said, forming the words carefully. "Might return."

"Ohhhhh, noooo!" Quisfahr crumpled into a heap and sobbed, hammering one fist on the earth. "It's so unfair!"

"It's gone," Mischa said. "It must have scented something something that spooked it, though whatever could spook *that* thing –"

"By the Great Horn! What is all this?"

At the voice, Mischa started and Quisfahr flinched. Ariana could not move, but was jolted by shock as well.

Another man, a tanned elf with a dark brown ponytail, stood above them on a hilltop amid the trees. He had come seemingly from out of nowhere. He held a nocked bow in his hands and wore the sensible soft leathers of a huntsman. A knife and an ivory horn hung at his belt.

"Is it Denethel?" Mischa asked in his halting Emerinian.

"You flatter me, stranger, and insult the god. Who are – Quisfahr?" There was no joy in his voice as he spoke the name. On the contrary, he drew back his bow and took deliberate aim. "On your feet, monster-maker. Else I will shoot you as you kneel and you'll die like the lowly worm you are."

"Leave me be, Obriel." Quisfahr did not lift his head.

"Now, wait, look here," Mischa said. "By grace of the gods I just healed that man, and I'd rather you didn't undo my work."

"You are friends of Quisfahr?" Narrowed brown eyes impaled them. His accent was like his appearance, brusque and leathery.

"We found him here, not long ago. Someone had beaten him near to death. Was it you?"

"Beat him? I'd prefer to stay at bowshot's distance and not dirty my hands, though I'd begrudge the waste of a good arrow on his vile flesh."

Ariana uttered a low groan, the only sound she could make as the paralysis spread into her throat and chest. Her lungs labored to draw breath.

"Whatever's between you and him, I neither know nor care," Mischa said. "My friend needs help. Please. She's an elf. One of you."

Obriel whistled in perfect imitation of a birdcall. More elves, archers and huntsmen similarly clad, melted out of the underbrush. "Take these two to our camp. That horse must be theirs."

"What of Quisfahr?" one of them asked.

As she was gently lifted from Mischa's arms and wrapped in a fur-lined leather cloak, Ariana saw the Lenaisians – for so they had to be by their accent and their dress – looking at the mage with undisguised loathing. Several sets of fingers yearningly caressed feathered fletching. Quisfahr, uncaring, stayed where he was.

"That man is ill," Mischa said. "I healed his physical wounds, but there's something else –"

"Oh, there's plenty else," Obriel said. "Nothing that an arrowhead to the heart can't cure."

"Then do it and get it over with," Quisfahr said, speaking to the earth. "You've wanted to kill me for years, Obriel. Go on. Have your fun. Someone's already killed my baby, and without him, I have little reason to live."

"We saw no baby," Mischa said. "We saw no one but him."

"His *baby* is no infant," an elf with reddish braids said, grimacing. "It's his familiar."

Obriel nodded. "He once told me that he feels its hurts as if they were his own. How was he when you found him?"

"He'd been bashed in the skull, and run through . . . run through . . . his familiar, you say? What manner of familiar?" Stricken dread filled Mischa's voice. "Was it . . . something like a dragonfly, only larger? With a . . . tail? Like a scorpion?"

Now Quisfahr straightened up. His eyes, so pale that they were nearly colorless, found Mischa. "You saw my baby?"

A hard grin curved Obriel's mouth. "*You* killed it?"

"It attacked us! I had no choice!"

"Earless murderer!" Quisfahr shrieked.

He dove at Mischa as if meaning to personally rend him to bits, but those of Obriel's men not carrying Ariana tackled him and bore him to the ground.

"Bring him," Obriel said. "As he said, I've waited years to kill him . . . but I can wait another day or so. With his crimes, a swift death is more than he deserves. And there's something he needs to tell me."

"Never! I will tell you nothing. She's *mine*. She was always mine. You stole her from me, but I took her back, and you'll never see her again."

"Silence him."

Despite Quisfahr's writhing and pummeling, they quickly trussed him hand and foot, wedged a gag in his mouth, and bound him hanging from a long pole. Those who had touched him scrubbed their hands on their clothes as if they'd come into contact with something foul.

A sharp-featured, fair-haired man with soft brown eyes had been examining Ariana, his hands gentle, his touch skillful. "It's venom indeed, Obriel. I'd say it was that of a blue viper, but it's progressing much too rapidly."

"It wasn't any snake," Mischa said. "It was . . . gods know *what* it was. Can you help her? She . . . she's of a noble house, and . . . on a mission for the king. In a manner of speaking."

"One of Quisfahr's *creations*?" Obriel scowled, and then his stony visage softened. "A girl . . . another girl lost to Quisfahr's evil magics? I will not have it. Lievve, do your utmost."

"I shall," the fair-haired man replied.

"We're in your debt," Mischa said, offering his hand. "The monster scented you and fled. If it hadn't, you would have found strewn limbs from here to Perras Peliani. Look what it did to Ari's horse."

Obriel clasped Mischa's forearm and gave it a rough, friendly shake, then turned to look where indicated. He paled as he got a better look at the carnage. "Denethel's Bow! What manner of monster was it?"

Mischa shook his head. "The most hideous thing I've seen in all my days. Quisfahr called it –"

Quisfahr's warning outcry was muffled by his gag.

"– Shedra," Mischa finished.

A dead silence fell.

"Shedra," Obriel said flatly. His men murmured in horror and denial. "Well. That answers one question."

"I'm . . . sorry?" Mischa said. "I don't understand. What . . . what is Shedra?"

"Not what. Who. Shedra . . . was my woman."

* * *

CHAPTER FIFTEEN

Stand between a man and his love only at your peril.
– Elwyndas, King Daharan, Act II

Ariana woke to the most luxurious feeling in the world, that of someone brushing her freshly-washed hair.

That made no sense. The last thing she recalled was grimly fighting to hold onto consciousness as the paralysis seeped deeper into her body.

Now she was on a cot, covered in a warm soft fur, that terrible slack numbness gone. Instead of dangling swamp-moss, she was looking up at a roof of crisscrossed leafy twigs.

While someone brushed her hair.

She murmured a wordless question, and tried to move her head.

"Awake at last, I see." The voice had the same Lenaisian accent as Obriel and his followers, but was youthful, sweet and feminine. "Lievve's medicines did their magic."

The elfmaid, when Ariana turned to regard her, was the same. She had masses of curly nut-brown locks tumbling around a pretty face, and wide guileless dark eyes. Her fawn-colored tunic was trimmed with tiny disks of polished antler. She sat on a stool beside the cot, Ariana's long silver tresses draping her lap like a blanket as she gently ran a brush over them.

"Where am I?"

"Our camp. I've been looking after you."

"Thank you." Ariana sat up, and the fur fell away. She saw that she had been bathed, and dressed in a simple long-sleeved cream-colored shift, with a pattern of autumn-leaf embroidery around the collar and hem. It made her think dourly of Mischa knowing the answer to the riddle. "I don't envy you the task of washing me, Lady . . . ?"

"Riella, though no lady by title." She twinkled a smile. "And yes, you were in a state. Covered with muck, the both of you."

"Mischa, my friend, is he –?"

If anything, the twinkle brightened. "Fine and well, and I daresay he cleans up into a much more handsome fellow than I ever would have thought on first look."

Ariana laughed. "Don't let him hear you say that, or he'll pursue you like a hound after a fox."

"As if I'd mind."

"You . . . you wouldn't? Oh . . . yes . . . you're Lenaisian."

"Though I'm sure Obriel would have quite a bit to say about it," Riella said. "Brothers can be *so* trying. Our parents died when I was very young, you see, and he's had to raise me. Left him a bit on the overprotective side. And after –" Riella broke off her amiable chatter as cleanly as if she'd been slapped. A desolate sorrow darkened her eyes.

"After Shedra?"

"You know of that?"

"It was the last thing I heard before all went grey and I woke here. Obriel said she was his woman? What happened to her?"

"That's what we'd like to know. Quisfahr wanted her for his own since the day he joined us, but Shedra had eyes only for my brother. When she and Obriel announced their engagement, Quisfahr went mad. He stole her away on the eve of their promise feast. Kidnapped her from our very camp."

"But the creature that attacked us . . ."

"I had no idea that such hideous magics even existed." Riella blinked away tears. "I'm sorry . . . I don't think I can bear to tell it."

"You said Quisfahr joined you. He's Emerinian, isn't he? A shaper-mage. Like Drea."

"Drea?"

"She of the riddles and the Tests." Seeing only blank confusion in the girl's eyes, Ariana tried again. "Mistress of the bird-creatures . . . accompanied by a faun? At Towering Tree?"

"But this is Towering Tree."

"What? We've come in a circle? How? And how is it you do not know of Drea?" Ariana looked at her wrist, but it was bare. "I had her token, here, on my arm."

"That poor soaked and bedraggled thing? I cleaned it, and set it to dry with the clothes you'd been wearing. Obriel sent some men back to retrieve any of your belongings that could be found – Mischa told us what had befallen your horse – but for now, this overtunic of Shedra's should fit."

She held up a loose, sleeveless garment of many colors, gold and red and orange and brown, its pattern shifting and moving like a tree bending in the breeze.

"It's lovely, but I cannot . . ."

"Please. If not for you, Obriel might never have found Quisfahr. If this is the path that will bring Shedra back to us, I doubt she'd mind."

Ariana accepted the tunic and inclined her head in thanks. "So . . . Quisfahr . . . enspelled her?"

"And not the first time he's done such a thing. He's a madman. Always seeking to *improve* animals by changing them to other forms, or melding them two into one. He first told us that he left his fellow shapers over rivalries and disputes, with himself ever the unfairly accused victim. But he later confessed that it was this unnatural dabbling that led to his exile."

"You took him in, and this is how he repaid you?"

Riella nodded, then brought Ariana a pair of doeskin slippers. "You must be hungry, and the others will be pleased to know you're feeling better. Obriel has many questions."

"As do I, so I'm sure we can come to some arrangement."

Although Riella had called this their camp, the wooden structure in which Ariana had wakened was more of a hut, with a sense of durability and hominess that led her to believe the Lenaisians of Obriel's band had been camped here for several years. This impression was confirmed when Riella pushed open a curtain over the doorway, and led her out.

A modest collection of similar huts nestled in a valley between two long lumpy ridges, in the shadow of a high, rough cliff. There was a thriving garden, and a clay bread oven, and a communal firepit surrounded by log benches. It had the look of a small village, bustling with midday activity.

Then Ariana got a better look at the cliff. And the ridges. She had mistaken them for earth and rock, but . . . "Towering Tree?"

The ridges were roots, hunching up out of the earth like any ordinary tree roots would do, but no ordinary tree roots would have been so immense. The trunk above them ended in a sheared-off stump two dragonlengths above the ground. Ariana could not even guess how high that tree must have been in its prime.

"So it was once called, by the maps," Riella said. "Kayella says it fell some fifty or seventy years ago. The rest of it lies to the east of here."

The legend had said that the princes went through the Towering Tree. And true enough, the mighty stump was cleft in the middle by a gap wide enough to let two wagons pass side by side. She and Mischa had been wrong before. Not Drea's tree. Drea's tree would have been a stripling compared to this giant.

Several of the Lenaisians cast curious but friendly glances at Ariana as she and Riella walked by. Most of them were fit, rugged men of Obriel's aspect, though they had a few women and even some children among them. No one was idle. Everywhere she looked, she saw people dressing out game, cooking, stretching hides on large racks, fletching arrows, carrying wood, and dozens of other activities.

Many animals, falcons and foxes and spotted kit pantera, shared the camp. Unlike tame Emerinian pets, these looked as wild as if they'd come from the forest only moments ago. Mischa's horse was tethered beside a hut, rubbed down and content, and currently being fed the cast-off ends of carrots by two blonde-braided little girls.

Another tree, this one an oak that would have been majestic in its own right if not dwarfed by the remains of the one that was probably its ancestor, rose in bough-spreading profusion on the far side of the firepit. Rope-and-wood ladders hung from its upper reaches, where wooden platforms provided vantage-points for keen-eyed archers on watch.

At the base of the tree were Obriel, two of his men – Ariana recognized the fair-haired one as Lievve, him who had tended her – and Mischa. All of them sat on leather mats stuffed with rushes, around a low wooden table. On the table were dishes and trenchers and flagons, a half-eaten roasted fowl, a haunch of venison, a bowl of plump purple berries, bread, stew, and other hearty fare.

Quisfahr was there as well, but far less comfortable. He was still gagged, and bound to a sturdy stake with a rope around his waist, more tying his ankles, and his wrists tied behind him. His near-colorless eyes met Ariana's in silent appeal . . . or demand. She was Emerinian, like him, those eyes said. She should help him, side with him against these ill-mannered barbarians.

"Ariana!" Mischa did not get up, but waved. Even had he not been the only human in attendance, he would have stood out from their woodland-clad hosts in his blue silk shirt and black trousers sashed in gold. "Fine and well?"

"Fine and well," she said, and bowed to Obriel. He, and Lievve and the other elf, had risen. "And thankful for the kindnesses your people have shown us."

"Lady Ariana," Obriel said, touching her offered palm. "Mischa has been telling us of your journey. You are both welcome in our camp for as long as you care to stay."

He introduced her to Lievve, and to Falerian, the other one. Through the greetings, she didn't miss how Riella's gaze tilted coyly to Mischa, or his smile in return.

"So *this* is the Towering Tree," Ariana said as they all sat down again around the table. She accepted the plate Lievve passed her, and began filling it with meat and berries. "Did Mischa tell you of our mistake?"

Falerian, who was dusky and dark-haired, nodded. "I know of this Drea . . . cousin to yonder accursed Quisfahr. The madness runs in their bloodline. Why she should talk such nonsense, riddles and guardians, I cannot guess."

"Perhaps humoring you with tricks," Lievve said. "Telling you that which she supposed you hoped to hear, playing what she saw as her part. But she is no servant of Denethel, Lady Ariana."

"What would she have done if we had lost the riddle contest?" Mischa saw Riella reaching for a flagon, and that did inspire him to move, to refill her goblet with wine. "Could she have done what she threatened?"

"It is well you did not have to find out," Obriel said.

"Now, at least," Ariana said, "we know we are truly on the right path."

"To Karria's Temple?" Lievve asked.

"Mischa, did you tell them *everything*?"

"They wanted to know what we were doing way out here, so far from the city," he said. "And we had long hours to pass, while we waited through the night to see if you'd be able to throw off the effects of that venom. I had to say something."

"We know of your quest," Obriel said. "You seek the Emerald. Even in Lenais, we had heard of it. In our land, the Hunter is lord of the gods, where here Valannin is set firstmost. I do not know why, therefore, such a relic should be here and not in Lenais . . . but . . ." He shrugged. "I am a huntsman. The ways of the gods are as mysterious to me as are the ways of magic."

"I don't mean to steal it, or sell it," Ariana said. She told him of her father, his unjust banishment, and her desire to see his name cleared. "And the Emerin does need a king. If this can help decide it, so much the better."

"And in the hands of a king, this gem has great power? Power enough to undo even Quisfahr's enchantments?"

She saw the sudden awareness spread to Riella, then Lievve and Falerian.

"Perhaps, but I do not know. And even if it did . . ." Ariana trailed off.

"We have no king among us," Riella said.

Obriel, stoic, nodded as if he had not dared let himself hope.

"Pardon my ignorance," Mischa said, "but why not have Quisfahr himself undo his spell?"

"Because he will not," Obriel said, with a cold look of hate in the mage's direction. "He would sooner doom Shedra to that fate than see her returned to me."

"If he claims to love her," Ariana asked, "how could he do such a thing to her? How could he transform her so?"

"I should very much like to know that myself," Obriel said. "We dare not ungag him to ask such questions, and risk having him enspell us all. Myself, I would happily assume a monstrous form if it meant being with Shedra, but I doubt Quisfahr would be so obliging. And whatever became of me, I would not see any more of my people changed."

"We'd be toads, or worse," Falerian said.

Above his gag, Quisfahr smirked.

Riella plucked at a bit of bread, shedding crumbs onto her lap. "What are we to do with him, then, now that we've captured him? Kill him, and Shedra might never be restored. We cannot force him to use his magic, and we've no assurance he wouldn't turn it on us if we gave him the chance to speak! Some other mage might be his equal, but those of the Emerin have little interest in the barbarians of Lenais . . . and any of sufficient rank and power would want fees that we could never afford to pay. We are snared neatly as any rabbit."

"It's not as bad as all that, sweet Riella," Mischa said, chucking her under the chin. "I'm sure Ariana can help. It's the least we could do."

"Me?" Ariana cried.

"You're a mage, your father's an Archmage, your grandmother is Lenaisian. Why not?"

"My father may be an Archmage, but I'm barely more than his apprentice. I still have much to learn. Quisfahr is of Magelord ranking. I doubt I could counter any of his castings."

A derisive snort of agreement came from Quisfahr's direction.

Mischa leaned toward her and whispered in Thanian, "Ari, I think this pretty little elfmaid likes me. If you can help her brother so he's in a jolly and grateful mood, I might stand a chance without coming out on the wrong end of an arrow. You have to try. For me!"

Lievve, on Ariana's other side, leaned in as well. "You do realize," he said, also in Thanian, "that we had to cross the Northlands to get from our home to the Emerin?"

"Ah." Mischa grinned sheepishly. "No, I hadn't realized that."

Fortunately for him, Obriel's attention was on Ariana. "Have you any advice?"

"I may have an idea," she said, a thought forming. "You said you dare not remove his gag to speak with him, but what if you could? What if you could question him and he had to reply, honestly? I know a spell that will compel him to be truthful. He would have to say whether or not it is even possible to restore Shedra to her normal form. It might help us understand what to do next."

"You can do this?" Obriel asked.

Quisfahr made a muffled, indignant noise. He had not been struggling against his bonds this entire time, but now he strained.

"He does not like the sound of that, I think," Lievve said.

"I believe he's protesting because the spell I would cast on him is, in the Emerin, considered forbidden magic," Ariana said. "But then, so is what he's been doing. I doubt he'd have much of a legal leg to stand upon.

"This is what happens," Mischa said, "when your father is an Archmage, but your mother is a thief. You pick up odd lessons in morality."

"I care nothing for the morality of it," Obriel said. "Not if he can tell us how Shedra might be freed."

"For your knowledge, Mischa," Ariana said, poking him in the ribs, "as the duke's advisor, my father finds that spell rather handy at court. Please do not be so quick to blame my mother for that one."

Obriel smacked a fist into his hand. "Then let us do it without delay. Falerian, clear the camp . . . I want only a half-dozen archers left behind. Riella, go with him, my sister, and let your merry spirit keep the rest at ease."

"And me?" asked Lievve.

"You, my most trusted friend, I would have by my side. But I would also not risk you unduly, for I'd wish you to lead in my stead should anything befall me. I leave it to you to decide."

"I am with you, Obriel, as always."

"Without delay?" Ariana asked as Falerian hurried off. "You want to do this now?"

Quisfahr squirmed and made more muffled noises. Obriel looked at Ariana, and the expression in his brown eyes was answer enough.

"Go with them, Mischa," Ariana said, giving him a little push after the departing Riella. "Help keep Riella's spirit merry."

"If her brother takes exception to a human –"

"These folk are Lenaisian. In their land, humans and elves and elfkin live and love equally. But here. Take this. It is my mother's dragon-ring. If this fails –"

"If he turns you into something gruesome, you mean?"

"Yes, if that . . . then go to my parents. And don't think I'm doing this for your sake, to better your chances with Riella. Whenever Obriel speaks of Shedra, there is a fire about him. He loves her in a way that would consume the earth and skies. I have to help, if I can."

"I've heard of loves like that, Ari. The poets write of them and the minstrels sing of them. But it seems to me that anything that can make a man look as Obriel does cannot be good for you. Too grueling, too demanding, too intense by far." He kissed her on the cheek. "Still, if it means so much to you, do as you will, and gods go with you."

The *Morvalan*, the southern elves, had the reputation for being hasty. But the speed with which Obriel's orders were obeyed might have impressed even them. The camp was soon cleared of people and animals, crafts and chores abandoned half-done without a single query or complaint. All that remained were Obriel, Lievve and Ariana before the captive Quisfahr, and a half-circle of archers at a discreet distance. Obriel had given them their instructions, and though they were clearly unhappy about the prospect of facing Quisfahr's sorcery, they were too loyal to abandon their leader.

Wondering how she had gotten out of Drea's clutches only to find herself in this mess, Ariana approached the bound Quisfahr. His eyes were like glass darts, sharp and clear and colorless, stabbing at her. But she read fear in them as well. A mage would have the greatest knowledge of and respect for magic, thus had her father always instructed her. Quisfahr would have a much better understanding than anyone else here of what she might be capable of doing to him.

"You may make this easy on yourself, Quisfahr," Ariana said. "Speak of your own will, and you'll not have to be compelled by mine."

She pulled the gag from his mouth. He coughed and spat. Around her, the Lenaisians tensed, and half a dozen arrowheads were fixed on Quisfahr's chest.

"You wish my cooperation?" His voice was dry and dusty, and haughty despite his undignified position. "After your brutish human slaughtered my baby? What threat could you make, what pain could you promise, that could be greater than I've already suffered?"

"I warrant I can think of some," Obriel said, with a growl.

Ariana waved him back without shifting her gaze from Quisfahr. "Tell me about Shedra. Why did you transform her?"

"I love her."

"You don't know the meaning of the word." Obriel tried to step forward, but Lievve grasped his arm.

"Speak on, Quisfahr," Ariana said.

"I will say no more to you, nor feel any need to justify myself before these barbarians." He clenched his jaw and turned his head away.

Ariana sighed. "The hard way it is, then. *Lartei.*"

The *aether* flowed from her, encountering the barrier of Quisfahr's struggling, stubborn will. For a moment, she was in doubt, but then his resistance broke in a watery sob.

"Tell me about Shedra," Ariana repeated.

"I followed her that night as she went to bathe," Quisfahr said, his miserable, tear-filled eyes downcast. "I meant only to beg her to love me, to win her before it was too late. I never meant to harm her. Not for all the world would I have done that. But when I tried to speak to her, she ran from me! She ran into the marsh. I . . . I heard her scream. When I reached her, a blue viper had bitten her. Its fangs were wedged in the bone of her wrist. In her panic, she fell into the water. I tried to pull her out, but an alligator attacked. It was savaging her, savaging her with its teeth. Killing her."

Obriel groaned as if the agony Shedra must have felt was his own.

"She was dying . . . the poison working in her even as she bled. There was no time. I did the only thing I could do. I merged them. To save her. To make her immune from the venom. I *healed* her. I saved her life. But she still lashed out at me. She fled into the swamps. I have been searching for her ever since. Calling her, summoning her. And I found her, finally found her, only to have *you* get in the way . . . again!"

He flung the last words like stones at Obriel, who had gone ashen beneath his tan. Lievve was supporting him, looking pale himself.

"Can you undo your spell?" Ariana asked, maintaining the compulsion that forced him to speak true.

"Yes," he said, slumping dispiritedly in his bonds as the admission was wrenched from his lips. "I can return her to her natural form."

"Then we must find her," Obriel said, his tone that of one who dared not let himself hope too much just yet. "Where is she?"

"Where?" Quisfahr looked up with a strange little smile. "Why, she's here. I called her, and she is here."

One of the archers shrieked, but his cry was lost in an enraged roar as Shedra hurled his torn body through the air.

* * *

CHAPTER SIXTEEN

The mercy of the wildlands is by quick tooth and claw.
– Elwyndas, Song of Lenais

She was upon them, and the lightning-fast reflexes of the hunter-elves were useless in the face of their horror. They couldn't even draw back their bows, let alone aim and fire. Helpless, rooted to the spot, they only stared and screamed and ran as the monster rampaged into the camp.

"Yes!" Quisfahr cried. "She comes to me! My darling! She knows she is mine."

Ariana saw Obriel get his first clear look at what had become of his beloved. It was as if a candle whiffed out in his eyes. The light of his mind was gone, snuffed, nothing left but a thread of smoke. He sank to his knees. One shaking hand reached out toward Shedra in imploring desperation, or denial.

Lievve dashed to Quisfahr, drew his knife and slashed the ropes that had bound his wrists behind the stake. "Restore her. Do it."

"When she's finished, when she's finished," Quisfahr said, crossing his arms insolently.

"Now." Lievve set the blade to Quisfahr's throat.

"Kill me, and you'll never –"

"Kill him," Ariana said, startled at the hard edge in her own voice. "We'll find some other way."

"All right!" Quisfahr blurted. "All right, I'll do as you bid. But she must be subdued first. I need time and peace to work my magic."

"Hold your arrows!" Obriel shouted at his men. "Nets! Snare her. Bind her! Shedra! Shedra, no, we are your friends!"

The hideous head whipped around toward his voice, and then she was coming closer, arms thrusting at the ground, tail coiling and propelling her along. One of the archers raced up with a net. Shedra screeched, swung her claws. He got an arm up to save his face, but before her blow hurled him backward in a shower of blood, that arm was severed.

She halted before Obriel, her scaled breasts heaving and blue foam running freely from her fangs. If there was a spark of elven consciousness left in her, Ariana could not see it.

"Shedra. Oh, gods, my dear Shedra."

In a heartbeat, she would strike . . . she would bite into Obriel's skull as easily as Ariana had bitten into the tart purple berries. Quisfahr was laughing despite Lievve's knife at his throat. None of the others were near enough to help.

Before the deadly jaws closed on his head, Obriel sprang into action. He seized up the fallen net and flung it over Shedra, entangling her upper half. Her tail lashed out and struck Obriel square in the chest. He crashed into and through the side of a hut, which collapsed, burying him in splintered wood. The net parted like fine thread under her claws. Shedra tore partway free, voicing her rage and triumph in a dreadful roar.

"Obriel!" Lievve turned to the remaining archers. "Shoot her! We cannot stop her now without slaying her, shoot her, in Denethel's name!"

"No!" Quisfahr's legs were still tied, but the rope drooped like the coils of a dead serpent around his feet. Another length secured him to the stake at waist-level. He was wrenching his body back and forth, working the end out of the ground like a loose tooth from the gumline.

"Wait!" Ariana thrust out her hands, thumbs touching, fingers spread like fans toward Shedra. "*Niahan!*"

A cold, cold force built in her, then rushed out. Freezing wind, bitter as any winter's blizzard, issued from her hands. Howling, swirling with ice and snow, the wind engulfed Shedra. Her next shriek was of shock and outrage. Within a seething white funnel, her frenzied movements began to slow.

"Yes!" Lievve said, eyes wide. "She is more reptile now than woman . . . the cold weakens her!"

The spell took all of Ariana's own strength, and still Shedra was fighting. She could not let the snowstorm lapse. But the opal *ilgilean*, meant for just such an occasion, was with her other clothes. Riella had removed it when bathing her. Its stored aether could do her no good from here.

"Too much," Ariana said. "I cannot . . . maintain . . ."

And still Shedra fought. Her stuggles were becoming sluggish, but it was not enough, not enough. Already, the icy wind was slackening. Ariana could barely stay upright. A bone-deep ache spread through her body as the magic took its toll on her living flesh. She was cold, so cold that her skin felt coated in frost.

"Hah!" Quisfahr thrust his arms in the air. "You cannot stop her! She'll outlast you!"

"Mayhap not." Lievve embraced Ariana from behind, holding her as he brought his head alongside hers. His lips brushed her earlobe, his breath hot. "Let my strength be yours. Take of it freely. *Sala Lor.*"

Ariana gasped as Lievve's spell took effect. He became as a living *ilgilean*, pouring his energy into her. She seized upon it as gratefully, feeling it flow into and through her, warming her as a draught of strong tea might warm her on a winter night. At once, her hands grew steady, and the chill wind blew with more force than ever before.

Shedra faltered and swayed, her limbs stiffening. As Ariana had hoped, she was slowing, her reptilian body entering a lethargic state as the cold permeated her blood. Shedra fell like a toppling tree and landed with a heavy crash on the ice-caked earth. She was barely breathing, eyes half-lidded and a scum of venom frozen on her lips.

"It is done." Ariana leaned against Lievve, trembling all over.

"No!" wailed Quisfahr. He had gotten free of the stake and ran to Shedra, trailing ropes. "Shedra, my darling, no!"

Obriel, scratched and gouged and bleeding from his violent trip through the wall of the hut, got there first. His fist closed in Quisfahr's pale hair and jerked him up short an instant before he could touch Shedra. Splinters, some the size of arrow shafts, pierced Obriel in several places, but he appeared oblivious to the pain. He kicked Quisfahr's legs out from under him, forcing the mage to his knees near Shedra's motionless form.

"Work your spell, Quisfahr."

"Never! She is mine! Mine, curse you! I –"

He would have ranted on, but Obriel's knife flashed and sliced off the tip of his ear. Quisfahr's squeal was so high-pitched that crystal might have shattered. Lievve, still holding Ariana, winced and tightened his arms around her.

Grim and steady despite it all, Obriel bent and poked the severed bit on the dagger's point. He brought it before Quisfahr's disbelieving eyes.

"Do as I say," he said, "or this shall be just the beginning."

"I'm all right," Ariana said. "Help the others."

Lievve let go of her and hurried to the fallen men, some of whom were likely already far beyond help. The unhurt or barely hurt survivors flocked close, standing ready at Obriel's side. Quisfahr, mewling and blubbering, did an awkward hitch-crawl toward Shedra with Obriel's fist still clutching him by the hair. He laid his hands on the twisted, tortured, scaled figure.

A marshfire-green glow spread from his fingers to envelop her. Bones cracked. Flesh shifted and flowed like warm wax. Scales melted into skin. The long tail dwindled and split, while another tail, knobbed and ridged, extruded from another spot. Limbs appeared as if sculpted by an unseen artisan.

The glow around Shedra brightened until it was painful to behold, yet Ariana could not look away. This was magic that put anything she could do to shame. The mass of the body was drawing apart into three distinct forms, two large, one small. Then the marshfire-green diffused into nothingness, and it was over.

They lay all in a row. The snake, its head and back speckled with blue markings. The alligator with its teeth nestled in the nooks and crannies of its jaw. Between them, naked and so very fragile, was the body of an elfmaid. All three were motionless, paralyzed by the deep cold, but it was Shedra that moved first.

She shivered on the icy earth, and sat up, wrapping thin arms around herself. Dazed and dreamlike, she looked from one face to another.

"Shedra . . ." Obriel said.

Her gaze found him, and her mouth hesitantly, silently formed his name. He knelt and with great tenderness gathered her to his chest. Her thin arms crept around his neck. As he stood, he turned to Quisfahr.

Shedra recoiled against Obriel at the sight of him. Quisfahr stared at her yearningly, seemingly unmindful of his maimed ear and the blood streaming down the side of his neck.

"Please . . ." he said in a cracked, imploring tone. "You are meant to be mine. Please, Shedra. All I ask is your love."

"Stand aside, Quisfahr," Obriel said. "She is not yours and will never be."

Quisfahr hung his head. "Yes . . . I see now . . . you two belong together."

A dark wave of premonition swept over Ariana. Though she was still weak, she locked gazes with Lievve and tried to send him an urgent, unspoken warning.

"And so," Quisfahr went on, "you *shall* be."

Lievve's eyes flew wide in understanding. He reached for his knife but the sheath was empty, the blade dropped at some point during the confusion.

Green mist formed a sphere between Quisfahr's palms. He looked up at Obriel. The marshfire glow cast an eerie radiance over his face, making him look as mad as he truly was.

"Eternally together," Quisfahr said.

Alarmed cries burst forth as the rest realized what he intended, but no one was close enough to intervene.

"*Firalel!*" Ariana barely got the word out. Pain twisted through her, bored into her like rusty metal and broken glass. She was too weak yet for even a child's spell. To do this, to shield them both, was a tremendous demand.

Lievve leaped at Quisfahr, who shrank back, his brow furrowed in concentration as he sought to keep control of his casting. Just before Lievve collided with him, he threw.

The sickly green sphere streaked through the air, directly at Obriel and Shedra. A hair's breadth before striking them, it curved in its flight. Curved, turned by Ariana's spell, it sailed past them to explode in a bright flare against a tanner's rack.

Quisfahr's outraged, infuriated curse was cut off as Lievve, lacking weapons, wrenched his head to the side and snapped his neck.

"There," Ariana murmured, and closed her eyes.

* * *

Low whispers and giggling wakened her, and Ariana was not immediately sure where she was. The place seemed familiar, and the whispering, giggling voices sounded familiar, but . . .

The cot. The hut. No one was brushing her hair this time, though. When she turned her head, she saw Riella and Mischa sitting side by side, heads close, fingers interlaced.

Ariana smiled. "I am loath to disturb you two, but perhaps I should leave and give you some privacy?"

"Or stay, if you'd rather," Mischa said with a wink. "*I* don't mind."

Riella blushed and straightened her tunic, which had somehow come a trifle disarrayed. "How do you feel, Ariana? My brother hoped to see you once you'd revived. We are all so grateful."

"I think I'm fine," she said after careful consulation with her nerves. "I've never taxed myself so before. But I only needed rest, to replenish. What of everyone else?"

"Obriel lost two men." Mischa sighed. "Gods keep them. But only two, considering how it could have been . . ."

"And Quisfahr is dead," Riella said. "He'll work his foul magics no more."

"I saw Lievve kill him," Ariana said. "He had no choice. I would have done it myself, if I'd been able, but I had to shield them from Quisfahr's spell."

Riella nodded. "Lievve told me what happened. Biraine had two rabbit pelts and a dun-striped pantera hide stretched there . . . but now the furs and the frame of the rack itself are all . . . enmeshed. They cannot be separated. That would have been Obriel and Shedra, had you not diverted his spell. We're many times in your debt."

"Among friends, there is no need to keep such accounts," Ariana said. "Now, do excuse me, for I am famished."

"We'll be along in a while," Mischa said, sliding an arm around Riella's waist.

"I'll not hold my breath." Ariana ducked out of the hut.

The camp was hushed but not solemn. Relief and joy could be seen on every face, even those of the archers who had been wounded in the attack. Although two men had died, these Lenaisians were not strangers to the harsher realities of wildland life, and better accustomed to dealing with death than were their Emerinian counterparts. Thus, they remembered and honored the dead, while those who yet lived were all the more thankful for having been spared.

Ariana had not been being untruthful about being famished. Her last meal had been interrupted, and the casting she'd done had left her ravenous. Once she'd come out into the rich smells from the cookfires, her hunger deepened. Soon she was enjoying herb-roasted venison swimming in rich gravy, crusty brown bread, baked apples with a spicy sauce, and cup after cup of wine urged on her by Lenaisians wishing to toast her their gratitude.

More than a little light-headed, she finally found Lievve at the bedside of the most sorely-hurt survivor. Mischa had done what he could to repair the grievous wounds caused by Shedra's claws, but even the powers of Talopea could only accomplish so much. Bandages wrapped his torso, and a cast of birchbark – wetted to conform to his shape and then allowed to dry into a hard cast – encased him from shoulder to wrist. But he was young, and awake and in good spirits.

"Hail, silver lady," the archer said.

"Hail, brave hunter," she replied. "How do you fare?"

"I've found reason to praise the viper's venom after all. It dulls the pain better than a mother's kiss."

Lievve grinned. "Khoray is a merry sort. It would take far more than near-death to dim his light."

"I'm pleased to know it. What of Obriel and Shedra?"

"As well as can be. Obriel barely seemed to notice his injuries, the healing of them, or the medicinal tonic I made him drink, though normally the taste of it makes even him fuss and complain like a willful little boy. Shedra has little memory of her time as the beast, which I count as a blessing. The shock has left her unable to speak. But she knows, and cannot escape the knowledge, that she inflicted these hurts on her friends. That weighs heavy on her."

"Surely no one faults her for it."

"No, never." He socked Khoray playfully on his good arm and told him to rest, then walked with Ariana toward the largest of the huts. "We all know who was to blame. She was as much a victim of evil as were the viper and the alligator, and we released the both of them unharmed."

"And you, Lievve?"

"You wonder if I suffer guilt for the death of Quisfahr." He shook his head. "I have killed men before, I'm sorry to say. Never an elf until now, but then, if any were unworthy of the name, it was Quisfahr. Had he been put to Obriel's justice, one of us still would have had to be the one to sink arrow into his heart. What I did, I did to save my friends. I would do so again without question."

"I have led a sheltered life," Ariana said. "I have trained, I have studied . . . but until a few scant weeks ago, I had never known true combat. Never been placed where life and death depend on my actions, nor had to take such responsibility. I do not know . . . if I could have done what you did."

"Yet you knew it had to be done. And I tell you this, Ariana . . . you acted with courage and cunning this day."

"What . . . what was done with his body? Despite all that he did, I wouldn't like to think that he was left for the scavengers."

"We do not use full rosecloth wrappings and crypts as you Emerinians do," Lievve said, "but I agree, even Quisfahr deserved the respect accorded the dead. We anointed him with rose oil and entombed him in the forest earth."

He rapped on the hut's door, and Obriel's voice bade them enter.

Shedra rose from a chair as Lievve and Ariana came in. She was tall and very thin, and on first look was not what the poets of the Emerin would call any great beauty. Her shoulder-length hair was light brown and softly feathered around a face a bit too oval, her mouth a bit too wide, her nose a bit too long.

Yet, although she was far from the elven ideal, there was something about her . . . a sweetness in her cloud-grey eyes, an innocence, a gentleness . . . that made Ariana understand why men should love her so dearly. Even men as deranged as Quisfahr.

Lievve had said she could not speak. Ariana could see her struggling to form words, and went to her instead. She was younger than Shedra by several decades, yet felt older, and protective. They embraced like sisters.

Obriel went to one knee before Ariana. "Lady –"

"Please, no," Ariana interrupted. "To see you rejoined with your love is all anyone could wish. It gladdens my heart to have been able to be a part of it."

"You risked much for strangers."

"As I told your sister, for *friends*." She drew him to his feet. "Let us be friends, Obriel."

"Our home, wherever we may wander, shall always be open to you."

"And mine the same, whether it be in far Gamelin, or here in the Emerin."

She and Lievve sat, and took wine – not that Ariana needed more wine – with Obriel and Shedra. The way the two of them kept gazing at each other, as if they could not look enough, could not fill their sight, made Ariana's heart well with emotion.

"Soon," Obriel said, "we will be putting this place behind us. We have stayed in this spot far longer than originally intended. Our path lies eastward to the sea, if you and Mischa would care to travel with us."

"If I did not have business to the north and in Perras Peliani, I would be happy to. Perhaps someday, I will reach the sea and meet you there."

"You'll be welcome," Lievve said. "And you'll at least stay a few more days? We have a long-delayed promise feast to celebrate. Don't we, Obriel, Shedra?"

"I'd not miss it," Ariana said.

As they finished the wine, Lievve and Obriel discussed plans for a hunt the following day, in preparation for the promise feast. Shedra, with an achingly sweet and dear smile, sat and listened, and her hand kept straying to touch Obriel's arm, hair or face as if she could not believe she was really herself again. That she was reunited with her love, against all odds. It made Ariana think of her own parents, and the powerful love they shared. She wondered what it must be like. Whether she herself would ever find it, know it, or be able to withstand it if she did.

"A long day indeed," Ariana said, later, as she and Lievve emerged from Obriel's hut. "It's just as well that I am no huntress, to rise at dawn. Tomorrow, I'll follow Mischa's example, and sleep until the sun climbs high."

"I'll walk back with you to Riella's, then, and say good night."

But when they got there, Ariana stopped, eyebrows raised. There was no mistaking the sounds coming from within Riella's little hut. "It seems she has other company tonight."

"So it does." Lievve smothered a chuckle. "She chooses her times well. Obriel, I'm sure, has far better things to occupy his mind than worrying what his sister is up to. What will you do?"

"After a day such as this has been, the thought of a bedroll on the bare ground is almost as appealing as would be a feather bed." She glanced sidelong at him in the firelight, feeling bold from the wine. "Unless you have any other recommendations?"

"I may . . ." he said.

"I've not forgotten how it was to be held by you, nor the feel of your breath in my ear."

His hand stole into her hair, parting the silver strands. "This ear?"

Ariana sighed as his fingers traced the rim. "That very one."

"As it happens," Lievve said, "my hut is quite close."

"Good," she said.

* * *

CHAPTER SEVENTEEN

And yet that threat hangs over us, even in the hour of our revelry.
– Elwyndas, The Queen's Lament, Act XIV

"Well, well," Tiercel said. "This is an interesting development indeed."

He looked down at the festive Lenaisian camp. Some sort of celebration was underway, looking like a primitive and barbaric variation on the betrothal feast he had so recently attended in honor of his nephew and Liana Riachlain. He could hear their music and lively laughter, smell their roasting meat and heady wine, see their cavorting shadows as they danced around the fires.

"Curious hadst thou been, to where Mirida's daughter had so suddenly departed."

"Yes . . . she left without a word even to the High Steward, and certainly without broaching her mysterious business with the Council. Now we find her here. What does that tell you?"

"That alone in thy notion were thou not, the Emerald to retrieve."

"I don't know how she learned of it, and I certainly don't know what made her deem herself worthy to go after it. With her *human* in tow."

"Of Karria's Temple, a base defilement it would be." A black-gloved hand caressed the ruby pommel of a sword.

Tiercel watched Mirida's daughter, her hair flaring behind her like the silver banner of the Order of the Eagle, her face alight and fair as she danced with some disheveled blond huntsman. The daughter of an Emerinian nobleman, down there with the barbarians. What would her father make of that?

Then he remembered, sourly, that her father had thrown over the exquisite Alinora Elyvorrin in favor of an elfkin bedmate. Obviously, Arien Mirida would not be in a position to say much about his daughter's choice in partners.

"Swordmaid, upstart, exile's child . . . what could *she* want with the Emerald? Profit? Power?

And what are we to do about it? We could destroy that camp, you and I."

"Nay. Though corrupted doth be their blood, the Lenaisians still elvenfolk are. And mayhap, bold Tiercel, underestimate them thou dost. Thine eyes may no armor see, but warriors hardened and honed are they."

"Their arrows might fly true to the mark, but we can both shield. Between Discordant and Baleful Gaze, we would cut through them as if they were made of parchment."

"If there to fight thou goest, thou goest alone. On innocent elves, I'll not whet my blade."

He turned to retort, perhaps even to challenge, but the words died on his lips as he saw something emerge from the brush. His companion took notice of his gaze and likewise turned, then breathed a single word, at once oath and prayer.

"Kaledhol!"

The creature stood out well against the black and green of the forest night, its hide a greasy pallid white in color. Its form was that of a large dog or a wolf, but it was hairless and hooved and rat-tailed. Its eyes were pink-red and bulbous, set narrowly above a protruding piglike snout. Beneath the snout was a wet cave lined with inward-curving spines of teeth.

Tiercel drew Discordant, which hummed in eager anticipation of combat. He dared not use its potent shriek, and bring down the Lenaisians upon them. This fight would have to be done in silence.

Baleful Gaze slid from its scabbard, the dark blade nearly invisible in the shadows. Sparks of red fire winked from the jeweled eyes of the silver basilisk-shape of its hilt.

The dog-thing advanced, head swinging back and forth as if it was trying to decide which of them to devour first. Tiercel settled the matter by lunging, Discordant's point outthrust in perfect extension, meaning to spit the thing's foul heart and be done with it.

Discordant sank into flesh without meeting resistance, passing through as if it had pierced nothing more substantial than mist. Tiercel, unprepared, was left open for its attack. A ring of teeth clamped down on his sword arm, penetrating his chainmail effortlessly. What felt like a thousand burning needles drove into him.

Only his will kept him from crying out. He tried to jerk his arm away and failed, dragging the teeth in widening gashes.

A smooth swing from Baleful Gaze would have cleaved the dog-thing in two, had the sword not passed through as harmlessly as Discordant had done. It chopped into the earth instead and wedged there.

"Impervious to our weapons it is!"

Tiercel braced his other hand on the dog-thing's jaw and pushed with all his strength. He could touch it, but he realized with sick horror that he could *feel* its pasty hairless skin against his. As if he wore no gauntlet at all.

"And our armor," he said through gritted teeth. "To all metal. We may as well be unclad."

"Then by hand must we combat it."

Together, grappling it by the head and jaws, they forced its mouth open to let Tiercel free his lacerated, bleeding arm.

He threw himself flat on his back and kicked out. His boots, good heavy leather, struck the beast's side. Yes, it was solid enough, so solid that the impact vibrated up Tiercel's spine. And so tough that he didn't budge it, didn't feel a single rib crack beneath his heels.

"*Ha-nah!*" his companion called. "Kaledhol, to Thy servant, grant Thy Might!"

Maroon light, death-rose light, bloomed around black gloves as they locked, one on the upper and one on the lower of the dog-thing's jaws. One sudden convulsive wrenching, with strength ten times that of any elf, and bone split asunder.

The lifeless body thudded to the ground.

Only now did Tiercel permit himself to groan in pain, hunching over his arm. He stripped off his cloak and his surcoat. His chainmail was woven in the way that only the elves could do, not linked clumsy rings that would allow arrows to wedge between them but a supple, flexible, almost impenetrable mesh. By most weapons, anyway. It was unmarked, undamaged, his blood filtering through.

When he removed the top half of his armor, the sleeve of the cloth undersuit was sodden and in shreds. The same could be said for his skin.

Like most professional soldiers, he had fair first-hand experience and education in field medicine. Having also the advantages of a noble upbringing, a decent degree of the talent and a familial connection in the secretive world of the physicians, he had supplemented his training with a bit of healing magic on the sly. Now, pushing the pain to the back of his mind, he concentrated and cast.

"*Salahin Roas*," he said.

At once, a soothing balm washed over him. The smallest of the many gouges drew together, leaving just tiny pinkish scars that would soon fade. The larger ones, the deep cuts that he'd earned from trying to pull free, slowed in their leaking.

"To all metal, a phantom," his companion marveled, prodding at the corpse. "Yet to wood or stone or flesh, as substantial as thee or I doth it be. From whence came it, I wonder?"

"I'd very much like to know that myself." Tiercel set about wrapping his arm in bandages. "We're not far from the Enclave. This must be the work of the shaper-mages."

"Threatened enough are our people, without new threats devising."

"The music has stopped. Did they hear us?" Tiercel put his armor back on, thinking that the familiar weight of it did not seem so comforting and protective now.

"Disturbed the Lenaisians we seem to have not," came the report. "Only an end to their feasting have they called, and to their huts retired. Though not, I daresay, will sleep be soon for many."

"And they are camped at the very base of what's left of the Towering Tree," he said, disgusted. "To do this in full accordance with the legend, we should go *through* the tree, not around it. Still, as you are unwilling to fight them and I won't fully trust my sword arm until tomorrow, it seems the choice is made for us. We wait."

*   *   *

Chapter Eighteen

And tumbling waters do cascade, necklaces of jewels.
– Elwyndas, Ryvali (ballad)

"She's not in the habit, you see, of leaping into bed on short acquaintance." Mischa spoke as if to the rainy forest around them, not looking over at Ariana.

She rolled her eyes. "You bring my words against me, is that it?"

"When it seems fitting."

"I'm amazed you've left it wait this long to mention."

They had left Towering Tree several days before, heading north following Obriel's admirable directions. Thus far, they had stayed clear of more swamps or any other hazards. They'd loaded their belongings onto Mischa's horse and hiked on, as fast and far as they could manage in each day's march.

"Why Lievve? May I ask? How could he seduce you in one day, when I've failed week after week?"

"Perhaps *I* seduced him. Perhaps you try too hard. Perhaps there was more between us than you realize."

"Oh? Do tell!"

"We shared magic, Mischa. When he lent me his strength to complete my spell, it was unlike the manner with which I'm familiar. The Emerinian method is to be detached, apart. This was different. In that exchange, I knew him as if I'd known him for decades."

"Does that make you fall in love with him, then?"

"No," she said. "There was a closeness between us, that's all. Why does this strike you so strange? Is it so odd that I should take a lover if I wish to?"

"Of course not. It's just odd –"

"That I haven't taken you? I know this will cut you to the quick, Mischa, but in truth, I've come to think of you more –"

He held up a warning finger. "Do not say 'as a brother,' Ari, I beg you. Not that. Anything but that, any words but those."

"Then there is nothing I can say. Why does this nettle you so? Do you honestly mean to tell me you've won *every* woman you've ever pursued?"

"Well, yes, as a matter of fact," he said. "And every man. Well . . . but for Yolanda Martane, and that was purely a matter of timing. I was to meet with her when you and Tal arrived, and forgot all about her the moment I set eyes on you."

"So you've never been denied?"

"Never. Perhaps I do try too hard, at least with you. Well, then. Consider me henceforth uninterested." He folded his arms across his chest. "There."

Ariana laughed. "Oh, Mischa. You don't truly think that'll work? Besides, I thought you'd finally lived out your dream, the purpose for which you came to the Emerin."

"Riella, I grant you, is a lovely girl and I could nibble on her ears from now 'til Wintersfest. But she is still only one elfmaid. I came to the Emerin with grander hopes than that."

"I hope you didn't speak of 'nibbling her ears' in front of her brother, or the rest of the camp," Ariana said. "That's rather indelicate talk, you know."

They had stayed for the promise feast, but the following morning, something had happened that made Ariana want to resume their journey as soon as possible. Two of the Lenaisian children had caught a peculiar bird, a bird that had proved to be no bird at all. It had been one of Drea's little subjects, and Ariana was sure that it had been sent to follow her. Perhaps tracking her by seeker-magic, perhaps even by the very token Drea had supposedly given her as a sign of her victory in the riddle game.

She had even less reason now than before to trust any kinswoman of the likes of Quisfahr. Or, indeed, any shaper-mage, if they were even half as mad. And if Drea took it in mind to avenge her cousin . . .

The bird-creature had been caged and given into Lievve's custody. He told Ariana he would release it once they had broken camp and gone on their way. The green braided cord bracelet, she had tied around the neck of a rabbit and turned it loose to go hopping off into the woods. Let Drea track that, if she wished.

"Oilskin tents . . . oilskin cloaks . . . do you think they knew when they gave us these generous gifts that the weather was going to turn, or was it just happenstance?" Mischa said as the rain intensified.

"I'm certain they knew." Ariana concentrated a moment, maintaining the spells that kept the two of them dry. "Be thankful I learned water magics at my father's knee, else we'd be as drenched as your poor mount here, oilskin or no oilskin."

Between the din of the steadily pounding rain and the increasing roar of the *Fenne-dar*, conversation soon became too much of an effort. They trudged on, Ariana's spell protecting them admirably against the downpour but not at all against the water that collected on leaves and in puddles, or from the spray when the horse gave a good shake.

When it began to get dark, prematurely dark thanks to the clouds, they stopped for the night. Mischa agreed to set up camp while Ariana paced off the line she would use as the limit of her protective wards.

She returned to find Mischa rocking back on his heels in satisfaction. "There. Who would have thought that I, Mischa Narrin, would grow so adept at this? If only Rayle and Josef could see me now!"

Ari nodded approvingly at the sight of their two tents set up so that the openings faced one another, with their oilskin cloaks suspended on poles between them to allow a covered expanse in the middle. A circle of stones held sticks and kindling, just waiting for her spell to ignite them.

"We'll make a woodsman of you yet," she said.

"I never *wanted* to be a woodsman." He stood under the rain, and grinned as the drops turned into fine mist before touching him. "As welcome as this is, how am I supposed to rinse the mud from my hands?"

"Wash them in the river. Half a moment, and I'll join you. I want to see if we're at all near the ford on the map Falerian showed me."

"I'm so glad that we're not stuck with directions from a two hundred year old book anymore," he said, with overdone innocence. "A map only not yet half a century out of date is so much the better."

"We found the river, didn't we?"

"Had you but asked, we could have had a Lenaisian guide to show us the way, and provide fresh meat for the fire into the bargain. Lievve, for instance. I'm sure he would have offered."

"As a matter of fact, he did offer, and I declined."

"Mmm-hmm," he said. "There's a surprise."

She secured the horse's feedbag, checked to be sure the reins were tied so as to prevent any wanderings, and turned to Mischa. "By your tone, I suspect you have more to say on the matter?"

"No, not at all. I've come to a realization about you, Ariana. I understand you now. You're terrified of commitment. More so than am I, and that, I must admit, is saying something."

"That is preposterous!"

"Rubbish. You fled Tradersport to escape this Gavin fellow. Talus Yor, well, all the Northlands know he'll *never* wed, therefore he was a safe choice. You only took Lievve as a lover because you knew you'd both be going your separate ways soon. No entanglements. No risk. You just keep running."

She was so astounded that when the slight mental signal came warning her that she needed to exert a moment's thought to maintain her spell, she utterly missed it. Cold water sluiced over them both, making her gasp and him yelp.

"You did that on purpose," he said.

"I didn't! And I'm not running from anything. Don't be a fool."

"It even explains why you wouldn't share my bed. After all, traveling together for months, you were fearful of falling in love with me but knowing that I'd never return it in that manner. So you've kept me at arm's length."

"Your arrogance knows no bounds, Mischa!"

"You give of your body when there's no risk to your heart," he said with a shrug. "The rest of the time, you play the ice maiden. Hiding your quicksilver passions and tempers beneath a mask. Because you don't want anyone to get close."

"This is the most inane, absurd, ridiculous prattle I've ever heard." She turned around and stomped back to camp, telling herself that she wouldn't be able to see a ford in the rain and the gloaming anyway, and it could just as well wait until daylight.

As she went into her tent and tied the flaps with such hard yanks at the knots that they nearly snapped, she could hear Mischa's laugh. She only barely resisted the urge to call up a few spells and demonstrate to him that a little rain wasn't so bad. Not compared to hail, or, oh, just for the sake of argument, a jet of pure freezing frost.

That notion brought her up short. That it would come to this, that she would be reduced to trying to silence him by physical and magical threats . . . just what did that say about his argument?

Subdued and thoughtful, she swapped wet clothes for dry and re-braided her hair into a thick cable. As she was putting her comb away, she found her mother's dragon signet, which Mischa had returned to her. She held it in one hand and her opal *ilgilean* in the other and looked back and forth between them.

"Livana," she said softly. "I *am* my father's daughter. He lived a century cold and alone. Yet what he did, he did in remembrance of pain, and overcame it. I have no such remembrance, but still . . . can it be? Could he be right? And Mother . . . who gives so openly of her heart . . . did I inherit so little of her trust?"

Her mind mulling on it, she placed the ring on her finger and the *ilgilean's* chain once more around her neck.

* * *

They spent a quiet night, Ariana lost in her own contemplations and Mischa perhaps thinking he'd said too much or pushed too far.

Dawn came grudgingly, the fog so thick that it was as if a cloud had settled to earth. That heavy hanging mist permeated everything, rendering Ariana's rain-shielding spell useless and turning the fire that they'd kept burning so cheerily into a dispirited flicker.

"Mischa," she said over a breakfast of half-cooked porridge and dried fruit, "I owe you an apology."

"It's all right, Ari. You needn't –"

"Yes, I do." She leaned forward and covered his hand with hers, looking urgently into his hazel eyes. "You were right. What you said last night was true. I wanted to deny it, but it's true. I have been running. Though not all in avoidance. With part of my heart, I'm . . . searching."

"For that great poetic love?" he asked. "Like your parents have, or like Obriel and Shedra?"

"And yet, at the same time, I'm afraid that I lack the strength to suffer and endure such a love. I watched my father and learned to be composed, when I should have been watching my mother, and learning to be strong."

"You are strong, Ariana. You'll see. Now, eat your porridge. It's good for you."

"And I must also apologize for . . . for the way I've thought of you, and treated you. I never guessed you could be so insightful."

"If you swear not to tell, lest it ruin the Talopean reputation . . . they do teach us more than the art of loveplay. Before we can minister to the desires of the body, we're taught to listen to the needs of the soul. Most of us just hide it. Maybe a bit too well."

"Why? Why cloak this wisdom, why let all the world believe that your entire faith cares for nothing but pleasure?"

He chuckled and shook his head. "Such questions are for higher-ranking priests than me. Have you ever met a priest of Galatine? Or the Helianites? Followers of Blackmoon? Any faith that is built on deprivation and self-punishment, on always striving to placate demanding gods . . . all I know is that every one of them I've ever met is too anxious of body, too weighted of mind. They are so wrapped up in what they *must not* do that they give themselves headaches and delicate digestion. Talopea is kinder."

"I *have* met priests of Galatine and Helia," she said. "They denounce your faith most vehemently, for the reverse of the reasons you gave."

They broke camp, loaded their possessions on the horse, and descended to the river. By the time they reached its banks and found the ford, the mist had lifted, but the sky overhead was still dark and threatening.

"Falerian's map showed the ruins of an old keep on the other side," Ariana said. "If our luck holds, it'll be sound enough to shelter in. We'll be in for another wet night otherwise."

"Sleep *indoors*?" he gasped with exaggerated awe. "Inside real stone walls? Gods' truth?"

"I don't promise. Still, we can look." She picked her way to the edge of the river, where she halted in dismay.

Maybe it had been a ford, five decades ago when the map had been drawn. Now it was merely a shallower, wider part of the river. Downstream, the water churned into a white froth as it raced into a chute formed by granite outcroppings. Upstream, it leaped over rapids and slick stones.

"Don't tell me we have to swim," Mischa said. "It looks cold."

"It is cold," she said, after bending to dip her fingers. "But I have a better idea."

Their baggage was uncomfortably bulky beneath them, and the precariousness of their perch – Ariana astride behind Mischa, and clinging to him – would have made it an impossible feat for any great distance. The horse, having perhaps gotten used to not having to bear any riders, let alone two, whickered and tossed its head as Mischa urged it closer to the water's edge.

"*Nia Aras*," Ariana said.

The toll was immediate and draining, for a horse was a far larger target than a single person would have been. She sensed the horse's blind animal resistance to her spell and overcame it with ease, envisioning silver-blue energy running down the big body and making its hooves shimmer. When the first hoof contacted water, it did not sink in, and the horse blew a startled breath through its nostrils.

Slowly at first, they moved out onto the placid surface. Their reflections paced them, distorted by ripples and raindrops and the occasional leaping fish.

"We must move faster," she said. "I cannot maintain it long, and when it ends . . ."

"Splash?"

Their pace quickened, the horse more sure now, the jolt of hoofbeats muffled as if they rode across a padded, wet carpet. More fish flickered past and beneath, as if crowding to view this astonishing thing. Ariana felt the last of her strength slip into the spell and drew upon the *ilgilean*. She knew it would be close. Still two yards from the bank, it let go. They plunged into water belly-deep on the horse, alarming it so that it leaped forward. Then they were ashore, the horse prancing about unhappily, she and Mischa soaked to the knees.

"Sleep indoors, you said," he reminded her.

"If we can find the keep."

A fruitless hour of searching later, as Ariana was about to admit that fifty years, while not a long time in the life of the typical elf, could wreak destruction on something that had already been a crumbling old ruin, Mischa turned and peered at her from under the hood of his oilskin cloak.

"This seeker-spell of yours," he said. "Can't you seek the keep?"

"I've never been there. Maybe a true seeker-mage could, but . . ."

"So we go on looking."

Mischa led the way, kicking cautiously at the ferns as if mindful for snares, though in all likelihood, had there been any, his method of testing would have surely gotten him caught. The horse paused to sample some leaves off low-hanging branches.

At last, they came to some old paving-stones half buried in the wet earth, and something that might have once been a road marker. They followed these until a shadowed bulk loomed ahead of them. What had once been a proud tower, not circular in the usual elven style but hexagonal, was now a tumble of masonry and jutting timbers, overlaid with the growth of several decades.

Ariana knew a bit about fortifications due to her lifelong association with the Chastain brothers, and saw that the keep's door had been located on the second floor. It would have been reached by means of exterior stairs, long-since destroyed. A fragment of the door's frame remained, indicating that it had once been a hexagonal opening bordered in carved marble. The opening itself was choked with rubble. But on the ground floor, part of the wall had given way, leaving a gap wide enough to admit even a horse.

"Dare we go in?" Mischa asked. "Or will the rest of it come crashing down on our heads?"

"As long as we do not jar the walls or timbers, it should be safe," Ariana said. "Anything that was to fall of its own accord surely has by now."

Summoning a mage-light, she stepped gingerly around outflung blocks of broken, blackened stone and looked through the gap. She was expecting to see a kitchen, perhaps. Or a great hall, or guard barracks, or the remains of a storage pantry. Instead, she was looking into a six-sided room with a ceiling of beaten metal that gleamed with a strange, dull shine that was not silver, not steel, and not gold. A thick, curved rim of the same metal rose from the floor. It resembled the basin-wall of a fountain, except that there was no fountain to be seen.

Nor were there any doors or windows or chimneys. It was a room without entrances or exits . . . except for the hole in the wall. And by the way the stones were scattered outside, she had the oddest impression that the wall had been broken down from within. Burst outward, by someone or something very strong, very powerful, and in a hurry.

* * *

CHAPTER NINETEEN

In times of need, oh cousin King, we shall all be at your beck and call, though the miles are long between us.
– Elwyndas, The Mages Royal, Act XXIII

"I wish my father were here," Ariana said as she ran her fingers over the metal. Brass? Bronze? It had been worked with considerable skill, which indicated either dwarven craftsmanship or metal-shaping, among the rarest of spells. "He's much better at this sort of magic, the magic of knowledge, than I am."

"But you're certain it's safe for us to stay the night in here?" Mischa asked, leading the grateful horse into the room.

"There are no living perils and only residues of magic," she said. "Spent spells and undone enchantments. Nothing that should harm us."

"I'll take you at your word."

Beneath gods-knew-how-many years of grime, a miniature scene was impressed into the metal like a relief or sculpture. It showed a city. Buildings and bridges and gardens and archways, shops and marketplaces and schools and . . .

"Mischa, look at this. Is it what I think it is?"

"I'd say it's a depiction of a temple, and priests conducting some sort of ceremony. But, Ari, you told me the elves have no priests. And what are those short figures, there? They don't look like elves at all. These ones do, the tall slender ones, but not these others."

"Dwarves," she said, feeling a creeping sense of awe and wonder. "In all of our long history, only once did dwarves and elves live side by side. In a city. The City of Gold. Govannisan."

"Is that where we are?" he asked, eyes round with amazement.

"It cannot be. The elves fled the destruction of Govannisan, fled north to the safety of the forests. This keep must have been one of the places they settled, before the Emerin became a kingdom. They must have abandoned it thousands of years ago and moved to Perras Peliani."

"I am no tracker," he said, "but those marks do not look thousands of years old to me."

He pointed, and Ariana lowered her magelight to examine the floor. There were scrapes in the stone that might have been made by errant sword strokes or arrow strikes, spatters that might have been dried blood, charred patches as if from intense scorching flame. A glint caught her eye. She bent and pried it up, brushing it against her cloak.

It was a silver-plated piece of truesteel, decoratively formed in a pattern suggestive of feathers, with a blackened, rippling streak across the jagged edge.

"What is it?" Mischa asked.

"Part of a helm, I think. The Order of the Eagle, knights who are expert in war magics, wear helms with silver eagles upon them. If there was a magical battle or duel in here, it would explain much. Bolts of magefire or lightning could have left those scorches. A magical blast could have blown out the wall."

"Who, though? And why? And how did they get in here in the first place?"

Borrowing the magelight, he crouched, then knelt in the dirt and sifted through it. Ariana allowed herself a smile. The Mischa Narrin she'd met in Thanis would not have recognized himself now. Battles with monsters, trials in the swamp . . . the habitual expression of vain self-indulgence replaced . . . no, he was not at all as he'd been.

She joined him in the search, but all of their efforts turned up nothing more than a few more tantalizing scraps of truesteel . . . scales torn from an armored corselet? Finally, tired and frustrated, they set up camp. To be sheltered and dry, warmed by their fire as the rain made its ceaseless drip and patter outside, was welcome.

Settling back in the muted orange glow of the coals while Mischa's breath deepened into sleep, Ariana let her gaze roam the chamber while her thoughts drifted. Around the top of the walls, where they met the domed ceiling, was a border pattern of complex intertwined and interwoven designs. The longer she looked, the more they invited the mind to lose itself in contemplation.

Then, with no warning, something in her head shifted with a nearly tactile click, and the patterns made themselves into lettering. Antique, runic, archaic letters. She blinked, sure that it would prove to have been a trick of the light or of her weariness. But the letters remained. Once seen, they could not be unseen.

She deciphered them as best she could, forming them into words that made little sense to her. *Ryval . . . Cecres . . . Relah . . . Gethrillian . . . Larenla . . . Tuvei.* Another language? An older speech? They were meaningless . . . and yet . . . some were not unfamiliar.

Ryval, for instance. She knew of a place called Ryvali, the Drowned City, lost to floods long ago. And doomed Larenlan, a township far to the south that had been devastated during the war.

Something else clicked. Elwyndas. The master poet and playwright of the elves. Wasn't there one of his works with characters whose names were similar to the ones inscribed above her? A lesser-known play, an unpopular one, not looked on with favor in the Emerin as it had shown too many important personages in too poor a light.

She sighed, disgruntled. Here was that lack of a proper Emerinian education rearing its ugly head again. Her father would have known.

Feeling that she was sitting right atop the key to a very important mystery, she finally sank into slumber.

By morning, the clouds had gone. The crumbled hole in the chamber's wall admitted clean sunshine, birdsong, a refreshing breeze and the rain-washed scent of the forest. The strange metal still had that same dull gleam, even when Ariana rubbed at it with a bit of cloth. She was more sure than ever that the city was a representation of Govannisan, that this place had been built when Govannisan's fall was still more memory than legend.

"I still see no other way in or out of here," Mischa said. "Unless they did it by magic? Sybil told me how your father was able to help them escape Castle Selbon. Could this be like that?"

"Teleportation, you mean?" Ariana pondered, looking again at the raised rim of metal.

Not a basin . . . almost like a barrier, though . . . could Mischa be correct? She had heard rumors of enchanted gates that could transport a person between two locations in the blink of an eye. It was said that the Archmage Feyna had such a gate, connecting his home at Feyna Rel with Perras Peliani. There were, she knew, farspeakers that allowed communication over a distance . . . a gate seemed a reasonable next step.

"There were several of them," she said, thinking aloud. "The play, the Elwyndas play, it had something to do with six Archmages, each of whom built his own fortress in some far corner of the Emerin . . . and then dispute broke out among them. What if this is one of those fortresses, Mischa? What if this was the home of an Archmage, thousands of years ago?"

"Then we should count ourselves lucky to still be alive. Who knows what wards or traps we might have triggered?"

"It's nullified, though," she said. "Broken. Dead. If ever there was an enchantment on this, it is gone now. Destroyed. Someone came here and destroyed it." She took the shard of truesteel from her pouch and examined it again. "Not all that long ago, and possibly at the cost of his own life. Was it by accident, or by design?"

She stepped over the raised rim of metal, her magesense open to its fullest, searching for any flicker or residue of power.

"Ari, don't. What if you're wrong? What if you disappear on me?"

"I told you, Mischa, the active magic is nullified. There is nothing here that can –"

The toe of her boot touched something that sank with a gritty, grinding click. Even as she sprang back with an exclamation, the floor dropped away beneath her. She had a brief moment to chide herself – for all her blather about wards and magical traps, she had forgotten every lesson her mother had ever taught her about mechanical ones.

Amid a hail of dirt, pebbles, dead leaves and debris, Ariana plunged into a deep shaft. She heard Mischa's echoing, distant shout as the trap door through which she'd fallen swung closed again, sealing her in blackness.

A dozen awful fates flashed through her mind. A blade in the shaft, spikes at the bottom, all the lethal devices that had made dwarven dungeon-tales into elven doom-stories. Oh, *now* she remembered everything her mother had said, all of it in diamond-sharp recall and intense imagery. Now that it was too late.

Her feet hit a solid surface, the impact jarring her from heels to head. Just as she was daring to catch her breath and assure herself that she was all in one piece, there was a creak and a damp gust as the floor fell away again, and down she went.

Shifting blue-green radiance surrounded her. She gasped in a lungful of cool, moist air. Instead of a shaft this time, she tumbled into an open space that was full of a glowing, sloshing, rippling luminescence. Before she could even begin to see where she was, she splashed into water.

Ariana surfaced, flinging her hair back from her face, swiping at her face. The water rose to the middle of her chest. She looked around, looked down, saw the sources of the eerie blue-green light, and went rigid.

They ranged in size from a handspan to the length of a man, translucent and boneless jellylike globs moving through the water. Their shapes were inconstant as they oozed and stretched and flowed. Each had what seemed to be a head at one end, with a pair of gently waving antennae on the top and a dangling, undulating proboscis below. She thought of leeches she'd seen in Tradersport physicians' offices, and of slick, tentacled jellyfish in tide pools along the shore.

Ariana held perfectly still as one of the blue-green glowing things cruised past her. Its antennae twitched briefly in her direction, inquisitive. The trap door above her had already closed, leaving her no escape that way.

The room was long, low-ceilinged, and rectangular. Its walls were of drab, dark stone streaked with moisture. At the far end, she could just discern a double row of biers or platforms, their tops rising above the lapping, rippling surface of the water.

A cold, clammy, repulsive jelly folded around her leg. She could feel it even through her Silversilk. Others were converging on her. Drawn by her warmth, her movement, mayhap even the rapid thunder of her pulse . . . she did not know, did not care.

Flailing in a motion that was neither swimming nor running, Ariana fought her way toward the biers. She had to get out, had to get out of the water before they enfolded her and drew her under. She didn't want to know what they were or what they'd do to her. She only wanted to get away.

A radiant, glistening mass humped out of the water. Its head broke the surface. Its antennae quivered in her direction. Its proboscis, tipped with some sort of needle-fine quill, elongated and flexed obscenely.

Her knife had somehow gotten into her hand. She jabbed and slashed at anything that came near. When she pierced the gelatinous sacs, the wounds released murky blue-green billows. The attacks made them recoil long enough for Ariana to scramble atop the closest bier, which rose like a low island. She realized instantly that it was made of some glassy-smooth stuff, slippery and treacherous. One misstep, and she'd fall back in.

The glowing blobs swarmed around, but could not quite get at her without rearing themselves up like beaching whales. They would eventually try, but for now her knife had taught them to keep a careful distance.

Ariana summoned a magelight. It shimmered across the water and enabled her to see just what she was standing upon. Horror drained away her will, weakened her knees.

The bier was like a crystal tomb, a hollow space filled with strange, thick liquid. An elven male was immersed within. He lay naked and pale, curled on his side like an unborn infant. Long coppery hair floated and drifted around his ears. His eyes were closed. His fingers and toes had a wrinkly quality she associated with long soaks in a tub.

But the worst was what shared the space with him. One of the blue-green globs, its inner glow extinguished, lay along his back. It was molded to him, partially engulfing him. Its head was pressed against the nape of his neck, the proboscis seemingly buried in the base of his skull.

The man's chest was moving. It rose and fell in a slow, steady rhythm like breathing . . . only not breathing. No air passed between his slack lips. She saw faint currents in the liquid surrounding him.

He was taking that into his lungs. Beneath closed, bluish-grey lids, his eyes moved as if in a deep dream.

He was alive, somehow alive in there. Alive, with that . . . that *leech* attached to him.

She pushed against the substance of the bier. It was not glass, not crystal, not ice. If anything, it was water . . . water made solid . . . the way her spell had made the river solid to the horse's hooves. A similar magic, perhaps. One beyond her skill. It indented beneath her fingertips, but no matter how hard she tried, she could not force her hand through.

The smaller swarming blobs had begun to lose interest, forgetting her once she was out of their reach. Some of the larger ones remained, but none had yet tried for her. Ariana judged the distance between this bier and the next, and decided she could make it. She stepped across, and shone her magelight down, already dreading what she knew she would see.

There, too, was the naked form of an elf. This one was a woman, her classical and elegant beauty mostly obscured by cloud of blue-black hair. Another of the leeches nestled against her back, and Ariana thought of how she and Lievve had slept, their bodies curled together, in the warm furs of his bed. She shuddered.

She found a child in the next bier, her heart wanting to break as she gazed down at the small face, the thumb tucked securely into a rosebud mouth. A tiny infant, barely more than a newborn, was in the one after that. Both were paired with blue globs of lesser size. The adults had been bad, but the children . . . the children were so much worse!

The next held the body of an elderly male with finespun white hair and a commanding visage, even in this unnatural death-sleep. His eyes were closed, his hands crossed to clamp on his upper arms. On one of his fingers, Ariana saw a ring reminiscent of the Magelord's ring Quisfahr had worn. Quisfahr's had been truesilver. This one was made from purest opal.

A mage's ring. An Archmage's ring? Could she be looking upon the very face of . . . ?

No. That was impossible.

Even the larger leeches had forgotten about her. Either that, or they knew she had no way out and were content to wait. Feeling more surefooted now – almost a promise that she would soon slip, she thought, and told herself not to get too confident – Ariana moved on from bier to bier. Some stood empty, but a few others were occupied.

Here was a mature male who resembled both the elder and the first man she'd seen, though they had looked nothing alike. A bridge between generations, perhaps? Son to one and father to the other? Beside him was a woman of the same age, her serenity marred by an expression of shame, as if she knew herself to be unclad and exposed. Next in line was, to Ariana's astonishment, a black and white tagga-dog. Even the tagga-dog had its own parasite, as large as it was, like a bloated tick grown to incredible size.

At the end of the room, she saw a flight of stone steps leading up to a door. It was beyond stepping distance from the furthest bier. Possibly beyond leaping distance, as well.

Several things in quick succession startled her. A muffled yell, a thud, and the creak of the trap door heralded the sudden and graceless arrival of Mischa Narrin. Arms crossed over his face, he plunged headfirst out of the shaft and into the water.

He had, Ariana saw, tied a rope at his waist and secured the other end to something up above, and it was a miracle he hadn't tangled himself in it, or had it wrap it around his neck and hang him, on the way down.

"Mischa!" she cried as he came up, coughing and sputtering. "Mischa, look out!"

"Ari? Ari! Thank Talopea – what are those?!" One glimpse was all it took to make him, in a truly amazing display of hitherto unsuspected strength and agility, skitter up the rope until he was suspended well above the surface. He swung there, dripping, gulping as he stared at the glowing forms circling below him.

"You came to rescue me," Ariana said. "That was very brave."

"Yes, well, now who's going to rescue *me*? I cannot dangle here like a worm on a hook all day."

She thought of the empty biers and shuddered again, having no difficulty imagining herself and Mischa submerged and senseless, their hair floating around them and their fingers slowly wrinkling from the water as the leeches throbbed cold and vile against their flesh.

"My arms are about to pop from their sockets, Ariana. Get me down from here."

"On the contrary, Mischa . . . hold tight. Be ready to climb."

"Climb? And what of you?"

"Remember the horse, and the river?" She cast her spell.

Most of the creatures were beneath Mischa, enticed by his struggles and chancy grip. Only a few stubborn holdouts remained by the stairs, near Ariana. They surged eagerly, making her think of goldfish seeking breadcrumbs in the pools and fountains of Hampton Gardens, where her grandmother used to take her. Ariana rested a foot on the water. Just before they reached her, she sprang over them and broke into a fleet run.

"Mischa, hold tight!"

"Ari, you're not . . . ahh!"

The water under him was churning with radiant blue-green, the globs jostling and overlapping each other. Ariana threw herself over them in a long leap, colliding with Mischa and setting him a-swing like a spinning pendulum as she clung to him with arms and legs wrapped snug around his body.

He gave her a sour look. "This is not quite as I imagined it."

"Climb up!"

"Climb? I can hardly hold on! You've got to go first."

As she scrambled over him, he gave her several boosts to help her along . . . or so at least she told herself, when he braced a hand firmly against her bottom. She seized the rope and climbed swiftly into the shaft.

Many long and shoulder-aching minutes later, they hauled themselves through the upper trap door and collapsed.

"Mystery after mystery," Mischa said when he could speak again. "Ari . . . those things . . . didn't that Drea woman say something about leeches? Mind-leeches?"

"'An empty, breathing shell . . .'" She shuddered. "That does describe what I saw in there. Lievve said she was a madwoman, but she knew about Shedra, and now this. She knew. Drea knew of this place. She spoke of Shedra, and mind-leeches, and . . . what else?"

"Dire-hounds," he said. "She said something about dire-hounds, whatever they are. Ari, who in the name of the gods *was* she? How'd she know so much?"

"I don't know," Ari said. "But if ever we're back her way again, I mean to find out."

* * *

Chapter Twenty

And there shall come a time of testing, and those unworthy shall have their limbs rent asunder and their spirits cast into oblivion.
– Elwyndas, Prophecies of the Elder Days

The gentle hillside before them sloped into valley divided by a meandering creek. It was a scene of peace and beauty, marred only by a wide swath of bare bone-white earth, where nothing grew and no animals ventured.

It put Ariana in mind of ruined Keyda, where elven war-magics and dwarven weapons had clashed in a terrible destructive force that scoured the land bare.

But this, if the legends were true, was from something far more momentous than any mere act of magic or war. This, if the legends were true, was where the god of the minotaurs had been struck down and denied his prize by the very hand of Denethel.

At the edge of the blighted spot was a flat slab of stone, a suitable sacrificial rock if ever there was one. Beyond it was the Temple of Karria.

"This is it," Ariana said. She felt curiously disappointed, saddened, and did not quite know why. "We've arrived."

Mischa stopped beside her. "That's . . . it? That's all?"

Four white marble steps rose to a half-circle terrace, where columns of dark green stone supported a curved roof. The building itself was a windowless square block, with an opening in the roof to allow the living trunk and boughs of a stately tree to emerge skyward.

Ariana could think of nothing to say.

"I was expecting something a bit grander," Mischa said. "Where are the mosaics? The windows of colored glass? The fountains and statues? It looks nothing like anything we saw in Perras Peliani, and even less like the temple sculpted into the metal back in the keep. There are no living quarters for priests, not much room for rites or ceremonies of any kind –"

"Karria dwelt here alone," Ariana said. "It wasn't for that purpose."

"Well . . . what next? Is it safe? What of the Tests?"

She shook her head. "Haven't our wills, wits, and strength been tested enough already just by the getting here? Whatever Drea might have known, I refuse to believe that she truly has anything to do with this place. And whether safe or not, we've come to it, and it would be foolish to turn back now."

Without waiting for his reply, she held her back straight and her head high as she descended into the valley. The grass whispered around her knees, the breeze stirred a few strands of hair that had come loose from her braid. It made her recall something her grandmother had told her. She undid the braid, and combed out her silver locks with her fingers.

"What are you doing?" Mischa asked.

"Grandmother Miralina had an old saying that it was best to go humbly before the gods, head bared and hair unbound. It seems right. More natural, somehow."

"By that reasoning, then, shouldn't you also go naked?"

"Grandmother certainly never said anything of that sort."

She could feel the sad and violent history of the land, this ancient battlefield, where truesteel arrowheads and elf-jewels were embedded in the earth alongside the brass horn-tips and gold nose rings of fallen minotaurs. Would poor, war-ravaged Keyda be like this, centuries hence? Would there be places where no grass would ever grow again? Places where the ground was scarred so badly that no one dared even walk upon it?

They skirted the sunken, desolate patch and came to the flat stone. Ariana rested both hands on its weathered surface. Here was where Karria had been bound as a sacrifice, where she had blown upon the horn and summoned her godly lover to save her.

Now they were very close to the Temple itself. Drifts of dead leaves were heaped against the outer walls and strewn across the terrace. The grass grew high around the steps, some of which were chipped. It had an air of neglect and deterioration that should not have been surprising, after thousands of years, but nonetheless seemed wrong to her.

"Wait here," she said. "Let me go first."

Mischa didn't argue. He hung back, holding the horse's reins, as Ariana moved toward the steps. She set one foot upon the lowest, and stopped as a low growl drifted from within the shadowed doorway.

A shape emerged, a sleek pantera-shape nearly the size of a horse. A greenlion. Its muscles rippled with strength beneath its lush verdant pelt. A mane dark as moss, but much softer, framed a proud face and direct golden eyes. Its dagger teeth, jutting down from the upper jaw, were twin curves of green-tinged ivory.

Stunned immobile by its magnificence, Ariana ignored Mischa's fervent but hushed prayer. She gave no thought to spell or sword. *This* was a fitting Guardian for Denethel's only Temple.

It approached her with the lazy power that only pantera seemed to possess, not hurried, supremely confident. At the top of the steps, it stopped. Ariana still stood with one boot on the bottom step. For a long moment, she and the greenlion regarded each other. It gave a slight, amused twitch of its moss-tufted tail.

Then it roared, a sound so enormous that the world itself might have cracked. Its hot, meaty breath blasted her face, blew back her hair.

Ariana cried out as well, though her voice went lost and unheard. Jarred from her near-trance by a sudden rush of fear and self-preservation, she drew her sword.

The greenlion's eyes flicked indolently to the blade, and a resigned expression seemed to come over its noble features. As if it were thinking, *This again? When will they ever learn?*

She let the point lower toward the earth, then let the entire sword fall. It landed in the overgrown grass at the base of the steps. Ariana held out one hand toward the greenlion, fingers curled and spread just *so*.

Was it her imagination, or did those golden eyes sparkle with understanding.

"*Radanis*," she said.

The *aether* rushed from her. She braced herself for what she was sure would be formidable resistance. Yet the spell found none at all. The spell had no effect whatsoever.

Ariana silently called herself a fool. "I should have known better," she said, meeting that golden gaze. "Magic to calm and befriend wild animals works only *on* wild animals, only on beasts of base intelligence. Not on the likes of you, Guardian."

"Still," said the greenlion in a voice that was growls made into words, "you did choose to try *that* rather than attack me. I have been met with weapons and war-magic and other threats too numerous to mention. Yet only those who gesture with friendship may pass without feeling the fury of my claws and teeth."

Ariana bowed. "It would have been an affront to dare try stripe your pelt with scarlet, even were it in defense of my own life."

The greenlion preened, and Ariana reflected that no matter the size, all cats were the same at their hearts. Excepting her mother, who bore the name and stealth and agility of a cat, but none of the vanity and pride.

"Princes have come here and not been so well-spoken. And so, moon-silver swordmaid, you may enter."

Then, without so much as a puff of wind to mark its passage or disturb a single blade of grass, the greenlion was gone. Gone, as if it had never been there at all . . . though she knew that it had.

And the Temple had changed. The dark green columns were revealed now in their full splendor, shining smooth and of the same banded gemstone that had graced the end of Quisfahr's walking-stick. The plain, weathered terrace came alive with mosaics, the tiny colorful chips laid in painstaking detail to depict trees and flowers, glades and groves, all the bounty and beauty of the forest.

The arched doorway was wrapped with living vines, laden with the ripest, most tantalizing berries Ariana had ever seen. A curtain of the finest, sheerest moss parted around her like a whisper as she passed through. Just within, two basins flanked the entrance, brimming like springs with clear, pure water.

Inside, rays of sunlight were filtered by the leaves of the tree that rose through the ceiling. Dappled shadows danced across the figures of the animals within, making them at first seem to move. Then she saw that they were statues, exquisitely sculpted of purest white marble. They were arrayed to either side of a central walkway. Stags and does, pantera of all types, bears, foxes . . . every kind of woodland creature stood in reverence, facing a raised platform at the base of the tree.

Upon the platform was a final statue, and just by looking upon it, Ariana knew that Karria had ordered it done to show him exactly as she remembered him. Denethel, seen not through the eyes of a scholar or priest, but through the eyes of a young lover.

A bow was slung over his shoulder, a quiver of arrows on his back. A horn hung at his waist.

One hand was curled near his chest, while the other was outstretched, the way a man might offer his hand to a lady . . . a lady standing just before him, to assist her in stepping up onto the platform.

This was a temple. This was a holy place. The elves *had* once worshiped, *had* once served the gods. And had the gods, in turn, bestowed favors on their faithful? How had they lost their way? Was it too late to find that path again? Too late for the Emerinians?

A new and unexpected feeling swept over her. She thought of Karria, who had given up her royal birthright without a single glance back, devoting herself to this place and this god forever and with devotion.

"Denethel," she said in a low voice, dropping to her knees. "Denethel the Archer, Denethel the Huntsman. I kneel before you to beg forgiveness. The quest that brought me here was an unworthy and selfish one. I thought it was for my father, for my family, my bloodline and my name. But it was not. It was for my own stubborn pride. I came to take the Emerald that was token of your love to Karria, to use it to force the Council to grant my request. But what does it matter if one small holding is returned to my family, when all the Emerin is in need? If you will allow me, I would still take the Emerald, to see that it *does* find its way to the hands of the rightful king."

Kissing her fingertips, she brought them to her brow. Then she rose and took a deep breath, instinctively knowing what came next.

She reached up, grasped the statue's outstretched offering hand, and stepped onto the platform.

As she did, she could see that which could not be seen from the floor. The statue's other hand, the one curled near his chest, held a vibrant green brilliance. The Emerald of Karria.

Only a swordmaid or a king.

Was she swordmaid enough?

Scarecely able to breathe, and not without a tingle of apprehension, Ariana touched the jewel. It was cool under her fingertips. She gingerly lifted it free, and turned it this way and that in a dazzling beam of sunlight to watch it sparkle.

It was the size of a young apple, perfectly round, polished smooth rather than faceted. Every imaginable shade of green was contained within its translucent heart. The palest tint of the cloudwillow, the nightpine's darkest hue, and everything in between could be found in the stone she now held.

Acting on impulse, she kissed the unmoving lips of the statue, and would not have been entirely shocked to feel them warm and soften and respond. They did no such thing, of course, and she smiled at herself as she stepped down.

It had all changed again. The mosaics were chipped, faded almost colorless. A few wisps more like cobwebs than moss hung from the archway, where the brittle threads of long-dead vines were all that remained. The statues of the animals were cracked, broken, half buried in dusty drifts of years or centuries worth of fallen leaves.

Catching her breath, Ariana turned to look at the statue of the god again.

The platform was empty. A marble base showed where it had been, but only a few dry leaves skirled across it in an eddy of wind.

Yet the Emerald was in her hand. Undeniable and real. She passed her other hand over it and murmured, "*Ralavi*," and the Emerald came alive in her magesight like some spectacular lightning-storm. Its power wasn't refined and structured and neatly channeled, as enchanted items were. This was raw and intense, as untamed as the depths of the wild woods. Yet, underlying that, tempering it, was a gentle, almost feminine aura.

Mischa was waiting for her where she had left him. He asked her what had happened, but Ariana could only shake her head. She did not know how to speak of it, not yet. She walked almost like one in a dream, following as Mischa led her and the horse toward the edge of the valley.

"You've done it," he said. "You've done it, Ari. The Emerald of Karria. It's beautiful."

Before she could stop him, before she even knew what he intended, he caressed the Emerald in her hand.

There was a burst of blinding green light. The gem bucked like a maddened steed, jolting Ariana and leaving her arm numb to the shoulder. Mischa was hurled back against a shrub and nearly skewered himself several important places on its thorny branches.

"Mischa!" She rushed to him. "What were you thinking? Remember the legend? Only a swordmaid or a king, and you are neither! Are you hurt?"

He groaned. "I'll live, but just 'twixt me and thee, I'd almost rather not. Have you ever had your foot fall asleep?"

"Of course."

"And you know how it is when it begins to wake, and you must be so very careful not to move it or the sensation worsens? Imagine that, but head to toe, and ten times as intense."

She tried to keep a sympathetic look, but it was all she could do not to laugh.

Mischa picked himself up out of the thornbushes, heaving a world-weary sigh at the new rips in his clothes and the new scratches on his skin. It took some time to settle the skittish horse, secure their belongings on its back, and resume their homeward course.

"If it does that to elves as well as hapless idiot humans, no one's going to be able to make a false claim for the crown. I'd like to see Council try passing that around the room. What will they make of it, do you think? And what will it make of them?"

Another voice cut in before Ariana could reply.

"Don't trouble yourself to wonder, human. *I'll* deal with the Council."

* * *

CHAPTER TWENTY-ONE

My word is my oath and my oath is my soul.
– Elwyndas, Sir Blaine's Last Battle (ballad)

All these dangers, all these tests, Ariana thought as she turned. *And now here's another . . . the worst one yet.* His voice and his words had told her that much, and the look in his eyes confirmed it.

He presented a striking figure, with a swordsman's lean grace of build. His black hair was cropped short in the military style, to not hinder the helm that currently rested under his arm. Golden lions danced around the rim of that helm, the design echoed in the buckle of his white belt. He had sharp, almost severe features and high, proud ears. Over meshed chainmail, he wore a charcoal-grey tunic edged in midnight blue to match the cloak that flared from his shoulders. He wore two swords, one glorious and golden and bejweled, the other dark and ominous.

Ariana looked at the crest embroidered on the breast of his tunic, then back into those ice-blue eyes that met hers with unconcealed contempt. He was waiting, she knew, for the two of them to erupt in questions, explanations, or perhaps pleas. But she had seen this before. Some things did not differ all that much from one kingdom to the next.

She raised her chin to inform him that she was prepared to let this game go on until the stars went dark, if that was what it took.

"I believe I have the advantage," he finally said. "You are Ariana Mirida, daughter of a discredited House. I am –"

"I know who you are," Ariana said. "Sir Tiercel Reyes, Order of the Lion, bearer of the sword Lionheart, bestowed on you by a grateful Starleaf Council for your actions during the war."

Tiercel's brows drew together. "How is it that you, no citizen of the Emerin, know me by sight?"

"I am passably well-versed in things heraldic." She nodded toward the crest on his tunic. "Your blazon is known even in Gamelin."

"Then you know also that as I am a member of the Starleaf Council –"

"An advisory member," Ariana said. Her heart was hammering despite her outward appearance of calm, polite interest. Why a man such as this, a knight of the realm, a war-hero, should be *here* of all places . . . at *this* of all times . . .

It might not have seemed possible for his eyes to go colder, yet they did. "Enough of these pleasantries. I charge you to deliver the Emerald of Karria to me. At once."

"How did you –?" Mischa took an indignant step forward.

"Silence, *human.*" This time, he gave the word an even more deadly inflection.

Cowed, Mischa did fall silent.

"As for you, girl," Tiercel said, returning his attention to Ariana, "give me the Emerald. I will not ask you again."

"You have not, in truth, asked me before."

"Mirida's daughter," he said with a sneer. "You'd get on well with Idelhar, the both of you cut from the same cloth. Spare me your clever wordplay and maneuverings. We both know how this will end."

She couldn't let him sense how she was quaking inside, could not show him an iota of fear for he would pounce upon it and destroy her at the slightest sign of weakness. "With the Emerald where it rightfully belongs. Why must we be at odds in that, if we both have the Emerin's best interests at heart?"

"You are not of the Emerin. You have trespassed here. You have stolen a relic and desecrated a holy place –"

"I have done no such thing!" And here it was, the quick temper her father had cautioned her against. Taunting a knight of his reputation – and even if the accounts were twicefold exaggerated, Tiercel was a swordsman of incomparable skill – was an unwise path to take. Yet neither was she about to just hand over her hard-won prize to him. Not when distrust coiled in her like a snake.

"My patience is at an end." Tiercel let one hand fall to the hilt of Lionheart, and reached out with the other. Barely constrained wrath made his fingers tremble, perhaps with the urge to cuff her across the face. He was flushed with fury, his jaw clenched so tightly that each word seemed bitten in half. "I will have the Emerald, now."

Ariana let her shoulders slump forward and bowed her head in defeat. "As you will. Here."

She held it out. He snatched at it.

Green light exploded between them. The shock rocked Ariana back on her heels, but she maintained her grip on the jewel. Tiercel flew from her as if kicked by a warhorse, all but knocked from his boots. He struck the knotty bole of a tree, slid down it, and lay with limbs sprawling and his eyes rolled up in his head.

"If I should have known better, he certainly should have," Mischa said, laughing.

"Let's be gone before he revives."

"Yes, I think so." He swung up onto the horse, which was skittish from all the flashes of light and violent commotion. It pranced and stomped.

Ariana thrust the Emerald into her belt pouch. She took a step, and was brought up short by a black-gloved hand that closed with implacable strength on her shoulder.

"A goodly effort thou hast made, but outmatched are thee."

The voice was soft, not unkind. But it chilled Ariana more than Tiercel's contempt and anger ever could have done. The accent . . . the pattern of speech . . .

She turned.

The woman before her was young and lovely, with dark hair that fell in wings about a heart-shaped face. Her eyes had the deep, rich hue of amethysts. But the shapliness of her form was covered in armor of deep red and black, decorated with emblems of roses and basilisks . . . symbols of death. Her cloak was a sweep of blood-red, the color of mourning. Ruby studs in the shape of roses glittered in her earlobes, bringing Ariana's hands involuntarily to cover her own ears.

As the two of them studied each other, Tiercel clambered painfully to his feet. "Allow me to present," he said, "my companion. Kai Tilanne."

Ariana wasn't sure what was worse . . . the title, or implications of this association. "*Morvalan. Rhunvala.*" Not just a dark-souled elf from the southern forests, but a blood-knight, a warrior-priestess of their terrible, vengeful god.

A *Rhunvala.* Here. In the Emerin. In the company of a man who was supposed to be a loyal knight, a hero.

"Such by Kaledhol's grace have I the honor to be," Tilanne said. Her eyes turned truesteel-hard as she shifted her gaze to Mischa, then back to Ariana. "Down from there get the vermin."

"Stay as you are, Mischa," Ariana said in Thanian, fear for him suddenly outweighing all her other concerns. Even that of having heard the name of the dark god spoken. "Your life's not worth a bent mark to a *Morvalan.* She'd kill you as soon as look at you."

Tiercel had brushed himself off, recovered from his encounter with the Emerald. He glared at Ariana, no doubt hating her all the more for having caused and witnessed his humiliation. "They die so soon at any rate," he said. "Why prolong their miserable lives?"

"They die so soon at any rate," Ariana threw back, "why go to the trouble of killing them?"

"I assure you, it'll be no trouble at all." He drew his sword, not Lionheart but the other one, with a hilt of rough-hewn crystal that made her eyes hurt to see. "They are a nuisance, are they not, Tilanne?"

"Overbreed and overrun all the world if not curtailed shall they," Kai Tilanne said.

With no pause for thought, Ariana struck Mischa's horse on the rump. Spooked, it reared up, hooves flashing near the *Rhunvala's* head. Tilanne ducked away, releasing Ariana. The horse came down running, with Mischa somehow still managing to stay on.

"Ride, Mischa! Go!"

He looked back once, incredulous and horrified, as the horse bore him into the woods. Tiercel spat a vile curse, but he carried no bow and if he knew any war-magics, he did not have the time to cast them before Mischa was out of range. Then man and horse were gone, the thunder of hoofbeats fading.

Ariana and Tilanne locked eyes. She felt that hers must be blazing-hot, sapphire flame. Tilanne's were steady. This *Morvalan* woman, Ariana knew with a sudden surety, was far more dangerous than quick-tempered Tiercel would ever be.

He was upon them then, rumpled and dusty and furious. He swung his arm backhand, striking Ariana across the face. She staggered, the skin over her cheekbone split by a jeweled ring he wore. "She-pantera! You are fortunate that you have more value to me alive!"

She touched the wound and winced at the thin trickle of blood. "That must be some value indeed, now that I've witnessed your treachery and betrayal of your people. Consorting with the *Morvalan*? Should the Council learn of that –"

His hand rose again. Then, with great visible effort, he brought himself under control. He stalked a few paces away, as if he did not quite trust himself to be within blade's reach of her. Standing with arms crossed and mouth set in a stony line, he said, "Tilanne, deal with her. You are a swordmaid. Put it to use. Get me that gem."

Ariana moved faster than she ever would have believed herself capable of. She whipped her sword from its sheath, whirled, and brought it around in a whistling, lethal silver arc.

To meet Tilanne's black-bladed sword with a resounding clash.

The *Rhunvala* might have been standing there waiting for all the time in the world, knowing exactly when and where Ariana's blow would land, even before Ariana herself knew she meant to launch it.

"*Ha-nah*!" Tilanne cried. A wine-red light blossomed around her as she struck.

Not at Ariana, but at her weapon. It shattered as if made of glass, leaving Ariana holding a hilt from which a few shards of metal still jutted. The rest lay in pieces around her feet. Her hand stung and smarted. She ached from fingers to backbone, and could not entirely believe she was alive.

The black blade was leveled unwaveringly at her throat. She heard a moan of dread, and realized it had come from herself.

Then Tilanne lowered her sword, and smiled. Actually smiled at her. "Once, when young and impetuous I was, thy father my life did spare. That kindness owed to him, I to thee repay. No harm from my hand shall thee befall."

"These oaths of yours are getting tiresome, Tilanne," Tiercel said. "Stop shy of slaying her if you must, but do not wax sentimental, and weaken on me now."

"Hither the Emerald to carry thou didst bring me," Tilanne told the fuming Tiercel. "That shall I do, but neither my own pledge nor mercy's debt shall I disregard."

"Very well," he said. "I'll do it myself."

Astonished by their exchange and by the mention of her father, Ariana backed up. "So the *Rhunvala* shows more honor than the hero of the realm . . . and a knight of the Emerin offers me more peril than does a *Morvalan*."

"Allow me to correct you." Tiercel held up the dark crystal-hilted sword, which glittered with malevolent purpose. "I am first and foremost *Morvalan*. And I do not offer you peril . . . I *insist*."

With her own weapon broken and naught but a knife left, magic was her only defense. Tiercel advanced, sizing her up not as a warrior about to meet a worthy foe but as an artisan contemplating a blank canvas or untouched block of stone. She had hoped he would rush in, anger-blinded and reckless, but understood now that such a man never could have survived long in the war.

She raised her left arm and concentrated on the command that would briefly transform it hard as iron, to deflect Tiercel's attacks. Her right hand crackled with frost. At a gesture, she would send daggers of ice flying at his face. If he was shielded, as she had shielded Obriel and Shedra . . .

If he was, he was. She would know soon enough.

He clasped his sword in both hands and his eyes narrowed in an intense burst of will.

A shrill, jangling, deafening, jarring torrent of sounds poured from the vibrating blade of his sword. It drilled into Ariana's ears, assaulting her senses, assaulting her mind. Both of her spells blew apart like ashes in a high wind.

Shrieking but unable to hear herself, she was driven to her knees by the noise. Covering her ears did nothing to diminish it. The very bones of her skull and body seemed about to shiver into splinters.

One last fragment of rational thought struggled to the forefront. Everything else in the legends had so far been proven true . . . it was her last hope . . .

She thrust her hand into her pouch and pulled out the Emerald of Karria. With a desperate, unschooled, semi-coherent pleading prayer to both Denethel and Livana, she sent her energies at the stone.

Cool green silence, the peace of a shadowed glade, surrounded her. The cessation of sound was nearly as shocking as the attack itself. She raised her head, and found herself at the center of an opaque dome of light.

Now what, Ariana? she asked herself. She had fought the good fight, but weaponless and nearly bereft of energies, she was running out of options.

The Emerald's shield faded and winked out. The world was quiet again, moreso than it had been before, because every bird and animal nearby must have been as overwhelmed as she'd been by that horrible keening-shrieking howl. Perhaps more. Perhaps to the point of death.

Kai Tilanne lowered her hands, which had been cupped over her ears and shining with that same wine-red glow. She glanced at the Emerald with the reverence of one who understood and respected such artifact.

"It seems," Tiercel said, "that the direct methods remain the best."

He spoke from behind her, having circled while she was in the protective dome of green light. He kicked out, the hard heel of his boot meeting her wrist with immediate crushing pain. The Emerald was catapulted into the air and all Tilanne had to do was rotate her hands outward, still cupped. It dropped neatly into them.

The rough-crystal hilt slammed into her back, striking between her shoulderblades. Ariana was driven to her knees, cradling her injured wrist against her breasts. Then the flat of the blade rang against her skull, and she knew no more.

When her eyes opened again, she found herself lying on her side in an unfamiliar shadowy clearing. Her ankles were lashed together and her hands – hurt wrist and all – wrenched around and tied behind her back. She saw the remains of a campfire, and two tethered horses, and the *Morvalan* woman some distance away, in the final stages of packing up their supplies and traveling gear. A padded, fur-trimmed black pouch hung from Tilanne's belt. By the rounded bulge in it, Ariana supposed she knew where the Emerald of Karria was.

Tiercel's boots strolled into her line of sight. The tip of that hated, horrible shrieking sword prodded under her chin, lifting it, making her have to meet his gaze.

"All things considered," he said after a long, evaluating inspection, "you are not un-pretty. You should do nicely for what I have in mind."

"Never," she said. "You'll see me in rosecloth before you ever see me in *your* bed."

He scoffed. "You flatter yourself. I have trials enough with women as it is. No, there is another who would very much like to make your acquaintance. How, though, am I to ensure your cooperative captivity? You seem the sort who'd endeavor to escape at the earliest opportunity. Even if kept bound and gagged, you may be skilled enough with some magics to use them without word or gesture . . . or slip your bonds. Given your . . . mother's tutelage?"

Ariana winced. Cat, or even Tal, might have already gotten free of the cords. Cat would have already gotten free of the cords, cut the strings of Kai Tilanne's purse to retrive the Emerald, and been gone away into the shadows like a whisper of smoke. Her father could have used any manner of magics with nothing more than a thought.

What *had* she been thinking, to undertake this? Arien was right . . . they had all been right. She was too young, too inexperienced and unschooled . . . too impetuous for her own good. And see what it had brought her to! Trussed up like a calf at the feet of an enemy.

"I could smite you unconscious again," Tiercel went on, "but it is a long journey, and repeated ministrations might leave you crippled or blind or permanently witless, if not dead. So, fortunately for your sake, there is another way."

He held up a small box. It was made of pale wood, intricately carved, and inlaid with knotwork lines and patterns in the richest, most vibrant gold she had ever seen. Truegold, could it be? A thousand times more rare than truesilver. Truegold, so powerful in *aether* that it could carry magic even into areas deprived of it. Some said that possession of a bit of truegold could even allow one who was not a mage to weild magic.

Tiercel opened the box and plucked something from within it. His face contorted in a spasm as he did so, not as if he was precisely hurt, but as if whatever he touched was unpleasant to the point of loathsomeness.

What he held out for her to see was a hook of dark bluish-black metal, an oversized thorn-shape as long and flat as her thumbnail. The tip was razor-sharp and tiny barbs lined the sides, leaving a blunt curve at the widest end.

"What is that?" She hadn't planned to give him the satisfaction of responding, had meant to let him have his smug rant while she tried to think of ways out of her plight. But that little barbed thorn was too ominous and unsettling to behold.

"This," he said, turning it this way and that as if to admire its indigo sheen, "is a dwarfmetal that the folk of Montennor call *manathricite*. We name it *gilthanat*. It is rare, expensive, and very, very powerful. Do you know what it does?"

Ariana shrank back as best she could. She had thought her threshold for horror already reached to its limit. Now she knew that those limits could be exceeded. She had heard of the metal he held. Heard of it, but never expected – and never wanted! – to see it.

"A . . . *nagilea*," she said. "An *aether*-diminisher."

"Not precisely. An *aether*-nullifier. Even so small an amount as this can strip the talent and spellcasting ability of a mage. Any mage, from apprentice to Archmage. So long as it touches the flesh or is worn too close to the skin."

That was why he had made that grimace when he'd picked it up. That was why he carried it in a truegold-laced box, so that the effects of the one would counter the other.

He grabbed her by nape of the neck and hauled her halfway to her knees. In one smooth, fast motion, he thrust the thorn-shape's point into the hollow valley just above her left collarbone.

She screamed as the razor edge sliced deep. Tiercel set his fingertip in the blunt curve at the wide end and pushed hard, burying the entire barbed fang in her flesh.

The pain was nothing compared to the hideous feel and sound of it . . . metal grinding and grating on bone. And the feel and sound were nothing compared to the immediate and awful sensation of her magic being snuffed out like a candleflame.

Now she could not even scream.

Her talent was gone.

She could not sense the *aether* that she *knew* was all around her, could not detect her *ilgilean* as anything other than a normal necklace, a useless opal bauble on a chain.

Her knowledge of spells and theories was intact, but she knew that she could cast all she wanted and nothing would happen. The energies would be absorbed even as they were summoned, absorbed into that hateful blue-black metal.

She realized Tiercel was speaking to her, and forced herself to focus on him.

"One drawback," he said, "is that it keeps *all* magic from you. Even spells cast by another, be they beneficial or malign. Thus, you cannot be healed."

Only when he said it did she realize that blood was running down the slope of her breast, soaking into her Silversilk. It, too, was robbed of its magic . . . now no more than fine-woven cloth. She couldn't see the wound itself, but knew it must be gouged, swollen, and ugly. It throbbed like an infected tooth.

Tiercel released her, and Ariana flopped to the ground. She felt tears flow, and could not hold them back, though she was able to at least keep from sobbing.

Many years ago, her father had suffered a near-fatal blow that had left his powers blocked. He had tried to describe it to her, but Ariana had never fully understood. Until now.

"As it happens, you're in luck," Tiercel said. "While I'm no accomplished physician like my nephew, I had a bit of experience with field surgeries during the war."

He showed her a needle and thread, and showed her his teeth in a cruel little grin.

* * *

CHAPTER TWENTY-TWO

Whoso carries chains within their heart shall always be a prisoner. But whoso invites freedom to dwell therein instead, shall never be in chains.
– Elwyndas, Joraic the Third, Act I

The stars were glaring balls of white fire that burned her eyes to look upon. Night-blooming flowers filled the air with an overpowering reek. Every rustling leaf sounded like wood being coarsely filed close to her ears, and the low conversation of her captors was like the gladiatorial din and thunder of the Sand Pits of Tradersport. An insect, alighting on her skin, was like the touch of a hot coal. She shivered, shuddered uncontrollably from a cold so biting it gnawed down to the bone.

The rolling, rocking motion of the horse was worse than any ship at sea. The saddle beneath her might have been made from hard iron, and the ropes holding her in place were like vines of stinging nettles.

Ariana hurt everywhere, everywhere, except for in her arms. Still bound behind her back, they had become deadened, like twin padded sticks no longer attached to her at all.

She was parched with thirst, the inside of her mouth feeling like baked, cracked clay. But when they gave her water, the taste of it was like the harshest orc-brewed whisky, like drinking acid that dissolved away her tongue and throat. Her stomach cramped with hunger, but a single bite of bread doubled her with violent nausea.

How long had gone by? Was this the first night? The second? The *tenth* since she had fallen into Tiercel's hands? How long since he had braced his knee on her chest to hold her down while he jabbed needle and thread through her skin, stitching the wound closed, stitching the hateful *gilthanat* into her flesh?

"Reacts badly to the *gilthanat* does she," Tilanne said some unknowable amount of time later, when they stopped. She helped – nay, she lifted Ariana down from the saddle. Supporting her as if she were a child, or a frail elder. "Fevered, she is."

Her voice was so loud! Like the screeching of a rusted gate, like a nail being drawn from a stubborn oak plank. Ariana wanted to beg them for silence, but knew that her own voice would bellow inside her head with bone-cracking force.

"Yes, I've seen it before." The clamor and thunder of rocks bouncing down a stony hill, Tiercel, shouting into her ear. "The stronger their talent, the worse it affects them. It'll pass. Another day or three, and she'll be over the worst of it. How is her wrist?"

They lowered her onto what was probably a pile of folded blankets and furs. To Ariana, it felt as if she was sinking into a bed of crushed glass. With all the gentleness of a torture-master, Tilanne untied her arms and brought them around to the front of her body. Fresh agony erupted in her shoulders, and hot sparks ran in runnels to her fingertips. Tilanne probed at her wrist and might as well have been beating her with an ironwood club.

Whatever they decided about her wrist, she did not hear. She drifted into a grey fog, dimly aware of the familiar sounds of camp being set up. For a moment, she could almost let herself believe that this was some miserable dream, and she would wake to find Mischa puttering about building a fire.

Then the bleak reality hit her. Mischa, for all that he'd escaped her fate or an even more dire one, was on his own. On his own in the forest, knowing even less woodlore than *she* knew. He would have the horse, and whatever had still been in the saddlebags, but how would he survive?

For a while, she did dream, and when she woke, her rioting senses had largely returned to normal. She saw morning light that did not spear into her eyes, and smelled kofa that did not reek like an open sewer-trench. The noises she heard were much more like birdsong now, and much less like the shrieks of people ruthlessly cut down on the battlefield.

She was in a large red tent, a round pavilion of the sort that Gavin and Galen Chastain kept for when they rode to compete in tournaments in neighboring duchies. It rose to a peaked central roof, and the flaps were folded back to give her a view of a tidy encampment.

Ariana found that her arms were still untied, and also that she did not want to move them very much. It was enough to let them lie beside her. It was enough to not hurt all over, from the crown of her head to the soles of her feet.

A shadow blocked the entrance. Kai Tilanne stepped in, holding a steaming bowl. Her dark brows arched when she saw Ariana awake. She set the bowl on a flat patch of earth beside Ariana's bedroll. The steam rising from it smelled of strong mint and bitter herbs. Ariana's stomach gave a queasy warning lurch.

"I'm not hungry," she said, in a weak sickbed whisper.

"'Tis not food." Tilanne knelt beside her and folded back the blanket. She had the competent manner of a nurse, changing a dressing over the place where Tiercel had embedded the *gilthanat* thorn and bathing Ariana with a cloth dunked into the hot, medicinal liquid.

"Where are we?" Ariana asked. "Where is Sir Tiercel?"

"Gone ahead a ways he has, our path to scout."

"You're not afraid I'll try to get away?"

Amethyst eyes only looked at her, and Ariana flushed a little. She tried to sit up, expecting Tilanne to stop her, and was surprised when Tilanne instead helped, and slid one of the saddles behind her to lean against. Now that she had her wits more or less about her, she was able to take stock of her condition. The wrist Tiercel had kicked was snugly wrapped in a bandage but only gave the barest of twinges when she moved her hand. She was clean, her hair lying over her shoulder in a long silver plait.

The clothes she had been wearing – and her Silversilk – were gone. She was dressed in a cloud-colored tunic trimmed in striped black and grey fur, and dark red leggings. Both were too large for her, but of a feminine cut.

"I'm getting tired of this," she said, more to herself than to Tilanne. First waking to find Riella brushing her hair and lending her Shedra's garments, and now borrowing from Tilanne's wardrobe?

"So thou hast thy spirits and wits recovered," Tilanne said. "Good."

"Why is he letting me live?" Ariana supposed that if anyone would appreciate bluntness, it would have to be a Morvalan. "You have the Emerald now, and he has to know that if I get a chance, I'll tell the Council everything. So why keep me alive? Who was he talking about, that would like to make my acquaintance?"

"Thou knowest not, whose Household Tiercel serves? Thou knowest not he is to Count Elyvorrin beholden?"

Ariana closed her eyes. "Oh ... oh, of course. That's what he wants with me. He's going to give me to the count. The tool of Elyvorrin's revenge against my father. A daughter for a daughter. He'll be the one to kill me, mayhap to see me die as Alinora did? Is that it?"

"To the count's plans am I not privy, but either that or ..."

"Or what?" She opened her eyes again, needing to see Tilanne's expression.

It was sober, troubled. "As bait Elyvorrin might use thee," she said, "the better a more personal vengeance to exact."

That was a horror too great to contemplate. Ariana refused to let it happen. Whatever else might come to pass, she would not let Alinor Elyvorrin lure her father back to the Emerin.

"You knew him," she said. "You were there, weren't you? At the fortress in the southern lands, where Solarrin was creating that construct."

"A girl there I was," Tilanne said. "In fire and blood, my father, my brother, and many of my people did die."

Which meant, Ariana realized, that Tilanne had likely also seen the others who'd been with Arien that night. Unca Alphonse, Greyquin . . . Cat. Her chest tightened. Better not to talk about that after all, perhaps.

"Is there anything to drink?" she asked instead.

Tilanne brought her a cup of watered wine, and when that stayed down, a cup of broth. Both were weak and mild, but almost more than her *gilthanat*-addled senses could stand. The meaty flavor of the broth was overpowering, the wine more potent than gnomish brandy.

As Ariana was finishing the broth, feeling sleepy and full and half-drunk, they heard Tiercel return and call for Tilanne. She left, and Ariana was alone. Escape would have been impossible in any case, for not only was she exhausted from the mere act of sitting up so long, she had noticed that one of her ankles was secured by a strap, the other end of which had been tied to a stake in the earth. Tiercel was taking no chances with Count Elyvorrin's prize.

If she'd had her magic, though . . .

Bracing herself, she brought her right hand across her body to probe beneath the dressing and blindly explore the spot where Tiercel had viciously inserted the *gilthanat*. She was glad she couldn't see it, couldn't see the swollen, scab-crusted lump with knots of thick thread holding it together. He had stitched her with no finesse, like a soldier and not a seamstress, caring only for getting the job done and not for neatness.

The pain, which had been largely quiescent, flared anew at her touch. The flesh there felt hot, puffy, bloated. Pressing it, even lightly, sent agonizing darts lancing out through her entire body.

Do it, she told herself. *Take it out.*

But the thought . . . clawing open her own skin, burrowing deep to find that awful blue-black thorn, drawing it out while the barbs shredded a wider path . . . no, no, she couldn't. There was no way she could bring herself to do it.

The wine and broth eased her into a hazy sleep through which dream-fragments of memories flitted – her mother, her grandparents, herself and Brianna and the twins as children, the long-dead but dearly loved Unca Alphonse, the glorious day on which she'd learned that she did indeed have a father after all, the tragedy of a lost babe that would have been a younger sister, the joy of her brother's birth after her parents had tried so long, the sorrow of her grandfather's death.

At some point while she wandered through that gallery of the past, Tiercel and Tilanne had come into the pavilion. They had brought food. They wanted her to try and eat. To her surprise, she was almost hungry. To her further surprise, the evening breeze told her that many hours had gone by.

There was no dried meat and porridge for the likes of Sir Tiercel Reyes, oh, no. They dined on puffed whitebread filled with mellow cheese, tender cuts of meat with a variety of sauces, a dessert of thinly-sliced fruit sprinkled with crushed nuts and sugars.

Ariana let herself be propped up, and accepted what they gave her. She did not want to enjoy the meal, the sumptuous flavors and delicate textures, but could not entirely conceal her appreciation. Tiercel, an Emerinian born and raised, was clearly accustomed to traveling with all the comforts. Enchantments of domestic magics provided a well-stocked larder even out here, far from the city.

When the meal was done, Tilanne checked her dressing again. If she noticed that it had been disarranged by Ariana's inquisitive probing, she said nothing.

"You overly concern yourself with her care," Tiercel said, looking on. "You *do* know what she is, don't you?"

The cool, maliciously playful note in his voice alarmed Ariana, countering the lulling effects of the food. He was not focused on her at all, but on Tilanne as he spoke.

"Our enemy, she is not," Tilanne said. "Obstacle, adversary perhaps, but no enemy."

"Tilanne, Tilanne . . . I forget sometimes how little you truly know about the distinguished Arien Mirida. You build your opinion of him from a remembered kindness he once showed an untutored girl, and pay no mind to the vile, perverse truth."

"Stop it," Ariana said.

"You would not have me tell her? You would keep it the shameful, shameful secret that it is?"

"I am not ashamed!"

"Aren't you? Proud of your elfkin mother, are you?"

Tilanne's amethyst eyes seemed to darken. She did not move a muscle, but her knuckles went white and the blood seemed to drain from her complexion.

"Elfkin," Tiercel said again. "Half-human. Tainted and impure. So you needn't be so charitable toward her."

"True is this?" whispered Tilanne, her deep violet gaze searching Ariana's face.

Tiercel sat back and poured himself another cup of wine. "Well, I could be mistaken. Mirida *is* wed to an elfkin, that much is beyond doubt. But perhaps, like mules, they are unable to breed. Perhaps the illustrious Lady Ariana here is the product of some other liaison. I hear his Lenaisian mother-in-law shares their home."

"Dung-eating *toad!*" Ariana cried at Tiercel. "You know *nothing* of my father, my family!"

"Thy mother elfkin is? Thy blood the filth of humanity doth carry?"

"My mother is elfkin," Ariana said. "It is no taint, it is not filth, it is not perversion. You are wrong."

"Full elven she doth seem," Tilanne said, turning to Tiercel with what was almost a beseeching tone. "Touched her, I did. The Temple she entered, the Emerald she handled. Pure *must* be her blood."

"Whether a taint is in her blood is yet to be determined, but surely there is taint upon her soul. You heard her *defend* them . . . and let us not forget the human lover she dared bring into the very Emerin to commit their acts of obscenity."

"Mischa is not my lover," Ariana said. "Truthsay me if you have doubt of that."

Tilanne shook her head. "Such power Kaledhol grants me not."

"And we could not truthsay you at any rate," Tiercel said, tipping his cup as if making a toast to the *gilthanat.*

Tilanne sat silent and thoughtful. Ariana did not like the expression of pensive speculation that had come over her at this revelation. She had not considered Tilanne a friend, or even an ally, but at the very least preferred and trusted her over Tiercel, strange and unthinkable as that was. Now, though, whatever kindly feelings Tilanne had felt toward her had been washed away. The memory of Arien's mercy was corrupted by the knowledge that Arien had married an elfkin. Did Tilanne remember Cat? Had she seen her, that night? Would she go from crediting Arien with sparing her life to blaming Cat for the deaths of her father and brother?

Abruptly, she rose. "On this, I must needs further think and pray." She left the tent in a swirl of dark red cloak, letting the flaps fall shut in her wake.

Tiercel lifted his cup and his eyebrow to Ariana. "Nicely done. I had to make her see that you, and those of like mind, represent as much of a threat to the Emerin and the elves as any dwarven army. The *Morvalan*, and in particular the *Rhunvala*, are a double-bladed sword. They despise the other races, but are too quick to afford trust to all elves solely because they *are* elves. Tilanne must learn that simply *being* an elf does not make one deserving of trust."

"Then she should look more closely at you," Ariana said.

"I do what I must for the sake of my people and my kingdom." He kept his tone light, but there was ice in his gaze.

She turned her head away from him, blinking away furious tears of impotent rage and frustration. Only a hitch in her breath betrayed her.

He chuckled. "Do not make the mistake of thinking you can soften my heart with your tears. Fairer ladies than you have tried and failed."

"I do not weep, and even if I did, you'd must needs *have* a heart to be softened." She spoke without looking at him, managing to put just the right amount of disdain into her voice.

"You play well," he said, amused. "You must be half out of your mind from the pain and the fear and the *gilthanat*, but still you play well."

* * *

Part Three:

Chambers and Dungeons

CHAPTER TWENTY-THREE

No blade cuts deeper than a loved one's unkind word.
– Elwyndas, The Patriarch, Act V

A long, trying evening meal had finally ended, and Alinor Elyvorrin gratefully escaped to the solemn cool silence of the family crypt. Not that its atmosphere was much of a change. Dinner had certainly been an ordeal solemn, silent, and cool. His daughter-in-law Faessia, far from being the blushing betrothee, had spent the entire meal morose, pushing food about her plate with barely a word to anyone.

He supposed she had her reasons; in the weeks since the promise announcement and exchange of rings, Faessia had been besieged by Tavalara Ilhedrion, Tiercel's sister. That eager lady had leapt headlong into the planning and arrangements with unseemly haste. Lacking a daughter of her own, with her niece still decades away from being of age and the mother of her son's bride-to-be having all the privilege of planning those festivities, she had fully embraced this task. Just as Tiercel had said she would.

It was a relief to Elyvorrin but a trial as well, for the good lady was determined to gain his approval of every detail, no matter how slight. Also, he suspected, it was going to be an expensive affair. As if Tavalara was determined to outdo Liana Riachlain's mother in every possible regard.

His mind had been further troubled by worry over his absent knight. How did Tiercel fare with his quest? Would it be successful? Would he return in time, before the Council came to some other decision? They had delayed too long already. Soon, they'd have no choice but to cast their votes, and the likely outcomes of such a vote consumed Elyvorrin's thoughts both waking and sleeping.

He could only escape them when he sought refuge in the marble-and-gilt crypt in a wooded copse behind the manor. Thorny rose vines planted by his ancestors had grown to entwine most of the structure, with long-ago spells ensuring that there were deep red blooms year-round.

Donystria, wrapped in rosecloth by his own grieving hands, no longer lay in state in the front hall. She had been moved here, into the eternal darkness touched with mourning-scent. Near to her son, and two of her daughters.

Elyvorrin regarded the casket without much emotion. The rich wood had been carved with scenes from Donystria's life, and bordered in painted roses. The lid was shaped in effigy of how she'd looked in her prime, before time and loss had lined her face, before the illness to which she'd finally succumbed had marked her with haggardness.

He rested a hand upon it and sighed, then turned and moved further into the crypt. Here was his only son, slain in the war, and here a daughter dead from a senseless riding accident. At last he came to a casket of pure white wood that almost gleamed with its own mellow and serene light.

The grief he had not felt when standing beside the earthly remains of his wife struck him now, lessened not a whit by the decades. It was akin to a woolen cloak, heavy and enveloping, dragging the shoulders groundward with weight. It was a dagger, sharp and piercing.

The effigy atop the white casket showed an elfmaid of divine perfection, roses clasped in her slim hands, a crown of jewels circling her brow. It had been shaped by the Emerin's premier craftsmage, to Elyvorrin's excruciating specifications, and still failed to capture her full beauty.

Over one hundred and thirty years ago, he'd seen his Alinora laid to rest.

Or so he had thought.

Thanks to Tiercel's inquiries, he now knew the truth. The child he'd believed to be dead, the Alinora so bright and full of shining life, had been enspelled into a state like death, sealed alive into her tomb, left to endure a century and more of the most dire loneliness.

Elyvorrin bowed his head until it touched the effigy's folded hands. He sought comfort and found none, because not even his daughter's bones rested within. The casket was empty as a broken heart.

Bad enough that his daughter had been snatched from him. Worse still that it had been no true, clean death but a thing of nightmares. And worst of all, that she should be stolen away from her resting place. Stolen and forced into a life of shame as the mistress of he who should have been her rightful husband. For years, she had endured that fate, only to die in fiery madness and be buried in damp earth far from home.

Alive! Alinora had been *alive* all that time, and he had never known. How often had he come to this very crypt, wept bitter tears over her rosecloth-wrapped form? Never suspecting that she was held not by death but by enchantment, never daring to dream that he could have woken her from it.

He clutched at the effigy as if the pale wood might by some miracle transform, grow warm beneath his hands. That the closed eyes might open and look once more on the father that sorrowed so.

It was not to be. This casket held only dust, crumples of rosecloth, a few dried petals.

A soft creak made him raise his head. The door was swinging open, admitting first moonlight and then a slender robed form.

His heart locked in his chest. A wild, irrational hope welled up within him. Just as that hope was about to spill itself from his lips in a joyously-cried name, the figure stepped into the crypt and raised one mage-lit finger.

The features revealed in that pale light were not a fraction so exquisite as Alinora's. The hair that was drawn back in a loose bun was misty beige, not the hue of spun-diamonds that had graced Alinora. The eyes were not newleaf-green but grey and serious.

She did not see him, concealed as he was in the shadows that lay deep in the crypt. He sat silent, watching, as she went to Donystria's casket. Her lips trembled as if she might speak or weep. She did neither, but sketched a design in the air. The magelight on her finger left a sparkling image of a rose that sank slowly onto her mother's effigy. Then she covered her face, and her thin shoulders shook in quiet grief.

"Lionnen," Elyvorrin said, unable to keep the harshness from his voice.

His only surviving daughter flinched, then slowly turned to look at him. "I . . . I came, *Valanor*."

"How good of you to pry time from your schedule. A pity you couldn't have managed months ago, when she wrote begging you to visit. Or to pay your respects as her body lay in state. Still, here you finally are, and that is all that matters, is it not?"

"I came as soon as I could," she said meekly. "When her letter arrived, I was committed to a project with Magelord Gloriander Dane. Until we completed the casting, I could not leave else it would ruin all the work."

"Well, what is a dying mother compared to that?"

"*She* would have understood," Lionnen said, and it might have been a rare show of fire from her had she not murmured it barely above a whisper.

"Would she? I suppose she might, at that. She understood when you abandoned this family to pursue your studies. She understood that we only ever saw you at weddings and funerals. But would she understand that you missed hers?"

"I never abandoned the family," she said, the magelight reflecting unshed tears that turned her grey eyes to rainclouds. She dared not meet his gaze, instead staring at Donystria's casket. "Being accepted to study at Feyna Rel is the greatest honor a mage can achieve. I'm learning to use my talent to its fullest. What is the harm in that?"

"The harm is that you willingly gave up all ties to this family. You cannot inherit, you cannot bring us useful alliances by marriage –"

"Stop!" she cried in a broken sob, slicing her hands through the air and leaving a streaky trail of magelight. "That was never my path and you know it!"

He regarded her through narrowed eyes. "Is this what they teach you at Feyna Rel? How to speak so to your father, who only ever wanted the best for you?"

Lionnen's brittle laugh was far older than her years. "The best? I may not be worldly, but neither am I a fool . . . I know full well what you wanted for me. Half the time you sought to turn me into Alinora, and the rest you ignored and despised me for not being her. When I was young, oh, how I sought to please you, but it never mattered. Nothing I could do would be good enough, for I was not and could never be *her*."

"How dare you say such things to me?" His lips were cold and tight.

"When she died, the part of your heart where she lived died with her, and there was very little left for the rest of us. Why not say it aloud, *Valanor*? I've heard it in your silence. Go on and speak the words. 'It should have been you, Lionnen, it should have been you to die.' That is what you believe, so speak it! Even now, look at you . . . it's not Mother you mourn at all. Her passing is but an excuse by which you can brood here over Alniora!"

"Lionnen!" His voice was a whipcrack in the marble tomb.

It was as if he had struck her, struck her with the realization of what she'd dared say. With an anguished cry, she whirled and gathered her robe around her, and fled.

Elyvorrin uncurled his fists with effort. His breath was hot and angry in his lungs, his blood simmering. It subsided slowly as he looked on Alinora's image, her face in repose as a balm at once soothing and sour.

As he emerged into the brisk night air, he saw Kysander Feyna's personal carriage parked beneath the arch that spanned the driveway.

So, this was how Lionnen had come to pay a visit. It seemed that this long, trying evening was becoming a long, trying night.

Elyvorrin closed the crypt's door and locked it – not that locks had done much good when it mattered most, not when that vile Mirida had made off with poor dear Alinora's body – and made his way across the grounds back to his home.

"Milord count," a domestic said as he entered, "the Archmage Feyna is come to call. He awaits you in the back study."

By the time he had made himself presentable for guests, Feyna would have been kept waiting a goodly while. That would not rest well with him, but it suited Elyvorrin fine. Arrive at a man's home uninvited and unannounced? A house in mourning? One could not very well expect to be danced attendance upon, under such circumstances.

When he reached the back study, though, he found that Faessia had already seen to their distinguished guest's comfort with a glass of wine and a plate of fruit and sugared flowers.

"Archmage," Elyvorrin said. "An unexpected pleasure."

"Neither expected, nor welcome, I am sure, but I will take only a little of your time," Feyna said. He placed a wax-sealed envelope on the table. "I wanted to apologize for the lateness of Lionnen's return. This letter from Magelord Dane similarly expresses his condolences and regrets."

"And where is Lionnen now?" Elyvorrin asked, filling a glass for himself and taking the seat opposite the Archmage.

"We had a tiring journey. She seemed a trifle overwrought. I thought it best that she wait in the carriage with my aide."

The rest of it spun out unspoken between them. Elyvorrin knew that Feyna was sitting there waiting, just waiting for him to ask why Lionnen was staying in town rather than here, at the house, with the family. Not that she would be welcome. Not that he wanted her here at all, the disloyal thankless wretch. But she was his daughter, curse it all, his and not Feyna's.

"I trust her studies are progressing well," he said.

"She is an apt and diligent student. Not the most innovative, but reliable and exceptionally well-disciplined of mind. A credit to her calling. I take it that you still do not agree with her choice of schooling? You had no objections before."

Elyvorrin regarded him. "Before, I had another daughter and a son to carry on the family line."

"I do understand, and I am sympathetic."

"If you were so sympathetic, you would release her from Feyna Rel."

Feyna laughed and helped himself to a bit of fruit. "My dear count, you make it seem as if we hold your daughter captive."

"She is now my only surviving child. Release her from her oaths, allow her to return here and resume her duties as is proper."

"Even were it possible in the eyes of the law, I doubt she would agree."

"What of it? I am her father."

"She is of age, has completed her apprenticeship, and has severed her legal ties with the

Elyvorrin family, though by custom she still has the name. Yes, you are her father, but you no longer have say in how she leads her life. Lionnen would not be willing to give up Feyna Rel in order to come back here. You know she was not happy, Alinor."

He bristled. "Which you'd dare to say is because of me?"

Feyna spread his hands. "I may no longer have children of my own, but with grandchildren, nieces, nephews, cousins and kinsfolk to the varying degree, I know better than to criticize."

"She feels I have treated her unfairly, that I never thought she could measure up to her sister. Yet is that so unreasonable? Alinora was the best and brightest maid in the Emerin. How *could* any measure up to her, least of all Lionnen?"

"Why, then, do you even want her back? You still have Celinar."

"And if something should happen to him? Should he die young, as my children seem fated to do? I need Lionnen. It is her place, and her duty."

He did not add that, should he, Alinor Elyvorrin, become king of all the Emerin, Celinar would be needed to succeed him. Who would rule the county then? He could not give it up, not hand it over to some grasping distant relation, or in-law. The very idea! Intolerable!

Feyna leaned forward, hands folded. "I cannot do what you ask. The law prevents it. Believe me, Elyvorrin, in my time as Lord High Archmage, how I have come to hate that law, that foolish, timid, short-sighted law!"

"Of course you have," Elyvorrin said. "It's all that keeps you from being a count in your own right."

"Gods forbid that a mage should have political power as well," Feyna said, and snorted disdainfully. "Gods forbid that there should be seven rather than six voting members on the Council, and end those tiresome evenly-split ayes and nays."

Elyvorrin rolled his eyes. "That in itself would be a wonder to behold."

"And all because some long-ago king was afraid of magic and easily swayed by the wills of others," Feyna said, shaking his head. "A strong-minded king would change all that. Instead of being held back and hampered by these archaic traditions, we might see our land change for the better."

"Are you saying that if the law were to be changed, someone might . . . for instance . . . be a High Mage and hold a county as well?"

"Imagine it. Our children would no longer have to choose between their families and their talent. It goes both ways, those who've lost their lands to that silly law, and those who've denied their gifts for the sake of inheritance and arranged marriages. The wastefulness of it!"

"But the same law that bars High Mages from holding lands also exempts you from many of the kingdom taxes," Elyvorrin said. "How many of your precious Magelords would agree to that burden?"

"Bah, taxes," Feyna said, with a dismissive wave. "If you had any idea how lucrative the art of enchantment is, you'd resent us even more for having not shouldered our fair share."

His melancholy mood had departed, as had his irritation with Lionnen. He eyed Kysander Feyna, not quite sure he believed what he thought he was hearing. Could the Archmage truly be suggesting . . .

"Speak plainly, Feyna," he said. "What is it that you have in mind?"

"Is that how you wish it?" Feyna asked. "In plain-spoken words? Very well. I would lend my full support to any candidate for the throne who pledged to change that law."

It sent a shiver through him. "Oh?" he said, striving for noncommittal interest.

"I already know that Bethelyn Fistrel would never consider it," the Archmage added.

"But you are an advisory member of the Council only, lacking a vote. How would your support make a difference?"

Though, of course, they both knew full well how monumental a difference it could and would make. Of all the advisory members, Kysander Feyna was far and away the wealthiest, the most influential. A single word from him carried a great deal of weight.

"Come now, Alinor," Feyna said, smiling. "I thought we were speaking plainly here."

"You know, Kysander, you are right. It is high time this law was changed. If it should ever come within my power to do so, I would not hesitate."

They shook on it, and then opened a fresh bottle of wine.

* * *

CHAPTER TWENTY-FOUR

Mages' secrets are best left to be, for they are beyond your grasp.
– Elwyndas, Nidarn's Warning (poem)

A ring in the shape of a lightning bolt flashed golden sparks as Zanyssa Feyna's hand moved across the parchment, etching letters that were each as jagged as lightning bolts in their own way. When she reached the bottom, she scrawled her signature. Satisfied, she sprinkled glittering dust across the page and watched as the ink faded from view, leaving the parchment as blank as when she'd begun.

A soft thumping sound made her rise from the sitting room desk to peek through one of the adjoining doors. The bedroom window was ajar, curtains stirring in the breeze. The sole occupant slept on, motionless and undisturbed. On the floor beside the bed was the source of the noise, lying where it had fallen with its big onyx eyes staring blankly up at the ceiling.

It would, she thought, probably explode in a most spectacular burst of fluff if she flung a bolt at it. The prospect was so tempting that her hand curled, one finger outstretched. But she couldn't. The resulting hysteria, tearful sulks and tantrums would be more than she could bear.

A High Mage had no business still needing a *plachee*. Such toys were usually the sole province of children, enchanted with minor spells of comforting to ease their cares whenever parents or nannies weren't at hand.

This one vaguely resembled some sort of dragonish creature, olive-green with a long tail and wings like those of a glider-squirrel. Its velvety pelt was worn thin and faded almost white in places, and it had probably seen more than a few repair spells over the past century.

A keepsake. A cherished childhood plaything.

Her hand tingled. One bolt, just a small one, just enough to smite that irksome toy into a smoldering pile of stuffing.

She quelled the urge.

After all, it could be worse. At least the girl did not insist on toting it everywhere she went. At least she had the sense to keep it in her room, and a shy mouse like that certainly never needed to worry about having to explain such a peculiarity to any lover.

Best of all, she did not coo baby-talk at it, or make everyone around her pretend that it was an actual, living, feeling creature . . . the way little cousin Zandi did with her *plachee.* And could Zandi become most haughty, imperious and indignant should anyone refuse to play along? Oh, could she ever. That was one child bound to become impossible in a few more years.

Zandi, however, was not Zanyssa's concern. Her concern of the moment was Lionnen Elyvorrin, sleeping there with her pillow still tear-damp and her breath still having that watery quality that came from hours of weeping.

Zanyssa picked up the toy and placed it back on the bed. As she did so, her ring gave off a sudden snapping flash snapped so bright and loud that Lionnen whimpered and stirred. But rather than wake, she reached for and found the toy, murmured a sigh, and tucked it close to her chest.

Closing the window, closing the door securely behind her, Zanyssa returned to the sitting room and ran her thumb over her ring, sending a magical signal in response to the one she'd just received.

"*Cados na Hassa*," she said, tracing an arc in the air with both hands.

Energy crackled from her fingers, making her hair stand out in a short white-blond corona. A miniature thundercloud appeared in the middle of the room. It expanded into a swirling cyclonic vortex, a stormy portal ringed with sizzling extrusions of lightning.

Kysander Feyna stepped through the portal, smelling of good wine and looking immensely pleased with himself.

"I take it your meeting with Elyvorrin went well?" she asked as she ended the spell, letting the storm dissipate.

"Very well indeed. How fares Lionnen?"

"Sleeping." She made a face. "With her *plachee*."

"We cannot all be as confident and self-reliant as you, my niece."

"I finished the message you wished sent to Drea," she said, indicating the seemingly-blank parchment. "I hope your faith in her usefulness is justified. If you ask me –"

"Which I did not. I know as well as you do, Zanyssa, that our family tree has some decidedly odd branches." He shrugged with resigned ruefulness.

Zanyssa sniffed. "That's what you get when you breed people for mage-talent the way they breed tagga-dogs for the color of their fur. Every now and again, a freak or two turns up. Too many more like Drea, and we're done for."

"That is why it is so important that we succeed in getting the law revoked," he said. "We need fresh blood. Too many children born to the old families today have negligible talent –"

"Spare me the lecture, Uncle," she said. "You've told me often enough, and I agree."

"Strong talent and sane minds. Is that so much to ask? If we're to have any hope of reclaiming the Gates . . ." Here he gave her a grim look. "The ones that are left, at any rate."

"I tried to stop Zanderian. He nearly killed me!"

"And you *nearly* killed him. Zanyssa, *tried* and *nearly* aren't good enough. Your brother destroyed one of the last remaining Archmage's Gates. We cannot get close to the one in Larenlan, which leaves us only Ryvali . . . and Ryvali may as well be beneath the deep blue sea . . ." He broke off, and exhaled. "You see my frustration. It does me no good to have the king, or the future king, in the palm of my hand if one of my own is running about undoing my plans. Zanderian of all people, my own nephew! Ever since the war, ever since Larenlan, he's not been himself."

"I'll find him," she said. "Next time, he'll not get away. As for him no longer being himself, talk to your mind-mages for that. None of the ones they tampered with were right afterwards."

* * *

"I learned something of interest today," Idelhar Fistrel said as he entered the room where his father and uncle sat on opposite sides of a Towers board.

By the looks of it, the game had not progressed much beyond its opening moves, although the domestics informed him that they'd been in the study the better part of the afternoon.

"As did we," his father said. "It seems Kysander Feyna is now backing Elyvorrin's claim for the throne. Which, needless to say, bodes ill for us indeed."

"Not to mention for the Emerin," Bethelyn said, rubbing at his temples. "I do not wish to become king myself, not for my own ambition, but I cannot in good conscience stand by and see Elyvorrin take it. By Valannin and all our ancestors, the man is half-mad with grief! He's not been in his right mind for, what, a century and a half now?"

"Near that," Aethelyn said. "I doubt I'll ever forget his rants to King Shaelan. He all but demanded the head of Arien Mirida on a platter."

Idelhar raised a hand. "My lords, if I may?"

"Oh . . . oh, yes, nephew, go on." Bethelyn ran fingers distractedly through his hair and then studied them as if he expected strands of it to have come loose in his grasp. "Some disconnected good news to distract us from these bleak prospects would be appreciated."

"It's not entirely disconnected, I fear," Idelhar said. "Did either of you know that Arien Mirida's daughter came to the Emerin?"

They exchanged an identical glance of consternation.

"This is the first we've known of it," Aethelyn said. "When?"

"Several weeks ago," Idelhar said. "I heard of it from the High Steward, Vangier. The lady, by name of Ariana, claimed to have urgent business to discuss with the Council. Further, she told Vangier, and he had every reason to believe her . . ." Idelhar smiled wryly and waggled his fingers in the tell-tale manner of a truthsaying spell, ". . . that her father is now the Archmage of Gamelin."

"I had heard the human duke appointed an elven Archmage," Aethelyn said. "Your sister Virine mentioned it to me some time ago. But why was the visit of his daughter not made known to the Council?"

Bethelyn shrugged. "Vangier is an obedient steward, and would not interrupt unless it was some vital business indeed."

"Vangier was given most stern instructions to keep her visit a quiet matter," Idelhar said. "He was told that someone else, someone of rank, would bring it to the attention of the Council. And then, not but a day or two thereafter, the lady left unannounced and unexplained, except to send a note to the High Steward by way of one of the pages, thanking him most kindly for his courtesy."

"Given instructions by whom, nephew?"

Idelhar raised one corner of his mouth in a wry smile. "None other than my old friend, Tiercel

Reyes. Who also, as it happens, has been gone ever since."

Bethelyn Fistrel sank his chin onto his fist, a scowl knitting his forehead. "So a Mirida returns to the Emerin . . . why?" He laughed sharply at himself. "Why indeed! To protest Elyvorrin's actions. We all knew that his demands were out of line, but King Shaelan complied for it seemed of little consequence. After all, Mirida had not set foot in this land for over a hundred years, showed no indications of ever doing so, and had no kin to speak on his behalf."

"And how very well-entwined are those involved," Idelhar said. "Elyvorrin, Riachlain, and Reyes, all bound together. Elyvorrin's widowed daughter-in-law is of a sudden betrothed to Tiercel, Tiercel's nephew is betrothed to Riachlain's daughter, and Riachlain holds the lands and the seat on the Council that were to have been Mirida's. And now *Feyna* throws his support behind Elyvorrin . . . ?"

"Something must be afoot," Aethelyn said with a heavy sigh. "Whether we'll find out what in time to do anything about it is another matter entirely."

Bethelyn stroked his chin, musing. "Could Elyvorrin have the Mirida girl secreted away somewhere? I'd not put it past him to take revenge on the father by threatening the daughter."

"If he does, I've yet to know of it," Idelhar said. "All else I've heard is that the count plans to hold a grand party next week, in belated honor of his grandson's birthday. Many of the pages, squires, and younger ladies are to be invited."

"A pity you cannot pass for a page or a squire," Aethelyn said.

"Or a young lady," Bethelyn added.

Idelhar smiled. "As it happens, one of the pages is the orphaned child of a friend of mine, with no ties to any of the Council or noble families. I can see to it that we have a listening ear at that party, if you wish it."

"See to it, then," Aethelyn said. "The more we can unearth about Elyvorrin's plans, the less he can spring unawares on us at the next meeting of the Starleaf Council."

* * *

CHAPTER TWENTY-FIVE

You cannot hide your true self from me.
– Elwyndas, *Lost Loves (poem)*

The estate was awash in magical rainbow lights, the air filled with bright laughter and music and excited, youthful cries. A carnival of activities and games had been set up throughout the gardens. There, for the delight of all, were mounted acrobats, jugglers, minstrels, a menagerie of rare beasts, a comedic play performed entirely by the spells of illusion-mages, and hosts of other entertainers.

Alinor Elyvorrin stood with his hands laced behind his back, watching from a balcony as his grandson led the pack. Celinar's adopted manners of adulthood, taken on in the past weeks, were now cast aside in the simple joyous revelry of this night. In cloth-of-gold garments and a circlet, the lad might have already been prince of all the Emerin. His mother, observing the festivities from her balcony, looked pale and drawn and pensive, but her mood went unremarked by Celinar and the others. Faessia's happiness or unhappiness was of as little consequence to any of them as it was to her father-in-law.

The banquet tables set up beneath a silken tent positively groaned beneath the weight of dishes and delicacies. There would be many an aching belly in the morning, many a draught of medical cordials forced down protesting throats by well-meaning mothers and nannies. Although the guests brought birthday gifts to honor Celinar, each of them would go home with lavish trinkets and remembrances of their own, so that the generosity of the Elyvorrins would be muchly remarked upon.

This was a party that none of the youngsters would soon forget. Elyvorrin had made certain of that. They would take back to their elders nothing but glowing reports, reports that the Household of Elyvorrin could host a gathering fit for any king's court.

Nodding in satisfaction, he went back into his rooms, and nearly sprang from his skin when he found someone waiting for him.

"Tiercel?"

"Sire." He bowed. "My apologies for this unannounced intrusion and unheralded return. Given all that I must relate to you, I felt it best not to make my presence known. Tongues may wag, and I would rather give them no reason."

Although the knight showed signs of having taken some pains to make himself presentable, he still wore the weight of long weeks of travel. He looked exhausted. Without waiting to be offered, Tiercel betook himself to the sideboard and filled a crystal glass with amber liquid. He drained it at a single draught, then refilled it and sat in a chair well-removed from any windows.

"How, if I might inquire . . . ?" Elyvorrin asked. "I had thought my guardsmen and domestics lax and lazy, to be sure, but not entirely blind."

"I have learned to make use of certain hidden rooms and passages of this manor," Tiercel said. "Thus did I come to you without being seen."

Elyvorrin frowned. "I trust all this secrecy has good reason, and good cause. Your quest was successful?"

"As you know, milord, when I left to seek the Emerald, I could not hope to do so alone. The conditions put forth by the lore of the Emerald demand a king or a swordmaid."

"Yes . . . ?" His frown deepened. "This begins to sound of excuses, Tiercel. You *do* have the gem?"

"I do, but as I said, I required help. The help of a swordmaid. I was able to enlist the aid of one such, who proved able to handle the Emerald safely."

"That must have been a challenging task, knowing Emerinian women. Swordmaids are few and far between among our ladies."

"Indeed, sire." Tiercel stared into the swirling brandy. "As it happens, they are even rare among the *Morvalan*."

"So," Elyvorrin said. "At last it comes out. You are finally ready to confess to me that you follow the southern ways?"

Tiercel's startled gaze flicked up. "You . . . you know?"

"This is my home, my family's home, and I have dwelled here boy and man for over five centuries. I have been aware of your disappearances below, your absences. I know the hidden passageways of which you spoke. How could I not? Following your departure, I chose to investigate. It was most . . . enlightening."

"The shrine and the crystal?" He had gone very still, watchful. "You found those? You knew what they were, what they meant?"

"Not entirely, but I am not an uneducated man and I am not a fool, for all my sight has been clouded by grief. How long have you been *Morvalan*, Sir Tiercel? Or is it . . . Kai Tiercel?"

"I've not yet earned the title of Kai," he said. "As for the other, I discovered my . . . heritage, as it were . . . several years ago. Before the war."

"Then all this time . . ."

"All this time," he agreed. "I have lived two lives. Yet you must know, you must understand, what the *Morvalan* truly *are*. They . . . *we* are not the monsters legend would make us out to be. We do not drink blood, we do not sacrifice virgins or children. We do what we must to keep that which is ours. To protect the elven people. Sometimes . . . oftentimes . . . from themselves. That is my task, milord. To save the Emerin from itself."

"By turning it to *Morvalan* thinking?"

"To stir our people from the stagnant pool of tradition. To not permit the Lesser Races to swarm over the land while we elves sit like indulgent overfed housecats, and watch, and do nothing, until all that was ours is lost and despoiled."

"Do nothing?" Elyvorrin echoed. "We have just come from a war, man!"

"A war we lost. This world should be ours. It once was, and we let it slip through our fingers. We are the most gifted of any race to walk upon it, and should be its rulers. Yet we dwindle and die, shut away in our woods with blind eyes and deaf ears. We lost our king, we lost our prince, we lost thousands of fair elven lives and untold resources . . . and for what? Our people would put the past score and a half of years behind them, to return to the life they led before as if the war had never taken place, to forget it happened. Does that not dishonor the memories of the men who fought and died? Does that not make their deaths for nothing?"

"Men such as my son," Elyvorrin said. He could not bear the fevered, urgent, almost mad light in Tiercel's eyes. They were like the harsh glare of a winter sun on ice. He looked above the mantle, at a framed portrait of his family done in bygone, bittersweet days. Himself, and Donystria, and their children. When all of them had been alive. When none of them had been lost to him. "Yet how could it honor his memory to corrupt our people with *Morvalan* ways?"

"The *Morvalan* are not foes of the Emerin," Tiercel said. "Nor am I. This is my birthplace, my homeland, and you must believe me when I say that I only want what is best for it. I knew that the Emerin needed a king who would not be afraid to act . . . who might be more open to accepting a different view. To lead us into a new era. I chose you above all the others because I felt and hoped that you would be that king. Sire."

Did he hear some implied threat behind Tiercel's words? Surely not. And yet, Elyvorrin could not deny that the young man's entire manner had changed. Where was the servile, complimentary, flattering Tiercel of before? Where was the Tiercel so eager to please? This was a colder man, a harder man.

Or it was weariness from his travels that made him seem brusque.

Best to let that go, for now. "Tell me, then, of your *Morvalan* swordmaid."

"For her, the title Kai is warranted. She is the first and thus far only female to attain the rank *Rhunvala*. She came here in secrecy, hoping to learn more of the Emerin and help bridge the chasm between our peoples."

"And she helped you retrieve the Emerald from its resting place?"

Tiercel finished his brandy at a swallow. "Thus would have been my plan, had we gotten to the Temple first. As it happens, another swordmaid had taken it upon herself to attempt the same mission. No *Morvalan*, this one, either. She planned to use the Emerald as a bargaining token to force the Council to overturn a recent ruling."

"What? The gall! To force the Council?" It pushed all other considerations and concerns from his head in an instant. "I am astounded and appalled, Tiercel. Who would dare do such a thing? Some foreign trollop, some Lenaisian she-barbarian perhaps? Who is she?"

Tiercel's slitted eyes almost seemed to glow with blue flame as he met Elyvorrin's gaze. He smiled. "Milord count, you won't believe me when I tell you."

* * *

At the center of a cluster of onlookers, Kevan Brindani rattled the eight-sided dice in his closed fist. "If I roll six flames, I beat your six trolls."

"Such'll never happen," Jen said. "Six flames in a single throw? Pah!"

"How can you play this awful game?" Wistria Dorne tossed her long hair and mimicked her mother's haughtiest court eyeroll. "You do know Trollbones was invented by the dirty humans, don't you?"

"No, it came from Montennor," Jen said. "The dwarves –"

"The dwarves, oh, is that what you think, Jennic Perraine?"

"Look at the symbols, though," chimed in a girl Kev didn't know. "Flames, trolls, axes, diamonds, stones, mugs, caves, and coins. It's *got* to be dwarven, hasn't it?"

"I think she's right," Kev said.

The stranger girl, who was quite pretty and fair-haired, gave him a dimpled smile. She had large blue eyes, almost-but-not-quite the exact shade as the sapphire ones of Lady Ariana, the eyes that haunted his dreams. He smiled in return, almost forgetting about the dice in his hand.

"What does it matter?" Jen said, giving Kev a scathing look. "Go on and throw, loverboy, and I'll have your money. If you can keep your mind on the game long enough, that is."

Kev tossed his handful of dice onto the velvet. As they came to rest, several heads leaned to see what symbols had come up. Just then, a muffled but furious bellow rang from the house behind them, followed by a crash as an upstairs window exploded outward. Something, glittering and twinkling as it revolved in the light, streaked down into the midst of the group gathered around the Trollbones table. They leaped every which-way. The pretty girl with the blue eyes was rooted to the spot, but Kev pulled her to safety just as a crystal glass struck the table and shattered.

Domestics rushed over, and other party guests wanting to know what had happened. When the mess was cleaned up, and the excitement died down, Kev realized he still had his arm protectively around the shoulders of the pretty girl.

"That could have hit me," she said. She was gazing up at him with awe and gratitude, and all of a sudden it didn't matter so much if those big eyes weren't quite the right shade of blue.

"I wouldn't have let it," he replied. "Kevan Brindani, yours to command."

"My name's Meliara."

Braced for teasing, Kev glanced around for Jen, who always got so highly irked whenever Kev went to mush over a girl. But Jen was nowhere in sight.

"Would you like to walk a while with me?" he asked.

"I'd like that very, very much."

* * *

Was this how her father-in-law planned to impress the noble families? Was this how he planned to begin his reign as king, if indeed that amazing and daunting prospect should come to pass? Hurling things out windows into their midst? It was a miracle none of them had been hurt.

Winding her courage to the utmost, Faessia Elyvorrin stalked up the hall. She would march in there and give her father-in-law a piece of her mind –

Just before she reached his door, it was yanked open from within, and she was face to face with the stranger she was supposed to marry. The stranger whose shrew of a sister had not given her a moment's peace since the announcement had been made.

His eyes did not in any way light with warmth at the sight of her. He regarded her first with surprise and annoyance, and then with cool disinterest. As if she were no more than a domestic, and a lowly one at that. "Good evening, Faessia," he said.

A bright lance of dislike so sharp that it was almost hate pierced her heart. She felt the ring he had indifferently given her burning on her finger like something made of fire and acid.

His eyes, though, his eyes were so cold! Winter-sky eyes, freezing her to the core. She could not bear the thought of seeing those eyes across the table every mealtime for the next several centuries. Could not, *would* not. And all at once her despair and frantic grief boiled up inside her, pouring forth before she could stop it.

Her hands shook as she fought to wrench the ring from her finger. "I'll not marry you! Never! Not in a thousand years!" It wouldn't budge, wouldn't come off, was stuck against her knuckle.

Then Elyvorrin was there as well, looming at Tiercel's shoulder and looking down on Faessia in every sense. His brow was stormy with rage. "Enough of your silliness, Faessia! You *will* and you'll be thankful. Now quit making a disgrace of yourself. I am weary of being plagued by troublesome women."

The ring came free, scraping across her skin and drawing blood. Before she could hurl it at Tiercel, he had seized her hands in a crushing grip. His face lowered toward hers, his icy eyes narrow and relentless.

"We'll discuss this later," he said in a voice no less dangerous for its softness. "For now, no one is to know I've returned."

He pushed the ring back into place, scraping her again and drawing more blood, as if sealing some unholy pact.

Elyvorrin pushed past them, as if she, and their little exchange, was of no further interest. He went to a large painting, some drab landscape of the wine country hung by an ancestor. The count reached out as if he meant to knock it from the wall, having come to the same realization of its drabness, but instead, he braced the heel of his hand against the corner and pushed. It swiveled inward, revealing a dark opening in the wall.

"No one is to know of *that*, either," Tiercel said, now sounding almost as irritated with Elyvorrin as he was with her. "Go back to your room, Faessia, and keep your silence."

"Let go of me." She meant for it to be a command but it emerged as a plea, and a weak one at that. "Let go of me, I despise you."

His grip tightened until the small bones of her hand felt as if they might splinter. The ring that she had given to him – her own dead father's ring, and given under duress! – dug painfully into her flesh.

"What you think of me matters not in the slightest," he said. "These affairs are far greater than you could ever possibly understand, and more hinges on them than you'll ever know. Do your part and you will have a prosperous and luxurious life."

"My part? Marry you? When there is no love between us? How can I dishonor my Celin's memory by giving myself to –?"

His sudden laugh was harsh. "Is *that* what concerns you? I'll never touch you as a husband touches a wife. Our marriage shall be in name only."

"Even a marriage in name only would be intolerable!"

"You are a playing piece, Faessia. Not a player. You'll do as you're told."

"What if I refuse?" she asked shakily.

"That is something you do not wish to even contemplate." He released her and followed Elyvorrin into the passageway without so much as a glance back.

The painting swung closed behind them. Faessia slumped down the wall until she was sitting with her knees pulled to her chest and her arms wrapped snug around them. She dropped her brow onto her forearms and began to weep.

* * *

CHAPTER TWENTY-SIX

By striking at his armies, you strike where he is strong. But his heart . . . ah, that is another matter.
– Elwyndas, Vaithric, Act IX

Ariana's relief at sitting on something other than a baggage-laden horse, a rock, a stump or the bare ground was undiminished by the fact that the chair had seen better days. It didn't matter that the cushions on the seat and armrests was lumpy, the fabric worn thin and threadbare, or that the whole thing wobbled due to one leg being shorter than the others.

It was a chair. And it was indoors.

Indoors . . . in a windowless, subterranean chamber below the manor of Count Elyvorrin. A cool, stone-walled room smelling faintly of old wine, mildew and musty mouse-fur. Furnished with old cast-offs scrounged from the manor's storerooms, it had served as Tilanne's secret lair. For how long, Ariana did not know. The *Morvalan* could not go openly among the elves, not with her earrings and her accent that would so quickly give her away.

For good or for ill, she was at the end of her bizarre journey. Somewhere above her, hearing the news from Sir Tiercel even now, was a man who held her life in his hands. No more waiting and wondering, which had thus far been the worst part of her captivity.

That aspect did diminish a large portion of her relief.

Ariana closed her eyes and quelled her dread. She would need her mind clear, her emotions serene, to face what lay ahead.

The worst of her physical reactions to the *gilthanat* had worn off. No more fever, no more nausea, no more excruciating sensitivity to even the mildest stimulus. But she was very conscious of the lump of hateful foreign matter buried in her flesh, absorbing her energies even as she tried to summon them, rendering her feeling more helpless and vulnerable than ever before.

Her hands rested in her lap, wrists bound with cords over a wrapping of cloth to lessen their chafing bite. Every surreptitious attempt to wriggle free had only shamed her and made her think in envy of how her mother, grandfather, or brother might have slipped so easily from the bonds.

Silence and inward-turning thoughts had been her most constant companions during her captivity. They had led Ariana deep within herself, making her contemplate the many natures of strength and search for the nature of her own.

Tiercel's was the strength born of extreme and perhaps undue confidence in his own physical prowess and cleverness . . . and should he be outmatched, Ariana suspected he would quickly falter. Tilanne, though . . . the *Rhunvala* was another matter. Her strength came from unswerving faith, in her god, her cause, and her people. That could not be stripped from her.

And what of Ariana herself? She knew now that she lacked her mother's fierce heart, and had not had time to fully develop the mental discipline that was her father's greatest advantage. Those might come in time . . . if she *had* time. Yet she had learned other things from her parents. From Arien, she had learned distance, aloofness, coldness. From Cat, watchfulness and when to know the moment to strike. Those would have to do.

A new scent reached her, a dusty smoke-and-perfume scent that tickled her nose and made her want to sneexe. She opened her eyes.

Tilanne was holding a small round box in one hand and its lid in the other. Both were glossy black, painted with scarlet swirls. She sprinkled some of the contents – a red-grey powder – into a goblet, then closed the box and set it aside. She added wine, and stirred.

"I'll not drink that, whatever it is," Ariana said.

"For thee it is not," Tilanne said, without even looking at her let alone sounding impressed by this show of defiance. "Medicine it is. Ash of blood-rose. Upon it, my life relies. Not without price was my becoming *Rhunvala*."

Ariana felt, and immediately quashed, a sense of sympathy for her. She did not want to like this darkly beautiful, queerly noble elfmaid. She was *Morvalan*, she was the enemy. Never mind that Ariana had witnessed more evil from Quisfahr, more cruelty from Tiercel, more madness from Drea . . . and those Emerinians all.

So she kept telling herself. And yet, as they had traveled south, it had become harder and harder to cling to any sort of animosity towards Tilanne. She was, in her way, admirable. By the time they had reached Perras Peliani, all Ariana could still dredge up was the heartsick memory of Mischa. This was the woman who would have killed Mischa with all the pity and satisfaction someone might have shown a rat or a roach. Not because of anything he had done. Solely because he was human. Something lower than vermin to a *Morvalan's* eyes. Something that should not be permitted to live.

All she could hope was that the end had come swiftly for him. She could not bear the thought of him in terror and misery, perhaps starving, perhaps with injuries that were slow to bring death but too severe for even the power of his goddess to mend. What if she had done him a disservice in helping him escape? Tiercel and Tilanne would have at least slain him swiftly.

Unbidden, a horrid image arose of poor Mischa, sprawled pale and dead on a bed of rain-sodden leaves. She vividly saw nsects creeping across his skin, his body gnawed by scavengers, with stiffened fingers clenched around the Talopean pendant that had been his last comfort.

She shuddered and a soft sound of grief escaped her lips.

Tilanne gave her a glance that was not without compassion. Had she known that Ariana grieved for a human, and not for the hopelessness of her own situation, Ariana didn't doubt that even such a gesture of comfort would not have been forthcoming.

Footsteps approached.

Ariana sat up straight, determined not to worsen the pitiable picture she knew she must already present.

The door opened and Tiercel preceded another man into the room. Ariana knew him on sight. Count Elyvorrin was tall and imposing, with striking features and pale golden hair sheened with grey. His eyes were a direct green, and as they fixed on Ariana she could feel them pierce her like emerald needles. His spine was rigid, his shoulders tight, his fists curled so that the knuckles were bone-white.

Any hope she might have harbored of being able to find a way out through discussion and diplomacy, faint though such a hope may have been, died without a murmur. He hated her. Hated her as much as one living being had ever hated another in all the history of the world. He'd never even seen her until now, but that meant nothing. He hated her, and he would gladly see her dead. Only a stiff-necked pride kept her from dissolving into weakness and perhaps even tears.

Elyvorrin's penetrating gaze searched Ariana's face, and then lingered on her hair. The long, silver hair that, though tarnished and tangled from travel, distinctively marked her as a Mirida. As her father's daughter.

"I should entomb you alive," he said in a voice that might have been pleasant were it not seething with venom.

Tilanne shifted, setting aside the drained goblet. She looked ready to step between count and captive, should Elyvorrin show any signs of lunging for Ariana's throat. Tiercel nudged her with his elbow, and shot her a stern glare from under one angled eyebrow.

"Sire, allow me to introduce Kai Tilanne," Tiercel said. In a lower voice and as an aside to Tilanne, he added, "Your oath is only that you *personally* take no elven life, as I recall. Any debts you feel you may owe this woman must be considered minor in the greater scheme of our plans. If the continued goodwill of the future king requires her death, so be it and you shall not interfere."

As unusual as a meeting of this sort had to be, the count barely acknowledged the Rhunvala before returning his attention to Ariana.

"Wrap you in rosecloth," he said. "Just for a hundred years or so. Let you lie, alive yet helpless, in a cold tomb while a century passes by."

"It will not bring her back," Ariana said, astonished at how steadily she spoke. "I know that your hatred for my father is great, but to make him suffer as you have suffered will not ease the hollowness in your heart. Instead, you will forever be less than him. What he did, tragic and misguided as it was, he did for love. What you do, you do only for revenge."

His already pale face went bloodless. "You have the sheer unchecked temerity to speak to me so?"

"If you wish it, sire . . ." Tiercel said, setting hand to Discordant's hilt.

"I would not give Mirida the comfort of knowing she died quickly. Nor would I grant that gift to this insolent she-pantera. I would pay back tenfold what my dear Alinora endured . . . nay, a hundredfold!"

"Wouldn't you rather have *him*?" Tiercel grinned. "She would make rather attractive bait."

"I would give all that I have and all that I stand to gain for the chance to exact my revenge upon Arien Mirida with my own two hands. And just the knowledge that his darling daughter was my prisoner would surely wrench the very soul from his body, even should he prove too cowardly to face me."

Ariana bit back an outraged cry as her worst fear became plan.

"These might aid in convincing him," Tiercel said, holding up the black dragon signet ring and the *ilgilean* that Ariana had worn.

"Yeeeesssss," Elyvorrin said, drawing out the word as if savoring the implications. He cradled the ring and the opal with avaricious glee. "He would have no choice. He would come. And witness for himself the fate that befalls his daughter. I will let *that* be the last sight to fill his eyes before I finish him forever."

Unable to look at them, Ariana glanced at Tilanne. The *Rhunvala's* expression was deeply troubled, disapproving, but she did not speak out against this proposed dual murder. Nor did she return Ariana's glance with any promise of help. Plainly, she meant to stand by and let these events run their course, no matter how abhorrent she might find them.

"In the meantime," Tiercel said, "we cannot risk keeping her here. I know a place where she will not be found and shall have no hope of escape, and guards who are my own sworn men."

Elyvorrin considered this news. "Your own sworn men, Tiercel? Other *Morvalan*, in the very Emerin itself?"

"Not *Morvalan*, but men loyal to me at any and all costs. They served under me in the war, and each owes me more than his life."

"You are certain? I would not have Fistrel or any of the others on the Council know of this. How do you plan to keep that wretched father of hers from finding her by sorcery?"

Tiercel explained the *gilthanat*, yanking open Ariana's collar to show the healing scab and the knotted stitches. She twisted away from him, biting her lip to keep from telling him that he was underestimating her father if he thought one little chunk of dwarf-metal would stop a man touched by the powers of the Avantari. And he was forgetting her mother altogether. The prison had not been built that could defeat Cat Sabledrake.

If she said any of that, though, they may well decide to kill her anyway. A dungeon cell and armed guards were far preferable to rosecloth, and the tomb.

"Then I leave it in your capable hands, Tiercel." Elyvorrin sighed with contentment as he regarded Ariana again. "For the first night in nearly a century and a half, I shall sleep well, though not nearly so blissfully as I'll sleep once this matter has been concluded. Take her from my house."

"What of the other matter, sire?" Tiercel asked. "The Emerald?"

"One triumph at a time. I'm afraid I may have distressed some of Celinar's friends with my earlier outburst, and I should placate Faessia. Return once our bait is safely sealed away, and then I'll expect an entire accounting of your journey."

"As you command. Tilanne, I believe I should handle this next step on my own."

She nodded. "Remain here shall I . . . with much to pray upon and Kaledhol's guidance to seek."

* * *

"Oh, lady, lady, please do not cry," Jennic Perraine said.

Faessia Elyvorrin may have tried to stifle her sobs, but it seemed her worn-thin nerves would have none of it. She lay crumpled across her bed, still weeping as piteously as she'd been when Jen had found her in the upstairs hall.

"Lady, please," Jen tried again. "Tell me what happened. Who threw that glass down among us, and why? I see bruises forming on your wrist, and your finger bleeds . . . who has done this to you? Who has hurt you?"

"I cannot fight them," she whimpered into the pillows. "What can I do? What can I do? Lionnen was right. He cares for no one but the dead."

With uncertain hands, Jen patted her arm. "Who?"

"*She* thought she'd won her freedom," Faessia said. "She even had freedom from this place for a time. But now he'll draw her back in, poor Lionnen. Trap her. As a spider binds a fly in its web. That's all we are to him. It may seem a safe cocoon, kept for a while, made to feel secure . . . but in the end, he drains and discards us all. Takes what he wants and leaves only dry husks. Poor Lionnen! Poor Faessia!"

"The count? Do you speak of Count Elyvorrin?"

"If *she* couldn't get away, what hope have I? He'll use me up, just as he will Lionnen. Make her the countess once he becomes king, but she'll still be under his thumb. Pinned and crushed. His and Feyna's both."

"Here, my lady." Jen offered a cool, damp cloth and Faessia gratefully blotted her tear-drenched face. "The count and the Archmage? Do you know their plan?"

She sniffed and nodded. "Lionnen told me. Lands and titles for the High Mages. She's as much a playing piece in this as am I. Oh, to be made to marry Tiercel Reyes . . . to let him raise my son . . . ah, no!" A fresh spate of weeping overcame her, but she forced words through it. "And they . . . all say what . . . a fortune . . . fortunate woman . . . I am."

"Surely Sir Tiercel would never let you or your son be mistreated."

"Oh, surely not . . . not by anyone save the count and himself!" She thrust out her arm. "*He* did this! Tiercel. To whom I am supposed to pledge myself as wife!"

"Truly? No, lady, no, it cannot be. That Sir Tiercel would do you harm . . ." Jen was too aghast to finish.

Faessia's eyes suddenly cleared, and she looked around with dismay. "And I should be telling you none of this. They bade me tell no one. You must swear to me to keep this to yourself."

"I . . . I . . ."

"If not for me, then for your own sake. Should they suspect I told, should they suspect anyone else knows of their plots and passages, they will take terrible action. I know they would!"

"What plots? What passages?"

"Swear to me."

"You cannot bear this alone, lady. Others can help."

"No. This must go no further. I charge you, make me this promise. Are you not a young man of honor, to deny the plea of a lady? Swear thusly to me."

Jen exhaled slowly. "Very well, then . . . on my honor as a young man, I so swear."

Faessia nearly wept again, this time in relief. "It is for the good of us both. I could not bear to see harm come to you because of my unwisely-said words. Now, go, and swiftly, lest they return and find you here and guess that you know more than you should."

"Yes, lady." Jen went to the door, opened it enough to peer out, and saw no one. "Should you have need, I offer –"

"No," she said. "Do not offer me your service. Do not even tell me your name. It is best and safer that you forget this ever happened."

Rather than returning to the ongoing festivities in the gardens, which had not been much deterred by the bombardment from on high, Jen instead crept quietly upstairs. The spot where Lady Faessia had been huddled on the floor was between the door to the count's sitting room and a large and, in Jen's opinion, extremely ugly and poorly-done painting of the wine country.

Still, no one was around. The domestics were all busy at the party. Knowing that an inquisitive page was good, but a too-inquisitive one was asking for trouble, Jen nonetheless listened at the sitting room door. Then, when all proved silent . . .

"Jen?" Kevan Brindani spoke from the hallway, making Jen jump. "There you are. What are you doing?"

"I could ask the same of you," Jen said, at once relieved and alarmed. "Sneaking about like that."

"I was looking for you. I wanted to tell you that I was leaving to walk Meliara home."

"Oh, *were* you?" Jen said.

"When I couldn't find you anywhere, I finally had to seek you." He waggled his fingers. When they'd been younger, it had been impossible to best Kevan in any games of hide-and-seek. "Are you mad, snooping about the count's private chambers?"

"Kevan, listen to me . . . there's much I must tell you . . ."

"Shh," Kev hissed. "Someone's coming. Oh, now we're in for it . . ."

"Hide," Jen grabbed Kev's hand and yanked him into the sitting room, closing the door as quietly as possible.

A long brocade sofa was set in one corner, angled against both walls. The space behind it held a round-topped table, but there was room for a pair of agile pages to worm down on either side of the table. Kev's elbow struck a delicate vase but Jen was able to steady it before it could fall.

They hunkered down in the cramped space, being careful to keep their heads below the level of the sofa's back.

"Wonderful," Kev whispered around the table's single leg. "Now what?"

The door opened again before Jen could reply.

* * *

CHAPTER TWENTY-SEVEN

When found, he was more animal than man.
– Elwyndas, Shoral's Rival, Act VII

At midnight, the walls of the palace of the Elvenking were illuminated by globes of maroon light, as if in honor of the spirit of mourning that still lay heavily on the people of the Emerin. Those who held the night-watch moved like specters through the reddish glow and the swirling fog that drifted down from the treetops. The palace was still but for their hushed conversations.

Tiercel passed through the gates recognized and unchallenged, greeted with respectful murmurs and knowing looks when the sentries noticed at the cloaked shape of a woman at his side.

Ariana wondered what would happen if she tossed her head to fling back the hood that concealed her face, revealing the gag. Or if she pushed her arms forth from the cloak, displaying wrists still bound. They would see then that this was not a case of the heroic knight sneaking one of his conquests into the palace to consummate some clandestine affair.

She resisted the impulse. For all she knew, these were more of his 'own sworn men.' And even were they not, they'd be far more likely to accept whatever tale he wove than believe anything she might claim. She could see the admiration in their eyes. This was Sir Tiercel, of the Order of the Lion, a general whose valor had been the talk of the wartime. She was unknown, and if the Mirida name was recognized at all, it would be with disdain because of the charges Elyvorrin had made and successfully carried out against her father.

So she let herself be led, head down and posture demure, through the gates, and then across darkened courtyards and along empty corridors and down long flights of stairs.

Tiercel never once let down his guard, reminding her by way of a painful grip in the juncture of shoulder and neck – on the other side, thankfully, than that which bore the painful wound – that any sudden valor on her part would be something she would greatly and swiftly regret. Even had she been courageous or foolhardy enough to try, she knew that, bound as she was, her only option would be to try and kick him senseless. Which was no real option at all.

The further they went into the depths beneath the palace, the less well-kept it became. Not that it was by any stretch of the imagination decrepit or gloomy, for the walls were still made from smooth and creamy stone and the torch-sconces were intricate and gilded. But dust had gathered in the corners, and the torch-sconces were dead and unlit. The air was not foul, but neither was it fresh as in the upper reaches. Few domestics, Ari guessed, had reason to tread here.

Nor would many others had reason to come this way either. The laws of the Emerin were founded on fines and restitution and social ostracism, rarely on threat of imprisonment or the more physical punishments. Execution was all but unheard-of. There was little poverty and need among the elves, and as such things were the seeds from which crimes tended to sprout, few criminals. Emerinian life was not a matter, as her father had once said, of the haves and the have-nots, but of the haves and the have-mores.

Thus, the few jails in Perras Peliani were nearly always empty, and most citizens were probably wholly unaware that their royal palace even *had* a dungeon. Those who lived and worked here might not even know of it. Tiercel meant to keep her in the perfect place, all but literally beneath the very noses of the Council.

Lower and lower, steep stairs like a stone throat, descending into a black as complete as a moonless night. The single magelight Tiercel had summoned only made the shadows seem to encroach more hungrily.

Lower still. It was as if the stairs formed a loop, an endless loop that they walked and walked, rotating in vast and silent space.

After what seemed ages, they reached a landing, where flights of steps split off in two directions, each as ominous as the last. Here, Tiercel paused and removed Ariana's gag. She coughed as the dry wad of cloth was removed.

"It would be useless to scream," he said. "No one above would hear you, unless as the distant cry of some night bird."

The smugness of his tone infuriated her. Had he been preceding her on the stairs, she might well have kicked him anyway, hoping that the fall would shatter his skull. Tiercel saw some of that in her eyes, for his confident smile gave way to a mocking grin. He pushed her toward the leftmost staircase, which was even steeper than the one they'd been on. She grabbed frantically at the banister with her bound hands to keep from living out that fate herself.

The risers were narrow, calling to mind the ledge that she'd inched along in the ruined keep, in the aquatic lair of the mind-leeches. Without the ready use of her arms, she was hard-pressed to keep her footing. A draft, chill as the exhalation of a grave, stirred her hair and made the cloak flap around her legs.

"We are above an underground river here," Tiercel said as he started down behind her. He sounded at his ease, almost chatty. "There are fissures in the walls that give onto it, hence the draft. None are wide enough to admit even a slender thing like yourself, should you be contemplating a swim. Even were they, the water is so cold would stop the very pulse of blood in your veins."

The air was moist and colder now, and her breath fogged in a nimbus around her head. Down and down, lower and lower. As if she was climbing into a well and at any moment the inky water might lap at her toes. Then, far below and seemingly straight down because of the sharp angle of the staircase, firelight flickered.

She saw some of the fissures that Tiercel had mentioned, thin mouths yawning on the sides and ceiling of the steep tunnel, their edges glistening. Drips splashed her, the water so icy its touch seemed to burn like acid.

Shivering, her teeth trying to clatter in her jaw, she continued down. Her fingers were numb on the banister. Though made from magically-preserved wood, it may as well have been a single long and continuous icicle. Her feet, clad in thin shoes of kidskin rather than her own boots, were growing numb as well, making her lose trust in them.

Her breath puffed dense cloudlets like steam in her eyes. She fancied she could feel the weight of the bedrock and the palace above pressing down on her. Then a few tentative threads of warmth caressed her legs. She heard the crackle of flames, smelled no smoke, and understood that the fire was a magical creation that required no fuel to burn. Low voices, distorted into incomprehensible mutterings, came from below.

She reached the end of the stairs. A short tunnel opened onto what looked to be a water-carved cavern. Ariana sank to her knees, her legs shaking badly from the descent. The orange glow of firelight and delicious heat enveloped her. When the discomfort of stone and dampness soaking through the knees of her leggings, she rose . . . and found herself looking at two shining arrowheads trained on her chest.

The bows were pale wood with darker striations, things of beauty and craftsmanship, well cared for and well-handled. The men holding them wore the uniforms and swordbelts of the palace guard, with the added concession of fur-lined capes against the cold.

As Tiercel appeared behind her, they relaxed and lowered their bows.

The shorter of the two was brown-haired and had a quick, foxlike way about him, with dark dancing eyes that sparkled in high amusement. The taller was blond and lithe, his features so elegant that he could have passed easily among the nobility. But as he turned to greet Tiercel, Ariana saw with horrified pity that his right ear was only a snarl of scar tissue. He heard her gasp and swiftly jerked his head to the side, making his hair tumble to cover the maiming.

The cave soared to twice their heights overhead and was as nicely appointed as any hunting lodge. Ariana saw shelves of books, a table for a Towers game, the blazing fire, provisions, beds, blankets, and more. She realized that these men must live down here for months at a time, for Tiercel couldn't afford to let these secret guards come and go and perhaps be noticed, perhaps be followed.

On the far wall, a massive door was set flush with the stone. Its lock had a plate as big as her hand. There was a metal wheel in the center. A lever, with truesilver handle in the form of a sinuous wyvern, jutted from the wall beside the door.

"I've brought a new guest," Tiercel said.

"As a captive?" the foxlike one asked, askance. "A lady? Here?"

"I trust, Pahelin, that you shan't be swayed from your duties by a fair face."

"No. No sir, I shan't. Of course not."

"She's not to be touched by either of you, is that understood?"

"Sir!" the blond said. "We are not humans to abuse prisoners."

"I meant no offense, Retharn," Tiercel said.

Retharn was not placated. "Just because we no longer walk among normal elves does not mean we no longer *think* as elves."

Tiercel looped an arm around his shoulders and led him off a few paces, his words unclear but the apologetic tone plain enough.

Pahelin stared at Ariana. "Why are *you* down here?"

"Why are *you*?" she returned. "Why do you give your loyalty to this man?"

"I owe him," he said, but he dropped his gaze. "If not for Tiercel Reyes, I'd be dead or worse. I'd lay down my soul for him."

"Do you not know what he is, what he's done? How he's been corrupted?"

"Not corrupted." Pahelin shook his head vigorously. "Enlightened. He's seen the way things must be, and has shared his vision with us."

Ariana gaped at him, at the uncanny hold Tiercel had on the hearts and minds of these men. Her eyes flicked toward the stairs. Only her eyes, no twitch of her body betraying her, but Pahelin raised his bow again as if she'd shouted her intent at the top of her lungs.

"This is a truesteel arrowhead with double-honed razor edges," he said. "Sunk into the back of your knee, it can leave you hamstrung and crippled."

"With my hands tied," she said, showing them to him, "I'd never be able to climb that stair anyway. Still, do you fault me for wondering?"

A corner of his mouth tweaked up in reluctant acknowledgement. "No. I'd most likely do the same, were I in your spot."

Tiercel and the mollified Retharn returned. The knight slapped his palms together briskly as if to knock dust from them. "Now, then. Gentlemen, we'll be offering Lady Ariana the finest suite in the house." He gestured toward the door. "Your key."

Pahelin fished a fine silver chain out of his collar. A miniature key, so small it could have rested on Ariana's thumbnail without touching the edges, dangled from the chain. She looked again at the lock, the keyhole of such size that her mother could nearly have slipped her clever thief's fingers inside and worked the tumblers that way. But rather than approach the door, Pahelin took down a flat box from a high shelf and unlocked it. Within was a much more respectable key.

Tiercel pulled her, with no great gentleness, over to the door.

"You don't mean to leave me bound, do you?" she asked.

By way of reply, he drew a knife and slashed the cords, though the cloth remained wrapped around her wrists and would still take some struggling to unwind.

The key clicked. Then Pahelin took up his bow again, while Retharn turned the wheel and the door groaned open. Nothing rushed out of the widening slice of darkness, but Pahelin was tense enough to show that he clearly *expected* something to.

A tremor of apprehension ran through Ariana. "What's in there?"

"Go find out," Tiercel said, and shoved her through the door.

The floor beyond sloped precipitously. Ariana cried out in surprise as she plunged forward, the soles of her slippers skidding across the stone as if it were waxed. She nearly went headlong, recovered, and then slammed into metal bars with bone-jarring force.

The door closed behind her before she even caught her breath. Before it latched, enough light came through to let her see that she was in some sort of a cage butted up against the door, and on the other side of the bars was a river-hewn cavern even larger than the one where the guards lived.

She huddled by the bars, working her hands free of the winding cloth. As it started to come loose, she sensed that she was not alone. This knowledge came not through anything she saw or heard, but sensed by some cat-whisker alertness.

Something was out there, something in the dark, stalking stealthily closer.

Nor was it altogether dark in here. A faint glow came from somewhere, as if seeping through the seams in a hooded lantern.

From deep in the wall behind her came a grinding clunk that she instinctively knew was the sound of the wyvern-shaped lever being thrown. At once, a section of bars in front of her rose like a portcullis. Unprepared, she toppled through the gap and lost her footing, pain flashing through her awkwardly-held and still half-wound wrists as she tried to break her fall.

She scrambled upright again, blinking as the blackness began to yield to shades of purple and grey. Still she sensed that something was near her.

As the handle had been in the shape of a wyvern, or perhaps a dragon, she would have been alarmed but not particularly surprised to hear the lazy flap of leathery wings and the tick of claws on stone as the denizen of the cave came out to investigate.

She tried to comfort herself with the reminder that they planned to kill her in front of her father – and the fact that such a thought was comforting showed her that her situation was dire indeed. Finally, she shook loose the last of the cloth and was able to move her arms apart for the first time in far too long. Her joints crackled like those of an old woman as she stretched.

Her extended fingers brushed against warm, living skin.

The startled scream that tried to explode from her throat was cut off in a gust as powerful arms seized her up. She was crushed against a bare chest that felt as wide as a wall and as muscular as a warhorse. Her ribs creaked and gave as if about to snap.

"I wondered when they'd think of trying this," someone growled in her ear.

It was Emerinian elven, but spoken in a voice so deep and resonant it could have belonged to a Perrifaulian thunder-singer. And yet no elf ever had such a voice, nor such breadth of shoulder and chest. Human? Elfkin? Some shaper-mage thing? What manner of creature held her in its grasp?

With her newly-freed hands, Ariana grabbed blindly where she estimated the man's head must be and found a thick mane of silky-coarse hair. Then ears, elven ones. Large, tapered, and by the feel, exceptionally well-shaped.

She heard her mother's advice as clearly as if Cat had been standing behind her. *Fair fighting is fine and well for duels and tournaments, but should someone ever grab you in a dark alley, forget the niceties.*

This was a cave, not an alley, but she wasn't in a mood to quibble. She clenched one ear in each hand and yanked.

He hissed in pain but did not drop her, only tightening that crushing hold.

"So help me, I'll rip them off! I will! Like drumsticks of an overcooked fowl," she said.

"I could break your spine in two," he said, squeezing harder.

Gritting her teeth, she wrenched and twisted his ears for all she was worth. This time he *roared*, his spice-scented breath blowing back her hair. He flung her from him.

Ariana landed solidly on hard stone, slid on her backside, and collided with a hanging curtain or blanket. She caught at it to stop her slide and pulled it down half-atop her. Candlelight rushed eagerly out, painting her with its pale glow.

He came slowly into the light, tense and wary, moving with a stalking predatory grace. She thought of the greenlion at the Temple, the way it had moved.

She rose into a crouch. Her gaze traveled up and up. He was the tallest elf she had ever seen, and by far the most muscular. His long legs were encased in snug butter-soft leather. His feet and torso were bare. His hair fell midway down his back in tawny-gold waves.

"I've anticipated this move," he said in that deep, resonant voice, "and it will not succeed."

"Who are you?" she asked. "What 'move?'"

"Ah, so you're taking that stance, playing at ignorance. It makes no difference. You and your fellow conspirators are wasting your time."

"I do not know what you mean. I am no conspirator, but a captive."

"Naturally. That is what I am supposed to believe. You will play at innocence, so that I'll come to trust you, confide in you. Then you'll betray me. I am not a fool."

He crossed his arms and looked down at her, and she saw that his eyes were the rich gold of a newly-minted coin. The same hue, the same sure expression, as she'd seen in the eyes of the greenlion.

"Hear me," she said. Standing, she discovered that he still towered over her, and she was not a small woman. "I do not know who you are. I am no part of these . . . schemes you imagine. I have been jailed here against my will by a vile and deceitful knight –"

"Tiercel Reyes, of course," he said. "So that we'll seem to share a common enemy, thus encouraging me to more readily accept *you* as a friend."

"He *is* my enemy!"

"You are a superb actress, I must give you that. Most convincing. However, don't think I'm such a fool as to fall for it."

She uttered an inarticulate cry of frustration.

"Although," he went on, "I suppose you could be telling the truth."

"Finally!"

"In which case, he would mean for me still to befriend you. He knows that I cannot be swayed by threats to my person, and might hope that to spare my *friend* the agonies of torture, I would submit to his will."

Ariana paused. "That does fit with what I've seen of him. Yet I still do not understand . . . who *are* you? What does Tiercel want from you?"

He shook his head. "Either you are in league with Tiercel and already know these things, or you are a bystander he hopes to use as a lever against me and so the less you know, the better. Whichever it is, I'll not play along. I will tell you nothing, and you shall mean nothing to me."

* * *

CHAPTER TWENTY-EIGHT

Look to the children, for they are honest and without guile.
– Elwyndas, The Seven Apprentices, Act III

Kevan's leg was cramping, but he dared not shift it for fear the count would hear the movement.

He and Jen had been trapped behind the couch for better than an hour while Elyvorrin stormed about the room acting the madman. He wailed, he raged, and then finally he basked in malevolent joy at the prospect of his revenge against Arien Mirida and that daughter of his.

Even if a clear and unobstructed path had opened up between Kev and the door, even if he had the utmost assurance of safety, he would not have left then. Not once he'd heard that. Something dreadful was afoot and it involved the Lady Ariana. He would not leave now, not for all the world.

Jen, who had seen Kev's reaction, tried to communicate by gestures just how great an idiot Kev was being, smitten already for some lady he'd met only a few times.

And still Elyvorrin went on. He was unable to stay in a chair longer than a few moments. Several times, he had seated himself at a desk to begin a letter to Ariana's father, but couldn't decide on how to address it, tossing out choices ranging from formal to filthy.

One such effort, addressed to 'Archmurderer of Gamelin,' had been crumpled and batted away and rolled beneath the couch, where Jen had stealthily picked it up.

Having pitched his brandy glass out the window, the count was bolstering his strength with wine straight from the neck of the bottle. Kev was appalled to witness a good and expensive vintage being gulped down with neither appreciation nor finesse.

"What now?" Jen mouthed.

Kev mimed drinking and lolled his head to the side with his tongue hanging out.

Jen looked distressed, knowing as Kev did how hard it was for an elf to drink himself into oblivion. Even if Elyvorrin went through that bottle and two more, it might not fell him. They couldn't wait that long.

Someone rapped at the door, and Kev's spirit soared with hope. It would be a domestic, come to investigate, who would gently usher the count off to bed. It would be Celinar wanting to show off his costly birthday presents. It would be –

"Sire?"

It would be Sir Tiercel.

The excited flush Kev used to feel at being in the presence of one of the Emerin's greatest heroes was now a hot coal of anger, for he understood from Elyvorrin's rantings that Tiercel was a part of this as well. Tiercel was involved with whatever had happened to Lady Ariana. If they had harmed a silver hair on her head . . .

Jen poked him warningly and Kev subsided, realizing that he was growling under his breath.

"Tiercel . . . faithful Tiercel," the count said. "I've been struggling with this letter and having little luck. It must be *perfect*, and in the fire of my emotions, I'm ill-prepared to write it. Has she been dealt with?"

"She has," Tiercel said, and Kev's heart plummeted to his toes while his stomach rose and tied itself in a knot just below his throat.

"I am pleased to know it. I'll confess, Tiercel, I had a qualm or two about exacting my revenge in this manner. But you heard her insolence. You heard how she spoke to me. To *me*!"

"I can see from whence those qualms may have arisen, for you are a good man and inclined to believe the best of others. Yet this Ariana is not the dear innocent that was your Alinora. She defied and insulted us both, and might even be said to bear some direct responsibility for Alinora's doom."

"How so?" Elyvorrin asked in a harsh whisper.

"Given that Mirida spent precious little time mourning Alinora, rushing off nearly the very next day . . ."

"He could have arranged her death, ridding himself of my precious daughter in favor of his foul mistress and bastard child, is that what you mean to say, Tiercel?"

"I know not, sire. It seems unthinkable, and yet . . ."

Kev wanted to pop up from behind the sofa and make them answer for these vile deeds and slanders, make them answer with swift steel. Would that he was older, his training complete. As it was, he had to hold his tongue and keep his place and simmer.

"I know what must be done," Elyvorrin said. "Fear not, Tiercel. Qualms shall not grow into doubts. I *will* have my peace. When I look into Mirida's eyes as he watches his daughter burn, burn alive and screaming and plunging to her death as my Alinora did, yes, I will have my peace."

"I look forward to that day."

"As do I." He sighed lengthily. "Now, then. I fear my emotions in this matter have overrun the *true* purpose of your mission. Did you bring it?"

"In this bag, sire. I . . . am not worthy of its touch. Tilanne bore it hither from the north, but we agreed I should be the one to bring it to you."

Kev heard a clunk, and turned to Jen with quizzical eyes. Jen shrugged helplessly.

"Gods and ancestors," Elyvorrin breathed. "I have never beheld such splendor."

Curious to the point that it overcame even their sensible caution, Ken and Jen ever-so-slowly peeped their heads above the back of the sofa. When Tiercel stepped to the side, Kev saw what had so held their attention. Wonder transfixed him at the sight of the spherical jewel. He knew it instantly for what it was, from legends he'd heard since the very nursery, and many things became clear to him in a single moment of flashing understanding.

"Take it up, my lord," Tiercel said. "Prove to me that my hopes have not been unfounded. Show to me and all the world that you are the next true and destined king of the Emerin."

Elyvorrin stared at the Emerald. "I *am*," he said. "Yes. I must be. Long live King Alinor." He reached out.

Searing green fire filled the world.

Kev ducked and threw himself flat. Something heavy slammed into the sofa, driving it back. The table behind it tottered, almost snapped as it was squeezed between the back of the sofa and the wall. The vase that had been on the table fell, smashing into crescents that rained into Kev's hair. He heard glass breaking – there went the rest of the windows – and a thunk as Jen's head hit the wall. Jen groaned and slid down beside Kev, unconscious.

Then all was still.

Through the decorative fringe that hung down from the bottom cushions, Kev could see an outstretched leg and one dangling arm. Elyvorrin's. The count had been thrown clear across the room to land senseless on the sofa. The back of his hand rested on the floor. Wavering greenish-grey smoke rose from the half-curled fingers.

Beyond, a pair of stylish black boots moved toward the count. "Sire?" Tiercel said. "My lord?"

Not so much as a grunt came from Elyvorrin. Kev cringed as the boots came closer yet. Then Tiercel dropped to one knee and took up Elyvorrin's wrist, testing for a lifebeat.

"Alive," he said, and now the proper and dedicated tone that had priorly underlain his voice was absent, replaced by something cold and sly. "But unworthy. There's a relief. It would have been a fine jest on me, had the Emerald accepted you. If you are to be king, it must be by the destiny *I* make, not by the will of the gods. A king of lies, ever doubting, ever needing the assurance that only I can give."

Kev's hands ached, so tightly were they formed into fists. Fists that yearned to plow into a nose, blacken an eye or two, knock loose a few teeth. He felt as if his hair might begin to smolder from the hot fury of his brow.

Tiercel chuckled. "What now shall become of this gem, this national treasure? Your pride couldn't bear to give it over to the Council, could it? Not when it might –"

Elyvorrin's fingers twitched, and Tiercel immediately adopted his former tone.

"My lord? I pray you, speak to me."

Kev nearly gagged.

A flurry of footsteps and voices brought Tiercel to his feet in a bound. He uttered a word that Kev had never dared speak aloud – a gentleman wasn't even to *know* such words! – and fled to lock the door a bare moment before the handle rattled. Tiercel rushed to the table, where Kev couldn't see his actions, but guessed that he scooped the Emerald back into its sack.

"Count Elyvorrin?" a nervous voice cried, rattling the doorhandle again. "My lord?"

"A moment," Tiercel called. "There has been a mishap." Lower, he said, "It *would* rouse the entire Household . . .

"Grandfather! Stand aside, let me through, get out of my way!" That was Celinar; Kev knew his imperious voice instantly.

Elyvorrin moaned. "What –? Tiercel?"

"Go along with what I say, sire, and all will be well. I must let them in before someone takes it into his head to panic and break down the door."

From his hidden vantage point, Kev saw many feet crowd into the room. A babble arose as everyone began speaking at once.

Tiercel commanded their attention, then with well-feigned abashedness wove a tale of how he had attempted to work some bit of minor magic but was not nearly so well-versed in sorcery as he was with a sword. Oh, and how he most earnestly regretted the results! He would have sooner thrown himself from a high tower than brought any discomfort to his lord.

To all of this, Elyvorrin, still half-fogged, agreed. An accident, these sorts of things happened to every mage now and again. Even the great Kysander Feyna could miscast a spell. No harm done, certainly no blame harbored against his most loyal, excellent and dedicated knight.

Kev felt ill, wondering how anyone could believe them. Yet, had he not known what he knew, he might have been similarly swayed. Who would think to question the honesty of a count? Or of a knight so well-renowned as Sir Tiercel?

Celinar, the domestics, and what few other guests had drawn by the noise soon filed out, and Tiercel shut and locked the door firmly behind them.

"So," Elyvorrin said. "That is that." His tone was at once bleak and heavy.

"That is what, sire? Oh, *that?* Nay, I pray you, put it from your mind."

"How can I? It could not have been made plainer had runes of flame appeared in the sky. The Emerald rejects me. I am not to be king."

"My lord, it is not so. Perhaps . . . perhaps . . ."

"You see, Tiercel? Even you, always with such a ready answer, cannot change this turn of events."

"The stone might merely recognize *bloodline.* Yes. Bloodline. It might only accept Karria's own kin. How could it be expected to understand that the direct royal line has ended? It means nothing, sire, nothing." Tiercel paced in front of the sofa and Kev watched his boots go back and forth. "Would that I had never found the accursed thing, if I'd known it would cause you such despair. You would have been king without the Emerald. Why let it ruin that?"

"*You* said that producing the Emerald would secure my claim to the throne."

"Such did I believe." He wrung convincing anguish from every word. "I was mistaken . . . not of your right to the throne, no, never that. But of the power of this jewel! The legends are meaningless. We ought not put our faith in old legends. You are *not* unfit to rule! You are wise and just and could lead this land to a new greatness. Emerald or no Emerald."

"Then what am I to do with it? I cannot take it before the Council. Suppose that each of them should demand to touch it? Suppose that it might choose one of them instead? I could not bear that, Tiercel. I could not!"

"I'll leave at once to return it to its resting place in the Temple –"

"No!" Elyvorrin cut in. "No, suppose one of my opponents should come to the same conclusion as we did, and find some swordmaid to fetch it on his behalf? Mirida's whelp thought of it and surely she can be no more cunning than the Fistrels. Can you not envision the terrible shame, if I were to lose my crown in such a fashion? Destroy it."

"Destroy it?" Tiercel gasped, in emotion that for once seemed unfeigned. "But it is the Emerald of Karria, the only divine artifact of which we know. It is a part of our history, our lore, of the very soul of the Emerin."

"You just called it an accursed thing, and said that the old legends were meaningless. Shatter it. If it cannot proclaim *me* the king, it shall proclaim none other."

Tiercel floundered. "My . . . my lord, please. We cannot harm this holy thing. Have we Emerinians not turned our backs on the gods enough already? To do such a blatant act would be blasphemy that could not be ignored. And I do not know if it even could be destroyed –"

Elyvorrin moved rapidly. Kev saw his feet bear him very close to Tiercel, so that he must have been looming threateningly in the younger man's face. "Do you not hear me, Sir Tiercel? I will have it broken, shattered. I will have it cease to exist. Think of a way."

There followed a long, weighty, thoughtful pause. When Tiercel spoke again, it was in the manner of a man contemplating some new and hitherto unexpected possibility.

"I can think of one way," he said. "But . . . no, it is too dangerous."

"I care not how dangerous; I would hear it and then decide. Tell me."

"It is said that the breath of a true-blooded dragon of the Elder Races can destroy *anything*, no matter how enspelled. Even the ancient magic of Govannisan could not defend against dragon flame."

"A dragon," Elyvorrin said. "Where would one find a dragon? Tiercel, your face betrays you. What do you know?"

"I do know where the lair of such a wyrm is. Racandros the Sixth, who lairs in a spent volcano far to the east, near the sea. The *Morvalan* have had dealings with him in the past."

"But would this Racandros be willing to do such a thing? Dragons are creatures of great greed, and the Emerald is a thing of great value. Should he wish to keep it instead –"

"If so, that might be good enough," Tiercel said. "No one could reach it then."

"That, then, is what we shall do. I charge you and Kai Tilanne with this task, Sir Tiercel. You will go with all haste. In the morning."

"So soon? With matters as they are in the Council?"

"I need you to ensure that no one else can come forward and steal from me what is mine. As for the Council, I've made some other arrangements during your absence that will strengthen my case. I've gained support from an unexpected quarter." Elyvorrin crossed to the sideboard and cursed as a rain of broken bottles fell out, more victims of the Emerald's violent backlash. "I need more wine. Come, Tiercel. We'll let the domestics see to this mess, and I shall tell you all."

When they had gone, Kev shoved the heavy sofa away from the wall. He sat up, broken glass spilling out of his hair, and and shook Jen.

"Lady, please," Jen mumbled. "Who has hurt you? My honor as a young man . . . honor as a young man . . ."

"I think your head's been addled," Kev said. "Can you stand?"

"Plots and passages." Jen blinked and looked up at Kev with wavering eyes. "Idelhar? Is that you?"

"You need a physician." He half-coaxed, half-dragged Jen after him. "We'll tell them you took a fall on the terrace. But, Jen . . . you must tell *no one* of what we just heard and witnessed. *No one*!"

"On my honor as a young man," Jen said, then stumbled against Kev. "I'm going to be sick."

"No, Jen, not here," Kev pleaded. "Outside. We'll blame it on the banquet. But not here, in the count's chambers."

He wasn't sure if Jen obeyed or if the urge abated, but they were able to get outside without seeing anyone before Jen did throw up. Kev felt more than a little like being sick himself. Tiercel's treachery, Elyvorrin's revenge, Ariana's peril, Emeralds, dragons, kings . . . it was all too much to take in so soon, and whirled round and round his mind with dizzying speed.

Only one thing was clear. He knew where his duty belonged. Not with pretenders to the crown, not with traitors masquerading as heroes. Like any true knight . . . well, squire . . . well, page in training to be a squire . . . his duty had to go first to his lady.

They had her locked away someplace, that much was certain. Someplace where no one would ever think to look, where no one would ever be able to find her.

No one . . . except, perhaps, a seeker-mage.

*   *   *

Chapter Twenty-Nine

Adversity forms bonds, or severs them.
– Elwyndas, Fianna's Song (ballad)

"How long have you been held here?" Ariana asked when she could stand the game of silently ignoring one another no longer.

On the other side of the fire pit, where a bank of embers shed warmth from beneath a layer of dark ash, her cellmate stopped what he'd been doing, which was swinging a whittled length of wood as if it were a practice sword. He looked at her for a long, evaluating moment as if deciding whether or not to bother with a reply. Then, with a slight shrug, made up his mind. "Eight years."

"Eight years! Eight *days* for me and I'm ready to lose my wits." She pulled the blanket more closely about her shoulders. "Why? What did you do to make Tiercel your enemy?"

Without answering, he started in with the length of wood again.

"Oh, yes," she said, voice dripping with scorn. "Either I already know, in which case my questions will only lead to prying, or I'm an ignorant victim and you mustn't risk becoming attached."

"That sums it up," he replied, moving into a series of lunges and thrusts that would have awed any weapons master in Gamelin.

"You've barely said a word to me since I arrived, save to tell me where the foodstuffs and other supplies were kept. I do not even know your name."

"Don't you?"

She sighed and sank her head into one hand. Her words came out in a clipped series. "I . . . am . . . not . . . your . . . enemy."

"Anyone they'd send would go to great pains to present such a front. And if you *are* innocent, then the less you know, the better."

"If I *am* innocent – which I am – and that louse Tiercel means to torture me anyway in hopes of getting to you, I'd at least like to know the name of the man I'm being tortured for. Irksome and tiresome though he may be."

Casting aside the mock sword, he scrubbed his face with a scrap of cloth and then slung it around his neck. "You may call me Rell, if you must."

"Rell. Fine. Thank you. I am Ariana. Under the circumstances, you'll forgive me if I do not say what a pleasure it is to meet you."

He chuckled dryly. "Tiercel must be more clever than I guessed. I'd have thought he would choose some fainting delicate damsel, armed with blushes and tears."

"Someone you'd feel obligated to protect and shelter?"

"Certainly not an abrasive shrew armed with contempt and insults. It adds a note of realism. I wonder if you could lie your way around a truthsaying, even were I able to cast one? Without magic, we may never know."

"*Gilthanat*?" Her hand crept instinctively to her collarbone. "He inflicted it upon me as well."

"Inflicted it?"

She described, flinching at the memory, how Tiercel had embedded the barbed metal thorn in her flesh. Showed him the scar, the ugly scrawl of scar still with scraps of thread knotted into it.

"Not so with me." Rounding the firepit, he turned his arm and showed her a scar of his own, an uneven circle the size of a half-mark coin. "Dwarven crossbow. Went through my armor as though the enchantments meant nothing. The tip lodged in the bone and broke off. There were no surgeons handy, so it had to stay in, and I never got the chance later to have it removed."

"You were in the war?"

He regarded her for another long moment. "Order of the Gryphon."

"The Gryphon!" She didn't try to hide the degree to which she was impressed. "You were a belted knight as both swordsman *and* warmage? Orders of the Lion and the Eagle?"

"I was," he said, and stalked beyond the reach of the candlelight as a clear sign their conversation was done.

Ariana drew up her knees and folded her arms across them, then rested her chin on her forearms. Her gaze wandered idly around the cave, though she already felt she knew its every nook and corner as well as she'd known her childhood bedroom.

The curtain, which Rell had re-hung shortly after her entrance, concealed the living area from the cage and the door. She reasoned that he did not want the guards able to gawk in at him, and wondered how long it had been since they, or Tiercel himself, had clapped eyes on their long-time prisoner. If they were expecting to find him weak and unfit from his confinement, they were in for dire disappointment.

At the rear of the living area was a deep pool, possibly a spring, possibly fed by the subterranean river Tiercel had mentioned. The clear water was certainly frigid enough to be the latter. There was no furniture, but the cave was well-stocked with preserved food, bundles of wood, furs and blankets, wax candles, basic medicines, and other necessities. She thought of the one time she'd toured the duke's prison, on business with her father. The cramped cages, the stink, the rats . . . filth-caked men in rags chained to the walls . . . catch-all pottage slopped twice a day from a bucket into cupped hands . . .

She knew humans who did not live a fraction so well in their free lives as she and Rell did in their captivity. They would not starve, nor would they freeze, and even if the supplies suddenly stopped coming, there was enough piled up to last for many more years.

According to Rell, every six months or so, the guards would shove a new load of supplies through the outer door, then close it and open the portcullis so that he could retrieve them. These deliveries sometimes included other items, such as eating utensils, books, assorted articles of clothing, and other odds and ends that all seemed to have been diverted from their appointment with the rubbish heap.

Ariana had, with Rell's indifferent permission, made herself a bed in a floor-hollow near the firepit. Piled with furs and covered with three blankets, it was far cozier than a bedroll in a forest clearing but nowhere near as luxurious as the bed she'd enjoyed during her previous stay as a guest in the palace.

She had been determined to outlast her sullen and begrudging cellmate, but after a week in the company of Tiercel and Tilanne followed by her unpleasant chat with Elyvorrin, she was weary to death of silence and wars of words . . . or not-words. Which wasn't to say that speaking with Rell proved to be overly rewarding either. He spent most of his waking hours engaged in grueling calisthenics and mock swordplay. At first, the savage intensity and *constancy* of these exercises had unnerved her, but she soon realized that none of his animosity was directed at her. There had been no recurrences of the ear-twisting and back-crushing altercation that had marked their initial meeting.

"Eight years?"

Hardly anything by elven standards, though there was quite a difference between eight years of carefree ordinary life and eight years of solitude and imprisonment. She had already felt for herself how the time seemed to slow to a crawl. To Rell, it must seem as if he'd been here half a lifetime.

"So, as you seem to be in a talkative mood," he said, startling her by pushing aside the curtain and coming back into the living area. "What supposed tale of woe is the reason you're here? What grievous crime have you allegedly committed?"

"You'd not believe me whatever I said. Why should I bother?"

He dunked a rag in the bucket they kept at the edge of the firepit and wrung it out over his upturned face. "I've had no news of the world since that door slammed behind me. Even if everything you tell me is false, it would at least be something to hear."

She watched runnels of water trickle down his chest and privately admitted that, though boar-stubborn and as irritating as a rash, he was quite a figure of a man. More fit even than Gavin and Galen, when she might never have thought such a thing was possible. "Where should I begin?"

"How did you make the acquaintance of the noble Tiercel?"

"He captured me outside of Karria's Temple and took the Emerald from me."

Rell coughed. "False is one thing. Try not to make it *outlandish*."

"It. Is. True." She bit off every word crisply.

"If I wanted fanciful stories, there's a book of children's bedtime tales in that box."

"You asked to hear this."

"Very well, very well . . . even if packed with lies, it's bound to be amusing. So tell me. Whatever were you doing with the Emerald of Karria?"

"I needed it in order to convince the Starleaf Council to hear my petition, which was to have my father's name and lands restored to our family. He was removed from the Book of Lists, wrongfully so. Further, I came to hope that the Emerald might cut through all the ridiculous bickering and political maneuvering by helping them choose the next king. According to legend –"

"I'm familiar with the legend," he said. "A swordmaiden or a king. So I take it that the war must be ended if the counts have time for squabbling over the throne?"

"Five years ago." She told him of the Treaty of Jeline, the devastation in Keyda, all that she knew of the last days of the war. And then, once she began and he seemed to truly be listening, she was unable to stop. She told him of her parents, of Alinora, and the count's revenge. Of Mischa, Talian, Vangier, Kevan, Drea, Quisfahr, Obriel, Shedra, Lievve. The ruined keep and the watery entombed horrors beneath it. The greenlion and the Temple. Tiercel and Tilanne.

When she finished, she went to the pool and dunked a dipper. The icy-cold water soothed her parched throat. Rell sat watching her as if his truegold eyes might pierce her soul.

"If you spin lies, they are seamless ones," he finally said. "I once thought myself to be a not unskilled judge of a person's honesty. Though I am out of practice, that instinct tells me to believe your words. Then again . . . I trusted Tiercel."

"Why has he done this to you? What did you do to stand in his way?"

"I would not give him that which he craved. My loyalty, my . . . conversion. He sought to influence many of those who held some positions of importance in the army. Warmages . . . the king's personal guard . . . he wanted them won over to his cause."

"To *Morvalan* ways?"

His golden gaze took on a faraway look, perhaps as faraway and long ago as the battlefields. "The Tiercel Reyes that I remember was a swordsman beyond compare. Bold . . . *too* bold, as if he walked in certain sureness of his own invincibility. Yet time and again, his most daring and risky ventures were successful. He was admired, even adored."

"He still is," she said darkly.

"Who would ever have suspected that he was *Morvalan*? That his main purpose during the war was not to defend the Emerin, not to defeat the dwarves, but to keep the fighting going as long as possible, drawing more and more of our human allies into it, drawing them to their deaths?"

"Instead, he was rewarded for his valor. The brave hero."

"The men who swore themselves to him saw only that side of him," Rell said. "Many of them were men whose lives he had saved, who felt they owed him everything."

"Retharn," Ariana said, thinking of the maimed guard.

Rell unconsciously and uneasily touched his own ear. "I was with him that day, two years before I learned the depths of Tiercel's treachery. The dwarves did not often use ambushes. They preferred the solidity, the security, of their shield lines, formations and war machines. But some were so fearless, so reckless, as to try an ambush. They took us by surprise, killed half our company. Retharn fell and we thought him among the dead. We had to leave them. Yet he lived, and when the dwarves realized it . . . they meant to carve both ears from his head."

Ariana shuddered in sympathetic unison with Rell.

"We heard his scream . . . I cannot describe it, you cannot imagine it. Tiercel went back for him. From then on, Retharn was his. Blaming the rest of us for leaving him, or for escaping with our ears intact, who can say?"

"Did he know Tiercel was *Morvalan?*"

"None of us did. Even when suspicion should have rooted, his presence was too bright and fierce and radiant to allow it to grow, as the summer sun's most glaring heat scorches the tender shoots."

"So he corrupted them," she said. "Winning them to *his* cause without letting them know of his southern ties . . . seeking to strike at the humans and . . . and what? Have his own small force of loyal men once the war was over? Why did he fail with you?"

"Because I came to see him for what he truly was." He closed his eyes, speaking with undimmed pain and difficulty. "And I came to suspect that he bore some of the blame for the death of the king."

"No," Ariana said. "That cannot be. Not even Tiercel . . ."

Rell sprang up, then threw himself prone and began doing push-ups with such fervor he almost looked as if he meant to tunnel through the floor. "There was to have been a meeting. A treaty. Peace. But apparently one group of soldiers never got the word. Apparently, they mistook Thane Konrad's approaching truce-party as assassins. They attacked. Killed high-ranking dwarves, wounded the thane. The dwarves cried treachery."

"That group of soldiers were Tiercel's men?"

He didn't seem to hear. His face had taken on a starkly haunted look. He sped up, as if by sheer physical exertion he could outrace the past.

"And such an outcry came forth from the dwarves! They'd been holding back their most horrible weapons, but loosed them on us then. Shells of iron, launched from catapults and filled with deadly poisons. Powdered rock that exploded into white flame. Clouds of gas that burrowed into the skin like acid, or made men gush blood from every pore, or cough their own lungs from their mouths. The sky was black from smoke, the earth ran red, the world was fire and ash and death."

She could barely move, held spellbound by the images that filled her mind.

"We rallied with our magic," Rell went on. "Our warmages . . . hundreds of them sacrificed themselves to stop the war machines. Our archers made the air sing with arrows. It was disarray . . . it was chaos. And in the midst of it . . . dwarven axe-troops fought their way through to the king's own guard. It was to have been a firm stand. But fully half of those men melted away. Without striking a blow to defend him."

He stopped, arms shaking and body streaming with sweat, and sprang up again. He grabbed the length of wood and swept it viciously through the air. It struck with a thunderous crack against a limestone formation. He kept on, punctuating his words with blows as if the column had taken on the aspect of his enemies.

"Tiercel had convinced them that the king was prepared to surrender rather than throw more lives away, and his death would make all of the Emerin scream for revenge. Their pride . . . the same stiff-necked elven pride that had refused to relent even after we'd learned that all of this had been caused by the mischief of Solarrin . . . would not let them accept the possibility of surrender."

"Solarrin was years dead by then. Oh, how pleased he would be to know his evil lived on!"

"So they stood back," Rell said, as if he hadn't heard her. "Stood back, and let the king fall. I was there that day. Retharn held me back and told me grimly that I should not let myself be killed. I . . . I smote him."

"Good," Ariana said.

"Put him flat and senseless. And ran . . . I was so near . . . near enough to see but too far to reach him in time . . . I saw his horse cut from beneath him, saw . . . saw the axe descend. He was so aged and frail . . . he should not have been there."

The limestone column had been the thickness of her waist at its narrowest joining point. Rell's next blow smashed through it, showering her with damp chips and leaving stalactite and stalagmite seperated by a gap a handspan wide.

"Oh, and then, *then*," he said, "who should appear with a great rallying cry? Who should seize up the king's standard? Who should lead the charge? None but Sir Tiercel Reyes!"

He bellowed the name and spun, flinging the length of wood end-over-end into the cave. Ariana heard it clatter against stone. Rell's chest heaved, his fists worked as if aching to close around a neck.

"The men that had fallen back now surged forth," he said in a more even tone. "Not a one of those dwarves survived. Tiercel himself bore the king's body behind the lines, to the safety of the camps. And *wept* as he delivered him to the physicians."

He trembled as if he were about to do the same, reliving that terrible day. Ariana reached out, but no sooner had her fingers touched his skin did he jerk away from her.

"No. I'll have no comfort. Not from you."

"I would not have believed I could loathe him more than I did. Then, I wanted only to kill him . . . now I should like to see him die in a manner slow even to an elf."

"I'll have no comfort from anyone," he said. "I hold fast to my fury. It hones me as a blade. I must let nothing dull it, so that when I meet him again – and I shall – the strongest of armor will be as useless to him as the king's enchanted mail was against the *gilthanat*-edged axe that snuffed his light forever."

"Let me help you," she said. "He's not wronged me a tenth so much as he has you, or a hundredth so much as he has the Emerin, but I –"

"I have seen too much betrayal."

"Rell, listen to me."

"Do you not understand? I can trust no one, least of all you."

"Look in my eyes and tell me you cannot."

With a sound more snarl than sigh, he seized her by the shoulders. His right hand pressed down on her wound so that metal scraped against bone and sent a twitching spasm down her arm.

He brought his face close to hers, gold eyes glaring into her as if he would strip away the layers of her mind, truthsay her, magic or no magic, *gilthanat* or no *gilthanat*.

* * *

CHAPTER THIRTY

Most of all, I dread to walk alone.
– Elwyndas, Forever's Heart (poem)

Faessia Elyvorrin paused as she approached the gate, and even stole a furtive look about to see if anyone might be watching her.

Silly notion. Who would be watching? There was nothing suspicious in her going out for the day.

She had left with the excuse of prowling the shops, an easily-accepted lie. Hadn't she been doing much of that lately? Usually in the company of Tavalara Ilhedrion and one or two of her friends, being dragged from one store to the next while the ladies oohed and ahhed over gowns, jewelry, shoes, and engagement gifts she might anticipate.

But lately, Tavalara had been in a state of annoyance. Her younger brother Tiercel had *deliberately* ruined all her hard work and planning by coming home only to dash off again on yet *another* mysterious errand, and didn't he *ever* stop to think that he might have other obligations? Social obligations? He was disappointing his sister so grievously . . . and his bride-to-be, too, of course . . .

Faessia had heard this tirade thrice already since Tiercel had been gone, and it was with great relief that she'd received the news that Tavalara had cancelled today's planned luncheon date.

Left to her own devices, she'd made her excuse and gone out. Just in case anybody happened to see her and later mention it, she did make a point of browsing a bit through the shops, but what goods she looked at failed to make any impression on her mind. She lunched at a lovely shaded cafe, a light meal that she barely tasted, then hired a carriage to take her to the Fistrel estate.

And here she was, poised at the gates, but hesitating as if she could hear her father-in-law's icy voice demanding to know just what she thought she was doing, consorting with his rivals. He would never believe that she was here on a mission of duty and mercy.

Assuring herself once more that she was doing nothing wrong, she entered the garden and followed a blue flagstone path made to look like a wandering brook. Some of the stones were inset with tiles in the shape of fish, and the path was lined with delicate reeds and flowers that bent their heads in hopes of catching their own reflection.

The manor itself was long and low, two stories and built in a flowing curve like the sweep of a bay. Nary a tower or turret in sight, an unusual construction that nonetheless managed to appeal to the eye.

A man opened the door as she mounted the steps. She recognized him by his ash-blond hair, his ready grin, and of course the striking resemblance he bore to both his father and uncle.

"Good day to you, Idelhar," she said. "I doubt you'd recall, but I attended school with your sister Virine. I am –"

"Faessia," he replied, descending to clasp her hands. "Of course I remember. I grieve for your loss. Celin was a friend, and I am sorry I wasn't able to attend his funeral."

"There have been . . . many funerals," she said. "So many . . ."

"Won't you come inside?"

"Oh . . . I don't mean to be a bother . . . I was wondering if you could tell me something?" She retrieved her hands from him and twined them together, looking down to avoid having to meet his kind eyes. "The night of Celinar's party, there was an accident. A page was hurt. I feel some responsibility, and when I asked at the palace, I was told he'd been brought here."

"Jennic, yes," Idelhar said. "The Perraines were very dear to me. When they died, I promised to look after their child. My ward, one might say. "It was a serious wound. Our physician was not able to heal it completely, and poor Jennic sleeps often, though must be woken every few hours. Perhaps you should come in, Faessia, and see for yourself."

Something in his voice alarmed her and she looked up. There was still kindness in his eyes, but awareness, too. Even suspicion, or some strange knowingness.

She trilled a little unsteady laugh. "He took quite a knock to the head. I do hope he hasn't said anything too preposterous."

Idelhar captured her left hand and studied it, rubbing his thumb over the knuckle of her third finger. The bruised swelling of her wrist and the scrape caused by the ring were gone, tended by a closemouthed physician – Tavalara's own son, as it happened. No sign remained of the injuries, except the invisible marks on her soul. Yet it was as if he knew. As if he *knew*!

Faessia pulled away.

"Jennic told me what happened," Idelhar said, and took her hand again.

"I do not know to what you might be referring." She started to turn away, but this time he would not let go.

"Jennic told me *everything*, Faessia."

She bowed her head and murmured, both sourly and in an odd relief, "So much for oaths."

"Some things are more important. Your welfare, for one. You should not have to live in fear in your own house, nor have your life dictated to you by others."

"That is simple for you to say. It is different with your family, Idelhar."

"I thank the gods and all my ancestors that my family is different from Elyvorrin's," he said. "He cannot make you comply with his wishes."

"Has your time in the Northlands made you forget?" she asked. "My parents are gone. I've no other kin. There is only Celinar, only my son. I *must* do as the count wishes."

"Come inside," he said, and this time she did not pull away from his gentle coaxing grasp.

"Jennic has been worried for you as well. Set a young mind at ease."

She allowed herself to be led inside. "What did he tell you?"

"That you are ill-used by both Elyvorrin and Sir Tiercel, who, caring nothing for your feelings and showing no respect for your state of mourning, forced you into this arrangement too soon and against your will."

"But as the count points out, I was initially wed to Celin over my objections –"

"Do not defend him, or take his words as your own," he said. "I know that you believe you have no other recourse, but he cannot control you."

"Why not?" Her laugh this time was jagged as shards of glass. "He seeks to control everyone else. He'd be king, you know."

One corner of Idelhar's mouth turned down wryly. "How well I know. He'd use you, and Lionnen, and anyone else in order to do so."

"Jennic told you about Lionnen?"

"And the Archmage. But I'd hear it again, from you. As you said, Jennic was hit in the head. I should like to be certain that what I heard was in truth what was said."

"How did it happen?" she asked. "How was he hurt? Please say he wasn't found out, wasn't punished. I would wish him no ill will, no pain, even if he did violate his promise to me."

He sighed. "If I prove to you that Jennic did not violate the letter of that oath but only the spirit, would that mollify you?"

"I have no desire to be mollified. A child finds me in my weakest of moments, I unburden my soul on assurance of an oath, and now it may as well be open talk in the marketplace."

"Faessia." He held her by the upper arms and turned her to him. "As the son of one ambassador and the brother to another, you must realize that I do not dispense open talk. I *sent* Jennic to Celinar's party with the purpose of finding out what the count might be hatching. Duty to me came before that promise to you. Only I have heard of it. Do *you* feel that Elyvorrin would make a good king? You need not say it aloud, for I see it in your face. He is a tyrant to his very family, so how could he be anything but a tyrant to his people? Then *tell* me. Tell me what he plans, so that he can be undone."

Haltingly, glancing now and again into his eyes for encouragement, she relayed to him all that she'd heard from Lionnen as they walked through the halls. "And I fear he and Tiercel have some other plot," she finished, "but I do not know what it is."

"One of Jennic's friends, Kevan Brindani, is missing. His family assumed he was still at the palace minding his duties, the steward thought he'd been called home to his family, and now I find that no one has seen or heard from him since that night at Elyvorrin's. I have one page hurt and one missing, and both may have been in a position to overhear something they oughtn't have."

"Let me see Jennic. I must be certain he's well. Oh, that this could be my fault –"

"Mine as well, for I sent Jennic there. But I must stress, Faessia, so that you'll hold no ill will in your heart for the breaking of that oath . . . Jennic broke only the *letter* of it, not the *spirit*."

"How could he not break the spirit of it? He swore on his honor as a young man."

Idelhar pushed a door open. Faessia stepped within, looking at the child with the bandaged head, curled sleeping atop the bedcovers.

"*Jennica* Perraine cannot earnestly swear on *her* honor as a young man," Idelhar said, smiling.

"A . . . girl? A *girl?*"

"The daughter of my dear friends, a brave child who volunteered to be disguised as a boy and placed as a page. None outside of this Household know, except for you." He unfolded a blanket that lay at the foot of the bed and shook it gently over the girl.

"The poor, poor child." Faessia curled a lock of Jennica's strawberry-blond hair around her fingers. "She tried only to be kind to me, and it came to this."

"She said it broke her heart to see you in such pain," Idelhar said.

"Orphaned so young, and she thinks of *my* pain . . . would that I had a daughter so loving. I always wished for a second child, but Celin was called away to war, and there was never time." A tear rolled down her cheek. "And now . . . I cannot bear the prospect of having more children, not *his* children. Oh, he may say that he means never to touch me as a man to a wife, but how am I to believe anything he says?"

He shepherded her from the room with a gentle arm around her shoulders. "Then do not, Faessia. Do not believe him, and do not agree to this marriage."

More tears overspilled. "If I refuse, the count will send me away, and I shall never see my son again. Celinar is all that I have left, all that I have left, and already he loves Tiercel best. I have seen it. To be Tiercel's squire is his fondest wish come true; to be Tiercel's *son* is greater than anything he ever dared to dream! He forgets his father by the light of Tiercel's cold star, and would as soon forget his own mother."

Idelhar held her as she sobbed, murmuring wordlessly to her as if she were an infant until the storm had passed.

"I have lost my parents, my husband, and my freedom. Now I lose my son, and myself. Please, Idelhar, if you can . . . please, help me!"

He pressed a soft kiss to her brow. "We shall help each other, Faessia, I promise. On that, you have *my* oath as a young man. And that, I assure you, I mean in both the letter and the spirit."

* * *

Alinor Elyvorrin leaned back in his chair and regarded what he had written. The crumpled results of countless abortive attempts were strewn around his feet, but at last he was satisfied.

To the esteemed Archmage of Gamelin, greetings.

Your presence is requested at the earliest convenience to discuss a matter of some urgency pertaining to your daughter Ariana.

Settling her petition would involve overturning of a verdict passed by the Starleaf Council with approval of the lamentably deceased King Shaelan Perras. In order for such a course of action to be considered, restitution for the original crimes resulting in said verdict must be made.

As head of your Household, this duty falls to you. Should you fail to attend to it promptly, it shall be assumed that your daughter is hereby authorized to represent you to the fullest extent of the law.

To assure you that this message is in earnest, you will find enclosed two personal effects relinquished by your daughter upon the event of her being taken into custody.

On behalf of the Emerin, allow me to express my hope that you will accept your long-delayed responsibility.

It would be a shame to see history repeat itself.

Signed this 36th day of the Season of the Hunter in the year 7904 S. F. E.,

Alinor Elyvorrin, Count of Shanlen

"Yes," he said. "That'll do nicely. No insults, no accusations, threats merely implied . . . all properly legal. So much more effective than a rant that would make the very ink smoke upon the parchment. Would that I could see his face as he reads this!"

He folded the letter and sealed it with his crest, then placed it in an envelope along with the *ilgilean* and the onyx signet, and similarly sealed that. The swiftest courier he could hire without resorting to Feyna's magical means would be dispatched to Tradersport to deliver the letter. Mirida would then be given ample time to contemplate what his daughter might have endured while it was in transit.

He rang for a servant to make the arrangements. Then, with a lightness in his step that he hadn't felt for over a century, went down to dinner.

* * *

"Support *Elyvorrin?* " Denryl of Marrion slapped his thigh. "I must commend you, Archmage . . . that's the finest jest I've heard in a century. Support Elyvorrin, indeed."

"I assure you, I am in earnest," Kysander Feyna said.

"Preposterous madness. You'd have me put my vote behind that man? After what I said in the Council chamber? Unless by some chance the Emerald of Karria has been sought out in its distant resting place and sings at his touch to herald him the true king, I said. Unless the Ring of Twilight shines upon his hand, I said. Have these unlikeliest of things come to pass? Would you have me go back on my word?"

"Your word, which was spoken in the heat of anger, as I recall. None would fault you for a change of heart once time and wisdom had allowed your temper to cool."

A colossal thump from overhead made Feyna instinctively curve his hands in a shielding-spell gesture. Denryl laughed, unconcerned.

"Only the children, Archmage. It is only the children."

"Ah, yes." He relaxed, but only a trifle. "I saw a throng of them as I came in."

"Throng, an excellent word. My own four youngest, the grandchildren, my sister's brood, my brother's pair, three cousins, and a couple that I'm not even sure from whence they sprang."

Feyna shook his head, impressed. "A bountiful Household."

"A noisy Household." He paused as a thunder of footsteps charged down the stairs. From below, a door banged open, then slammed shut. Denryl exhaled. "Now, as we were saying . . . you may be right that I'd be excused for a change of heart, but why Elyvorrin? If I were forced at arrowpoint to choose between him and Bethelyn Fistrel, I know which my choice would be. Am I alone in worrying for Elyvorrin's sanity? The man is all bowstrings drawn too tight. He'll snap at any moment, and when he does, woe to any in reach of the whipping strings. Is that truly the man that should be on the throne of the Emerin?"

"He has been under great strain lately, yes . . . the loss of his son and wife have not been easy for him. Yet I believe he can overcome these trials and accomplish much for this kingdom."

"Fistrel could do more. He has strong ties to the Northlands –"

"Precisely . . . do we *wish* strong ties to the Northlands? Do we wish the Highlord poking his nose about in Emerinian affairs? Do we wish all the world to know how direly hurt we were by the war?"

"Well . . . yet I *cannot* support Alinor Elyvorrin."

Feyna sighed and fixed him with a look. "Can't you?"

Denryl frowned, as if beset by a sudden fog of perplexity. "Can't I what?"

"Think on it, Denryl. Aren't you letting your personal feelings for the man stand in the way of what's best for the Emerin?"

"I may be . . ." he said.

"His is a very valid claim," Feyna said. "A majority of the other members are inclined toward him . . . he may well become king even without your support . . . and then where will you be, if you are known to publicly oppose him?"

"That . . . that would not be wise of me . . ."

"No, it would not. The wisest and most prudent course would be to flow with the current, set aside your grievances."

"Wisest," he agreed.

"After all, you've a large family to think of, and it would be best for them to be in favor with the crown . . . in a score or so of years, Elyvorrin's grandson will be of an age for betrothal . . . you do have many eligible young ladies in your House. Imagine one of your daughters or granddaughters as next queen of the Emerin."

"Hmm . . . now that you mention it . . ." He chuckled. "Very well. You have my agreement. I will support Elyvorrin . I must say, you're very convincing, Feyna. Did I not know better, I might suspect you were using forbidden magics to affect my mind."

Feyna chuckled with him. "The Master of Feyna Rel, using forbidden magics? What would this world be coming to?"

* * *

CHAPTER THIRTY-ONE

As single spark to sudden flame, two lives shall never be the same.
– Elwyndas, The Song of Shannia, Part Four, Verse Eleven

Face to face in the dungeon cave, Ariana and Rell stared at each other. She would not drop her eyes first and let him call it deception, but poured forth the full force of her honesty that he might know she spoke the truth. However insane it might sound, she did speak the truth.

Golden gaze, hawk's gaze, dragon's gaze. Fixed and riveting. His expression unwavering, distrustful.

An abrupt warm glow suffused her, racing outward in all directions from her center. Ariana drew in a startled breath as her knees weakened, her ears tingled.

Before she could even begin to question or deny the flushed arousal that crashed over her like a wave, she and Rell were locked in a kiss. Their mouths were open and hungry and demanding. Matching wordless needful moans arose from low in their throats.

Her hands plunged into his tawny mane and found his ears, not in a fighter's grip this time but a lover's, cradling the back curves, flicking her thumbs over the rims. She was being crushed against his chest again, of her own accord as she pressed to him with impassioned fervor. One of his arms encircled her waist, holding her tightly. He slid his other hand up from her shoulder and caressed her ear in a slow stroke from lobe to tip and back down.

Oh, melting, she was melting, yet filled with a gathering aching tension that pleaded for release. The faint clamor of her thinking mind was drowned and swept under by her consuming need.

The few layers of cloth between them now seemed a wall, blocking and barricading, keeping them apart. She had to be rid of that wall, rid of it at once, had to feel the heat of his skin next to hers.

His lips moved from her mouth along her jawline, paused tormentingly as his warm breath teased. She brazenly pushed back her hair, exposing her ear to him fully. He brought his lips to it. The first touch of that intimate kiss made her grow dizzy, and as he searchingly explored the tender curves and folds, she nearly fainted. He dropped both hands to her hips, pulling her more firmly against him. She could feel the hardness of his flesh beneath the softness of leather.

Rell broke away from her with such suddenness that she fell and had to catch herself against the lower half of the broken limestone column. His eyes seemed to blaze.

Between ragged gasps, he said, "What are we *doing?*"

"You haven't been down here that long," she said huskily. "You must remember."

"This is wrong."

"I know. Oh, gods, do I know. And yet . . ."

"And yet," he agreed yearningly.

"We shouldn't."

"Mustn't."

"Want to."

"More than I can say."

"Then what harm?" She held out her arms.

"Ariana . . ."

The sound of her name spoken in that deeply melodious voice of his made the blood rush to her ears all over again. "Rell . . ."

His expression was purest agony. "No!"

He whirled from her and in two great strides was at the spring. He plunged his head into it, immersing himself to the shoulders in the icy water.

Ariana gasped as if she'd been the one doused, and slapped herself smartly across the face. She turned away, trying to bring her wild desires under control, trying to quell the flutters that beset her loins like a wingstorm of butterflies.

"What did you do to me?" Rell asked unsteadily.

"You blame *me*?" she said without turning around.

"Some trick . . . it must have been a trick."

"You kissed first."

"I beg to differ. I'll not fall prey to your wiles."

"What wiles?" She spun to face him, incensed. "This was none of *my* doing."

"You were clearly trying to seduce me and gain my trust."

"You are the most irksome fool I have ever met."

"And you must think me a fool if you imagine I'd be taken in by such a contrivance."

"I did not try to seduce you."

"You leaped at me like a starving pantera!"

"You leaped just as fast!"

"As I said . . . some trick, some sorcery."

"I cannot *use* sorcery!" She tore the collar of her tunic open to reveal the *gilthanat* scar, but in her wrath she tore it far more violently than she meant to and revealed an expanse of moon-pale cleavage.

"You still seek to tempt me with your beauty." He moved swiftly, swept her into his arms again. "Perhaps I should take what you offer."

"I'd not offer it were you the last man alive." Yet even as she said it, she was returning his rough embrace, caught up once more in the storm that raged all the more furiously for her anger.

He bent his head to her chest, in so doing bringing the point of his ear within reach of her mouth. She licked at it, alternating quick darts with savoring caresses. His arms closed more crushingly around her. He groaned against her.

"Vile temptress," he said, his voice muffled.

"Arrogant beast," she retorted, then drew the tip of his ear between her lips.

"I'm truly beginning to hate you." One of his hands was cradling her buttocks, the other pulled aside the rent fabric of her tunic even further.

"I positively *despise* you." She ran her tongue down the rim of his ear.

A grinding creak heralded the opening of the outer door to their prison cave.

They sprang apart as if scalded, both immediately wary and alert despite their breathless condition. Rell seized up a length of wood and moved with catlike stealth to the hide that blocked the living area from the doorway. Ariana did likewise.

Firelight streamed through the open door. A shadow of a head and torso leaned in briefly, then withdrew.

"Making certain we're not plotting an ambush," Rell whispered. "It's not yet time for a delivery of supplies, so . . ."

"They're come for me," she finished. "Can Elyvorrin's letter have reached my father so soon?"

The clunk of the lever being thrown made them both jump. The portcullis began to rattle upward, and the man-shaped shadow reappeared.

"That's not right," Rell said. "They never open both at once."

"Ari? Ariana! Are you there?"

Dumbstruck at the sound of the voice, she couldn't answer.

"Thanian speech?" Rell glanced suspiciously at her. "What is this?"

"Ariana!"

"Mischa!" she cried. "Is it really you?" She ran forward though Rell tried to hold her back.

Mischa Narrin, alive and well, stepped into the cave. When he saw her, a huge smile of relief and joy lit his face. "Praise Talopea, we've found you at last."

"You're alive," she sobbed, flinging her arms around his neck. "I thought sure you'd die in the forest, yet you're alive. And . . . what are you doing here? How did you . . . oh, I am so pleased to see you!"

"A human?" Rell paused as he stepped out of the shadows, taking in the sight of Mischa. "So you did speak true."

"You've got company," Mischa said, raising his eyebrows. "My, my, Ariana! Did I . . . interrupt?"

"No!" Ariana and Rell chorused, too vehemently.

Mischa grinned. "Time enough for that later. We'd best go if we're going to. The guards won't stay occupied forever. And Kev is waiting upstairs."

"Kevan? You brought Kevan into this?" Ariana asked, horrified.

"He found *me*," Mischa said. "But there's time enough for that later too."

Ariana followed Mischa into the guard room, and stopped short, her eyes feeling as if they might pop from her head. "Oh, dear gods . . ."

Rell came up behind her and froze in astonishment.

"Shh," Mischa said, putting a finger to his lips. "Don't disturb them."

All of the blankets from Pahelin and Retharn's beds had been hastily thrown together on the floor. Armor and clothing were strewn all over the place. The two guards were entwined on the blankets, oblivious to everything but each other.

Ariana blinked, and that action seemed to force her eyes back where they belonged. She turned her incredulous gaze on Mischa. "Are you responsible for this?"

"Well, I couldn't very well *fight* my way past them, now, could I? So I begged Talopea's intervention, and She visited them with a compelling desire for one another."

Pahelin glanced up, and concern briefly furrowed his brow, but then he gave a shrug and went back to what he'd been doing. Rell kept shaking his head in short, sharp jerks as if trying to dislodge something. Most likely, to dislodge this entire scene from his mind.

"Mischa, how could you? To force them like that –"

"No, Ari, no, you misunderstand . . . Talopea only works with what She finds. If they weren't interested, nothing would have happened and I'd have had to think of another way."

"You called this down upon them, such an overpowering urge?" Rell asked.

"By the grace of my goddess, yes." Seeing the way they suddenly looked at each other, the flush of guilt, the torn and disheveled state of Ariana's tunic, Mischa's grin widened. "There might have been a . . . wider range of effect than I expected."

"Never mind that," Ariana said brusquely. "I am more than ready to see the last of this dungeon."

"I, too," Rell said. "I'd planned, should I ever escape, to slay Retharn myself . . . but how can I attack a man . . ."

"In his position?" Mischa winked.

"Still, we must do something," Ariana said. "When they've . . . finished . . . they might sound an alarm." She picked up a discarded swordbelt and secured it around her waist. The weapon was heavier than she was used to, but she would make it work.

"And they must be made accountable for their treason." Rell lashed out with one foot, kicking over a table. It upended, spilling the remains of two meals and half a bottle of wine to the stone floor with a crash. "Retharn!"

The two lovers were jolted from their pleasure-daze and leapt up with the reactions of trained soldiers, though Ariana was fairly certain most trained soldiers weren't often called upon to defend themselves while nude. "You're not to be out," Retharn cried. "How –?"

"You have wronged me, Retharn, and now you shall pay." Rell overturned a chair that was between them and went at the maimed elf.

As the two of them grappled, Pahelin backed rapidly away, holding his hands a span apart. Ariana reflexively tried to summon a shielding-spell, but could not. In a matter of moments, Pahelin was holding a small sphere of dark-veined rock.

She hadn't time to be awed – earth magics were among the most difficult to learn – and charged him as he made ready to throw.

The missile shot from him just as she closed to a blade's reach. It struck her left arm with numbing, bruising force and her swing went wild. Pahelin ducked under the sword and kicked, missing her knee.

They squared off, Ariana favoring her hurt arm, Pahelin casting about for a weapon. He found an arrow and threatened her with the truesteel point.

Mischa came up behind him and swatted him stingingly across his bare backside with the flat of his sword. Pahelin yelped in shock and sprang forward. Ariana dodged to avoid being skewered by the arrow, and brought her pommel down hard on his head.

He pitched face-first to the floor and lay motionless.

Ariana glanced at Rell and saw that he'd battered Retharn senseless with no weapon but his powerful fists. "Do not kill them," Rell said. "I will see them answer to the Council for all that they've done and be punished accordingly." He seized Retharn by a handful of hair and dragged his unconscious body to the door of the prison cave.

"This one knows earth magics," Ariana said, indicating Pahelin. "He might be able to shape the stone from within and craft a way out."

Rell shook his head. "This place was once meant to hold mages. It has been stripped of its *aether*. Even without the *gilthanat* that hampers us, we would have been able to work no spells within. They'll keep."

While Rell carried the prisoners into their new accommodations, Ariana quickly scavenged through the outer chamber. She replaced her torn tunic with one from a trunk, found no boots that would fit her and was thus resigned to the slippers for a bit longer. She added a knife to her belt, slung a bow over her shoulder and a quiver across her back.

Conversely, while Retharn's boots would fit Rell, the tunics were a lost cause. He settled for covering his bare torso with a fur-lined cloak, and took a sword of his own. They locked the door and Rell kept the key, putting it in a pouch along with something that briefly flashed cool lavender in the firelight.

"My first rescue effort," Mischa said. "None too shabby, I daresay."

"You did splendidly, Mischa, even if your methods were a bit unusual."

Rell agreed with a snort. "I did on occasion let myself dream of rescue. Yet, somehow . . . it was never quite like this."

"How in the world did you get here?" Ariana asked. "I was certain you'd never survive the forest alone."

"Oh, I survived. That woodlore I was so proud of learning? Making camp, building fires? Saved my life. It wasn't *pleasant*, mind you, and I'd rather not dwell on it. But it saved my life. Those cursed *Morvalan* left a trail that even I could follow, though I never managed to catch up. I was almost to civilization when another horse came along. I hid, but the rider came right to me."

"Our young seeker-mage," Ariana said, understanding. "He could not seek me for the *gilthanat*, and so found you instead."

"Anyone else might have believed you dead. I know I was half-convinced of it myself. But Kev wouldn't give up. He's much to tell you of that snake Sir Tiercel."

"There's no new depths to his treachery that could surprise me."

"We'll see about that after you've heard what Kev has to say. Anyway, he still couldn't seek you, so we puzzled it out bit by bit. He overheard that they'd locked you up somewhere. He smuggled me into the palace and every night, we've been following passages that might not have known the tread of a foot in thousands of years. We finally found this one."

"What of Tiercel?" Rell asked, snarling as he spoke the hated name. "Where might he be found?"

"Apparently," Mischa said, "Sir Tiercel left again some days ago. Another secret errand for Count Elyvorrin. You're not going to like it, Ari."

"What? Has he sent *Tiercel* with the message for my father?"

"No, he's sent Tiercel to destroy the Emerald of Karria."

"What? " Ariana and Rell exclaimed together. "He *wouldn't!*" Ari added.

"I'll let Kev tell you the rest." He headed for the stairs, producing a magelit coin. "Courtesy of your young admirer, Ari. What he'll think when he hears the state in which I found you, I shudder to wonder –"

"Are there more guards above?" Rell asked.

"At the gate," Mischa said. "I passed them with Kev's help, but they might find something amiss in the way you two are dressed."

"Then we find another way out." He brushed past them and took the lead.

"And all this time," Mischa muttered to Ariana as Rell began climbing the stairs, "I thought *I* had a remarkable rear!"

"Hush!"

*   *   *

CHAPTER THIRTY-TWO

Take from me my lands, my properties, my very name . . . but never my true self.

– Elwyndas, Nalnarennian the Exile, Act XII

The stairs had seemed long on the way down; now they stretched to the very stars themselves. Ariana ascended them almost as a ladder, her hands pattering on the steps ahead of her. Mischa was right behind her, making remarks about her rear as well. Glad as she was to see him, if he kept snickering like that, she was liable to back-kick him all the way down.

Up and up. Soon they were nearing the final landing. Mischa hid the magelit coin, casting them into darkness but for a thin line of light across the bottom of the door.

They could hear nervous humming on the other side. Ariana could even identify the tune – *Dance by the River*, one that had been popular since the last years of the war.

Rell threw the door open and burst through, pouncing on the lone figure in the hallway with the speed of a trapsand spider and the strength of a pantera. By the time Ariana rushed out, Rell had the struggling Kev in a grip that threatened to break the youth's neck. But he realized his error almost at once and turned Kev loose with a brusque apology.

"My lady," he gasped when he saw her. "By my ancestors and all the gods, you are safe."

"Thanks to you, my brave one," she said, clasping his hands and urging him to his feet. "You have saved Mischa's life and mine, and hopefully my father's as well."

"I've much to tell you. Horrible news and dire tidings indeed. Oh, lady, Sir Tiercel is a lying traitor. But then, you know that much . . . the Emerald . . . he means to make Count Elyvorrin the king, not destiny's king but his own . . . Racandros the dragon . . . destroy the stone . . . *Morvalan* . . ."

"We mustn't dawdle," Rell said. "Guards could come along at any moment. We'll take the old siege tunnel."

"Who's he?" Kev rubbed his neck."What siege tunnel? What's he talking about?"

"This is Rell, of the Order of the Gryphon," Ariana said, knowing there was no more sure path to impress the young knight-to-be. As she'd expected, Kev's eyes widened with awe as he looked again upon the newcomer.

Rell set off at a brisk stride, and they had to hurry to keep up. "It's in the oldest part of the palace. Storerooms, armories, and an escape route that leads out of the city. It was to be used in case the very palace was beseiged. We're not outfitted for travel, so must equip ourselves there."

"Travel?" Mischa said. "I thought we only needed to get as far as the authorities. Someone else on the Council . . . Kev's father . . ."

"Not yet," Rell said. "We have no way of knowing which of the Council have been corrupted."

"*My* father would never –"

"We have no way of knowing," Rell repeated. "If we went to the wrong person with our tale, we could end up *wishing* for the dungeon."

"Who put him in command?" Mischa asked Ariana.

"I outrank the rest of you," Rell said. "That puts me in command."

"Wait, wait." Ariana circled around in front of him. "There *are* those on the Council who can help us. Elyvorrin's chief rivals, for instance. Or we might seek the help of my kinswoman, Talian."

"If that is your will, that is what you may do. *I* am going after Tiercel, to make him answer for all that he's done and retrieve the Emerald before he can do anything to it."

"It's madness to follow him," Ariana said. "He bested you once and he's most likely not alone. The *Rhunvala* will be with him. She has powers that you cannot hope to defeat, especially without your magic."

"He did not *best* me," Rell said. "He did not have the honor to face me in a fair fight, but took me captive by trickery and deceit."

"He'll be back. Why chase after him when you could denounce him and wait? Let him return to a criminal's welcome instead of that of a hero."

"And let him destroy the Emerald?"

She recalled how she'd felt in the Temple of Karria, what she'd said to Denethel. "You're right. He mustn't be allowed to do that. So be it, Rell. I'm with you."

"Ari, what?" Mischa blurted. "Why?"

"We have to stop him, Mischa. I know you've had far more hardship than you bargained for, and should you wish to return to Thanis, I understand. But you above all should know that we cannot let something of the gods, perhaps the only thing we elves have of our gods, be harmed."

He heaved a sigh. "More adventure. How could I refuse? Just please do bear in mind that I don't live as long as you elvenfolk, and I'd like to relax sometime before I'm too old and grey to enjoy it."

"You'll need a seeker-mage to track them," Kev said.

"Oh, Kev, no –"

Rell spoke over her. "Join us, Kevan, and be welcome." He offered his hand.

Kev reached out, looking up into Rell's face. Then his eyes flew wide and his mouth dropped open. "I know you."

"He's been imprisoned for eight years, Kev," Ariana said. "You would have been little more than a toddler."

"No, lady, I *do!* From a portrait."

"Ah," said Rell, looking uncomfortable. "*That* portrait."

"What are you talking about? Mischa asked. "Who are you?"

He answered Mischa, but it was Ariana he looked at as he did so. His golden eyes met hers directly. "My true name is Wyndrel Perras. Son of Shaelan."

Her jaw dropped. "But that would make you . . ."

Kev went gracefully to one knee. "Rightful king of the Emerin."

"I thought you were killed in the war," Mischa said. "The prince's body was never recovered."

"Because I did not die that day. Wounded, yes . . . and then spirited away and jailed by Sir Tiercel, who sought and failed to convert me to his cause. He did not kill me because he hoped I might be won over to his cause. All he would need to do is convince me, and then devise some story to explain my absence. A blow to the head that undid my memory, perhaps. Imagine, then, the adoration the people would hold for the noble hero who found and restored their prince."

"Not to be the skeptic of the group," Mischa said, "but do you have any other –"

"Proof?" Rell – Wyndrel – reached into his pouch and withdrew the item that had winked lavender fire. It was a ring of truesilver set with an oval gem, neither amethyst nor sapphire but *mihran*, crystal tears wept by the evening star. "I have the Ring of Twilight, given me by my father."

Ariana reeled. She had been imprisoned in a dungeon with the lost true king of the Emerin? She had . . . oh, dear gods, what had she done? Her lips, and her ears, still tingled from it.

"This changes all," Kev said. "Long live the king! An end to the Council's bickering, no more need for them to argue amongst themselves. Let us go to them now, tonight. I'll rouse one and all from their beds. I'll rouse all the city! No elf in the Emerin shall greet the dawn without knowing that the king has returned."

A half-smile crooked Wyndrel's mouth. "Not so fast, my impetuous young friend. I will not present myself yet."

"Why not?" Kev asked. "If even a page can recognize you, surely you cannot think the Council will doubt your claim. And should they by some madness do so, there are spells to verify what you say. *And* you have the Ring, which was thought lost forever. How could they deny you?"

"They will wish to know where I have been all this while and why. To answer them, I must bring accusation against one of the most beloved men in the Emerin."

"Truthsay –"

"Would not be done until such time as Tiercel himself could be brought present to hear the charges. News of this treachery will shake the faith of every elf in the land. They will question and doubt and wonder . . . unless I can produce Tiercel himself to answer for his deeds." He took Kev by the shoulders and looked somberly down into his face. "This must remain secret for now. Do I have your word on it?"

"My word and my life, for my king," Kev swore, eyes shining.

"Couldn't you just send soldiers after Tiercel?" Mischa asked.

"Unknowing which of them might be more loyal to him? He is the great hero, recall. Many will be unwilling to believe anything less of him. No, if this is to be done, *I* must do it." His golden gaze moved to Ariana. "Are you yet with me?"

She felt faint with embarrassment. She had been kissing the king of the Emerin! Had hurled herself at him like a starving woman, had climbed him like a tree, had chewed on his ears! But if he was willing and able to let all that be in the past, a lapse, an aberration brought on thanks to Mischa and Talopea, so could she. They both had scores to settle with Sir Tiercel Reyes.

"I stand by what I said before," Ariana said.

Mischa heaved a sigh. "Oh, fine . . . count me in. I just hope that when it's time for the formal coronation ball, you'll permit a lowly human to attend the festivities."

Wyndrel led them quickly through a maze of darkened, lesser-used halls, finding his way with a surety that could only have come from a lifetime spent living in the palace. They emerged from a discreet corner door into the very throne room. There, amid the tapestries and other paintings, Ariana saw the one that Kev must have meant. It showed King Shaelan and his son, both of them in fine new armor, looking as if they were prepared to march off to war. It had probably been the last piece of artwork done of the king and prince before they did that very thing.

She studied the image of Wyndrel. Yes, the features were the same, save that his jaw was now firmer. The unusual golden shade of his eyes had been rendered perfectly by the artist. His form, though, that had changed greatly, the result of eight years with little else to do but hone himself into a strong and lithe warrior.

From the throne room, they followed Wyndrel through an even more mazelike series of passageways designed to confuse and addle the mind. He slowed, but in the end unerringly brought them to the siege tunnel he'd described. Vast storerooms opened off of it, holding enough foodstuffs and supplies to last an elven lifetime.

They all equipped themselves as well as they could. The armor and clothing were at least eight centuries out of fashion, but preserved from rust and moths and general decay by domestic magics. Kev and Ariana had the best luck, though after being accustomed to Silversilk, Ariana felt weighed down and confined in a truesteel corselet that glittered with jewels.

"Whose was this?" She ran her hand over the cool, curved metal. "When in the Emerin did women wear armor? I feel odd about taking it."

"It may have belonged to my father's first wife, Nyrialle," Wyndrel said. "She was the daughter of the commander of the Order of the Horse, and a fair lancewoman in her own right. As for taking it, all of this is mine to do with as I please, and thus I arm my allies. Wear it, Ariana. It is yours."

"Thank you . . ." she broke off and laughed. "I know not what I should call you. Rell, Wyndrel . . . Your Majesty?"

"I have no need of titles just now. Wyndrel will do, or Rell if there is need to conceal my identity."

She saw that Kev and Mischa had moved out of earshot, and lowered her voice. "What happened before . . ."

"We were the hapless victims of what affected the guards," he said.

"Yes."

"Caught up in the same unexplainable, undeniable compulsion as they were."

"Yes."

"Forced to act in a way contrary to –"

A throat cleared. Mischa had approached with sly diffidence. "Pardon, but that's not what I said. Talopea cannot *create* desire where there is –"

Ariana's head whipped left and Wyndrel's whipped right. Under the combined ferocity of their glares, Mischa had second thoughts and retreated.

"I'm relieved there are no misunderstandings," Ariana said.

"None whatsoever," Wyndrel replied. "It shall not happen again."

"Absolutely not."

* * *

Far to the south and east of Perras Peliani, Tiercel Reyes rested his back against a tree trunk and peered up at the stars. "I wonder how our prisoners are getting along?"

"Dost thou not fear that Elyvorrin of the other might learn? Thy captive prince?" Tilanne asked. The Emerald of Karria was tucked securely away in a purse held fast to her belt not by cords or thongs but leather straps made strong with metal.

"Even if the noble count does find out, his part in this has gone too far now," Tiercel said. "He has done too much, condoned too much. No, he'd do nothing."

"Thy intent remains, the Emerald to destroy? Pains me that does, Tiercel. An artifact of the gods, it is. As such, not lightly should it be taken, nor lightly to dragon's fire condemned."

Tiercel nodded. "My very thoughts, Tilanne. But your people have had dealings with Racandros, and with other dragons. He'll keep it for his hoard. I expect he'll even offer us something more valuable in return."

She sat up straighter, eyes narrowing into amethyst slits. "Of what speakest thou? From his hoard, what would thou wish? Wealth thou hast, and enchanted blades *two* to wear. What more couldst thou seek? The Helm of True Thought? The Allsong Harp?"

"Have you heard of the Phial of Sevarre? My uncle Tanneivan told me of it, when once I asked him if he knew of any great weapons against the humans. Bane-swords, I meant, but he did me one better. According to my uncle, the contents of the Phial can cleanse this world of the taint of humanity. Think of it, Tilanne. The Mountain King would no longer be a threat to your people. The *Morvalan* would no longer be constantly fighting to survive. They could achieve the same glories as have those of the Emerin."

"This Phial of which thou speakst, what is it? Whence came it?"

"Does it matter? What matters is that it was made by elf-magic, by some Magelord whose home was so beset by humans that he needed to be rid of them."

"Yet safe is it for elvenfolk?" she demanded.

"Perfectly safe." His lips curved in a cold, mirthless smile. "Though I'd think – hope – the impure elfkin would die as well. I do not know how it might affect the orcs and gnomes, but they are really of no consequence. It is the humans, always the humans, who pose the greatest threat."

"To rid the world of humans a goal most worthy is," she said.

He clapped her on the shoulder. "We shall see Kaledhol's vision made fact, and one day . . . one grand day . . . the world will thank us for it."

* * *

The End

The ElfLore Trilogy
Book II

Knight
of the
Basilisk

Prologue

As she dismounted, Kai Tilanne touched the rounded weight of the Emerald of Karria in her belt pouch, and sighed.

"A great and grievous shame it is," she said. "Already thy people have so far from the gods their sights turned. To of this deprive them, the last and only token and proof that once among them faith was strong . . ." She shook her head, wings of rich dark hair falling around her face.

"It must be done," Sir Tiercel said. He sat down on a moss-cushioned fallen log and stretched out his long legs while their horses browsed among the tender grasses. "Much as we both might regret it, it must be done."

They were deep into the wilds of the eastern Emerin, a land that had been left largely unexplored for thousands of years by all but the hardiest of souls. If any had crossed this way before, Tilanne knew, it had been long ago.

"Folly doth it seem, such an artifact willingly into the claws of a dragon to offer."

"If we hope to claim the Phial of Sevarre, which elixir might hold the hope of all the elves within its deadly venom, we must have something of value to trade. Racandros is an old and canny beast. He wouldn't part with one of his treasures for some mere trifle."

"Other items must there be that would a dragon's fancy take," Tilanne said. "Do not of their enchantments the mages of Feyna Rel boast?"

"Often," Tiercel agreed. "But there is another side of this that you've not considered. Why did we seek the Emerald in the first place? Not for Count Elyvorrin's sake. I knew there was no way under the many stars that the Emerald would accept him and prove him king. Or, at least, so I hoped. Ha! What a prank on me had it been otherwise."

"Why, then? Why didst we to the Temple go?"

"We were but the first to think of the Emerald. It would have been only a matter of time before someone else on the Starleaf Council had the same idea. It might have proved a chore indeed, finding a swordmaiden in the Emerin. But I'd not have put it past the Fistrels to try. We had to be rid of it before someone else came to the same conclusion."

"Not the first were we to think of it," Tilanne said. "Ariana Mirida –"

Tiercel chuckled at the mention of the name. "She did us many favors that day, delivering herself into our power as readily as she turned over the Emerald. Quite a useful creature, that one."

"As bait you've left her to be used, that Elyvorrin might her sire summon."

He grinned, a hard and cold grin that imparted only ice to his pale-blue eyes. "Count Elyvorrin means to murder Arien Mirida's daughter before his very eyes. Likely by setting her afire and pushing her from a high place to avenge his precious Alinora. But I have reason to believe the good count sorely underestimates Mirida."

"Begin do I now thy true intent to fathom. Thy hope it is that Mirida shall Elyvorrin slay. Leaving thee, to the widow Faessia betrothed of the count's grandson and heir his sworn guardian. Of the estate as regent wouldst thou be in full command."

"Not only of the estate. If all goes as it ought, the Council will name Alinor Elyvorrin as king. Said office shall then very shortly thereafter fall to Celinar."

"So as king of the Emerin in all save name shall Tiercel Reyes be."

"And with the attendant fortunes and influence thereof, I will help our people. No longer must the *Morvalan* live in constant threat from the Mountain King. No more will the humans be allowed to encroach upon our borders and sully our world. That, as always, is the greater goal, Tilanne."

On that subject, she could only agree with him. All *Morvalan* knew how great a threat the humans were. Yes, some few rare and trainable examples might be useful as mine-slaves and laborers, but as a whole, they were vermin in need of extermination.

While Tiercel roamed off in search of fresh fruits and berries to supplement their magically-preserved and provided larder, Tilanne busied herself with seeing to the horses. The animals had weathered the journey well thus far, despite the lack of roads. The going was bound to get rougher as they continued eastward, toward the isolated peaks of the Stepstone Mountains that poked in rocky and snowcapped points above the dense green. The territory beyond that was a blank on the maps, known even to the far-roaming Lenaisians simply as the Forest of the Great Unknowns. And somewhere by its eastern coast, rearing higher than even the Stepstones, would be Mount Racandros.

There, they would find the dragon who shared that name. If all went well, he would treat with them, but if they transgressed and offended him – the arrogance and spite of dragons was as legendary as the wealth of their hoards – he would have no compunction against searing them to ashes and fishing the Emerald from amid the blackened shells of their armor.

In her belt pouch was a holy artifact, an item of great power and worth. She did not covet it, bore no greed in her heart for its possession, would never have wanted to keep it for her own. But neither did she like to see it be given away to a dragon and taken from the elves. No matter the reason, no matter how good the cause.

She could not help but pity the *Alvalan*, the Emerinians, those elves who had long ago turned from the gods. Her heart hurt to take from them this piece of heritage, even if they no longer held it dear.

A cry of alarm jabbed into her thoughts like a thorn. The shout was followed almost at once by the high and piercing cacophony that was Tiercel's sword Discordant, unleashing its punishing magical scream.

Tilanne sprang up, drawing Baleful Gaze. But she could take only a few steps in the direction he had gone before Discordant's shriek became too painful to bear. She had to re-sheathe her weapon and cup her hands over her ears, praying to Kaledhol to shield her.

Rose-colored light bloomed in her palms. She could still hear the sword's cry, but was no longer laid low by weakness and shrill pain. She heard also the sounds that underlay it. They were the sounds of combat, and a bestial snarling roar.

She ran after Tiercel, swift despite her armor.

He had come upon a black-backed bear by surprise. The beast loomed over him, driven to madness by Discordant as if a swarm of bees beset its head. But rather than flee, or fall dazed, as most living things did, the bear lashed out with heavy paws and sickle-sized claws.

Tiercel was flung backward. He kept hold of Discordant, its blade dripping. Tilanne saw deep gashes across the chest and shoulder of the bear. But still it kept coming, lumbering toward the fallen knight. Tiercel rose shakily, winded but seemingly unbloodied thanks to his meshed mail. He lifted his sword again.

Tilanne gripped Baleful Gaze in both hands and called out a prayer asking that the strength of the god augment her own. "*Ha-nah!*"

As she struck, more rose-light shimmered briefly along her arms. The blade plunged into the bear's back, ripping through shaggy hide and shearing deep into flesh. The bear reared up in reaction to the pain, and Tiercel drove Discordant into its belly.

Still, the beast would not die. The ground beneath it grew sodden with blood, but the deadly swipes of its paws landed hard as ever. Tilanne thought her corselet might buckle at the blows. She staggered back against a sloped wall of crumbling stone. Another two paces to the left and she would have been knocked into the dark gap of a cave mouth.

The bear charged at Tiercel, who thrust Discordant straight out. He meant the blade to slide between the gaping jaws, but at the last moment the bear raised its head and instead was impaled through the neck. Discordant was ripped from Tiercel's hands, its shriek instantly stilled. The resultant silence was almost as deafening.

The force and momentum of the bear's dying charge bore Tiercel down and trampled him flat. So determined was the animal that even in its final throes, it was trying to come around for another pass at its slayers.

The valiant effort failed. The bear's legs faltered and went all askew. The weight of its body crashed to the earth. The shaggy bulk heaved once, trying to rise. Then again. After one final effort, it collapsed with a shudder. But from the way its sides rose and fell like a smith's bellows, Tilanne could see that it yet lived.

The ground where Tiercel had been overrun was dense with springy grass and a layer of last fall's leaves turned to mulch by snow and thaw. He had not been crushed, did not even appear to have any broken bones. He was only bruised and groaning, except for a wound on his cheek where a claw had caught him.

Tilanne held out a hand, and pulled him to his feet. "For bear-sign didst thou not look?"

He shot her a glare through his suffering. "Of course I looked, but I am no barbaric Lenaisian hunter, to read volumes into a single bent twig."

"Dangerous this is," she said. "Rife with hazards are the eastern forests. A guide, perhaps, or at least one with woodslore skilled, we might have brought."

"Forgetting for a moment that you are not only *Morvalan* but *Rhunvala*, believed by all outside the southlands to be a blood-drinking, soul-stealing monster . . . and forgetting for a moment that I have engaged in acts that could possibly be construed as treasonous, and forgetting also for a moment that we are on a mission to be rid of the Emerald of Karria, where do you suppose we might have found such a guide?" He strode to the bear and wrenched his sword from its pierced neck, then finished the job with two swings to decapitate it. "At the least, we have fresh meat. While neither of us are Lenaisians, we Emerinians can do some things better. Watch."

The bear's den was on a hummock of land, the hill dropping away sharply only a few paces from where the dead bear sprawled. Now that her ears no longer rang with magical sound, Tilanne could hear the burble of a creek somewhere nearby, and something else. A rattling, hissing noise that made her first think of dry reeds in a wind.

Tiercel took a small wooden box from a pouch on his belt. Within, nestled in pocked nests of soft padding, were a collection of spherical semi-precious stones, marbles of jasper, carnelian, and agate. He held one aloft. His eyes narrowed. A ripple of barely-seen magic flowed from his hand to the bear.

As Tilanne looked on, the hide was stripped off and the carcass neatly dressed out in mere moments, as if an entire band of invisible butchers armed with flaying knives had stopped by to do the deed. The edible portions were sorted aside, the inedibles cast into a heap.

The ground sank slightly at this rearrangement of weight, and sudden unease filled Tilanne.

"Tiercel, beware!"

"*This* is the way we do it in the Emerin." He took a step forward, meaning to retrieve the choicest pieces of meat for their meal.

The shelf of earth crumbled away beneath him, dropping the tidily arranged remains of the bear into a shallow gully.

"Gods sunder it!" Tiercel swore, struggling to stay upright as the ground shifted beneath his feet. He gathered himself to leap, but before he could, the section upon which he stood fell away to join the rest. Tiercel was spilled into a mess of disturbed earth and no-longer-tidy bear meat.

Tilanne heard the hissing she'd noticed earlier. It had intensified into a frightful whistling, and now she recognized the sound. Her unease flashed into fear. "Tiercel!"

His expression of disgust was nearly as sour as his voice. "What?" Then he heard it too. She saw the awareness in his eyes. The awareness, but not the understanding. "Snakes?"

"Thine eyes! Close them!"

"Close them? Are you –?"

"Not snakes," Tilanne said, tightening her grip on the hilt of Baleful Gaze. "Basilisks!"

He gaped at her, and then a small, reptilian form slithered-crawled into view at the periphery of their vision. A glimpse of it was enough to convince him. Tiercel not only shut his eyes but clapped his hand over them.

That first one was followed by a second, and a third, and then a writhing flood. The basilisks came boiling out from a lair that had been twice disturbed, once by Discordant's shriek, and again by having a wagonload's worth of dirt, debris, bear meat and one elven knight crash down into their midst.

They were not the kind with which Tilanne was most familiar, not covered in glittering red-

and-black scales. These were more rust-and-grey in hue, duller. But basilisks they assuredly were, six-legged with long barbed tails and the leathery flaps of vestigial wings folded against their spined backs. They only the size of largish rats, but even so she would have rather upset a dozen more bears than this nest.

"Climb!" she shouted to Tiercel.

But he, not daring to look and on such an unsteady heap of terrain, could not manage more than a single step without falling to his knees. The basilisks, their deadly ink-black eyes shining, swarmed toward him.

Tilanne jumped down. The nearest ones scattered, almost in astonishment . . . nothing in its right mind would willingly come *toward* a basilisk, a defense that they had grown most accustomed to and comfortable with. Even as they ran from her, their long necks craned to fix their unblinking, unflinching stares upon her.

She felt the lethal power pulsing from them. Such was their magic, that any creature looking into their eyes would be overcome with a paralyzing effect that stopped the heart, shocked the brain, and led to almost immediate death. But Kai Tilanne, sword in hand, looked back at them equally unflinchingly. This confused them further, for they milled about in a storm of hissing and chittering.

"Tilanne?" asked Tiercel in a low voice.

"Here am I," she replied in the same tone.

"Even I cannot fight this many of them with my eyes shut."

"To the edge shall I lead thee, and then climb thou must, climb for all thou art worth."

Moving slowly and with great care, Tilanne led him to the base of the crumbled hill. Tiercel, feeling his way, began the ascent.

Then, with a snarl of challenge, the boldest and largest basilisk darted at Tilanne. She could nearly read its thoughts: if it could not fell this intruder with its stare, it would fell her with its venom. Although she sidestepped, its fangs screeched across the blackmetal plate covering her boot, leaving streaky trails of poison.

Sorry as she was to do so – they were Kaledhol's creatures – she kicked out and lofted it into the bole of a tree. But its charge had emboldened the others. She was surrounded.

More of them sped past her and sprang high, their myriad of claws and teeth catching into the fabric of Tiercel's cloak. He was pulled back down by their weight, landing face-up. His eyes flew wide for a startled instant, fixing briefly on Tilanne's, and then he snapped them shut again. The basilisks pinned under him squirmed and squealed.

As she moved to help him up again she saw one of them wriggle its head out from beneath his shoulder. Its fangs sank into the unprotected side of his neck.

Tiercel went rigid in pain, back arching. Tilanne stabbed down and skewered the basilisk. She seized Tiercel's up thrust arm in her other hand, and in desperation cried out to Kaledhol.

"*Ha-nah . . . hanahia!*"

Power surged through her, a tide of greater potency and duration than she called upon in brief spates during combat. The god-strength, which could enable her to shatter an opponent's weapon in a parry or counterstrike, was now all through her body and wreathing her in a red glow.

She pulled and flung all in one motion. Tiercel, for all that he was larger and heavier than her, was yanked flying from the ground and thrown bodily to the edge above. Tilanne was spun by the effort and stumbled, and as she dropped to one knee, Baleful Gaze was jolted from her grasp.

At once she slammed her own eyelids shut, no longer protected by the enchantments on her sword. Her ears seemed to become preternaturally sharp, letting her hear every hateful hiss and snarl as the basilisks, cheated of half their prey and enraged by their injuries, came at her in a group.

Tiercel was calling to her, not daring to look and see what was happening, but Tilanne could not spare him an answer. She groped blindly over the tumble of stones, finding bear-bones and the skinned-off hide, finding the tail of a basilisk – it whipped around and teeth slashed across the backs of her knuckles, splitting her leather glove and drawing blood.

And then, there. The hard metal of Baleful Gaze's silver hilt. She closed her fist around it and opened her eyes in time to see three of the basilisks leap at her face.

She ducked aside and swung, the edge chopping one in half and carrying through to take the tail from a second. The third hit Tilanne in the shoulder and gnashed its jaws, missing her flesh but catching a mouthful of dark hair. She snatched at it and got it by the neck, a clump of hair tearing free as she hurled it from her.

After that it was a grim business of swordplay, over in moments as the surviving basilisks fled from this strange prey-thing that did not succumb to either of their weapons. When the last of them had disappeared into the underbrush, Tilanne climbed to where Tiercel had come to rest.

Her heart sank as she looked at him. The venom was already working fast through him. He was pale and shaking, with beads of sweat on his ashen face. The side of his neck was swollen, an ugly red deepening to purple. His winter-sky eyes rolled toward hers, and in them she saw both misery and fear.

"Done are they, or gone," she said. "But bitten were thee, and swiftly the poison in thy veins does course. Not much time have we."

"If I am to die," Tiercel said, "I would . . . that it be by steel."

"Such would any warrior prefer," she said. "But die today, thou shall not, Kaledhol willing."

With the bear dead and no indications it had mate or young, its den would have to suffice for shelter. She moved Tiercel into the cave and ran to fetch their horses from the grassy glade where they'd initially stopped. He made a few muttered protests but did not resist . . . and soon enough, could not resist.

She took a box from her saddlebag. The box was black and painted with roses of rich hues. She shook some of the gritty powder within into a goblet of wine, and stirred the bitter concoction with a twig.

Tiercel, swaddled in their sleeping-furs as well as both of their cloaks, nonetheless shivered until his armor sounded like the rattle of dice in a bone cup. He watched unseeingly as Tilanne brought the wine to him.

"Drink this, thou must." She held it to his lips. He recoiled from the scent, which was heavy with roses and soot. "Help thee it might, or kill thee it might. But dead art thou otherwise, and so our only choice it is."

He drank, and subsided into an uncomplaining fog as Tilanne examined the bite. She grimaced, but even in her dismay was somewhat relieved – had the fangs pierced either of the great vessels in his neck, he would have been dead before she could have gotten to him. As it was, he would not last the night unless she could cleanse the wound, and hope that the ash of blood-rose would gird his system against the venom.

Working as quickly as extreme care would allow, she built a fire and heated a thin truesteel dagger until it glowed. Then she made a short, deep incision between the crusted-over fangholes. When she broke the skin of that swelling bulge, fluid spurted out, watery and pinkish. Tiercel twitched, but did not cry out. Tilanne pressed the sides of the wound until no more would flow from it, neither blood nor serum nor venom. She spread the sides of the incision and flushed it with water, then sprinkled more of the grey powder into the raw flesh.

All the while, she sent silent prayers to Kaledhol, and wished not for the first time that the god of protection and destruction offered His faithful powers of healing. It was not right, was terribly wrong somehow that *human* priests could work such wonders, wonders that the magic of the Emerin and the prayers of the *Rhunvala* could not match. The elven gods, the elven people, had been first and greatest . . .

She set aside such thoughts of injustice and covered the wound with a clean bandage of cloth. It now remained to be seen how Tiercel's body would react.

Tilanne sat back and exhaled, weariness tugging her shoulders earthward. But there was still much to be done, and with a sigh she made herself get up and do it. They would have to camp here until he was well enough to travel – or so ailing that she had no other option but to lash him to the saddle and bear him to the nearest settlement where they might find help. How she, a *Morvalan*, would win the aid of any Emerinian townsfolk was a daunting prospect, but she would find a way.

The cave was roomy enough to admit the horses, so she tethered them near the opening where they could reach to crop and would alert her if anything came near. She brought their belongings inside. After a careful check of the area revealed that the basilisks had not returned, she descended again to bring back the bearskin and some of the meat to rinse in the creek.

She also retrieved the bodies of the dead basilisks, saying a few words in honor of the bravery with which they had defended their lair. They were too valuable to leave to rot, the venom-sacs and skin and claws all having their own uses.

Because Tiercel was, to the opinion of the *Morvalan*, in many ways a spoiled and pampered northern *Alvalan*, he traveled with all the comforts he could carry. From the enchantments on his cloak that kept him cool when the day was hot or warm when the night was cool, to the metal rod tipped with a jeweled beetle-shape that made insects avoid their camp, he bore with him magical conveniences aplenty. Among these was a case the size of a small chest, which kept all foodstuffs inside it free from decay. If it worked on mutton and fish, Tilanne reasoned, it should work on these carcasses. She wrapped them in oilcloth and tucked them well away from the edibles.

With all of that done, she had little to do except wait. Tiercel regained consciousness at dusk, and she was relieved to see that he had already shown much improvement.

"But you were bitten too," he said, noting the bandage she'd tied around her hand. "Why. . .why does it not affect you?"

"Told thee have I," she said, "that not without price was my becoming *Rhunvala*. Bitten by basilisks have I been, and survived. An immunity to their venom did it impart me, it seems." She stayed his hand before he could bring it to the side of his neck. "Touch it thou must not, Tiercel, else irritate it and worsen it thou shall."

He clenched his fist and lowered it, but his arms quivered from the effort of keeping them at his sides. "Very well, but I may go mad. Gods, how it itches!"

"Bind thee, I can, if the only way it is."

"No!"

"Then resist thou must. And remember, although terrible the itching must have been, Ariana did not at her injury scratch."

His jaw firmed, and she knew she'd hit upon just the right sore spot. Sir Tiercel of the Order of the Lion, hero of the Emerin and bearer of Lionheart . . . Tiercel Reyes of the southlands, son of a distinguished line and bearer of Discordant . . . in neither guise would he willingly be outdone by some elfkin-born interloper.

Tilanne cobbled together a meal, musing on that last fact. Ariana Mirida . . . as tall and graceful and as silver-haired as her father, who seemed in all ways to be as pure an elf as any Tilanne had ever known . . . how could such a one be the daughter of an elfkin? The grandchild of a human? How could she be, and show no taint of it?

Tiercel tried manfully to eat, but she knew by the sickly tinge of color in his cheeks that the battle of blood-rose against venom was leaving him nauseous. After that initial complaint, he bore his sufferings – the nausea, the itching, the hot-quicksilver pain of the poison – with a stoicism that would have made even a dwarf proud.

"Some days might it take, the medicine its course to run," she said. "If worse it becomes, to a town and a physician must I take thee."

"I'll be well," he said, leaning weakly into the pillow she'd made from a saddle padded with blankets. "We must go on. And if I cannot, *you* must. Our purpose is greater than both of us, Kai Tilanne. The *Odan Rhunvale* knew that when they brought us together."

"Something to which at the time, thou were most opposed," she reminded him with a tight smile.

Tiercel chuckled ruefully. "I have since repented that. But can you fault me? Even your own people never knew what to make of you, a female *Rhunvala*. And yes, if it is a confession you wish to hear, I was envious. *I* should have been Terindor's heir and squire."

"To become such was never of my design," Tilanne said. "Nor would it have been his, had not death so near at hand to him been, had not the night been so dire. Someone, *anyone*, the Kai needed. By chance alone was it I to happen upon him. Believe it could I not myself, when this token he did give me."

She drew the ruby from within her collar. The jewel swung at the end of a blackmetal chain that was too thick to serve as a woman's necklace, and the flickering fire brought a heart of bright scarlet alive in the shape of the basilisk.

"I think it is time," Tiercel said, his voice a mere rasp now and his eyes heavy-lidded as he watched the ruby twirl in the firelight, "that you told me all of it. Not how he died. I know that. But the rest. What happened . . . after?"

Tilanne fell silent, regarding him for several moments. "A long and oft difficult tale it is. Truly dost thou wish to hear it?"

"If it will take my thoughts from this terrible, maddening itch like ants burrowing in me, I would hear any tale. Even the bleakest of Elwyndas' epic tragedies would be preferable to lying here waiting to see whether I live or die."

She took a deep breath and let it out slowly, and began to speak.

* * *

Part One:

Blood and Fire

CHAPTER ONE

Rough hands seized and shook her. Tilanne Murres came awake with a start and a cry. She sat up flailing her limbs, and had clouted the man kneeling over her twice before she recognized him as one of her own.

Her first thought, feeling those hands upon her, was that it was the orckin. Having finished Kai Terindor, he would now slay her, but wanted her awake to die. Or that it would be the silver-haired *Alvalan*, him whose eyes had carried such a freight of sorrow and empathy, having decided that she must be slain after all.

But it was neither of those. She looked upon Ilantisian, the broad-shouldered scribe and teacher whose assistant she had been. His greying hair was singed and scratches laddered his face, but he smiled with joy despite her pummeling at him.

"Tilanne, alive thou art. Praise Kaledhol!"

Groggily, shaking off the effects of the spell with which the *Alvalan* had struck her, Tilanne let him help her to her feet. She chronicled her pains as she did.

Although her arms felt as if they had been battered to shards by the blow of the orckin's flail she had turned with the Kai's shield, they did not seem broken. She was bruised and aching from head to toe, but compared to those around her, such hurts were minor indeed.

Cliffcave Fortress was in ruins. Smoke rose from the wreckage of the stables and a heap of wood and bones that had been a funeral pyre. Some of the sharpened tree trunk posts that made up the wall were still blazing like giant torches. More smoke drifted from the sunken shell of the fort proper, where the very stones seemed to have melted from the intense heat. The rising sun shone thinly through that brownish-black pall in the air. Tilanne could hear sobbing, moans of pain, and the mutter of voices in distress and confusion.

"Worried was I, child," the scribe said, and smoothed the disarray of Tilanne's dark hair as if she were a toddler. "Dead is Kai Terindor. Dead also are Marona of the Crown and all of her Circle. Thy father as well, and of the Kai's soldiers every last man excepting Corandir, who sorely hurt is. What is to become of us now, I despair to think. Even the orcs deserted us have, though to that say I that better are we without them."

"Leave here we must," Tilanne said. "Betrayed by the Horned One we have been, and tainted now is this place."

He patted her shoulder. "Trouble it not, child, we shall –"

Tilanne reached into the collar of her tunic and brought forth the chain and pendant. Ilantisian's words dried up as he stared at the ruby basilisk depending from blackmetal.

"How came thee by that?" he asked. Those gathered nearby, who had been busy tending their own injuries, looked to see what made him speak in such an offended tone. Eyes grew wide all around as they beheld the gem.

"The Kai himself around my neck did place it," Tilanne said, trying to sound strong and brave as she knew he would have wanted, even if the burden of its implications threatened to crush her into the earth. "For all that a girl I am, of not even thrice ten years, he did bid me his message deliver, and in his stead to safety lead thee."

A chorus of disbelieving outbursts met this, but Tilanne stood her ground. This sorry band of survivors was neither wizards nor soldiers. These were the folk like Tilanne whose parents, siblings, spouses, or children had served Marona and Terindor. They had come to be with their families, to care for their needs and support their cause, and now the reasons for it all were gone. Dead. Gone to ash on the pyre, buried beneath the collapsed roof of the fortress.

Their grief had not even begun to set in yet, still lost amid a wash of shock and horror. All had gone awry in a single night. Everything was destroyed, dozens of *Morvalan* lives had been cut violently short, and a *Rhunvala* lay dead before them.

That last was perhaps the worst blow of all. There were so few who were called to serve Kaledhol in that way, and fewer still to survive the rites needed to be worthy of the sign of the basilisk. They were held in respect and awe, nearly revered for their closeness to the god. To have one die was bad enough . . . to have one die to an orckin was unthinkable.

Tilanne scanned the courtyard, where many elven and orcish bodies still sprawled. She saw the spot where the orckin had fallen, the stain of his blood dark within the imprint left by his massive body, but he was gone. So too was the silver-haired *Alvalan.*

"Escaped they did?" she asked, but needed no answer. There were none here able to stop them, and if Kai Terindor had not been able to, perhaps no force on earth was.

"Our lives they spared," said Ninthar, who had been one of the cooks and servants. He had a sword belted to his waist and wore it uncomfortably. "To me the *Alvalan* did say that to go we were, once fit to travel were our wounded. That take only what we needed we should, and the hall of the wizards avoid. Then departed did he and the orckin."

"And leave we shall," Tilanne said.

"Thee to follow?" Falana's face was strained, her eyes reddened, but she did her best to stay composed for the sake of the three children huddled around her. The eldest of them could not have been more than seventeen years, the youngest too young to understand that his father would never return. "How are we *thee* to follow? A mere girl?"

"So I am, but the Kai did as his chosen heir name me." She curled her fingers around the ruby, and pointed to the sword that lay near where she had slept. "This did I accept, and so Kor Tilanne am I now."

"Saw it did I." That was Jedriel, the younger of the scribes. "To the Kai's side she did rush in battle, and would have his death avenged, if interfered had not the *Alvalan*. True it is."

Now Tilanne saw a wanting-to-believe in many pairs of eyes. She knew how they felt, for their place in Kaledhol's greater Cause had always been to be obedient and led by those such as Marona and Terindor. Without one to lead them, they would be at a loss, all still joined by the common bond that made them *Morvalan* but unsure what to do. Unsure how best to serve their god and His purpose.

Oh, and there were so few of them left. A painfully quick count showed her a bare score of elves around her. Of those, half a dozen were children under twenty and three others were so badly injured they could not walk. Only one wore a uniform of the Kai's soldiery, but most of his head was swathed in a bandage that covered the wadding where one eye had been – Corandir had been half-blinded by an elfkin.

Tilanne's own brother, Vandil, had been the one to tend Corandir's wound. Seeing his handiwork reminded her that Vandil's blood still stained her hands. She had tried to hold in his shattered ribs after the orckin's deadly flail had staved his chest. Her soul screamed with rage and loss, for all of her people but mostly for her brother and their father. Now, of all their family, of all the seven children her mother had born, she and one sister were all that remained of the Murres line.

The rest of the *Morvalan* voiced no further arguments, all too stunned and soul-sore to think clearly or care. Whether Jedriel's words had convinced them or not, they were eager to quit this tragic place, to leave the sights and scents of death behind.

"If able thou art," she said, drawing confidence from the Kai's ruby, "much is there that must be done. Our dead to Kaledhol properly sent must be. What horses live, bring hither that supplies and the injured they might carry."

Her words set them in motion, slowly, but with faint relief at having tasks to perform. Some dragged elven bodies to the still-burning heaps of wood and cast them within, adding rosewood oil from a few crocks that hadn't been already emptied or broken. Others looked after the hurt and the children, while the rest combed the ruins for anything that they might need.

Tilanne went to the body of the Kai. He had lost his breastplate, and the links of the mail beneath had been fused by magical fire, slashed by glass. Helmless, his hair burned away, his face blistered and covered in dried blood, there was little left to remind her of the striking and noble figure he had been. With the help of Corandir and Sahen, she carried him to the pyre.

"Over thy soul, Kai Terindor Reyes, may Kaledhol vigilant and proud be," she murmured, having heard similar words said by her father when the commander of Deepwater had been laid to rest. She hoped it would be sufficient for a *Rhunvala.*

Blinking back tears so as to show no weakness, Tilanne tipped the jar of rosewood oil over the wood and stepped back as Corandir set it aflame. Her brother had been one of many to burn in the night and her father would remain where he had died in the casting chamber, so she could only stand the fire-watch for this man. This man, who had not spoken a dozen words to her before this night, but had forever changed her life.

She stood there as the sun climbed and the fires finally dwindled. Around her, she was aware of the others moving about, gathering what they could. Exhaustion etched deep hollows beneath their eyes.

"Sleep we need, rest we need," she said. "But here, we cannot stay."

"The intruders, we should follow." Sahen was a few years older than Tilanne, and had been serving as a general squire and attendant to the soldiers. She noted that he had armed himself–excessively, perhaps, for what need would he have of three swords, two bows, and so many quivers of arrows? Further, he had taken from somewhere a soldier's cloak of midnight and crimson. Its hem dragged behind him, but his expression was filled with a hunter's hunger.

"Follow?" she echoed. "Follow, for what? That die we might as did our kin?"

"That avenge them we might. Are we our necks humbly to bend in defeat?"

"Nay!" Reshelli cried, and brandished a spear with truesteel point. "Such did I say before and gainsaid was, but vengeance ours should be."

"And said before did I," Ninthar put in, "that to attack them a sheerest folly would be. Four of them there were, four only, and all of this they wrought. Against wizards and soldiers and *Rhunvala* all. How might *we* fare?"

"Too few are we, and too hurt," Tilanne said. "No more lives can we risk for revenge."

"And *thee* the Kai his heir named?" Sahen's lip curled. "Corandir, a soldier thou art . . . surely must thou sayst that this cannot be."

Corandir studied the jewel around her neck for what seemed an eternity, lifting it before his remaining eye. At last, he nodded. "To Tilanne, the Kai has this honor passed, and for now, heed it shall I. As should thee. But warned be, Kor Tilanne . . . the *Odan Rhunvale*, the Citadel of the Basilisk, much on this might have to say. Deny thee, they might. For never in all our history has a woman *Rhunvala* become."

"That must I face when comes the time," Tilanne said. "Now, from this place shall we go, and in the shelter of the forest our refuge seek in sleep."

Sahen did not move, merely stood regarding her scornfully as everyone else busied themselves hefting the sacks and packs that held what scant provisions they'd been able to salvage from the ruins of the fort. They had precious little in the way of foodstuffs or weapons, not that many of them could use the latter in any case.

Tilanne took no sword, knowing that the large knife she wore at her belt would have to do. She had torn her cumbersome skirt nearly to the waist to free her legs for movement, and now it was so stained and tattered it was almost impossible to tell what color and material it had once been. After some deliberation, she shed it in favor of a pair of dark leggings and a man's crimson tunic that fell to her knees.

As the two horses that had been calmed by Vennan were being laden with bundles, Alarice called to Tilanne.

"A cart," she said triumphantly, brushing her long white-blond hair from her face and leaving a smudge of dirt. "Damaged it was, but with my spells did I mend it. Now Findaire and the younglings ride might."

"Well done," Tilanne said, feeling suddenly odd as she sensed Alarice was looking to her for approval.

There had been a time not that many years distant when they had been playmates, schoolmates. But then Alarice's budding mage-talent had drawn her toward the Crown Magics, while Tilanne had wavered between healing and teaching, and still had chosen no path. Now a destiny she'd never even dared consider had been dropped upon her, while Alarice's master and teachers were gone.

Findaire had escaped the fires largely unburned, but for a singing crispness at the ends of her hair, but the heat and smoke had seared her lungs. Tilanne could hear the tortured laboring of her fluid-filled breath even from ten paces away when she went to tell her Alarice's news. The sound of it made her wonder if the woman would live long enough even to need the cart.

Jedriel glanced up, and shook his head almost imperceptibly, his dark eyes grim. Young Ninare missed the exchange, bent over her aunt and helping her to lean forward as more spasms of coughing wracked Findaire's body.

"Alarice a cart has found and mended," Tilanne said.

"Of no use will it be. Dead already am I."

"Say such things not," Ninare said. "A physician shall thy hurts tend, I know it."

"A physician we have none," Tilanne told the girl as gently as possible, pierced anew by the loss of Vandil. "And far from here is the Valley of the Cloudflowers."

"Another town . . ."

"Closest is Jewelgreen," Jedriel said. "Even so, many days' travel is it."

"Leave me, thou must," Findaire said, her voice a weak and bubbling whisper. "Here should I stay, in the company of my kinsfolk to rest. If thou wilt, Kor Tilanne, swift mercy grant me."

Ninare sobbed, and Jedriel drew her comfortingly into his arms. Tilanne stared down at Findaire, hardly able to believe what she'd heard. She could not do what Findaire was asking. How could she do such a thing? Take steel and end a woman's life?

"You see?" Sahen spoke from her elbow, when she had not even seen him come near. "Suffers, she does. Thy duty should it be, but the stomach for it thou hast not. Unfit art thou to command us, if this one small thing thou cannot do."

"Small thing? A matter of squeamish stomach this is not," Jedriel said, still holding Ninare. "Couldst *thou* do it, Sahen? Couldst thou?"

"Died already have so many, and so few are we," Tilanne said. "Findaire, please . . . live."

But Findaire could not answer, could only fight for breath into her drowning lungs and look up at Tilanne with pain-shadowed sea-green eyes, mute in her appeal. She was dying, might have died even with a physician to tend her.

"I could and I shall, if too weak is this pretender *Rhunvala*." Sahen reached for one of the swords he'd claimed, but before his hand touched it, his wrist was seized in an iron grip.

"Thy place, it is not," Corandir said. "Unless by the Kor ordered."

"Order me about she cannot! Her elder am I, and war-trained besides."

"Enough!" Tilanne cried. "Sahen, enough. Findaire suffers, and relief must be granted. Corandir, wilt thou?"

The half-blinded soldier nodded soberly, and released Sahen's wrist with a brusque push that staggered the youth. Ninare pressed her face into Jedriel's chest, but did not object as they heard steel sing as it was pulled from its sheath.

Nor did Findaire object. With the last of her strength, she mouthed her thanks and set her hands upon her breast, thumbs and forefingers framing the area just above her heart. Tilanne could hardly bear to watch, wished to turn away as Ninare had done, but stood firm as Corandir delivered a single swift thrust.

"Thy task it was," Sahen said in a low, deadly whisper to Tilanne. He was about to say more, but the back of Corandir's glove slapped the words from his lips.

"Not for thee is it to say what her tasks are. Not for thee is it her place or her fate to say. For the *Odan Rhunvale* to decide it is. Not thee, not me, none of us. Until then, we follow."

"But wrong it is! Only by luck that closest to the Kai was she. Any of us it could have been, another of us it *should* have been –"

"But Tilanne it was," Jedriel said. "And better so, for jealousy and ambition such as thine a doom to us all would surely be. Hast thou the Cause forgotten, Sahen? Before one's own desires comes one's family, and before one's family comes the Cause. So has it been, so must it be. If thyself thou wouldst put first, go then to the north and a selfish *Alvalan* become."

Sahen gaped at him, the young scribe's speech having done what even Corandir's slap had not. He seemed to struggle for something to say, failed to find it, and lowered his head to scurry away before any of them could meet his gaze.

Tilanne sighed deeply and made gestures of thanks to each of them. She helped Ninare take Findaire's body to the pyre, and stood with the girl as Ninare poured the rosewood oil over the embers. The dying flames leaped up in renewed energy, crackling and bright orange.

When the fire had consumed Findaire, Tilanne raised her voice to announce it was time to leave. Her small band of refugees formed slowly, in protective groups and pairs.

Olithiana and Carenar were so tightly embraced that they might have been one being. The husband and wife stayed a bit apart from the rest, as if knowing how bitterly their good fortune might sting the new-made widows and widowers. Ilantisian, Jedriel, and Alarice, all of them among the best-learned, stood together. Vennan would not move far from the horses, and Ninare seemed to have taken two orphaned boys under her wing, holding three-year-old Parcian while eight-year-old Hastinar pressed close to her side.

Tilanne might have expected to find Ninthar and Reshelli together, as both were cooks and if fortress rumor was to be believed, occasional lovers. But they were far apart; Ninthar with the silent and hollow-eyed craftsman Deverall, while Reshelli with her spear had placed herself beside Sahen.

"Mivana, where hath gotten thy brother?" Falana demanded irritably as she secured her infant son's carry-basket amid the bundles in the back of the cart.

"In there," the ten-year-old girl said, aggrieved. "Told thee that already did I, *Vali*, but listened wouldst thou not, and now *me* for his disobedience thou'll blame."

Tilanne felt a raw, chilly horror seep from her marrow when she looked where the child pointed. "Falanar in *there* hath gone?"

Falana paled. "Nay, such a thing would he not have done. Too dangerous it is . . ."

"Went there he *did*," Mivana insisted, and pointed more firmly at the central building of the fortress, where the Circle's casting chamber had been housed.

* * *

CHAPTER TWO

A stillness and dread settled over the elves, broken only by the dying sizzle of the flames. As if their very attention had brought it on, a new sound came in the form of a shifting, rumbling groan. One of the fortress walls sagged inward. A gout of eerie purple fire licked up, and from somewhere within that blackened, smoking mess came a cry of pain.

"Falanar!" his mother shrieked.

No one seemed able to move, and in that instant Tilanne fully understood that it all fell to her. She had not been able to save Findaire . . . she could not lose another of them.

With that thought foremost in her mind, she headed for the ruin. Corandir tried to stop her, but one even look from her was enough to make his hand slip free from her arm. He let her go on unhindered, while the rest looked on in dismay.

Each step that brought her closer was a step Tilanne would rather not take. She could see it more clearly now, the damage and the danger. A shimmering bank of heat rose from the stones, which themselves looked softened, melted. Here and there, half-buried by tons of rubble, protruded charred sticks that had once been elven limbs.

From within, Falanar cried out again. "Mother . . . someone . . . help!"

"Where art thou, Falanar?" Tilanne shouted.

"Tilanne, nay, come back," Alarice rushed after her.

"Alarice, stay! Find him I shall."

Even the least experienced hunter would be able to follow the boy's fresh tracks in the ash, which led toward a gaping and uneven opening. It was like a mouth, a dragon's mouth, all darkness and heat with a reddish wavery glow underlying the shadows. Jagged, burnt stumps of beams were the teeth, and a slab of marble was the tongue.

The fortress shifted again, things sliding heavily and unseen. Falanar's call became an agonized scream, echoed by one of desperation from his mother.

Tilanne flinched back as chunks of stone tumbled from above. The moment they stopped falling, she squinted against the waves of oven-warmth and held her breath against the vile fumes that issued from the forbidding opening. She plunged inside.

Now she knew what the Torments would be like. Terror and confusion and pain beat at her from all sides as she made her way into the malformed remains of a once-lovely fortress. Everywhere she looked she saw death. Elves robbed of their long lives, robbed of their beauty, robbed of their hope and promise.

Timbers creaked and stone squealed against itself. Tilanne could hardly see but dared not attempt to feel her way, knowing that a single brush against a beam might bring it all down upon her head. She groped with her toes, eyes stinging and watering from the stench of death.

As she pressed deeper, seeking the source of Falanar's voice – he had progressed now to incoherent moans and sobs, perhaps understanding that no one could reach him – Tilanne felt something new and upsetting. The *aether* was disturbed.

She was no sorceress as was Alarice, but any elf could sense the patterns of *aether*. The force that was the lifeblood of magic was as constant and taken for granted as the very air. But in this place the air itself was twisted and treacherous, laden with poisons that dizzied her when at last her aching lungs compelled her to sip short breaths of it. So too was the *aether*, twisted and strange, made poison.

Wiping futilely at her streaming eyes, Tilanne saw shafts of discolored daylight ahead. Had she gotten turned around? No, she couldn't have been, because Falanar's moans still came from somewhere up ahead. Then she remembered the way the explosion of warped fire had roared through the roof, raining down on the courtyard. Picking her way toward the light, she came at last to what had been Marona's casting chamber.

Her foot struck a corpse, a woman whose body was half scorched to a cinder. The unmarked side of her face was locked in a grimace, and the tattoos along her scalp as well as the multiple piercings marching the rim of her ear proclaimed her as one of the Crown Mages.

Candlewax formations of rock, which had melted and then cooled to congeal in strange shapes, turned the floor into a hostile landscape. Shards of thick glass had been driven into the very walls, in one case having pinned the skeletal remains of a robed elf through the chest.

Among the bodies were several in armor, though the black metal had been deformed almost beyond recognition. And the bodies themselves, those ones, looked wrong to her eyes. Even allowing for the damage the fire had done, they looked wrong.

She could not take the time to look further, for she had found Falanar. Or at least she saw part of him, one feebly moving hand over a pile of rocks and debris. A balcony wall had collapsed atop him, the balcony itself resting in nearly perfect condition as the lid to a tomb, in which the boy was imprisoned alive.

Tilanne scrambled over the uncertain footing. "Falanar!"

"Ti . . . Tilanne?"

"Be still, Falanar. Help thee I shall."

"My father . . . sought did I my father . . . only wished did I to find him . . . to the pyre bring him . . . not buried in stone like a dwarf should he be . . . not left to rot . . ." He coughed, a horrible, wracking cough too terribly reminiscent of Findaire. Too hurt, too hopeless.

She reached the pile and grasped his hand. His fingers closed on hers with no more strength than an infant. Blisters were rising in white bubbles on his skin. Two of his nails had been torn away to the quick, threads of blood trickling from them.

By moving one of the few stones that did not seem to be supporting any of the others, Tilanne was able to see his face. His eyes were dark holes, pits of fear, and he looked so very young. Seventeen, no older than she'd been when her father had been assigned to Cliffcave Fortress. Too young to die at all, let alone such a death as this.

"Falanar . . ."

He heard what she couldn't bring herself to say, and shook his head in negation. "*Please*, Tilanne. Leave me here thou cannot!"

"If more of the stones I remove, shift shall the balcony atop them and surely crush thee. How severely art thou injured? Able art thou at all to move?" She spied a few other pieces that did not seem to be weight bearing, and pushed them aside. They bounced and rolled in a clatter, and she bared Falanar's arm.

He did not reply, did not need to when she saw the dismay in his eyes. He was trapped and paralyzed, and the rest of the walls might come down at any moment, and she did not even have Corandir here to do what she could not bring herself to do.

"Lost already so many lives," Tilanne murmured, touching the knife at her waist. "I cannot. . .Kaledhol forgive me, I cannot."

But neither could she leave him to a slow and miserable death. Finding larger chunks and parts of beams, she tried to brace up the balcony while pawing away the heap that held him. He watched her like a rabbit in a snare, helpless. Findaire had been resigned, accepting. Falanar was terrified. He wanted to live.

Tilanne cast desperately around the chamber, seeking something else to help hold up the balcony or pry away the stones. Her gaze took in the scattered ring of armored figures again, crumpled in a regular pattern unlike that made by the bodies of the mages . . . almost as if they had fallen before the explosion . . .

A familiar wink of color caught her eye, and Tilanne caught her breath as she recognized the yellow star sapphire set into the pommel of her father's sword. Dragon's Eye, that blade was called, and it had been one of her mother's last gifts to him before death-in-birthing had carried Vandanne Murres from this world.

She stood, then dropped back into a crouch and shielded her head with her arms as a hail of pebbles pelted her from above. Wincing in expectation, she waited for the inevitable larger missiles. A rock the size of a bird's egg struck her forearm, another hit the floor and bounced up to crack smartly against her kneecap.

A sliding rumble shook the room. Falanar wailed, and distantly from outside Tilanne could hear the rest of the survivors calling in alarm.

When the room did not immediately collapse in on them, Tilanne risked rising again. She picked her way across the littered floor and came to the glinting yellow gem.

"Dragon's Eye," she breathed.

The sword was still sheathed across her father's back as he sprawled face down. The finely tooled leather of the sheath had become made of ashy-black flakes that fell apart as she touched it, but the weapon itself appeared undamaged.

There was no time to waste, but she had to look one last time on her father's face. As horrific as it might be to see him so, she *had* to.

She set the sword aside, grasped him and turned him over. The warped metal was hot even through her gloves. Steel clanged dully on marble as she rolled him to his back, and a scream lodged fast in her throat.

She had been prepared to see him burned, thought she was ready for such a sight. But that which greeted her was so different, so horrible, that for a moment Tilanne was rooted to the spot and oblivious to all around her. The acrid smoky air ceased to bother her; the threatening grind and shift of stones went unheard.

He *was* Forantil Murres . . . and yet he wasn't. Not this ancient, wizened husk. Her father's hair, what strands of it had escaped from beneath his helm, was the color of parchment-ivory when once it had been as coppery-red as Vandil's. His skin was etched with wrinkles, blotched with age-spots, and shrunken against the contours of his skull. His lips were drawn back in a rictus, exposing teeth from which the gums had receded. And his eyes, wide-open and frozen in a glassy stare, were filmed in milky cataracts.

Rare indeed was the *Morvalan* that lived out his or her natural lifespan. Warfare took the males, birthing took the females, injury and illness took one and all. They did not have the luxury of their spoiled northern cousins, to while away centuries.

The oldest living being Tilanne had ever seen was the sorceress Ensinameline of the Scepter, who dwelt in Deepwater where Tilanne's sister's husband was stationed. That diminutive, white-haired woman had seen nine centuries, yet she would have looked young and vital compared to this . . . this *thing* before her that showed her father's features in that shriveled mask of age.

She stared as if spellbound, horror creeping insidiously along her every nerve. After an untold amount of time, at last her surroundings filtered back into her consciousness. Falanar was hitching and whimpering, plaintive and desolate sounds that said he thought himself to have been abandoned again, left to die slowly and alone.

This thought gave Tilanne the strength to tear her gaze from her father's desiccated visage. Clutching Dragon's Eye, she backed away from his body.

"Be thou brave, Falanar," she said, unnerved at the shakiness she heard in her own voice. But it soothed him, and he quelled his whimpers as she returned to his prison.

Using the sword as a lever, she worked it into the heap and pried apart the larger stones. Soon Falanar's shoulders and head were unburied, and he clawed at cracks in the floor in an effort to pull himself free. To no avail. Tilanne peered as best she could into the shadows that held him, and saw the rear edge of the balcony pinning his legs.

Her mind was all a swim now, from shock and the impure air. A crash from elsewhere in the fortress shook the ground, and sent new cascades of debris into motion. The opposite wall broke apart with the slow grandeur of an iced-over waterfall giving way to the spring thaw.

Falanar cried out, loud and despairing and doomed. Sensing immediacy, Tilanne let go the sword and seized his outstretched arms. She pulled with all her might. The boy's body moved slightly, him shrieking as bones were wrenched and skin was torn.

A boulder-sized piece of the opposite wall fell, bounced, passed close enough to Tilanne to whip her hair in the breeze of its passage, and smashed into the corner. The pile that had held up the balcony slid in a jittering and cracking avalanche.

She saw her name on Falanar's begging lips, the sound of it lost in the hungry roar of the shifting stone. She threw her weight backward, no longer caring if she dislocated his arms or scraped all the skin and flesh from his legs, meaning only to get him out, save him.

The balcony slammed down, its leading edge hitting Falanar just below the shoulder blades and driving him into the floor. As if that wasn't enough, it teetered side to side, grinding him beneath tons of marble.

Tilanne screamed with him, and sustained hers long after his was abruptly lost in the gout of blood that spewed from his gaping jaws. He went rigid, his hands beating against her in thoughtless panic. She clutched at them, caught one as he went limp. The other slapped against the floor with a lifeless smack.

His eyes slid briefly toward her, but there was no comprehension in them. And even as she leaned forward, shaking her head in mute denial, the spirit drained from them and left them blank, empty orbs.

Numbed and uncaring that the room was continuing to shake itself to pieces around her, Tilanne kissed the back of Falanar's hand. Only when a careening chunk of stone struck beside her with enough force to batter itself into dust did she suddenly and with a wail of despair and rage come back to her full senses.

She snatched for the hilt of Dragon's Eye and the hilt was all she got, the blade having snapped off. Tilanne whirled toward the exit and saw that it was heaped with rubble, only a narrow gap remaining at the top. She ran at it all the same. She scrabbled up the slope, dislodging several stones and almost sending herself to the bottom in a rockslide, and wormed through the gap with her back scraping against the underside of the arched doorway.

The inrush of air had breathed new life into the smoldering fire. Beams and slabs lay at haphazard angles across a long blazing pit, and the ceiling overhead was streaked with jagged, spreading cracks that sifted dust down onto her.

"Kaledhol, please," she said without realizing she spoke aloud. "If Thy will it is, let me this place escape. Swear to Thee do I that never by my hand shall elven life be lost, and pledge do I always elves to defend."

Tilanne stepped onto the end of the nearest beam and crept out over the expanse of hot orange, all too aware of what a misstep would mean. The wood smoked beneath her boots and she could feel the heat through the soles. Her quick, light breaths turned the lining of her mouth and throat to something that felt as dry and baked-shiny as a pot in the kiln.

As she reached the end of the beam, it dropped with a jolt and she went with it. The heavy end kicked up a shower of sparks and flame, and not hearing her own terrified scream, Tilanne leaped.

She landed on a marble slab. It tilted toward her, the slick surface giving her scant purchase as she slipped inexorably back toward the pit. A chance look upward showed her a dangling lattice of wood. A lunge, a grab, and she was suspended above the inferno as the thin slats cracked under her weight.

With no more prayers and no more screams, her jaw clenched tight, Tilanne swung from hand to hand along the untrustworthy lattice, splinters from it sprinkling her hair. She got her feet over another slab, this one at a steeper angle but textured with sculpted reliefs of Crown Magic runes. Not bothering to worry what spells she might unleash by stepping on the symbols, she scaled it as if it were a rough hillside. She reached the top and saw a clear expanse of hallway leading deeper into the cliff side, and a partially blocked rat-warren of a hallway leading the way she wished to go.

She chose the blocked way, squeezing past and around and under the obstacles. Ahead was daylight, dimmed again by dust and smoke. Her shoulder bumped a beam. Tilanne dove forward as a tremendous deadfall crash jolted the hall, and looked back gasping to see that the beam had missed her by a margin too close to consider.

There was no time to congratulate herself, for the ceiling was quaking and spilling steady streams of gravel. She sprang up and dashed forward although her every muscle strained and hot stitches dug into her side.

The ceiling caved in with a coughing roar, and Tilanne was thrown headlong into the courtyard in the midst of a billowing cloud of dust and soot. She struck with bone-jarring force and was barely able to cover the back of her head before she was overwhelmed by a flying shower of wood and stone.

Gradually, she realized that she was still alive and that the sounds of destruction had diminished, like a thunderstorm passing into the distance. She heard voices calling her name. Dazed and aching, she couldn't answer, could only stay where she was as the others frantically pulled debris off of her.

The next thing she knew, she was being helped to her feet by Corandir and Jedriel. She swayed and they supported her, and she gagged and spat to clear her gritty mouth.

"Falanar?" someone asked.

Tilanne shook her head, tears streaking the dust that coated her face. "Trapped he was, and save him I could not."

A mournful, anguished sob burst from Falana. She fell to her knees, rending her hair and keening her grief, as young Mivana looked on without comprehension and Vanfal cried in his basket.

"For his father's body had he gone, who like mine a soldier had been," Tilanne said to Corandir. A convulsive shudder went through her. "In the casting chamber . . . dead were they, Corandir, dead and unspeakable before even the fire came. What . . . what to them was done?"

"Know do I not," he said, and touched the bandage over his eye. "Resting in the infirmary was I then, when summoned by the Kai were the rest."

As if for the first time, Tilanne looked at him and *saw* him, saw how he was consumed by pain and refusing to show it. She steeled her own spine and pushed the ghastly image of her father from her mind.

Jedriel took her by the upper arms. "Tilanne, that thou shouldst not have done. Too great a risk was it. Lost as well thou could have been."

"True he speaks," Olithiana's voice was shrill. "Better a man had gone."

"Gone would I have," Sahen said huffily. "The chance I had not, so quick and impetuous was she."

Reshelli snorted. "Man, not boy . . . and what of it? At least alive Tilanne emerged. The same would I have done."

"For thee, Reshelli, fine it is thy life to throw away," Olithiana said. "Barren thou art anyway, and thus no true woman. But Tilanne young and vital is, and best shall her people serve as a woman ought. By marrying, by bearing many children our numbers to replenish. Now more than ever, needed is such."

Sahen pounced on that, while Reshelli sputtered in indignation. "And so, plainly, no *Rhunvala* should she become. A *Rhunvala* marries not."

"Kai Terindor wed was," Corandir said. "Died long ago did his wife, but live on still do his children. No law is it."

"Different is it for women," Olithiana said. "Hazardous enough is childbirthing, and moreso if with combat she life and limb endangers. Thus is no woman to arms training permitted."

Reshelli, still fuming, thumped the ground with the butt of her spear. "If so great a proponent of motherhood thou art, why no children yet dost thou have, then?"

"No compassion have any of thee?" Falana stormed into their midst. "Dead lies my son! Unsafe is this place, cursed is this place, and away from it we should before more of us into death my poor Falanar follow. Two children have I yet, and not a moment longer here will I keep them."

"So it is," Tilanne said, although every fiber of her being cried out for a rest. She brushed herself off, only then discovering that somehow she had tucked the broken hilt of her father's sword inside her tunic. "Leave for Jewelgreen we must, and now."

Vennan led the horses, with the children perched in the cart while Ninare walked alongside. Sahen insisted on leading the way, and with Ninthar's help was able to wrestle the heavy gates open enough to admit them. Tilanne was the last one out, and turned to look at the fortress that had been her home for over a dozen years. She would have given much to be able to blink and have it back as it had been, to be able to go to the apartment she shared with her family. To have life be as it always had been, when her most pressing problem was the very one that Olithiana had voiced–which prospective suitor her father would choose for her, and how many of their children would survive. But she did not waste time wishing for the impossible.

"As was thy wish, noble Kai, so shall I do," she promised in a whisper. "Fail thee shall I not. Though know do I that thou might otherwise have wished it, I do pledge thy trust to earn, and that cause to regret thy choice shall thou never have."

* * *

CHAPTER THREE

The land around the fortress had been cleared in a widening ring over the past ten years, as the Horned One's orcs spent their time chopping wood and making desultory efforts at growing their crops – ryegrass, onions, peas, and potatoes. Aside from a few orc-shacks, there were no other signs of civilization except for the road. A crude path, hacked and stamped by the orcs, disappeared off into the Forest of the Many Brooks to the west.

Tilanne had heard that this path led beyond the boundaries of the Emerin, past Greydrake Ravine, and ultimately to the human land called Goldenfields. Her own people had used it occasionally for trading, the orcs more frequently for raiding, but in either case the use was never much and consequently, it was so overgrown as to be almost impassable.

They never would have gotten the cart along it, but fortunately they didn't have to. Another road, this one cut through the woods long ago by the *Morvalan*, wended its way north toward the snowcapped peak of Mount Cauldron.

To follow that road would bring them to Deepwater, once Tilanne's home. There, the black opals were mined and the wyrm-singer could call forth the dragon that dwelled in the bottomless spring-lake that gave the settlement its name. There, Tilanne's sister Forana lived, with her husband and children.

She would have given much to strike out for Deepwater and see her kin again, even if it meant having to bring Forana the dire news. But Deepwater was far by the road, which curved snakelike through and around the wooded granite-boned mountains, and sometimes climbed steeply over them.

The Valley of the Jewelgreen, resting in its gentle meadow, was closer. The way to it was little more than a trail, but it was smooth and grassy and wide enough for the cart. There would be towns in Jewelgreen, towns to take them in and welcome them.

The death of Falanar had been the final blow, snuffing what little of their spirits that had remained. That first night had been spent in a bleak and solemn silence as each of them tried to come to terms with all that had happened. With all that had been lost.

For Tilanne, the dark hours seemed endless. Sleep eluded her like a wily prey-beast. When at last she caught it, she was swallowed by a morass of nightmares.

Rising early, as the night's chill was condensing to dew in the pearly light of the dawn, she stirred the embers of their campfire into renewed life and set about brewing tea. Ninthar rose shortly thereafter and had hot porridge ready by the time the others awakened. Over this simple breakfast she reaffirmed her decision to take Jedriel's advice and make for Jewelgreen.

No one argued, not even Sahen. And so their march had continued, through cool verdant shadow and golden sunlight, serenaded by songbirds. Once, when a summer-fat doe bounded across the path, Reshelli raced after it and brought it down, clumsily but fatally, with her new spear. Standing over her kill, the domestic-turned-huntress shouted triumph to the clear blue sky, and streaked the doe's blood on her cheeks as if she were some barbaric Lenaisian.

Barbaric or not, that did not stop anyone from feasting on the kill. Strangely, the venison did what their carried provisions had not been able to do – it reminded them that they were all still alive, grieving and alone but *alive*. Ninthar roasted the meat to perfection, and Deverall took the small curled horns and fashioned them into a matched pair of rings, which Reshelli wore proudly on her forefingers.

That second night was better, with conversation around the fire and some pairing off – Olithiana and Carenar, of course, but also Reshelli with Corandir and Alarice with Vennan. Seeing Jedriel glance speculatively at her more than once, Tilanne realized that she, too, could have companionship did she so desire.

She was tempted for a moment or two. Jedriel, with his silken firegold hair pulled back in thin braids from his temples and his dark eyes that shone like polished obsidian, was certainly handsome. She had never considered him a prospective lover before, nor seen a hint of interest from him until now. But too many worries consumed her thoughts to allow for such distractions.

Worries . . . Falana watched her remaining children like a hawk, and went into fits of fright if Mivana was out of her sight for even an instant. Sahen was still sullen and unpleasant, though the effort of marching with all of his scavenged swords left him too weary to make trouble.

And Ilantisian . . . he tried to hide it, but it soon became clear that he was ill. He lagged behind, barely able to keep up.

"No," he said when Tilanne inquired. "Fine am I . . . tired only."

"Heat-bright are thine eyes," she said, reaching for his brow. "And flushed is thy skin."

He moved his head away. "Fine am I, in truth."

She persisted and found him fearfully hot to the touch. A qualm fluttered in her heart, for if there was one thing the *Morvalan* dreaded even above the armies of the Mountain King, it was sickness. Especially fever, especially the lethal *kholi* fever.

Tilanne had assisted Vandil enough to know some of the signs. She was relieved when she did not see the telltale crimson fire-roses of *kholi*, but only partially. That symptom might still arise. Yet what was she to do? She could not isolate him from the others, not in this situation. Nor could she have him ride in the cart, for children were most susceptible and weakest.

She had Vennan unhook one of the horses that Ilantisian might ride. With wet compresses and cold teas brewed from medicinal herbs, she did her best to tend him.

No one spoke of it, though the same dread worked within each of them. Tilanne could see it in their eyes when they stopped for a rest. They feared they would never reach Jewelgreen, but she silently vowed that she would see them safely there, even if the cost was her own life.

As they made camp for the third night, Carenar and Corandir approached her. The wounded soldier was mending and in less pain, clearly so as evidenced by his vigorous bed sport with Reshelli the previous evening, but his jaw was tight and his one blue eye was serious as he hunkered down across from Tilanne.

"Carenar feels that followed we are being."

She glanced up at Carenar. Olithiana's husband was thin and diffident, with finespun hair the color of a sunset. Soft-spoken and thoughtful, he did not look like much. But she knew there had to be more to him than showed. He had spent seven years as overseer of the Horned One's orcish troops, answering only to the *Alvalan* known as Donnell Silverhand.

"Elvenkind?" she asked without hope.

"Nay," Carenar said. "Heard have I several times the call of a rock-owl, but not until full dark do they from their lairs stir. When hunting the orcs birdcalls and beast-sounds as signals use. Expected would I not that this way they'd come, but rather west, or south into the mountains." He shrugged. "Mistaken was I."

"A threat to us they may well be," Corandir said. "No love for elves they harbored. Without Silverhand, blood-mad with vengeance for their own, attack us they might."

Tilanne let her gaze roam the camp and knew that even one armed and determined orc could likely make short work of them. "Corandir, thy advice?"

"Fight can I still, if fight I must," he said. "But not as well, and doubt do I that one-eyed as adept with a bow would I be. Some few of the rest, warrior's courage have . . . but optimistic would I not be for our chances, Kor Tilanne."

"And thee, Carenar?"

"Some spells I know," he said. "Spells of pain, that I might Silverhand help the orcs discipline. As a dog the hand with the whip does fear, so did they fear me. But despise me as well."

"Alert we must be," Tilanne said. "Although weary we are, guards at night must we post. All, save the children and Ilantisian, must their turns take. In pairs."

"So be it," Corandir said, with the air of one who would have been doing that all along but hadn't felt it to be his place to mention it.

Tilanne reddened in chagrin, but also in annoyance. How did he expect her to know what to do? She had never aspired to battle. Concern and compassion, rather than bravery, had brought her to the Kai's side that fateful night. Was she to have absorbed the Kai's knowledge as easily as he dropped the chain around her neck?

She let the flash of annoyance pass, for if the fault was anyone's, it was hers. Not Corandir's. *She* had been given this duty, and should have been asking his opinion all along.

So it was that they posted guards, to some mutterings and grumblings but no real complaints. Even those mutterings and grumblings might have been avoided had she told them the reason, but she suspected that the idea they might be hunted by orcs would send them into a panic.

Ilantisian worsened during the night. Tilanne sat up with him until well past midnight, taking away the compresses when they seemed about to steam on his head. By daybreak, he was burning with a hot, sweatless fever. He never descended into delirium, but when speech failed him and all he could do was look up at her with those plaintive eyes, she was reminded of Findaire and Falanar. She had failed both of them, no matter how they silently beseeched her for help. Her resolve strengthened even as she was forced to admit that there was nothing she could do for Ilantisian either. He was so feverish that the horse sidestepped and nickered when they attempted to get him into the saddle. All of Vennan's patience and cunning were needed to hold the steed in place.

They set off again, but hadn't gone far when Sahen, in the lead, halted with a surprised exclamation.

"One more step, *thrulk*, and this spits your gizzard." The harsh utterance was as much glottal bark as spoken words. The language was Thanian, the human speech of the Northlands, though the orc's malformed jaw pushed the sounds out in a strange accent.

Tilanne saw Sahen slowly raise his hands to shoulder-height. An orc blocked the trail in front of him, and several more melted from the underbrush to take up positions of readiness. They were nearly identical in their ugliness, these orcs that had been sent to the fortress by way of the Horned One's magic portal. Lumpy features were covered in yellowish-green skin that somehow looked at once leathery and slick with toad slime. They had low, sloped, beetling brows and massive outjutting shelves of chins, with ivory tusks jutting up from the lower jaws. Their hair was coarse and oily, black or in shades of drab brown. They were almost of a height with the elves, but far wider and bulging with corded muscle.

The leader, being the tallest and most broad-chested, had a dwarf-make crossbow trained on Sahen. The point glittered with deadly promise. A double-bitted axe, tipped with a finial spike of hammered bronze, was strapped across his back. A knife of all serrations and razored edges had been thrust under his belt without benefit of a sheath. Like most of his company, the leader hadn't escaped the fortress unscathed. Dirty bandages showed through rips in his sleeves, and a festering burn scar seethed on the side of his face. His eyes were as dark and sharp as flints poking out of the earth.

"Zorak." Carenar joined Tilanne, his fingers curled in some gesture of sorcery.

A flicker of unease passed over many an orcish face as he moved into view, and one or two shrank back a pace. But the one called Zorak stood firm, and hatred lifted his upper lip away from his tusks.

"*Master* Carenar." He sneered. "You give over your foodstuffs and weapons, and we let you live. You do not, and we have them anyway by striding over your corpses to get them."

"Fled in fright did thy orcs," Carenar said. "Thus did our alliance end. Finished our dealings with the Horned One were when destroyed was the construct and slain were the mages. If neither time nor forethought didst thou take, thy orcs to properly equip, no concern of ours is it."

"Orcs take what we need," Zorak said, with a snarl low in his throat. "You *thrulk-toh* would have given us nothing."

"And still nothing shall we give. Get thee hence and from humans raid thy stores." Carenar raised his hand, which was wreathed in greenish marshfire.

At the sight of it, the orcs murmured and flinched. Even Zorak eyed Carenar with wariness now, rather than contempt. But then, as his flinty gaze flicked over the rest of the *Morvalan*, his sneer widened into a mocking smile.

"You have your hurt-power, but you are one and we are many. These other *thrulk-toh* are soft and helpless. Can you, alone, stop all of us, *Master?* I think not. I think we take your food, one way or another." Zorak's snout of a nose wrinkled. His tusks ground against his upper teeth with a hideous noise. "And her. That one there. The *thrulk* sow with hair like sunshine."

Tilanne did not need to turn to know he meant Alarice, and heard by her startled gasp that she knew it too.

"Why her?" Carenar demanded.

"Because," Zorak said, shifting his crossbow to Carenar's chest, "she . . . reminds me of another . . . and it's that other's fault that I was sent here. I'll settle up that debt with *her*."

"Never," Tilanne said with a courage she did not feel. "Neither provisions nor prisoners shall we yield thee. Go now, and spared might be thy lives."

Zorak bellowed a laugh. "Another sow! And this one with a flapping tongue. I'll have that tongue out, and toast it over the fire for my supper. Who are you, *Master* Carenar, that you let such a she-piglet speak for you?"

"Kor Tilanne am I, by the Kai himself chosen in his stead to lead." Tilanne let her hand come to rest on the hilt of her knife. She couldn't take her gaze from Zorak to look, but she sensed others coming up to stand with her. Reshelli and Corandir first, and Jedriel, and even Alarice with faltering steps as she neared the orc. Sahen, still ahead, tensed like a pantera about to spring.

The crossbow swung to point at Tilanne. She could all too clearly imagine what it would feel like to have that barbed shaft tearing into her flesh. At so close a range, it might even pass through her, shearing a gruesome channel. But she continued staring at the orc, staring him down, challenging him with what she hoped was the cool, confident amethyst of her eyes.

"I'll have what I want," Zorak said, and pulled the trigger.

In that instant, many things happened. A tumult of voices rang out at once, shouts and warnings and battle-cries. Sahen lunged at Zorak, pushing the crossbow up so that the bolt whistled high into the boughs. Carenar's spell flew in a blur of swampy light and engulfed the both of them. Corandir charged the other orcs, sword flashing. Reshelli, with a primal shriek, ran at the nearest and drove her spear at his belly. And Tilanne, knife in hand, rushed toward Sahen.

He and Zorak, glowing green, both writhed on the ground. Elf and orc alike were screaming as if being devoured alive by carrion-wasps. Neither had a mark on him, but such sounds of unendurable pain would have been heard nowhere else but one of the Mountain King's torture chambers.

More crossbows twanged. Carenar howled as one sank deep into his side and another skewered his upper arm. A third hissed through Tilanne's hair, grazing the back of her scalp in a thin, stinging line of fire as she bent toward Sahen. Alarice responded with a magical blast of air that blew two orcs completely off their feet. Corandir was engaged sword-to-sword with a hulking brute whose bald, stubbled head was a rash of blisters and scars. Vennan needed no urging to put his bow to good use, nocking and releasing in a fluid beauty of motion and seating arrow after arrow into their foes. Ilantisian's horse reared at the sudden commotion, and the ailing scribe tumbled from the saddle to lie motionless in the grass. Ninare covered the children with her own body while Falana, impelled by maternal instincts, clouted an orc with a length of wood.

Zorak, shaking off the effects of Carenar's spell, rolled and snatched the axe from his back and came up onto his knees and swung at Tilanne, all in one movement. She avoided the blow with a breath and a promise to spare. Against such a weapon, her knife would be worse than useless, so she cast it aside and seized one of the swords from Sahen's belt. He, still wracked with pain, did not notice.

Holding the heavy sword in both hands, Tilanne backed away from Zorak and circled around to draw him further from Sahen. The orc stalked her, yellowed teeth showing in a malicious grin.

"Skinny she-thing," he said. "Not even worth a *fhokk.*"

Trying not to grunt from the effort, Tilanne raised the sword and brought it down in a clumsy chop. Zorak dodged it easily. Her arms were almost wrenched out of joint. She couldn't stop the blade before it hacked into the earth. The orc planted one boot on it and laughed, and for all her struggles she couldn't pull it out from under him.

He drew back the axe with leisure and anticipation. Tilanne let go the hilt and scrambled away, but tripped and landed atop Sahen, who had lapsed into unconsciousness. She somehow got a hold of another of his swords, but the angle was bad and she couldn't free it from the sheath.

Zorak stood over her, savoring the kill and possibly thinking he'd slay two elves with one strike. As his arms bunched with strength, an arrow pierced his thigh from behind, going through layers of boiled leather and tough orcish hide to emerge partway on the other side. Zorak's leg buckled. The axe blow that would have cleaved Tilanne and Sahen in two instead carved a vicious gash in the dirt.

The sword finally came loose. Tilanne chopped at Zorak's other leg as if trying to fell a sapling. The impact of steel against bone jarred the weapon from her grip, but the damage was done. Zorak crashed down on his side, roaring more in astonishment than pain.

She found her own knife as if by magic and leaped upon the downed orc. Perhaps the Kai might have honorably given him the chance to get to his feet and continue the fight fairly, but the Kai had been armored and trained. So, with only the merest twinge of conscience, Tilanne did her best to slash Zorak's throat.

He divined her intent and ducked his chin, so that the blade scraped along that bony shelf. With a heave of his arms, she was airborne, landing hard on her hip and shoulder. The breath burst out of her in a gust. As he came at her, hunching along on hands and one knee, another of Vennan's arrows found him. The sharp-tipped shaft went clear through Zorak's meaty arm and vanished into the bushes, and Zorak toppled straight toward Tilanne.

Unable to get out of the way, she angled her knife up at him. The pressure of his crushing weight ran him onto it to the crossguard, a gush of blood soaking her as she was caught beneath him. He bit at her, tusks gnashing against teeth only a handspan from her face. She twisted the knife deeper, aware that she was screaming in revulsion and anger.

The orc's huge callused hands found her throat and encircled it. He pinched off her breath. She tried to brace for the sudden brittle crack of her neck. Before it came, Zorak jumped as if from a blow, then went abruptly slack and loose and dead weight, smothering her as he collapsed atop her.

She could not budge him, could do little more than kick her feet helplessly because even her arms were trapped, hands wrapped around the knife-hilt that was jabbing into her stomach like a spike.

But then Jedriel and Alarice were there, managing between them to lift Zorak enough for Tilanne to worm out from under. Drenched in vile orc blood, she got up and almost fell down again from dizziness. Jedriel was there to hold her, and leaning against him while clasping Alarice's hand, Tilanne looked around for the others.

"No," she breathed, as the scene embedded itself forever in her memory.

* * *

Chapter Four

Carenar was dead, impaled by two crossbow bolts and with his head laid open by the edge of a sword for good measure. The orc that had slain him was itself dead, his one-time master's fingers digging into the meat of the orc's shoulders.

Ninthar was slumped against the bole of a tree, head bent as if peering in amazement at the spill of his own entrails that filled his lap. Ilantisian still lay where he had fallen, as did Sahen. Olithiana was also on the ground, but it seemed she had only fainted. Corandir was standing, his forearm pressed into a wound on his side and his sword's point held beneath a captive orc's chin.

Reshelli was splattered in gore from the tips of her ears to the tips of her toes, but appeared to have sustained only scratches. There was a wild, exultant light in her eyes that Tilanne didn't care for at all. For the first time, she wondered if the destruction at the fort might have irreparably harmed Reshelli's mind.

Falana, too, was one about whom Tilanne could harbor similar worries. She still stood over the body of an orc, beating it with her weapon of wood even though it was clear the orc would not be getting up again. With each strike she voiced a savage little noise more suited to an enraged she-pantera. Her daughter regarded this strange apparition of her mother with wide-eyed alarm from over the edge of the cart, resisting Ninare's efforts to shield her vision from the carnage.

Jedriel had a line of blood oozing from a cut on his cheek, but Deverall, Alarice, and Vennan were untouched. So too were the children and Ninare.

Four orcs, in addition to Zorak, were numbered among the dead. The rest had fled, but were hardly unharmed judging by the liberal splashes of blood that marked their trail. The only living orc still among them was Corandir's captive.

"Kaledhol," Tilanne said softly.

"With us indeed was our god," Jedriel said. "Else never could we so few untrained elves have so many battle-ready orcs overcome."

"But behold how costly this victory." Alarice could not herself behold it a moment longer, covering her face.

Jedriel's dark eyes were laden with sorrow. "Costlier still might it have been. Only the greatest of fortunes is it that any of us yet live."

Corandir, barely able to stay on his feet, looked at Tilanne. "This one . . . slain or bound do you wish him?"

"Slain," Tilanne said, without hesitation. "No use have we for captives."

With a curt nod, Corandir plunged his sword through the orc's throat. Reshelli dashed up to help, stabbing her reddened spear into the body, teeth bared in savage joy. With the deed done, Corandir dropped his weapon and clung to the side of the cart. Tilanne hurried to him. When she persuaded him to move his arm, she sucked in a breath as she saw the rent in his chain mail. The gash beneath was long and deep.

"No bandage will for such a wound suffice," he said, not needing to look. "Thy brother would have sewed shut . . ."

"Deverall!" Tilanne called as Corandir went grey and doubled over. She caught him, lowered him to the ground as carefully as she could.

The craftsman came in response to her summons, then blanched when she told him what she wanted him to do. He tried to argue, but Jedriel put his crafter's kit into his hands. The calfskin case was filled with implements of all types, for Deverall's skill was limited to no one specialty. He had chisels for stone sculpting, woodcarver knives, the minute and delicate tools of a jeweler, and a box of fine steel needles and threads in a rainbow of colors.

"Leatherwork thou hast done," Jedriel said. "Cloth thou hast stitched. No different is this."

"A physician he needs," Deverall said, averting his face as Tilanne ripped away the soft cloth shirt beneath Corandir's armor. "Injuries might there be within, and bleeding."

"Likely so there are," Tilanne said. "But sooner he will die if closed this is not. Sew it, and to reach Jewelgreen he might survive."

Alarice brought forth water from the air to lave the site clean. Deverall, unable to muster any more protests, got out his longest and strongest needle and threaded it with sturdy black thread. Tilanne and Jedriel turned Corandir onto his side, and held him in place as Deverall gingerly prodded at the torn edges of skin. His face twisted in a grimace as he poked the needle in. Corandir, still insensate, nonetheless jerked.

Once he'd gotten past the initial jab, Deverall's nervousness deserted him and his hands moved with their customary speed and skill. Eleven small, even stitches closed the wound, reducing the blood to a seeping rather than a streaming. Tilanne covered it with a padding of cloth, and then wrapped a long narrow strip of linen around Corandir's waist.

When there was no more to be done for him, Tilanne returned her attention to the others. Sahen was awake, shaken but no longer suffering the painful effects of Carenar's spell. He stood by Reshelli, listening as she regaled him in vivid detail about the battle. Falana had come out of her own fit of rage enough to be comforting Olithiana, who sat on her heels beside Carenar in stunned shock.

But Ilantisian . . .

Alarice, who knelt by the scribe's side, looked up at Tilanne as she approached. There was such anguish in her wintergreen eyes that it brought Tilanne to a halt.

"His back," Alarice said. "Broken it is . . . his legs he cannot move."

"It is as if gone they were," Ilantisian said in a hoarse croak. "As if severed was I, below my chest."

A strong and not entirely unattractive urge seized Tilanne then, an urge to just throw herself to the grass and give up. Two more elves dead, one crippled, and one sorely hurt . . . and the Jewelgreen still many days away. They would not make it. They would die out here alone, one by one, until finally their bodies simply rotted where they fell.

Alarice touched her hand. "Into the cart I can with my magic lift him."

"Strong enough art thou?"

"Strong enough shall I make myself be."

Although they had only come a short ways from their previous night's camp, there was no discussion of going further on that day. While Reshelli and Sahen stood sentry, Tilanne and Deverall collected wood for a pyre. Ninare and Jedriel found a wild rosebush, and gathered blooms and twigs from it so that the dead would have the proper treatment. Olithiana could not be persuaded to leave Carenar's side until the time came for him to be borne to the pyre. She dissolved into tears, unable even to look as his body was consigned to the rose-scented flames.

With the help of the horses, Vennan dragged the dead orcs back down the trail and tumbled them into a rocky, bramble-filled gully to leave them for the scavengers. They had been carrying little of value except for their weapons and a sampling of coinage of various realms. These, Vennan saved. But the enameled ornaments the orcs wore around their necks on cords, flat disks of dark red with the white image of a bull's head inside an eight-sided design, he left on the bodies.

The night passed slowly, every sound an ominous warning. There was little sleep for any of the elves that night. All of them lay wakeful braced for another attack that never came. Once it was light enough to see clearly, Tilanne gave the order to continue on. Both Ilantisian and Corandir were unfit for walking or riding, so Alarice used her spells to float them into the back of the cart. This did not leave room for most of the children, so Ninare put Mivana and Hastinar onto the other horse and led it by the reins.

They pressed on, leaving that sad spot with its bed of cooled ashes. Tilanne tried to take solace in the knowledge that Carenar and Ninthar were with Kaledhol now, reunited with all who'd died in the fortress.

The path took them up and down rolling hills, into lands where the denser forests had given way to lighter dottings of trees and sun-dappled glades. They could see Mount Cauldron looming to the northwest, and the Forest of the Wandering Lost to the southeast.

Tilanne paused, a shiver going through her as she looked at that dark green, almost black, sea of foliage. The Forest of the Wandering Lost lay in a sunken valley half-ringed by towering mountains that rose in a semicircular range to the south. The carpet of the treetops was flat as a still pond, unbroken by any glimpse of roads or habitations.

Somewhere down there, somewhere beneath those trees and hidden from all outside sight, was the *Odan Rhunvale*. The Citadel of the Basilisk. The castle-temple-home where the *Rhunvala* were trained. The place where their armor and weapons were forged with blackmetal mined from the roots of the Dragonheights, forged by volcano fire, and cooled in the ink-dark River of Time.

Somewhere down there . . . that was where she would have to go.

A thousand fears rose up clamoring in Tilanne's soul. She feared the forest itself and all she'd heard of it – the deadly plants and animals, the paths that shifted as if by magic to lead the unwary into traps. But she also feared the Citadel and its occupants, and what might befall her when she dared venture there.

"Tilanne?"

She gasped, and realized that the rest had gone ahead while she lingered, her gaze drawn as if enspelled to that distant dark forest.

Jedriel peered at her in concern and spoke her name again. "Tilanne, well art thou?"

"Am I, Jedriel?" she asked. "Never in all our history has a woman *Rhunvala* become, and not even a woman yet am I, still only a girl. Of weapons and warfare I know nothing. Why should I to the Citadel go? How can I hope that ever would they find me worthy?"

"Only they, and Kaledhol, can that answer give." He put his hand on her shoulder. "And thee thyself, Tilanne. Chosen by the Kai thou were, but thou art still allowed to choose. If another destiny thou wouldst have, thou needst but say. What was it thou hadst planned to be? A teacher of the young? Still and always are teachers needed. As are wives and mothers. As are *Rhunvala*. For thee it is to decide, Tilanne, how best thy life might our people serve."

"A teacher, a wife, a mother, yes, all of these things had I planned and hoped to be. But . . . to me did this sacred duty come, even if unintended and unmeant. Strive I should to at least prove the Kai's choice, and his memory honor."

"When all the rest of us did cower and hide, thou alone bold enough were Kai Terindor to approach." He ran his finger along the blackmetal chain at the side of her neck, brushing lightly against her skin as he did so. "This token he gave thee, but to keep it or not is now thy decision."

She looked up at him, liking the way the sun turned his hair to living flame and struck darts of blue light from the sapphire teardrops dangling from his earlobes. He was not that much older than her, perhaps forty or forty-five.

"Why is it thou didst never a soldier become?" she asked, falling into step with him as they set off after the others. "Fit and strong thou art, and brave. Wondered long have I, but never dared to ask."

Jedriel looked down at his hands, at the calluses on his fingers that were made by familiarity with quills rather than weapons. "Not for lack of desire was it. My father, his brothers, my mother's brothers, and my brothers all had soldiers been."

"All the more reason –"

"That I should not," he interrupted. "Or such the will of my mother was. Her youngest-born was I. So many of her kin in war had perished that a vow she swore, that spared such a fate should at least her last son be. That one of her sons a chance at long life might have, that she might grandchildren someday see. A promise from my father she extracted, that never would I at arms be tutored, no matter how I might beg. As no talent for crafting or sorcery had I, a scribe I became." He gave a rueful laugh. "Forgotten had she, perhaps, how many women soldiers as husbands prefer."

Tilanne smiled sympathetically, knowing he was right. Every *Morvalan* girl grew up knowing that swordsmen and archers made the most desirable mates. If such were unavailable, weaponsmiths or fortificationists were second-best. If not one of those, a wizard or physician might be sought after, and a huntsman or stonemason of sufficient skill might be deemed an acceptable choice if all else failed. Most other professions – farmers and orchard-tenders and vintners, teachers and scholars and artists – were considered more the province of women. Tilanne knew that Ilantisian had only become a scribe when an accident in the smithy had left him unfit for such grueling work. Deverall the craftsman was *chani*, a male who had little interest in women, and therefore didn't care that his choice of work left him a bachelor.

"Good and kind art thou, Jedriel. Saw did I how well thou consoled Ninare, and how patient with the young ones thou hast been. A fine teacher wouldst thou make. Thy situation the very opposite of mine doth seem."

"Perhaps together we belong," he said, his mouth grinning but his eyes holding hers in a more serious way. "Know do I that never would I have on thy father's list of suitors been, Tilanne, but much is changed now."

"Yes, much is changed. Too much and too soon." Tilanne sighed. "Dead are my father and brothers, so that choice, too, mine own is. But of marriage and families I dare not think, not until I have to the *Odan Rhunvale* gone."

* * *

CHAPTER FIVE

The Valley of the Jewelgreen was a wide, shallow bowl, ringed by low hills and rounded mountains. Two fortresses faced each other across the hazy span of the valley. A stone-paved road between them neatly bisected the valley one direction, while a sparkling ribbon of water flowing from north to south bisected it in the other. At the point where road and river crossed, in a green patchwork of farmlands, orchards and pasturelands, nestled a town.

Reaching this bastion of safety at last was a welcome blessing to Tilanne's weary, grieving band of survivors. They arrived at the westernmost of the two fortresses just before twilight, and soldiers rushed out to meet them.

Tilanne could have wept with relief as she felt the burden of responsibility being lifted from her. No more wilderness. No more constant dread that at any moment more orcs might burst from concealment and finish what they'd started. No more fear that she would be wakened in the night with the news that either Ilantisian or Corandir had succumbed to death, or that someone else had been hurt or fallen ill.

The Jewelgreen. They had made it. Elves surrounded them, a babble of questions and concerned voices. Someone summoned a physician. Someone took charge of the horses. Someone else led the children away to feed and clean them.

"Led us did she," Reshelli said.

Tilanne turned, and found herself facing the fortress commander. He was tall and striking, with dark hair worn short in the military style and eyes the color of kofa. His uniform was red and black, cut at severe angles. The well-worn hilt of a businesslike sword was at his hip.

"Commander," Tilanne said.

His gaze moved past her and sought out the men in their party, particularly Vennan and Jedriel. "True is it, what this spearmaid claims? A girl doth lead you?"

Sahen jutted his chin and looked about to say something, but Alarice quelled him with a severe look.

"Such was I by Kai Terindor bade to do," Tilanne said, and held up the ruby basilisk.

Ripples of consternation and awe passed among the soldiers. The commander reached out suddenly, as if he meant to snatch it from her and cry blasphemy, and Tilanne closed her hand around it.

"Kai *Terindor?*" the commander said as if he'd misheard. "Terindor Reyes?"

"Given this was I by a *Rhunvala*, and not until by a *Rhunvala* am I so ordered, shall I remove it," she said, willing her voice to stay steady.

"So it was," Jedriel said. "When fell did Cliffcave, and dead or dying all others were, did the Kai this young woman as his successor choose."

With dismal foreboding, Tilanne knew that she was going to be encountering this very same situation in every town and at every fortress from here on out. The prospect was daunting enough to almost make her change her mind. How much easier it would have been to remove the chain, give it to the commander, and go back to being Tilanne Murres rather than Kor Tilanne! But she did not do it, could not do it. Nor did she, down deep at the core of her heart, truly want to. If it was Kaledhol's will that she become *Rhunvala*, so be it . . . and if it was Kaledhol's will that she not, so be that also.

"Later, of more of this shall we speak," the commander decided. He began issuing sharp orders to his men.

With all haste and courtesy, the refugees were shown to a building where they might rest. Food was brought and offered, a simple meal of bread, jam, salted fish, and cheese. Soldier fare. But after so many days of living off of their meager provisions, augmented by whatever game Vennan and Reshelli had been able to catch or what fruits and berries were in season, soldier fare was as good as any banquet. Best of all, there was wine. The wine cellar at Cliffcave had been buried beyond reach, and they'd been making do with water. To have wine again, the sweet dark-violet or hearty indigo vintages of the Valley of the Growing Vines, was a pleasure above all others.

Before she could let herself sit down and enjoy the meal, Tilanne made sure the others were doing well. Corandir and Ilantisian were at the physician's home, and the matronly aunt of the commander had taken Ninare and the other children under her wing. This left Falana to stay with Olithiana, the two of them having become close as sisters in their shared grief . . . though they did carry on sometimes as if only *they* had lost loved ones, when there were none among them who hadn't.

Sahen disdained relaxing, strutting about the fortress bragging to all who would listen about the battle with the orcs. Tilanne noticed how he always seemed to neglect to mention that he'd been smote by Carenar's spell the entire time, and hadn't struck a single blow. Yet he always described how Tilanne had been trapped beneath Zorak's corpse, implying that *he* had killed the orc and she had merely gotten in the way. It did not matter much to Tilanne. Sahen could say whatever he wished, but in the end, he would have to stand before Kaledhol as all *Morvalan* ultimately did. At that moment, all of his life's deeds would be made clear, and Kaledhol would decide the fate of his soul.

Like the food, the beds were simple fare. But they were indoors, and raised off the ground, and there were blankets of laundered Singing Valley wool for each of them to offset the evening chill. Tilanne slept better than she had since before the intruders came to Cliffcave, and woke refreshed.

After washing up and making herself presentable the next morning – though still in trousers and tunic rather than a skirt – she went to the commander's office. In this small closet of a room tucked between the kitchen and the barracks, the only nod to luxury was a fine leather chair.

Commander Ellorn folded his hands on the cluttered desktop and studied her, saying nothing. Tilanne did not presume to ask for a seat but stood as expectantly as any soldier, waiting to be asked a question.

The silence spun out and became some sort of contest of wills. Tilanne thought of the gem around her neck and took strength from that, refusing to be intimidated.

From across the courtyard, she could hear the rhythmic tones of a smith shaping a piece of metal, perhaps a sword blade. She counted the strikes, each with so regular an interval between them that it might have been the tolling of some odd clock.

Fifty musical clangs had drifted through the air when Commander Ellorn relented, and spoke. "So," he said. "To soldiery thou wouldst presume."

"Nothing do I presume, Commander. Although a soldier my father was, and one of my brothers also, never did I to such a position aspire. Set upon me was this task, and to my best of abilities shall I see it to the end."

"What end? To safety thou hast thy survivors brought, and so thy task is done."

"The Kai did Kor Tilanne name me," she said. "Until unsaid by other *Rhunvala*, until taken back by them is that name, to his words shall I abide."

"Some of what at Cliffcave happened have I been told. I would from thee hear it as well. Sit."

She lowered herself into a chair and relayed to him what she knew of the goings-on of those last few days. She told him what she had heard about the intruders, how the *Alvalan* had eluded Donnell Silverhand only to return and slay him, how the casting chamber had exploded, what the Kai had said to her, how the orckin had fought and bested the Kai. She told him what had come after, of the deaths of Findaire and Falanar, and the fight with Zorak's orcs. When she had finished, she rested her hands on her knees and waited.

"For how much of this dost thou blame thyself?" he asked.

Tilanne blinked at him. "The best that I could do, untutored as I am, I did. To save them, to help them, I tried. Anything would I have given, better to have done."

Commander Ellorn rose and went to a cabinet that barely fit in the small corner of the room. He opened it, and removed a long oilcloth-wrapped shape, which he placed in Tilanne's hands.

"My sword this was when as a squire I trained," he said. "Thine it is now, if to wield and to use it you wish to learn."

Tilanne unfolded the oilcloth and admired the old, well-used weapon. It was not fancy, not grand. The scabbard was plain leather rubbed shiny in places, and the steel fittings were scratched and dull. The hilt was unadorned, bound in leather and wire. The blade itself was nicked and pitted. But it was *hers*, given to her by a commander, and in that instant no weapon could have been more splendid.

"To study arms and swordplay, you will permit me?"

"Permit thee? Stop thee I could not, if thy will it was. If truly a Kor thou art, then equal in rank to a fort commander or Circle mage thou art as well. Only a Master of the Circle, or a full *Rhunvala* or *Dhanvala*, would thee outrank."

She sat not quite able to speak, the sword resting across her lap.

"The youth Sahen," Ellorn said. "Told am I that a squire-general he was. A post here he wishes to accept, if thy permission he has."

"*My* permission?"

"Nominally, under thy command is."

Tilanne had never given a moment's thought to rank, or commands. Or to having any say over what another did with his or her life. Could she truly have gone from being a girl whose future depended on her father's whim in choosing a suitor, to being able to give or withhold permission over where a squire was to serve? Small wonder Sahen had been so outraged! A sense of whirling trepidation swept over her, and only by biting hard on her lower lip was she able to gather her wits enough to speak.

"All the best I wish Sahen. Never would I from such an opportunity keep him. If *thy* will it is to have him."

A tight smile flitted across Ellorn's stern face. "Arrogant and outspoken he is, and filled overly with pride. If ever a proper soldier he is to become, these traits must from him be purged. Known am I for a firm hand at discipline having."

She wanted to ask if Sahen knew any of that. Would it make a difference to him? Or was he so eager to get out from under the command of a lowly girl that he would agree to anything and leap at any chance, sight unseen?

"If willing is he and willing are thee, no objections have I," she said. She thought back to when she had been no more than seven, and her elder brother Fordanne had gone off to his first post, and dredged from her memory what her father had said and done. Because if she had such power over Sahen's fate, surely she had other responsibilities for it too. "Under thy banner accept him, with my blessing. Weapons he has already, and for armor and his keeping I shall a purse of silver provide."

Commander Ellorn's eyebrow arched appreciatively. "Accepted."

The announcement was made later that day, and everyone congratulated Sahen on his good fortune. He, puffed with conceit, could hardly wait to exchange his travel-worn clothes for a new uniform.

That night Tilanne visited the physician's quarters to see Ilantisian and Corandir. She found the scribe recovering from his fever, propped up in bed with a writing-desk balanced across his lap. Although his legs were still paralyzed, he had the use of both arms and his flowing script had not suffered, and the commander's wife had wasted no time enlisting his aid in catching up on her letters to her extensive family.

"Decided I have," she said, sitting on a stool between him and Corandir. "The Kai's legacy shall I carry out, as best I am able."

"Well it is," Corandir said. The fortress physician had reopened his wound, drained and cleaned it, then packed it with medicinal herbs. The bandage over his missing eye had also been changed for a smaller one. "Proud would thy father be, although dare I say some surprised."

"Surprised am I also," Tilanne said. "But right it feels."

"How soon dost thou mean to leave?" Ilantisian asked.

"Soon. Not large, nor well-stocked enough is this fortress to so many of us hold, and the town proper is but an easy day's journey. Came did I to inquire what thy wishes were."

"Here must I a while more remain," Corandir said. "Until fit to travel am I, and the physician says that some ten days or more it may be. Spread and burrowed deep had the infection, and lucky am I that uncorrupted were my organs."

"This great girdle," Ilantisian said, rapping on the birch bark that had been molded damp around his body from shoulder blades to hips and left to harden as it dried, "cannot my broken spine mend, but neither does it from being moved prevent me. If abed must I lie, rather in a town than a fortress would I be."

The next morning, Tilanne bade farewell to Commander Ellorn and his wife, to Corandir and Sahen and the rest of the soldiers. With the sword the commander had given her strapped to her waist, she led her small procession out through the gates and into the Valley of the Jewelgreen. The day gloriously golden, the sun shining beatific warmth on the waving plains of tall emerald grass. They had done much of their traveling under tree-shade, so Tilanne wasn't the only one to tip her head back and revel in the clean light falling on her face.

"Raised was I in Jewelgreen," Jedriel said, walking beside her. "My brother Jedren there is captain of the town."

"Willing he might be, a girl in swordplay to instruct?" Tilanne asked.

"Ask him shall I."

She glanced down at the scabbard beating softly against her hip with each step. "So little of the *Rhunvala* do I know. Is there anything more, Jedriel, that thou hast heard and canst tell me?"

To either side of the road, the grass rose to almost chest-height. Jedriel extended his arm and riffled the tall sheaves of it as he passed. "Little too do I know. Only that even more to the god than we are they sworn, and in them is Kaledhol's duality made one. The Protector, the Destroyer. As is fire itself. As is the basilisk, His sign. Fierce is that creature in defense of its own, deadly to all others."

"Fatal is its gaze, to all save its own kind," Tilanne said, conscious of the smooth, hard press of the jewel within her tunic.

Behind them, Reshelli raced after a brace of pheasants that their passage had flushed from hiding. She went jabbing with her spear and laughing maniacally as she tore through the grass and left a trampled trail in her wake. She missed both fowl, and lost them, and was still laughing when she returned to the road.

They continued on, deeper into the valley, soon reaching the farm-fields and orchards. On such a bright and warm summer's day, many elves were out at work and came to meet them curiously.

The town, despite being snug in a mountain-ringed valley, despite having its only passes guarded by forts, was walled and guarded as stoutly as if it had been alone and out in the open on the plains. It was laid out as many such settlements were, in concentric circles with wide avenues and rows of shops and lodgings, all centered around a temple. Unlike at the fortress, there was ample space to take in refugees. The optimistic ancestors who had designed and constructed it had not foreseen what a constant struggle it would be for the *Morvalan* to even maintain, let alone increase, their numbers.

Dusk had come by the time Tilanne saw to it that the others were housed in vacant chambers, and fed from the communal food-stores. Clothing, too, and other goods were made available to them.

"Enough," Alarice said when Tilanne began pondering how best to go about finding adoptive parents for the young orphaned boys. "Tomorrow or another day can it be done. For tonight, with Falana they are."

"And Ilantisian, him to a physician I must see –"

"Already done is it. We are all of us well settled, save thee. To sanctuary, thou hast seen us safe.

Absolved now is thy responsibility. To us, at least."

Looking into Alarice's pale green eyes, Tilanne realized it was true. She had brought them to safety, although not without losses. But the majority of them had made it, and now their fate and their future did not rest upon her shoulders any more.

Yet strangely, it wasn't as comforting as she might have thought. Without all of them to worry about, she was entirely freed to face the prospect of the *rest* of her responsibilities. The rest of the duty and inheritance the Kai had left to her.

She was too tired to think on it more. Embracing Alarice, Tilanne whispered her thanks and made her way to one of the unoccupied single-room dwellings.

Built connected in thick-walled rows as they were, the lodgings had only arrow slits for windows, and iron bound doors that could be barred. In such nice weather, though, most of the people of Jewelgreen left their doors propped open that breezes might circulate. She passed several families preparing or eating or cleaning up their evening meals, smiling at the sight of children playing in the cool shade of the avenues.

The room she had chosen wasn't terribly large, and had only a few simple furnishings. There was a rope bed with carved wooden posts, the empty skin of the leather mattress-bag hanging over the end. A small round table was flanked by two chairs. A washstand and basin stood beneath a polished-steel mirror affixed to the wall. The hearth was lined in baked ceramic tiles, making an eye-pleasing pattern of colors.

Even as she was setting down the satchel full of items she'd taken from the communal stores, a brisk tap sounded on the open door. A pair of youngsters, a boy and a girl so closely resembling each other that they had to be siblings, came in carrying a bale of dried grass between them.

"For thy bed-stuffing, Kor Tilanne," the boy said, staring in awe at the ruby resting on her tunic.

"Fill it for thee, gladly shall we do," the girl added shyly.

"A kindly act that would be of thee," Tilanne said.

Working together efficiently, they broke apart the bale and stuffed the soft, sweet-smelling grass into the mattress and heaved it onto the bed frame. She had two blankets – a light one of quilted silk, a heavier one of wool – and spread them on the bed. From the satchel, she removed a pouch of dragonspice soap-powder, a pewter drinking mug, half a loaf of bread, a wedge of sharp cheese, a jar of fruit-preserves, a full wineskin, a comb, a washrag, and a change of clothes, all of which the communal stores had provided.

She was tired, and eager to crawl into that fragrant bed and pull the blankets high. This might be the first fully restful sleep she'd had since the night before Cliffcave had burned. But first, unconcerned about passers-by and the open doors, Tilanne undressed and wrapped herself in a thin linen shift, and walked along the inner avenue until she found the bath-house.

Despite the lateness of the hour, she could hear voices and splashing coming from within. As she entered, warm steamy air enveloped her. Several other elves were relaxing along the shallow edges, nibbling at fruit and sipping at wine as they chatted. A few stood waist-deep in the places where the currents flowed most strongly, lathering and rinsing. One or two, out in the deepest center, swam or floated or climbed onto flat-topped marble pillars to jump and dive.

Tilanne slipped out of her shift and, wearing only the blackmetal chain with the ruby basilisk, descended the steps into the water. She was very aware of being watched, of being talked about in low tones and whispers.

She paid them no mind. They had good reason to talk, and she knew that had the situation been otherwise, she would have been doing the same. All she cared about now was how good the water felt, liquid warmth massaging the tension from her bones and muscles. She waded out until it reached her shoulders, and tipped her head back to thoroughly wet her hair.

There had not been occasion for a proper bath since leaving Cliffcave. They had been forced to make do with stream water, and what few spells of cleaning that Ninthar, Reshelli, and Alarice knew. Though the cleaning spells were powerful, and would have long since rid her of the residues of battle, Tilanne still imagined she could smell soot and blood caked into her hair.

She scrubbed with her washrag and the foaming, gritty paste of wetted dragonspice until her skin was tingling. She scoured her hair and used her fingers to work the snarls from its dark length. At last, finally feeling clean, she sank to her chin in the current and let the water course around her.

Gradually, the other elves drifted off, until only Tilanne remained. She swam a bit, then floated on her back and watched the ripples of reflected magelights playing on the arched marble ceiling.

Then, obeying some impulse she didn't understand, she closed her eyes and just drifted there, alone in the darkness of her mind. The sounds, the echoing lap of water on the rim, the gentle susurration of the hidden currents, first seemed magnified and then faded away, barely impinging on her consciousness. She felt as if she were suspended in nothingness, apart from the world, turning inward.

Her breathing slowed, and the thump of her heart likewise slowed. And at once it didn't seem she was aware of either. Not of her breathing, not of her heartbeat. She should have been startled, should have gasped, but Tilanne remained curiously calm.

And then, light.

Her eyes remained shut, but she saw light. Strange auras in colors for which she lacked names. As she concentrated on them, she saw their source. They welled from within an uneven spire of rock crystal, flickering over a base of rough stone.

"Tilanne."

* * *

Chapter Six

"Tilanne."

The voice did not speak her name, but intoned it. Invoked it.

Tilanne attempted to sit up, forgetting that she was floating in the deep center of the pool. She submerged, choking on a mouthful of water, and thrashed until she regained her wits and control of her limbs.

Swimming to the nearest pillar, she pulled herself out, and only then saw what she'd already known – she was still alone in the bath-house.

But she had been called. A voice had spoken her name.

Even if she'd wished to, she could not deny that call.

She dove from the pillar, swam to the edge, and emerged from the pool. A row of dragon-head sculptures jutted from one of the walls. When she stood before the gaping jaws, a gust of warm air came out, drying her skin. She combed her still-damp hair, letting it fall free about her shoulders, and put on her shift.

Barefoot, she left the bath-house, and realized at once that it was far later than it should have been. How long had she floated, unaware, basking in the unseen light from that strange crystal? By the position of the stars, and the sleeping silence that reigned in Jewelgreen, she knew it must have been long indeed.

Only the night-watch guards were about, patrolling the walls with a vigilance that would have been no different if they were on one of the border fortresses standing between the Mountain Kingdom and the rest of the *Morvalan* lands. The fact that they were in this spot, defended and safe, was no excuse for shirking. As their attention was focused outward, none of them noticed her as she left the bath-house, returned first to her room and then crossed the inner avenue.

She approached the temple of Kaledhol, the silver moon's radiance throwing her shadow on the wall. The tall, slim, black image paced her, wrapped in a diffuse cloud of linen as the moonlight shone through her shift, and its shadow-hand reached out for her own as she pushed the door open.

Within, the temple was somehow both humble and grand. The room was a square, windowless box, the walls unadorned stone and the floor herringboned of ebony and cherrywood. Directly at the center, a circle of obsidian pillars supported a domed rotunda over a circle of mosaic floor.

The inner surface of the dome was painted with a stormy sky. The suggestions of shapes and figures within the roiling black clouds showed an armored elven form holding fierce dragons at bay. The mosaic was all in red, black, and silver. It depicted basilisks, a double line of them, head to tail and gripping claws, so as to form a twisting chain around the edge.

At the center, beneath the dome and amid the pillars, was a circle was a raw chunk of stone half Tilanne's height. A tall, jagged crystal rose from its top, pointing up at the undercurve of the dome. The crystal was dark, brooding. But as she entered, violet and amber sparks twinkled within its smoky core.

Part of the stone in which the crystal was set jutted out in a vaguely rounded shelf, and that part alone was smoothed into a satiny basin.

Tilanne raised her hands. Cupped in them, winking dim fire, was the Dragon's Eye that she had pried from the hilt of her dead father's broken sword. She had gone back to her room to fetch it, obeying the same half-understood impulse that had led her here in the first place. Perhaps it was even the same impulse that had brought her to Kai Terindor.

She knelt, the mosaic cold and pebbly against her bare knees, and gazed into the crystal.

"Kaledhol the Protector, Kaledhol the Destroyer," she said. "Guardian, Undoer, Defender, Avenger. God of my people, unto Thee am I pledged. Unto Thee this token I bring, as offering. Accept of it, accept of me, and by Thy will I shall all my days and nights to Thee be sworn and dutiful."

She kissed the gem, and placed it upon the rounded altar shelf. As she did so, more lights came alive within the crystal, whirling and dancing, fireflies of blood-red, swampfire green, indigo, the burnt orange of the sunset. From somewhere, nowhere, everywhere, there issued a deep vibrant humming that penetrated Tilanne's bones and made her very soul shake in sympathy.

Her pulse was racing, racing. Her breath came in quick gasps. Her nerves quivered with energy. And yet she felt utterly calm, utterly at peace.

Now the light shining from the crystal was all one hue, the dusky wine-red of roses. The color that to the *Alvalan* meant death, and mourning. But to the *Morvalan*, it was strength, the strength of their people, the strength of their living blood.

Brighter, brighter, that glow, and brighter still, until tears leaked from Tilanne's eyes, but she did not close them. Did not look away. For in the most intense moment of that rose-red brilliance, the Dragon's Eye vanished.

Gone.

Taken.

Accepted.

Kaledhol had accepted her offering and taken it unto Himself.

"Kaledhol," Tilanne said, clutching the ruby around her neck. "If truly Thy will it is that *Rhunvala* I should become, I pray some sign to give unto me. Not for all the world would I Thee offend, and presume too much."

The hard, lifeless jewel moved against her palm. Tilanne looked down as it writhed and twitched. Its hard, smooth surface gave way to a scaled hide and a warm, living body. The miniature, scarlet basilisk craned its neck, looking up. Before she could think to close her own eyes or look away, its gaze had fixed on hers.

She stared, transfixed and oddly feeling no fear. The creature scuttled around in her palm, vestigial wings fluttering along its back, long tail twining between her fingers.

The tiny basilisk looked up at her again, and still Tilanne was able to meet its gaze without fear, without pain, without death. And then, after cocking its head as if to be sure it had her attention, it nipped the tender pad of her thumb.

Tilanne cried out as the diminutive needle-teeth pierced her flesh. She jerked her hand away, and the basilisk swung on the blackmetal chain to bump into her chest. She grabbed at it, hoping to get it away from her skin before it could bite her again . . .

. . . and it was a ruby.

Gemstone. Lifeless. Yet twin droplets beaded her thumb, as red as the ruby itself.

"Thy will be done, Kaledhol," Tilanne whispered.

She pressed her bloody thumb against the crystal, leaving an oval print. The blood hissed on a surface turned suddenly and searingly hot. Tilanne drew back with a cry. The two tiny wounds were cauterized, and the smear of her blood was charred black.

She stood, and for the first time since Kai Terindor had summoned her to him, finally and truly felt that this *was* what was meant to be. The pact was sealed. The oaths would be kept.

"Kor Tilanne am I," she said. "And by Thy will, one day shall I Kai Tilanne be."

So saying, she bowed before the crystal, and left the temple.

She returned to her room, noting that the hour had grown even later. Somehow, most of the night had passed while she was in the bath-house and the temple, and the morning star already glimmered on the eastern horizon. She closed the doors to her dwelling and slid between the blankets.

Sleep found her in a strange place, standing alone on a high tower. The sky overhead was an inverted blue bowl stretching to the golden haze of the horizons, and the unobstructed view filled Tilanne's heart with an unknowable fear. No trees, no mountains, cradled her in a sheltering, safe embrace. All was openness, endlessness.

Below her, a great and empty city sprawled in ruins. Once-proud spires lay in pieces. Parks and gardens were smoldering heaps of ash. Cracked stone walls bore scars that suggested gilded plates had been stripped from them. Entire buildings were broken apart, like eggshells, that something had split to dig out the contents.

Only scavenger birds and low beasts poked among the wreckage. Far in the distance, a dusty plume rose from the body of the vast plains. Other trails, marks of hasty flight, stretched out from the gates.

Even in her dream, she knew what she beheld. Govannisan, the Golden City, ancient home of the elves and dwarves at a time when the Elder Races had lived and worked as friends. Until their wealth had drawn the jealous, greedy fury of the dragons down upon them. Destroying the city. Scattering the survivors.

And forever thereafter, blaming Him for failing to protect them, all other elves but the *Morvalan* had turned their backs on Kaledhol, and stricken even the name of a god from their Book of Lists.

* * *

Chapter Seven

Tilanne arose the next day with a surety of purpose that she had never known before, not once in her life. Others could see it on her. She could even see it herself, when she regarded her face in the polished steel of her mirror. It was her face, the same violet eyes looking back at her, but she seemed to have changed somehow. Grown, perhaps.

Doubt was gone. Uncertainty was no more. There had never been any question of accepting the destiny the Kai had so suddenly dropped into her lap, but that first morning, and each morning thereafter, she woke feeling the rightness of this new path.

Already, the survivors from Cliffcave were settling in, making themselves useful, finding things to do. Vennan befriended several sling-hunters who ranged the valley and foothills in search of game. Deverall could have had his pick of the local crafters to work with. Alarice decided she was willing to change her emphasis from Crown to Scepter and accept an offered apprenticeship with Jewelgreen's resident Scepter Mage. There was no shortage of families willing to take in the orphaned children. Most of all, there was no shortage of eligible men who would be waiting for Olithiana and Falana to finish their time of mourning . . . or be waiting for Reshelli to choose a husband, or for Ninare to reach marriageable age. Here, as in most settlements, unmarried women of childbearing years were eagerly sought after. They would not merely be welcomed, but encouraged, to stay.

Tilanne was very aware of the way gazes followed her, as well. They were not quite the same as the looks the ones the others drew. Word of her unusual circumstances had spread through Jewelgreen. No one would come right out and ask if she had taken leave of her senses, but what could she be thinking? A girl her age, ripe for a husband and children? Seeking to become *Rhunvala*?

She felt their skepticism, understood it all too well.

But she did not let that stop her, some few days later, from seeking out Jedriel. She found him with Ilantisian in the lodging chamber they shared. They were in the midst of some argument when she walked in, and both broke off to turn to her, appealing for her intervention.

Jedriel caught sight of Tilanne and rolled his eyes thankfully. "Perhaps to thee, he might listen. Unable am I to convince him that more rest he needs and not yet from the fever is he recovered. Out and about he would go, in that contraption he bade Deverall to build."

The contraption in question was a chair fitted with wheels and footrests, so that Ilantisian could propel himself around the room with his capable arms. "Refuse do I," he said, "like an invalid to be treated! If a useless burden on my people am I to be, better that thou thy sword take up, Tilanne, and through my heart run it."

"That could I never do," Tilanne said. "Yet right also is Jedriel. No rush is there. Barely just arrived have we."

In the end, the argument was won not when Ilantisian agreed, but when his fatigue caught up with him. He fell asleep sitting up in the wheeled chair, and it took both Tilanne and Jedriel to ease him back into bed without waking him. Once that was done, Jedriel permitted himself a grin, and mimed wiping sweat from his brow as he and Tilanne went out.

"Glad am I for thy timely arrival," he said. "Ever more difficult and obstinate has he been."

"Well it is that his spirit and strength he keeps despite his infirmity," she said. "Too easy would it be for him into blackest despair to fall."

"And far worse had he a soldier been." Jedriel paused to watch a pack of children run by, Hastinar among them. "Even before, when he a smith was, and injured, his spirits he kept high. Resilient is he."

"As are we all, as we all must be," Tilanne said. "No good of brooding comes, and while grieving must be done, with living must it not interfere."

"And thee, Tilanne? To thy course, thou art set?"

"I am. Kaledhol my offerings have accepted, and thrice now of the Lost City have I dreamt. Thus, Jedriel, if thou wouldst, I would with thy brother meet."

She sensed a reticence in him, but he nodded.

The main garrison for the town watch stood on the easterly side of town. A fenced-off yard was bordered on three sides by the barracks, the armory and the captain's lodging. At mid-morning, the yard was bare except for an elderly domestic. Despite having one lame arm, he handled a broom adeptly as he swept dust and windblown leaves from the packed dirt surface.

As Tilanne and Jedriel drew near, the door to the captain's lodging opened and a man stepped out. He bore such a striking resemblance to Jedriel that Tilanne would have known their blood bond even had she not been forewarned. But where Jedriel was lean and slight of build, Captain Jedren's profession was proclaimed in his broad shoulders, in his stance, and in his precise, controlled manner of movement.

The brothers shared the same honey-and-flame hair, though Jedren's was worn short to better fit beneath a helm. His eyes were not the piercing obsidian of Jedriel's, but were blue-grey with darker striations. An old, pale scar ran along his jaw line, from the lobe of his ear to the ball of his chin. He wore a hoop of polished grey-black stone in one earlobe, on the side opposite the scar.

He descended the front steps to meet them. "Greetings, little brother. Come at last to visit, have thee?"

"Come at last. Jedren, might I Kor Tilanne present?"

Tilanne, expecting a less-than-cordial reception, was startled when Jedren grasped her hand in a warrior's greeting.

"Well met indeed," he said. "Of thee, much have I already heard."

"Then perhaps thou might know what I would of thee request," Tilanne said.

"Kor Tilanne, at thy service am I." He had not released her hand. The pressure of his grip somehow changed, manacling her wrist. And the quality of his gaze changed as well, boldly assessing her.

She caught a flicker of reaction on Jedriel's face, quickly masked. There and gone before she could be certain of what it was. Anger? Resignation? Jealousy? Resentment? It was as if he'd seen this moment played out many a time before.

"Commander Ellorn this sword gave unto me." Using her words as an excuse, she freed her hand and patted the weapon at her hip. "But how to use it, I know not. If I am to the *Odan Rhunvale* to go, prefer would I at least something of armsmanship to know. Wilt thou the benefit of instruction grant me?"

"Gladly would I instruct thee . . . and in *all* things," Jedren said, raising an eyebrow while the hint of a smile played about the corners of his mouth. "I doubt not that an excellent student I'll find thee."

Nonplussed, Tilanne glanced at Jedriel, but he was staring down at his ink-stained hands with a faint scowl. The set of his shoulders was stiff. Clearly, he did not care for his brother's flirtatious attentions toward Tilanne. She did not care much for it herself. She should have been flattered, of course. He was the captain of a garrison, an accomplished swordsman, handsome and fit. But she was not here for the purpose of flirtation.

"I charge thee, Captain, to as strict with me as thou wouldst with any other student be. No quarter show me because a girl I am, and no undue accord give me because this basilisk I wear."

Jedren took a long, re-evaluating look at her. His smile turned a bit more sly. If he was surprised, or disappointed by her lack of reaction, he did not show it. "When wouldst thou thy training begin?"

"Even now, if time thou hast."

"So be it. Brother, wilt thou stay?" There was a challenge and more than a hint of mockery in his tone. "To watch?"

Jedriel bristled a little. "If Kor Tilanne objects not."

"No objections have I," she said.

Jedren's smile widened, but the warmth of it did not reach his eyes. They had gone chilly and slate-grey. He called out, "Jedina!"

At the summons, a wisp of an elfmaid popped her head from an upper window. "Yes, *Vala?*" The same red-gold hair her father and uncle shared crowned her as well, as a tumble of loose ringlets hanging nearly to her waist.

"Jedina, Kor Tilanne this is. To the armory show her, that she might a suit of quilting find, and practice blades."

"At once, *Vala*." She disappeared from the window.

"How grown she is," Jedriel said. "And so like her mother she looks. But for her hair, Helina reborn she could be."

"Yes, very like her mother she is, in all ways. Excepting Helina's willfulness. That, my Jedina lacks. A fine and obedient daughter is she."

"Uncle Jedriel!" The girl scampered out to them. She must have been nearly twenty but looked far younger. She stood on tiptoe and still could not reach Jedriel's cheek until he bent to let her kiss it. She flung her slim arms around him. "Heard had I that home thou'd come!"

Jedriel clung to her for a moment, then set her back and patted her affectionately on both shoulders. "Jedina, *tashti.* Barely more than an infant when for Cliffcave I left, and now look at thee!"

"Time enough later for these reunions shall there be," Captain Jedren said. "A task I've set thee, child. About it be, at once."

The girl approached Tilanne, shyly regarding her with wide-eyed awe. "Truly a Kor thou art?"

"Truly." Tilanne showed her the ruby, which made Jedina's dark eyes widen further.

"Heard such had I, but believed it I did not," she said as she led Tilanne toward the armory. "How came such a thing to be?"

Tilanne told her of it, while Jedina moved around the interior of the well-stocked room. The shelves were laden with sheathed swords and knives, bundles of arrows, oilcloth wrapped bows, and armor in all descriptions. The quilting, as it was called, was an outfit of padded cloth, the trousers snug with laces along the cuffs, the tunic long-sleeved and high-collared, with a hem that fell to midway down Tilanne's thighs. Over the tunic, Jedina had Tilanne strap on a breastplate of soft leather. There were knee-high boots and flared gloves to match. A leather-and-quilting full-helm that covered her face except for a cloverleaf cutout through which her eyes and mouth were exposed. She changed into the bulky, cumbersome stuff, feeling a bit silly. Her limbs seemed clumsy, thick, and hard to move. But she knew that this was nothing compared to the weight and constriction of full armor, and she had better get used to it.

"So exciting it is," Jedina said. "A woman, *Rhunvala!* Never did I think the likes to see, and especially not by my own father being taught! Told me, did he ever, that war the province of men alone was."

"And for the most part, right he is," Tilanne said. "Not by my choosing was this, but as come to me it has, to be worthy of it shall I strive."

Though shields were not commonly used, neither were they unknown. Since Kai Terindor had favored one, Tilanne supposed that she ought to as well. She chose one that was far smaller than the one she'd carried for Kai Terindor. Before the orckin had landed a blow on it that nearly broke both of her arms.

The practice weapons were of wood as well, soft willow shaped around a core of ironwood to give proper weight. Blows from them might not kill, but would surely be bruising enough. That much, Tilanne knew from her own father. Training had to hurt, or a soldier wouldn't take it seriously, and be caught off-guard by the pain when a true wounding happened.

Armed and armored, feeling as if she was encased in some hot, stifling cocoon, Tilanne followed Jedina back out. By now, word of what she was doing had spread through the town. Enough had decided to put aside their work and come watch to make it a good-sized crowd gathered around the garrison yard.

She saw Jedriel among them, and raised her heavy wooden sword at him in a salute. The gesture brought a grin to his face, but the grin was tinged with envy. She regretted it at once. Jedriel would never, by virtue of the promise his father had made, be allowed to be where she was now. To do what she was doing now.

And his brother was very aware of it.

Captain Jedren had changed from his scarlet and black uniform into a suit of quilting similar to hers. The sword he'd chosen was heavy and thick. Tilanne could already imagine the punishing blows it would deliver. The padding would hopefully keep her bones intact, but she knew she would come out of her lessons well purpled.

So it began, her training at arms. In that first session, she did not even come close to hitting Jedren, and suspected she would come to hate his sharp, imperious voice as he commanded her, corrected her, instructed her. But she endured it, mostly by reminding herself that Sahen would be receiving like treatment from Commander Ellorn.

Jedren pulled his strikes, a mere tap sufficient to show when she was letting her defenses lapse, leaving herself open. He circled her, seemingly unhindered by the armor – which he doubtless was. To him, this was a decrease in weight from the metal he would wear in actual battle. It made him lighter on his feet, quicker in his motions.

Still, Tilanne felt that she comported herself adequately. Perhaps many of the onlookers expected her to give up, or cry, or more likely both. They might have even been over there placing wagers on her. Gritting her teeth in grim determination and telling herself that she was born of good soldier stock, chosen by the Kai and the god Himself, she refused to do either. Fail, she might. But quit, she would not. Nor would she show them any tears.

When it was done, her arms felt so leaden she could barely lift them to shoulder height. She was wringing with sweat, tendrils of her hair having escaped her helm to lay in dark, wet strands stuck to her face. Her limbs shook from exertion and strain, and her muscles throbbed in unison with her laboring heart.

Yet she was standing, and Captain Jedren's nod was one of approval. "Promise thou hast, Kor Tilanne," he said. "And spirit, undeniably."

Her throat was choked with dust, so she could not answer except to bow her head in thanks. She was so weary that it was all she could do to stay upright as Jedina led her away and divested her of the armor. Tilanne wanted nothing more than a long hot soak, followed by hours upon hours of sleep. She felt choked with the dust that had been stirred up by the scuffling of their booted feet in the dirt of the yard.

When she emerged in her tunic, the crowd had dispersed but for Jedriel. His obsidian eyes were gleaming with pride and admiration. "Knew did I that thou wouldst do well, and quite a surprise thou didst my brother give. In time, and not much of it, I expect thou'll his better be, Tilanne."

Alarice hurried up, and she'd had the foresight to bring a wineskin. "Parched must thou be," she said.

"Parched am I," Tilanne agreed, and let the cool, sweet wine run down her throat.

Flicking at the sweaty clumps of Tilanne's hair, Alarice said, "And a bath thou dost need as well."

"Join us, Jedina, wilt thou?" Tilanne asked.

A fey, strange look flitted across the child's face. "With others am I not permitted to go. Only with my nurse do I bathe. On the morrow shall we see thee, Kor Tilanne?"

"Thy nurse? Still thou a nurse hast?" Jedriel asked. "At thy age?"

As if the mention had called her into being, a mature woman came up to them. She had hair like midnight and eyes like emeralds, and would have been lovely had her skin not been heavily marked with old burn-scars. One of her ears was a melted and misshapen stub mostly hidden beneath a silken kerchief. She had a timid, scurrying way about her, reminding Tilanne of an oft-kicked but still plaintive dog.

"Come, Jedina," she said, taking her by the elbow. "Wander not."

"Hardly is she wandering," Jedriel said. "Her uncle am I."

"And friends are we all," Alarice said, her tone one of mild offense-taking. "Think you that with us she'd not be safe? Here in the very middle of town?"

Without replying, the nursemaid all but whisked Jedina away, leaving the girl time for just one backward, apologetic and wistful glance. And for the briefest of instants, hauntingly, Tilanne saw something in her eyes that seemed familiar.

But the aches in her body would not let her mind contemplate much more than finding an ease for them. She went into the bath-house, and with Jedriel and Alarice undressed and slipped into the deliciously hot water. They had the place to themselves at the middle of the day. She groaned as the heat sank into her body.

"Now understand do I," she sighed, "why so often my father and other soldiers to Vandil came, seeking oils and massages the pains from their muscles to work."

"Oils they have," Alarice said, pointing at a high shelf filled with an array of bottles in colored glass, poised above the jutting heads of the wind-dragons. "And although little of it do I know, I shall for thee attempt it."

"Something of it do I know," Jedriel volunteered. Half his mouth quirked up in a grin. "Though perhaps too soon do I speak . . . what fool am I, when a fair beauty to a dark beauty does such a service offer? When instead, watch I could?"

Alarice looked at him curiously. "Art thou not *chani?*"

Tilanne slipped and inhaled water. Trust Alarice of all people to say what was on her mind, to voice rumors that had gone around Cliffcave for years. Not that Tilanne believed them herself, nor had she since she had caught him giving her those long, considering looks. Coughing and choking, she shot Jedriel a glance but wry and amused.

Jedriel did not look nearly so outraged as might have been expected. He sighed, as if it was hardly the first time he'd heard such a charge. "More that scant opportunities otherwise to prove have I had," he said, and got out of the pool to fetch a pot of oil. If more proof were needed, it was plainly evident that being in such proximity to the two of them had had a distinct effect.

"Sorry am I," Alarice said, bright pink and trying not to giggle. "Mean did I not . . ."

"If from head to toe one great aching misery was I not," Tilanne said, "such an opportunity thou might have. Alas!"

"Alas!" Jedriel seconded with feeling.

Sorry as she was to leave the comfort of the water, Tilanne managed to pull herself out and hobble to a bench so artfully shaped that it did not feel like hard stone at all. She stretched out upon it, rivulets streaming from her hair, and groaned again as Jedriel skillfully worked the oil into her tormented back and shoulders.

"Magic are thy hands," she said, turning her head so that her cheek rested against the marble.

"Magic is thy shape, lovely Tilanne," he replied.

Alarice, having lapsed once in her discretion and not about to do it a second time, silently and quickly gathered up her things and slipped from the room. She shot an impish smile at Tilanne as she left, and closed the bath house door behind her.

Lulled, relaxing, the wine seeping through her inhibitions as the warmth and oil seemed to seep into her flesh, Tilanne said, "Very fond of thee I am, Jedriel. Known to thee, that is, I hope?"

His hands stilled. "The same of thee could I say."

"Why, then, didst thou seem to think that thy brother I would prefer?"

She heard his wince in his indrawn breath, felt it in the way his grip tightened.

"So obvious was I?"

"No, but clears my mind does the steam, and loosens my tongue does the wine. What did not before, now seems clear. Saw did I how thine eyes darkened when we met."

"My brother he is," Jedriel said after a lengthy, weighing pause. "And love him I do as brothers must. But not always close have we been, not always friends. And sometimes, our differences we have had." He moved to massage the backs of her legs. "Jedren, the older, the swordsman, the captain . . . always the first and the best of all seemed to have. And to know it, and never fail to remind me."

"How unfair to thee it is."

"Unfair or not, it *is*. And so has it always been." He reached her feet, and Tilanne all but dissolved in the pain-pleasure as his thumbs sought out the tension in her soles and heels. He huffed, a noise not quite a chuckle. "Helina . . . his wife . . . when young we were, loved her I did and would her husband gladly have been. But to Jedren did her family marry her. For he, the soldier, better prospects offered than could a lowly scribe."

The Cause, then the family, and lastly one's own desires . . . yes, thus was the *Morvalan* way. If it served the Cause, the people and her family best for a girl to marry elsewhere than where her heart led, she could not go against that tradition.

There may have been nothing she could say to give comfort and ease his pain, but there was certainly something she could do.

Tilanne turned over, and raised her arms to Jedriel. He looked at her in bewilderment for a moment . . . but only a moment . . . before accepting her invitation.

* * *

CHAPTER EIGHT

The black moon – Kaledhol's Fist, Kaledhol's Heart, dark companion orb to Livana's bright chariot – tracked many a full course of the heavens while Tilanne studied at Jewelgreen. As the skies turned toward autumn, the constellation of the hunter-god rose earlier and earlier each night. Leaves changed. Crops ripened.

For Tilanne, sometimes the days flew by at hawk's speed, and sometimes they crept by so slowly a snail might have outraced them. She felt that she would *never* master all that she needed to, and she felt that her head was *already* full to bursting with the skills and knowledge she'd gained.

In addition to her training-at-arms with Captain Jedren and his men, she learned to care for her armor and weapons, to keep them well and make minor repairs as needed. From Thoraine, an aged soldier – a rarity deserving of the utmost respect – she learned of battle-strategies and tactics. From his son, a fortificationist, she learned of castles and defenses, of sieges and dwarven war-machines.

But to be *Rhunvala* was not solely about warfare, and the folk of Jewelgreen were eager to contribute. Her survival, and her success, would benefit their people as a whole, and to have nurtured her knowledge would be a credit to their town. So, under the tutelage of many, she studied woodslore, tracking, the care of horses, history, medicine, languages. Although her mage-talent was not great, Alarice helped her to a better understanding of the ways and capabilities of sorcery.

Often, she despaired and might have been tempted to give up, had she not been so sure that the Kai, and Kaledhol Himself, willed this to be. Her regular visits to the temple at the center of town only reinforced her determination to prove herself worthy of the destiny she had been offered.

Jedriel, too, encouraged her with his gentle wit and teasing, his unshakable belief in her abilities. He continued to lodge with Ilantisian, but passed many of his nights with Tilanne.

By first harvest, her sword was no longer a strange and awkward tool in her hand but almost a living extension of her arm. Her shield was a well-appreciated defender. She had always been tall and slim, shapely, but as the practice and exercise went on, her limbs lost their softness and became lean, taut.

By last harvest and first frost, she could match Captain Jedren stroke for stroke, without going short of breath or even breaking much of a sweat. True to her request, he treated her no differently than he would have treated a man.

This did not, however, mean that he forgot she was female. His hints and attentions grew more obvious as winter set in. Yet there was something in the quality of his interest that made the tender skin behind her ears tighten in unease. It was, perhaps, the veiled contempt in his voice whenever he spoke to, or about his brother. Jedren made no secret of his disapproval when he heard that Tilanne and Jedriel were bedmates.

She did not dare spurn Jedren outright, but neither could she pretend to encourage him. Her best path seemed to be one of polite reserve, never responding to his remarks or invitations, and maintaining as cool and businesslike a demeanor toward him as was possible. When they were not training, she kept her distance, though could not avoid him entirely. Nor did she wish to . . . for Jedina's sake.

Before Kai Terindor's dying legacy had fallen upon her, Tilanne had always expected to become a teacher. To devote her life to the care and raising of children, her own and others. The more she saw of Jedina – which was infrequent enough – the more she wondered and worried on the girl's behalf.

"Shy she is," Alarice said, one evening when the two of them strolled the high walls in a softly-falling snow. "In that there is no harm."

Tilanne shook her head. "Seen hast thou not, how never with the other children is she? Never with them does she school or play, but always at the garrison stays. Rarely without her nursemaid is she seen."

"Perhaps ails she does?" Alarice suggested. "Sickly she seems not, but weakness and illness a subtle mask can wear."

"Nothing of the sort has Jedriel mentioned."

"As if know he would." She tossed her head, her silvery-blond hair a shimmer in the snow as the long plait flipped from one shoulder to the other. "Barely anything of her does he know. Hardly has he seen her. Thou art more often around the child than he, her own uncle."

"Old wounds and bad blood between the brothers lie," Tilanne said. "Discourages does Jedren any closeness. Cruel it seems. Cruel to Jedriel, and to Jedina also."

"A good soldier he is said to be, and a good captain," Alarice said. "But such a coldness there is in him. Told me did Tandira that ever so has it been, since died did his wife in birthing. By now, remarried he should have but has not. And has, so is said, no interest in another woman shown. Until now."

Tilanne stopped. "Alarice, what is thy meaning?"

"Full well thou knowst. For thee he hungers, Tilanne."

"Hungers . . . a goodly word. As hungers does the wolf, or the bear." Tilanne pulled her cloak around herself to ward off a deeper chill than that which came from the frosty air. "Not with passion's warm light do his eyes glow, but something else. Something that much sharper and more dangerous than passion is."

"Knows does he, as do we all, that Jedriel thy bedmate is. Away from him might Jedren hope thy affections to win. Not so much for desire of thee – though comely thou art, my friend, comely indeed – but for desire his brother to hurt, and another victory in their rivalry claim."

"No part of any rivalry do I ever wish to be. And if such is their contest, has not Jedren already won? The woman Jedriel loved, Jedren himself for a wife did have."

"But gone she is, long years gone to roses and ash," Alarice said. "Here, now, art thee, vital and alive and by Jedriel loved. From him, Jedren would win thee, if he could."

"Loved?" Tilanne's breath escaped in a mix of laugh and sigh. "Great fondness and affection have I for Jedriel and he for me, but wed are we not. Nor shall we be. Not if I am to the *Odan Rhunvale* to go."

Perhaps Jedren came to that realization himself, for as the winter progressed his pursuit of Tilanne lessened. He seemed to take delight in mentioning at every opportunity that when spring came, there would be no more for Tilanne to learn at Jewelgreen. It would be time for her to depart, and continue her studies elsewhere.

Then spring did come

"As well trained as any soldier art thou, and better than most," Jedren said, stripping off his helm and raking gloved fingers through his short hair. The ring in his ear winked grey-black darts of light in the afternoon sun. "The *Odan Rhunvale* must now thy tutelage complete."

They were in the garrison yard, having just finished a practice bout in which she had turned his every blow by virtue of either her shield or her sword, remaining untouched by the tarred length of wood. And she, moving with deft speed, had succeeded in marking him three times, once to each arm and a killing blow to the chest.

A crowd had gathered, as one so often did to watch Tilanne take on the captain. She could see Jedriel among them, his dark eyes shining with pride. And with something else . . . sadness? Loss? Alarice was beside him, her smile bright and cheerful. Up above, peeking down from her window, was Jedina.

"My gratitude is thine, Captain," Tilanne said, saluting Jedren. She turned and repeated the gesture at the crowd, her gaze finding and holding in turn the various others who had helped her. "And all of thine as well."

"To celebrate," Jedren said, "I would invite thee with myself and my undercaptains to dine tonight."

To refuse would be a deliberate slap, an insult of the gravest sort. But his undercaptains would be there, and Jedina would likely be there. She would not have to be alone with Jedren. No one could mistake this for a romantic dinner in any way.

She went directly to the bath-house, but there was no solitude to be found within its walls. Too many people were eager to congratulate her, swept up in the excitement. There had never been a female *Rhunvala* before, they reminded each other. Think of the renown it would bring to Jewelgreen! Kaledhol was sure to smile on them as well.

Even when she left the bath-house, there was no surcease of visitors and well-wishers. She found herself in the uncomfortable position of being showered with gifts, gifts she could not refuse without hurting the feelings of those who gave them. It was an embarrassment of riches, items made new and just for her rather than being taken from the communal stores. A scarlet cloak trimmed with the softest black silkmole fur, a sword belt with silver buckle worked into the shape of a rose, an oilskin pack with many cunning compartments, a set of eating implements made from the antlers of a deer slain by Reshelli, a creamy-white doeskin tunic embroidered with red roses and black basilisks, other treasures.

As she was leaving for the garrison, dressed in the new tunic, she saw Jedriel waiting. His eyes still wore that shine of sadness and pride, but he summoned a smile for her as he approached.

"I, too, a gift for thee have. Kor Tilanne. Never did I doubt thee."

"Until now?" she asked, tilting her head to the side.

"No. Thee I doubt not, and never shall."

"Then what is it, Jedriel, that troubles thee?"

"Too well do I my brother know. His ways, his persuasiveness."

"So frail of will dost thou find me, that as helpless prey to his seductions shall I be?"

"Frail? Thee? Not in any way, Tilanne, art thou frail. Still, know do I Jedren, and trust him, do I not. The status and respect he doth command –"

"Thy brother might a captain be," she said, placing a hand on his arm, "yet the better man thou art, Jedriel. In thee do I thy kindness and thy caring spirit see. These things, Jedren lacks. Circumstance did prevent thee from a soldier becoming, but not thy fault is that. Thou wouldst any woman a fine and worthy husband make."

"Even thine?"

"Were I not otherwise beholden," she said, meeting his gaze squarely. "Were I not to this course sworn. But my path from here leads on, Jedriel, in strange ways that to me are yet unclear. I must that path follow, above all else. For guidance have I often prayed, and a sense have I that . . . that my place in the southlands, *out* of the southlands might be."

He touched her cheek, let his fingers roam from there to the sensitive side of her neck and into her hair. She had resisted shearing her dark locks like a soldier, instead pinning them up tight in a coronet of braids when she needed to confine them beneath a helm. Loose and gleaming now, it fell in sable waves around her shoulders.

"Every woman I care for, I am to lose," Jedriel said softly. "Unkind is our god, a second love to grant me and a second love wrest away."

She set her palm over his heart. "Love remains, always. Gone are our parents, yet love them still we do. Apart am I from my sister, yet love her still I do. And when apart we are, Jedriel, love each other still shall we do as well."

Jedriel covered her hand with his own and held it there firmly, against the steady drumbeat of his pulse. His eyes were somber, both of them knowing that they might never meet again. She was not *Rhunvala* yet. For all either of them knew, the process of becoming so, of being tested, might itself kill her before any enemies of the *Morvalan* even had a chance.

"As before I said, a gift have I for thee." He brought out a small box, opened its lid, and held it out to her.

The twin ruby earrings were not dangling jewels nor hoops, but studs meant to rest flush against the skin. They had been painstakingly shaped in delicate detail into two perfectly matched roses.

"Beautiful they are," she said. "Gladly shall I wear them."

Jedriel brushed back her hair, exposing her ears, but they were alone on the avenue with no one near enough to see such a bold act. "And beautifully on thee shall they sparkle."

Tilanne tilted her head back and welcomed his kiss, welcomed his gentle caress. She could feel the love of this good man radiating from him, and understood what he meant–Kaledhol could be unkind. No person and no power was forcing her to go on. She *could* lay aside sword and shield, forget the *Odan Rhunvale*, if that was her wish. She could marry Jedriel and bear him strong sons and clever daughters. She could do all of that and the god would permit it. . .but would think less of her. As would the spirit of the Kai and everyone else who had come to believe in her, to believe in Kor Tilanne.

Jedriel stepped back from her, and she could see that knowledge in his sorrowful, steady gaze. She was tempted to forget the feast that was being laid out at the garrison, forget the company of swordsmen and warriors, and spend the rest of the night in the arms of a scribe.

"Thou'd best go," he said. "Late thou'll be."

"When done it is, later," she said, "shall I to thy lodging come?"

"Ever to thee is my door open." Jedriel ran his fingertip in a feather-light stroke along the rim of her ear, making her tremble.

Something in his voice, though, made her think that he did not expect to see her, that despite everything that they'd said and that had passed between them tonight, she would still greet the dawn from the tangled sheets of his brother's bed.

*   *   *

Chapter Nine

Tilanne left her cloak and sword belt with the raven-haired, scarred woman who seemed to serve not only as Jedina's nursemaid but also as the sole cook, housekeeper, and domestic for the captain's household. Her name was Selmaire; she was long-widowed . . . but even after all this time in Jewelgreen, that was all Tilanne knew of her.

Captain Jedren had taken pains to dress well for the occasion. His trousers were darkest blue, his boots shiny black. He wore a doublet of iron grey with subtle threads of silver and black woven through the fabric, and the clasps down the front were truesilver in the form of dragon claws.

"Kor Tilanne, a pleasure," he said. "Delighted am I that join us thou couldst."

He ushered her into a dining room that was small but finely furnished. The hanging lamps glowed with magelight, a green and gold tapestry covered the floor, and place settings of pewter and jade adorned the pristine white tablecloth.

"My undercaptains Bairdan and Renveil, thou knowest, and of course Thoraine."

She greeted them all, having studied a time with each. Bairdan was an axeman, perhaps having become so because for an elf he was uncommonly broad through the hips and torso, a build better suited to the weight and swing of an axe. Most of what he had taught Tilanne was a deep respect for the weapon, and a hope that she never came up against one in the hands of a foe who knew how to use it.

Renveil, by contrast, was tall and wiry, with deceptive strength hidden in his slim frame. He was naturally gifted with all manner of weapons but most of all with the bow, able to draw and nock and fire so fast that the eye could barely keep up. Unlike Bairdan, whose brown hair was cropped so short that pink scalp showed through, Renveil wore his flaxen hair in a single plait that reached nearly to his belt.

The other soldiers all regarded Thoraine with something akin to awe. He had been of the profession his entire life and still lived to tell the tale. Seeing one's six hundredth year was occasion enough for any *Morvalan*, but for a warrior, it was impressive indeed. He had been witheringly scornful of Tilanne, certain that no mere girl could grasp the complex strategies of a battlefield. Of all her teachers, she had endeavored most to win a nod of approval from him. Not even her first triumph over Jedren had been quite so sweet as Thoraine's grudging admission that perhaps, after all, she *did* have a head for tactics.

"Jedina joins us not?" Tilanne asked as Jedren showed her to a seat.

"In her room she dines. No place is this for a child."

The conversation tended toward military matters, Tilanne's progress and that of other students, news from the fortresses, news brought by travelers from neighboring settlements, the constant rumors of invasions by the Mountain King's forces and marauding bands of orcs from the Dragonheights. Tilanne was reminded of dinners when she was small, listening to similar conversations among her father and brothers.

Selmaire brought a salad of fresh shoots and greens tossed in a spicy oil. It was followed by a hearty soup of beef broth with shredded meat and slivers of root vegetables, and next a platter of sliced breads, cheeses, and jellied meat. For the main course, she brought each of them a plate holding a whole pheasant, which had been stuffed with mushrooms, herbs, and breadcrumbs before being roasted golden brown.

Tilanne had not enjoyed such an elaborate, carefully prepared meal in a long time. She ate with appreciation, but paused when she lifted her goblet. To go with the pheasant, Captain Jedren had poured a pale golden wine from the Valley of the Growing Vines. As she was about to sip it, she caught a whiff of a strange and hauntingly familiar scent.

Pretending to drink, she sniffed again at the wine. The scent was there, faint but distinct. It put her in mind of one of her brothers. Of Vandil, the physician.

Nhallaia leaf? Had her wine had been laced with extract of *nhallaia* leaf?

Vandil used the extract when he was required to perform some difficult, painful procedure on an injured person. It worked slowly, relaxing the body and the mind, inducing a state of calmness and disconnection and leading to a pliant semi-consciousness.

Her shock and anger were overwhelmed only by her sheer astonishment. He meant to drug her senseless! To do what he liked with her while she was helpless, insensate. She would wake with no memory of what had transpired. What manner of man was he to even think of such a thing? Was he so determined to have her, so desperate, that he would stoop to such measures?

She glanced at Jedren. He was laughing at some joke of Bairdan's, but Tilanne saw him watching her out of the corner of his eye. She pretended to take a deeper drink, then lowered her goblet and complimented him on such a fine wine. He smiled, a wide and crafty smile that made her lose any lingering doubts she might have had.

But what to do? If she did not drink, he would notice. He might try some other ploy that she could fail to recognize until it was too late.

Thoraine, having finished three goblets already, was in a voluble mood. It took little effort on Tilanne's part to get him to tell one of his favorite war-stories, of a battle that had taken place one harsh and brutal winter long before any of the rest of them had been born. As he spoke, relating the adventures and dangers his company had faced from starving wolves and pantera and orcs, losing a dozen men before even seeing the face of one of the Mountain King's soldiers, Thoraine's gestures became more dramatic, more expansive. All eyes were on him, and Tilanne seized the opportunity to stealthily empty her wine into the soup tureen, mixing it with the dregs of the broth.

Bare moments later, Selmaire came in to clear away the dishes. Tilanne breathed a quiet sigh of relief when the tureen was borne from the dining room. Recalling the effects of *nhallaia*, she took care to make her movements seem slower, more languid, more relaxed, as Thoraine finished his story and launched into another.

Dessert was a brandycake soaked in honey and then sprinkled with sugared nuts and candied fruit, heavy and too sweet. Especially for Tilanne, who had not been accustomed to such decadence even before adhering to the simple, healthy diet of a soldier. She begged off after only a couple of bites, feigning a lassitude she did not feel.

"To the study shall we for some games or amusements adjourn?" Jedren said.

Tilanne could have declined, to see what he would do if she tried to leave. Would he let her go? Would he try to find some other way to get her to stay? But she was curious, and she was indignant. How dare he do such a thing? To her or to any woman? She had heard of humans sinking to such despicable deeds – or worse – but one of her own people? An elf? A *Morvalan*?

So she joined them as they went to the study, and watched the undercaptains play darts while Jedren and Thoraine faced off over the Towers board. She was careful to continue her ruse of becoming ever more relaxed, aware that Jedren was keeping a close and watchful eye on her.

Through it all, her anger continued to burn. That he would drug her! For one awful moment, it occurred to her to wonder if the others were in on it as well, but she quickly dismissed that notion. Thoraine, Renveil and Bairdan seemed oblivious.

And Jedren seemed to grow more and more impatient for the other men to go. He lost badly at Towers – she was certain he had done so on purpose, and had to work hard at it, given how drunk Thoraine was. He refused when Bairdan suggested that they all sit down to a friendly game of cards.

She knew why he was so eager for them to leave. He wanted them well gone and out of the house before she fully succumbed to the *nhallaia*. Yet they were not cooperating, and he was trapped. If she were to slump unconscious, their concern would interfere with his plans. One of them would insist on sending for a physician. How did he plan to separate her from the other guests?

"Retiring soon shall Jedina be, Kor Tilanne," Jedren said at that moment. "If goodnight to her thou didst wish to say, know do I that greatly would it please her."

"If no objection have thee, Captain," Tilanne said.

He rang for Selmaire, and when the domestic came in, directed her to take Tilanne upstairs. Tilanne followed, maintaining her pretense of languidness in case Selmaire was a part of his treachery. She did not want to think so, but could not afford to lower her guard in the slightest.

Jedina's small but tidy room was on the second floor, overlooking the garrison yard. The door stood half-open, a candle within shedding a soft light over the desk where Jedina sat in her nightdress, drawing on parchment with colored charcoal-sticks. She looked up, a slim wraith all in white with that cloud of long curly red-gold hair, and joy suffused her little face.

"Kor Tilanne?"

"Came did I goodnight to say to thee, Jedina." Tilanne kept her words slow, her voice mild, her movements languid as she drifted over to the desk.

Selmaire left them, but did not close the door all the way. Her footsteps receded down the hall.

"For thee did I draw this," Jedina said, and with huge hopeful eyes held out the picture she had been drawing. "If not to thy liking, dispose of it thou canst –"

"Oh, Jedina," she said. To her surprise and abashment, it was a picture of her. But not Tilanne as she was now. Tilanne as she might – Kaledhol willing – someday be. In black-enameled armor and mail, helm beneath her arm and hand resting on the hilt of a sword that was stuck, point-down, into the earth. "Not to my liking? Very much to my liking it is! And very skilled thou art."

Jedina smiled, a shy and unbearably sweet smile. "An artist someday I hope to be," she said, as if confessing some long-held and most secret dream.

"Hast thou not yet apprenticed been?"

Her smile was erased as abruptly as a cloth swiping a chalk mark from slate. "No." She gathered up her charcoals, aligning them neatly in a wooden case.

Holding the picture, Tilanne sat on the end of the bed and regarded the girl, who seemed determined to avoid her gaze. "Jedina . . . wondered have I why so rarely with the other children thou art seen. Why is it that thou dost not school with them, or play? Ninaire, who from Cliffcave with me came, thy age is and would a good friend for thee make. Jedriel, thy uncle, would gladly have thee visit, but even he sees thee not often."

The smile tried to reappear, wavering. "Wish to I that in Jewlegreen with him, thou couldst stay. Loves thee, he does."

"Yes . . . behold what this very night he gave me." She brushed back her hair from the sides of her head, showing Jedina the ruby rose earrings.

"Oh, so lovely they are! Often wished have I that old enough was I my own to have done. But too young still am I, my *Vala* says." She heaved a wistful sigh. "When older I am, many piercings do I mean to have. And here, in this jewelry case, my mother's earrings are."

Tilanne admired the collection. "Pretty they are."

"This one, my favorite is." She held up a complicated arrangement of truesilver studs and loops. The piece would fit through many piercings along the rim of the ear, to be joined by graceful drapes of chain from which tiny diamond teardrops hung.

"Bearing thee thy mother died?" Tilanne asked.

Jedina shook her head, the earring she had held up to the side of it jangling and getting caught in her hair as she did so. "Sick she fell, when still just a babe I was. Remember her do I hardly at all." She tugged, the delicate chain pulling and in danger of snapping.

"Here," Tilanne said. "Caught thou art. Let me."

She moved behind the girl, and carefully unwrapped strands of hair from the snagged chain. As she did so, she swept the long ringlets aside out of the way, revealing the back of Jedina's neck and the loose collar of her nightdress. A spidery-fine ridge of scar climbed above the lacy trim.

"Please say that break it did not," Jedina said. "My favorite it is!"

"Break it did not." Tilanne spoke without hearing herself, without knowing for certain whether the earring had in fact broken or not. She hooked a finger into the collar and peered down, drawing in a horrified breath between her teeth. "Jedina –"

With a sudden fearful gasp, Jedina tore away from her. She whirled and pressed her back to the wall. Her face had gone paler than usual, her eyes large and dark as forest pools at night.

"Thy neck," Tilanne said. "Thy back."

"Nothing it is. Nothing."

"That I might see, turn and show me."

Jedina's chin quivered. "Nothing it is, told thee did I."

"Then in my looking, no harm is there. Turn."

She said it perhaps more sternly than she meant to, the iron in her tone surprising even her. But it worked, and with a faint fawn-like shudder, Jedina turned and bowed her head.

Tilanne parted her hair, and hooked a finger into the collar again. The spidery white line was a scar, an old one. A crisscross of similar scars descended Jedina's back, marring her white skin in slashes and ropy weals. They looked like the marks left by a switch, struck mercilessly hard against tender flesh. And then ill-treated, left to heal on their own rather than being given the attention of a physician.

"By these, how came thee?"

The girl's trembling increased, and her only answer was a mewl of terror. From downstairs, Tilanne could hear men's voices. Hearty. Boisterous. Making their farewells.

"What to thee did this? *Who* to thee did this?" Tilanne asked, turning Jedina again to hold her by the upper arms and look her in the face. "Tell me thou must, Jedina."

She shook her head, a short, quick motion.

"Thy father it was." She did not ask it, knowing it with a deep and true sureness. "Thy own father."

"Promise he made me that no one should I tell, not ever." Jedina's voice was so low and meek that even standing right in front of her, Tilanne more had to read the words on her lips than hear them aloud. "Swore did I. Please, Kor Tilanne. This secret thou must keep."

"Thy own father with a switch did beat thee? Why? How could he such a such a monstrousness to his child do?"

"Deserved it did I. Something bad must I have done when small I was, for him so to punish me."

"This is why he'll not let thee to the bath-house go, why he here in the house has thee stay. Beats thee does he still? Even now?"

"Hardly ever, and only when deserve it I do!"

Her anger at her own treatment had been utterly eclipsed by a white-hot rage greater than anything she had ever known before. Children were precious, so very precious and vital! They were to be treasured and protected, cared for with the utmost love and attention. Yet this was Jedren's love and attention, here before her eyes. His daughter, his only child, beaten until she was striped from neck to knees with scars. Kept her away from others her own age, denied the company of friends, a virtual prisoner in her own home so that this horrible and shameful secret was not brought into view . . .

At that moment, she had cause to bitterly resent the vow she'd promised unto Kaledhol. At that moment, she could have spilled elven blood, could have taken an elven life, and been glad to do it.

"Please, tell him not that thee I told. Furious will he be!"

"Furious am I already! Innocent thou art, and not a hand upon thee shall he lay. This do I swear. Away from him and away from this dreadful house I'll take thee . . . now, this very night."

"Loves me he does, my *Vala*," Jedina said, tears flowing unchecked. "Loves me he *must* else care he would not, else correct me he would not. Loves me he must, or matter would it not to him if good or bad I was. Leave him I cannot. Punish me he would, worse than ever."

"No more," Tilanne said. "To that shall I see. Never again shall he hurt thee."

She started for the bedroom door, intending to march Jedina down the stairs and out of the house, pausing only long enough to grab the girl's cloak and boots on the way. When she stepped out into the hall. Selmaire was blocking her path.

"Go thou must," the older woman said. "Out of this house."

"Yes," Tilanne said. "And with me goes Jedina."

"Permit that I will not." Hate twisted her features, combining with the livid, ugly burn scars to make a grotesque mask.

"Knew thou didst. Knew of this, and thy silence kept. Allowed him this child to harm, and not a word to any other soul did say. Why? How couldst thou such a thing in all conscience condone?"

She flapped a hand at her devastated countenance, the melted lump that had been her left ear. "*This* enough of a warning was the captain never to cross."

Tilanne reeled at this fresh revelation of horror. "That, to thee, he did as well? Maimed thee? Disfigured thee? Against him, then, thou shouldst and *must* speak –"

"And a worse fate suffer?" Selmaire's laugh was that of a madwoman.

"*Vala* that to thee did?" Jedina asked in a faint, whispering whimper. "Thy face, thy ear, he burned, Selmaire?"

"No more of his tyranny shall this house abide," Tilanne said. She attempted to move down the hall, but Selmaire continued to block her way.

"Wise thou wouldst be," Selmaire said, "not an enemy of the captain to make. Wise thou wouldst be thy cooperation to give. And then, unmarred, unmaimed, thou might from this place depart."

"After he has of my unwilling body made use? The *nhallaia*, that as well, thou didst know and his accomplice was."

"Into thy cup at his bidding, I placed it, yes. Wants thee, he does, and what he wants, always and without fail, he has."

"My cooperation, my body and my silence he'll have not." She advanced on Selmaire, and the domestic, perhaps seeing the grim intent in Tilanne's eyes, shrank back. Still with Jedina in tow, she headed for the stairs.

And halted, as Captain Jedren appeared at the top of the landing.

* * *

Chapter Ten

Tilanne set herself between Jedren and his daughter, hearing the girl's moan of dismay.

Selmaire gave Tilanne a heartless, vindictive look, one of evil gladness and spite and more dislike than she had ever seen on another face before. Now, that look said, now this uppity warrior-maid will be made to pay for poking her nose where it doesn't belong.

"So, Tilanne," Jedren said. "Well enough alone thou couldst not leave. And remarkably awake art thou, too."

"*Nhallaia* known to me is," she said. "Failed did thy plan."

"On thyself didst thou such drastic measures bring. My overtures thou didst ignore, and so more direct means was I forced to take."

"Thy overtures I ignored because I desired thee not."

He sneered. "My *brother* thou dost prefer? Pah! Man enough for the likes of thee, Jedriel is not. Weak he is, and soft, and a foolish, girlish, *chani* dreamer. But let Jedriel be forgotten. Thee, Tilanne . . . this trespass I can forgive. Let us anew begin."

She stared at him in disbelief. "And let be forgotten, let be unseen all that I have this night learned and witnessed? Never, Jedren. Vile thou art, moreso than any human. No true elf art thou."

"Thus dost thou seek thy vow to circumvent? By unelven calling me?" He punctuated it by making a gesture at his ears, a rude, contemptuous flick. "No good, Tilanne. Elven am I, as elven as thee. Thy vow yet binds. Selmaire, Jedina to her room return –"

As the woman moved to obey, Tilanne held her hands, palms out, at the height of Selmaire's chest. Not touching her, not pushing her, but ready to do so. Selmaire stopped short, her gaze darting uncertainly between Tilanne and Jedren.

With a slow, deliberate singing of steel, Jedren drew his sword. Tilanne had a moment to regret leaving hers in the cloakroom; out of courtesy to her host, she had come unarmed to his table. He leveled the blade at her, magelight from the hall lamp running along it like molten silver.

"*Vala*, please," Jedina said in a whimper.

"Stand down," Jedren said, ignoring the girl. "Stand down, Kor Tilanne, else the consequences pay."

Tilanne did not. Her hopes of getting out of this unscathed and without hurting anyone dwindled. And yes, vow or no vow, part of her yearned to lash out at him. To strike down this monster, this deceiver, this horrid thing that called himself an elf.

"Thou wouldst a Kor attack, Captain?" She tried not to make it sound like a challenge, tried to get through to him in hopes that he might suddenly realize the evils he'd done. But she saw by the hardness in his expression that any such hopes were in vain.

"My house leave at once, and perhaps lenient shall I be. Remain, persist, and harshly with thee must I deal."

"I leave, but with me goes Jedina. And for thy deeds, for thy crimes, thou wilt answer. A beater of children, thou art . . . a maimer of women . . . to thy uniform a discredit and to thy people, to thy *god*, a disgrace."

He was flushed and quaking with rage, all semblance of handsomeness lost. A bellow burst from him as he sprang. The narrowness of the hall prevented a swing, so he plunged the point of his sword at her in a thrust meant to skewer her through her unarmored ribs.

She could not leap out of the way. Jedina was behind her. Tilanne slammed the heel of her hand sideways, hitting the flat of the blade and driving it into the wall. It skidded and squealed along the wood, then wedged fast. Jedren lost his grip. The sword fell, and then she was upon him. They grappled in the close space, no practice bout this time but brutal hand-to-hand combat in deadly earnest.

Tilanne shut her mind to Jedina's terrified and protesting screams, to Jedren's curses, and concentrated on delivering one blow after another. She felt his fist glance off her cheekbone, blurring the eye on that with tears. She bloodied his nose and made the breath gust from him with a hard punch just below the breastbone. But as he staggered backward, he seized her tunic, and they tumbled together down the flight of stairs.

The descent was jarring, bone-clattering. Both of them fetched up at the bottom, dazed. Jedren recovered first, dragging Tilanne to her feet.

"Slay thee I will," he said, spraying her with blood as he panted into her face.

"Didst thou thy wife murder as well?" Tilanne asked through clenched teeth. "A great warrior against women and girls thou art, Jedren!"

The accusation made him go rigid with shock. She wrenched loose, pounded his arm into the banister, heard something snap – his elbow? – and then rammed her knee up full-force between his legs.

He went down again, curled into a tight wheezing knot and cradling his arm. Jedina ran down the stairs past them and out the front door, shrieking fit to wake the dead. Selmaire, howling like a scalded cat, threw herself on Tilanne. A single hard blow to the chin dropped the woman, her eyes rolling up.

Grabbing Jedren before he could regain his breath, Tilanne flipped him onto his belly and bound his arms behind him with his own belt. Her strength amazed her as she hauled him to a chair and flung him into it.

"Thy vow . . ." he choked.

"No elven life to take, and to all my best efforts elven lives to defend," she said. "So I slay thee not, justified though it surely would be."

A thunder of running footsteps and shouting voices filled the night. The door banged open and people filled the room. They gaped at the sight that met their eyes. Captain Jedren, bound and bruised and bloodied . . . and Kor Tilanne, only slightly less the worse for wear, standing over him.

Renveil pushed his way to the front. "What madness this?"

"Madness indeed!" Jedren cried. "Hers! Attacked me, she did, in my own home."

"Evil mischief have I here discovered," Tilanne said.

She told them everything. The drugged wine, Jedina's scars, Selmaire's confession, everything. As she was speaking, she saw Jedriel come in with Jedina pressed to his side. He was stark with horror and shock, looking from Tilanne to his brother to Tilanne again. His hand stroked Jedina's hair as she sobbed, inconsolable.

"True is this?" Jedriel asked the girl. "Jedina . . . thy back . . . ?"

"The scars show them," Tilanne said. "All right it is. Over, it is."

She clutched at her nightgown and glanced at Jedren, chewing her lip.

"An outrage is this," he said. "Forbid it, do I, Jedina!"

"Swear to thee by Kaledhol's might do I," Tilanne said to Jedina, "that safe from him now and evermore thou'll be."

Jedriel cupped Jedina's face. "*Tashti*, the truth tell me. Hurt thee, has he?"

Eyes brimming, she looked up at Jedriel. A hush fell as every ear strained to hear the whispering words that fell from her lips.

"Hurt me . . . he has. Yes. Many times, hurt me, he has."

She unlaced the front of her nightgown, then drew it over her head and gathered it in a bunched wad to her scant, budding bosom. A universal gasp arose as the scars, the criss-crossed latticework of them, were exposed. They ran from the nape of her neck to the drawstring of her plain white smallclothes.

"Jedina!" Jedren roared. "Disobey me, you *dare?*"

Tears rained down Jedina's face. "Sorry am I, *Vala* . . . so . . . sorry."

"No!" Jedriel ripped a drapery from the wall, the rings breaking and flying in bits all over the room. He folded the cloth around Jedina and dropped to his knees. "No apology do you owe him, Jedina, not ever. Jedren, why? In Kaledhol's name, *why?* Thy own daughter?"

"Even now, thou knowest not?" Jedren's laugh was a cold, sneering hatefulness. "Even now, *brother?*"

Everything flew together in Tilanne's mind then, as if Kaledhol Himself had given her the answer. "His daughter she is not," she said. "But *thy* daughter, Jedriel, thy daughter, she is."

The silence in the room could have been carved from the air, so thick was it. The color slowly drained from Jedriel's face, while at the same time it rose in a scarlet tide in Jedren's, as if the familial blood they shared was somehow being transferred from the one to the other.

"Mine?" asked Jedriel. "But . . . it . . . *mine?*"

"Thy lover Helina was," Tilanne said. "Yet to Jedren was she wed. Knew did he, or suspected, that the child was not of his seed conceived. For this, Jedina, merely for being what she is, he has ever since given punishment."

The girl's eyes were enormous. Those eyes, obsidian-dark. Jedriel gazed into them, and must have finally and for the first time seen that they were his own. A murmur went around the room as if everyone, seeing it, wondered how they had possibly been so blind.

"True it is." Jedren said. "Oh, yes. True it is. My wife she was, yet with him dallied, and her wretched ill-got whelp to my house delivered, expecting that as my own I'd raise her. And I did! A home for Jedina I provided. But I could not the mockery and faithlessness of her mother bear, and so, her neck with my own two hands I wrung."

The admission stunned the room into another complete silence. Mouths hung open in astounded gapes. Then Jedina, understanding only one thing, burst into renewed tears. She made to flee from the room, but Jedriel caught her and held her close.

"Hates me he does!" the girl sobbed. "Hates me, my own *Vala!*"

"No, child . . . thy father, thy *Vala*, I am," Jedriel said. "My daughter thou art. Thy mother with all my heart I loved, and thee as well." He touched the damp corner of her eye, then his own. "See? Thine eyes and mine? How alike they are? True it is."

Renveil, although moving with the sleepwalk-slowness of one unsure if he was waking or dreaming, brought some of his men to surround their captain. They all looked as bewildered as Tilanne felt. What were they to do? Jedren was one of their own, not some outsider, not some orcish raider or invading human from the Mountain Kingdom.

"Thou didst thy wife kill?" Thoraine asked. "Pretty Helina? But thou didst love her."

"All for naught," Jedren said. "Loved her, yes, but loved she me in return? My brother she loved, despite all, and him . . . him have I ever loathed!"

"What have I to thee done? Loved thee all did I, admired and envied thee, and all my three brothers." Jedriel looked as if the heart had been torn from him and was being slowly crushed before his eyes. "Adored thee. But if thou didst hate me so, why thy rage on Helina, on Jedina, vent? Why not on me?"

"Thou canst bald faced *ask?*" Jedren lurched forward as if meaning to launch himself at his brother and rip out Jedriel's throat with his teeth. Renveil held him back. "All thy life, pampered and coddled by our parents . . . from the pains and miseries of soldiering spared, while the rest of us made to suffer it were! A safe and easy life they gave to *thee!* Precious baby Jedriel, *Vali's* favorite. Too special *thy* skin in battle to risk. Despised thee for that we did, all of us, I and our brothers. Died hating thee did they!"

Jedriel, wracked with shudders that were very nearly sobs, retreated to a bench and collapsed upon it. He clung to Jedina as if she were a branch thrown to a drowning swimmer.

"What, then, is there to do?" a soldier named Garain asked. "Never before . . ."

He trailed off, and Tilanne wasn't the only one to nod. Never before. Never before had something like this happened. Never before had someone acted so brutally against his own people. They had no jails, no judges, no juries as did their northern kin. There had never been a need.

They regarded Jedren with revulsion, horror. He returned their gazes with a flat and reptilian hostility. And madness. Utter, hateful, shining madness.

What *was* there to do?

Tilanne looked at the undercaptains, at the elders, at Tandira of the Scepter. The ranking leaders in Jewelgreen . . . yet, with sudden consternation, she realized that *they* were looking to *her* for an answer. Not only had she exposed this evil, but her rank was highest. Desperate for some solution, any solution, they would agree to whatever she decided.

The power and responsibility stole her breath. She held Jedren's fate in her hands. She held his very life, and could crush it as easily as she might crush a butterfly in her fist. She could order him exiled, or imprisoned, or even executed, and they would not protest.

And oh, how a part of her yearned for just that! For the sake of Jedriel, Jedina, poor dead Helina, and even Selmaire, she did not so much want justice as revenge.

"Summoned must be Commander Ellorn," she said. "His wisdom would a more fitting judge make him. Until then, detained and under guard must Jedren be kept."

* * *

Chapter Eleven

The soldiers led Jedren away to secure him in a storeroom. Reshelli appointed herself among his guards, lest any of the captain's men take sympathy on him. None would, Tilanne was sure. None could. Not after what they had beheld. But she did not say as much to Reshelli, who had come to fancy herself a spearmaid and warrior.

Alarice took charge of Jedriel and Jedina, both of whom were numb, speechless and stunned by the many shocks the night had hurled upon them. Vennan and another rider volunteered to leave at once for the fortress, to fetch Commander Ellorn without delay.

At last, the crowd had dispersed and the garrison lodging was quiet. Only then did Tilanne realize that in the confusion, Selmaire had slipped away. Listening intently, she heard movements from upstairs. A scrape, a thump. Hasty packing? Where did the woman think to go?

She called for Selmaire, but there was no answer.

If they did not know what under the stars was to be done with Jedren, how could they know what was to be done with Selmaire? Surely something did have to be done, for she was hardly blameless in this. She had known of the beatings. For long years, she had known and said nothing. Even after the horrendous mutilation she had suffered. And had she known, as well, of the circumstances of Jedina's mother's death? Had she kept her silence about murder?

Tilanne climbed the stairs down which she had so recently fallen. It reminded her of her bruises, but none of that was important now.

Their struggle had made a ruin of the upper hallway. Furniture toppled, a long ragged gouge along the wall where Jedren's sword had –

The sword. The sword was not where it should have been. Not where it had fallen.

"Selmaire?" she called again.

Apprehension tightened her nerves. She grasped the hilt of her own sword, which she had belted back on. She could not believe that Selmaire of all people would attack her. But why else remove the sword from where it had lain?

At the end of the hall, a door stood open. The small room beyond – even smaller than Jedina's, a domestic's quarters tucked beneath the eaves – flickered with sputtering candlelight. She could see the end of a narrow bed, a bit of threadbare rug.

"Selmaire, step out."

Tilanne advanced, senses alert, poised to react to the first hint of a threat. As she came closer and saw more of the room, she noticed that it was neat and ordered. No half-packed satchel on the bed, no strew of clothes and possessions.

Selmaire knelt by the window, steadying Jedren's sword with both hands. The pommel was braced in the angle where wall met floor. The point rested below her breasts.

Comprehension brought Tilanne to a gasping halt. She knew, instantly knew but could not bring herself to believe, what Selmaire intended.

That ruined face turned towards Tilanne. "Loved me, he did. Loved me, made love to me. Told me did he that my hideousness mattered not. That grateful should I be . . . and grateful, ever, I was." Selmaire's emerald eyes were so empty and dead that they might have already been the eyes of a corpse.

"No!" Tilanne sprang across the room.

But she was too late. Selmaire threw herself down, impaling her body on the blade. She screamed as sharp steel plunged through flesh with a wet and gruesome sound. The back of her nightgown was poked out in a tent of cloth, cloth that immediately flooded deep crimson.

More crimson gushed from Selmaire's screaming mouth. Her hands slapped-fluttered, leaving bloody marks on the wall and the sill. She fell onto her side, thrashing, gurgling.

Alive, she was still alive, the stroke had not been a single clean kill and she was dying in terror and agony.

"Selmaire!" Tilanne dropped beside her, in an agony of her own.

The wound was fatal. She knew that. No magic and no medicine in all the world could have saved Selmaire's life. But she was not yet dead, and in such suffering . . . there was no way to save her, but neither could Tilanne give her mercy . . . how *could* she give her mercy when it went against her sacred vow? Did the god test her, challenge her, even mock her with trials such as this? What was she to do?

The cloth had torn, the blade sliding out glistening and red as Selmaire writhed and clawed at the wall. Tilanne caught one of those flailing, clawing hands and held it. She felt Selmaire squeeze it tight, saw the same pleading panic in her gaze that she had seen in Falanar's and Findaire's . . . how many would die as she watched? How many? Was there nothing she could do?

Selmaire's bloody lips moved. "For . . . give . . . please . . . forgive . . ."

"That can only Kaledhol do," Tilanne said.

The fingers clutching hers clamped down harder than ever. Selmaire trembled all over. Her other hand rose, splayed and searching, as if reaching up for something only she could see. With a final bubbling exhalation, her arm dropped. Her grip went slack in Tilanne's.

She stayed beside the body, her mind lost in thought and prayer, until a worried Alarice came looking for her.

"Help her I could not," Tilanne said. "Save her I could not."

"But save Jedina thou didst," Alarice said, coaxing her to let go of Selmaire's cool, dead hand.

"A family destroyed."

"A family restored!"

"To Helina, tell that."

Alarice pointed a stern finger into Tilanne's face. "Not for Helina canst thou any responsibility claim. Knew her thou didst not, long ago it was. Selmaire her own choice did make, a bad one, a wrong one, but *hers*, Tilanne. Not thine. Weight enough on thy shoulders thou'll have without all the world's woes as well! Thou didst this night a child from dismal circumstances save, and to a good man the greatest of all gifts did give."

She let herself be led from the sad room, the sad house. She let Alarice clean Selmaire's and Jedren's blood from her hands and her new tunic. "Jedriel and Jedina, how fare they?"

"Time they both need, all of this to take in," Alarice said. "Yet each other they have."

A pale dawn had already colored the horizon pink and gold. The entire night had passed without her knowing it. As she emerged from the garrison, Tilanne became conscious of what a long night it had been. Weariness dragged at her limbs, and aches gnawed into her muscles.

"Someone must to Selmaire's body see –"

"Done shall it be. For thee, Tilanne, time it is and overdue for sleep."

"Sleep? Alarice, sleep I cannot."

"Sleep thou canst and shall, even if enspell thee I must. The rest of this, leave to us. When arrives does Commander Ellorn, well-rested must thou be."

With no further protest, she acquiesced. Her last foggy recollection was of Alarice drawing a blanket over her, and then all was a dark and dreamless nothing until Bairdan woke her late in the afternoon with the news that the riders had been sighted, and were expected to reach Jewelgreen soon.

Tilanne got up, washed and dressed, and had a quick meal of cold kofa, bread and preserves. From what she observed as she went about these minor errands, the previous night had rocked everyone to the very soul. None of the shops were open. None of the crafters or farmers or hunters were at work. The soldiers went about their duties in a half-hearted daze. Everywhere, it seemed, people simply gathered in groups and took comfort from each others' quiet company while each of them tried to come to terms with these terrible, tragic turns of events.

Commander Ellorn rode in with Vennan, the other rider, and a small party of his own men. Even Corandir was among them, a patch now covering his missing eye and otherwise fully recovered. The fortress soldiers came armed and armored, as if they were not sure just what they would find. Perhaps they had been unable to believe what they were told. Who could blame them? A captain, accused of deeds almost too unthinkable to name?

The commander dismounted in front of Tilanne and Bairdan, and pulled off his helm to regard them. He also took in the solemn gatherings of people, and the swags of dark wine-red fabric with which some had adorned their doors. "Told we were that alive he was," he said. "And until our arrival, under guard being held."

"So he is," Bairdan said, after a brief, perfunctory salute. "Undercaptain Renveil his custody personally oversees. For another are these signs of mourning."

Once he had heard all, Ellorn insisted on seeing Jedren at once. He did not let his shock and revulsion get in the way of his interrogation, and Tilanne watched him almost as closely as she watched Jedren's responses. Kaledhol forbid she should ever have to do anything of this sort again . . . but if she did, she would need to know how.

Jedren, now in actual manacles and chains instead of merely being bound with his belt, stood wrathful and unrepentant before the entire town. His glare, as fierce as that of any basilisk, shifted from one person to the next as if forever marking them in his memory, and holding each of them singularly accountable for his downfall.

"Grievous deeds has he indeed done, and to them confessed," the commander said. "But, for punishment, correct thou art, Kor Tilanne . . . none of us such authority have. To Kaledhol, and Kaledhol alone, must he answer."

"What, then, can be done?" Bairdan asked.

"We must to the temple take him," Tilanne said. "Fit is he on such ground to tread?"

Ellorn nodded. "When upon the altar-stone his hands Jedren doth set, when pricked are his palms that the blood might from them flow, to Kaledhol shall all his sins in their entirety be shown."

"Never!" Jedren, who had remained motionless and sullenly silent in his anger, moved fast.

He spun, striking out with his manacled wrists at Renveil. The heavy chain smashed the undercaptain's jaw and pitched him backward to sprawl in a scattering of his own teeth. As other soldiers rushed to restrain him, he went into a frenzy. He kicked at one man, bit at another, and was overborne fighting frantically to the ground. More men – and Reshelli – leaped into the fray. Though he lashed out with strikes born of frantic rage, striking many a severe blow, in the end, they proved too much for him. Jedren was hoisted aloft, still struggling.

Sickened, sickened by all of it, that it should go this badly, that the situation should exist in the first place, Tilanne wanted to turn away. Wanted to *run* away. She wished to see no more of this. Yet she firmed her spine and followed as half a dozen men carried Jedren toward the temple. Reshelli led the way, her lip split and her eye blacked but holding her spear up with all the pride of an army's standard-bearer.

As many of the folk of Jewelgreen as could fit crowded into the temple, staying beyond the ring of obsidian columns, beyond the mosaic of the red basilisks twining in their endless circle around the floor. Tilanne saw Jedriel among them. His face was pallid, his dark eyes hollow, as if he had not slept in days. But he had Jedina with him, their hands clasped in a trusting unity so earnest it nearly brought Tilanne to tears. She would not allow herself that indulgence. Now, more than ever, she knew that she had to be at her strongest.

Jedren lost all his fighting will when he was borne between the black columns. He did not resist as the soldiers set him down – rather ungently, slamming him to his knees – on the mosaic ring of basilisks. His gaze was fixed on the chunk of rock and the dark crystal rising from it. He was quaking, as if that was no crystal at all before him but some dragon or nightmare beast come to devour him in slow, agonizing bites.

Renveil, his jaw shattered, had been taken away by the physician, so it fell to Bairdan to unlock the manacles. Corandir held one of Jedren's wrists, and one of the commander's men held the other. Jedren seemed barely to notice as they extended his arms with the palms turned upraised.

"Kor Tilanne," Commander Ellorn called.

With feet that felt mired in deep mud, Tilanne moved to join him. He drew a sharp, thin dagger, reversed it, and extended the hilt toward her. His nod was grim.

She took the dagger. With her other hand, she touched the ruby basilisk she wore around her neck. No sense of rightness and purpose filled her this time as she stood within the circle of columns. No welcoming lights danced within the dark crystal. She could sense Kaledhol's presence. Watching. Judging. Stern. Relentless.

Yes, she had to be at her strongest. She knew that she could not afford to be weak. Not now.

Jedren came alive again when she approached him. "Let it not be her!"

Bairdan held him down by the shoulders, forcing him to stay on his knees. Corandir and the other soldier would not let him pull his arms away. He clenched his fists into tight balls, hiding away the vulnerable palms.

"Rather wouldst thou some other this deed performed?" Bairdan asked, pitching his voice in a low whisper as if hoping to spare his former captain this one last shame. "Perhaps thy brother?"

At that, Jedren's features contorted with revulsion. He grudgingly uncurled his fists, opening them to Tilanne. He would not look at her. She stared down at his hands. Hands that had shown her how to hold a sword, a knife, a shield. Hands that had throttled the life from Helina, held the switch that striped Jedina's tender back with scars, hurled fire into Selmaire's face.

"Thy god, thy Cause, thy people and thy family thou hast offended, Jedren," she said, speaking loud enough for all to hear. "For Kaledhol it is, thy soul to forgive or thy soul to condemn."

She sliced his palm, drawing a dark line of blood. At the sight of it, the last of Tilanne's hesitation fell away. She did the same to his other hand, moving surely even when he uttered a sudden violent scream and began yanking wildly at the men that held him.

"No! No! Do this thou cannot!"

Tilanne stepped back. Corandir and the other soldier, with Bairdan's help, dragged Jedren upright and then pushed him forward, a hard shove that sent him tottering toward the chunk of stone. On pure instinct, he thrust out his hands to stop his headlong fall. His bloodied palms landed full against the dark crystal.

It flared alight, umber and indigo and a deep throbbing red, violet and forest green. The colors spun through the temple in revolving beams. They flowed over the walls and floor, gleamed on obsidian columns, played across pale faces, glittered darkly in pair after pair of wide elven eyes. As one, they all sank to their knees. Parents and children, husbands and wives, soldiers and crafters, mages and domestics, all kneeling in the strange, shifting hues.

Tilanne grasped the ruby basilisk again, and found it warm in her hand. Warm, and beating with a pulse that matched the thundering of her heart. It matched, too, a steady thrumming beat that seemed to emanate not from the crystal, not from the stone, but from everywhere. From the very air around them, from the very earth beneath their feet.

Jedren's arms tensed and bunched so violently that the seams of his sleeves burst apart, cloth hanging in folds from his shoulders. Yet his hands remained as if bolted, as if *fused* to the stone. He scrabbled with his legs, to no avail. He could not pull himself loose.

And now the light, that terrible, wonderful, godly light no longer just emanated from the crystal but *welled* from it in droplets, like moisture beading on the skin, like sweat issuing from pores. Running down its uneven, faceted sides . . . flowing thick, light like honey or slow tree sap made of dark rainbows. Living, liquid light.

"Protector god, destroyer god," Tilanne said, barely hearing herself above that drumming pulse. "In Thy mercy, in Thy wrath, Kaledhol this man's fate decide."

The crystalline dark rainbow liquid light reached Jedren. It pooled around his fingers. He shrieked, a cry so high and shrill it sounded more like bird than man. The substance, like cold living lava, coursed over his trapped hands. Slowly, slowly, it oozed and seethed and flowed its way up his arms. Dazzling deepwater blue, maroon, cloudy silver, burnt-orange . . . it flowed over and encapsulated Jedren as if he were a fly caught in amber. Defying nature, it ran uphill over his chest, to his neck, to his head. When it covered his mouth, his screams were not muffled but abruptly cut off, a totality of silence.

He was engulfed, head to toe, unable to move, suspended in an uncanny cocoon of swirling radiance. Tilanne could see his eyes, wide open and conscious, aware, seeing her through that thick, translucent barrier.

The colors began to turn darker. The light was fading, the thrumming beat slowing. A glow, a wine-red glow, swelled from nowhere and everywhere. Tilanne had to squint and shield her face as it grew painfully, blindingly bright.

With a deafening pop, a sensation that pushed at the eardrums and sucked breath from their lungs, Jedren disappeared. Just as the Dragon's Eye had done when Tilanne offered it to Kaledhol. He and his crystalline cocoon vanished into nothingness, taking the wine-red glow with them the way a heavy stone, dropped onto a floating circle of cloth, might pull the cloth after into the lightless depths of a pool.

And Jedren was gone.

Gradually, in the absolute stillness that reigned in the temple, Tilanne felt her pulse and her senses return to normal. All around her, she saw the same expressions on others that she was sure she must be wearing on her own face – a profoundly humbling reverence and awe, mixed with fear.

They were all looking at her, looking at her as if she could explain what they'd just witnessed.

"Took him did Kaledhol," she said. Her voice was so husky that she could barely recognize it as her own. She rubbed her thumb against her forefinger, remembering the sharp little bite of the ruby basilisk and how she had pressed her own bloodied thumb to the crystal. "Took him . . . took him while yet he lived . . . the Torments to endure."

A great general sigh arose, and in it Tilanne heard acceptance, relief, weariness, sorrow, and a host of other emotions combined.

"To the Torments," someone said. "To the Torments has he gone."

The day was still bright outside, the autumn sun a rich golden ball in a bed of blue and the trees dripping leaves like garnets and topaz. Yet it felt like it should be night, dark, cold.

Taken by Kaledhol. He had been *taken*, just as an offering might have been.

"Heard have I," Commander Ellorn said, breaking the spell of silence that hung over the group, "that once, when died a great *Rhunvala* did, his body to the temple was carried and there to the god given. Kaledhol did him take up, armor, weapons, and all."

"I too, that story remember," Tandira of the Scepter said. She was Alarice's new mentor, an elegant woman with buff-colored hair worn in a netted twist, and a design of climbing flowered vines tattooed like a frame around the edges of her face. "But never before a living thing. Never of that have I heard."

No, none of them had. But, as unsettling as it had been, there was an odd comfort and security in it. Kaledhol had made His wishes known in a way that could not be questioned, could not be denied.

Tilanne understood that even better than the rest of them. Not long after, even before the ashes of Selmaire's funeral had cooled, she announced her intention to leave Jewelgreen.

She knew that if she did not do it soon, she would find it harder and harder to go with each passing day. There could have been a place for her here. Commander Ellorn would have gladly named her undercaptain to the newly-promoted Bairdan, had she wished it. With Jedriel and Jedina, she could have had more than just a place. She could have had a home, a family. She ached to leave Alarice, Ilantisian, Reshelli, Corandir, and so many friends both old and new.

"Thought had I once that on thy journey I might accompany thee," Jedriel said later that night, when they lay close and entwined in her bed. "As far, at least, as might be allowed. The Citadel itself would to me be forbidden, but –"

She nuzzled her face into the warm hollow of his neck, her breath caressing the curves of his ear. "Welcome company wouldst thou indeed have been, Jedriel. Here, though, here art thou more needed."

"With us Jedina could come," he said. "Greatly fond of thee she is."

"Of her, also, am I. But a home she needs, Jedriel. Too many dark memories and old pains must she conquer, or else to her a haunted place this will seem. Here she must stay, and new memories make."

He sighed and kissed her brow, and rolled one of her earrings between thumb and forefinger. "When first the Kai this destiny granted thee, so pleased was I, so proud, so happy for thee. Never did I think that *we* would be, or that between us that, thy destiny, would come."

The good folk of Jewelgreen insisted on making her departure an occasion, with a lavish feast and still more gifts. Commander Ellorn came from the fortress to see her off, and even brought Sahen with him. Tilanne had not seen Sahen since leaving him in Ellorn's charge, and she was almost as surprised by the changes in him as he was by those in her. Discipline had been good for him. Gone was his sneer, gone was the imperious tilt to his nose.

The wine flowed freely. They feasted and danced until long after both moons had set. It was nearly sunrise by the time Jedriel fell asleep, his red-gold hair tangled across the pillows, his face serene with the faintest of smiles.

Tilanne was reluctant to leave the blankets that had been warmed by their bodies. But they had said their farewells in the best possible way, and she would rather leave with the memory of that happiness than look back, and see sorrow in his dark eyes. She kissed him so lightly that he did not wake.

She slipped from the bed and dressed, then went through her lodgings collecting the last few items not already packed. Last of all, she paused at a small curtained alcove where Jedina slept, and spent a few moments gazing down at the dreaming child.

"Fare thee well, Jedina," she said. "For me, thy father look after."

Aside from herself, all that moved on the avenues was a drifting fog. A damp chill lingered in the air. Tilanne went to the stables, glad for her cloak and boots and gloves. Her horse – another extravagant gift, this one from Commander Ellorn – was black as midnight. She had named the mare Morai in honor of an ancient warrior.

The guards at the eastern wall did not speak, but they saluted at her approach. She returned it. The soft, muffling fog swallowed the grinding of hinges as they opened the great gates for her, and swallowed the clop of Morai's hooves as she rode out.

Before her, unwinding like a spool into the mist, was the road that would ultimately lead her to the Forest of the Wandering Lost, and to the *Odan Rhunvale*.

* * *

Part Two:

Descent into Darkness

CHAPTER TWELVE

"Firsthome," she said. "Morai, Firsthome soon we'll see, if still exists Firsthome does."

She had taken to talking to the horse on her journey, and what of it? Morai had proved to be good company, steadfast and fearless, undaunted even when Tilanne herself felt a qualm as they came to each new settlement to go through a repetition of the same welcome.

And it was the same, always the same. Her reception was initially one of curiosity, for few people traveled much at all and hardly ever alone. Least of all a woman. When she turned out to be an armed and armored woman, a woman bound for the Citadel to try and become *Rhunvala* . . .

Well, that too was always the same. They thought she was jesting, then they thought she was mad, and then they thought she was a rebellious and impertinent upstart. A girl, *Rhunvala*? A *girl*? That skepticism always lasted until she demonstrated her skills and knowledge, showing them that she did have the strength and speed to make a warrior. Her quiet but sincere devotion showed that she also had considerable faith.

And so, settlement after settlement, she had won their acceptance. Not always their approval, and sometimes the acceptance was most grudging. She had been subjected to more than one well-meaning attempt to dissuade her, by those who claimed only to be trying to talk some sense into her. For her own good, they said. So that she did not go putting reckless ideas into the heads of other impressionable young girls, they said.

Was it any wonder, therefore, that she had come to prefer the conversation of her horse? Morai never tried to talk sense into her. Morai never recoiled in shock and demanded to know just what her mother would think of this foolishness.

Not that she'd stayed long in any one place. Only in the Valley of the Cloudflowers had she truly been tempted to linger. The blue-bladed grass, the cloudflower vines with their eruptions of soft white blossoms . . . riding across it was like riding across a summer sky filled with puffy white clouds. The valley itself was ringed with small fortress-spires, to protect the rare plants and the physicians who lived and trained here. Their homes were aloft, a village of platforms and huts and bridges constructed up in the high branches of trees with silvery bark and indigo leaves. Her brother Vandil had apprenticed at Cloudflowers, and being there had reminded her of him with more power and poignancy than any other place since Cliffcave.

From the Valley of the Cloudflowers, she had journeyed on to Southvale Fortress, the last occupied outpost of the *Morvalan* lands before the vast reaches of the Forest of the Wandering Lost. The road was little-used, descending from the fort in a series of switchbacks down steep mountainside.

Tilanne was aware of the sentries on the high wall behind her, growing smaller as she left Southvale behind. Had they placed bets on how far she'd get before turning tail and coming back to the security of stone walls and archers? It would have come as no surprise, and nothing new.

She was just glad that she had thus far given no one any satisfaction in collecting on such a wager. She had not turned back. Had not retraced her steps. Even when the weather had grown ugly or the way had grown hard, Tilanne and Morai had pressed on, undeterred.

"Kaledhol my path guide, Kaledhol my heart make strong," she said.

The Forest of the Wandering Lost looked no less forbidding from up close than it had from when she'd first gazed out over it. The canopy of leaves stretched to the rising snowcapped spines of the distant Dragonheights. Under a slate-colored sky of low-hanging clouds, the expanse was so dark a green as to look black. As black as an ink-dark lake.

Even now, she could hardly believe she was going to see Firsthome. Like ancient Govannisan, it was a name she'd heard in legends and stories since she was just a little girl but not anything that seemed as if it could possibly be real. Not anyplace that a person – any person, let alone ordinary Tilanne Murres – could ever truly go.

"Govannisan home to all elves was," she said to the horse. "And to the dwarves besides, both races side by side in harmony dwelling. Firsthome, though . . . Firsthome only to the *Morvalan* belonged. By *Morvalan* hands built, by *Morvalan* blood defended."

And the *Morvalan* had made the same fatal mistake as their predecessors. Safety in numbers, some had said. All our eggs in one basket, others had countered.

"They, the latter faction, the ones proved right were," Tilanne said. "Never all together in one city should they have settled. Protected from the dragons they may have been, but to other dangers, far more vulnerable they were. In the deep forests, crops they could not grow and herds they could not tend. When illness came, and plague, like wildfire through them it spread."

And when the Dread Beasts had been loosed . . .

Tilanne pushed that thought from her mind. The Dread Beasts had been long ago. They were no more. The *Morvalan* had seen the error of their ways and spread out into smaller communities so that no one threat could eliminate them.

The first spatters of rain came down as she and Morai neared the bottom of the switchbacks. Tilanne was thankful it held off that long; she wouldn't have cared to make such a steep and tricky descent over slick stones and slippery mud.

Vennan had taught her that one of the first rules of the wilderness was to never eat what one had brought, if one could eat what one could find. She gathered nuts and a few apples as she collected firewood for her solitary camp. Better to save her provisions for a time when nature might not be so accommodating. Tilanne cracked nuts between stones, eating some and throwing the rest into her cookpot to simmer overnight with a handful of grain. By morning, she'd have a hot pottage that she and Morai could share.

It sometimes astonished her how readily she had adapted to her harsh new life. The armor that had once been so uncomfortable was now a thing she unbuckled with reluctance and set aside each night before she crawled into her bedroll. She stood no watches, for she had to sleep sometime and there was no one else with whom to alternate. If trouble came, then trouble came, and all she could do was be ready.

She woke to a very different world, the clouds having rained and blown themselves out while she slept. Sunlight slanted through the trees, making sparkling jewels on the damp foliage.

Over the next several days, as she progressed further into the woods, the darker it became. At first, Tilanne thought that it was because the canopy was getting thicker, blocking the rays of the sun. She soon realized that wasn't the only reason. The plants themselves were getting darker as well . . . *darker* in a literal sense. The tree trunks she'd seen when she entered the woods had been brownish-grey. Now they were a much darker brown. The overall color of the leaves had deepened beyond rich green toward black.

The undergrowth was a dense tangle. If there indeed had been a road, however many dozens of centuries before, it had been reclaimed. She finally had to dismount and led Morai by the reins, picking her way in a slow, frustrating path that she could only hope was still taking her in the right direction.

Others did come this way. Others had to come this way. *Rhunvala* and *Dhanvala* had to get to and from the Citadel somehow. Unless she had gotten lost.

"Not for no reason is this the Forest of the Wandering Lost known," she said to Morai.

As for Firsthome, if the woods had reclaimed the road, might they not also have reclaimed anything left of the city?

After one particularly vexing afternoon, in which she'd become certain she was going in circles, she made camp early and took her bow to see if she could have meat for the fire. Her skill at archery, despite Renveil's instruction, was never going to be great, but she did manage to shoot a rabbit.

She did not, however, manage to kill it with that shot, and her supper bounded feebly off with her arrow still sticking out of it. Tilanne grumbled and gave chase, reminding herself that rabbit or no rabbit, she had best not go too far or she might make matters far worse.

A crumbling stone wall covered in moss and vines and creepers loomed ahead of her.

The rabbit was forgotten. Supper was forgotten.

She had come to Firsthome.

The forest *had* made an effort to overtake it, but hadn't completely succeeded. She could make out the lines of walls, the shapes of buildings. Silver-shot grey marble. Alabaster pillars, some broke, a few still miraculously intact. Mosaics of semi-precious gems in green and red and magnificent blue in angular knotwork patterns. Roofs made from overlapping disks of slate, and the verdigris-tinted shine of one peaked roof made of metal.

The city must have been immense. Far bigger than any town, fortress or settlement in all the southlands. It staggered her imagination.

"In the thousands they dwelled here," she said, amazed. "In the tens of thousands, all together, all in one place."

What must such a place have been like at its height? When every home and shop and building was occupied, when craftsmen did their work, and shopkeeps hawked their wares, and children played and lovers argued and soldiers trained? What must it have been like?

Noisy, she decided. Noisy and hectic.

Yet there would have been love here too. Love and family and companionship.

She fetched Morai, moving her camp to a grassy nook within the ruins. Any thoughts of a hot meal had fallen out of her head by wonder. She nibbled on bread and a hunk of cheese as she wandered, awestruck, through what must have once been avenues and courtyards and marketplaces.

In one such marketplace, a vast square that could have held everyone in Jewelgreen and both its guardian fortresses combined without them feeling the least bit crowded, she came to a stunned halt.

It must have been a fountain once, a huge and glorious fountain. Water-channels led off from it in six directions, but she barely paid them any attention. The sculpture . . . the sculpture took her breath away.

Carved from purest white stone – or shaped by earth-magics? – were a dozen elven figures, half again as tall as life. They faced outward in a ring, nude men and women holding ewers tipped over the fountain's main basin. At the very center of the ring of statues, towering over their heads, rose a slim tower with a railing around its top and steps spiraling up the outside.

The whole sculpture was worn and weathered, damaged with chips and cracks, but Tilanne had never seen anything more beautiful and incredible in all her life. She knew crafters, yes. But function always came first, always, and to make something artful as well as useful was indulgence enough. The idea that her people had once been safe enough, leisurely enough, to build anything so extravagant as this . . . she could hardly believe it.

She slipped between two of the figures without hesitation and climbed the steps to the very top of the tower. At the railing, she traced with her gaze each of the water-channels, and tried to guess the purpose of the various structures into which they had flowed. Bath-houses? Laundries? Watering-places for animals?

Then she saw the temple.

It was built of darkest marble, nearly black. A peaked roof of tarnished silver was held up by two ranks of fluted columns. And there, before it, many times the height of a man and carved from flawless obsidian, was a statue of an armored warrior.

Tilanne unthinkingly went to her knees.

An image of Kaledhol? A statue of the god? A depiction of Him? She'd never heard of such a thing, never seen one. No one was to know what the god looked like. How could they? He was a *god*, able to take whatever form He chose. To attempt to capture His image, limit Him the way the orcs and humans did with their false gods . . . who would dare presume such a thing?

Yet . . . if she had been asked to say what she thought a statue of Kaledhol might have looked like, her answer would have come very close to that which she now beheld.

She climbed down from the fountain tower at a careless breakneck scramble, and rushed through the ruins until she was at the very base of the magnificent statue.

Sword in hand, shield held at the ready. Head high, wary, alert. A face all planes and lines, a sharp face, elven yet *more*, brows lowered over watchful eyes as if having just sighted an enemy in the distance. On the breastplate, the suggestion of roses.

The statue stood on a round dais, the edge of which crawled with carvings of basilisks and inscribed lettering. Tilanne could only decipher a bit of it, enough to tell her what she already knew – Kaledhol the Protector, Kaledhol the Destroyer, the great guardian, the dark and avenging blade.

She tipped her head back to study the face. How had they known, those ancient artisans? *Had* they known, or had they guessed? And if they'd guessed, how had they been sure that doing so wouldn't offend Kaledhol and bring down the Torments upon them?

Her heart wrenched as a closer view showed that even the statue and the temple had not escaped the ravages of the centuries. One entire wall had caved in, and a hair-like snarl of growth choked the opening. Wide, low steps marched up to the doors, one of which hung by a single hinge and the other of which had long since been torn away. The gap was so overrun with vines that a ropy green curtain barred her entrance.

"Not by vines shall I be deterred," she said.

As she went to push through them, the vines came alive like a nest of disturbed snakes. They whipped around her, tangling her arms and legs, yanking her off her feet to hang suspended and ensnared like a child's string-puppet. Thorns that she hadn't noticed pricked and clung at her clothes, her hair, the exposed portions of her skin.

* * *

Chapter Thirteen

Something stirred in the unseen depths of the temple. It made a slithery, nasty, sound. Wet. Slapping. Slick. Horrid.

In a burst of sudden strength, Tilanne ripped herself free of the grasping vines. She stumbled back and they swayed out toward, reaching, wavering. She could hear their raspy rustle, and the squishing, repugnant noises from within.

Outraged and appalled, she drew her sword and began slashing. Here of all places, Kaledhol's own temple? Invaded by some loathsome terror, some malevolent menace? She would not allow it! Not unchallenged, anyway!

The remaining vines recoiled as if in pain, as if understanding what her sharp-edged blade could mean to them. The severed pieces seeped a thick greenish fluid from their ends. The ones on the ground continued to writhe and flex like dying serpents.

Her heart was hammering, her ears tucked all but flat to the sides of her head, her eyes wide. She itched in the places the thorns had drawn blood, itched like a frenzy. A quick glance showed her that the skin around the scratches was already reddened, puffy.

She could see through the waving tendrils of vines to the interior of the temple. It was far larger, far grander than anything they had in Jewelgreen or any of the other settlements. Perhaps those could only properly be called shrines, while this, this was a true temple. At the far end, she could just make out another image of the god, a face over what seemed to be an altar made to resemble cupped, gauntleted hands.

Emboldened by her faith and her fury, Tilanne stepped forth again and hacked at the vines. She dodged them when they snaked toward her, and cut high so as to slice them from the doorway.

Those that sought to twine about her boots, she kicked away or stomped. Once she'd cleared an opening, she plunged into the temple's shadowed interior.

The vegetation was deep and dense in here, vines piled one atop the other, a teeming nest of the hateful grasping things. The thickest were as big around as her thigh, their thorns like knives. Others, quicker and thinner, rose up like snakes about to strike.

Somehow, by luck and sheer determination, she kept her footing despite vines that tried to snag her boots and trip her. If she fell, she knew, it would be her death. She kept laying about her with the keen steel blade. At last, she won through to the outstretched stone gauntlets.

The vines could not seem to reach her. There was a wide swath where they did not go, did not grow. The floor was bare, clean. It glistened. No dust, no dried leaves or withered bits of vine. Indeed, the floor looked almost . . . wet. Shiny. As if freshly washed.

The floor was slick, too. Moist and slick beneath the soles of her boots.

She heard the horrid sucking and slurping noise again. Slowly, against her will, Tilanne turned to look at the thing that came oozing from between a pair of flanking pillars.

It churned and rolled over itself as it moved, overlapping like a slow tumble of glue-mud or vomit. Featureless, lacking limbs or head or any discernible parts, it was sickly yellowish sludge, mottled with black and a rusty brown-red. A smell clung to it, faint but revolting.

"Lung-rot," Tilanne said, for that was what it reminded her of.

She remembered her mother's elder sister dying of it, when Tilanne herself had been barely more than a toddler. The clots and globs spewed up by the dying woman had been of exactly these hues, when in the extremity of her illness she had begun shedding parts of her own corrupted flesh. The disease had been all through her in the end, spreading from her lungs down into the soft tissues of her viscera, eating away the lining of her mouth and nose. They'd all had to wear cloth around their faces to keep any in the house from inhaling the pestilence her aunt had coughed into the air.

This thing, this hideous squelching thing, could have been the disease personified and brought to some hideous life of its own.

Without realizing what she was doing, Tilanne pulled the collar of her tunic out from under her armor, to shield her mouth and nose.

Eyeless, earless, it nonetheless came unfalteringly at Tilanne. Perhaps it detected the warmth of her body. Perhaps it sensed her by some means she could not understand. However it found her, she realized its intent was to swarm over her, engulf her. Just as Jedren had been swallowed up by the crystalline substance, except there was none of Kaledhol's power at work here. This was no manifestation of the god, no chosen warden to protect the temple from intruders. This itself *was* the intruder, hungry and mindless.

A Dread Beast . . . still a Dread Beast here after all!

She retreated as it surged toward her, but had few options. The vines would tear her apart, or hold her immobile while the lung-rot monstrosity overpowered her. A sword would be no use against a creature whose gelatinous body would merely part around the steel and then re-form in its wake. She tried anyway. Each cut carved a deep line but drew no blood. The thing did not even seem to notice her attacks.

Tilanne dove to the floor and rolled-squirmed-crawled under the upraised altar-hands. Her armor scraped and grated against stone, but she rose up on the other side, the hands now between her and the creature. She could never chop her way through the vines in time, and her only other way out was a hall that led into the deeper recesses of the building.

Or it was no way out at all, and she would be trapped.

She ran down the hall anyway, stirring up the dust and debris left by tens of centuries of abandonment and neglect. The walls were coated with moldy grey-green growths. The first door she came to was barricaded as stoutly as any fortress gate. The ironwood timber socked into the brackets on the door was spongy with age but still so heavy that it would have taken two strong men to lift it, and the dampness had swollen it so that it might not have lifted free even if there had been two strong men handy to try.

To her left, a flight of stairs descended into a cellar. A bitter, rancid odor drifted up, a reek of old decay but far preferable to the ripe, fetid stink of the lung-rot. She saw white objects below, white objects and the faint glint of metal.

Bones? Bones and armor?

Her mouth dry with horror, Tilanne went down the steps until the remains became more visible. Two bodies lay sprawled in contorted positions. An iron lever, three burnt-out torches and other tools were strewn around them, as if they had managed to pry open the door at the bottom before dying.

Something about them . . .

She took another step, frowning. Something about the bodies . . . something about the width of their ribcages, and the shape of their skulls . . .

Understanding came to her like a dousing of ice water. The bones were not those of elves. They were human. Human bones. Human bodies. Humans had been . . . had been *here!* In Firsthome! And not just in Firsthome, but in Kaledhol's own temple!

By the way they were positioned, Tilanne surmised that they had opened the door, preparing to go in, and something had struck them dead where they stood.

Humans, here! Here in Firsthome, here in the *Morvalan* lands!

The bitter offense made bile rise in Tilanne's throat. She could guess from whence these men must have come. Spies of the Mountain Kingdom, no doubt. Seeking plunder or scouting ways to sneak their armies against the settlements. Well, they had paid the ultimate price for their trespass here. It served them right.

What, though, had killed them? Not the vines. The creature? Some old remnant of warding-spell on the door?

Confident that no such spell would hurt her, she drew the door open. Hinges groaned like a living thing in pain, and the lower edge stuttered across the floor with such a din that anything with ears would know where she was.

Beyond was a catacomb, stretching cold and long as far as her eyes could see. The walls of it were lined with stone chests . . . no, they were . . . strange as it seemed, they were caskets. Stone caskets, worked with designs of rose-garlands all along the rims.

She knew what she was seeing, though she hardly understood it. This was a burial-place for the dead. Rather than being decently consumed by clean fire and rose-oil, elves had been buried here, entombed in their coffins of stone.

Worst of all, their rest had been disturbed. More bones littered the floor, these ones were ancient and gone mostly to dust. Scraps of cloth – rosecloth? – and strands of hair were mixed with the bones. Some of the caskets were askew, their lids off or their contents dumped out, trampled and pawed through for some reason she could not comprehend . . .

But then she did, and her bitterness turned to a soul-aching venomous pain. The humans. During the time of Firsthome, the elves had entombed their dead instead of putting them to pyres, and the humans had come looking to plunder those graves for jewelry and treasures.

She was gladder than ever that they'd died for their deeds. Then her thoughts faltered as something else occurred to her.

Two bodies. Three torches.

Two bodies outside this room, trying to get in. No third body inside.

Did that mean there had been another grave-robber? One who had survived long enough to do this damage, this desecration? One who had gotten away?

Lost and forgotten in a pile of dust, she found one treasure that had been overlooked – a single grape-cluster earring of truesilver leaves and amethyst beads. It was broken, caked with tarnish and dirt.

Her vision had blurred, but she didn't realize until tears dripped from her chin that she was crying, crying for these poor elves whose final rest had been so cruelly disturbed.

Not all of them had been. Some caskets were untouched, festooned with cobwebs and a layer of dry moss. Thick white flaky patches of moss, white patches speckled with black dots.

Pah-kena. The tomb was growing with *pah-kena* moss.

She still had her tunic's collar pulled up, but she stopped breathing just the same.

This chamber, sealed for untold centuries after the elves left Firsthome. Cold and dank. The moss growing, growing. Thriving in the airless dark.

And then, so many years later, along had come the humans. They'd wrenched open the door, and a gust of the poisoned air had rushed out at them. The nearest two, in the brunt of it, would have dropped on the spot, died instantly.

But a third person, farther back? Seeing his companions fall, for no visible cause . . . but not close enough himself to share their fate.

Close enough to let himself in for a worse one. He'd breathed in the spores stirred up by the rushing air, and they had taken root in his lungs. Given him the lung-rot . . .

Which had become something more. It hadn't just killed him. It had continued to grow, long after he was dead. The rot gradually encompassing his entire body, until nothing human was left. Only the cancer. Only the lung-rot. Living a monstrous new life of its own. Feasting on what it could find. Vermin, insects, unwary animals that wandered too close.

Tilanne shuddered, and her chest throbbed with spears of fire. She needed to breathe, didn't dare, could all-too-clearly imagine the same thing happening to her. But hadn't she already inhaled of the air down here? It could be too late.

She would not let herself think of it. On unsteady legs, she went out of the door and closed it behind her, stumbling through the scattered bones and tools. The spears in her chest had become a vise, crushing her. Her throat felt drawn to a pinhole, her jaws and lips locked. Her head pounded, and red sparks shot across her sight.

The third human must have gone back in when he deemed it was safe, gone in and touched the moss. Stirred up the spores. She had touched nothing . . . well, the earring, which she had picked up with the intention of putting it into the nearest casket . . . she still held it.

Staggering now from lack of air, she reached the top of the stairs and looked yearningly at the ironwood-barred door. A waver of greenish light played across it, and in her head-swimming state, Tilanne did not immediately realize it was a glimmer through a high, small window in the opposite wall. The sunshine filtered through leaves, but they did not look like the vines. She hoped they were not.

Was the opening large enough for her? She'd have to trust in Kaledhol's good will.

Releasing her held, burning breath in short puffs but not yet daring to take in any new ones, Tilanne dragged a discarded slab of wood and leaned it against the wall as a makeshift stepladder. She was about to clamber up it when a squishing, slithering, unwelcome noise made her whirl around.

The rest of her hoarded breath came out in a revolted cry. She had thought the hall was too narrow for the creature to fit, but she had been wrong. Lacking bones, lacking any sort of real shape at all, the lung-rot monstrosity could ooze through almost gap.

The hallway was filled, blocked, by the quivering mass. Tilanne threw herself up the slab, hearing the half-rotted wood squeal, feeling the mushy sag of it as it threatened to give way. She struggled to haul herself up and out, and felt something sticky latch itself onto her boot as she hung, half-way and head down, above a long drop onto hard earth.

A skull-smashing plunge was by far the lesser evil. She yanked and kicked with all her might. There was a slurping noise as her boot pulled loose of the thing. Tilanne twisted her body and thrust her arms upward. She grabbed onto an overhanging eave. The roof, metal and rough, sliced through her gloves and into her fingers when the full weight of her armored body hung by nothing but her hands. Gritting her teeth against the pain, she pulled herself the rest of the way up and onto the peaked, tarnished metal roof. She ran along it despite the dangerous tilt, until she came to a safer place to drop down.

The creature had not followed her out. Her only guess, her only hope, was that the sunlight was somehow painful to it.

Tilanne coughed experimentally. She feared but expected to hear the clogged rasp of lung-rot already infesting her. Though she was breathing hard from her exertions, she felt fine at the moment. But only time would tell.

In the meanwhile, something had to be done. Not only because it was vile and monstrous but because it had once been *human*. There was no way that any *Morvalan*, especially one bound to become a defender of her people, could allow it to have charge of a place sacred to Kaledhol.

By morning, when her lungs were still clear, she let herself begin to believe that she might have come through untouched by the spores. As she investigated more of the ruined city, trying to think of how to destroy the creature or at the very least get it out of Kaledhol's temple, she caught a faint whiff of smoke. Just a wisp of it, blown on the breeze . . . but it was followed by the snorting whinny of a horse that was not Morai.

Her armor did not lend itself to perfect stealth and silence, but she crept as quietly as she could in pursuit of the scent and the sound. She spied the cookfire some hundred paces beyond the farthest edge of Firsthome. As if they had not quite dared make their camp within the walls.

Humans.

One, burly and bearded, dumped dirt on the fire to extinguish it. Another, slim as a whip, was packing up. They wore scrounged, ill-fitting armor and had the rough, tough, leathery and scarred look of the Mountain King's people. The burly one had an iron mace at his belt. The lean one carried a sword much like him – long, sharp, quick. They had a trio of horses and two small but sturdy ponies, currently laden with nothing but a pile of empty sacks.

A third human, an elder with distinguished silver-grey hair and intelligent eyes, stood apart from them as if menial work was beneath him. He leaned on a staff, and studied the ruins with an expression of anticipation and greed.

Her belly seethed with venomous outrage, but she stayed put and listened to what she could hear of their conversation. They spoke the patchwork dialect usual to the Mountain Kingdom, made up of bits and pieces from a dozen human languages.

The grey-haired said, "Now, remember, watch your step. I lost three men here last time and was lucky to escape with my life."

"What killed 'em?" the burly one asked.

"Bad air."

"How come it didn't take you?" the slim one said.

"*I* had the good sense to stay outside," he replied haughtily. "I told them to tie ropes to the door handles, pull from a distance, and wait while the good air mellowed and diluted the bad. But they were so hot to get their hands on elf-silver and jewels that they paid me no mind, and paid for it dearly."

"I don't care me none for silver and jewels," said the burly one. "Well, not that I'd snub me nose at 'em. But it's weapons what I want. Elf-steel, and magic."

"Leave the magic to me, Horald," snapped the grey-haired one. "Stick to that at which you excel."

Horald snorted. "There's no one here for the killing."

"No people, mayhap," said the slim one, cinching his sword belt. "But beasts, there'll be beasts. Bears, or woods-cats. Maybe a dragon."

"Nonsense," said the elder. "I doubt we'll see anything larger than a wolf. What I meant was, you two just be ready to lift and carry."

"We's fighting men, not burden-bearers," the slim one grumbled.

"On this jaunt, Gelvin my lad, you're burden-bearers."

"The king said –" Horald began.

"That you were to obey my every instruction as if they were his own."

They made sour faces, but neither argued further. Tempted though she was to leap out and chop them to pieces before they knew what happened, Tilanne stayed hidden as they approached the ruins. The elder's mention of magic made her cautious. There were human wizards, she knew, as appalling a notion as it was to think that such a gift should be visited upon any of that benighted, miserable race. She'd have to see what the man was capable of before she went at him with sword and shield.

Though Horald and Gelvin wanted to go off their separate ways and explore, looking for treasure they'd not have to share, the grey-haired elder directed them to the temple. Following, Tilanne didn't try to hide a hard-edged grin when she thought of the vines, and of the other surprise they'd find waiting for them. Let them be slaughtered by one of their own. Let this wizard see what had become of the last man he'd brought here, and left for dead.

Even so, it nearly killed her just to see them set foot upon the temple steps.

"What's this?" Gelvin bent down. "These vines have been cut –"

"Don't touch those!" cried the elder.

The vines snaked up, coiling around Gelvin's arm. He yelled, blundering backward. Horald seized the vine and tried to pull it off. He was snared at once. The vines lashed the men together, pressed together like lovers meeting after a long absence.

Their armor protected them from the worst of the thorns, but they must have been well aware of how ridiculous they looked, and cursed frightfully as they struggled.

"Hold still, hold still, a burning pox on you!" The third man spoke potent words in a language that Tilanne had never heard before. He gestured at the tangle of green.

The vines unwound themselves in a flash. They seemed to be striving away from the men, straining and quivering at the furthest distance they could reach without uprooting themselves. This left the doorway unobstructed. With watchful looks and ginger, tip-toe steps, Gelvin and Horald preceded the wizard into the temple, and out of Tilanne's sight.

She counted her heartbeats.

One . . . two . . . three . . .

Male voices rang out in screams of shock, horror, and dismay. The wet slap-squish-slither of the lung-rot creature was everywhere.

Drawn almost despite herself, Tilanne climbed the steps, keeping a wary sidelong eye on the vines. They were still repelled, still held at bay, so she looked in.

There, under the merciless stone gaze of Kaledhol, she saw a sight both gruesome and spectacularly satisfying. Horald, or at least his legs and feet, flailed. If he cried out, it was beyond all hearing, for he was embedded from head to waist in the gelatinous substance of the yellow-black nightmare. Gelvin was dancing about with alacrity and agility, too fast for the questing pseudopods to strike him, but his lightning-fast swordplay was of no more avail to him than Tilanne's had been to her.

The wizard had his back to the wall and staff held in front of him in what looked like a useless gesture of defense. He chanted more words of power. Orange light flared around his staff, then a jet of fire shot from the end of it. Flame sizzled and seared the air, hitting the creature. It heaved and lunged. With a sickening noise, it spat Horald from itself.

Gelvin raced to his aid and reversed with even greater speed as he saw what was left of the other man. Horald's lower extremities were untouched. But the rest of him, the upper half of his body, was nothing but steaming bones and stringy clots of slime. His corselet was pitted and smoking from the acidic soup of digestion.

The wizard shot another volley of scorching flame-bolts. Gelvin put his speed to good use and ran for his life, dodging nimbly out of the way.

The creature reared itself up in a cresting cancerous wave. Even as its midsection bubbled and boiled, it loomed forward, forward, more and more of itself flowing up into a top-heavy bulge. Gelvin saw the danger in time to save himself, but the wizard was not so quick.

The wave crashed down on him and bore him under.

* * *

Chapter Fourteen

Even buried beneath the thing, even with his flesh surely being melted away, the wizard's magical fire kept burning. Tilanne could see it, ablaze within the creature like a candle flame inside of an inverted, ugly pottery bowl.

Gelvin backed toward the door, shaking his head, making inarticulate croaks that might have been meant to be words.

With a crackling hiss, the entire mass of the creature ignited like jellied oil and then exploded. The burst of brightness and heat was so intense that the nearest vines curled into crisp black strings. Gelvin, his hair afire, whirled and dove straight through the doorway. He flew past Tilanne, struck the stairs and tumbled to the bottom like a disjointed doll.

She spared one last glance inside – globules of fire everywhere, and in the midst of it a stick-man form thrashing, slowing, going still.

Her eyes, for one fleeting but soul-thrilling moment, touched those of the stone visage of Kaledhol and it seemed that they *saw* each other, god and girl. She nodded, and turned to go after Gelvin.

The man was rolling in the dirt, scooping up handfuls of damp leaves to push against his blistered face and scalp. He finally fell onto his back, smoke rising from his clothing, and lay there with chest heaving.

"Get up, human." She forced the hateful speech through her lips.

He jerked, hearing her voice, hearing his own language with her accent. He sat up. When he saw her, and a multitude of expressions jostled for position on his face. Surprise was chief among them, but bewilderment, a tinge of fear, and an utterly repugnant lustfulness were there too.

"Who . . . who are you, elfwoman?"

Her sword answered for her, singing its song of steel as she drew it from its sheath.

"Hold . . . wait." He raised his hands, palms out. "What are you doing?"

"Slaying you."

Gelvin dove to the side as the blade whickered through where he'd been. Even scorched and battered from his fall, he was fast, and came up into a fighter's stance. "I'm unarmed."

"Your fault and failing, not mine." How ugly their words were. How clumsy and coarse.

"It's dishonorable –"

She slashed at him again, and although he sidestepped, she scored a shallow cut to his leg, where only leather protected his flesh. "You trespass in our land, defile temple, and talk to me of *honor?* Servant of a murdering lord, you know nothing of honor!"

He clapped a hand to his wound and stared at the blood on his palm. "Wait, stop, listen to me! There's something in there, a monster. It killed my companions. We should band together, in case there are more."

Tilanne lowered her sword and looked at him.

He, seeming to take this as an encouraging sign, offered her a tentative smile. "What do you say?" he asked.

Again, she let steel answer, with a vicious backhand swing that tore a diagonal gash from his shoulder to waist. Metal screeched as her sword sheared through his corselet. The force of it knocked him onto his back with blood leaking from his chest.

Gelvin was up again almost as soon as he'd fallen, and all pretense at friendliness was gone. He held himself tense, alert, his body swaying in a manner that reminded her of a pantera's tail as it was poised to spring.

"All right, she-dog, if that's how you wish it," he said.

"What did the Mountain King want with this place?" she demanded, as they circled each other, scuffing boot-tracks in the dirt. "Mere treasure? Weapons? What secrets would you steal from my people?"

"You think I'll tell you?"

He feinted, but she was not taken in by it, and her return thrust would have spitted him through the throat if he hadn't evaded.

"I think –" she said.

Gelvin kicked a spray of dirt and gravel at her. As she raised her shield to keep it from her eyes, he rushed in, close, grappling for her sword arm and punching her in the face. Her lip split against her teeth. They fell, and she slammed up her knee as they went. She hit him in the upper thigh, not the groin as she'd been hoping, but it was enough to convince him to roll off of her.

Tasting blood, so covered in grit that she must have looked like a breaded piece of meat ready to be fried, Tilanne attacked again. This time, Gelvin let her come, ducking away from her sword and grabbing her arm again.

They were face-to-face. He had tight hold of her, and her shield was hampered by the press of his body. With a violent forward butt of her head, Tilanne smashed the front of her helmet into his forehead. The impact jarred through her, and she thought her clenched teeth might shatter from it, but Gelvin reeled back. He stood wavering for a few moments. Then his eyes rolled up so that all she could see were the whites and the bottom rim of brown iris. He crumpled.

He'd barely hit the ground before Tilanne caught up a handful of his hair and raised his torso enough to give her a good clear shot at his neck. Two swings decapitated him. The flood of scarlet was amazing from his neck. With a wordless shout of triumph, she held his severed head aloft. Her first kill . . . the first human to fall to her sword!

The wild exultation drained from her as suddenly as it had come. She let the head drop, with a grimace at the feel of his hair, so greasy and wiry even through her gloves. The glazed eyes fixed on her as the rolling head came to rest. With the toe of her boot, she nudged it over so that she wouldn't have to see that gruesome death-rictus.

Wiping her blade on the rough wool of his cloak, Tilanne went up the temple steps again. The vines made no move to hinder her. Most were charred, their leaves withered into ashy husks. Only a few still moved, and those with the sluggish, mindless pain of dying things.

She peered within. The lung-rot creature was gone. Only a reeking puddle of sludge, like something from a pot left too long to boil over, gave testament that it had ever been. Horald remained as she'd last seen him, hideous and half-dissolved. Of the nameless wizard, only a few bones remained, and the staff. It, intact and apparently undamaged, lay in the middle of the smoldering puddle.

The battle was over . . . but as Tilanne looked around the temple, she realized that the real work had not yet begun. Was it always thus? The conflict of war both glorious and short, and then the long, dismal, tedious aftermath of cleaning up and setting-to-rights?

It took her three full days before she had taken care of matters to her satisfaction. She could not work as fast as she wished, for the next morning she woke up stiff and aching from the fight. Her arms and shoulders ached from climbing and from swordplay. Her split lip was puffed. A line of purple-black showed where the rim of her helm had bit into her brow when she'd slammed her head forward into Gelvin's. She brewed medicinal tea and rested frequently, seeking solace and strength in prayer whenever she did. And, slowly, she made progress.

The bodies, even the old bones from the catacomb hall, she left for the scavengers beyond Firsthome's walls. The burnt vines, she chopped down and piled and burned again. She was none too eager to go anywhere near the remains of the lung-rot beast, fearful of its acid and its pestilence. Several pails of water, toted from the nearest creek, served to sluice away the worst of the melting gobbets that remained.

While retrieving the staff, she found something that must have been in the belt pouch of the elder wizard. It was an earring, truesilver and amethyst, the mate to the one she had found before. These, she returned to one of the caskets. The staff, and everything else worth salvaging from the humans' camp, she kept. Even the foodstuffs. She did not relish the prospect of eating it, but she could not bring herself to throw it away.

The weather turned cold, rain becoming a heavy and wet snow, before she was ready to leave. She not only had Morai to look after now but the three other horses and the ponies, all tethered together.

Not even the vestiges of any sort of road led south from Firsthome. She found the humans' backtrail easily enough but disdained it. They had not come through the Forest of the Wandering Lost but apparently skirted it, and her destination lay somewhere at its deepest, darkest center.

The going was slow, but she trusted to Morai's instincts and let the mare go at her own pace. The others followed in a placid line, their breath making faint plumes around their noses in the cold, damp air.

Tilanne saw game everywhere as they moved further into the dense wilds. Rabbits, foxes, deer . . . once, a slinking, golden-eyed pantera. She refilled her waterskins at fast-flowing, crystal-pure streams and gathered wild grapes that had grown a rime of ice around their plump purple skins. Overripe, they were almost unbearably sweet and heady.

Eventually, she realized the forest floor was descending in a slow, gradual slope that showed no signs of rising again. The trees seemed to stretch taller and higher than ever, their branches and leaves interlaced so thickly that most of the snow was caught before it could reach the ground. Every so often, something would bend or break, and an avalanche would plummet from those hidden heights.

Still downward, downward, the slope steepening, the trees towering.

Tilanne recalled how the forest had looked from a distance. The tops of the trees had all seemed mostly a shallow, nearly flat basin, an expanse of darkest green. There was no way of knowing, from out there, how it truly was inside. How the land here was lower, but the trunks loomed ever higher, so that they seemed to reach to the same level in the end.

The boles of the trees seemed to be even larger around the farther she went. She had the uncanny impression that she and the horses were shrinking, smaller every day, instead of the trunks getting bigger, the branches higher. The foliage overhead was so dense that hardly any light, and no snow at all, could reach the ground. The underbrush was first sparse, then scant, then vanished altogether beneath a bed of old leaves and needles.

The humans' horses and ponies didn't like the change, but Morai remained calm. They saw fewer and fewer other animals, the cries of birds above seeming impossibly distant.

Camping at night, Tilanne used lengths of firewood that had been bound to one of the ponies. There was hardly anything available to collect from the forest itself, without using an axe to try and hew chunks from one of the massive trees. The firelight made odd, dancing shadows on the towering trunks.

Some of the roots, almost as big around as a grown man, humped up out of the earth so high that Tilanne could walk under them without ducking her head. Huge red-orange mushrooms covered the bark in shelves and ridges as big as dinner plates. Others, a beeswaxy-yellow, nodded their bulbous heads on thin stalks taller than Tilanne. It once more made her feel as if she'd somehow shrunk while everything else remained the proper size.

Soon, the canopy blocked the sun so utterly that she could no longer tell day from night. She saw everything in shades of purple and grey. The trees rose so high they seemed able to reach the moons, and accordingly wide. Cracks in the bark were almost large enough to admit the horses, and the monstrous roots bulged beneath the earth in mounds like hills.

Nothing else moved down here. Nothing else made a sound. The silence was deathly, tomblike. Tilanne almost felt as if the very air was pressing down on her with an overpowering weight. She labored to breathe. Her heart pounded harder than her activity called for, as if it found it more and more difficult to move her blood through her veins.

Then even the purple and grey gave way to a blackness so unrelieved she could have been struck blind. No light at all penetrated to the ground.

She summoned a magelight. Its faint glow seemed only to emphasize, rather than banish, the darkness. She couldn't have felt more confined had she been underground, in some cavern-deep where only the dwarvenfolk dared go. Above her, an unfathomable height above her, leaves waved in the breeze. But whether they were kissed by sunshine or rain or snow, or whether dusk had already fallen or dawn had come, she could not tell. She had lost all sense of time in this strange, eternal night.

The horses had, too, and crowded close to each other in a constant state of nervousness. Even brave Morai nickered and puffed, and bumped her nose against Tilanne in a quest for reassurance.

Surprisingly, it wasn't cold down here. Cool, yes, but like in a cave, the temperature held at an even degree no matter what might be going on with the seasons of the upper world.

In fact, as she continued – it was simple to avoid going in circles; all she had to do was keep heading downhill and she knew she wouldn't be retracing her steps – Tilanne decided that her senses were not playing tricks. It was getting warmer. Warmer, yes, the air tinged with a faint mineral-sulfur scent that reminded her of certain hot springs like those at Deepwater. And smoke, not wood-smoke but coal-smoke.

She kept moving, not wanting to think about how far below the sky she must be. The bark of the trees was black, the ground was black, and in the shine of her magelight the only colors she could see were those of the things she'd brought with her.

And then, light. Quick and fleeting, a pale streak across a gap in the trunks.

Tilanne drew her sword almost before she knew she intended to. Her nerves were tight as harp strings. The scrape of the blade leaving its sheath was a loud shout, the sheen of metal an eerie phantom-silver in the magelight.

Again, the light. A swooping pale radiance. Enormous. Dazzling.

This time she saw the source of it clearly, and her mouth dropped open. It was like no bird she had seen or heard of in her entire life.

So large that it could have borne away a man in its talons as easily as an eagle might a hare, it had the angled wings and sleek head of a predator. But it was white, uniformly white. Not albino, either . . . it glowed with its own phosphorescence that seemed to emanate from every feather. Its eyes, above a bone-white hook of beak, were bright as stars.

Its great wings flicked lazily. It flew almost without sound, gliding a weaving course around the trees. She had seen dragons, from a distance, but not even a dragon was as fabulous and strange and inexplicable as this huge, glowing bird.

The ponies whinnied in fright and tried to flee. Their movement tangled the tether that held them to the other horses. One of them, an ill-tempered gelding, nipped a pony on the flank. Morai held her ground, but Tilanne could feel the mare trembling beneath her.

The bird cruised over them, cocking its head curiously. A noise, more of a coo than a screak, rose at the end in bird-speak questioning. It seemed more inquisitive than hostile, at least, at first.

The tether snapped. The endmost pony, bleating in terror, bolted.

If the bird hadn't known what they were before, the sudden flight of obvious prey told it enough. Its wide-spanning wings beat the air as it wheeled in pursuit. Tilanne felt the downdraft blow back her hair.

The other horses and ponies panicked. Tilanne clung to reins and lead rope, and only hoped as Morai broke into a trot that the mare knew what she was doing. She glanced back, seeing the pony by the reflected aura of the bird. Talons, each as long as her forearm and curved like boat hooks, raked and grabbed. The pony squealed once, then again, but the second squeal was cut off as the bird's head dipped, the beak scissoring. That had been the pony carrying most of the foodstuffs and the bulk of the firewood, but at the moment she did not have time to bewail the misfortune.

The bird must have had more interest in feasting than giving chase, because they left it behind. Tilanne was finally able to slow, calm and untangle the others. Miraculously, none of them had stumbled and broken a leg, or lost their bundles. Hoping that if they could not see another such bird – if there were other such birds, and if there was one, there probably would be more – they would not run, she blindfolded them with lengths of cloth cut from the spare garments that had been in the humans' saddlebags. She left Morai's eyes uncovered. The mare tossed her black-maned head and snorting with aplomb, as if to say it would take something much larger, and much scarier, than that to get *her* galloping off like a frightened colt.

As she remounted and continued on, Tilanne was beginning to despair of finding the *Odan Rhunvale*. Had she gone the wrong way? Surely the *Rhunvala* did not live down here, in this place of unremitting darkness. How could they live? With no light, with no crops and no food?

But, not knowing what else to try, she resolved to press on, at least a little ways more.

The smells of sulfur and smoke intensified as they continued inexorably down, down into the deeper and heavier black. The air got considerably warmer. And more humid. Tilanne had removed her cloak and gloves, but could not bring herself to take off her armor. Soon she was bathed in sweat that formed on her skin in a moist, close-fitting garment, and did not evaporate in the hot, moist air. She thought of bath-houses and steamy kitchens and the dank, moist chambers where she and her sisters had gone to wash the family laundry in great copper kettles over beds of coals.

She wiped her face and the back of her neck with a handkerchief again and again, until the handkerchief was sopping and she was still no drier.

Ahead, her magelight illuminated something new. Lacy black curtains of moss, layer after layer of them, hung between the trunks of the trees. The blackness was speckled with tiny silvery-blue flowers shaped like fairy-bells, and a plaintive, sweet scent issued from them.

The moss waved and billowed gently, like becalmed sails, or sheets hung on a line in a mild breeze. As they moved, parting and falling back together, Tilanne saw hazy gaps of light on the other side.

Cautious, mindful, remembering how the vines at the temple had come alive and seized her, she approached. The moss made no move against her, even when she poked at it with her sword. The blade did not dissolve, the strands did not suddenly whip around her arm and yank her from her feet to dangle and kick helplessly. The moss merely stayed there, inert.

She took another step, and touched it with her hand. The moss was silky and fragile, black gossamer and tiny bellflowers, and parted like cobwebs between her fingers.

Glancing over her shoulder at the placid, blindfolded horses, she saw a pale blur gliding in widening circles. The bird, perhaps searching for them to finish its meal. Or perhaps its mate or some other. It decided her.

Using her sword like a physician's scalpel, she cut careful slits in the moss and proceeded through, a layer at a time, leading Morai and the other animals. The moss fell together behind them, hiding them from the eyes of the bird.

Her initial, hopeful thought had been that the light she'd glimpsed through the moss was sunlight – that they'd somehow come through to the other side. She dismissed that wistful fancy as it steadily brightened, very much unlike sunlight. Not firelight, either. The glow was too steady, and the color was wrong. But nor was it magelight . . . not any kind of magelight she had ever seen.

She pushed her way through the last few layers of moss and that eerie light fell full upon her. She was bathed in damp heat. The scene before her brought her to an immediate halt, which was just as well because one more step would have taken her over the edge of a precipitous drop and sent her plunging straight down into the midst of a world like nothing she'd ever imagined in her strangest of dreams.

*   *   *

CHAPTER FIFTEEN

The chasm, the trench, extended in a bending curve to the left and right as far as her eye could reach. Tilanne stood on a rocky outcrop at the very edge of it, an outcrop jutting from loamy-looking soil like burnt, soggy kofa grounds.

As wide as it was, the monumental trees growing on both sides of it were still so vast at the tops that their spreading branches meshed together enough to blot out the sky.

She could see it all. She could see more than she wanted to see.

Jets of blue-orange flame hissed up from rocky cones like miniature volcanoes all along the base of the trench. Vents in the stone issued plumes of gas that sporadically ignited into fiery cyclones. Other volcanoes belched continual gouts of black or yellow smoke. Hot springs bubbled with water or seethed with boiling mud. Some spouted geysers, scalding streams shooting high and raining down.

The air was vile, rank. Breathable, for now anyway, but the fumes made Tilanne's head pound and her stomach slippery with nausea. The taste of it coated the inside of her mouth and nose. It was rotten eggs and skunk-musk and swamp-mire. Poisonous? Even if not, certainly unhealthy.

Yet things lived here. Somehow, incredible as it was, things lived. The trench teemed with bizarre life.

Plants, uncanny and unfamiliar, grew in abundance. Tufts of greyish grass poked up like strange fingers. Pale hedgehog-flowers, bristling with spines, clung to the sides of the trench. The largest of these was as big as a cottage. Ferns swayed and rustled, ferns with pure white leaves around a rising central stalk like a blood-red bottle brush. Some huge, fleshy blossoms waved thin tendrils tipped with glowing bulbs, and when some hapless bird or insect came close to investigate, the blossom's maw would clamp shut like a bear trap.

She saw long, low creatures with white carapaces, scuttling around the vents clacking their pincers at each other. Segmented white worms many times the length of a man rolled and wallowed in the hot mud. A host of pale, multi-colored and glowing insects a hand span or more in size were under constant peril from smaller versions of birds like the one she had seen only a little while before.

A herd of deer-like creatures with stunted forearms and powerful hind legs grazed on the grasses. The males had ash-grey antlers rising from their shaggy white manes. They kept watch on a low-slung hunter that looked to be part pantera and part lizard, with a tufted tail and a rill-crest of skin around its head. This hunter, sprawled indolently on a flat-topped boulder as if basking in the heated gas, yawned to expose a double-row of sharp teeth.

Tilanne clung to Morai's bridle, overwhelmed.

This could not be the elvenwood. This could not be the Forest of the Wandering Lost . . . no one could be *this* lost, so as to have come into some world altogether different and abnormal. This was some Otherplace, like a place of the Torments. This was some hallucination. This could not be real.

Above, in the open space between the trunks that flanked the chasm, the larger birds spiraled and soared. Not only birds. She saw draconian things there too, with long scaled tails lashing and leathery white wings catching the heated updrafts.

Her heart in her throat, Tilanne did her best to fade back into the concealing caress of the hanging moss. She might be brave, especially for a girl, but she was not foolhardy. A single sword could not deal with those terrors, did they decide that Tilanne and her horses were prey. Further, the sides of the chasm were nearly sheer, and she could see no path down, no path through.

She was braced for the moss to come alive *now* and stop her retreat. It would have parted easily before to lead her in, only to trap her once it was too late. But it gave way with no greater effort than before, and fell closed behind her as she led the horses out.

After the weird light of the fire-plumes and volcanoes, her poor stunned eyes adjusted slowly to the return to darkness.

What now? How was she to possibly find the Citadel now? As if it hadn't been an impossible enough task already?

But no, it couldn't be an impossible task, an impassable way. The *Rhunvala* had to come and go, didn't they? And they rode on horses, or walked afoot, just like anyone else. They couldn't just sprout wings or send themselves through the air with a thought.

There *had* to be a way.

So telling herself, Tilanne followed the outside edge of the curtain of moss. She kept her eyes open and scanning the air, lest the bird or one of its cronies decide to make another pass.

Before long, she was tired. Beyond tired. Exhausted. The heavy air, the heat, the fumes, the pressure and the tension and the unending weight of her assorted concerns wore on her, slowing her steps. She had no idea whether it was day or night, how long had passed since last she ate or slept. All she knew was that her legs felt leaden, her stomach was a knot that had even given up growling, and her mouth and throat were parched. Her hair straggled around her in limp black strings, and she knew that she must be filthy, stinking of sulfur.

A crook of roots at the base of one of the colossal trees formed a perfect shelter, three wooden walls and an overhanging spur that could serve as a roof. Not that she was worried about rain, no, not at all. Rain, she would have welcomed. The fear of being seen, being stalked . . . that was what made her crave shelter.

She situated the horses and the surviving pony inside. Spiking a sheet of oilcloth to the root and into the ground so that it covered the opening, she made a snug little hut with an oilcloth door. She undressed, her clothes wringing wet from sweat, and used half of a waterskin sponging herself off and trying to rinse the smoky rotten-eggs smell from her hair. Clean, but not much cooler, she donned a fresh tunic and trousers.

The air lent a bad taste to any food, so Tilanne barely could muster the appetite to choke down more than a few bites. She spread her cloak on a bed of old, soft leaves in a cradle formed by a curve of the root.

"Kaledhol my path to guide," she said as she closed her eyes. "A way there must be, if find it I can. Lead me, oh Protector, that I might to Thy Citadel come."

She slept far better than she might have expected, and woke feeling rested and refreshed, though still with no inkling of the time and no better appetite. She made herself eat anyway, merely fueling herself for the continuance of her journey.

Some time later, still following the curve of the moss-curtain and ducking through every so often to see if the chasm was still there – it was, each time, still as deep and still as unnerving and still populated by plants and creatures that made her very mind hurt – she fancied she heard voices.

She saw no one.

She'd been alone now far longer than most *Morvalan* ever were in all their lives. It was not their way to be solitary. Would it be any wonder if she turned peculiar, all on her own and removed from her secure role in society? Would it be any wonder if she thought she heard things that weren't there? Saw things that weren't there? Was that the explanation? Had her journey robbed her of her wits?

But then, plain as could be, she heard laughter and knew it was real. Male laughter, two elven voices sharing amusement.

Still, she saw no one. Then she realized that the voices had come from *above*.

Tilanne craned her neck back, peering into the hidden heights of the trees. Seeing a glimmer, she doused her magelight and blinked, reacquainting her eyes with the totality of the darkness.

And yet, the darkness was *not* total. There was a light, high in the boughs. Swinging back and forth, the way a lantern might swing held at the end of a striding person's arm.

"Up in the trees they are," she said, her voice low and wondering. "Up in the trees!"

Far above her head, she could just make out the branches that grew together in a twisted braid-work, forming a path. A bridge. A roadway above the earth, as high as any span between towers, as wide as any avenue.

She rushed, excited, to the nearest of the trees that seemed connected to this forest bridge. But even if she could have climbed it – which she doubted – there was no way to bring horses, no way to carry anything.

The laughing lantern-bearers vanished, headed in the direction that she believed was south. The direction she'd been going, the way that led to the hot, fuming chasm. But their roadway, their tree-way, would take them over it. Over it . . . and to the Citadel?

It had to be. Those men might have been *Rhunvala!* Well, no, that was never something she'd heard Kai Terindor do. But perhaps they served at the *Odan Rhunvale* as smiths, masons, or in other capacities.

Excited and filled with renewed hope and purpose, Tilanne fetched her train of horses and followed under the high bridge. She went back in a northerly route, moving from tree to tree in search of some way up. There had to be one, and if she was forced to go all the way back to the edge of the Forest of the Wandering Lost, what of it? Better she spend another *year* retracing her steps than try to make her way across that chasm.

She did not know how long it took. Only that she was perilously low on food and had been giving the horses most of the dwindling supply of water. And that she had trudged far enough back uphill out of the depths to barely able to perceive a diffuse lightness to the air, though nowhere near far enough to see the sun.

In that faint, dim, perpetual twilight, She came to a tree that from a distance looked like it was being crushed in the coils of a gargantuan snake. At first, she thought that was what it was. Which wouldn't have surprised her, not in this place.

But, closer, she saw that it was a snake formed of wood. And not really a snake at all but a ramp, a slanting ascending way that led from the roots up to the branches. There, it looked to join with the bridge.

Even Morai was none too keen about this new demand. In the end, Tilanne had to re-blindfold the pony and the humans' horses, and coaxed Morai with every bit of desperate persuasion she possessed. Up they went, spiraling higher and higher around the trunk of the tree until at last, Tilanne stood upon the high bridge made of twisted boughs. Nothing so useful could have come about by nature's accidental design. The hands of her people had been at work here, plant-magics to shape the wood and encourage it, and make it strong. Though she was still far from any other elves, she no longer felt quite so alone.

She walked the horses, going slowly as her feet and their hooves became accustomed to this new path, with its occasional bumps and knots and boles. The bridge led from tree to tree, and in several of the trunks, she found to her delight that dwellings had been shaped into the living wood. Each was a comfortable hollow, an overlarge bole like a squirrel's den, cozy and secure. Along the way, also, were cisterns brimming with rainwater, fed by hollow reeds rising up to the unseen topmost branches.

The horses did not care for any of this, but Tilanne was delighted. It did her much good to feel so at home, in a shelter that had been crafted by elven design. She slept almost as well as she might have done had she been back in Jewelgreen with Jedriel warming the blankets beside her.

When they moved on, she always led her horses in the center of the bridge. Blindfolds or no blindfolds, they seemed to sense the precipitous drop to the forest floor so far below. Of course, as deeply cushioned with leaves and needles as that floor was . . . Tilanne smiled at the mental image of horses bouncing to a soft landing.

It began to get darker again . . . not night but the darkness, the high bridge sloping not as steeply as the ground but sloping all the same. The bark's hue darkened through shades of brown to midnight-black, and her magelight was the only glow in that eternal, smothering shadow. It was like walking endlessly through nothingness, suspended on this thin ribbon of wood with open space around her on all sides. Only coming to the next tree, occasionally finding another knot-bole shelter or wide platform, proved that there was anything else in the world.

Yet she still did not go back to feeling so alone. Now and then, she found signs that others had used this path before her. Not long before, either, only a few days. The lantern-bearers she'd seen, perhaps. Here, a fresh bed of ashes in one of the dwelling's hearths. There, wood-voles quibbling over a dropped crust of bread.

At one point, sensing a fathomless depth beneath her and detecting the hint of sulfur and smoke rising on the air, she knew they were passing over the chasm. The bridge was so high that she could not perceive even the faintest glimmer from the fiery jets. Trepidation wrapped tingling, cold fingers around her. She watched her steps more carefully than ever. If she fell from here, fell for what would seem like forever only to drop into that teeming morass of rock formations, hot mud, and gaseous fumes, she would die on impact. And count herself lucky, because a thousand times worse than dying in the fall would be still being *alive*, to be devoured by the strange, pallid things living there.

Shortly after that, the bridgeway began to climb as gently as it had previously descended. There was at first only a vague grey, not much brighter than the darkness, letting her distinguish her hand before her face but not much else. Then the air around her took on a pleasant verdant tone. She could see birds and scampering furry creatures. Flying pantera glided by in the cool green shadows, the loose folds of skin stretched out between their fore and hind legs as they played out their dramas of predator and prey still far beneath the interlocked, dense canopy. Tender leaves provided food for the horses. Clusters of hard-shelled nuts, berries, and the occasional eggs raided from nests replenished Tilanne's all-but-gone supplies.

She rounded another of the mighty tree trunks and a startlingly clean, brilliant-white shaft of light speared down through a gap in the leaf-cover, bathing the bridge ahead and piercing deep into the dusty blackness below.

Tilanne walked slowly forward into the glorious ray. She tipped her head back and stared up at a blue patch of sky. Sunlight, she had come through to find sunlight again. She felt radiantly uplifted and continued her journey with a less plodding tread.

The Citadel was close now. She could feel it, feel it like a song in her very bones, calling to her. She did not delude herself into thinking that once she'd reached it, all of her troubles would be done. Oh, no. She knew better than that. Her troubles might only be beginning. The rest of her people might, after some initial consternation, be able to accept the idea of a woman as *Rhunvala*, but would the *Rhunvala* themselves?

She slept that night in yet another of the shaped bole-dwellings. She dreamed of herself as she had appeared in Jedina's picture. Kai Tilanne, stalwart and fierce in her glossy black armor. Yet she also dreamed of herself as the Tilanne that could have been, with Jedriel by her side and their children growing up clever and strong.

The next day, she woke to the secret sound of rain. The horses had finally grown accustomed to this unusual route, and stood calm as she loaded them with their burdens. Morai nudged Tilanne hard with her nose, as if to ask when her rider planned to make proper use of a steed instead of trusting all her travel to those two silly legs. Tilanne rubbed the sides of the mare's face affectionately.

The day after that, she saw more sunlight, thin rays of it piercing down through sparse leaf-cover. From above, from a distance, the canopy might have looked unbroken, the forest as deep and dense as ever. But the giant trees were more widely spaced, and valley clearings spread around their bases like lush skirts. Smaller trees grew in groves far below.

And then . . .

"Oh," Tilanne said. She stopped in her tracks. Morai gave her an impatient snort and a toss of the head.

A mountain of black rock rose from the valley floor. Its cliff-like sides were riddled with openings and walkways, as if a castle had been carved or shaped from the stone itself. She could see tiny figures of men and horses moving about, and bonfires burning on the parapets.

Welcome though those sights were, they were what held her spellbound.

It was the crystal that did that. The dark, rugged, smooth-sided crystal. Like the one at Jewelgreen, it was alive with swirling color and light – violet, indigo, amber, maroon. Like the one at Jewelgreen, it emerged from the top of the rock like something being born into the world.

But the one at Jewelgreen had stood no taller than the height of a man. The one she saw now, though still towered over by the trees, could have rivaled the tallest castle ever built.

The Citadel of the Basilisk.

She had come to the *Odan Rhunvale* at last.

* * *

Chapter Sixteen

All of her trials thus far had led to this. All would be decided, now and forever, in these next few crucial moments.

Tilanne strived for outward calm as she waited and watched them come.

She had not crossed half the valley before galloping riders had swarmed from the Citadel's gates to surround her. As they approached, she reined in Morai and sat, waiting. The other horses and the pony, glad to be down on solid earth again, grazed unconcernedly. But Morai could detect Tilanne's tension, and pranced in place, flicking her ears and tail.

At a glance, she could see that this hidden vale was lush and prosperous, with grazing herds and pure springs, orchards and farmlands. Of the River of Time, which was said to have waters dark as the space between stars, she saw nothing, but sensed somehow that it coursed in lightless channels far below this sacred place.

Sacred, yes . . . she could feel it. Like a temple, but moreso, as if the crystal voiced a silent call that penetrated to her very soul.

The first ones to reach her looked like . . . like anyone else. Ordinary men, healthy and fair. They wore ordinary clothes, as well, proclaiming them as having interrupted their work in the smithies or orchards to come hurrying in response to the sentries' alarm. They were not soldiers, did not train arrows on her as they came. Only a few were even armed beyond the standard belt-knife.

Tilanne made sure to keep her hands in plain sight and away from her sword. They would not know what to make of her to begin with, and the last thing she wanted to do was give them some reason to mistake her intentions as hostile.

Their horses fanned out, surrounding her. No one spoke. She could feel their gazes, their suspicion and dubiousness as they took in her armor, the weapons she wore. Perhaps taking in as well the line of her jaw, the look in her eyes, the strength uncharacteristic of a woman that showed in the way she carried herself even in her weariness. And her youth? Yes, that too.

She studied them, as well, revising her earlier impression. Though they did all look like men of ordinary professions, there was something . . . otherly about them. A self-assurance, an inner ease and balance. She noticed that although they had no particular uniformity of dress or coloring or hairstyle, many of them wore an unusual gemstone, either as earring or set into a necklace, ring or circlet. Had Kai Terindor worn such a gem? She couldn't recall.

The evaluating silence stretched out, becoming a torture. Tilanne wanted to speak, found herself wanting to hastily blurt out an explanation and an apology. She did not, but only by exerting a monumental effort of will.

So long without anyone but herself and Morai to talk to! So long without seeing other elves, when she'd never previously before been alone a day in her life! She was nearly frantic to be among people again.

What if they sent her away? What if all they said to her was to tell her to go? She did not think she could stand it, returning back through the Forest of the Wandering Lost. It would break her spirit, break her mind.

The nearest row of men parted, allowing a magnificent iron-grey stallion to approach. At the sight of the tall, scarlet-cloaked rider, Tilanne inhaled sharply.

The eyes that regarded her with a weight like stones were the uncanny lavender-blue of the sky at twilight. A thin scar ran beneath one of them, hooking upward at an angle. An onyx hoop pierced one earlobe, a rough varicolored gem the size of a pea was in the other. His hair was drawn back from his face and clasped at the nape of his neck. The color of it was almost as silver as that of the *Alvalan* who'd spared her life, but darker, a burnished pewter with a faintly steel-blue shine. His body was broad through the shoulders, tapering to lean hips and long legs. Over blackmetal chain mesh, he wore a black tunic belted in silver, with a scarlet-embroidered basilisk on his chest.

The *Rhunvala* nudged his horse toward her. Morai, as impressed by the iron-grey stallion as Tilanne was by the rider, nickered softly and shifted her weight to give him room.

"I thee greet and welcome, sister," he said after a lengthy pause in which she felt sized up and evaluated. "Thou art to the *Odan Rhunvale* come."

She reached into her collar, drew out the blackmetal chain, and the ruby basilisk sparkled as she brought it into the light. Though the men gathered around still said nothing, she saw them stir, and glance around at one another. On their faces, she read surprise, consternation, offense, anger, disbelief, bafflement.

"Kor Tilanne am I," she said, aware of the renewed reactions that her title incited. "Come am I our god to serve, if worthy He finds me this symbol to bear."

She saw the *Rhunvala's* gaze dip to it, then rise again to stare intently at her, as if he could see through her eyes and into her very thoughts. "By that, how came thee?"

"To me it was by Kai Terindor Reyes given." She paused, not liking to have to deliver such news but knowing that it had to be said. "Before claimed by death was he."

Now the others did not stay silent, but murmured with grief. The *Rhunvala* bowed his head and sighed.

"Kai Peredur Denisse am I," he said when he looked up again. "Well known to me was Kai

Terindor. Yet not known to me was it that a Kor he had chosen."

"Only in final extremity did he," Tilanne said. "Injured he was, and dying, but before his foes he faced again, this last measure he took." She touched the ruby basilisk.

Another man pushed forward. He had a curly mop of blond hair and merry blue eyes, which did not fit well with his scowl. "And thee, the only one about were? Thee, a girl?"

"I, a girl. Yet sought have I ever since, through many passages of the dark moon, the Kai's last wish to honor. And so, yes, to the *Odan Rhunvale* am I come, myself as Kor to present."

They were all looking her over again now, more intently than ever. Most surveyed the contours of her body, though not in the manner of men assessing a woman. They did so in the manner of warriors assessing her potential and ability.

"At warfare and swordplay thou hast studied and trained?" Kai Peredur asked. "Under whose guidance and where?"

"At Jewelgreen," she said. "Tutored was I by many there, and my skills by Commander Ellorn of West Jewelgreen Fortress were tested."

"Never has a woman *Rhunvala* been," the merry-eyed blond said. He dressed like a craftsman, but spoke like a person of considerable rank. A master at his craft? "Unheard of is such a thing."

Kai Peredur plucked the basilisk from her chest, the blackmetal chain suspended in an arc between the two of them. He pressed the ruby between his thumb and forefinger, eyes closed. She had the strangest feeling that he was somehow communicating with the gem, as if it could somehow prove the validity of her claim. Then, recalling her vision in which it had seemed to come alive and sink its fangs into her that she might seal her pledge to Kaledhol with her own life's blood, she realized that more was possible than she knew. Perhaps he was. Perhaps he was, after all.

"Truly she speaks," he said. "From Kai Terindor this ruby came. With his blood and hers has it been touched, and within it still resides undimmed the power of our god. Abandoned it has He not, and thus denied her has He not."

"Peredur! To accept this thou propose?" The blond man would have to be a person of importance indeed, Tilanne thought, to so openly criticize and doubt a *Rhunvala*.

"I do," Kai Peredur said. "As thou shouldst, Master Dael."

Dael accepted the rebuke with remarkably poor grace, sniffing in what was very nearly a snort, but said nothing more.

"Full aware am I," Tilanne said, "of the difficulties and irregularities by this matter presented. No desire have I trouble to cause, but desire I *do* have this path to follow, for so long as Kaledhol doth permits."

The *Rhunvala* seized her chin between the same forefinger and thumb with which he'd held the ruby. His grip was firm, not quite painful. He turned her head side to side as if studying, memorizing, every line of her features and what unseen things he could read behind her eyes. A qualm, like a living thing, scuttled in the pit of her stomach as if making a nest for itself, but she met his gaze as evenly as she could.

"To the Citadel I'll take thee," he said finally. "Told to all the Kais and Masters here gathered thy full tale must be. For them shall it be thy fate to decide, when once to Kaledhol for wisdom we all have prayed."

"I thee thank for thy welcome," Tilanne said.

A hint of a smile softened Kai Peredur's face. He had seemed handsome yet forbidding, able to smite dread into the hearts of an opposing army with nothing more than a look, or inspire his command to seemingly impossible feats of bravery by nothing more than their fear of failing him. But when he smiled, a warm light entered his eyes, and Tilanne could see through to the man beneath. That man, she understood without knowing how the knowledge came to her, was similar to, yet in some fundamental way quite different from, the cold and stern Kai Terindor.

"Thy full name, young Kor?" he inquired.

"Tilanne Murres."

"Master Dael Swordbright is this," he said with a gesture to his left, at the blond-haired man. "Weaponsmith and armorer. Savillan Angen, yonder that dark and brooding fellow is, our quartermaster who in generous food and more generous wine keeps us."

The "dark and brooding fellow" he indicated was not much older than Tilanne, and laughed with a self-deprecating grin. The Kai went on to introduce each of the other men that had come to investigate. Most of them were – as they seemed to be – farmers, hunters, and craftsmen. Tilanne greeted them all. One took charge of Tilanne's string of additional horses, clucking to himself over the shoddy workmanship of their gear and prompting her to explain that she had taken them from a trio of humans.

"Humans?" Kai Peredur asked, his smile melting back into that forbidding look. "Where didst thou in our lands humans encounter?"

"Firsthome," she said, to understandable uproar and outrage. "In the service of the Mountain King they were, and with a wizard traveled, the city of treasures and magic to plunder. But slain were two by a creature that had the temple inhabited, and the third to my sword his head bade farewell."

Kai Peredur had to signal for quiet, when questions burst from every pair of lips. The only one who did not comply was Master Dael, whose blond brows raised skeptically.

"*Thou* didst a human slay?" he asked.

"Yes," Tilanne said. "But others, too, before them had come."

She told the story, not elaborating and certainly not trying to make her part in it sound any grander than it had been. When she had finished, a somber anger had descended over the group. Kai Peredur sent them to go back about their duties, and then with Masters Dael and Savillan, fell in around her.

"So, alone through the forest ways thou didst come," Savillan said as they proceeded toward the mountainous Citadel. "How didst thou Lowfire traverse?"

"The chasm, its name that is? Where burning gas from the earth into darkness doth erupt, and where dwell the pale beasts?"

"Lowfire, we call it," the Kai said. "Surrounds this valley it does, a barrier that most intrusion prevents. Few so far into its strange heat and darkness are willing to venture, and fewer still the attempt survive."

She explained how she had heard laughter, and seen a lantern-light, and those things had led her to discover the high bridge through the trees.

"Most impressive it is," Savillan said in a tone that seemed deliberately chosen to needle Dael, "that thou didst alone through so much of the wood pass, and still in health arrive. Not many grown men better could have done. Brave indeed thou must be."

"Brave? Terrified I was," she said, and then wished she hadn't. What was she thinking? To admit her fear in front of the very people whose favor she'd come here in hopes of winning?

Now she'd told them she was a coward!

But Kai Peredur only smiled. "Terrified, yet persevered thou didst. Thus bravery is, Kor Tilanne. Thus true bravery is."

Out in the open midst of the valley, Tilanne looked up at the sky and it seemed as if the heavens were light green rather than blue, with that screen of leaves stretching on the widespread boughs of the encircling ring of trees. She could see the castle made from the rising outcrop of stone, its bonfires ablaze even in the daylight. Up close, the battlements and walkways were more readily apparent.

"Many are there who the Citadel call home?" she asked.

"No," Savillan said. "Most of us unmarried are, or to our professions wed. An honor here to serve it is, a great honor. But no place for families, for children, is this."

"Only so many can this valley support, and able must those be themselves to defend," Kai Peredur said. "Ordan Quaide to our fortifications sees, and Neterian Kelda with his wife Leiata all other crafts supervise. Kinnon Faer of the Scepter and Idrasanna Denisse of the Crown our High Mages are."

"So . . . some women, some wives, there are?" She hadn't thought before how her arrival might upset the careful balance of the *Odan Rhunvale*, but knew that she did not want to become an object of competition and dividing jealousies, or bitterness. She was glad, therefore, to hear the female names.

"Some few," Kai Peredur said. "Not many."

"Just as well, it is," Dael said sourly. "Women a distraction are."

"How true." Savillan winked at Tilanne. "A distraction most pleasant."

She demurred with downcast eyes, hoping she was not foreseeing trouble. In a place such as this, she could not go about taking a lover lightly, and that was not why she was here in any case. Had she wanted a mate, a husband, she'd left a perfectly good one behind in Jewelgreen. But here, where eligible women were even scarcer than elsewhere in the *Morvalan* lands, she could become the center of much attention whether she wished it or not.

"And the *Rhunvala*?" she asked to change the subject. "Of them, how many are here?"

The Kai shook his head. "Not many *Rhunvala* there *are* at all, and few here remain. Most to fortresses go, or where needed they are. At present, myself and Kai Maltanar in the valley dwell. Maltanar aged is, here his last years in peace and comfort to pass. Then, Kor Lothairal there is." He paused, a troubled expression there and then gone before she could be fully certain she'd seen it at all. "With him, thou'll be training –"

"If accepted she is," Dael said.

"If accepted thou art," Kai Peredur said. "Verily."

They reached the bottom of the sheer-sided mountain. Thanks to the rushings-ahead of some of the others who'd come to meet her, Tilanne's presence must have been made widely known, because several curious pairs of eyes peeked down from windows and battlements. She dismounted, stretching the kinks and aches of her long journey from her bones, and handed Morai over to a wide-eyed stablehand.

To enter the Citadel proper, she followed Kai Peredur and the two masters up a flight of wooden stairs to an entry a full floor above ground level. If danger threatened, it would be an easy matter to bring the people inside to safety, fire or dismantle the stairway, and leave an enemy with no ready entrance. Meanwhile, archers could be raining arrows from the upper levels, and she did not doubt that the Citadel itself was so well stocked as to resist a siege for decades.

The interior of the Citadel was arranged in concentric circles, except as the halls followed the contours of the mountain, the circles weren't perfectly round. Chambers along the outer wall had windows, some with balconies or doors giving access to walkways and battlements. The enclosing stone had a weathered, old, welcoming feel to it, and was cheered and brightened and warmed by ample use of tapestries and woven mats. There were many hearths as well, so that no chill lingered even in the mountain's heart.

Some of the rooms they passed, or passed through, were filled with such fascinating items that she wanted to stop and look around, but she told herself there would, Kaledhol willing, be ample time for that later. There were libraries, for one . . . whole chambers given over to books. Most of their lore was handed down in told-stories, and she had never seen so many books in one place. Artwork, as well . . . when she'd been in Firsthome, she'd wondered at those ancestors for wasting time in such frivolous pursuits. Here were many beautiful works, perhaps brought from Firsthome, perhaps even saved from Govannisan itself.

Kai Peredur brought her at last to a large oval-shaped room. At the very pinnacle of its domed ceiling, a gap in the stone opened not onto the sky but onto dark crystal shot with colors. Tilanne caught her breath, knowing that she was looking up at the underside of the great crystal that rose from the top of the stone mountain.

The walls of this room were a mural of mosaic, a panorama that gave way smoothly from one scene to the next. She saw ocean beaches, plains of grass, forests, snow-capped peaks, every landscape of the world that she'd ever heard of. There were animals of all sorts, as well as images of elves, and even a few dwarves and dragons depicted.

The floor was sunken in the center in two places, making two side-by-side circular sections. In one, curved and cushioned benches encircled a stone-ringed fireplace. An inverted, conical metal chimney hung over it, splitting into two pipes that vanished into the walls. In the other, similar benches covered in oilcloth ringed a deep pool.

Around the edges ran a stone walkway lined with a red carpet. Several arched doorways, all outlined in dark stone intricately shaped with knotwork patterns, interrupted the mosaics. They were hung with crimson curtains.

"This, the main chamber of the *Rhunvala* is," the Kai said. "Each of those doorways to a bedroom leads, and this common area we all share. As too the pool . . ." He paused, looking at her as if for the first time musing over the problem of having a woman bathing alongside the rest of them. When no conclusion apparently sprang readily to mind, he shrugged and went on. "Our meals, in the main dining hall with the others we take. And there, down that hall, our main temple is."

"See it may I?"

"Prefer wouldst thou not first to rest?"

"Oh, no," she said. "Weary I am, yes, and travel-grimed, but before all else should I the temple see, if only for a moment."

Smiling at her eagerness, he said, "At least thine pack set down."

As heavy as it was, in her wonder and delight at seeing the *Odan Rhunvale*, she had all but forgotten she carried it. She slid the straps from her shoulders, and left it on one of the benches near the fireplace, along with her cloak. She put her helm there too that she might enter the temple bare-headed.

The long hallway was unlit by any magelights or torches, and yet it was not dark. A splendid chorus of ever-shifting radiance danced along the walls and floor, which sloped upward at a gentle angle. Tilanne's pulse quickened as they neared the end, as they entered the spill of colors.

"Here," Peredur said, and stepped aside to let her precede him.

Tilanne did so, with hushed and reverent steps.

This place was not so much one of ceremony as of solitary worship and meditation. Rather than being a building, it was a bubble, a hollow in the bottom of the crystal, so that she was standing in it, amid it, surrounded by it. The colors swirled and played about her, sometimes passing over her. As they did, she could feel them, each a different texture, each seeming to carry with it a secret hint of scent and sound as well. When she was bathed briefly in indigo, she smelled night-blooming flowers and felt a caress like that of softest silkmole fur. When the vibrant forest green lit her, she smelled the woods after a rain, felt cool damp grass. The amber light was warm as a homey fire, and brought with it the aroma of baking bread.

She reached up with both arms, awash in these sensations, and wept with amazed joy at the wondrous, welcoming feeling that enveloped her. She could have stayed there forever, overwhelmed, but at last Kai Peredur gently led her from the chamber.

"It . . . it . . . so wondrous . . ." Words failed her.

He nodded as if he understood. "Truly, Kor Tilanne, here dost thou belong."

* * *

CHAPTER SEVENTEEN

If the gifts with which she'd been showered upon leaving Jewelgreen had seemed an embarrassment of riches, at least her room at the *Odan Rhunvale* gave her a fitting place to keep them. It was by far the most opulent chamber in which she'd ever contemplated trying to sleep. The heavy furniture was of rosewood, an ancient but still plush wealth of hanging tapestries covered the walls, the washbasin magically brimmed with clear water, the fireplace had an unusual chimney that branched into two flues with a framed mirror inset between them.

The wardrobe had glass doors etched with climbing thorny vines of roses. Her collection of clothing did not even fill a quarter of its racks and drawers. Nor did she have much in the way of books or knickknacks to occupy the shelves over the desk. She hung her armor, sword belt, and helm on an armory rack provided. Brackets set into the wall supported her shield.

By the time she was done unpacking, the room still seemed empty and expectant of a new guest. Tilanne stood at the center of it, on a thick rug, and tried to imagine this as her home. An entire family could have lived comfortably in this space, and here it was all for her.

Not only that, but she had the outer chamber with its pool and far grander fireplace at her disposal. And, according to Kai Peredur, very nearly the run of the entire Citadel.

She decided she'd best make use of that pool, and see to it that she was presentable before the evening meal. At it or after it, she knew, she was to be introduced to the other ranking *Morvalan* here. It wouldn't do to go before them when all she'd had during her travels were makeshift sponge-baths.

Tilanne gathered her bathing-things and stepped out into the main chamber. She had it to herself, Kai Peredur having gone off to make arrangements for the addition of a new squire-in-training. The pool was heated and pleasant, soapsuds and dirt carried away by circulating and purified currents of water. She immersed, sighing, and laved the travel-grime from her hair and body.

As she did, she finally let herself believe that it was true. She was here. She'd done it. She had reached the *Odan Rhunvale*, and been taken within. Welcomed. Accepted, if only thus far on a tentative basis.

Part of her had harbored the deep but nagging fear that even if she was able to find the place, they would turn her away at the gates. They would deny her, possibly with a scornful laugh or even a thrashing for presuming to think that a woman could ever aspire to such an honor as becoming *Rhunvala*. Whether she was able to succeed and earn those things to which she aspired was another matter, but if she didn't, it would be because of her own failings and not because she'd been forbidden the opportunity.

A sound, a step, caught her attention as she was basking in the pool. She turned, water lapping at her collarbones, and there stood Kai Peredur with his arms laden.

"Some things for thee I've brought," he said.

"Kai, no, such thou needst not –" She stammered and stuttered, appalled to think that a *Rhunvala* was fetching and carrying on her behalf like some domestic.

He chuckled and set the parcels on one of the benches. "Learn must thou, Kor Tilanne, that while *Rhunvala* may we be, still men we are. Or, women, as may the case be. Respected are we, if such respect deserved is, but revered we are not."

"But . . ."

"Wouldst thou wish, Tilanne, revered to be?"

Tilanne blinked, taken aback. "No, but only a mere girl am I . . ."

"No 'mere' is there about it," he said. "For a 'mere' girl, much trouble would I have had in proper attire for thee finding. Few ladies have we, and thus, few lady's clothes. Yet as one of us thou art to be, best thought I it that in trousers and tunic thou didst dress. Of those, aplenty we have. Books also have I for thee brought, for thy lessons in history and philosophy."

"My thanks, Kai Peredur. When do I my lessons begin? The morrow?"

He made a dismissive, nonchalant wave. "Only just arrived hast thou, and long years thou'll study. A day or two matters not. Much there is, Kor Tilanne, for thee to learn."

"Well aware of that am I." She dipped her head.

"But ample time for thee to learn it. The dining-hour almost upon us is, and eager are the others thy acquaintance to make."

"Likewise am I to make theirs." Tilanne climbed the steps from the pool, and picked up a drying-cloth.

She felt rather strange, being naked before a *Rhunvala*. This wasn't like the communal bath-house at Jewelgreen, not at all. She couldn't suppress a blush as she dried her body and wrapped her hair. The fact that Kai Peredur observed her with amusement at her blush and appreciation of her nudity did little for her composure, and she did her best to avoid meeting his eyes as she hastily donned a robe, collected the parcels he'd brought, and took them to her room. But Kai Peredur followed along, leaning in the doorway to talk to her as she dressed.

"Of a usual day, meals at Second, Sixth, Tenth, and Fourteenth Bells are," he said. "The night-watch at the Fifteenth Bell begins, and so on the night through. Grueling shall thy work here be, fearsomely so."

"Expected such did I." She slid her legs into a pair of black trousers that fit like a second skin.

"But not such a harsh taskmaster as some am I."

"'Tis thee, then, that shall the training of me have?" The cream-colored silk undertunic had long sleeves with tiny onyx buttons down the front and at the cuffs. A lot of tiny buttons, and she could not for the life of her seem to get them into the correct loops with him standing there, smiling at her.

"Even so," he said. "Though advised by Kai Maltanar I'll be. Kor Lothairal only a short while under my tutelage has been. I doubt me not that swiftly thou'll catch up. From dawn until dusk, with lessons and with prayers, shall thy day be filled."

She put on the overtunic, which was of soft scarlet wool. Sleeveless, it had outward-pointed shoulder pads, and laced up the front with black velvet cords. The hem of it was a triangular shape, the points front and back coming to just above her knees while on the sides, the garment was cut to her hips.

"Good it is of thee this chance to give me," she said, securing her sword belt around her middle and buffing the dirt from her boots.

"To thee, I gave it not. To thee, Kai Terindor and Kaledhol did give it." Kai Peredur shrugged, and his smile nearly became a grin. "Pleased am I this chance to have. Often have we spoken, other *Rhunvala* and I, and in speculation wondered whether a woman the training could survive. But never the opportunity to find out did we expect to have."

Her own smile in return was somewhat strained. "Survive?"

His grin widened. His eyes twinkled. "That any woman would such horrific rigors wish to undergo, an unlikely eventuality seemed. Yet here thou art, Kor Tilanne."

"Not much at all like Kai Terindor art thou," she said without thinking, and touched her fingertips to her lips. "Mean do I no offense!"

The grin became an outright laugh. "Taken is none. Of different disciplines were Terindor and I, as thou'll find."

"Different disciplines?"

"Of fire, think," he said. "To thee, what means it?"

Puzzled, Tilanne did so. "Fire warmth gives, and food cooks."

"True indeed." He nodded. "But also does it not burn and consume?"

"It does . . ."

"Dual of purpose it fire, dual of discipline. So too Kaledhol is. The Protector, the Destroyer. We each of us, we *Rhunvala*, must one of those Ways to emulate choose . . . or the other."

"To protect, or destroy?" she asked, frowning, and pulling the cloth from her hair to brush it out.

"Which we choose doth our powers determine. Kai Terindor the path of Destruction chose. Powers as weapons against others he had. Those like myself, who have the path of Protection taken, powers are granted ourselves to make stronger, that better might we those in our care defend."

Tugging at a stubborn tangle, Tilanne considered this. "Which am I?"

"Most Kors at some point in their training are to one Way or the other drawn. But thee, Kor Tilanne . . . thee, I think, are already to one path pledged."

She twitched, pulling harder than she meant to on her hair and wincing. She hadn't told him, hadn't told any of them of her vow. But he spoke it as matter-of-factly as could be. And as he did, she knew he was right.

"To the path of Protection am I called," she said. "Feel it do I, in my soul. Already an oath to Kaledhol have I sworn, no elven life to take, and in all my best elven lives to defend."

"Such it is," Kai Peredur said, and she detected approval in his tone. "And so dost thou see why different in nature, different in approach, were Kai Terindor and I. But not only a difference in these paths was it, of course. Always more dour and intense of nature was he, while I more light of heart. Becoming *Rhunvala* means not that we our true selves give up." He clapped his hands together briskly, looking her over. "But starved am I, and time for evening meal it is, and presentable thou art. So, to the dining hall, let us go."

"Presentable truly?"

"Lie would I?"

"No, never."

"In our vows is no pledge of truthfulness required, Kor Tilanne. But in this, I lie not. Most presentable thou art, darksome-lovely and strong and a delight upon which to look. The others shall no fault in thee find. Well, excepting Dael."

"Meant did I never the Master to offend."

Kai Peredur patted her shoulder. "Simply Dael it is. Adverse to change is he, even moreso than many an elf. In thee, an unwelcome challenge he sees. Never before, I warrant, has he armor tailored to a woman had to make."

Tilanne couldn't help joining in his chuckle, but hers was flavored with anxiety. "Never a warrior-woman has there been, a swordmaid, *never?*"

"None since Firsthome." His mirth faded. "By plague and peril so reduced were our numbers that all the more precious our life-giving women became, that they might enough children bear our people to replenish. Since then, custom has it become. Not that wholly restored are our numbers, nor likely ever to be, for perish do too many good soldiers, and far swifter than replacements born and raised can be."

"Suggested to me has it been," Tilanne said with a sigh, "that of the oppositions to this calling I'll face, for that reason most of all shall it be. That these years I should in childbearing spend, not training, and not my life-giving life in battle putting to risk."

"If Kaledhol's will it is that better our people thou might in this method serve," he said, "then for the greater good of the Cause shall it be."

She fell in beside him as they left the chamber. "Such hope do I, such pray do I."

A man came hobbling toward them, supported by a staff of oak nearly as gnarled and seamed as the walnut-knuckled hand that gripped it. He had gossamer-thin hair of purest white floating like dandelion fluff around his head. Only the sagging droop of flesh hanging from his stooped bones told of the powerfully built man he must have once been. His eyes were a faded wash-yellow, the eyes of a scarred old tomcat that had lived through many nines of lives and many a midnight tussle.

Yet despite his age and obvious infirmity, he carried himself with a presence that would have drawn notice even without the sign of the basilisk sewn in red on his tunic. In addition to the staff, he still wore a sword, and it looked to be just as battle-worn and experienced as he was.

"Kai Maltanar, good eve to thee," Kai Peredur said. "My privilege it is to thee Kor Tilanne to present."

Those yellow eyes found her, bored into her. In them, she saw all the hardness created by centuries of warfare, centuries of fighting. She was reminded of Thoraine, back in Jewelgreen . . . Thoraine, an old but still hale soldier. Here was one even older, and far less hale. Here was a man with a bone-deep weariness of walking this world, and the sadness that could only have come from having outlived everyone he'd ever held dear. Wives, siblings, children, friends, war-companions . . . all dead, all gone, and in these, his declining years, he had only the church to see him through until he was finally done with this life.

But then he smiled at her – toothlessly, but it was a smile – and some of those layers of sorrow peeled away. "Kor Tilanne, is it?" His voice was firm, not cracked and wavery as she might have expected.

"Pleased am I thee to meet, Kai Maltanar," Tilanne said.

"To what comes this world, Peredur, when the tasks of grown men are by slips of girls taken up?" He shook his head ruefully, but the smile did not fade. "Modern women."

He was . . . he was *teasing* her. These men were *Rhunvala*, at the very *Odan Rhunvale* itself! And they were friendly, they spoke to each other with the casual familiarity of long affection, they joked and teased and . . . and treated her like . . . like she was one of them.

"Alas, unlikely it is that a sweeping change this will herald," Kai Peredur said.

"More's the pity. Said before have I and say it again I shall, far better off would we all be if more females in this old pile of stone dwelt."

"Beware, else like my mother thou'll sound," Kai Peredur said. He adopted a nagging matronly tone. "All of us wives should take, and the Citadel with the pitter-pat of children's footsteps echo."

"Not at the Citadel some man's wife to become is *this* sable-haired beauty," Maltanar said, chucking Tilanne under the chin as if she were a toddler in pigtails. "Correct am I?"

"Correct are thee, *Nantor*," Tilanne said, using the term of fond address for an elder. Only after she'd said it did she realize it might have been the wrong thing to say to a *Rhunvala*. Once again, she brought her hand to her lips. "No disrespect did I mean."

But rather than be angry, Maltanar's smile returned, and a mist of tears touched his eyes. "*Nantor*," he said. "Long has it been since I've by that title been called. As *Nantor* at any time mayst thou address me."

He fell in with them, and both Tilanne and Kai Peredur slowed their strides to allow for his more sedate pace. Down the hall they went, down a wide and curving flight of steps – Maltanar took these even more slowly, using his staff to prod ahead as if he were testing for hidden traps and pitfalls – and finally, into a long, low-ceilinged room that rang with lively conversation.

The tables filling the dining room were large and round, each one appearing to be a slice from the trunk of one of the great trees. The rings of tree-age were visible beneath coats of clear varnish. The seats were like roots, curving out from the thick supporting post of each table and then flaring out into saddle-shapes that looked awkward but were, as Tilanne discovered as soon as she sat down in the one Kai Peredur indicated, very comfortable.

Several others were already at that table, all elves of rank. She recognized Master Dael Swordbright, who scowled and then went back to a discussion with a black-haired man. Savillan Angen raised a hand in a friendly wave.

One of the ranking elves was a woman. The moment she saw her, Tilanne guessed who she must be. A tall, elegant-looking lady, she sat straight despite having a silver-topped black cane resting at her side. Her hair was the same pewter shade as Peredur's, feathered with a lighter silvery-grey at the temples and caught up in an elaborate coronet of braids. A knotwork-pattern tattoo followed her hairline and descended down the sides of her neck to vanish beneath the high collar of her indigo gown. She wore the multiple earrings, cuffs, and delicate linking chains popular among High Mages. More jewels and precious metals glittered on her fingers.

"Thy mother this must be," Tilanne said.

"My mother indeed this is," Kai Peredur said. "Idrasanna Denisse, Idrasanna of the Crown."

More introductions were made once the rest of the table had taken their seats. The black-haired man talking to Master Dael was Ordan Quaide, the fortificationist. The other mage, short and wiry, with a shaven head completely covered in a multi-colored tattoo picking out the orbits of the planets, was Kinnon Faer of the Scepter. Another man and woman having the aura and manner of a couple who'd been married so long and so happily that they'd begun not only to take on aspects of each other's personality but had also begun to look alike – slim even by elven standards, light brown hair, ready cheerful smiles – were Neterian and Leiata Kelda.

Last but not least, arriving just as the first course was being served, was a young man only ten or so years older than Tilanne. He was athletic and attractive, his manner was a strange smoldering cross of pent-up energy and lethargy.

He was introduced to her as Kor Lothairal, but barely acknowledged her or anyone else. He slouched in his seat and picked at his food in a listless way. A maroon cord, a sign of mourning, was tied in his dark-brown hair.

"Perhaps thy tale thou'll tell us, Kor Tilanne?" Kai Peredur invited as a tureen of thick mushroom soup was passed around the table.

A hush fell over the dining hall. Tilanne swallowed a bite of bread. Her hands wanted to tremble as she looked around. So many people. All of them watching her. All of them, listening to her. It was like Jewelgreen, like every other settlement where she'd stopped along her journey, but tenfold. Here, she had to tell everything. She did not have the luxury of leaving out the troublesome or painful parts. It was why she'd come.

She began speaking in a low voice, then gained strength and confidence from their quiet encouraging nods. She told them of her ordinary family, her ordinary childhood. How she had accompanied her father and brother to Cliffcave, and what had gone on there.

When she reached the part about the death of Kai Terindor, then and only then did Kor Lothairal's head come up. His hazel eyes fixed on her with unsettling intensity. She found his stare so unnerving that her voice shook as she described the final confrontation between orckin and knight, and her own small part in it.

Her voice and hands grew steadier as she described how she and the other survivors had made their way to safety, and what had happened after. Still leaving nothing out, she told them about Captain Jedren, what he'd done and what had happened to him. She told them of Jedriel and Jedina. She told them of her journey to Firsthome and what had gone on in the temple there. Lastly, she spoke of the woods, and how she had finally found her way.

She finished the tale when the main course – a baked dish of alternating layers of sliced mutton, mintleaf, pastry, and minced vegetables – was being taken away to make room for a dessert of berries and cream. Once she was done, she took a deep breath and awaited their reactions, awaited the inevitable questions and debate.

Master Dael continued to scowl. Kor Lothairal had returned his angry, indifferent attention to his place once she had finished telling of Kai Terindor's death, and would not look at her. The rest regarded her without rancor. Their expressions ranged from resignation to sympathy, and smiles.

"Well?" she asked when the hush grew unbearable. "Decided have thee? Permitted to stay am I?"

Idrasanna laughed like the music of bells. "Decided? Permitted? Not for us are these things to do. No tribunal needs there be, when certain it is that by Kaledhol's will thou art here. Between He and thee the decision rests. Drawn hither were thou, and here dost thou belong."

Dael's brows lowered, making his scowl even more fierce. "Yet," he said, "only a woman is she. Not even that. Only a girl."

"For shame, Dael," Leiata said. "Bore thee did a woman."

"If at sorcery every bit as skilled are women as men," Kinnon said, "at arms, why not?"

"Some more skilled are," Idrasanna said, giving him a wink. "But still, the weapon-master's point a valid one is. By long tradition has it been that we females for life-giving are meant. But no law is it that we cannot another profession manage as well. On me, look . . . ten living sons have I, and still a sorceress of some small skill."

"Ten living sons?" Tilanne thought her eyes might bulge out of her head. Her own mother had died after bearing seven children, and now only Tilanne and a sister had not been sent young to their pyres.

"Though," Idrasanna added with a sidelong look at her son, a look that was part loving and part exasperated and part teasing all in one, "thus far has only *one* of them wed, and grandchildren given me."

"Yes, Mother, heard this many a time have I and my brothers besides." Kai Peredur rolled his eyes good-naturedly. "That a woman *Rhunvala* there has never been, means only that never one has there been. Until now. If satisfied with Kor Tilanne is Kaledhol, otherwise is it for none among us to say."

* * *

CHAPTER EIGHTEEN

In the company of Leiater Kelda, the adolescent son of the craft-masters, Tilanne passed the next several days exploring the castle mountain from its height to its depths, learning all that she could of the *Odan Rhunvale*, its people and its workings.

The Citadel's highest point was the chamber she'd already visited, that hollowed-out cupola in the great crystal itself. The personal rooms of the ranking elves were on the upper floors, and just beneath them were the common areas devoted to the dining room, kitchens, libraries, and galleries. There was also a single great hall large enough for all of the inhabitants to gather for occasional celebrations and entertainments.

The lower levels provided lodging and workspace for the craftsmen, soldiers, and farmers. Deeper still were the storage cellars and the mint. The mountain sat upon a rich vein of silver ore, from which the *kaimora* coins were struck. Money had always been more of a novelty to Tilanne, a symbolic exchange rather than something of actual value.

Deepest of all were the forges and armories. There, blackmetal was heated and hammered and formed into a variety of armor and weapons. These were then cooled in the River of Time, which flowed dark and cold as the starless sky in a subterranean channel

Tilanne found Leiater to be good company, if dangerously accident-prone. When he offered to show her how one of the coin-strikers worked, he caught his hand in it. Though he escaped having the sword and the rose of a *kaimora* forever impressed into his flesh, in recoiling he knocked over a table, spilled a cask of unstruck coins to jingle merrily across the floor, trod on Tilanne's foot, and struck his own head a ringing blow on a low beam. Their first riding tour of the valley surroundings ended abruptly when a saddle strap came loose and dumped him headlong. Similar disasters followed him wherever he went.

By the end of each day in his company, Tilanne retreated thankfully to her room, wondering what possible profession his parents would be able to find for such a youth.

Her formal training began shortly thereafter. As Kai Peredur had promised, it was full and rigorous. What she'd sampled at Jewelgreen had only been the beginning. She was put through her paces until she ached so that she thought her limbs might fall off – and to think, she'd believed herself to be in some sort of fighting trim!

Because a *Rhunvala* was expected to know at least a little bit about every aspect of *Morvalan* life, including magic, Tilanne was assigned regular sessions with both Kinnon and Idrasanna. She was grateful for the informal learning she'd had from Alarice, though it did make her miss her friend all the more keenly.

"We of the Crown in Circles of many mages work best," Idrasanna explained. "Those of the Scepter, a more solitary craft pursue. From Kinnon, concentration and mental discipline shalt thou learn. While I, thy teaching of cooperative casting will have."

"But no great mage of talent am I," Tilanne said.

"Matters it does not," Kinnon said. "In fact, matters more does it, for one unskilled at sorcery must a better grasp of it have, the better able to defend against it to be."

After some initial skepticism and doubt, most of the various crafters and other ranking elves came to accept Tilanne as one of them. Those of lower rank followed their lead. Only Master Dael did not warm to her. She remained conscious of his disapproving glare, and did not look forward to her trips to the armories to be outfitted.

"If some consolation it is," Kai Peredur said when once she remarked on Dael's continued unfriendliness, "not specifically *thee* is it that offends him, not Tilanne Murres. Not even that Tilanne Murres, a girl, wouldst *Rhunvala* become. Around women in general, ill-at-ease is he."

"*Chani*, he is?"

The Kai coughed to cover a laugh. "Some *Alvalan* cousin, his heart did break. When abandoned him she did, without a word of farewell, so came he all women to distrust and at the feet of the many lay blame for the faults of the one."

"So . . . much trade and contact with the *Alvalan* there is?" she asked. "Told was I by Kinnon and thy mother that to the Great Homes of the Scepter and Crown Magics frequently mages from the north do come. And heard did I that our wine and goods to *Alvalan* merchants and markets are sold."

"Subtly is it done," he said. "Secretly, even. To most of our northern kinsfolk, a frightening mystery we remain. But elves we are, one and all. Though Kaledhol has from their lore been stricken, though diverse the ways of our peoples may be, yet one race we remain, and should never enemies be."

Even more shocking to Tilanne was to learn that some *Morvalan* ventured beyond the boundaries of the forest to trade and have dealings with the humans. Not with the Mountain King's hated, savage folk, but to the west, to the Northlands.

"Sometimes," Kai Maltanar said when she broached the subject, "a necessity it is."

"But our enemies they are," she protested. "Trade with them we do? Foodstuffs and goods that could *our* children be benefiting, we into human hands deliver?"

"How better of them to learn?"

"To learn of them, I care not! To stop them, slay them, for these things very much do I care."

"Not all of them slain are, Tilanne," he said. "Many as slaves or laborers in the mines and quarries do we keep."

"Here?! Humans at the very Citadel are?"

"No," Kai Peredur said. "Here, to my knowledge, never a human foot has stepped."

Through the course of her lessons and training sessions, she grew to see them both as people, not just as *Rhunvala.* She might have expected that such would cause her admiration of them to dim, but it did not. If anything, it was the opposite. The more she got to know them, the greater her admiration and fondness became. She never would have thought such a thing to be possible, having expected all of the *Rhunvala* to be as coldly, darkly forbidding as Kai Terindor had been.

In Kai Maltanar, she found a wise and sage mentor. His recollection of recent times tended to be fogged, and he might sometimes forget what he'd eaten for the previous evening's meal, but he could clearly recount adventures from centuries past. He treated her kindly, as he might have treated a favorite granddaughter. As she had never known either of her grandfathers, she took a welcome comfort in his affectionate teasing.

Kai Peredur was another matter. Tilanne tried not to think too often or too deeply about her feelings towards him. He was patient, and good-humored, and never made her feel like a fool despite her countless questions. In that, he reminded her of her brother Vandil . . . and of Jedriel as well. But in a vital other way, he reminded her of the gentle physician and gentler scribe not at all. Peredur was a swordsman, a warrior, a knight. Peredur was *Rhunvala.*

Kor Lothairal was often sullen and broody when they were brought together to study or train. At first, Tilanne had assumed it was because he resented her presence, resented having another Kor around. But his anger never seemed directed at her. She was left with the sense that he didn't care one way or the other that she was here. That he cared even less about her being a girl.

Nor did he seem to be envious of her. Such would have been laughable, anyway. It was hardly as if Tilanne had swept in and shown him up at every turn, outshining him in every aspect of their training. Far from it. Lothairal was far and away the better warrior. He fought, even in practices, with a single-minded and blood-hungry intensity that Tilanne doubted she'd ever be able to match.

The years ahead, which had been such a daunting and unknown future of mist, shadow, and uncertainty, no longer troubled Tilanne at all. Years, yes, it would be years until she was ready to undergo the final rituals necessary to earn her place in Kaledhol's sight. But she did not begrudge that investment of time, and looked forward to it more and more.

The *Odan Rhunvale* became so much like a home to her that it was soon hard to believe she had lived anywhere else. She threw herself into her studies with determination.

It became her habit in the evenings to retire to the main chamber shared by the *Rhunvala.* There, pleasantly sore from her day's exertions, she would rest with a book and a glass of wine or some other treat. Often, Maltanar or Peredur or both would join her, and they'd sit together reading in companionable quiet or talking, just talking, over any subjects that came to mind.

One such evening, she was alone, curled on the soft bench with the journal of Dyanavan Morestatali in her lap and a bowl of sugared almonds at her knee. She had heard the legends of how the founders of Firsthome had survived Govannisan's fall, but it thrilled her to read the story in Morestatali's own words, written by his own hand. She shivered as she came to the lines that described how Rigellian Morestatali, Dyanavan's brother, had been uplifted by Kaledhol and became the first Kai, and led his people to safety.

To us were the dragons' eyes made blind
For from their sight concealed us did Kaledhol
The trolls and beasts before us fell
For our aim made true did Kaledhol
The stone did part, the waters clear
For our spells made strong did Kaledhol
No fear held the wild, no dread held the night
For protected us did Kaledhol
The mountains and forests our people embraced
For such was the will of Kaledhol

Tilanne re-read that passage, remembering her own disastrous efforts to lead the survivors of Cliffcave. She had failed so many of them . . .

The sound of approaching footsteps and angry voices brought her back to her surroundings with a gasp. Nestled low on the cushioned bench as she was, the hanging metal cone of the chimney blocked her view of the doorway and similarly blocked her from view as the arguing men came in. She did not need to see them in order to know them, however.

"Know these things already do I," Kor Lothairal said. "Told thee that I did. Learned them already, practiced them already a thousand times I have! Why clear to thee is this not?"

"And told *thee* did I," Kai Peredur said, evenly but with an underlying sternness, "that with thy training back to the beginning must we go, so that assured am I that naught missed or overlooked hath been."

"Upon Kai Lothar doubts thou wouldst cast?"

The question was sharp as a blade in the gut, and the similarity of names made Tilanne go numb. Kai Lothar? *Lothar*? That could only mean one of a very few things.

"Nay, Lothairal, that never would I do."

"Said didst thou that sloppy and imperfect his training of me hath been."

"No such thing did I say. Only that–"

"Missed? Overlooked? Were those not thy exact words? With my own ears did I not just hear them?"

They had stopped on the far side of the hearth. Tilanne could not see their faces, the hanging chimney continuing to obscure them from the chest up. But she could see their stances, Lothairal's of coiled and fist-clenched wrath, Peredur's relaxed but ready.

"My words, yes, they were," Kai Peredur said. "Not saying am I that anything missed or overlooked *hath* been. Only that my duty it is thy capabilities and knowledge to judge."

"No infant am I. Thy hand guiding mine in forming my letters, like a third ear I need. So coddle me not."

"Never such was my intent."

"Then for a change, thy trust give. If not to me, to Kai Lothar and his memory give it. And of this, let us speak no more." Kor Lothairal stalked around the raised walkway, fiercely swept aside one of the curtains and vanished through the doorway of the room that was his.

Moving with quiet care, Tilanne sat up and unfolded her legs, putting her book and bowl on the floor. She leaned to peer around the chimney.

The Kai, only his profile visible from Tilanne's vantage, sank onto on a bench and slumped there with a heavy sigh. He massaged his brow with both hands. Without looking up, he asked, "Of that, how much didst thou hear?"

"Sorry am I. Meant to eavesdrop, I did not."

He glanced at the closed curtain through which Lothairal had gone. He seemed to be weighing the worth of going after the Kor, of trying again to talk to him. "Difficulties betwixt us there are, as doubtless didst thou notice."

"Is it that the other Way, he's chosen?"

"The Way of Destruction, yes, that a large part of our differences is. But not all, Tilanne. More, there is. To another Kai was he sworn before me. Died did that Kai, two seasons ago. Worse . . ."

"His father it was?"

Again, he glanced at the curtain, chewing at his lower lip. He stood and beckoned to her. Tilanne slipped from the bench and followed him. They went up the short, slanting passage that led into the rounded chamber in the very base of the dark crystal. Into that place of light, color, shadow and sensation.

"Kai Lothar a bold and brave *Rhunvala* was," Kai Peredur said. "None in battle more ferocious, more skilled couldst thou have in all our lands found. Against the Mountain King's folk a special hatred he held, for his wife – Lothairal's mother – was by their hands slain."

Tilanne made a wordless noise of sympathy, though she probably could have counted on the fingers of both hands all the elves she'd known whose family tree *didn't* contain at least one life lost to the Mountain King's armies.

"His own son as Kor, Kai Lothar took, and his training at once began. Too quickly, he began it, too ruthlessly. On matters of warfare alone was he centered, and other matters neglected. Lothairal too hard he drove, and of the boy too much demanded."

"Eager to please and make proud his father must he have been," Tilanne said. "The Path of Destruction, Kai Lothar followed?"

Kai Peredur nodded.

"And died, he did."

"Yes. Word we received that humans had into the forest come, raiders from the Mountain Kingdom. Kai Lothar against them a force of soldiers led. With him, he brought Lothairal, though not yet completed was the boy's tutelage. Disagreed with this decision did both Maltanar and I. Strongly. Yet heeded us, Lothar would not."

An aching pit opened in her heart. Kai Lothar's death must have occurred not long before that of Kai Terindor. To lose any *Rhunvala* was inevitable but sad tragedy enough. To lose two, so close in time together? That was a bleak and dismal turn of events.

"Wounded was Lothairal, but lived he did," Kai Peredur continued, gazing up into the swirling shadow-colors of the crystal. "With some scant few of the soldiers he to the Citadel returned. When healed and recovered he was, under me his training he resumed. Challenging it has for the both of us been."

"Help can I? In any way?" she asked.

"Already a great help hast thou been," he said. "Begun had I to believe that all the fault on my shoulders rested. But as such progress and improvements in thy efforts I see, know do I that not an abject failure as a teacher am I."

"No!" she said. "Kai Peredur . . . thy teaching . . ."

She was shocked to the core that he ever could have harbored such an idea, ever. It left her all but speechless, as she fumbled for the right words to assure him that he was *not* a failure as a teacher. No one could be taught who was not willing to learn, and if Lothairal was being obstinate and stubborn – as he was – then if there was blame to be laid, it was to be laid upon Lothairal for being a poor student.

Tilanne wanted to say all this, and looked up earnestly into Kai Peredur's eyes. They were the dusky purple-blue of twilight, and even if she had been able to speak she might have lost the power then and there.

She was lost in the play of the crystal's light and color across his features. A ray of rich amber flowed from his chin along the line of his jaw. It traced his ear in golden radiance, as if outlining the path that her fingertips might follow if she were allowed to caress him so familiarly.

Unbidden warmth kindled within her. A fleeting thought – what would it be like to make love *here*, in the very heart of Kaledhol's most sacred place? – flickered through her mind and brought a dryness to her mouth. It was followed by a franker speculation – what would it be like to make love to *Peredur*, here or anyplace? – and her knees went weak.

They were breathing in synchrony, the visible pulse in his throat matching the throbbing of her own. Their gazes remained locked. Her cheeks felt flushed, a tingle spreading down and through and along her limbs. She could not move, felt rooted to the spot.

The air around them felt charged as it might before a lightning storm. Even the colors spilling from the crystal seemed to spin more rapidly, shine more brightly.

Peredur raised one hand, slowly, and held it before her with the palm turned outward. Not aware that she had control of her body, Tilanne found her arm mirroring the motion. They stood almost touching, but that last bit of space between them seemed a gulf, a chasm every bit as real and impassable as the Lowfire in the darkest part of the wood.

Still slowly, their fingers bent together until the tips met. First the smallest – Livana's finger, the channel through which most magics flowed. Then Shannia's, with its nerves leading directly to the heart. Then Denethel's, without which a bow could not be drawn. And Valannin's, vital for writing and direction. Lastly, the thumb, Kaledhol's, most important of all in its versatility and usefulness.

There they stood, no parts of them touching but for those five tiniest of contacts, and Tilanne trembled because she doubted that the most intimate joining would have been so fraught with intensity. She could almost imagine their blood mingling, flowing from his veins into hers and the reverse, making them one.

Conflict warred in her soul, wanting him and fearing that wanting, trying to deny it. They were teacher and student. He was *Rhunvala,* and she would someday be. In their relationship was no room for desire, for passion, for love. Not of that sort.

As if coming to that conclusion in the same moment, Kai Peredur and Tilanne withdrew their hands and curled their fingers. His head turned one way while hers turned the other, breaking the powerful lock of their gaze.

She placed the hand that had so recently been touching his over her heart, felt its rapid thrumming through the fabric of her robe. She closed her eyes and stood where she was, listening to his fading footfalls as he walked rapidly from the chamber.

They could not allow that to happen again. Neither of them.

*   *   *

CHAPTER NINETEEN

Over the next five years of Tilanne's time at the *Odan Rhunvale*, she became someone who would have been unrecognizable to her family and friends, to all those who'd known her before. This taut-limbed, steady-eyed woman with a warrior's reflexes often seemed almost a stranger even to herself.

Gone was the unsure girl with no clear sense of where she belonged. This was where she belonged, this was what she was meant to do. To serve her god and serve her people. In whatever way Kaledhol required of her, she would follow His will.

During that time, the *Morvalan* lands enjoyed a brief respite from invaders. Those of the Mountain Kingdom were too caught up in warring amongst themselves to send many invaders into the forests. Some, Tilanne among them, even hoped that their old enemies would destroy themselves and spare the elves the trouble.

Alas, it was not to be so. When the smoke cleared and the dust settled, a new Mountain King had seized power. The raids began again. There were rumors of elves taken prisoner, tortured, forced to use their magic to do the new king's bidding.

His name was Durvan. A dwarven name, a dwarven-sounding title, but he and his forefathers had all been human.

His heir, though . . .

Durvanian.

The name alone was enough to make Tilanne shudder with revulsion and horror when first she heard it, and when first she understood what it meant.

"Time it is the battle to them to take!" Kor Lothairal's eyes flashed as he addressed the assembly that had been called in the great meeting-hall of the Citadel. "Too long have we in tight defense of our homeland sat and waited, like wary rabbits in a hole. Centuries overdue are we this festering canker of humanity to excise. Let the earth with their blood run red! Let of their dwellings only hot coals and ash remain! Destroyed they must be, for once and for all!"

His impassioned words stirred ripplings of agreement. Even Tilanne, sworn to the Way of Protection as she was, couldn't quell a bright flame of yearning in her heart. Yearning to swing astride her mighty armored and battle-ready Morai and plunge into the enemy lines with blade swinging. She longed to see the humans fall before her like ripened grain, to hear their dying screams, savor their agonies.

"The earth red with *our* blood would run," Kai Peredur said. "Against the Mountain King's army, too few are we his lands to attack. If ventured there we did, swiftly slain would we be, and no good accomplish."

"No good?" cried a pale, anguished man. "What of revenge? It would *revenge* accomplish! Raided and razed years ago was our Valley of the Moonglow, and where is revenge for those who there perished? When my Willene they . . . they . . ." Here, he choked and could not finish, but added, "Where is revenge for *this* which they did to me?"

He thrust out his right arm. It ended at the elbow in a bole of white scar tissue, and for all its ugliness, was perhaps the cleanest of the injuries he'd suffered during the attack and his subsequent captivity. He had only one eye, a gouged and horrible knot of flesh where the other had been. Both of his ears had been chopped off. The rest of the marks of his suffering were mercifully hidden beneath his clothes.

"Our men were for the amusement of the soldiers taken prisoner, maimed and mutilated," Lothairal said, hammering his fist on the table. "Foodstuffs and treasure they stole. Homes they did burn and animals butcher. But that not the worst of it is! Are we to these outrages ignore?"

"Let Erwille speak on," Peredur said.

There had been six of them, Erwille reported, his voice shaking and cracking. Six elfmaids, the fairest and prettiest in the settlement. They had been delivered untouched to the Mountain Kingdom as gifts for Durvan. When he had finished with them, he turned those that had pleased him the least over to his men. Those four had subsequently, and horribly, died.

The two others had not been so fortunate. Willene and Darissa, Durvan had presumed to call his wives . . . though Darissa had soon managed to still her heart with a stolen dagger.

"Willene, I am told," Erwille said, "was under constant guard kept that she might not Darissa's example follow. By their foul alchemy, drugged she was, and as a shell of a broken creature lived."

The few men who had lived through the attack and tortures had been kept in the Mountain King's dungeons. Several of them died of starvation. Some went mad. Some, like Darissa, took their own lives. Some were killed by their captors, either in sport or out of malice.

In the end, only Erwille and his brother had still been alive and more or less in their right minds when Durvan sent for them some two years later. They had not known what to expect when they were brought, fishbelly pale and nearly blinded by even the weakest candle flame, from their fetid cells up to the Mountain King's feasting-hall.

"Arawille, my brother, so terrified was that into a fear-stupor he fell," Erwille said. "With fire and knives they tried from it to revive him, but to no avail."

Erwille himself, though barely able to walk, had been revitalized by the sight of his daughter.

He'd assumed that she, like all the others, was dead. But there she was, his sweet and dear Willene. She sat near Durvan, looking as hollow and lifeless as a figure made of straw.

Roaring his great laugh, the Mountain King had come forward. Not, as it turned out, to order Erwille's death or subject him to more maimings. Durvan had heartily clapped him on the back, an act which in itself had nearly been enough to break bones, as weak and malnourished as Erwille was.

The pain, though, meant nothing to him when he deciphered the coarse language of the human speech and understood what Durvan was saying.

Congratulating him. On the birth of his grandson.

Once that terrible meaning became clear to him, Erwille turned his horrified gaze once more upon Willene. She, staring apathetically down at her folded hands, did not even seem aware that her father was present. But there beside her, a plump and grinning human woman was nursing an infant.

This nursemaid, this fat-hipped and unwashed slut, rose at Durvan's command and brought the child closer. She lifted the naked babe from its swaddling clothes. Erwille saw his daughter's honey colored hair, saw Willene's grey-green eyes. But the face was malformed, the ears stunted. Elfkin ears. The boy's brow and chin were heavy, his limbs thick. Like those of his father. Like those of Durvan.

"Durvanian, they called him," he said. "As if mocked us enough they'd not already done, a name in our elven style upon that atrocity he bestowed."

Erwille remembered the bellowing laughter of the Mountain King, the celebratory cheers of the gathered humans. He remembered an order being given to take him back to his cell, there to sit in darkness and think about what he'd seen. He remembered being led from the hall, glancing back to see Willene, ignored by all around her, gnawing at the skin of her wrist where it was parchment-thin above the pathways of veins. He remembered seeing his daughter's blood begin to flow.

"And then, all a blankness was, all a blur." He shook his head. "Even now, remember it can I not . . . yet glad I am. Would that all of it, couldst I forget."

The next thing he'd known was freedom, frantic and hard-won freedom. He knew that he must have slipped away from his guards somehow, escaped the castle, though he had no idea how he'd accomplished such a thing. The journey that followed was so terrible an ordeal that he wondered sometimes if he had been condemned to the Torments, but such thoughts never lasted long because he knew that Kaledhol, no matter how fierce His wrath, would never do such vile things as this.

"Near Kibos, we found him," Master Dael said. "To bring blackmetal ore from the caves below we had gone. Somehow, survived he did and able were we to the Citadel to bring him."

"Obvious is it," Lothairal said. "The battle to them we must take."

"Thousands of men the Mountain King has," Kai Maltanar said. "Ever outnumbered have we been, since first his ancestor that kingdom from the mountains carved. Humans, orcs, and dwarven slaves as well, they have. Like one vast and mighty fortress is that entire kingdom, the peaks like battlements rising. Into it can no army hope to penetrate."

Lothairal brushed that away as if it were no more than a bothersome fly. "For these most heinous of deeds can we not stand. Too many *Morvalan* have by these monsters been slain. Aware and prepared our soldiers are, that in this way they might their ends meet. But women? Children?"

"And now an heir he has," Ordan Quaide said. "Hoped we had that without issue, die would this Durvan. Aged by their standards he is, fifty years or more, and had he no son left, fallen to disputes and fighting might his followers have done. Now an el . . . now an heir he has." He swallowed thickly as if to hold his gorge down, and then rinsed his mouth with wine to counter the bad taste that must have filled it.

"Now an elfkin heir he has," Savillan said, his customary grin lost in a frown. "Believe do the *Alvalan* that never to adulthood can they live . . . perhaps in infancy or childhood this Durvanian shall die, and –"

"Not so," Tilanne said. "An elfkin, full-grown and faculties all possessing, among those who destroyed Cliffcave was. With my own eyes I saw it not, but others whose word is undoubted did."

"More like us than we wish to believe are they," Idrasanna Denisse said. "Some the talent for magic have, and centuries might their life spans stretch."

"Centuries," Lothairal echoed, looking around at them all in turn. "And magic . . . already the humans some wizards have, and this strange alchemy. Suppose that a sorcerer this elfkin is? Into such hands the Mountain Kingdom must *not* be delivered, else a time of war like no other shall we suffer. For certain is it that heavy upon us will his hatred fall, even moreso than might a human's."

"Why might he not peace with us seek?" Leiata Kelda asked. "His own mother's people we are, are we not?"

Erwille made a sound of agony.

Lothairal cut Leiata to the bone with a scathing glare. "Despise us he shall, of a certain, for that which he lacks is that which we *are*. Doomed he is to this half-life, and jealous of us shall doubtless be."

"And what welcome here would he find?" Ordan Quaide said. "No love for elfkin have we, contaminated as they are."

Idrasanna inhaled as if about to speak, but Peredur caught her eye and surreptitiously shook his head. Some silent argument sped between them that no one but Tilanne seemed to notice. In the end, the Kai won, and his mother subsided into a perturbed scowl most unlike her usual serenity.

"Killed he must be," Lothairal said. "The only way it is, the only answer. Killed while young and helpless he is."

"Couldst thou a babe-in-arms slaughter?" Leiata shot back.

"Did they such mercy to Moonglow's children show?"

"But human are they, brutes, savages. If to their level of murder we stoop, no better than them shall we be."

"Better than them in all ways, we already are," Lothairal said. "Murder it is not, no more than when a rat or some other vermin one kills. Extermination, it is. A cleansing."

"Whether right or wrong, impossible it remains," Kai Peredur interrupted. "The babe to reach, first the very castle of the Mountain King itself must fall. If every soldier in the *Morvalan* lands we gathered, if every able-bodied man and youth swords took up, still could we never succeed."

"Something must there be for us to do," Tilanne said. "Some way this threat to nullify or end."

"Too few are we." Maltanar blew out a breath and shook his head. "If triumphant had Kai Terindor been, at our disposal now would the armies of the Northlands be, fitting arrow-fodder in advance of our lines to send. If on better terms with the Emerin we were, perhaps to our aid might they come. But no good is it to dream of ifs, for intangible as morning mist are they."

"The Emerin?" Lothairal made a face. "Even if help us they would, useless in battle would the *Alvalan* be. What of war know they?"

"Gather do I," Peredur said dryly, "that more of it even now they're learning. Though wonder do I why against the dwarves they'd be fighting, when humanity a greater danger is? Together should the Elder Races stand, not at war with each other be."

"Matters does none of that," Lothairal said. "Spring upon us is, a mild winter over and little snow in the passes did fall. Vulnerable are we. Already near the ruins of Moonglow have the Mountain King's scouts been sighted. Another raid, we shall not tolerate!"

"With that I agree," Peredur said. "Action taken must be, and shall be. To Moonglow our forces I'll lead."

At this pronouncement, a globe of ice seemed to form in Tilanne's stomach. She did not let her dread stop her from drawing her sword and setting it on the table before him. "With thee am I, Kai Peredur."

"And I!" Lothairal said with vicious anticipation, his own steel ringing on the wood as he slammed it down.

"No." Peredur pushed their weapons back to them. "Not complete yet is thy training. Too few are we *Morvalan*, fewer still are we *Rhunvala*. Here thou'll stay, under Kai Maltanar's guidance."

"Not children are we!" Lothairal said.

"Need of us thou might have," Tilanne said. She found it odd to be on the same side of an argument as Lothairal for once, but did not pause to marvel at this wonder.

"On both counts am I agreed," the Kai said. "Children thou art not, and need of thee I may well have. But made up is my mind. If fail we do, if die I do, to thee shall it be left as *Rhunvala* to carry on."

That globe of ice within her grew until it seemed to Tilanne that she was about to freeze solid from the cold of it. But she saw the determination in his twilight-blue eyes, and knew he meant what he said. With nothing to be gained but his irritation by further argument, she picked up her sword and returned it to the scabbard.

Almost every soldier, hunter and able-bodied volunteer was outfitted for the journey. Tilanne had never truly realized just how small the population of the *Odan Rhunvale* was until she beheld them gathered into their makeshift army. They numbered only five-score altogether, yet the place would seem very echoing and empty without them.

Lothairal was livid and infuriated, offering no help to any and spending his time surly and brooding in his room. Tilanne, although she in some part shared his feelings, put it behind her and instead did her best to make herself useful.

Every man in the valley was given some perfunctory training at arms in addition to his other chosen profession. They were all fitted with scale shirts, and armed with swords and bows.

Those few staying behind watched and waved from the battlements as the small army, led by Kai Peredur and Kinnon Faer, set out across the grass.

Tilanne wished she'd had the chance . . . or the daring . . . to say more of a farewell to Peredur. A more . . . private farewell. Her spirit soared to see him, *Rhunvala*, a magnificent figure in his glossy black armor with a red plume sweeping from the top of his helm. He rode to do battle, rode to serve Kaledhol in the greatest glory of the Cause. He rode to defend their homeland from the Lesser Races that sought to pollute and defile it. All that was the very heart and soul of the *Morvalan* people was represented in that single tall figure.

And yet, she had also come to care very much for the man behind the rank. There had been no recurrence of that one moment when they'd let their fingertips touch in the shifting light of the sacred crystal. She had been careful ever since to make sure that her manner remained as was proper for a student, and his had never strayed beyond that of a dutiful teacher. The attraction, though, was there. Somehow, it was all the more compelling for never having been voiced, never having been acted upon.

She supposed that she loved him. And why not? He was everything she'd grown up believing to be the ideal of a man . . . a warrior strong and proud. Yet at the same time, his warm nature, thoughtful and considerate, appealed to her.

Yes, she loved him.

At last, they were gone from sight, gone into the surrounding forest. When there was nothing left of them to see, one by one the watchers left the wall and returned to their duties in the empty stillness of the Citadel.

Tilanne was last, and lingered, a foreboding chill creeping along the back of her neck. A premonition of danger brushed her, light as a moth's wing. She was suddenly sure that none of them would ever return, that they were heading off not to glory but to doom.

She told herself that she was worrying too much. There was no one in the world better suited to look after and lead that force than Kai Peredur. She'd pray for them, of course, but her prayers would be redundant. Kaledhol would be with His people.

When she went inside, she could already feel the oppressive silence of their absence. The smithies were cold and unused, the muted clang of forged metal no longer to be heard. No more singing drifting in through the windows as the farmers and orchard-tenders worked in the fields.

Those few who'd stayed behind whiled away the days in their various tasks, but Tilanne felt the same expectant anxiety from everyone. They were waiting, only going through the motions of their usual activities out of habit. It was as if there was some unspoken conviction that, so long as they kept up the routines as they should be, everything would turn out all right, and life at the Citadel would be back to normal that much the sooner.

Lothairal kept more to himself than ever. When not sulking in solitude, he tended to erupt into a frenzy of action. He practiced his swordplay ruthlessly, shredding several of the straw-stuffed leather manikins they used in training at combat. He pushed himself to the limits of endurance with too much exercise despite Kai Maltanar's words of caution and restraint.

Each night, before going to bed, Tilanne visited the chamber of the crystal and sent her well wishes to the ones who'd gone. She kept hoping to be given some sign that they were all right, but such a sign never came.

Until the evening she entered the chamber and was instantly beset by a powerful sensation, an urgent clamor seeming to come at her from all sides. The colors in the crystal were spinning, whirling, hectic. An alarm seemed to clang within her mind, drowning all other thoughts with its single demanding call.

She dashed from the chamber, blood racing through her veins, and nearly collided with Kai Maltanar. He, groggy and just-wakened, scrubbed a hand over his eyes and looked at her.

"Something . . . something amiss is . . ." she said, but did not know what.

"Felt it too, did I. Woke me it did."

Everyone in the Citadel had experienced it to some degree, though perhaps not so strongly as had Tilanne herself. By the time she reached the main hall, most of them were already gathered there, sleepy and cross in their bedclothes. They stopped asking each other what was going on, and turned to ask Tilanne.

"Warning us is Kaledhol," she said, not sure what she was going to say until she heard the words leave her lips. "Of danger, great danger, warning us."

"The others?" Idrasanna Denisse asked. She was pale, one many-ringed hand fluttering nervously at the base of her throat. "My son?"

Tilanne shook her head, only indicating that she did not know. She wanted to believe that if Kai Peredur *was* in harm's way, or had met some terrible fate, she'd have felt it. But who was she to presume so much? Not his lover, not his wife . . . only his student. And if even Peredur's own mother did not have a sense of his fate, how could *she* expect any different?

Kor Lothairal came plunging into the room wearing only smallclothes, his body soaked with sweat. "Attacked are we! Attacked is the Citadel!"

"Impossible," Neterian Kelda said. "Nowhere in the south safer than here is."

Tilanne did her best to shut out the babble of exclamations and arguments. She closed her eyes to the sights around her. Wrapping her fingers around the ruby basilisk at her neck, she opened her heart and her mind and begged Kaledhol for enlightenment.

At once, startling and exhilarating, an inner eye opened in her mind and she *saw*. Saw the *Odan Rhunvale*, the valley laid out around her at a strange angle as if . . . as if she could see it all at once, a full circle of view. Everything was oddly colored, shadowed in murky grey darkness, but at the same time she could make out every detail clearly.

She realized with a quiver of awe that she was seeing through the crystal itself, the great dark crystal rising from the top of the Citadel.

There, yes! The tree-canopy was silver-green in Livana's nearly full radiance, and silhouetted against it was a shape, a black shape, skimming above the leaves and churning them in its wake.

Even as Tilanne identified it, the shape broke through.

"Dragon!" she cried, her voice a clear peal that cut through everyone else and left them staring in stunned shock at her.

* * *

CHAPTER TWENTY

Tilanne whipped her head to face Lothairal, so fast that her braided hair swung from one shoulder to the other. "Thyself arm and armor."

He did not contradict her. Instead, a wild eager light burned in his eyes and his lips pulled back in a teeth-baring savage grin.

"Mad art thou?" A farmer named Shalanos grabbed at her arm, not heeding the startled gasps around him as he addressed a Kor in such a way. "Thy intention to *fight* it is?"

"In no danger are we," Neterian said. "Told thee did I, the Citadel impenetrable is."

As the debate raged among the others, Tilanne shook free of the farmer. She and Lothairal rushed to a high arrow slit-window.

The dragon was of some dark hue, not black but a deep grey or blue that couldn't clearly be defined. As dragons went, Tilanne knew, it was of no more than medium size. Still, even a dragon of *small* size was huge compared to a man, and it was not without some trepidation that she glanced at her fellow Kor.

And wonder of wonders, there in Lothairal's eyes Tilanne saw something she never would have expected to see. That wild light of eager bloodlust faded, and a very real and sensible dubiousness took its place.

"If here they are come, then dead must . . ." he said.

"Finish not that thought."

The dragon glided in a wide descending spiral. They could see a figure perched atop it like a rider on a horse. Dangling from the dragon's rear talons was a long knotted rope. More figures clung to that rope, clung to it for dear life. They were for the most part broad and bulky, and weapons hung about them like strange metal fruit.

Everyone else had come up behind them, and now Neterian touched them both on the shoulders. "No need for this is there, young Kors. Few we are, but secure is the Citadel and well supplied. No way is there that a danger to us they can pose."

"No way?" Tilanne pointed. "Upon the battlements the dragon can those humans and orcs deposit. Vulnerable we'll be, unless into the very bowels of the castle we retreat."

"Then so let us do," he said, shrugging. "Warriors we are not. Soon enough shall Kai Peredur and the others return, and with these intruders –"

"No!" Tilanne said, anguish wracking her voice. "If return they do, likely from battle wounded and weary they'll be coming. Wouldst thou have them unsuspecting into a dragon walk? For them it is, not us, that done must something be."

Neterian gaped at her. He wasn't alone in doing so. Tilanne pushed her way through that sea of open-mouthed faces, pulling Lothairal with her.

"Correct she is," Kai Maltanar said. He was wheezing, having been forced to hurry his old bones faster than he'd done in some decades. "On all counts, correct she is. Now each and all of you must some arms and armor take up. Prepared be the Citadel to defend!"

His was the voice of absolute authority, given weight by the respected factor of his age as well as his rank. With no more objections, they ran to obey. He called Leiater back, the youth stumbling over his own feet in eagerness.

"Yes, Kai Maltanar?"

The old Kai gave Leiater a heavy truesteel key, as Tilanne and Lothairal looked on in bewilderment. "Thy assistance in the lowest caves I'll need."

"The . . . the great doors?" Leiater took the key with a hand so shaky that he seemed likely to quiver the metal into pieces. He clamped his fist around it as if it were a lifeline, yet at the same time a lifeline that he was almost too afraid to clutch.

"Great doors?" Tilanne echoed, mystified. "Of what doors dost thou speak?"

"Go, Kor Tilanne," Maltanar said. "On the both of thee, must our salvation depend."

She still had not been outfitted with a full suit of black *Rhunvala* mail, such being the privilege and province that would await her when she underwent the final ritual necessary to complete her training. Her serviceable old armor had proven itself time and again, and she buckled into it now with the ease and comfort of familiarity.

There was no time to coil and pin up her hair as she usually did, so she simply thrust her helmet over it. With shield on one arm and sword drawn, she hastened from her room in time to see Lothairal, similarly attired and bearing Winterfrost, the blade that had been his father's, rush into the hall.

Tilanne followed, adrenaline coursing on the flood tide of blood in her veins. This was the first time since arriving here that she would face real combat, as opposed to training bouts or hunts, and she was both apprehensive and filled with wild excitement. Above all else, the desire to prove herself and protect this holy place blazed within her.

Despite Lothairal's head start, Tilanne caught up with him just as he slammed open one of the outer doors and let himself onto the battlements.

The dangling rope they'd seen couldn't have held more than a dozen men, but it looked to Tilanne like there were at least twice that number, engaged in and already pressing back the Citadel's meager numbers of unskilled defenders. Orcs or humans, they were equally brutish and violent in their relentless assault on the elves.

Where had they come from? It didn't matter. They were here, they were the Mountain King's folk, the enemy. For their intrusion, they would die.

Lothairal's thoughts must have mirrored her own. He charged at them, Winterfrost crackling with blue-white light and the blade encased in a sheen of ice. The nearest foes turned, one of them too slowly to prevent Lothairal from cleaving his arm from his shoulder.

The man staggered against the wall, screaming, and gaping in horror at the neatly hewn stump from which no blood flowed. A ruby-red blister of ice bulged there instead, the blood having frozen solid, the flesh around it gone the dead grey color of frostbite.

Tilanne spared not a moment to admire Lothairal's handiwork. She leapt at the closest foe, an orc of brownish hide and piggish snout that bristled with short whisker-like hairs. She thrust with the sword given her by Commander Ellorn, and was gratified to feel it pierce armor and flesh, sink deep, and grate on bone.

Their arrival, young as they were, swayed matters in the favor of the elves. The arrival of Idrasanna Denisse swayed it even more. Hair blowing back from her tattoos, the jewels of her many earrings catching the torchlight in splinters and twinkles, she flung her arms skyward, fingers splayed and bent in the knuckle-aching gestures of magic. Magebolts, brilliant blue darts of energy, leapt from her hands to smite the humans and orcs.

One prosaic craftsman, not bothering with anything fancy, shouldered two men over the wall. Dwindling wails rent the air as they plunged toward the earth. But more . . . there were more crowding in already. So many of them! Far more than Tilanne's mind insisted there should be. Where had they come from? Was an entire flight of dragons bringing an entire army?

She sustained a cut to the arm, shallow but painful, and whirled to face a human with glinting black eyes and a short beard. He swung at her again.

"*Jhe-nah!*" Tilanne shouted, and the incoming blade veered before it could touch her, knocked aside by a burst of wine-red light.

The man, shocked, faltered for the barest of instants before recovering. That instant was all Tilanne needed. She drove her sword through the face-gap in his helm, and he staggered back with a dying gurgle.

Lothairal stood nearby with one dead foe sprawled at his feet and another crumpled behind him. He was cutting a path through orcs to a knot of elves that had been backed into a corner. A human lunged at him, and he chopped the man down without pausing. The body landed at Tilanne's feet.

He had glinting black eyes and a short beard.

The man she'd just killed? It couldn't be. She had stabbed that man through the face. This man had been cut diagonally from shoulder to waist.

She dug her booted toe beneath another body and kicked it over onto its back. The head lolled, diffuse moonlight and magelight shining down on glinting black eyes and a short beard.

They were identical, all three. Down to the clothing they wore and the weapons they wielded.

She'd heard that sometimes humans gave birth in litters, like the beasts that they were – but that could not be the answer. Even brothers would not have been so identically dressed . . . and these ones, unlike the orcs, did not stink of sweat and onions and sour beer. They did not seem to give off any scent, any scent at all.

Illusion? But . . . no . . . they struck, they cut, they hurt. Her arm trickled blood thanks to one of them. That was no illusion.

Instinct spun her again, in time to see a man with glinting black eyes and a short beard *appear* before her, out of nothingness. Air pushed against her, confirming the solidity of him. No illusion, but something with substance, with reality.

Now she knew why there seemed to be so many of them. She was wasting her strength on false flesh rather than true foes. But she couldn't ignore these things, for even if they were not real, they were deadly enough to present a very real threat.

"Idrasanna! Constructs are they! Conjurations! Dispel them thou must!"

She shouted at the top of her lungs, but with the din of battle did not know whether the sorceress would be able to hear her or not. Then she felt a pulse surge through the *aether*. Human forms writhed in sudden contortions. The fell, losing shape, melting like men made of wax in a forge's searing heat.

In moments, only a few orcs and other humans, rough-looking men who did *not* have glinting black eyes and short beards, were left.

A voice bellowed in rage from above. Tilanne turned toward it, and caught her breath at the sight of the dragon very close. It was beating its great wings to hold itself steady on a level with the battlements.

The human rider was dark-haired and dusky-skinned, with heavy, arrogant features. His furious gaze fixed on Idrasanna Denisse. One hand guided the dragon by a complicated arrangement of reins and harness. The other held an oaken staff wrapped in gold wire, and tipped with a faceted yellow jewel. It was similar in design to the one Tilanne had taken from the human wizard in Firsthome, years ago. She'd given it to the mages, thinking that they might find it interesting or be able to learn more of human magic, and then she had forgotten all about it.

The dragon's eyes turned with almost lazy speculation onto Tilanne. She could see the striated dark gold orbs, each as big as half a melon, split by black pupils. The fire pouch, a loose wattle of skin along the underside of its jaw and front of its neck, bellowsed in the rhythm of the wyrm's breathing. Smoke curled from its fanged jaws with each exhalation.

Lightning jumped in a jittering bolt from the end of the wizard's staff, snapping the air with the sound of many tiny whips. Tilanne's hair tried to stand on end beneath the confinement of her helm. She smelled the hot ozone of its passage as the lightning streaked toward Idrasanna.

But the Circle Mage was shielded by her magic, so that the bolt shot harmlessly past her to leave a blackened blotch on the wall behind. She fanned a return volley of magebolts at the enemy wizard, striking him and the dragon multiple times.

At this, the dragon roared. Its head was only a few paces from Tilanne. The volume of the sound was almost a physical force, knocking her back a step.

The pouch below its jaw swelled, inflating. A dull orange glow beamed through the gill-like slits. The mounted wizard fought to control his steed, no doubt knowing as Tilanne did that a burst of fire-breath here would incinerate as many invaders as defenders. But the enraged dragon would not be denied.

"Down!" Tilanne flung herself flat in the shelter of the parapets, hoping the others would hear her, hoping they'd heed and be quick enough. Derethin, an orchard-tender, was lying wounded beside her. She covered his exposed face with her shield as she ducked her own face into a corner.

A torrent of seething flames billowed and churned over her, the heat trying to suck the very breath from her lungs. She heard screams, but it was impossible to tell if they were elven or not . . . it was impossible to tell if they were her own or not. In another few moments it wouldn't matter anyway, because they would all be prematurely sent to their pyres.

But then, with stunning abruptness and a solid thump of heavy impact, the flaming jet was snuffed. Tilanne sprang up with smoke wisps rising from her, expecting to see some proof of Idrasanna's work.

Instead, she saw another dragon. This newcomer, locked in mortal struggle with the first, was immense. Its color was a dusty plum-purple, the scales around its muzzle and ears white with age. It was covered in old scars and one wing edge was tattered like a wind-torn flag.

Astride the second dragon was a black-armored man whose red cloak flared behind him in the wind. Although his face was concealed by a helm, Tilanne immediately knew him by the set of his frail, but still proud, body.

"Maltanar!" she cried.

Initially caught off-guard, the younger and smaller dragon reacted with vicious fury. Claws flashed and jaws snapped as the two raked at each other. Their screeches drowned out all other sounds.

"Aid the Kai we must!" It was Lothairal, spattered head to toe with blood as he fought his way through the renewed battle on the wall to reach Tilanne.

"Whence came that dragon?"

"No time! To Maltanar!" Lothairal sheathed his sword and then, astounding Tilanne, vaulted over the edge. He uttered an incantation as he did so, slowing his fall – and astounding her further because she hadn't known he knew any magic beyond the most basic spells.

She had no idea what he meant to do, afoot and alone while the draconian combat was in the air above him, but that did not stop Lothairal from charging across the field. Then she understood. With their wings beating at each other as much as at the air, their flight had become a veering, erratic descent toward the distant valley floor. Lothairal was heading for the spot where he reasoned they must come to earth.

Lightning arced from the wizard's staff again. It struck black armor and burst in a dazzle of energy. Kai Maltanar was pitched from his perch on the dragon's neck by the powerful bolt. He plummeted.

A shriek of denial ripped from Tilanne's throat. Without thinking of the consequences, she jumped after Lothairal, only remembering when she was in midair that *she* had no way of slowing or stopping her fall.

She landed painfully but not as badly as she could have, or perhaps she was beyond noticing such mundane things as injuries. For all she knew, she might have shattered every bone in both legs. But all she felt was a twinge in her ankles and knees, and when she tumble-rolled to a stop, she smashed her elbow and shoulder on the corseleted chest of a broken-necked orc. She was on her feet again regardless. Silently beseeching Kaledhol's aid, she felt the pains dull to a bearable ache, felt her exhaustion slip from her. This was not true healing, only a temporary dulling, and she knew she would suffer for it later. If there was a later.

The younger dragon back-winged and clawed with all four feet. Its tail ended in a spade-shaped point, carapace-hard and blade-edged, that it tried to use to flay open the older one's underbelly.

Maltanar's dragon was canny to such a trick, clamping its jaws onto the tail just below that spade-shape. With a heave of its larger body, the plum-colored beast spun the smaller one in a circle like a stone in a sling. The human wizard and his saddle parted company, and another body was flung into the air.

The man somehow kept his wits about him and was able to cast a spell even as he was spinning crazily, for his fall slowed just as Lothairal's had done. He righted himself and landed on his feet, shaking a fist and shouting at the dragons.

Had he looked around, the human might have seen death bearing down on him at a full run. He did not, and Lothairal didn't slacken his pace as he swung. With the momentum of his charge behind it, Winterfrost cleaved the man in half at the waist.

The younger dragon twisted and doubled back on itself, as if it had the flexible bones of a stoat. It closed its jaws on the older one's wingstrut, crunching the bone. Crippled, the older dragon fought to stay aloft, but no amount of desperate fluttering with one wing would do. The great beast crashed to earth, and the smaller one soared high, pealing its victory to the skies.

"Lothairal!" Tilanne saw what her fellow Kor didn't . . . that, behind him, somehow, the human wizard was still alive. Still alive, and still gripping that deadly staff.

As Lothairal turned to see what Tilanne was pointing at, he was hurled backward by an incandescent yellow-white blast of lightning that lit the entire valley and ignited the sky with sizzling sparks.

The human hitched himself forward on one arm, not seeming to care that he was trailing his intestines in his wake. Lothairal lay dazed, perhaps already dead. He did not move. Then she saw his chest hitch. Still breathing. He was breathing, but already the wizard was leveling the staff at him and preparing for another blast.

Tilanne knew even as she raced the last few steps that she wouldn't be able to reach them in time. She would be too late *again*, always too late, always only in time to watch helplessly as someone she was supposed to protect died in agony.

A shape wreathed in wine-red light rose up as the human reached Lothairal. A battered and bleeding shape, black armor smoldering, red cloak charred to tatters. Kai Maltanar raised his sword, the hilt in both hands and the blade pointed down. He drove it with the last of his strength into the crawling wizard's back. It sheared through and pinned him, twitching, to the earth.

Arriving a bare heartbeat later, Tilanne caught Maltanar as he collapsed. Holding him was like holding a loose sack of bones encased in hot metal. Every part of him seemed to be broken. The wine-red glow around him glimmered and was gone. She understood that only by calling upon their god had Kai Maltanar attained that last surge of effort needed to slay the human, and save Lothairal's life.

She lowered him and removed the helm. A faint smile tugged at his lips as he looked up at her, then faded as he looked past her to the aged dragon. "To him . . . Tilanne," Maltanar said. "To him take me. Let us . . . together die . . . we old soldiers."

Tilanne did not question, but gathered him again into her arms. Her strength seemed more than adequate to the task without even having to call upon Kaledhol, and she carried him easily to the dragon's head. Its sides were heaving like a smith's bellows.

Kai Maltanar stretched out one shaking arm, and rested his hand upon the dragon's snout. He patted it the way a man might greet a faithful hound. Its eyes opened, milky-silver and shimmering like moonlight.

Tears ran unchecked down Tilanne's face. This was, somehow, right. Right that they should go together like this, a fitting end to their long lives. They had fallen in battle long after their days of combat were believed to be done, and earned all the greater glory from it.

She had not known the full and proper words before, could not say them for Kai Terindor there at Cliffcave. She knew them now. Kai Maltanar's gaze fixed upon her as she spoke. He managed a slight nod as she finished, the nod of a teacher well-pleased with a student for having mastered a difficult lesson. Then, his eyes closed and he settled into stillness. The dragon did likewise, a spectral wisp of smoke forming the visible cloud of its last breath.

Tilanne knelt beside them, but only for a moment. Lothairal needed her. Much as she had loved the old Kai, the needs of the living always had to be placed before honoring the dead.

She started to turn, started to rise, and that was when the ground shook. A warm wind that smelled of ashes blew back her cloak as the younger dragon fanned its wings.

It placed one clawed foot on Lothairal's motionless form.

* * *

Chapter Twenty-One

The dragon snorted as it looked over at her. It seemed to know as well as she did that one warrior with a single sword stood little chance against such a creature. The older one might have hurt it, but not so badly that it would be unable to take care of Tilanne with one quick blast of flame, or one quick bite from those jagged jaws.

Haltingly and without much hope, she tried to address it in the harsh, hissing, tooth-gnashing, glottal speech of dragonkind. Its head reared back on a long, sinuous curve of neck, and the dragon growled in response. One claw flexed, squealing across Lothairal's corselet.

"Have him, you'll not," she said, advancing a pace. "Not until dead I am as well."

Golden eyes regarded her. It lifted its paw off Lothairal, but not in retreat. It stepped over his prone form, stalking toward Tilanne with tail switching like that of a cat toying with a mouse.

The blessing she'd invoked to render herself briefly immune from pain was fading, and now she felt as if dwarves were slowly boring into her ankle and knee with augurs of iron. She had set down her shield at some point – when she'd caught Maltanar? She no longer knew – and she had only her sword to defend against a dragon.

It swatted. She dodged. The spade-tipped tail twitched. The golden eyes gleamed. Each of its teeth was long as a hunting knife, and sharper.

She could not glance back toward the Citadel to see if help was coming. No one could help her, and she did not want them to try. No more lives should be lost this day. Least of all, on her account.

The dragon swatted again. Tilanne met claws this time with steel, parrying. The blow numbed her to the shoulder. She jabbed, piercing a tender spot in the crook of its draconian elbow. The dragon yowled. As it jerked away, the sword, still embedded in its hide, was yanked from her hand.

Its long sinuous neck curled and it snapped at her with gaping jaws. When the teeth struck her armor, there was a rusty screech and a flurry of sparks. One pierced through to rip a gash along her side. The bite knocked her over, bringing her to earth with a bone-jarring crash. A sensation more like whole-body nausea than mere pain roiled sickly through her.

She thought she heard someone speaking her name, but her ears rang from the buffeting she had taken. Lurching up again, she was in time to see the dragon daintily bite the sword out from where it had stuck, like someone removing a thorn. It spit the sword the way she might have spit out a seed. Then that large head swiveled to regard her again, and with much less amusement this time.

Tilanne evaluated the distance to the weapon the dragon had spit out. Before she could even take a single step in that direction, the wyrm spun with a dancer's lithe agility, turning away from her. She had an instant to wonder if it was fleeing before she heard a low whistle, and realized what was about to happen.

The dragon's tail, limber as a whip, came at her with deadly velocity. The spade-shaped, sharp end of it, moving almost too fast to be seen, would do to her what Lothairal's sword had done to the human.

Rather than try to step back, she jumped forward, past the arc of the tip and into the path of the scaled limb itself. It was like getting struck by a tree. Catapulted head over heels, Tilanne landed flat on her back, staring up at the dark leaf canopy so high above. All of the breath had been driven from her, and her bones might have all been disconnected, so loose and disjointed did she feel.

The dragon pranced backward at her, neck bent fluidly back and around so it could see where she was, and commenced beating her into the ground with heavy slamming swipes of its tail. The sharp tip never found her, but each successive slam crushed Tilanne further. Her armor buckled. So did her ribcage. A glancing blow against her helm made her think that her skull had been cracked like a nutshell.

She lost count of the strikes, almost lost consciousness, but gradually became aware that she wasn't being smote anymore. She had been pounded so hard that her body had been driven into the soft ground, making an imprint of her shape.

Laboriously raising her head, an effort that made sunbursts of orange and white explode all through her, she blinked to clear her vision. She expected to see the dragon's teeth descending to pluck her from the grass and chew her up. Or to see it hunched over one of the others, enjoying a feast before it came back to finish the meal with her.

She saw Lothairal, smoldering and limping but up, ducking and weaving away from scything claws. Somehow, he had gotten up again. She had given him enough time to recover . . . though to what end, she did not know. To die on his feet?

Winterfrost's blade dripped with the hot red-black gore of dragon blood. The creature did not bother toying with him as it had with Tilanne. It was out of patience for these games, for these troublesome elves that would not stay down and stay dead like they were supposed to.

Every part of her a throbbing misery, Tilanne somehow clambered out of her shallow, open grave. Stripping off her gloves – each movement sparking renewed pain – she tottered forward, not sure what she was going to do. Then she knew, as if Kaledhol Himself had spoken it in her ear. She flexed her bare hands and tried to draw a deep breath. Needle-stabs of splintered ribs fore-stalled that at once.

The dragon was oblivious to her, all of its attention focused on Lothairal. She made her way toward it, along its side, under the folded jut of its wing. When its big head darted forth to bite, Tilanne was ready.

"*Ha-nah! Hanahia!*" Calling out to Kaledhol, invoking His strength and His courage, she threw her arms around the dragon's neck.

A blazing aura the color of roses, wine, and blood flared around her. She wrapped her arms tight, locked in a constricting, choking loop.

Nothing else seemed to matter. She no longer felt the tortures of her various injuries. All that existed was the red glow, the scaled flesh, the steady pressure as she squeezed, squeezed. As she felt the dragon's sudden panicked thrashing, the thunder of its lifebeat, and a crumpling-crushing-*give*. Tighter and tighter. But her strength was ebbing and still the beast lived, still the beast fought to shake her loose.

A hand touched her, closed hard on her shoulder. She heard Lothairal's voice raised in fervent prayer. She understood his words, knew what he was attempting. Something that she, in the Way of Protection, could never do. Something Kai Terindor had done to the soldiers of Cliffcave. To her father. He was draining the life force of the dragon, drawing the vital energy from it . . . and lending, channeling, that power to Tilanne.

He stole the dragon's own strength, sent it to her, and in a strange diminishing circle as the dragon's own power was used against it, used to kill it. Tilanne felt not a give this time but a deep, wet cracking like that of a sodden branch underfoot. Still, she did not relent, did not give up. Kept squeezing. Kept up the terrible mortal pressure as death-throes shuddered through the massive form. The scaled skin split, drenching her with hot blood. She strained harder, and suddenly wrenched her body to the side, twisting until she both heard and felt a grinding snap.

The dragon stiffened. Its spasming tail beat the earth. It went limp in her arms, slack and dead.

The god-given strength fled from Tilanne. In a rush, the pain returned. She sank to her knees, then to all fours, then flat onto her stomach. She held her head up just long enough to see Lothairal, looking grim but jubilant, retrieve his sword and plunge it into the dragon's chest to make sure of its death.

Tilanne raised half her mouth in what was supposed to pass for a smile. She lowered her weary, aching head onto her crossed forearms. But the gesture didn't end there. She dropped much further than that, tumbling into some internal well of darkness.

She spent a long time in that darkness. Sometimes there were hazes of light, sometimes the distant rushing murmur of voices like the echo of the breeze. Sometimes there was sensation, a whole-body throbbing as if she'd somehow been transformed into a taut-skinned drum against which some firm hand beat a rhythm.

But most of the time it was only the dark, only the silence. She could have been the only passenger on an ebony ship, sailing the cyclopean channels of some subterranean river. . .the River of Time with its inky waters, its soaring but unseen cavern ceiling. She could have been lost in the forest again, feeling her way blindly in the black.

At last, at very long last, Tilanne opened her eyes. The lids parted with a sticky, encrusted reluctance, and the soft magelight illuminating the room stabbed into her like spears. She grimaced.

"Awake, art thou?" an unfamiliar voice asked. "Thought did I that soon it would be. Sturdy thou art, and strong."

Turning her head seemed like too daunting an endeavor, so Tilanne shifted her eyes until they found the stranger seated beside the bed. He was an elf of middle years, perhaps three and a half centuries, with wavy salt-and-pepper hair and mild blue eyes.

A frightening thought came to Tilanne – was she supposed to know this man? Had her memories been stolen from her?

But no . . . she remembered all that had happened. Or thought she did. The Citadel, the dragons, Kai Maltanar, Kor Lothairal.

She tried to speak, but her mouth was so parched that the inside of it felt bumpy, coarse, and pebbled, like the hide of a lizard left to dry in the sun. All she could utter was a dusty croaking noise that might have made her laugh under other circumstances.

The man nodded sympathetically. "In thy own good time, Kor Tilanne. No rush is there. Sorely injured thou hadst been, and both slow and careful thy recovery should be. I'll some water bring thee."

Following him with her gaze as he moved from the bedside, she realized she was not in her own room. Nor was she in any other chamber she recognized. The walls were of the same sort of stone as the rest of the Citadel, and the *feel* of the place was the same, so that she knew she was in the same building. Just in some room she'd never been in before. Unfamiliar, though finely furnished.

The man poured a goblet full of water, and the sight and sound of the clear-flowing liquid filled Tilanne with greater yearning than she'd ever known. It was enough to enable her to pull herself partway up, bracing her back on the cushions. Just that simple act left her trembling with exhaustion, sweat sheening her brow.

She had planned to take the cup from him, but her hand was so uncertain that he covered it with his own and guided the rim to her lips. The first reviving touch and taste of the water was overwhelming. He removed it before she'd had nearly enough.

"Slowly, now," he cautioned. "Too much ill shall make thee."

Tilanne hardly considered a mere sip or three to be too much, but as he rationed the water to her in more of those careful, measured doses like medicine, she realized he was right. Before the goblet was half-empty, her stomach felt bloated.

Her head fell back against the softness of the pillows and she sighed. Now that she was awake and regaining her faculties, she was surprised that she didn't hurt nearly so much as she might have expected. She was not encased in a corselet of birchbark to hold her ribs in place. Neither arm was supported by a sling. What she could see of herself did not appear to be bandaged, or covered with the thunder-purple bruises she should have gotten from the dragon's pummeling tail.

What she could see of herself looked like it belonged to a stranger. So thin, so wasted, so pale and feeble.

"What . . . ?" she began to ask then changed her mind. "Who . . . ?"

"Physician Denisse am I," the man said. "Idran Denisse."

Looking more closely at him, she could see the resemblance, though he must have favored his father more than either his brother or mother. If he was half so adept at his profession as were the others of his family, Tilanne knew she was in the best of all possible care.

"How badly am I hurt?" she asked.

"Barely at all, now," he replied. "Grievous at first thy injuries were, and of course few magics for quick healing have we. But time its own healing brings."

"Time . . ." Tilanne, knowing more than a little about the physician's art thanks to Vandil, frowned. For mending wounds, especially those such as she must have suffered, she knew only one thing that would be a proven cure. "In a death-sleep was I, then? For how long?"

Idran's eyebrow rose. He seemed surprised by her knowledge, perhaps even impressed, but Tilanne was not interested in impressing anyone.

Even as she'd said the words, she knew them to be true. She had been in a death-sleep. Long enough for bones to knit, for bruises to fade. Long enough for the honed and muscular strength of her body to have deteriorated into frailness.

"For more than three years hast thou slept," he said.

* * *

CHAPTER TWENTY-TWO

Three years . . .

A very long time to sleep.

Kai Maltanar would have been long since sent to his pyre, he and the valiant dragon. What else had happened, what else had she missed? Who else had lived and died that day? She did not know. Those losses, the pain of which might finally be easing in the hearts of the others, would be as new and sharp to her as if it had only just happened.

She tried to ask, but all at once grief claimed her in a fierce grip. As thirsty as she'd been, as dry as she still felt, she wouldn't have imagined there to be any moisture in her available for tears, yet they over spilled her eyes in a sudden flood. She drew up the blanket to blot them.

When she lowered it at the sound of the door closing, thinking that the physician had left her in privacy, she saw instead that someone else had come in to joining them. This was no unfamiliar face, but one she knew well.

"Kai Peredur?" she said shakily. "Thought did I that died you had. Thought did we . . . that died you must have, you and the others all."

"Tilanne," he said, devouring her with his gaze as if he had feared he might never see her again. "Oh, Tilanne . . . among us again, at last, art thou."

"Told thee I did, little brother, that reviving she was." Idran gave him a stern look. "A little while only, Peredur. Her rest she needs."

"Rested for three years have I," Tilanne said.

"And rest more shalt thou have," he said. "I'll no arguments from either of thee hear, *Rhunvala* or no."

"From thee alone would I such orders take," Peredur grumbled.

"Well, from me and from Mother."

"Away with thee, Idran! If only a little while thou'll give me, have the manners not to with thy chatter that precious time take up!"

"Very well, very well. But tire her not, and distress her not."

"A Kor she is. Of sterner stuff than most she's made. Out." Kai Peredur all but pushed his brother toward the door, and closed it behind him far more firmly than was required. He took a deep, steadying breath before he returned to Tilanne.

She gazed at him, more relieved than she could ever express to see him here, whole and unharmed, unchanged from the Kai Peredur she knew. Well . . . not entirely unchanged. He seemed sadder, somehow. Older, perhaps . . . not that three years should make that much difference.

And her? What was he seeing as he looked at her? She had known people who'd emerged from lengthy death-sleeps before. Was that what he beheld? A gaunt, pallid face, all sunken eyes and prominent bones? A weak, spindly shadow of the strong and vibrant Tilanne he'd known?

"Prayed did I that Kaledhol thy safe return would grant," he said. "That not home to Him would he take thee yet."

"Likewise did I, for thee," she said. "The Moonglow –"

"Later." Kai Peredur sat on the edge of the bed and took her hand. His was warm, the grip firm but gentle. The touch left her feeling even weaker, though not at all in the same way.

"Hear of it I would. Of all that, in the death-sleep, I missed." Her voice was barely her own.

"When well again thou art."

"Hear it I would, Kai. Who lived did, who died did. Know it I must." She pushed herself up, wanting only to prove to him that she was not an invalid, and then somehow she was in his arms. Peredur held her to him, to his warmth and his strength, and because she had grown so frail, he seemed even stronger than ever. His head leaned against hers, his embrace the sort that might never want to let go.

"From Lothairal the whole story I had, " he said, in a low murmur very near her ear, making her shiver. "After the dragon thou didst slay, though sore hurt he himself was, he did to the Citadel thy body bring. Others forth to help him came. At first, certain were they that . . . that hope there was none."

"How many did that day perish?"

"Here? Five, among them our valiant Kai Maltanar."

"Five . . ." Tilanne closed her eyes and pressed her face to Peredur's shoulder. "Sorry am I . . . so sorry . . . tried we did but . . ."

"If the blame to anyone falls, to me it does," he said. "Sparsely defended I the very Citadel left. A trick it was, a trap. Expected did they, hoped did they, that we the majority of our forces would to Moonglow bring."

"The Citadel all along they intended to attack?"

"If presented itself did such an opportunity. The dragon they had, which was by a Hramadan wizard tamed. Knew did they that with it, the *Odan Rhunvale* itself could they strike while away our soldiers were. In league they are, the Mountain King and those of Hramad, an alliance long secret but now known, an alliance that to our people a most dire future portends. But of all that, another time we can speak."

"And thy mission, what of that?" she asked.

He had not released her, still held her. One of his hands stroked her hair, almost as if he did not realize he was doing it. His other arm curved around her back and supported her.

"Near the Valley of the Moonglow, encounter them we did. Costly was the battle, costlier for them than for us, Kaledhol be praised. Believed did we that triumphed we had. Until, under interrogation, admitted to us did one of them that a distraction it all had been. Of the alliance he told us, the wizards . . . the dragon. Set out at once we did. Through days and nights without sleep and with barely a rest we marched, and still, too late arrived. Already to his pyre had Kai Maltanar and the others been sent. Already . . . already in thy death-sleep didst thou lie."

"If not for Kai Maltanar, fallen would have we all," she said. Her own hand, faltering and hesitant as much from incapacitation as nervousness, crept up his broad back. Her fingers twined through his hair, still worn pulled back and tied. "The dragon he rode . . . whence came it?"

"Greatwing," Kai Peredur said. "Knew of him I did, of course, and how in his cave at the root of the mountain he laired, but a dragon can for decades, even centuries, sleep. In my time here, so infrequently did he wake that all but forgotten him had I, and most others. Locked were the doors, and the only key by Maltanar was held."

"Bravely and well together did they die."

"As would he have wanted."

"The body . . . ?"

"Of Greatwing? Maltanar's pyre he shared. Fitting it was deemed that with our venerable Kai should his venerable steed go. The other, the smaller that thou didst slay –"

"Lothairal and I," she said. "Not alone could I such a thing have done."

She felt his smile in the movement of his lips, which were against her cheek in what was not quite a kiss. "For the kill, full credit to thee Lothairal gave. When butchered it was – for such a bounty of meat and hide and teeth and claws to waste could not be allowed to go – the best parts were for thee saved back. And, of course, the pearl thy trophy is."

Tilanne tipped her head back enough to look at him. "The pearl? Mine, it is?"

Their faces were very close. His eyes . . . that stirring twilight-blue . . . had never been so deep.

"Kept it for thee I have," he said. "Not large is it, for young yet the dragon was. But a fine prize, opaline and iridescent."

"Honored am I."

"Earned it thou didst. And glad am I, Tilanne, so glad that at last returned thou hast to claim it." He clasped her to him again, with a breath like a mingled sigh and a sob. When he spoke, his voice had gone husky. "Never knew did I that three years such an eternity could be."

There was a discreet rapping at the door, which then opened. Idran Denisse peered in. "Brother?"

"Yet a while longer give me," Peredur said, without glancing around.

"Rest she must." He came into the room, the stately form of Idrasanna sweeping in behind him. "Expected did I that with me thou'd argue, and so Mother I've brought as well."

"Heed thy brother, Peredur," Idrasanna said. She surveyed them, and Tilanne was not certain what emotion she read in the older woman's eyes. Was she pleased? Dismayed? "The physician he is, not thee."

Slowly, reluctantly, Peredur released his grasp and eased Tilanne back onto the cushions. He bent over her. His lips brushed her brow, lingered there warm and sweet.

"Kai Peredur . . ." Words she dared not utter hung in her mind like suspended jewels. She could not have said them in front of his mother and brother . . . could not have said them even were they alone.

"Tomorrow I'll see thee," he said, giving her hand a gentle squeeze before settling it onto the blanket. "Provided thy watchdogs permit."

"When wartime it is, I thy instructions obey," Idran said. "Now upon my field of battle we are. Go and to thy duties attend. All here well managed is."

After one long look back, Kai Peredur did indeed go. Tilanne felt weariness seep into her like cold water. She could no longer lift her head and let it loll on the pillow as the physician fussed over her. Idrasanna Denisse came to the bedside as well, smiling down at Tilanne.

"How badly hurt was I?" she asked.

"Quite a scare thou didst give us," Idrasanna said. "So crumpled was thy armor that from thy body it had to be cut away before ever thy wounds could be seen to. When the extent of the damage we knew, I for Idran immediately sent."

"Many of thy bones broken were," Idran said. "Thy innards bruised and bleeding were, and thy head a most fearful blow had been struck. Though did I for a time that no hope was there for thee. That kindest would it have been thy lifespark to let extinguish. But hear of it would they not. And so all my skill I did on thee employ."

"In thy debt I am –"

"Nay, never that, Kor Tilanne."

She swallowed. "And . . . and Kor Tilanne am I still? To stand, to walk, I'll be able? To fight?"

"Not today," Idran said with a snort. "To thee I'll not speak lies and false comfort, and so tell thee I must that a long and miserable recovery wilt thou endure. Weak as an infant thou'll at first be. Thy body must even the simplest tasks relearn. Assistance thou'll need and should not be ashamed for such assistance to ask."

"But such assistance thou'll have, and no lack of it," Idrasanna said. "Cared for thee over these lost years have we, and care for thee we'll continue to do."

Tilanne wanted to question them further, but Idran made her drink a medicinal tea that relaxed her into the first natural sleep she'd known since the night before the dragon had come to the Citadel. The next day, as promised, Kai Peredur returned, and sat with her holding her hand while he related more of what had transpired during the past three years.

Lothairal had completed the final ritual and become a Kai at last. He had gone off with a few other *Rhunvala* to guard the borders of the woods. Not only was there this troubling alliance between the mages of Hramad and the Mountain King, but the Emerin itself was embroiled in a war with the dwarves. It seemed that the *Morvalan* lands were more surrounded by peril and enemies than ever before.

Another *Rhunvala*, Kai Estaran, was newly arrived at the Citadel. He followed the Way of Destruction, though he was, according to Peredur, much less volatile than Lothairal. He had come to them from Deepwater, a settlement that had been Tilanne's home before Cliffcave, and knew her sister. Tilanne was overjoyed to hear that Forana was fine and well, having recently given birth to a daughter. Estaran put Tilanne in mind of a storm cloud, ever dark and brooding. Initially, she believed that he shared Master Dael's mind regarding women as *Rhunvala*, because he hardly spoke to her. But she soon saw that he hardly spoke to anyone at all, preferring his own company and silence over companionship.

Others of the Odan Rhunvale were eager to visit her sickbed, and she had a steady stream of company. Leiater and his parents, Ordan Quaide, Savillan. Derethin, the orchard-tender whose life she'd saved by shielding him from the dragon's flame, brought regular gifts of succulent fresh fruits

Even Master Dael paid a grudging call one afternoon, perhaps if only to see for himself that she was truly among the living again.

The physician had been right in his prediction of her lengthy recovery and weakness. Tilanne was shocked to find that she very nearly had to learn to walk all over again. Just moving from one end of a room to another had her panting for breath, her legs as wobbly as those of a newborn fawn. The simplest things – bathing, dressing, eating – left her exhausted.

Now and then, she despaired of ever regaining all that lost ground. On nights when the pain was exceptionally bad, she sometimes caught herself thinking that perhaps she should give up, perhaps she should forget her wish to be *Rhunvala* and simply be happy she was alive.

Whenever such thoughts came to her, Tilanne pushed them away. She scolded herself sternly, remembering others who had come through far worse than this. She thought of Ilantisian, lifeless from the waist down. Or Corandir, missing an eye.

This infirmity of hers would not be forever.

It *seemed* like forever. A year went by, a year of tedious and aching daily exercises to strengthen her limbs and restore tone to her muscles. A year in which each day she pushed a little further than the day before. Physician Denisse kept a hawk's watch on her and intervened whenever he felt she was overtaxing herself. Though it vexed her to be so enforcedly idle, she dared not go against him. Not even Peredur could defy Idran for long when a matter of health was at stake.

"All thy sons so formidable are?" Tilanne asked Idrasanna.

They had taken to gathering in the evenings for wine and companionship in the outer chamber of the *Rhunvala* quarters, by the round hearth and the pool. Kai Estaran, who rarely bothered with that room, did not object.

"As formidable as these two?" She laughed. "Perhaps, though not as much as these two do the rest of them bicker."

"Any wonder is it?" Peredur grinned. "With a mother so formidable, no choice had we."

"Only bicker do we because together we are," Idran said. "As would any brothers do."

"When in Thanis with Peredin and Peredal I am, remember that I shall," Idrasanna said. "Bicker they do not."

"Peredin bickers not because Peredin, like Kai Estaran, speaks not," Peredur said. "And Peredal for nothing but his wines and vintnery cares."

"Thanis?" Tilanne frowned. "Is that not the city in the human lands? Why wouldst thou to such a place go?"

Idrasanna traced the line of knotwork tattoos at her hairline. "Some small auguries do we Circle Mages know. Foreseen have that Thanis a place of great importance is, and shall to all elvenkind be. I know not what, not when, but decided did we High Mages that necessary it was a set of eyes and ears in that place to have."

"Among the humans to live? Safe, such cannot be!"

"As safe there as here I'll be, with Peredin," Idrasanna said. "*Dhanvala* is he."

Tilanne blew out a low whistle. As rare as the *Rhunvala*, knights and warrior priests, were, the

Dhanvala were rarer still. Theirs was an order that disdained heavy armor and large weapons, for the entirety of their bodies were honed into weapons enough.

"And he the baby of the family is," Idran said, chuckling.

"Formidable, said I?" Tilanne shook her head with awe and admiration. "*Rhunvala*, *Dhanvala*, physician . . . what else?"

Peredur refilled the wine goblets, then counted off on his fingers. "One Crown Mage, one Scepter Mage, two soldiers, two metalsmiths, and a winemaker."

"But with all of that," Idran said, "still as a failing she sees it, for only Rasan married is and grandchildren has produced."

Tilanne blinked at Idrasanna. "Thou didst ten sons to such rank raise, a husband and household kept, and *still* a sorceress became?"

"Yes, and if so much could I capably manage, fail do I to see why my boys so difficult find it wives to attain."

"What woman wouldst wish *thee* as mother-in-law?" Idran settled back into the cushions and stretched his feet towards the hearth. "So intimidated are they by the meeting of thee that little will they have to do with us."

"Some harridan am I? Some shrew? Sifrina hates me not."

"Sifrina terrified of thee is. A single scowl from thee couldst into tears send her. Thou must this truth face, Mother."

"Never have I a single cross word to her said!"

"Nay, Mother, thy own fault it is," Peredur said. "For thy sons by thy very example, thou hast a standard set to which too few women could measure."

She swatted him smartly on the back of the hand. "A pitiful excuse for thy bachelorhood that is, Peredur Denisse. Surely in all the elvenlands must there be at least some other strong-minded and capable women who would of my sons be worthy!"

"With that," he said, casting a sidelong look at Tilanne, "I argue not. Rare, they may be . . . but exist, I know they do."

Her pulse raced, and her breath caught in her throat. They had not spoken of the way he'd held her when she had finally awakened from the death-sleep. She had known then that his feelings for her were deep, as deep as hers for him.

"Then thy feet quit dragging," Idrasanna said. "No younger are we any of us getting."

"My dilemma known to thee is," Peredur said. "As *Rhunvala* –"

"Not forbidden to thee is marriage. Rather, marry the *Rhunvala* should, and many children have. Only the finest and best of our people can *Rhunvala* become. Such blood and gifts and talent, passed on should be. Not in celibacy wasted."

"The life of any soldier dangerous is," he said. "Widows and children they leave bereft. For a *Rhunvala*, greater still is that risk. Wouldst thou have me a wife wed, only to a widow make her? Wouldst thou have thy grandchildren fatherless raised?"

Idrasanna sniffed. "The life of any *Morvalan* dangerous is. Our men on the battlefield die, our women in childbed die. Such risks, Peredur, we all of us must take."

He looked at Tilanne again, sighed, and then looked at Idrasanna. "Mother . . . perhaps marry *Rhunvala* can, and perhaps marry *Rhunvala* should. But marry each other, *Rhunvala* could not."

Tilanne closed her eyes. She could not quite believe that any of this was being said. A fluttering constriction seemed to have seized her heart. He did care for her, did love her and want her. He would marry her, this man, had matters not been as they were.

But matters *were.* She understood his full meaning, even if – as the stubborn set of her jaw evidenced – Idrasanna did not.

Understood it, and accepted it, and knew it to be true.

* * *

Chapter Twenty-Three

Slowly but surely, Tilanne's health improved. Her muscles hardened, her limbs became supple again. She realized that her body hadn't truly forgotten its skills, but had only let them lay dormant while she recovered from her years-long ordeal.

She was determined not only to regain that lost ground, but to surpass where she'd been before. She threw herself into her training with diligence and concentration. Within two years after waking from the death-sleep, she was more adept with sword and shield than ever.

And then, one glorious autumn day almost a year after that, she faced Kai Peredur in a practice bout . . . and disarmed him for the first time. His wooden sword went flying. Before he could react, she struck him a solid blow that knocked him off his feet.

Her instincts said she should press her advantage, get him at blade's point while he still sprawled there in the dust. But surprise rooted her the spot. She could not believe it. She had been striving for this, working toward it, and now that she'd actually done it, she was so stunned she could only stand gaping down at him.

"If an enemy I was, and dead I was not," he said from the ground, "a dagger or spell couldst I fling at thee whilst slack-jawed and defenseless thou art. Thy sword at the end of thy arm dangles, and thy shield by thy side hangs, and neither much help would be."

Hastily, she resumed a ready stance.

"Much better!" He sat up, then winced and rubbed his side. "A bruise from that, I'll have for certain. Well done, Tilanne. Think do I that fully learned thou art."

"Truly? Fully learned?"

He reached up. She set aside her weapons and helped haul him to his feet. He brushed himself off, then shoved back his visor. His face was shining with sweat, tendrils of hair plastered across his brow. His eyes and broad smile gleamed with a light of pride that tingled through her like a shower of sparks.

"The prayers and meditations mastered thou hast, the teachings and philosophies by heart thou knowst. And now, at combat thou art my match. Yes, fully learned. No more instruction can I to thee give."

Tilanne pulled off her helmet. For so many years, she'd been waiting and hoping that this moment would come. Now that it had happened, she did not know whether to laugh, cry, or shriek her joy to the very stars.

"Am I . . . at last . . . to *Rhunvala* become?"

"The full of the dark moon just three nights hence is," Kai Peredur said. "The final ritual couldst thou then undertake, if willing thou art."

"Willing I . . . I most . . . assuredly am." She was so choked with sudden emotion that she could barely say even that much.

"And Kai Tilanne thou'll be."

A laughing sob, a sobbing laugh, escaped her. She shook her head in astonishment. Although she'd spent so many years preparing for this, although she'd striven for it with every bit of her body, mind, and soul . . . somehow it seemed that it had all just happened, just burst upon her as a sudden, wondrous shock.

Laughing too, Kai Peredur threw aside his shield and helm. His hands descended onto her shoulders. He gave her a firm, affectionate shake. "So proud of thee am I . . . so glad for thee."

"Without thy tutelage, never could I have . . . oh, Kai Peredur, grateful am I beyond all words. A chance thou didst give me. Thy trust thou didst give me."

"Well earned it was." His hands were still on her shoulders, but his grip had softened. "But thy thanks and thy gratitude rightfully first to Kaledhol should go. Mayhap in desperation did Kai Terindor this legacy upon thee bestow, but Kaledhol's wisdom true as truesilver proved."

"If wise is the god, cruel also can He be," she said, gazing up into those twilight-blue eyes and feeling tears sting her own. "Knew did I that when to the *Odan Rhunvale* I came, all my past life and loves must I forsake. Knew did I not . . . dreamed would I never have dared . . ."

She could not finish. Peredur released her shoulders, and she started to turn away, calling herself a fool for having gone and spoken what should not have been spoken. Before she could, he slid his hands along the lines of her jaw, cupping her face.

"Tilanne," he said, almost murmured. "So many reasons there are that we should not . . ."

"So many," she agreed, trembling in his grasp. "Know them all do I. But this I tell thee, Peredur . . . at the moment, very unimportant do those reasons seem."

He caressed the bottoms of her earlobes with his thumbs. Even as she gasped with pleasure, a poignant thought of Jedriel flashed through her mind. He seemed so long ago now, so far away, and their time together as lovers had been so very brief. The earrings she wore were all she had left of him.

This man here before her, she knew far better than she'd ever known Jedriel, in all ways but one. They had been nearly constant companions for more than a decade, sharing their deepest thoughts and dreams, joined in their common purpose to serve Kaledhol's will and the Cause. They had seen each other, head to toe unconcealed, but had rarely touched. Had rarely *dared* to touch, both of them knowing that it might bring about something more serious.

As it seemed to be doing now.

She dipped her head to the side, bringing the fullness of her ear into the cup of his palm. Sensation thrilled through her, as much from the physical feeling as from hearing his low, yearning moan. His fingers traced the rim in a slow stroke.

Tilanne stopped questioning whether it was right or wrong to be doing this. She had gone too long without being in a man's arms, and this man, more than any other, was the one she wanted. Raising her chin, she found him already bending to her, and their lips met.

The kiss sent passion roaring through her. She needed him here, now, this very instant. But reason prevailed, reminding her that they were both disheveled and sweat-soaked, and that at any moment someone – Kai Estaran, Leiater, Master Dael! – might come out and see them.

Peredur realized this too, and stepped back from her. "Here we cannot stay," he said. His voice was unsteady.

In silence, keeping a careful space between them as if any accidental contact might be their undoing, they put away their gear, and returned to the chambers within the Citadel belonging to the *Rhunvala.*

Despite nearly overwhelming temptation, Tilanne kept her eyes averted as they bathed. She did not know why. She had seen him unclothed many times before. But those times, she realized, had always been with earnest admiration and wistful longing. It was different now. Wonderfully different.

She was aware that he was doing likewise, keeping his back turned. Only when they were both clean, clad in their robes, did they turn to face each other. His burnished-pewter hair was nearly black when it was wet, and combed back to reveal the full stately curves of his ears.

"Thy room or mine?" he asked, indicating the doorways.

"Thine."

His room was quite similar to hers, furnished in ornate rosewood. A candelabra, with candles of silver and magelit crystal flames, cast a gentle radiance. He poured wine for them both, and they settled before the hearth.

Peredur touched the damp sable fall of her hair where it spilled over her shoulders. "So lovely thy hair . . . glad am I that not for ease under a helm dost thou shear it short. For thee might I brush it?"

She nodded, then closed her eyes and leaned into the luxurious sensation as he drew a brush through her hair. When it was nearly dry, and smooth as finest silk, he embraced her from behind and moved his head alongside hers to kiss the side of her neck. The full length of their ears rubbed together, making her melt. Tilanne reached up, twining her arms over her head to embrace him, one hand finding his other ear and curling her fingers around the tapered tip.

Time and actions dissolved into meaninglessness. At some point their robes fell away, leaving nothing between them but the blackmetal chains and red stones of their necklaces, the glow of the rubies beating in unison.

She reveled in him and he did the same, molding her body with his hands as if discovering it for the first time. Every part of him was wonderful to her touch. Even the faint scars that raised his skin into seams and ridges only served to enhance the rest of him. They explored each other with a sort of patient, tender eagerness, bringing the most from each moment.

When at last they fully joined, he was kneeling back on his heels as she sat astride his thighs, facing him. Their gazes were locked, bringing their minds and souls together in a way every bit as complete as their bodies.

Tilanne had never known such a union, which was almost telepathic in its intensity. She knew him, she *was* him, and all of her was equally laid open to him. Even when she closed her eyes, that sense of connection persisted. She could see him without seeing him, hear him not only in the soft cries of his passion but in the whisper of his very thoughts.

They made love for hours, long past the time when sleep normally should have claimed them. This was more refreshing, more invigorating, than any amount of slumber. More fulfilling than the finest of meals. She could not get enough of Peredur, nor he of her.

But finally, sated, their desire ebbed and weariness took its place. They had moved from hearth to bed during their encounter, so it was a simple business to disentangle themselves from the fur coverlet and slide beneath it. The sheets were cool on their skin, and with the comforting weight of the blankets atop them, they curled together contentedly.

As she drifted toward sleep with her head cradled against Peredur's chest, she thought with bittersweet poignancy of Jedriel. Jedriel, so gentle and kind. Did he wait for her? She hoped not . . . she hoped that he had found another. She could not marry him. As sweet as their love had been, as good a man as he was, she knew that she'd found her soul's true mate in Peredur.

Therein was her trap, her doom. Peredur had been right in what he'd told his mother. The two of them could never marry. A male *Rhunvala* might wed, knowing that his widow would be there to care for the children if and when battle claimed his life. Even a female *Rhunvala* like Tilanne could have taken a husband . . . if she married a man like Jedriel, who would never go off to war.

But if both of them were *Rhunvala*? How could they bring children into the world when those children might be deprived of both parents? When they were almost certain to be orphans?

Yet . . . she paused in her sleepy thoughts, frowning. Was that not the risk all parents took? Fathers who were soldiers might be more in danger of death, but accident and illness could claim even a peaceful life such as Jedriel's. Women died in birthing all the time, as Tilanne's own mother had done. Idrasanna Denisse had been right, too. All *Morvalan* lives were risky ones.

But, with a sudden chill, she understood that her own particular situation was even more complicated than that.

No matter which way she looked at it, there was no way to escape the truth. She could never marry, could never have children. A man could be *Rhunvala*, and also a husband, also a father. A woman . . . a woman could not. The dangers of the battlefield *and* the dangers of childbirth?

A shudder wracked her as she finally and fully understood the price that Kaledhol demanded.

* * *

Part Three:

Prayer and Price

CHAPTER TWENTY-FOUR

Tilanne had thought that the *Odan Rhunvale* held no more surprises for her, that she had come to know the ins and outs of the Citadel quite well.

But she had been made to change her mind after realizing that she'd never even suspected the bulk of the mountain contained the enormous cavern lair where the dragon Greatwing had whiled away the decades in slumber.

Her lack of experience with Master Dael's domain was less surprising. He had given up his grumblings about her, at least openly, but they had never become friends. She had never been privileged to view much beyond the main armory. That, at least, was a known and familiar place to her. The vast, long chamber with rack after rack of armor, weaponry, and shields all of various designs and makes was one she'd visited many times.

"So," the swordsmith said, his lip a sour curl. "Sent thee here has the Kai, for thy final ritual thyself to arm."

"Yes," she said. "A weapon I'm to choose . . . or by one, to be chosen."

He indicated with an imperious gesture that she should feel free to look around. Tilanne did so, but with increasing dubiousness. There were many adequate weapons here and even some of exceptional quality. But none of them seemed particularly special to her, and the tone of Peredur's voice had suggested that this was a momentous decision she would have to make. Perhaps the most momentous in her entire life.

The armory's subterranean stone walls were filmed with moisture. From nowhere and from everywhere came a whispering, rushing sound. A tributary of the black-watered River of Time thundered in a cataract through some lightless tunnel below. She could feel its constant motion in the vibration transmitted through the damp floor to her bare feet. Had she been wearing boots, or even slippers, she might not have detected it.

A chill draft eddied up her legs. The hem of her simple shift stopped just above the knee. The sleeveless garment was belted with a plain black cord. Her hair was unbound, falling loose down her back. She wore and carried nothing else but for the ruby basilisk around her neck.

Without her armor, without good boots and a stout shield, she felt naked and vulnerable. She had not even so much as a dagger.

This, though, was part of the ritual.

"Well?" Master Dael hoisted a skeptical brow.

"More must there be," she said. "Others that not displayed with these are."

He scowled, and she supposed he had been hoping she would settle for grabbing the first sword at hand and letting that be good enough. When she made no move to do so, he stepped grudgingly to a blank stretch of wall and caused it, by some means Tilanne could not discern, to slide apart. Beyond was another chamber, a secret chamber.

Dael paused in the opening and raised one hand, a blaze of magelight hovering above his palm. As Tilanne saw what the light revealed, a thrill of excitement went through her. At the same time, a deep and venerating awe brimmed up from her soul.

This was much more like it.

The room beyond was far smaller than the long armory. It was round and dome-roofed, the floor a gently curving shallow bowl. A dozen pedestals curved out from the walls, each supporting a sword.

And what swords! Dael's magelight sparkled on jewel-studded hilts, ran like liquid along shining blades. Each was more exquisite than the last. There was magic here, too, sorcery and high enchantment that she could feel like a tangible aura radiating from them.

Conflicting emotions swirled in Tilanne. Here were weapons of incredible power, the products of the combined skills of expert craftsmen and mages . . . left here to do nothing but sit upon their pedestals and wait for a *Rhunvala.* Why were they not being used? Why were these fabulous swords not in elven hands even now, and smiting down their enemies?

Yet at the same time she understood why it had to be that way. A regular soldier might be far more effective with such a sword, but a regular soldier was also far more likely to die in battle and lose his weapon to the enemy. Such magic in the hands of the Mountain King's forces would be disastrous. So these weapons *had* to be kept here, kept safe, until they could be claimed by those who could use them with a greater chance of success.

Further, only a *Rhunvala* would be able to withstand the ritual that would link the enchantments of the sword to his or her life. She had not known of that aspect before, but Kinnon and Idrasanna had explained it to her. Tilanne remembered Kai Terindor, and the sword that she'd placed upon his breast as he was consigned to his pyre. At the moment of the knight's death, the magic would have fled from the sword. Had it been retrieved from the ashes, anyone else would find it still a weapon of exemplary quality, but no more than that.

Was one of these swords meant for her? For Tilanne?

The thought was enough to make her quiver, to humble her with reverence and awe.

"When thy sword thou've chosen," Master Dael said, sounding both bored and peevish, "through there thou must go."

Across from the portal where she and Master Dael paused was another egress, which Tilanne saw when she tore her gaze away from the dazzling splendor of the waiting swords. Twin columns of gleaming black supported an arch that was one seamless curve, like a crescent sliced from the dark moon. Hanging beneath it was what Tilanne first took to be a red curtain, but it rippled strangely in a breeze that was not there

The more she studied it the more she realized that it seemed to be flowing like water. Like a waterfall. A scarlet cascade . . . a blood-fall.

Blood. Yes. It was a flowing curtain of blood.

Master Dael was watching her, a smug little smile on his mouth, as if he expected her to recoil in disgust or turn squeamish. If she did, he would no doubt call her unfit for the ritual, and end her progress on the spot.

"What then?" Tilanne asked evenly. She tried not to imagine what it would feel like to be coated in that rippling sheet of blood, tried not to wonder if it would be cool or as hot as if it had just spurted from severed arteries. "After that, what must I do?"

Disappointed, Dael shrugged. "Different for each it is, or so am I told."

Kai Peredur had informed her that no two rituals were the same. What went on in hers was between Tilanne and Kaledhol. No one else would know what happened to her until . . . and unless . . . she emerged. Whether she spoke of it later was at her own discretion.

She turned her attention back to the swords. A shiver of presentiment gripped her and she suddenly knew that this was not simply a matter of selecting one by virtue of its appearance, by her preference. All of them were strongly magical, but not all of them were benign.

This was part of her trial, before she even reached the blood-fall. To take up the wrong blade meant failure . . . might even mean death.

The swords themselves gave no clue as to their intentions. Tilanne glanced at Master Dael, but he had gone, closing the door behind him and leaving his magelight burning unattended. His reaction would tell her nothing as she examined each particular choice.

Tilanne closed her eyes and sought to calm her mind. She would not let herself think of what painful or deadly curses might have been woven into the enchantments. She would not select a sword based only on what it looked like, because such could be deceiving.

"Kaledhol my hand do guide, that find it might that which it is meant to bear."

Her words rang oddly in the confined space, or perhaps it was because her hearing seemed intensified in her deliberate blindness. She waited at the center of the room, her right hand held slightly out in front of her and curled as if ready to accept the hilt of a sword.

The urge came over her to take a few steps to her left and she did so without hesitation. Odd images occurred – lodestone, dowsing rod, the instinctive questing of a flower toward the sun. She did not resist as she was drawn by this inner compulsion. The floor sloped up, letting her know she was nearing the wall, nearing the pedestals.

Tilanne reached out and felt the hilt of a sword. She grasped it, raised it from its resting place. She opened her eyes.

This weapon, to which Kaledhol had directed her, felt light and right in her hand. The blade was black as a sliver of midnight, with edges as sharp as shards of glass. It was not pure obsidian, for such a thing would have been brittle, but was fused with blackmetal, stronger than steel. The hilt was truesilver in the shape of a basilisk with glinting red eyes, its tail curled around a faceted ruby pommel.

The sheath that went with it was of dusky red-black leather, not dragonskin, but stitched from the hides of basilisks. The fittings were plain blackmetal. The runic letters of Oldspeech spelled out words in silver.

"Baleful Gaze," Tilanne read aloud. The name of the sword. The name of *her* sword, to which she'd been drawn and guided.

No terrible effects befell her. Nor were there any bursts of light or other signs to tell her that the sword had accepted her, but she sensed it in her heart. She could feel the power in Baleful Gaze. Carrying it and its scabbard, she moved toward the blood-fall blocking the door. She felt ill at ease in nothing but the thin shift, missing the comforting weight of armor more than ever.

"Thy will it is, Kaledhol," she said, standing before the pouring crimson flood. "Thy will be done."

She could smell the blood, fresh and dark. Not a trick. Not colored water, not wine. When she reached out, her fingers made indents around which the blood parted and coursed. It was warm, almost hot, as hot as if it pumped from a beating heart. Rills of it ran down the back of her hand, startlingly red against her skin.

Tilanne pushed her hand into it, hoping to find that the barrier was thin. But when she was elbow deep and still could not feel open space on the other side, she firmed her resolve and took a deep breath and stepped into the doorway.

The blood-current was not strong enough to drive her to her knees, but the pressure of it slowed her progress. The hot, liquid feel of it, tepid and thick, made her gorge hitch. She kept her lips sealed tight, her eyelids also.

At last, she was through. Open space surrounded her. Tilanne stood drenched in blood, her shift pasted to her body. Her hair was sodden, weighing heavily on her scalp. She could only imagine how gruesome she must look.

When she opened her eyes to confirm the worst, she was astounded. There was not a single stain on her. Every trace of the blood had vanished. Her shift and hair were dry, her skin clean. But the sword, Baleful Gaze, was gone.

With a startled cry of denial, Tilanne whirled, ready to plunge once more into the torrent of blood, frantic at the thought that she might have dropped it, lost it.

She spun and tottered an instant before her feet nearly lost their purchase. The doorway with its flowing red curtain was gone. Wheeling her arms, Tilanne caught her balance and did not fall from the narrow ledge upon which she now found herself precariously perched.

A pit gaped below her, and in the shadows of its depths, something large rustled and stirred. She heard a low growl that sounded as if it was born of some hideous, eager hunger.

Tilanne eased back from the brink and hazarded a look around. She was in a square chamber with no windows, the walls rough-hewn stone, with no features whatsoever apart from the pit, two torches burning in iron brackets, and four doors . . . each of very different aspect.

Two doors were in the wall to her right and two in the wall to her left, near the corners of the room. One gleamed as if made of solid gold. Another was of iron bars, almost more of a portcullis than a door. The third could have come from any *Morvalan* settlement, a plain and ordinary door. The last was of glossy, polished wood.

The rectangular pit took up the center of the room, and was surrounded by a walkway. Two flights of steps led down into a darkness that the sputtering torches could not banish. Tilanne could smell the odor of carrion wafting up from it, dank dungeon smells, and the incongruous fragrance of roses.

This, somehow, was her trial. This was the ritual. She did not know what she was supposed to do next, or what any of it was supposed to mean.

The nearest door was the one all of gold. As she approached it, she saw that the metal was embossed with images of dragons, all manner of dragons. Sinuous wyrms, tiny drakes, the bestial lesser dragons, the proud greater ones . . . dragons of every size and shape. Even the solid gold door handle was in the shape of a dragon holding its own tail in its jaws, wings folded along the sides of its body.

It opened easily and light poured out, almost as bright as the pure unfiltered summer sunlight she had not seen in many a year. Tilanne let go of the handle to rub at her eyes, which were so accustomed to the perpetual shade of the *Odan Rhunvale*. The door thumped closed behind her.

That was impossible; she hadn't stepped through. How could it have closed *behind* her, when she was outside of it?

But she was inside. Somehow, she had passed through the doorway and into the room, and the mystery of how such a thing had happened was almost immediately lost by amazement at what surrounded her.

Treasure. Coins were everywhere, coins as abundant as pebbles on a lakeshore. Silver coins, and gold. Gems, too. . .a rainbow of gems, all colors, all sizes. Strands of pearls. Golden statues, cups, platters, coffers, necklaces, scepters. She saw silver basins, bells, rings. Jewelry everywhere, enough to adorn a thousand queens.

And weapons, too. A greatsword of gold with a hilt that looked to have been formed from a single huge diamond. Knives made from pure jade, daggers carved from rubies. She saw a shield with a single rounded sapphire bulging from its center, reflecting cool fans of blue light onto a scattering of smaller baubles.

Why, just a handful of this would be wealth beyond measure. A sack of it would let her live out her life in the utmost comfort, lacking for nothing, wanting for nothing. With such riches, she could go anywhere, do anything. She could bid farewell to the endless, hopeless struggle that was *Morvalan* life and start anew anywhere, even in the Emerin. Her *Alvalan* cousins might have no great love for her kind, but who were they to argue with gold?

"No," Tilanne said, and it seemed her voice rebounded off of each coin, each gem. "My sword I seek, and that only."

But with this wealth, she could afford a sword even finer. One made to her own exact specifications, with whatever enchantments her heart desired.

She felt pain in her hands and looked at them, finding that they were clutching and unclenching so convulsively that her fingernails were gouging the tender flesh of her palms. Tension knotted the muscles of her arms. Her teeth ached, so tight was her jaw.

The temptation was awful . . . and beyond all reason. That *she* could be struck with gold-lust was insane. What use had she for treasure? Gold had not saved the elves when Govannisan fell . . . indeed, gold had brought about that downfall. If not for the gilded spires shining like beacons for the dragons, the city might have escaped destruction.

She wrenched free of the unwelcome urge and groped for the door. It would be locked . . .

It opened. She stumbled out into the central chamber again, remembering just in time to beware falling into the pit.

Did each door contain a similar temptation? Or was her sword behind one of them, and all the others meant to distract her from her true purpose here?

The next one along this wall was the one made from iron bars. A key was conveniently hanging on a peg beside it. Too conveniently.

When she opened it, the hinges gave a rusty squeal. A fat brown rat scurried out, brushing her bare ankle like the malicious caress of a disease. Wincing, Tilanne shied away from it and looked through. She saw a curving stone stairway beyond the iron bars. Recesses in the walls held glow-stones in a descending spiral. She could hear agonized screams, and the low mewling moans of such abject hopelessness that they could only come from tortured souls beyond even daring to dream of rescue.

Apprehensive, wishing again for armor, for weapons, Tilanne followed the stairs down. They brought her to a landing, a jutting tongue of stone overlooking a dungeon. One whole wall was a cage in which naked, pitiful figures huddled. More bodies were affixed to devices of pain.

Though they cowered and covered their heads in terror when she appeared, she could see them for what they were. Humans. They were humans all, some of whom she recognized. Some of the faces had been those of the men who'd attacked the Citadel, and the wizard and his henchmen she'd seen in Firsthome.

They deserved no less than this punishment! A quick death was too good for them. Let them writhe in their miseries and grovel in fear before her . . . they had *dared* to affront her . . .

Tilanne's thoughts broke off with a snap. Here was her new temptation, the temptation to enjoy the sufferings of these prisoners. This was a vicious and evil place, yet had its own horrid dark appeal. She could give in to the rancid delight of such sadism, becoming the cruel and merciless monster that so many others were willing to believe the *Morvalan* to be.

"No," she said again.

Her sword was not here.

She turned her back on the agonized humans in their devices of pain, and went up the stairs.

Skirting the pit, she came to the door of polished wood so similar to ones in the Citadel. When she opened it, she rocked back on her heels at a sudden joyous burst of applause. Tilanne stood with her mouth agape, staring around at a crowd of people. They were cheering for her, shouting her name with adulation and acclaim.

She knew them, knew all of them. Not only folk from the Citadel were here, but old friends – there was Alarice, and Reshelli, and Commander Ellorn. And Corandir, tears of pride streaming from his one remaining eye. Even Sahen was here, as exultant and congratulatory as the rest.

But . . . but she had done nothing. . .nothing more than open a door. Why were they here, why were they doing this?

Did it matter? She had won. She had won through, and they were here to celebrate it. To honor her. To shower her with the glory that she –

"No!" Tilanne cried. "Not for glory did I come!"

She fled from that temptation as well, revolted by the idea that anyone would seek to become *Rhunvala* for any of the reasons she'd seen. Not for wealth, not for acclaim, not to intimidate and terrify. She wanted none of those things, would never want any of those things.

Only one door remained, and Tilanne regarded it most warily of all. She did not know what might be waiting for her behind that humble door. She was afraid to find out. Yet she could not turn away.

It struck her like a fist to the belly.

Warm firelight rushed out at her, and with it came merry laughter. Two little girls, with dark hair and darker eyes, threw their fragile arms around her legs, chattering excitedly. Behind them, an older boy with reddish hair hung back shyly, waiting his turn to greet her.

She had never seen them before, did not know them . . . and yet . . . it felt as though she should. It felt as though she always had.

And then an arm slipped around her, and lips pressed a kiss on the side of her neck just below the ear, and Jedriel's voice said, "Welcome home."

Almost not daring to do so, Tilanne looked up at him. He was the same, just the same, with his obsidian eyes and that firegold hair drawn back from the temples, and Jedriel's kind, loving smile.

Home!

Without thinking of what she was doing, she knelt and opened her arms to the two little girls. They embraced her, sweet and warm and lively, still talking so rapidly that their words overlapped one another's. Tilanne could not make out any of it, yet the noise delighted her.

"Missed you we did, *Vali*," her son said.

She had come *home*. Home to her husband, her children, her family. Their love enveloped her and brought a lump to her throat, tears to her eyes.

But as she began to rise, holding the girls, she froze in woeful understanding.

Oh, cruel, most cruel of all! This temptation, not of what she might gain but what she must forsake, pierced her like a truesteel knife. She slowly set down the children, then rose, and backed away from them.

"No," she said, in barely a whisper that tore like a jagged edge. "If those others I deny, this too I must."

The confusion, the hurt, in their expressions was almost more than Tilanne could bear. Jedriel, concerned, stretched out a hand to her. The plaintive voices of the children begged her to stay.

Her soul felt ripped into pieces, but she fled from them, rejected this family that could never be. She swept the door closed behind her, sobbing. Her vision blurred, her eyes unseeing, she almost plunged headlong into the pit.

Stopping, Tilanne looked back – she knew she should not, that a single glance more might be her undoing – but found that the door was still closed. All of them were closed. She had come no closer to finding a way out, or finding her sword, or learning what she was supposed to be doing here.

Or had she? In seeing what she was willing to sacrifice to become *Rhunvala*, and in seeing what she did *not* want from that office, had it brought her closer to knowing what she *did* want? What did she expect to gain from this?

"To gain?" she said aloud. "Nothing. Not to gain is this, but to give. To serve. My people to protect. Kaledhol's Way to keep. Only that. Nothing more."

As she said it, new light grew. Flame, at the bottom of the pit, igniting in a round trench. It burned both ways in an expanding arc, and as it completed the circle and brightened, she saw a hill of earth at the center. Growing from the top of the earth was a rosebush, flowering in the color of death.

And caught in the thorny boughs of the bush – her sword.

* * *

Chapter Twenty-Five

So that was it . . . instead of giving in to the distractions and temptations afforded by the various doors, she was meant to turn away from all of them, and go into the pit instead.

The fiery ring blazed, its flames springing from no readily visible source. Mystic orange-red runic shapes reflected Baleful Gaze's shining black blade.

Tilanne moved to the nearest flight of stairs, recalling the sound she'd heard before. A shifting, a growling. The fire did not illuminate all of the pit, leaving its corners cloaked in shadow, but she knew that there was something alive down there. Something large, and hungry.

But her sword was down there as well, the chosen weapon to which Kaledhol had led her, and she meant to retrieve it.

The floor of the pit was hard-packed dirt, moist and redolent of root-cellar smells. Mushrooms sprouted from it, and here and there she saw the thin pale gleam of half-buried bones. Not elven bones, but the remains of small animals. Rats, perhaps, like the one that had slid so loathsomely past her ankles.

Her heart ached, felt twisted and wrung out as a damp rag. She cared little for wealth, less for acclaim, and not at all for power . . . but oh, how the loss of the family she could never have cut her to the quick!

Nothing sprang from the shadows to attack her as she neared the center of the pit, but there she stopped, faced with a new problem. The flames leapt high, no illusory menace but emitting a very real heat. They would sear her skin into blisters and blackened flaps if she tried to pass through. The hill of earth in the middle was tall, the spreading rosebush reaching well above her head.

Baleful Gaze was beyond reach, guarded by thorns. Her flesh cringed in anticipation of the sharp points.

Hssssssss!

A low-slung creature came into the light. Its body was sleek and reptilian, six-legged, with stubby vestigial wings and a long barbed tail.

No sooner had its shape impressed itself in her mind than Tilanne knew it for what it was, and clapped a horrified hand over her eyes.

Basilisk!

Her studies had taught her that there were many varieties of the deadly lizards, some smaller than the rat she'd seen, others the size of dogs. This one's hunched back came to Tilanne's waist, and its length exceeded that of a horse.

It was enormous.

Hssssssssss . . .

Menace beat from the basilisk in waves. Tilanne took a step, but the fire was too hot, lapping at her unprotected skin. She edged the other way instead. Blind, feeling her way with her bare toes, she knew that even if she did not look at it, she could not escape. Such a beast, with claws like daggers and a poisonous bite, did not need to see her to finish her.

Could she fight it? Unarmed, unarmored?

Should she try to strangle it as she'd done with the dragon? But a basilisk was the sacred symbol of Kaledhol! He would not approve of such an act. He would withhold the divine strength that had let her triumph that way before.

Determining by its continued hissing that it was now to her left, Tilanne chanced a quick look to her right. The opposite set of stairs was not far away. She kept her hand between her face and the basilisk, able to see the tip of its tail dragging in the dirt but not able to see its eyes.

Run for the stairs?

That would mean leaving her sword behind, fleeing, failing. She could not do that.

A second snarling basilisk, this one almost as large as the first, slunk into view. Tilanne had the barest of glimpses of its head swinging around to fix on her before she covered her eyes again. There seemed to be differences in coloring, and she suspected one was male and the other female. She was in their territory, their nest.

She came too close to the fire again and recoiled. The basilisks had her flanked, and she could not see where she was, could not see any route to safety.

"Faith my armor be," she said. "*Seh-ahna!*"

A glowing second skin appeared over her own, like a snug-fitting garment of sheer red silk. Not a moment too soon, for needle-teeth gnashed at her leg. Rather than rend her calf into bleeding meat, the basilisk's bite was deflected by the red glow as if it were not light at all but fine steel.

Would it protect as well against fire?

Tilanne did not pause to wonder. She silently thanked Kaledhol for His armor and leapt through the wall of flames.

Even protected as she was, she felt the intense heat. The ends of her hair were singed, the hem of her shift scorched. But then she was through, through and standing on the hillock of earth that gave way in crumbles beneath her feet and threatened to spill her back down.

She could see the sword, stuck high above her. The scent of roses was overpowering, the sound of the flames like a pyre. Yes, this must be what it would be like to experience her own funeral while yet living. To be engulfed in the fire, breathing the smoke. But she had not come this far to die . . . surely that could not be Kaledhol's intent.

Fire, roses, and basilisks. All representing death, but also all representing the god in His duality of nature. Fire warmed, fire burned. Roses were sadness, roses were transcendence. Basilisks killed, but defended their own.

And death?

Even death was a duality . . . death was an ending, but also a beginning.

To conquer these things, she did not need to fear them or fight them, but only to accept them.

A calm surety fell over Tilanne. She climbed the loose mound of earth, and although sharp-edged leaves scratched at her face, they drew no blood. The armor of faith around her turned away the jabbing thorns. She plunged her arm into the center of the rosebush, and took hold of the hilt of Baleful Gaze.

It came free effortlessly. Tilanne stood there with the flames and roses all around her, and pressed the cool black blade to her brow reverently. She kissed the crosspiece of the hilt, the truesilver like ice beneath her lips.

With a sudden rending crunch, one of the basilisks lunged through the fire and into the rosebush. It weight snapped and bent the thorny boughs toward her, but the face of the basilisk held all her attention.

Eyes like black diamonds snared her, a brief glance but deadly in that fleeting contact. Lethal power like silvery talons would reach into her mind, seize the part of her that let her heart go on beating and her lungs go on drawing breath, and still those parts forever.

Too late . . . she was too late again, this time too late to save herself. Tilanne belatedly closed her eyes, waiting for the moment when she would feel death take hold of her just as surely as she had taken hold of the sword.

She could not move, as petrified as she would have been if this had been one of the rarest breed of basilisks, the ones whose gaze turned living things to stone instead of slaying outright.

But her heart kept on hammering as rapidly as ever, and no pain seized her – she was sure there would be pain in dying, short perhaps, but all-encompassing. Just as she was beginning to realize that she was not about to drop dead after all, the entire uprooted rosebush crashed down atop her.

Stumbling, off-balance on the slope of earth, she fell. Fell into the fire-trench, landing half-across it and sending up a whirl of sparks like a cloud. The rosebush was on her, pinning her, thorns piercing and leaves slashing, blooms shedding a startled drift of petals onto her upturned face.

She was not hurt, not yet, the red shine of her armor still protecting her, but she was trapped. Trapped, and now the rosebush was catching fire as well. The pyre-scent was stronger, overpowering, as rose-oil seethed from the stems and stalks, as flowers charred and their perfume became ashes.

And her armor was fading. Her strength was waning. She had failed somehow, and was going to die here, immolated alive.

A hulking shape loomed over her. A basilisk. It was atop the rosebush that it had pushed onto her, part of the great heavy unbearable mass that held her down. The flames licked at it too, and any normal beast would have fled from the burning. But it was emboldened, or enraged, by the sight of its helpless prey below, and struggled to get at her.

Venomous saliva dripped from its jaws. Its eyes were pools of glassy midnight in which mirrored firelight danced like embers. Tilanne stared unbelieving into those eyes, still not falling victim to its power.

Then she understood. The sword, Baleful Gaze. With a name such as that, it must have the power to protect her from such magical effects.

The basilisk seemed to realize this as well, to comprehend that this elf-woman was not reacting as other creatures did. But its gaze was not its only weapon, and it bit her on the shoulder.

This time, the teeth found their mark. The pain was immediate and huge, exploding through Tilanne like some dwarven weapon of war. Her armor of light was gone.

She still held the sword, flattened to her body by the imprisoning weight of rosebush and basilisk. Now the thorns were impaling her her, now she was at the mercy of the fire.

Accept this? She could not . . . perhaps death could not be fought, but it could be resisted.

So thinking, through the haze of agony that engulfed her, Tilanne sought deep within herself and found a reserve of determination. Although she feared that the loss of her armor meant the loss of her faith – had she fallen to doubts? Had Kaledhol turned His back? – she beseeched Him for strength all the same.

"*Ha-nah!*"

And incredibly, the god answered. She angled Baleful Gaze upward, and thrust it through the skeletal tangle of burning branches, through roses that had grown petals of fire. She met opposition, a tough scaled hide, and pushed harder until the blade tore through it.

The basilisk screeched and thrashed, sundering the rosebush, sending smoldering parts of it flying. A red-black river gushed down the length of the blade to soak Tilanne, splashing onto her face. More spilled into the mangled wound on her shoulder, mixing with the poison like a dousing of acid. Tilanne screamed, but in opening her mouth to do so she choked on basilisk blood and the hot ashes of burnt roses.

Somehow, she wrenched out from under the basilisk. Its struggles grew feebler as its life's blood poured away. It raised its head to regard her again, this time without malice but with the mute pleading that she had seen before. In Findaire's expression, and Falanar's, Selmaire's. The body's look of misery so great, the body's look that said that death would be a blessing, though still the spirit yearned for life.

And still the gaze of the basilisk did not strike her down. Not while she held this sword.

She could end it now, finish it with one clean swing. That would be the kindest thing to do. But she would have to do it quickly, while she still could. The pain in her shoulder was spreading through the rest of her body, as if the flesh was being melted away. Beneath that terrible sensation was one almost as bad in a different way, a spreading poisoned heat like the stinging of a thousand ants.

Yet . . . if the gaze of the basilisk was fatal to all save its own kind, and its gaze was *not* fatal to her, did not that mean that *she* was its kind now, and it was hers? And was she not sworn to defend her own? Did her vow extend to this as well?

No.

She had sworn to take no *elven* life. And all else aside, this was a basilisk, not an elf. A symbol of Kaledhol, not Kaledhol Himself.

It hissed at her as she stepped closer, but that last show of defiance was too much for it, and the basilisk let its head fall to the floor. One inky eye rolled to watch her progress.

Now she saw the terrible cost of her vow. This was mercy, this was kindness. A mercy and a kindness she would be forever prohibited from giving to her own people, even if the need was there. But it also made her resolve all the more firmly to defend them, for in so doing she would be able to prevent them from needing that final mercy.

"For this lesson, Kaledhol, I thee thank," she said, and swept Baleful Gaze down in a swift arc, cleaving through the basilisk's neck.

As she did it, darkness swallowed her so suddenly that it was as if she were the one to die. When it cleared a moment later, she was in a new place, a place she'd seen before. In dreams.

But then, in the dreams, the city had been in ruins all around her, and now it was alive. Govannisan. Its golden walls were made silver-gilt by the brilliant spray of stars. Music drifted on the air, along with elven and dwarven voices in a tapestry of conversation. There were threads that clashed, raised in argument. There were threads that blended together subtly but smoothly, the murmurs of romance.

She saw them then, these ancestors of so long ago. They were tall and graceful and fair of face beyond belief, so much so that she looked upon them feeling as base and low as any human might when looking upon an elf.

The dwarves, as well . . . Tilanne had only ever met two members of that other Elder Race, but they had seemed as far removed from these noble-featured, silken-bearded denizens of Govannisan as she did from the elves.

They all passed her by without seeing her, as if they were utterly unaware of her presence despite the fact that she stood among them, they in their finery and she in the blackened tatters that were all to remain of her shift, holding a sword in one hand while the other arm hung limp and coated with blood. As if she was not, in fact, there at all.

The pain in her shoulder was raving and roaring. She could feel the basilisk's venom working its way through her. All she wanted was to collapse, but her trial was not yet done. She had to find out what was wanted of her here, in this place of legend.

Stumbling on legs that did not want to support her, Tilanne sought the tower she'd visited in her dreams. Then, it had been ruined, the great crystal spire that had arisen from its top shattered into broken shards that stuck up from the stone. Now it was whole.

Pleasant breezes stirred the boughs along the tree-lined avenues. She saw shops that were open late, elves and dwarves dining together on terraces. Grief speared her, seeing their friendship. What would be waiting for them after the dragons came? Millennia of distrust and blame, reclusiveness, animosity. Only to culminate in the war that was even now ravaging the Northlands, the war between the Emerin and Montennor.

Could she warn them? Could she tell them of the attack, of the flights of dragons drawn by the great and glorious gleaming of gold that called them from their far mountain lairs? Could she change what had been?

Was she even here?

Tilanne reluctantly concluded that she could not truly be in the time of ages ago, not truly in the Lost City. Thus, she could not change the past. She knew such travel was possible but such changes were not – Idrasanna Denisse had once told her of a mage whose entire career had been dedicated to trying to find a way to undo something that had been done in the past, but who had ultimately been unable to do so.

And even if it had been possible, she thought as she came within sight of the tall doors into the temple of Kaledhol, she knew that she could not do it, could not make decisions for all the elves yet to come based on what she knew of the future.

Did that mean she was dooming her own people, the *Morvalan*, to the life of vilification and struggle they would face? She passed through the open doors and inside. She came to a place that was familiar to her, not from her dreams now but from her studies.

Here was the very place upon which the first Kai, Rigellian of Dark Moon's Rising, had stood when he prayed for guidance and counsel. Rigellian's brother, Dyanavan Morestatali, had described it all so well that reading it made Tilanne feel she was truly there.

Now she was seeing it. That was the cloth, the sacred altar-cloth. The elves who would one day be called *Morvalan* had carried it from the destruction of the city. The dragons had come, the dragons had leveled Govannisan with their fiery breath, deadly claws, and powerful tails. In the wake of that, Rigellian and the other survivors who followed Kaledhol had taken refuge here. And here, from right before their eyes, Rigellian was taken as an offering might have been.

She caught her breath and the prospect of witnessing that moment, the taking and divine return of the man who would be the first of the *Rhunvala*. He who would lead his people to safety in the forests and mountains, while other groups of elves spurned Kaledhol's warnings and set off to live their lives by the principles of, if not in the worship of, the other gods.

But this was not that fateful day. The city was whole and unharmed, untouched by the wrath of the greedy dragons. Tilanne was alone.

Alone, and yet not alone. She sensed a presence here, directing her. Without pausing to question it, she stepped up onto the dais, onto the altar-cloth. She was in rags and ashes and blood, carrying naught but a sword, and yet somehow it did not seem to matter.

"I Thee serve, I Thee honor," Tilanne said. Her voice was harsh, her mouth still full of the foul tastes of roses and soot and basilisk blood.

Then the miracle that had happened to Rigellian happened to her. She was wrapped in color and light and jarring sound that hurt the ears with strange, not-quite-melodic tones. When it cleared, she was clean and healed, standing in what she identified as a throne room, although she'd never seen one.

Except there were five thrones, not one. Each was a different color, a different style. One was more a couch than a throne, draped in beautiful cloth. Another was silver-white and glowed like the moon. A third was made from living boughs, as if a tree had grown in the shape of a chair. The fourth was rigidly straight and severe. The fifth, the one in front of which she stood, was ebony, wide and sturdy as if built to support the weight of an armored man. And occupied.

Tilanne went to one knee and bent her head, even more afraid to look upon the man on the throne than she had been to look into the eyes of the basilisk. What she'd seen in that quick moment before her body obeyed her mind stayed with her – a suggestion of fair skin, dark hair, darker eyes, stern but compassionate features.

"Kai Tilanne," He said, and His voice seemed to reverberate through the room, far deeper and more commanding than that of any elf she'd ever heard.

Her soul leapt at the title, at hearing Him speak her name and bestow it upon her. In that instant, she knew she'd somehow succeeded, although she wasn't sure how it had happened.

"Truly now art thou *Rhunvala*," Kaledhol continued. "Yet not without price is thy privilege. For the rest of thy life, vital to thee and thy survival shall the ash of blood-rose be. And difficult still is the task that awaits thee."

She nodded, still not daring to raise her gaze above the metal-shod black boots.

"Thy place in the southlands out of them is," He said. "To the Citadel shall one come, answers to seek and a sword to claim. This attempt, allowed he must be, although *Rhunvala* he is not and not bound to him by life-linked enchantments shall that sword be. If successful he is, with him thou must go."

Tilanne started to ask one of the many questions yammering in her mind – who was this man, why was he to be granted the chance at a sword if not *Rhunvala*, where would he go, why would she go with him, what would her purpose and mission be?

But before she could decide which of these to ask, before she could muster the courage to do so, Kaledhol was gone.

All of it was gone. The throne room, the city, all.

For a moment, her world was a blank and terrifying nothingness. She fought to escape it, bursting up with a cry.

Her surroundings were familiar. Her own room. Her own bed.

At the sound of her waking, startled cry, Kai Peredur rushed in from the outer chamber. His expression was a conflict between worry and pride. Upon seeing her sitting up, bewildered but alive, joy overtook both.

Something heavy rested across her lap. She looked down at the sheathed sword. Baleful Gaze. How much had been real? How much had been illusion, dream, or vision?

But as Peredur helped her up, she realized that it had *all* been real, the parts that mattered.

Kaledhol had accepted her. This sword's magic was now linked to her life. She had taken that final, ultimate step.

She was *Rhunvala*.

* * *

CHAPTER TWENTY-FIVE

Tilanne, although now *Rhunvala*, was still only flesh and blood, and the cost of her ordeal was a heavy one. She spent a long recovery confined to her bed, during which time she was slowly able to come to terms with what had happened to her.

The ritual itself had not been physically real . . . from the moment she'd passed through the blood-fall curtain, she had been in a place that was neither here nor there, a dream-realm. Her mind and soul had gone journeying, not her body.

Yet the hurts she had sustained while in that other-place were somehow transmitted to her flesh. She revived to find a bandage and poultice on her shoulder and the neat stitches of Physician Idran Denisse's work beneath, revived to the news that as a result of the basilisk's poison, her health would indeed be dependent on a concoction of ash of blood-rose for the rest of her life. Without it, she would rapidly sicken, and might even die.

Kais Peredur and Estaran, as well as Kinnon of the Scepter and Master Dael, had followed and observed her progress through the trial. They had been aware of the temptations she faced, witnessing her reactions to them and rejections of them. They had seen her confrontation with the basilisks in the pit, where the rosebush bloomed in its circle of flame.

They did not, however, know anything about the final vision, that of Govannisan, and Kaledhol.

"To thee the god directly did speak?" Kai Peredur asked when she told him what she had experienced. "Such things, I've heard, before and to others have happened. To myself, never."

She related the god's words in their entirety to the other Kais. A stranger, not *Rhunvala*, that would come to the Citadel for a sword, without the binding enchantment? A stranger that Tilanne would follow out of the southlands?

The scar on her shoulder faded to a paler scrawl against her skin. Physician Denisse showed her the making of the blood-rose powder, told her how she might best mix it with wine, and provided her with an ample supply.

Once again, it took her some time and considerable effort to regain her strength and fitness. She trained, she exercised, she learned to handle Baleful Gaze until she might have never used any other sword.

"Not only immune to the stare of the basilisk does it render thee immune," Kinnon told her, "but against any similar attack or spell, be it by basilisk, mage or other means derived. The power it also has to a living being to solid stone transform, or like enchantments to undo."

Master Dael choked down the last of his protests now that she was in fact and undeniably a Kai. He might never like her, but he saw to it that she was properly outfitted. The armor he presented her with was at once functional and breathtaking . . . blackmetal and truesteel, with designs of basilisks and thorned roses. Her helmet was blackmetal as well, with a silver basilisk crouching on the crest.

"Restless thou art," Peredur said one night, rolling up on his elbow beside her. His hair was a darkish-silver tousle, sweat-damp around his brow, and his bare chest gleamed in the firelight.

Tilanne looked up at him, smiling. "Restless? Exhausted am I. Pleasantly so, to thy credit, but exhausted all the same."

They had not gone to any effort to conceal their status as lovers, though neither had they made any great announcement of it. Most seemed to regard it with mixed feelings – much as Tilanne herself did. Happiness for them, but also concern, and resignation, and sorrow. They could love, but they could not marry.

She wondered what Idrasanna Denisse would have had to say on the subject. But Idrasanna was gone, gone away to the human lands with her two youngest sons. The winemaker and the *Dhanvala*. Foreseen . . . was that not the word she'd used? Had Idrasanna been given a vision, a message, like Tilanne had?

Peredur's fingertip caressed the curve of her ear. "Entirely?"

"Mmm," she said, stretching, stirring like a lazy pantera. "Perhaps not *entirely* exhausted am I after all."

"And when together like this we are, content dost thou seem. Other times, though, noticed have I thy restlessness."

"A feeling I have." She rolled her head, bringing her other ear within his reach. "A gathering sense, like the air before a storm, within me builds. Someday, and soon, leave here I must."

He nodded. "Thy place in the southlands out of them is."

"But when am I to go? Where am I to go? North to the Emerin? Into the den of the Mountain King? West into the human realms as went thy mother and brothers?"

"Not into the Mountain Kingdom should any of us go alone."

"His plan for me, His purpose, what are they? Needed here, I am not."

"Always –"

"New Kors there are that thy teaching and Estaran's need. No longer thy student am I." She slid close to him and kissed his warm skin.

"In such matters as this," he said, running his hand down her back, "not much my student at all . . . and at times, my teacher."

Later, when conversation could resume, she said, "Thought have I that for a time, away from the Citadel I might go. *Rhunvala* am I now, and as *Rhunvala* do so should I do."

"What of the stranger for whom thou were told to wait?"

"Come he will, come he must, if Kaledhol's will it is. And in the meanwhile, Peredur . . . if truly the southlands I am to leave, if truly my destiny beyond our borders lies . . . my farewells I should say. My sister I should visit, and my old friends."

"Those at Jewelgreen?"

"Who first in me had faith, and believed that this course I could pursue, yes. Although over the years some messages there've been, some letters sent and received, the same it is not as seeing, as speaking."

"And they should in their faith and support rewarded be," he said, lifting her hand to his lips and kissing the knuckles, the fingertips. "When behold they do this Kai Tilanne, what a delight and a vindication to them it will be. What of thy past lover? What of Jedriel?"

Tilanne exhaled and burrowed her forehead against Peredur's neck. "Difficult will it be. My final and greatest temptation in the ritual, thou didst witness."

He stroked her hair. "A sensible husband he'd make for thee."

"Indeed, and yet . . . no husband at all am I to have, Peredur. No children. How could I? First and foremost, my duties as Kai must I uphold. Have I all this time and training undergone, that I in pregnancy my life should risk? To battle I could not gravid go and an unborn babe endanger. Armor would fit me not. To run and fight I'd not be able, not for two years or more. No . . . never am I children to have . . . and so, never husband should I take, either. Unfair to such a husband would it be." She closed her eyes and gave a soft, mournful sigh, rolling onto her back.

Peredur leaned over her. He pressed a tender kiss to each closed eyelid, then to her lips. "Perhaps not so bleak as all that may it be . . . say not *never*, Tilanne. Sacrifices our god doth require, but not so ungenerous is He that all our heart's desires He would from us withhold. Thy time for motherhood may yet come. Abandon not that hope."

She wished she could take more comfort from his words, but her heart still felt hollow whenever she saw Leiata Kelda playing with her infant daughter. There would soon be a wedding at the *Odan Rhunvale*, as well . . . Kor Hollisian had brought his sister along, and demure Lissia had broken Ordan Quaide's lifelong devotion to bachelorhood. Happy though she was for them, Tilanne could not entirely escape a glimmer of melancholy envy.

Savillan planned to lead a spring trade expedition, to replenish the Citadel's supplies and exchange news with neighboring settlements. Tilanne elected to ride along with his company rather than set out alone. Preparations were made, and on a fine morning when the air was redolent with the sweet scent of blossoms, they were ready to set out.

"Sorely missed thou'll be," Peredur said, holding her close. "By me most of all, but not by me alone."

"And thee most of all, I'll miss . . . but not thee alone. Return soon I shall. Here must I be when this foretold stranger arrives."

"Fare thee well, Tilanne. Kaledhol with thee go."

Faithful Morai had died long ago, but the good mare had left behind a foal – sired by Peredur's stallion, as it happened – that had grown into a steed every bit as worthy. Khian was likewise black, but named for the white blaze like a comet on her forehead. Tilanne swung astride, rather amazed that she was actually leaving the valley that had become her true home. Aside from a few brief forays into the forest and surrounding mountains, she had not been away from the Citadel since she'd arrived, all those years ago.

She could barely remember the unsure girl she'd been when making that first dark, lonely, frightened journey. That seemed a different Tilanne altogether. She had come not knowing what she would find at the end. Not knowing if she would be welcomed and accepted and allowed to stay, or turned back in disgrace. Her future had been a murky mystery then, a churning night-river along which she'd been swept like a passenger in a tiny boat. Unable to see ahead, only able to hold on for dear life and pray.

They rode out, and up one of the spiraling wooden ways to a high tree-bridge, half a dozen men and horses, and ponies laden with goods. Savillan was as merry and good-natured as ever, and insisted on filling their travels with songs, bright conversation and laughter. But even in the midst of their cheerful fellowship, they were on their guard.

Following the failed assaults on the Citadel and the Valley of the Moonglow, the Mountain King had made no recent moves against them. This was not as reassuring as it should have been. None of them could forget what they'd learned. He had human wizards now, these mages of Hramad, allies with an even greater hatred for the elves. Those mages might be using this time of quiet to work enchantments that would make the invading armies even stronger. The Mountain King also had his elfkin whelp, and might simply be waiting for Durvanian to be grown enough to strike against them himself.

Whatever the reason, Savillan's expedition was a peaceful and uneventful success. Tilanne traveled with them as far as the Valley of the Cloudflowers, where she visited with Physician Denisse. He received word on occasion from his mother and brothers, still away in the Northlands. They were, Idran told her, fine and well . . . having befriended some elves in Thanis. If he knew what Idrasanna hoped to accomplish there, and what possible role the human realms could play in the future of their race, he did not say.

From there, she retraced the route she'd taken, passing through the same settlements she had passed through before. She did not come as such a great surprise to them now . . . word of the only female *Rhunvala* had spread, her reputation preceding her.

Those who'd seen her before, though, were startled to recognize her now. Tilanne realized that she had changed far more than most over the span of years. There was a maturity in her features now that had been lacking when she'd left Jewelgreen. The soft roundness of girlhood and troubled innocence had been carved from her face. Sometimes, when she peered into the reflection of her own amethyst eyes, she saw depths in them that even she did not know.

Before, she had mostly met suspicion and disapproval as she'd traversed the southlands. Many people thought that she must be mad, she *had* to be mad. A girl, wanting to become *Rhunvala*? A girl, learning to fight with sword and shield? What was the world coming to? Women did not belong on the battlefield. Not that they should be helpless . . . no . . . they should readily be able to take up weapons to defend their homes and families if need be. But for a woman to deliberately place herself in harm's way?

Now, if the suspicion and disapproval were still there, they'd been well masked. Who would ever criticize a *Rhunvala?* Even a female one? That would be like contradicting Kaledhol Himself! Instead, and more troubling, she found awe. Awe of the very sort Kai Peredur had counseled her against.

She was still Tilanne, not to be held in awe by anyone. Respected, if respect was deserved. Not revered.

The blush of spring had given way to late summer's golden warmth as Tilanne came to the Valley of the Jewelgreen. She stayed the night at the eastern fort, and rode down into the valley itself the next day.

* * *

CHAPTER TWENTY-SIX

With the town in sight, a nervousness descended over her. Faces and names and voices flitted through her mind. The friends she had left . . . friends close as family after they'd fled the destruction of Cliffcave together. After they'd struggled and suffered and fought for their lives. She had led them here. It was a wonder any of them had survived at all, she knew. A wonder that so few of them had died along the way. Yet knowing that did not help. She still felt each loss and each failure keenly.

Was she ready to see them again? Ready to hear what had become of them?

She rode on, through lush farmland and orchards. They saw her from far off, and long before she reached the walls, she had collected an enthusiastic crowd. The day's work was abandoned without a second thought. Khian pranced and stomped in displeasure at the cluster of excited folk, the babble of their voices as they exclaimed and queried and called out.

"Calm, for Kaledhol's sake, be calm!" Renveil shouted above the din, as the impromptu procession made its way through the gates. But for his lack of teeth and a slight crookedness to his jaw, which never had set properly after being shattered, the undercaptain was unchanged. As rangy and keen of eye as ever, his white-blond hair still worn in its customary long single plait.

They settled down, a sea of expectant and eager faces turned up. Through a shimmer of joyful tears she tried to hold back, she saw more familiarity and friendliness than awe. They were pleased for her, proud of her. They did not come to her applauding and cheering, as she'd seen in the temptation of her trial. She was still Tilanne to them.

The town was unchanged as well, still with its stone walls and concentric circles of avenues. She saw the bath-house, the lodging that had been hers, the garrison. Just as it had been in her memories, in her dreams. This place that could have been her home. She could have been happy here, raised children here. A doleful note of what-might-have-beens shadowed her joy.

She saw Reshelli, grinning widely. Reshelli, still holding her trusty spear but also wearing the uniform of a guard! She saw Olithiana, who must have finished mourning Carenar and gone on to snare Captain Bairdan . . . they were arm in arm, and Olithiana's hand rested on the proud swell of a pregnant belly. There was Deverall, who stood so close to an unfamiliar but handsome young soldier that Tilanne instantly knew the *chani* crafter had found love and happiness of his own. And there, Vennan the huntsman, looking tanned and rugged and happy.

Could that lovely creature be little Ninare? Ninare, grown and preening and surrounded by attentive young men? And surely that wasn't Hastinar, who had been such a small and scrawny boy, towering a full head's height over Thoranian?

In the midst of the throng, she dismounted and found herself before a plump, round-faced woman with blue-and-gold star-shapes tattooed at her temples. Tilanne had to look twice before she gasped in recognition.

"Alarice?"

Laughing, Alarice threw her arms around Tilanne, then let go of her at once. "Thy armor against these matronly curves of mine hard and uncomfortable is, Kai Tilanne!"

"Matronly . . . so, married art thou?"

"And two children have," Alarice said. A stout toddler with chubby cheeks clung to her skirt, his thumb corked in his mouth. She patted his light-brown curls. "Alaric, my son, this is. And Corice, my daughter, is this year *ten*! Believe it, canst thou? Ten!"

"Corice?" Tilanne echoed. "Thou didst . . . surely thou didst not . . . didst thou *Corandir* marry?"

She dimpled. "Even he. Lieutenant to thy old friend Commander Ellorn he is, at the western fortress. How glad he'll be when word of thy arrival he hears! To stay, hast thou come?"

"No," she said, not without regret. "A visit only this is. To Deepwater next I'll go, but then back from whence I came. To the *Odan Rhunvale* must I return."

"And true, then, it is? Kai Tilanne thou art? *Rhunvala*, thou art?"

"*Rhunvala* I am," Tilanne said. "But Alarice, what news? Ilantisian, I see not . . . what of him? And what of –"

She felt a timid touch on her arm, looked down to see a small hand. Its owner gazed up at her, obsidian eyes framed in a tumble of red-gold ringlets. Jedina's mouth made a tremulous bow of a smile.

"As ever I imagined," Jedina said, "so thou art. Oh, Tilanne!"

They embraced, Tilanne mindful not to crush the slim young maiden against her armor. Jedina was no longer frail, but had a delicate and ethereal quality to her that suggested she might break under even a mild blow. Her tunic was streaked and spotted with paint, and there were charcoal smudges on her forehead and chin. Proof that she had kept up her artist's ways.

"Well met, Jedina," Tilanne said. "Where is thy . . . ?"

She saw him then, a few paces behind Jedina, and that last word went unsaid. Jedriel stood with a curled hand pressed to the base of his throat and his eyes, his dark, dark shining eyes, fixed on her as if he could hardly believe what he beheld. As if he thought she might vanish like a dream upon waking.

"Tilanne," he said.

The crowd that had been gathered around melted back in a wide ring, with hushed whispers and held breath. Jedriel moved through them as if oblivious to their presence, stopping arm's length from Tilanne.

"Jedriel."

"Even more beautiful than ever art thou," he said. "Beautiful and fierce as a dragoness, garbed all in night and fire."

The poetry of his words and the softness of his tone filled Tilanne's heart with love and remorse. In that moment she wanted nothing more than to go to him, put her arms about him, hold him as tightly as she could. To forget the rest. To forget the world. Here he was, her gentle scribe with his skin unmarked by battle-scars, his hands not callused by a sword hilt or arrow string.

She restrained herself, except to step toward him and extend a hand. Jedriel clasped it, and squeezed it firmly. His eyes never left hers.

"So pleased am I to see thee, Jedriel." She could not tell him what she had to say, not now, not here, not in front of all the town. Not when it would hurt him and dim the hopeful light she could see in his dark eyes.

Alarice had been looking closely at her, and Jedriel, at the both of them. She stirred, and smacked her hands together in a brisk attention-getting clap. "Let us not like statues stand about," she said. "Kai Tilanne to us is returned . . . let us a celebration prepare! A lodging she'll need, and for her horse stabling, and word must to Commander Ellorn be sent . . ." Issuing orders like any general, she bustled through the crowd, dispersing them.

Tilanne turned Khian over to Deverall's handsome young soldier, Erim. Her belongings were unpacked and settled in a vacant lodging. Alarice whisked her off to the bath-house, just the two of them, while others went about arranging a welcoming feast.

As she stripped off her armor and relaxed into the steaming water, Tilanne saw Alarice gawking at her.

"When Jewelgreen thou didst leave," she said, "already uncommon fit and strong thou were. Now I look on thee and . . . thy limbs so taut with muscle, thy balance like a cat's, thy movements . . . a formidable warrior must thou be, Tilanne." She regarded her own ample figure and laughed. "Whilst I, a great soft butter-pastry have become. Thankful am I that with my magic it interferes not, and that Corandir most happy with me is."

"Thee and Corandir," Tilanne said, shaking her head. "Never such would I have guessed. Still apprenticed art thou, or hast thou fully thy rank attained?"

"Alarice of the Scepter am I now, indeed." Her smile faded. "Asked me earlier for news thou didst . . . Tilanne, died eight winters ago did Ilantisian and Falana. *Kholi* fever through the valley swept, and several lives it claimed. Sahen dead as well is, by humans in the mountains slain."

They talked for a while more of what had gone on in Jewelgreen since Tilanne's departure, and then as they dried themselves in front of the air-spouting dragons, Alarice asked about the *Odan Rhunvale*.

"Splendid is it? Do many *Rhunvala* there dwell?"

"Only with poor and inadequate words couldst I the Citadel describe," Tilanne said.

Still, she did her best, not only then but after they'd dressed and joined the rest of Jewelgreen at the feast. Everyone was filled with questions. Tilanne answered those she could, demurred on those she did not feel right in answering, and talked until her voice had gone hoarse no matter how many goblets of rich indigo wine she drank.

At last, though, the celebration came to an end. If Alarice had arranged it, or it had just happened by chance, Tilanne was left alone with Jedriel. Even Jedina had slipped away. The two of them had the dark avenue to themselves, the guards above on the walls mere silent shadows against the night.

They walked without speaking for a while, walked until they had come to a low stone wall curving around a tree. Here, they sat, and she was conscious of his gaze upon her. Of the longing, and the sadness, in it.

"Love thee still, I do, Tilanne," he said. "Hoped had I that when completed was thy training . . ."

She covered his hand with hers. "That return I would and thy wife become, thy children bear? Thought . . . *hoped* for that too had I. Such a precious life would it have been, Jedriel! Such a precious life was I offered . . . shown to me it was, a vision, the fine son and dear daughters that our own family could have been. But . . . turned from it I did. Turned from it, I had to."

"Why?" he asked. In that one single word, she heard untold desolation.

"In birthing, do many of our women die," she said, gazing off across the quiet town. "In battle, do many of our *Rhunvala*. I, in both being, must both fates beware. If in battle I died, my children would be of a mother deprived. If in childbed I died, my people would be of a *Rhunvala* deprived."

"And greater, for our people far greater, the need for *Rhunvala* is," he said. He did understand, she could hear it, but she could also hear how devoutly he wished that it was not so. "Is there never to be marriage or children for thee?"

"To say *never*, am I not," she said, thinking of Peredur with a sharp, wistful pang. "Now? No. Someday? Perhaps, if Kaledhol's will it is."

"Yet more there is," Jedriel said, touching her cheek to turn her toward him. "More there is that said thou've not. The ruby-rose earrings I gave thee, still in thy lovely lobes are worn . . . but thy manner changed is."

"Long years apart we were, Jedriel. Much in such time might occur –"

She was *Rhunvala*, supposed to be brave, supposed to be strong, but she would have rather stared into the eyes of a hundred basilisks than see the comprehension and pain unfolding on his face.

"Tilanne, if to some other thy heart is pledged . . ." He swallowed, and took a deep breath. "Thou wouldst tell me, wouldst thou not?"

"Pledged am I to no one," she said. "Excepting Kaledhol Himself. But yes, Jedriel, yes, another there is. Though love thee I do, love him do I as well. Torn am I. The both of thee I love . . . and neither of thee can I have."

Jedriel put his arms around her, and they held each other with their brows pressed together. The thin fire-gold braids falling forward from his temples brushed against the sable sheaves of her hair.

*   *   *

Chapter Twenty-Seven

Tilanne stayed in Jewelgreen for most of a full cycle of the dark moon, but knew that if she did not leave before autumn, she would be tempted to winter there. And if she wintered there, she would want to stay longer . . . and then might never be able to leave.

It seemed that Jedina, in particular, had come to a similar conclusion and was determined to do everything within her power to convince Tilanne to delay leaving. Jedriel might understand, but his daughter would not listen. To Jedina, it was simple enough – they loved each other, and they should marry. They should have children. Tilanne should stay in Jewelgreen and be her stepmother. And they would all be happy. No one, not Alarice or even Jedriel, or Tilanne herself, could explain the situation in a way she would accept.

"When did she so willful become?" Tilanne asked Reshelli, after Jedina stomped off with her ringlets bouncing.

"A meek and beaten-down thing before she was, to be sure," Reshelli said, leaning on her spear. "When freed her thou didst from that brute Jedren, freed her as well from meekness didst thou. Thy own fault it is, Kai Tilanne."

At least she never had to worry about reverence from Reshelli.

The nearest settlement to Jewelgreen was the Valley of the Growing Vines, where a road led first to Opal Vale and then over Deepwater Pass to Deepwater itself, the town where Tilanne had grown up. The town where her sister still lived, and her nieces and nephews.

Unlike other settlements, where the buildings were clustered together at a single defensive core, the entire vast expanse Valley of the Growing Vines was surrounded by and dotted with individual farmhouses and wineries. The vineyards themselves were row upon row of grapevines climbing on stakes in the earth. Their leaves were varying shades of green, speckled with plump grapes of white, lavender, blue, violet, and dusty plum-black.

Tilanne guided Khian carefully until she found a trail wide enough to admit the horse. Twin ruts, left by the wheels of small carts, marked the rich soil. Riding through the vines was oddly like wading Khian through deep green water. The vines rose almost to the horse's haunches.

Elves, and slaves both human and orcish, moved through the fields picking the ripe fruits and filling the cart-baskets with their bounty. They all turned to stare at Tilanne, whose presence could hardly go unnoticed. When the elves got closer looks at her, at this solitary red-cloaked and black-armored rider passing by, she saw their jaws drop in unfeigned astonishment. Apparently, rumors of a female *Rhunvala* had not reached this more remote and rustic part of the southlands . . . or not been taken seriously.

Tilanne had thought she was fairly familiar with the many varieties of wine, but even so, her night's lodging at one of the winery farmhouses proved a treat. She was invited to sample several vintages she'd never tried before, and she had never eaten such a meal. Tender, delicately seasoned pheasants had been stuffed with grapes and wrapped in the large flat grape leaves, then slowly roasted until the meat nearly melted off the bone

In the morning, her hosts provided her with a full skin of wine, as well as a pouch of dried grapes that were flavorful and tart but so chewy they threatened to pull the teeth from her head. She thanked them and set out, on the road that led to Opal Vale.

The road took Tilanne high into the mountains, so high that some were topped with snow even now in late autumn. She saw gorges where narrow falls spilled plunging into churning ponds, whitecaps frothed around boulders, wreaths of mist caught rainbows in the air, and rivers ran in twinkling ribbons of water far below. She crossed bridges made by the combined effort of masonry and magic, some held up by tall pillars, some guarded by towers that looked too fragile to be made of stone.

Opal Vale was a mining town, rich with veins of silver, truesilver, and the black opals that the High Mages used for fashioning their *ilgileani*. The mountainsides around the town were honey-combed with shafts and tunnels. Scaffolds and ladders gave access to the openings of the various mines.

Tilanne knew that the most notable feature of all would be found at the center of town. There, a single black opal rose from the earth in a smooth, flattish bulge. Five elves with hands linked would have been needed to encircle it. According to the stories she'd heard, this black opal was a natural *ilgilean*, holding a concentration of magical energy that any elf could draw upon to work his or her spells. The first settlers had not dared try to move or mine this wonder, but built their town around it instead. Where a temple or fountain might have been in a more traditionally-designed settlement, here there was the black opal.

Opal Vale was home to two *Rhunvala*, Kai Farlan and Kai Aldevor. Tilanne had met Farlan once, several years before, when he'd paid a visit to the *Odan Rhunvale*. He was a gruff man in his fifth century, whose calling had come to him late in life when he already had a devoted wife and family. Aldevor was younger and hot-tempered, a high-blooded and lusty sort. Unmarried, he was a great favorite among the local women and quite a lot of the youngsters in town seemed to share his distinct hue of foxpelt-auburn hair.

"Orcs there are in the mountains, orcs in abundance," Kai Farlan told Tilanne over their evening meal. "And humans, as well . . . more than ever. Deserters and criminals from the Northlands they are. The war they flee, and think to in the Mountain Kingdom their refuge seek."

"But, for the mines, a bonus it is," Kai Aldevor said, lounging in his seat and swirling a glass of brandy. "Slaves aplenty we have. As many as needed there are, and more. If to the death they are worked, easy enough are they to replace."

She did see a slave train, which was being brought in as she was leaving Opal Vale. Orcs and humans, a chained shuffling line of them, perhaps thirty in all. They were filthy, stinking, and bloodied from beatings they'd been given by their brutish overseers – a trio of especially large and surly orcs, more than willing to abuse their own kind in exchange for favor from their elven masters.

At her approach, the slaves were ordered aside and out of her way by the elf in charge. He, a lithe man with a shock of brown hair and a couple of fingers missing from one hand, inclined his head to her as she passed.

Humans. Humans here in the *Morvalan* lands. She did not like that, had never liked it, would never get used to it. Yes, they had some value and usefulness as slaves, as beasts of burden fit for menial labor . . . but it was too easy to imagine them rising up in revolt. She remembered Carenar, whose orcish charges had hated him all the more for his magical hold over them. They had killed him as soon as they'd had a chance.

One of the humans, a grotesque hairy creature that looked like the result of a union between man and goat – with humans, she supposed it wasn't unlikely – openly ogled Tilanne as she rode by. He said something to his nearest neighbor, and although she did not hear the words, there was no mistaking the suggestive tone, or the lewd laughter that greeted his remark.

She reined in at once and pierced him with a glare. Those around him quailed and looked away, but the goat-man's leer did not vanish. If anything, it intensified. He made a crude gesture with his tongue, waggling it at her.

The brown-haired elf was there in three quick strides, and struck the man backhand across the face. Spitting and growling in the ugly Northlands speech, he said, "How dare you so much as look at her, you dog? I'll cut that tongue out and the eyes from your head."

"A better idea have I," Tilanne said. She drew Baleful Gaze.

As the black blade slid free, the goat-man flinched. He masked it almost at once – she had to credit him with that; he was bold, for all he was a fool – and stood defiantly as the men to either side of him strained as far away as their chains would allow.

The elf stepped back, deferential. The three overseers stared, eager to see blood, their heavy whips dangling.

"Go on, then, point-eared bitch," the goat-man said. "Kill me. Go on!"

"To kill you where you stand," Tilanne said, speaking slowly and clearly as she made her mouth form the ugly sounds, "would be no great matter. Nothing but the slaying of a rat that the bar of a trap did not break. But you are worse vermin than any rat. Death is too clean for you, and even slavery would be a generous fate."

She held the sword above his head. He tensed. She could read in his expression how he was trying to brace himself for the feel of that blackmetal edge shearing through scalp and then skull, and then cleaving into the soft brain beneath and ending his wretched human life. When she tapped him with the flat of the blade instead, a smart rap like that of a parent disciplining a disobedient child, his features twisted with shock and surprise.

And just as many a parent had warned their child not to make such horrid faces, lest they got stuck that way . . . his did. His face, open-mouthed gape and bulging eyes and all, froze. So did his body. He solidified, with a crackling, grinding sound as of gravel underfoot, into stone. Clothing and all, a perfect stone likeness wrapped all in chains.

Yelps burst from the other men. They fell all over each other with a clashing jangle of chains as they tried to flee. The overseers scrambled to get them back in order and in line, while their brown-haired master looked up at Tilanne, grinning and impressed.

"What wouldst thou have with this new statue of thine be done, *Rhunvala*?"

"As a lesson and reminder to these other slaves let it be kept," she said.

"At the entrance to the mine, we'll place it," he said.

The humans and orcs, unable to understand their speech, cowered together like sheep before a thunderstorm. They eyed Tilanne with skittering glances, as if each feared he might be next.

As she rode on, she looked back and saw with satisfaction and amusement that the rest of the slaves were now additionally burdened by carrying the heavy, cumbersome stone body of their former companion. If they dropped him, he would likely break apart. Given how clumsily they were handling him . . .

Tilanne laughed, and urged Khian into a burst of speed.

* * *

CHAPTER TWENTY-EIGHT

She reached Deepwater three days later, after spending her nights in a succession of way-houses. When at last she saw the perfectly round and mirror-flat lake, and the town with its buildings set along and often carved into the sheer stone walls of the cliff around it, she felt her spirits leap.

There were boats out on the water, their oars dipping and rising to the rhythm of drumbeats that floated dimly to her ears. Perhaps the wyrm-singer was out there, communing with the dragon that lived in the seemingly fathomless depths. Perhaps fishermen were bringing in their full nets. She thought of the taste of fresh deepfish, and shivered with the memory.

This last span of road was precipitous, descending the cliff in a wide sweeping curve. To one side, the rock face rose up to the skies. To the other, it dropped away straight down.

Dusk had fallen by the time she reached the gates. She had watched as one after another window twinkled into light, like fireflies emerging from the evening shade. She saw a sliver of the white moon rippling on the lake, saw the white-fire etching of one of Denethel's arrows streak across the reflected black pool of sky.

"Who goes?" a young but proud voice rang out.

Tilanne reined in and dismounted. She pulled off her helm and hung it from her saddle, then stepped into a fall of torchlight. Her armor gleamed. Above her, leaning out to scrutinize her, was a young squire-general. By the stiff and self-important way he carried himself, he was obviously still new to the rank.

"Kai Tilanne am I," she said.

"Tilanne? Didst thou say that *Tilanne* thy name is?"

He leaned further out, so far he was at risk of toppling from the wall, and in the inquisitive tilt of his head and his cloud-grey eyes, Tilanne knew him.

"Darantil? Nephew?" She had not seen him in a score of years or more, but Forana had that exact way of tipping her head when she was sure she had misheard something. "Dost thou not thine own aunt remember?"

"Aunt Tilanne . . . *Kai* Tilanne? 'Tis true, then? Heard had we that to the *Odan Rhunvale* thou'd gone, but hard was it to believe . . ."

"Yet true it is." She spread her hands and shrugged. "Completed is my training, hoped did I my kin to visit, and so here at Deepwater I am. If thou'll the gate open . . . ?"

Others had come out, hearing this exchange, and in a matter of moments the gate had been opened to let her lead Khian through. Darantil, all but dancing in place the way she had seen him doing when asked if he wanted a candy, grasped her hands and shook them with enthusiasm.

"*Rhunvala!*" he cried. "My aunt, my mother's sister, *Rhunvala* is! Mother overjoyed to see thee will be." He then visibly remembered that he was a soldier now, expected to conduct himself with some measure of control. He coughed and self-consciously smoothed his newly shorn hair. "To escort thee, Kai, honored would I be."

"I thee thank." She matched his grave tone, hiding her smile. She needed no escort to make her way around Deepwater.

He led her, puffed with pride and importance, through town. They drew many a look, and Darantil paused to tell anyone and everyone he saw that his aunt, the *Rhunvala*, was come home. She could no longer hide the smile, though by now was more than a little embarrassed by all the fuss.

"Darantil," she said, "before dawn should I like my sister to greet. If not too much trouble for thee it is thy pace to quicken?"

"Oh. Oh, yes. This way our lodging is, Kai Tilanne."

The sight of the old familiar structure, with its sturdy stone walls, many narrow windows and rooftop garden, brought a lump to her throat. The smells of her mother's climbing lilac vines, good woodsmoke, and frying deepfish wrapped around her like a cloak of warm memory. She could hear the laughter of children, the fussy howls of an infant. The sounds swelled as Darantil opened the front door.

"A surprise I have for thee!" he called to the household at large.

Tilanne gasped as there was a thunder of small feet and two little girls rushed out. Two little girls, like those in her trial . . . her temptation . . .

Then she saw that they were not the same ones, not her daughters-that-might-have-been. These were older. They had Forana's grey eyes, Daran's honey-colored hair. Her nieces. They came to an abrupt halt as they beheld her. She saw their eyes go wide, and wondered what she must look like . . . this stranger, this tall, black-armored figure standing before them. Little hands came up to cover little round-shaped mouths.

A surge of protective love filled Tilanne. These were her sister's children . . . in them was the continuance of her family line. None of them would bear the Murres name, true, but Murres blood flowed in their veins. If she could not contribute to the continuance of that line, she could at least do all within her power to see these children grow up safe and strong.

Darantil had run to fetch his mother. Tilanne could hear him insisting she come and see what surprise he'd brought. Forana protested that she had to tend the baby, but her protests died on her lips as she emerged from another room and saw Tilanne.

"Forana . . . sister," Tilanne said.

"By Kaledhol!" Forana had frozen, eyes wide, mouth round and hands covering it, exactly like a larger version of her daughters. "Tilanne?"

"None other."

She could all but read Forana's confusion, her uncertainty. What was she to do in such an instance? Her sister, her last surviving sibling was here . . . she should go to her, greet her with an embrace! But her last surviving sibling . . . her *sister*, and her baby sister at that! . . . was *Rhunvala*. One did not just go about embracing a *Rhunvala*.

Tilanne removed the debate from her by moving toward Forana with open arms. She was careful, as careful as she'd been with Jedina, not wanting to crush or bruise her sister against the hard blackmetal corselet with her fierce grip.

After a stunned moment, Forana's arms came up to return the embrace. She patted tentatively at Tilanne's back at first, then burst into tears and they clung to each other, laughing and crying at the same time.

Then, as if satisfied this was the same Tilanne she'd always known and, despite the armor, nothing else had changed, Forana set her back and swept her with a critical look. She made a slight noise – *hmf!* – and said, "So . . . this is how thou wouldst dress?"

"Ever the elder sister art thou! Wouldst thou have me in long skirt and bodice ride to battle?"

"Mother!" Darantil looked mortified. "Kai Tilanne *Rhunvala* is!"

"*Rhunvala* thou art," Forana said, shaking her head. "What to say, I know not. Suits thee it does, I suppose. But happy dost it make thee?"

How like Forana to say such a thing. "Of course," Tilanne said. "No greater honor could there be, that so might I our people and our god serve."

"Yes . . . well . . ." A faint frown pursed her lips. "Still unmarried thou art?"

"Mother!"

How like Forana to say that, too. "Still unmarried I am."

"Surely some prospects must thou have?"

"Sister, please, thy patience I beg," Tilanne said, striving to sound light-hearted, although inwardly she was pained. "No matchmaking do I need."

"But as gone are our parents, to me the duty of finding thee a husband falls –"

Tilanne set her hand on Forana's shoulder. "Reasons there are that wed can I not. Later shall I all that to thee explain. For now, come have I thee and thy family to visit."

The still-tucked and dubious set of Forana's mouth told Tilanne that they were not yet through with this topic of discussion, not by a long way, but she was willing to let it go for now.

And to think, a time or two on her journey here, she been worried that her own sister might be in awe of her. Pah! So long as Forana was there to keep her in her place, Tilanne knew that she need never worry about becoming corrupted by her power and rank.

"These Anada and Vanti are," Forana said, introducing the girls once Tilanne's things had been brought in and unpacked in a spare room. "Danfor the youngest is, and finally napping so him I'll to thee later present."

Darantil had gone, very much against his will, back to his post at the gate. Tilanne suspected that only the knowledge he'd be able to tell all the other soldiers about his aunt the *Rhunvala* had made it worth his while. She winced at the thought.

"And Ordanna?" she asked. Forana's eldest daughter had been born not long before Tilanne had gone with their father and brother to Cliffcave.

"Married, she is."

The clipped, curt tone of Forana's voice made the skin on the back of Tilanne's neck prickle. She had been slicing vegetables, and the knife clacked down with such quick, violent chops that Tilanne was afraid for Forana's fingers.

"Ordanna, married already . . . yet pleased thou art not?"

"Not to Daran's and my choosing was he."

Tilanne was speechless. While it was not law carved in stone that an elfmaid had to wed as dictated by her parents, it was rare that one would openly defy them and marry against their wishes. It was just not done.

Then again, she reminded herself, as the only female *Rhunvala*, she was not much of a one to talk.

Seeing her askance look, Forana grimaced. "Agreed to it we had to, else fatherless the babe would have been."

That degree of rebellion was more than rare, moving into the realms of outright unheard-of. Tilanne was still speechless, and it was perhaps just as well, because she could not imagine what might have come out of her mouth. Surely, it would have been unfit for the children's tender ears to hear.

"And now estranged we are," Forana finished in a voice as bright, brittle and false as glass fruit. "Her husband an innkeep is."

"An innkeep?" Tilanne cudgeled her brain for understanding and it finally came. "Mean do you . . . a way-house for money, as in the *Alvalan* lands they have?" An even more startling thought struck her. "*Alvalan* he is not, is he?"

"No!" The denial was loud and sharp, a whipcrack. Then Forana sighed heavily, and turned to Tilanne with doleful, admitting eyes. "But *Alvalan* his mother is. Not fully of our land or of theirs is he. Along the Larenlan road to the north they live, with no settlement, no walls, no fortresses their home to defend."

"Has she of her senses taken complete *leave?*" Tilanne shook her head. "Believe it I cannot, sister. Believe it I simply cannot."

"Tried did we to convince her this folly to reconsider," Forana said. She abandoned her kitchen-work, and sank down at the table with her elbows on it and her head in her hands. "Even offered did we, Daran and I, that here with us they might dwell."

Tilanne made a murmur of sympathy, knowing what such an offer must have cost her proud sister. To not only let her eldest daughter force them into accepting a marriage with some half-*Alvalan* innkeeper, but to take him into their house? At the same time, however, she understood why Ordanna and this still-nameless husband of hers had refused.

"Listen to us would she not," Forana continued. "Off with him she went. Beyond our borders and in the middle of a war to this *inn* of his she went, and my own grandchild have I never seen!"

Forana was seized by a storm of tears that brought her daughters on the run, seeking in vain to comfort her. Tilanne did her best to help, but what was there that she could do? It tore at her to see this rift in her family. They were all she had left . . . the only family she would ever have. As strange as it was to think of her sister as a grandmother, she could not stand back and do nothing while Ordanna broke her parents' heart.

"Perhaps to me she'd listen," Tilanne said.

Sniffling, Forana raised her wet-eyed face to look at Tilanne with a mixture of hope, appeal and doubt. "To thee? When thou hast of thy own accord against all convention gone?"

"But by Kaledhol led, not by rebellion and whim. At the very least, some effort at reconciliation would it be. To Ordanna I'll go, sister. My promise thou hast."

* * *

CHAPTER TWENTY-NINE

"Knew did I that my place in the southlands outside them was to be," Tilanne said, her tone light to offset the unease that was trying to gain a foothold on her nerves. "But never did I think that so soon that destiny would come."

She spoke to no one but Khian and Kaledhol, and the imposing northern forests.

Her nephew had begged to accompany her, but Forana would have none of it. See another of her precious offspring leave the safety of the *Morvalan* lands for the perils and mysteries of the north? No. No, not ever, not unless he wanted to slay his own mother dead as surely if he had stuck a dagger in her heart. Or so she had proclaimed, loudly, tearfully and at length.

Daran, his father, had not carried on in such an emotional – and, to Darantil, hideously embarrassing – way. But he had insisted that the young squire-general still had too much to learn about soldiering. Darantil's arguments that he could have no better teacher than a *Rhunvala* failed to bend his father's will.

As for Tilanne herself, she was just as glad to be going alone. This was challenging enough, daunting enough, and she did not want to seek to protect and reunite her sister's family by leading another of them off into danger.

When Darantil hinted that he could sneak away from his post with his parents none the wiser, she told him in no uncertain terms that if he did, she would return him to Deepwater bound and gagged and slung over her saddle.

From whence had sprung this contrary streak in her sister's children? Certainly none of her siblings had been like that when they were young. Even she, with her own departure from what was expected of a woman, was not because of her own willful doing. She was as shocked by

Ordanna's defiance and Darantil's rebellion as were their parents.

Yet neither did it seem to come from Daran's side of the family, all of whom were as steady and traditional and firm as the very mountains themselves.

Once she was there, the vague border realm between the southland and the Emerin did not seem all that frightening and unknown. It certainly far less dark, ominous, deadly and strange than the Forest of the Wandering Lost had been. These were . . . woods. Tall, green, and silent but for the ordinary sounds of nature making ready for winter.

She knew that somewhere ahead, somewhere to the north, would be the River Farelin and the Emerinian town of Larenlan. Not that she intended to go that far, no. The dividing line between the *Morvalan* and the *Alvalan* might not be so clear and so sharp as most elves believed or wished it to be, but even if traders and travelers from the south did occasionally venture to Larenlan, she could not imagine that a *Rhunvala* riding boldly in would be met with any sort of a friendly welcome.

Still, it would be well for the *Morvalan* to become better acquainted with their northern kin. Selfish and spoiled and flighty though those northern kin were . . . they were still elves. If ever they were to succeed in eradicating the Mountain Kingdom and the greater threat of humanity as a whole, they should ally.

Yes, she understood the good of such an alliance. She just . . . just did not much care for the idea of her own niece out here at the forefront of it. Married to a man who, if not entirely *Alvalan*, certainly seemed to have their leanings. How else could he have convinced a good, dutiful girl like Ordanna to put her own wishes before those of her family, or the good of the Cause?

If everyone did that, went around pursuing their own desires above all else, their society would fall apart. Everyone had his or her part to play, the way Kaledhol wanted and demanded it to be. Should they disregard that, it would be the downfall of the *Morvalan*.

When she camped, it felt strange to know that there was no surrounding defensive ring of mountains. She felt open, exposed. She was far beyond her home now, seeing places that few of her people had ever seen – and fewer still would ever want to. But the night sounds of the forest were much the same, and the winking stars seen through the high leaves were in their familiar patterns, and Tilanne slept well despite her unease.

She woke one day to a soft, cold morning, the air filled with moisture that was almost more mist than rainfall. It dampened her without ever really seeming to form drops. She found it revitalizing at first, but it palled as the day went on. By the time a cloudy, premature dusk descended, she was beginning to think that this inn must be all the way to Larenlan after all.

Her every sense came to sudden full wariness. Khian's ears flicked and the mare nickered, feeling it too. They were no longer alone. She slowed the mare to a walk.

There was a strange scent in the air, a scent she couldn't identify, absorbed by the mist almost before she could detect it. For some reason, she thought Master Dael scoffing that this was no fit rank for a woman . . .

Master Dael. The forges. Hot metal. Oil and smoke. That was what she smelled. But how could it be? Those scents, out here in the forest and far from any town, settlement, fortress or smithy?

Tilanne dismounted, walking ahead of Khian as she led the mare by the reins. She slid her shield onto her arm, and kept her other hand near the hilt of Baleful Gaze.

The road ahead . . . something was wrong, different, amiss. The earth there looked lumpy, recently turned. The scattering of leaves and twigs was too precise to be natural. Vennan had told her stories about how Lenaisian elves could trap a wolf, bear or even a pantera, Tilanne drew her sword and bent to prod at the disturbance.

She expected the tip of the blade to find a taut canvas or square of leather, but instead, it grated against metal.

A low, odd sound – *proing!* – came from somewhere off in the trees, and on its heels was a whickering *whish!* Something silvery and blurred swept over Tilanne, just above Khian's head and so close it riffled the mare's mane.

Although she didn't know who had put it there – this was no Lenaisian pantera-trap – or how, she divined its purpose. A scything blade, triggered by the metal plate buried in the road. Had she been in the saddle, it would have struck her in the back and removed everything from the shoulderblades up in one devastating swipe.

"*Chun'dakta!*" The voice was a coarse, rumbling bark, like someone speaking while chewing gravel.

Tilanne was so shocked at hearing the dwarven speech that it took her a moment to translate the oath. Then she wished she hadn't. Some things were best left untranslated.

What she heard next was less execrable, vile and obscene. But not much more welcoming. She turned around, sword in hand.

"Stupid leaf-eared stick insect! Look what you've done! Now I have to winch it back to its proper position."

The source of the gravel-filled voice was indeed a dwarf. The top of his shiny bald head came only as high as Tilanne's chest, but he was as wide as three of her standing side by side. To make up for the lack on his scalp, his beard began high on his cheeks and fell in well-groomed waves all the way to his belt buckle. That well-tended beard was the color of iron, blending in with the mail shirt he wore. A mace was thrust through his belt and the handle of a pick stuck up over his shoulder. His eyes, like pyrite-flecked chunks of ore, glittered at her meanly from beneath a single eyebrow that resembled a bristly grey caterpillar.

"Who are you?" she said, and now was when she'd find out if her command and pronunciation of their language was as good as she hoped.

He jumped a little, and peered more closely at her. "Why . . . you sound almost like . . . are you a *female?* Who are you?"

"I ask who *you* are."

"You're not *him*, then." He grunted, and spat a brown stream from the corner of his mouth. "All right. Good. That'll do."

"Not who?" Her throat was hurting already from the harshness of their words, the necessity to half-swallow and rasp them from the gullet rather than speak properly at the front of the mouth. "And what are you doing? What is this trap? You could have killed me."

"The trap was not for you. You were just in the way, skinny elfgirl. Now move. If he comes, if he escapes Hurkot, he will come fast."

The dwarf stomped past her and squatted. His short legs did not take much of a bending to bring him down to where he needed to be. He fiddled with the metal plate. Resetting it, she presumed.

"Who will come? Who is Hurkot?" Although she had no quarrel with the other Elder Race, she was beginning to see why the Emerinians might take umbrage at them enough to go to war, if they were all as unhelpful and abrasive as this one.

He ignored her, muttering to himself in such a low, irritable manner that she could hardly tell if he was speaking dwarven at all. He sounded like he was breaking rocks between his teeth. When he was satisfied with the plate, having covered it once more with loose dirt and debris, he trudged over to a tree beside the road.

Tilanne followed, saving her throat and her breath since he did not seem inclined to be helpful. But she still wanted to know what he was doing, why he should set some fiendish trap out here in the middle of nowhere.

When she looked up, she shuddered. The device suspended among the trees wouldn't have been visible to anyone riding or walking by, but from here she could see it clearly. The machinery defied her ability to make sense of it, and she could not determine how it connected to the plate in the road, but she had no doubt as to its purpose. When the plate was depressed, it caused the blade to swing down. And the blade . . . the blade was a huge, sharp, ugly thing that could easily chop an armored man in half.

"You cannot have this here." Over her initial shock, she was both angry and belatedly frightened. "Take it down!"

The dwarf, having just affixed long spikes to his boots so that he could climb the tree – he did this by kicking the spikes in, impaling the trunk, and hauling himself up by the arms with the help of a leather strap studded with smaller spikes – stopped and looked at her with pitying scorn.

"Listen, girlie . . . you are a south-elf, a dark-elf, whatever they call you people. We are not at war with you. So stay out of it."

"But the war is far from here. The war is in the human lands."

"True." He hitched the strap higher and kicked his climbing-spike in.

"Are you a soldier?"

"No." He grinned, that flash of white teeth startling against the dark iron-grey of his beard. "I'm a specialist."

"In what? In traps?"

"Traps, ambushes . . . that sort of thing." He heaved himself up, in slow progress that looked painful.

"If you are at war with them, why are you here? This is *Morvalan* land." How strange the elven word sounded mixed with the dwarven speech.

"Yes, yes," he said. "We have no fight with you darkwooders because you lurk in your shadows and do not try to attack Montennor with your unnatural magics. But one of *them* is coming *here*, gangle-shanks, and we were sent to stop him. Answer enough? Good. Now get out of the way. This is hard enough work without you looking at me."

"Stop who?" She was in desperate need of a drink to soothe her abused throat, but the raspiness made her sound more like a dwarf.

He rolled his eyes and snorted, as if impatient with a particularly lack-witted child. "Their new general. You know what that means, girlie-elf? General? Big army leader? If he goes back to the battlefield, he will be a powerful foe to us. We want to be rid of him before that can happen. Our spies learned that he was given a leave before assuming his duties, and then that he was coming south."

"I know what a general is," she said. Did he not see that she was armed and armored? Of course she'd know such a thing.

The dwarf paused and frowned, an expression that folded his forehead down on itself in deep wrinkles. "We did not know *why* he was coming south. Maybe it was to try and ally with you, get you darkwooder-elves to help fight us."

Then the rest of it dawned on her, this general, this general they'd be rid of. "You speak of an *elf?* This an elf you would be rid of him and murder with your traps?" She stumbled over the words in her urgency and bit her tongue hard enough to draw blood.

"Of course he's an elf." The dwarf eyed her. "You're not much of a one of those smart book-learning sorts, are you?"

"You cannot kill an elf."

His laughter smelled of smoke-weed and ale. "No? I have killed dozens. One more, ten more, it will not matter. But Hurkot will finish him at the inn. My trap is only a just-in-case, if by some mischance, he escapes. He rides this way, and . . ." He swept his hand through the air and imitated the sound the blade had made – *whish!*

Atrocity upon atrocity demanded Tilanne's mental attention. An elven general, these dwarven spies were planning to murder an elven general! If murder failed, they'd catch him unawares with this hideous device!

And . . . "Finish him at the inn? What inn?"

"Some inn, or so they call it." He waved up the road. "Shoddy place. Not a decent mug of ale to be had there, only that berry-squeezings you call wine. Terrible stuff. Sour. Gives me the dribbling squitters."

"You kill no more elves, not now and not ever," Tilanne said. "I am ending you."

He bellowed laughter again. "Even if you were a man I would not be afraid of you. Your magic cannot touch me, and no single elf can beat a dwarf in combat."

"Try this elf." She lowered her visor.

"Oh-ho, the willow-spindle elfgirlie is bold!" He chortled and slapped his leg. "She challenges Vezzok Ironclaw! Why? What is this north-elf to you? Do you know what they say about your folk? That you sacrifice to your hungry god and drink the blood of your babies. Why would you help him?"

"Right or wrong he is an elf and I am sworn." She lightly whapped the flat of Baleful Gaze against his shoulder. "Let go the tree or I stab you as you climb like a . . ." She didn't know any dwarven words for squirrel or other such animal, and was momentarily thrown by this.

Vezzok did not seem to notice, taking her threat seriously enough. He got down from the tree, casting aside the leather climbing-strap. "You are making a mistake, elf-woman."

"Yours was the first, and worst mistake."

He bent, and she thought he was going to unhook the spikes from his boots. But abruptly he uncoiled and came at her, far faster than she would have thought a dwarf could move. They might be stocky, and heavy, and their legs might be short, but he was amazingly quick for all of that. He snatched the iron mace from his belt and swung it.

She turned it on her shield, marking and appreciating the sheer physical power behind Vezzok's blow. She might have appreciated it more had it not been aimed at her with bone-smashing force. Once again, the folly of this entire war seemed to loom large. Elder races fighting each other? When it was the *humans* that meant to spread and expand and take over the world? They should be working together, elves and dwarves, to hold onto that which was theirs by right.

Now, however, was not the time for a philosophical debate. She could not allow these dwarves to kill an elf, certainly not a general. Even *Alvalan*, he was under her protection whether he knew it or not. Whether he wanted it or not.

Baleful Gaze came down again, not with the flat this time but the edge. It screeched against Vezzok's armor, sending up a shower of sparks. A particularly large one landed in Vezzok's beard and sizzled there, sending up a tendril of smoke.

He roared, not with pain but with offense. "My beard! You burn my *beard*, you careless nest-robber?"

Her shield shivered under the next crashing strike of his mace. She retaliated. They moved out into the road, metal clanging as they exchanged blows and scored minor but painful wounds. Tilanne tried, once, to use Baleful Gaze's power to transform him to the stone he already resembled. Nothing happened. It was true, then; the dwarvenfolk were resistant to magic.

But the gifts granted by Kaledhol were not magic.

As she swung, Tilanne cried, "*Ha-nah!*" and felt the answering surge of strength in a scarlet aura that flared around her.

Vezzok gaped, and raised his mace to intercept her descending sword. Although his mace was an ironwood haft with a solid steel head, it burst apart into splinters. There were more sparks, though these did not endanger his beard. Incredulous, he nonetheless remained quick, snatching for the deadly pick slung on his back. Tilanne closed with him, crowded him. She rammed her shield into his face and broke his nose.

He hit her not with the pointed iron head of the pick but with the butt of the handle, catching her just below the elbow at a grouping of nerves that made her arm spasm. She missed with Baleful Gaze. Vezzok kicked out –

She had forgotten about the climbing spikes still jutting from the toes of his boots. The spike pierced her leg, a sudden lancing pain that made her think it must have impaled her all the way through and come out the other side. She bashed with her shield again, knocking the over-balanced dwarf sprawling on his back.

In an honorable fight, now would have been the time to stand back, help him up, wait for him to be ready. But there was no such thing as an honorable fight, Tilanne had come to believe. Survival, and protecting one's own, those were what mattered. To those ends, anything went.

Tilanne drove Baleful Gaze point-first into Vezzok's belly, just below the ornate gold buckle of his belt. The mail shirt was strong, and there seemed to be a boiled leather jerkin beneath it, as well as the normally tough hide of a dwarf, but the blade still bit deep.

Hurt but not killed, he kicked at her again, clumsily. She deflected the boot-spike with her shield with a squeal of noise that set her teeth on edge. She was driven back a step.

Vezzok rolled, meaning to get to his feet. Tilanne felt a bit ashamed for doing it, but shame didn't stop her from driving the toe of her own boot – plated with blackmetal – squarely into the seat of his pants. He plowed a furrow in the dirt with his face.

"Yield, and thy life I'll spare," she said in elven, and then shook her head, scowling, and repeated it in his tongue.

He sat up, spitting out wet clots of earth. "Vezzok Ironclaw yields to no one."

"I feared you say so." Tilanne advanced on him again. She brought Baleful Gaze down in a cleaving strike aimed at the bald crown of his head, calling out the words of prayer. Kaledhol's strength was tenfold her own, the blade splitting thick bone.

Vezzok stiffened, his limbs jerking. His fingers clawed at the air. His jaw slammed shut so forcefully that teeth cracked into pieces, falling to pepper his beard with white chips.

Baleful Gaze was embedded in his head to the eyebrow. Tilanne, grimacing, had to brace her foot against his chest and push him backward to pull her sword out. The blade came free with a grisly sound that she could have done without. The dead dwarf flopped to the road, spread-eagled, staring sightlessly at the overlapping boughs. A leaf, delicate green with a lacy, scalloped edge, twirled down and landed on his broken nose.

Tilanne wiped clean her sword, exhaling in short puffs. Her various small wounds hurt, and the larger, impaled hole in her leg felt as if it had been packed with burning tinder, but she had no time to lose.

The general. Hurkot. The inn.

Ordanna. Ordanna and her husband and their child.

"Kaledhol grant that not too late am I!"

She leaped onto Khian, and spurred the mare into a gallop.

* * *

CHAPTER THIRTY

Before she came within sight of the inn, Tilanne knew that her last prayer was not to be granted. Perhaps it was not within Kaledhol's power.

She *was* too late.

Ahead, a roiling column of smoke unfurled above the treetops.

Tilanne exhorted Khian to greater speed, ducking low against the mare's neck and aware, if only as an unrealized thought in the cellar of her mind, that if Vezzok had planted any other traps along the road, she would be plunging headlong directly into them.

Now she could hear the clashing of metal, the terrified wails of a child, voices shouting in two different languages. One of the voices was that of an elfwoman, screaming, pleading.

Vezzok, who had called himself a specialist, had gone lightly-armored . . . for a dwarf. He had not even been wearing a helmet. Just that hauberk of iron rings over boiled leather. He was a trap-setter, planning to let his lethal machine do the majority of the harm while he stayed back to watch from a safe distance.

As she thundered on Khian toward the crossroads, the inn-yard and the burning building, she saw that Hurkot and his companions had come ready for battle. They were not here to set traps. Theirs was the sole purpose of killing. Each of the three of them was encased in heavy plate armor so thick that the full force of a dragon's bite might not penetrate. Their heads were covered by great-helms, their extremities with armored boots and gauntlets. Not a scrap of flesh was visible. Even their beards were tucked safely away beneath their corselets. They might have been not so much living things as machines, every bit as complex and deadly as the siege engines and vehicles of destruction they employed in war.

The one nearest Tilanne, whose back-slung iron shield bore the emblem of a clenched golden fist, held a double-shot crossbow trained on the elves, keeping them pressed against the wall of the inn some ten paces away. They could not dare move without being shot, though the structure was ablaze and the fire was spreading with ravenous haste.

She knew her niece at once, Ordanna's hair as sable-dark as Tilanne's own. So, too, was the hair of the child in her arms, the child that thrashed and struggled and wailed in its terror.

"No, please, no, hurt him not!" Ordanna screamed. "Irvynlin! Irvynlin, no!"

Ordanna's husband, fair-haired and handsome and determined as he stood between his wife and the crossbow, was not wholly defenseless. He held a slim sword poised, and his other hand was wreathed in the orange glow of magefire. Neither would be very effective against a fully armored dwarf, and by the hopeless set of his shoulders, he knew it. Still, he kept himself between the crossbow and his family. Despite her initial predisposition to dislike this half-*Alvalan* innkeeper for having lured Ordanna into defying her parents, Tilanne couldn't help but feel a certain grudging admiration.

The crossbow-bearing dwarf did not let his attention waver from Irvynlin, despite the duel going on halfway across the inn-yard. There, the largest of the dwarves – no doubt Hurkot himself – advanced with a morningstar whistling, the spiked ball whirling at the end of its chain. His shield's emblem was that of an odd, wingless dragon possessed of abnormally large front claws and a supple, stoat-like body.

His opponent had to be the general of which Vezzok had spoken, though the man did not appear much like what Tilanne's mind insisted a general should look like. He was young for such rank, perhaps not yet even to his centennial. Young, and strikingly handsome, with short jet-black hair, elegant ears, and eyes like cold-burning ice – she could see these features because his helm still hung on the saddle of his nervously sidestepping steed. He wore meshed mail, a truesteel breast-plate, and a surcoat of white embroidered with a gold lion

His fancy, bejeweled sword was a golden blur as he gave ground before the dwarf, deftly parrying each blow of the morningstar. Tilanne knew full well how challenging that was, how insidiously the whirling chain could entangle a blade. Had she not seen Kai Terindor fall to a flail? This stranger even reminded her of the Kai in an odd way. Something in the hard light of his eyes, the grim line of his jaw.

She saw the short-legged, shaggy ponies that must have brought the dwarves here, a fine horse that had to belong to the general. She saw the flaming inn, saw the tears of the child and the terror of her niece. She saw that the third dwarf likewise had his shield slung on his back to free his hands, but instead of any weapon known to Tilanne, he held some sort of lumpy head-sized chunk of what looked like raw ore. A leather loop had been wrapped around this, as if to turn it into a kind of throwing-hammer. It looked ungainly and strange.

She did not need to see more. Drawing Baleful Gaze, she urged Khian forward. None of them had noticed her until then, but her arrival now at full gallop was anything but subtle. To make sure their attention was on her, she yelled a full-throated wordless challenge.

The dwarf with the crossbow spun toward Tilanne and squeezed off a shot, which she shunted aside with her shield. Seeing her bearing down at full speed, he mustered his short stocky legs to scramble out of the way, but was too slow. Khian reared high and came down. Her forehooves clanged against his corselet and knocked him down. He reflexively pulled the triggers again as he fell. The second crossbow bolt sped at Tilanne. She felt it scrape the side of her helm.

Now they were all aware of her, this dark figure that had so suddenly appeared in their midst. Tilanne saw shock on elven faces and in dwarven postures. She read the questioning, astonished word *Rhunvala* on Ordanna's lips. And, even more surprisingly, on those of the young black-haired general as well.

The dwarf on the ground was rolling this way and that, trying to scrabble away from Khian's stomping hooves. Tilanne leaped from the saddle and landed on her feet, running toward the inn.

"Ordanna!" she cried. "Go, Ordanna, thy child take and *go!*"

"Ambush, Hurkot, ambush!" shouted the dwarf holding the lump of ore.

Hurkot, perhaps grimly deciding that he would at least fulfill the mission he'd come here to do, resumed his attack on the elven general with terrific ferocity. Tilanne had time to think that for all his crisp, clean, shining appearance, the *Alvalan* did know how to fight. She did not know many men who could have withstood such an assault for long. She did not know if she, herself, could have done it.

Ordanna, clutching her child, fled shrieking for the woods. Her husband, that poor unprepared innkeeper, was slack-jawed with confusion. He looked from the *Rhunvala* to the dwarves to the *Rhunvala* again, clearly not knowing where to sling the magefire in his hand.

As Tilanne changed course to bear down on him, the dwarf with the lump of ore twirled it on its leather strap and let fly. She raised her shield even as the general yelled out a warning, and at the last moment changed her mind to dodge instead.

The clumsy, lumpy thing hurtled past her and struck the wall of the inn. It exploded in a tremendous burst of heat, flame and sound. Tilanne was pitched forward by the blast as if swatted by a huge unseen hand. She tumbled, and landed stunned on the ground as bits of burning shingles rained down on her.

Dazed, her ears humming with a high and deafened buzz, Tilanne raised her head. She saw Khian, spooked, bolting off into the woods. The dwarf she'd been trampling looked battered but still whole, getting to his feet and unlimbering a pair of small but heavy hand-axes. The inn was an inferno now, fire roaring high beneath a choking tumult of smoke. The one who'd hurled the explosive reached for his belt, where he had a dragonhide poke that bulged as if stuffed with rocks.

So *this* was the horror the Montennor army unleashed upon the warmages of the Emerin. She could not imagine what it must be like out there on the battlefield, amid the colossal destruction that was being dealt by magic and dwarf-lore.

Irvynlin made up his mind and flung his magefire at the dwarf with the axes. Brilliant orange and yellow flame splashed over him in gouts, leaving a dull red patch of heat on his corselet.

Somehow, Tilanne was up again without realizing she'd arisen. She seized up Baleful Gaze from where it had fallen when she was knocked head over heels, and charged at the dwarf who'd just drawn a grape-sized lump of the same ore from his poke.

He flicked it at her the way he might have flicked a bit of stone at a pesky rat, a gesture more of annoyance than outright aggression. Tilanne, too close this time to dodge, got her shield in front of her face. The blast was smaller, but jarring enough to make her arm felt as it had when she'd blocked the orckin's flail for Kai Terindor. The front of her shield buckled inward as if horse-kicked.

She was aware of the other fights going on around her. Hurkot and the general were still trading blows, and though she could not hear anything, she gathered they were also trading curses and insults in the most colorful epithets the languages of Montennor and the Emerin had to offer.

Irvynlin, having bravery sufficient to make up for what he might lack in good sense, was attempting to take on the axe-wielding dwarf with his sword.

Baleful Gaze scored a deep scratch on plate mail but did not penetrate. Another lump of ore, this one as big as a bird's egg, came at her.

"*Jhe-nah!*" A wine-red shimmer sent it veering past Tilanne to explode against a tree. A smoking black hole appeared in the bark, and the trunk was instantly girdled in flames.

She was so close to him now that she could see slate-grey eyes and the blackish-brown bristle of eyebrows through the visor-slits of his helm. He yanked a short, broad-bladed knife from its sheath and rammed at Tilanne's stomach. Her blackmetal turned it but the breath was knocked from her.

Over the low head of her foe, she saw Ordanna's husband staggering back, his sword snapped off into a hilt and a stub. He raised his arms to defend himself as one of the axes whickered down. The curved edge sheared through flesh and bone, loosing a torrential spray of blood.

"*Ha-nah!*" Tilanne summoned Kaledhol's might and renewed her attack. Her first strike splintered the broad-bladed knife, her second carved a deep rent in his corselet, and her third split the dwarf's helm right off of his head. He reeled back a few paces and sat down hard.

Like Vezzok, he was bald, but unlike Vezzok, in his case it seemed to be by shaven-scalped choice, like an elven soldier cropping his hair. His beard was the color of freshly-turned loam, disappearing into the collar of his corselet. He blinked up at her, then slowly slumped over backward.

Skillful as he was, the general had managed to get several stabs through weaker spots in Hurkot's armor. Each hit was not itself enough to kill, or even truly hamper, but they added up. Slow, thick crimson trickled from seams and gaps, puddling around the dwarf's boots. But that morningstar had done its own share of damage. The general was limping, his surcoat shredded by the spikes on the chain-tethered ball, his armor pocked with dents and small holes.

Irvynlin had gone to his knees, so aghast at the sight of his severed forearm and hand lying in the dirt that he barely seemed aware of the pain or the blood. He was all but leaning against the burning inn, and seemed oblivious to the flames and the ominous lean of the wall as well. Nor was he aware of the dwarf stalking toward him, scraping both axe-blades together like a cook about to carve a roast at the table.

"Leave him be!" she shouted in the dwarf-speech, her words sounding muffled through the ringing in her ears. "No elf will die!"

The dwarf wheeled toward her. As he did so, Irvynlin's other hand shot out and closed on the rim of the shield strapped to that wide back. Heat, a huge and blistering heat, made the shield glow with the hot orange of a smith's forge.

Tilanne had to retreat, squinting, wincing. She could see the shield beginning to soften, the edges curling in on themselves and running like wax. The dwarf howled in agony, cooking alive inside his plate mail . . . the very armor that had been his best defense now his crematorium. Smoke issued from his visor-slits. There was a sizzle that Tilanne was glad she could only barely hear, and a stench she could not block out.

Irvynlin's hand, unburned, not even reddened, slipped away from the shield. He slumped to the ground. Blood continued to pump from his other arm.

"Behind you!"

She dimly heard the general's cry, and looked over her shoulder.

The one whose helm she had split was sitting up again. Looking at her with a hateful grin as he dipped his hand into a second poke, this one of leather reinforced with chainmail. When he pulled it out, he held something that looked like an iron pinecone wrapped in a wire net. Overlapping sections like petals formed a crude ball. The dwarf stripped off the net and the sections loosened a bit, relaxing in his grip. He handled it very gingerly, as if even he was wary of this particular menace.

Tilanne dropped Baleful Gaze, drew a knife of Master Dael's making from her boot, sent a silent prayer to Kaledhol to guide her aim, and threw. The knife struck the ball just as the dwarf prepared to lob it. The sections came apart, unfolding, opening like a metal blossom and freeing the contents.

A cloud of tiny dark specks, like a swarm of gnats or tiny stinging flies, issued out and mostly obscured the dwarf from sight. He thrashed about, flailing his arms, beating at his exposed face and head as the motes settled onto him. They were sucked by the hundreds into his nose and mouth, down into his lungs.

His contortions became a death-dance that seemed to go on forever . . . and at the same time were over almost at once. The cloud dissipated, the motes sinking into the dwarf's skin and seeping through the seams of his armor like water. He collapsed in a twisted, rigid posture. His face had gone purple-black. His tongue, also black, and gritty as if rolled in coarsely-ground peppercorns, poked out. His eyes had been dissolved away to runny black sockets like puddles of tar.

Tilanne dared not breathe as she waited to see if she would be next. It was some kind of poisonous dust or gas, some atrocious dwarf-weapon, yet another example of what must be happening all across those war-torn lands to the west.

But the cloud was gone. The metal pinecone lay open and empty by the dwarf's outflung hand.

A long and awful moment drew out as the rest of them – Tilanne, the general, Hurkot – looked at each other as if to ask what happened next. Did they continue? Or had there been enough for one day? Enough fighting . . . enough death?

Hurkot stared at the bodies of his companions, one hideously convulsed from the poison, the other a motionless husk mercifully hidden from view by his still-steaming armor.

"You are *Rhunvala*," the general said, looking at Tilanne. It was more a statement than a question, but the question was there, underlying it. "A woman, but *Rhunvala* nonetheless."

"Yes."

There wasn't much time for other conversation, as Hurkot decided he had little else left to lose. He came at them both, the morningstar whipping in deadly arcs. Tilanne moved forward, shielding them both, turning a flurry of ringing blows from the spiked iron ball. The general chose his moment with uncanny instinct, darting past her in a form-perfect lunge. The shining blade slid neatly through Hurkot's visor, skewering him through the head.

The dwarf stiffened. He took a few faltering steps backward, causing the blade to emerge from head and helm. It was slicked with blood. Beginning to shudder all over, Hurkot took a few more wooden steps. He stumbled into the wall of the burning inn, bumped along it like a bee trying to pass through a pane of glass, and blundered by through the doorway into a seething cavern of smoke and flame.

The roof creaked, groaned, sagged. Inside, a burning timber slammed down, sending up a cyclone of embers.

"He's still alive," the general said.

"Not for long shall he be. In there could nothing survive."

"Not him . . . the elf."

Tilanne glanced sharply around. She saw Irvynlin dragging himself along the ground, pushing with both legs and pulling with his good arm. The other trailed at his side . . . the stump a charred black and no longer bleeding. She remembered his hand gloved in magefire, and her admiration for this man her niece had married rose again.

The general ran to help him, just as the wall of the inn collapsed on them in a mass of blazing rubble.

*   *   *

CHAPTER THIRTY-ONE

"No!" Tilanne rushed toward them.

They had not been crushed, not been buried, not been killed. But beams had pinned them in place, and their clothes were igniting, and the smoke was everywhere, suffocating and thick.

A gate in her memory swung wide. It was Falanar all over again, Falanar trapped in the wreckage. Crushed and helpless. Trapped and dying . . . dying while he clung to her and begged her to save him. She had failed.

"Kaledhol, no, let this not *again* happen!" She threw aside sword and shield, and waded into the heaped, fiery debris. Her gloves smoldered as she lifted and shoved burning wood out of her way.

She reached them, found the general covering Irvynlin's body with his own in a futile attempt to ward off the searing heat. He craned his neck to look at her. Even in this churning orange-red-black nightmare, they were ice-blue, and cold.

Tilanne crouched. Her cloak was on fire. She slipped her arms under the beam that held their legs. "*Ha-nah,*" she said, her voice low, her jaw tight. "*Ha-nah*, Kaledhol, in Thy name, by Thy will . . . *Ha-nah . . . Hanahia!*"

Deep rose-red-blood-red-wine-red light engulfed her. She felt the divine strength infuse her limbs. With one smooth rising heave, she stood and hurled the beam aside, then stood gasping through clenched teeth.

The general scooped up Irvynlin, who was not moving, and carried him past the bodies of the dwarves well beyond the conflagration. Tilanne followed, the light around her fading and leaving her unutterably exhausted.

She sank to her knees and pulled off her helm. "Lives does he? Say that lives he does."

"He does, but . . ."

"A physician he needs. But the nearest in Deepwater is . . . so far, too far . . . survive the journey he would not. Cauterized the wound he did that no longer does it bleed, but other hurts he has, and infection risks . . ."

"Let me. I can help him." The general knelt beside her. Brushing her hands aside, he gripped Irvynlin's injured arm above the elbow and whispered, "*Salahin Roas.*"

She half-understood the words of magic, and knew a healing when she saw it. The few sluggish trickles of blood from Irvynlin's other wounds slowed, then stopped. His color improved. His labored breathing eased.

"A physician as well thou art?"

The general sat back on his heels and shook his head. "Only a soldier with some small knowledge of healing magics picked up on the sly. I'm not trained, but when there is no other recourse, it comes in handy. Here, you're hurt too."

She had come through this fight largely unscathed, but still bled from where Vezzok's boot-spike had impaled her leg. She had all but forgotten. The pain came back to her now, throbbing and deep.

"Your timely arrival was no accident of chance," he said when he had cast his spell again. "How did you know to come? How did you know they'd ambushed me?"

"A fourth on the road I met," she said. "A trap for thee he was setting, and interrupted him did I. Slew him as well did I, when of his intentions I learned."

He looked her over again, more closely this time now that they were not fighting for their lives, now that her helm was gone so he could see her face. "I was not aware that your order accepted females, Kai . . . ?"

"Tilanne. The only woman of the order am I." She eyed him as well. "Thou most clearly *Alvalan* art, yet of our ways curiously knowledgeable and of a *Rhunvala* curiously unafraid seemst thou to be."

"Well, I may be *Alvalan*," he said, making a bit of a grimace, "but I hardly think I'm typical of the Emerin. My family's roots spring from the south. I've visited before to explore my heritage. My name is Tiercel Reyes."

"Reyes?" she echoed, eyes widening. "Thou a *Reyes* art?"

"Yes, how do you . . . ah, of course. My uncle is *Rhunvala.* You must have heard of him, perhaps even know him. Terindor Reyes."

A mixture of emotions eddied through Tilanne. She took his shoulder in a grasp both consoling and firm. "Regret most deeply do I such news to give, but many years gone thy uncle is. With him at the end was I, and most bravely in battle he died."

Tiercel hissed in a long, slow breath and let it out just as slowly. "I feared it might be so. He once told me that few *Rhunvala* live to see old age. But then it is all the more fortunate that I found you here. If I am to succeed him, I –" He broke off. "What? Why do you shake your head? Why do you look so?"

"Before his death, a successor did he name." She touched her chest lightly, where the ruby basilisk was confined within her armor.

"You? But . . . but *I* should have been . . . I hoped . . . I meant to . . ." He cleared his throat gruffly. "Well. You were there and I was not, I suppose. Fire take it all, though, I'd intended to ask my uncle's help with the war. I thought he might intercede and win the support of the *Rhunvala*, and your people, to ally with the Emerin."

"This much right now I can tell thee," Tilanne said. "War with the Mountain Kingdom already we *Morvalan* have, and for centuries against that enemy have we our borders held. Sorely pressed are we. By a thread hanging, in truth. No troops have we to spare. If alliance were to be made and aid given, sooner here is that of thy people needed."

"Still, I would try to persuade them. Will you take me to the place of the *Rhunvala?* To your Citadel? Even if I am not to be my uncle's successor, I *must* go there. I know that I must."

Tilanne felt a sweeping chill of realization. She searched his coldfire-blue eyes. This man was the stranger, the one whose coming Kaledhol had foretold to her? This was the one who was to be given a sword? This was the one with whom her own fate was somehow intertwined?

"My arrival indeed no accident of chance was," she said. "Led here was I. Brought here not so much my niece and her family to save, but thee to find. And so, Tiercel Reyes, to the *Odan Rhunvale* take thee I shall."

* * *

EPILOGUE

"The rest," Tilanne said, "thou knowst."

Tiercel nodded. "You never quite agreed with it, though, did you?" he asked, cradling a cup in his hands. "The vision. You still wonder if I'm the one. Even after I made it through the ritual and emerged with Discordant."

"Agreed? Kaledhol's own word it was. To question that am I?"

He gestured with his gaze toward the purse at her belt, wherein was held the Emerald of Karria. "You shall see, Tilanne. Once we've accomplished our mission, we'll be able to rid ourselves of the humans once and for all. Under my guidance, young Celinar Elyvorrin will lead the Emerin back to the greatness it deserves. We'll rebuild Govannisan even better than it was, and this time we'll see to it that Kaledhol is properly acknowledge, respected."

She nodded now, for those were all worthy goals. But a feather-soft brushing of disquiet still stirred somewhere within her.

Exhausted by that speech, Tiercel sank onto his side. He had come through his battle with the basilisk venom and was well on the way to recovery, and had even been able to take and keep down several sips of broth.

She divested him of the cup before he could spill the dregs all over himself, and tucked his cloak more securely around him as a blanket. He mumbled something that might have been words of thanks, and subsided into sleep.

Such rest would be longer coming for Tilanne. She had talked herself hoarse, not so much recounting those years as reliving them.

Yes, they both knew the rest. How they had escorted Ordanna, her crippled husband, and her child to Deepwater. There, Ordanna had been reunited and reconciled with her parents, and Irvynlin had given up all thoughts of returning to *Alvalan* life.

Tilanne, after once more bidding her sister's family farewell, had ridden with Tiercel to the *Odan Rhunvale*. Along the way, she had occasionally been dubious of his motives – Tiercel's professed faith sometimes seemed to her a matter of convenience, a matter of how Kaledhol could further his ambitions rather than how he could serve Kaledhol.

Had he persisted and become *Rhunvala*, he would have been of the Way of Destruction. Discordant was the sword of his hidden but true self, the violent and devastating weapon he kept secret from the rest of the Emerin. To them, he was Sir Tiercel Reyes, a knight, a young but adept general. That Tiercel carried Lionheart, given to him by the Starleaf Council.

He had fulfilled both potentials during the many years of the war with Montennor, becoming a hero to his people and a vengeance loosed upon his enemies. Little did anyone on either side know that his ultimate goal had not so much been victory over the dwarves as it had been the devastation of the humans. To prolong the hostilities, to keep the battles raging across the Northlands . . . to see villages reduced to ashes and humans fleeing in beaten, starving, desperate droves . . . these were the ends towards which Sir Tiercel worked.

During that time, Tilanne had lived secretly among the Alvalan, observing them from concealment and shadow. She could never have masqueraded as one of them, not even had she wanted to. Such duplicity and selfishness was not in her nature. And she was no dissembler. Her accent, her earrings, her mannerisms and a thousand other things would have given her away.

She did not take part in the battles, but did venture forth now and then when she could to defend elven soldiers. If any of them saw her, a dark and unknown warrior-woman, they kept it to themselves. Perhaps they supposed no one else would believe them.

She had also been there, watching from hiding, on the day the Emerin's old king had fallen to the dwarven axes. Later, seeing that she was displeased, Tiercel had attempted to explain it away. It was all for the best, he'd told her. King Shaelan had been twelve centuries old and hopelessly set in his ways. He'd never bend to a way of thinking that might include and welcome the Morvalan. They needed the support of a younger king, fiery and headstrong and easily swayed. Such as Prince Wyndrel.

But that, too, had not gone as Tiercel anticipated. When Wyndrel proved unwilling to bow to Tiercel's will, it had very nearly been the end of him. Only Tilanne's intervention had saved Wyndrel's life, not that anyone – least of all Wyndrel himself – knew of the private battle of wills she and Tiercel had waged. In the end, Tiercel had decided that in time the king might change his mind . . . but to make sure of it, he'd arranged the "disappearance" and presumed death of the prince.

His eventual fate was of no consequence now. Of less consequence, if more personally troubling to Tilanne, was the knowledge that Wyndrel was no longer alone in his captivity. The silver-haired Ariana had been imprisoned with him in that secret palace dungeon. Ariana, who had seemed so elven . . . but whose blood was tainted and corrupt. The daughter of the man who'd spared Tilanne's life. That debt was now repaid, and she was glad. Indebted to a man who'd wed an *elfkin?* Who'd gotten children on an *elfkin?*

Worst of all, she, Tilanne, had not known. She had looked right at Ariana Mirida – tall, stately, beautiful Ariana – and never would have guessed. Had spoken with her, seen her do magic, seen her handle the very same sacred Emerald of Karria that Tilanne now carried. And she hadn't known. To her every sense, Ariana had seemed as elven as Tiercel, as elven as Tilanne herself.

Could it be so? Could an elfkin bear a true-born elven child? If so, what might that mean? Were the elfkin possibly not the irredeemable abominations that the *Morvalan* had always believed? Could they be brought successfully back into the elven race?

Not that Ariana's fate was of much consequence, either. Count Elyvorrin meant to use her to lure her father into a trap, and then would probably kill her.

Except . . .

It *was* of consequence, wasn't it? Tilanne had allowed Ariana to be given into Elyvorrin's clutches. But if Ariana was, in fact, as purely elven as she seemed . . . did that not go against her vow?

She sat by the fire as Tiercel slept, musing on these and many other thoughts. A rightful king, locked away from the world . . . for how long? Forever? And whatever the actual nature of Ariana Mirida, her father *was* true elven, and Elyvorrin would no doubt murder him.

Most worrisome of all, most pressing of all, was the Emerald. If it had to be placed forever out of reach in the claws of Racandros in order to give the Emerin a king that would help her people, then such had to be done. If it could be exchanged for something that could scourge humanity from the world, like this Phial of which Tiercel had spoken, so much the better.

But was there such a Phial? Did he know? Could she . . . this was the part that dismayed her the most, a thought she tried not to let herself think . . . could she trust Tiercel? She did believe and had never doubted his dedication to the elven people. He would do anything and everything he could for them. His conviction was as sure and unshakable as her own.

At the core of it, though, she was not sure she could fully trust him.

They had never quite become friends, she and Tiercel. He perhaps resented that she, and not himself, had been named Kor to Kai Terindor. That she, Tilanne, had somehow usurped his rightful place. She, in turn, had often feared that Tiercel would go too far in his overwhelming desire to triumph.

In a way, he had become almost a kinsman to her. Like some distantly-related and not particularly affectionate cousin, exasperating at times, impossible at times. But, undeniably, kin. They were connected after a fashion. They did have a common purpose, if differing ways of attaining it.

They had certainly never become lovers, which was just as well as far as Tilanne was concerned. She had struggled through more than enough complications of that nature. Even now, so many years later, she could not think of Jedriel without a bittersweet pang of regret. And Peredur . . . sometimes it hurt too much to think of Peredur at all.

As far as Tiercel was concerned, there being no attraction between them was even more than just as well. He'd told her that he'd narrowly escaped the clutches of a childhood betrothal and, as he'd put it, "a near-fatal brush with matrimony," and had resisted or avoided all familial efforts since to coax him into marriage. He was not *chani*, as far as she could determine, but he harbored an abiding distrust of all women and their manipulations.

Perhaps that was why it had amused her so when he'd been neatly cornered by Count Elyvorrin into an engagement to the widowed Faessia. That, she thought, was a courtship surely doomed to end in disaster.

They camped at the bear's den until Tiercel had recovered enough to be fit to travel . . . or at least until his fretting and impatience got the best of her. Reserving the right to bring their journey to a halt again if he seemed to be pushing too hard and imperiling his health, Tilanne agreed that they should continue on.

She did not tell him that she was impatient, as well. Or that she'd developed the oddest certainty that time was running out . . . and that the final destinies awaiting them at that dormant volcano so far to the east might not be what either of them expected.

* * *

The End

The ElfLore Trilogy
Book III

Truegold

PROLOGUE

He woke with a snort from dreams of fire and plunder. Raising his head, he turned it this way and that until bones popped in his neck. He peered about, blinking sleep from his eyes.

All was as it should be. Nothing was disturbed. Not a coin, not a gem, not a stray item out of place.

What, then, had awakened him?

Hunger? He consulted his belly. While some meat would have gone down well, he was not in great need of food. Just as well. His vision wasn't what it had once been in the old days, when he could tell an acorn from a beechnut at a half-mile's distance.

An intruder, then?

He pushed himself up from his bed and turned to the entrance. The cave's mouth was a gaping out-blown hole from which a wind-worn slab of stone protruded like a tongue. Outside, he could see only blameless blue sky and a puff of cloud.

His nostrils flared, testing the air. Dimmed his eyes might be; his other senses were as keen as ever. He detected first his own spicy-leathery-dusty scent, then that of the treasure surrounding him. Underlying those familiar odors was, as always, the smoke of sulfur rising through minute fissures in the floor. The mountain had long lain dead, but the last spark of its fiery life and breath lingered deep within.

The fresher air flowing through the opening brought him tantalizing whiffs of sea spray, green forest, rich earth salted with specks of precious metals, and the eternal dance of predator and prey in the vastness of nature.

His ears confirmed this, identifying the muted rumble from the old volcano's depths, the shift and creak of the mountain's stones, the slow churning of the surf, the more urgent rush and tumble of the waterfall, wind through boughs, bird calls, and the sounds of animals in all their variety.

Nothing seemed out of the ordinary, nothing that any of his senses could determine.

Still, he had been disturbed.

Shaking himself, hearing the patter of coins as they unstuck from his underside and rained down onto his bed of gold, Racandros lumbered to the entrance of his cave. His inner eyelids came down, further casting a veil over his sight but protecting his eyes from the glare of the sun.

The instinct of long habit made him fold his wings tightly against his scaled sides to spare them scraping along the walls. His long talons ticked and clacked on the stone. His tail swayed behind him, counterbalancing the length of his neck and the weight of his wedge-shaped head.

Aeons ago, mere impressions in the memory of his earliest ancestor, the mountain's restless fire had erupted in a fury that had not gone *up*, but *out*. The entire side had bulged like a boil until it exploded in a shower of roiling mud and ash that laid flat hundreds of wingspans of trees like so much straw. Burning rocks ejected from the upheaval had come to rest further away still, touching off forest fires where they alit. The sky had gone black with soot and smoke. Violent spasms had wracked the land, thrusting up a row of dark-veined grey peaks to the west and opening a deep ravine to the south. The sea had heaved and frothed. To the terrified beasts of the wild, it seemed as if the very world were coming to an end.

These things, Racandros knew not because he had been told but because they were buried in his very blood, bones, and scales. All that his progenitors had seen, learned, or done was within him, there to be called upon should some unexpected change in his environs demand it. Their experiences were his, just as his would have passed down to any young that he'd sired.

He came out onto the ledge, which was partly sheltered by stone outcrops. In the lee of these were heaps of bones from recent kills.

Above him, the uneven peak soared to a height that left it snow-capped even in the warmest times of the year. Below, sheer, undercut cliffs dropped away to a sloping scree of ancient condensed ash and mud, black-gleaming rivers of volcanic glass. A few stubbornly struggling trees poked up from this otherwise barren landscape.

That long-ago eruption had done more than reshape the mountain. It had brought water where there hadn't been water before. With the dim but unerring sense that let him understand the ways of the elements, Racandros knew that there was an immense lake trapped far beneath his home. A stone-throated channel, once made by rising columns of molten rock, now conducted water from the subterranean lake to a spot halfway up the mountain. It formed a bubbling spring wide enough for him to bathe in, but bitingly cold. From there, joined by rain and snowmelt, it funneled into a smooth-worn course and ultimately plunged over a cliff just beneath his ledge. The waterfall ate its way steadily backward, infinitesimal increments that had added up over thousands of years to carve out a vertical chasm where no outcrop or tree could take hold. At the far-below place where the plunging water met stone again, it had scooped out a pool so deep that not even Racandros knew how far down it reached.

He stretched his wings. They groaned from disuse as they unfolded to their vast span. Their membranes, so thin and fragile-seeming, shimmered an iridescent green-black. The sun fell on them, shone through them, cast a gauzy shadow striated with the network of his veins.

Racandros lifted his nose and sniffed again. A brisk breeze fluttered the loose folds and flaps of skin of his fire-pouch under his jaw. He surveyed his domain carefully for signs that his worst fear was coming true. The land was only so big, after all, and the other races bred so quickly. One day, he knew, he would look out from this vantage point and see smoke from their habitations as they dared . . . as they *presumed* . . . to settle in the shadow of his great sleeping volcano.

Sometimes he saw the sails of ships far out to sea. Sometimes when he flew out to hunt, he saw groups of humans and orcs, groups that gleamed and glittered with armor. And sometimes, rarely, the elves came. They hailed Racandros, brought him gifts, sought his wisdom, wanted to barter.

Humans and orcs, Racandros had little patience with. If he happened to be in the mood, he might sweep down on them exhaling blistering clouds of fire and send those who survived scattering, and usually burning, in all directions. Those who stood their ground and loosed arrows or spears at him – which glanced off his scales with never so much as a drop of blood drawn – he might pluck up in his foreclaws and drop from on high. How they would scream as they fell!

The elves, though . . . they were another matter. They and the dwarves had been a part of the world for long and long. Nearly as long as the dragons. They were often interesting and occasionally even clever. Worth listening to, especially if they came bringing him gifts of new treasure.

Once, their kinds had been enemies. Had not his own many-times-grandsire Racandros the First been among those who flew against the golden city, and leveled it to smoldering ruin? Had not the bulk of his hoard come from that time? Greed, they called it. Blind dragon-greed, as if dragons were no better than foolish birds attracted by the shine of gold and caring nothing for its worth.

Oh, but that was untrue. They cared *immensely* for its worth. They *understood* its worth in a way that the elves and even the deep-mining dwarves did not. Those races saw it as soft, pretty metal that could be worked into coins, into jewelry, into decorative works of art. They would sooner spend it or look at it, without knowing its true power.

Racandros chuffed in scorn, a wisp of smoke puffing from his mouth. It drifted up on the errant breeze and was torn apart. They had no idea. For all their knowledge, for all their vaunted civilization, they really did have no idea. Only another of his kind truly could know what his hoard meant to him, why he needed it, why he would kill to protect it.

Another of his kind . . . he paused. Might that have been what awakened him? It had been long since he'd last encountered a fellow dragon. Not even any of his own brood were welcome in his territory. None of them had amounted to an ember, anyway. All those breedings, and nary a one worth the Racandros name. If those savage, feeble-minded spawn turned up here thinking to claim his cave and his hoard for their own, they'd find that their sire was nowhere near too decrepit to put up a fight.

But there were no other dragons about. No females seeking a mate, no young males spoiling for dominance, not even another old relic like himself passing through on that long and final flight to the sea.

He could not find any cause for his abrupt wakening. Raising and lowering his wings to show his indifference, he went back into the cave. After the dazzle of daylight, its darkness was all the deeper. Racandros enlarged his pupils and opened his inner lid, and paused to proudly admire the sparkling treasure laid out before him. He was a proper old-fashioned dragon, not one of these wild younglings who threw everything in a pile and then wallowed in it. No, the Racandros line had always known how to keep a hoard.

The delicate and deadly items were carefully set in niches that had been chipped out of the cave walls by dragon-claws. What would be the sense in having a crystal statue of an elf-goddess if one tossed it in a pile and crushed it beneath one's weight? As for the the weapons . . . the last time he'd attended a gathering of his kind, Melandros had told him of a doltish young male who came across a fabulously jeweled and enchanted sword, added it to the heap of his bed, and promptly slew himself when he lay down upon it.

The rest made up his bed. Here were the coins and nuggets, some silver and lesser metals. Here were the gemstones, be they faceted in the way that only the elves and dwarves could do or polished smooth as the other races did. Here were mounds of jewelry and silver bars, breastplates or corselets worked from truesteel. Here were chalices, platters, goblets and bowls. Figurines of ivory and jade and bloodstone.

Mostly, though, it was a bed of gold. Gold coins, gold bars, gold pins and rings and brooches. Gold game pieces and a gold-and-onyx board that had once belonged to a dwarven thane. A golden circlet that had graced the head of an elven prince. Thin-hammered sheets of gold, crumpled by the weight of sleeping dragons, that the first Racandros had peeled from the gilded walls of that long-ago city.

Gold, more life-giving than food. Without it, he would first descend into brutish stupidity and then he would die. He would wither away into a skeletal husk and a few errant scales.

He stepped onto the bed, treasure grating and shifting as he pawed it around to make a comfortable depression. He lowered his body into it with a long gust of a sigh. His chin rested on crossed forepaws, and his tail curled around his side.

It had been, he decided as he slipped toward sleep again, some other sense that had awakened him. Some foreboding. He could, if he wished, cast his mind back through his own life and that of his sire, grandsire, and to the beginning of their line. It was an ability related to the way he could know at a touch the history of every item in his hoard. But on occasion, that natural gift had its unnatural side, whispering to his mind not the past, but the future.

Something was coming. Some change, some event. Not here yet, not even near yet, but coming. It might be one of those would-be successors. It might be some puffed-up hero desiring the glory of being a dragon-slayer. It might be that the mountain meant to explode into new fury and consume his home, his hoard, and himself.

His great eyes, as golden as anything around him, slid slowly closed. A growling snore escaped him as he burrowed down into the comfort of his bed and let sleep claim him.

Something was coming . . . but Racandros would be ready.

* * *

Part One:

The Town on the Lake

CHAPTER ONE

A curse on you, oh intractable beast!
– Elwyndas, Veriandor, Act III

"So much for your idea," Ariana Mirida said. "It seems we walk after all."

Wyndrel shot her a glare, but was too occupied in trying to catch his breath to retort.

The rest of them were little better off. All four were gasping, cross, bruised, and out-of-sorts. Their horses were gone but for the receding rapid thuds of hooves on the earth. The gear that had laden the beasts was a messy strew all along the path.

"It could be worse," Kevan Brindani said. The young page, barely a few years older than Ariana's little brother Tal, sported a scratch along one cheek from a low-hanging branch. He dabbed at it and looked, wide-eyed, at the blood on his fingertips. "Will I have a scar?"

"Half a moment and I'll see to it." Mischa Narrin got grimacing to his feet. He had taken the worst of it, having been thrown from his horse to land bone-jarringly in the road.

If, thought Ariana with brief amusement, the other priests of Talopea could see Mischa now, they'd scarcely recognize him. He still wore the corselet he'd donned in Thanis, but it was dented, and the sword at his waist was nicked from use. Gone were the silk shirts and impeccable grooming. He had not spared time to shave since their flight from Perras Peliani; his chin was thus darkened by stubble that gave him a highwayman's aspect.

Gone, too, was much of his self-indulgent attitude. The Mischa who had offered – nay, insisted – on accompanying her to the Emerin had been expecting a journey of leisure and luxury and had very quickly learned otherwise. Yet he hadn't voiced a word of complaint despite the fact that their new journey was even less likely to result in occasions for the pleasure and revelry that the Talopeans held dear.

Drawing herself upright and throwing her thick silver braid over her shoulder, Ariana supposed that she, too, bore little resemblance to the elfmaid who'd set out from her safe and pleasant home. The Silversilk, that marvelous weave of light that protected as well as armor and mended itself by magic, had been taken from her. So, too, had been her mother's signet and her *ilgilean*. Not that a powerstone would do her a whit of good just now.

Her hand crept to her chest, just above her left collarbone. She felt nothing but cold metal. The armor she wore was truesteel, crafted for an elven queen and adorned with jewels. It was strong and light, but after the Silversilk, felt cumbersome. It prevented her from touching the gouged and horrible wound where a thorn-shaped wedge of *gilthanat* had been driven into her flesh and robbed her of her magic.

"Yes, we walk," Wyndrel said.

In the scuffle, the rightful king of the Emerin had sustained a kick to the shin, a horse-bite to the shoulder, and abraded weals on both palms from trying to hold the reins. The only tunic he'd been able to find that would fit his broad shoulders was hundreds of years old, and under the strain the seams had split. Cloth hung around him in flaps. His hair was in his face, he was dirty and scowling, and despite all that – despite, too, her constant annoyance with him – he was an impressive figure of an elf indeed.

Their escape from the dungeons had gone unnoticed, largely because there were few in the palace who knew they'd been there at all. The guards who'd had the keeping of Ariana and Wyndrel were locked away in the very *aether*-deprived cell that had held the prisoners, and the man on whose orders they'd been jailed was the very man they now pursued into the eastern wilds of the Emerin.

The thought of Sir Tiercel brought a bitter taste to Ariana's mouth. Tiercel Reyes, the renowned hero. The brilliant young general whose bravery had been rewarded. The secret traitor who'd arranged the death of the old king and the capture of the new. The villain who'd taken her hard-won prize, the Emerald of Karria, and stabbed the *gilthanat* into her. Tiercel, whose traveling companion was not only *Morvalan* but a dread *Rhunvala*.

Tiercel, who was according to Kev, on his way to destroy that very Emerald.

They couldn't allow it. The Emerald would know the true hand of a king, and thus Wyndrel's claim could be undeniably proved to the Starleaf Council. The Emerald was an artifact of true faith, the only such that Ariana had ever seen. This gem out of legend, gift from a god to a princess of old, must not be allowed to be destroyed.

Revenge, though . . . that also had its appeal. Wyndrel wanted the Emerald safely restored, and his kingdom to be his as it was meant to be. But he also had expressed a wish to see Tiercel dead, and if anyone could do it, Wyndrel could. Possibly even with his bare hands.

Unless Ariana got to Tiercel first.

In most ways, she was her father's daughter. When it came to being wronged, however, her mother's quick temper and even quicker blade often served her better than Arien's cool logic.

"Can we catch them if we're on foot?" Mischa asked.

His command of the elven language had grown steadily, though his accent remained atrocious. He looked around at the encroaching thick-boled trees as he spoke, and rubbed his arms nervously. Prior to rescuing Ariana and Wyndrel from the dungeon, he'd been on his own in the forest for several days and was nobody's woodsman.

Wyndrel clenched his fists. Tendons and muscles stood out in sharp relief. His jaw was so tight his teeth ground together, and when he finally looked up, his tawny-gold eyes were dark and furious.

"That'll be a 'no,' then." Mischa turned to Ariana. "Well, what now?"

"We go on," Wyndrel said. "We find other horses if we can, we walk if we cannot. We crawl if need be. But we go on."

"He was speaking to me," Ariana said.

"It was my question to answer," Wyndrel replied.

Kev watched them anxiously, the tug-of-war between his allegiances plain on his face. On the one side, he had a boy's smitten fascination for Ariana . . . on the other, Wyndrel was his lord and king.

"We should have expected that the theft . . . excuse me, the *borrowing* of the horses wouldn't go unnoticed," Ariana said. "Kev's right in that it could have been worse. We were lucky to have time to unhook our gear. Instead of summoning them home, their owner could have sent someone after. A seeker-mage like him, perhaps." She nodded toward the boy, who bit his lip fretfully.

"Do you want to see Tiercel get away with this?" Wyndrel took a step toward her, blowing a sheaf of golden hair from his face with an exasperated breath. "Do you think we should go meekly back?"

"Meekly?" she echoed. "You're the rightful king, aren't you? Proclaim yourself and have all the horses you want, and an army to go with them."

His hands cut the air in refusal. "You know as well as I the time that would take. You know as well as I how the Council operates. They would do nothing until they were wholly satisfied of my claim. Even if every last man of them knew me the moment I set foot in their chamber, the matter wouldn't be settled until they'd all had their say, and come up with objections and disputes and all manner of other nonsense just so that all and sundry would be assured of their presence. That is one thing I mean to change, but I cannot change it now."

The force of his personality blazed forth like dragon fire. Mischa and Kev both recoiled before it, but Ariana, having faced up to his temper before, stood her ground.

"If we cannot catch up with him, we cannot stop him destroying the Emerald," she said. "Don't you know that eats at my heart? I held it, I felt its power. I know that to let such a thing be broken or lost would diminish us all. But if we walk, we'll be too late. If that is the case, we might as well wait and catch him off-guard when he returns. Believe you me, I hate that idea, but it may be the best we can hope for."

"In the storerooms, you said you were with me," Wyndrel said. "Has your mind changed? Ariana, you have no reason to stay. You have a home to return to, provided that you are able to avoid those in service to Count Elyvorrin. Indeed, you should go home if only to spare your parents the anguish of receiving this letter of which Kev told us. I, however, must to go on."

"Would you listen to me for a moment? One moment, Wyndrel?"

"I have listened. You're correct in that we probably cannot catch up. Nonetheless, I intend to try." With that, he stooped and picked up bundles and packs that had been so hastily unhooked and flung from the horses' backs.

"If you go alone, you're going to your death," she said. "Not that I'm saying the rest of us would make much difference against Tiercel and Tilanne, especially without our magic. Alone, though, it's a surety. You need us."

"I never said I did not."

"Yet you're willing to go it alone."

"It must be done."

Ariana yanked off the truesteel pot helm that matched her corselet, and rubbed at her temples. "I am trying to talk sense into you. No one can fault your determination, least of all I. But you must look at the facts. Among the four of us, we have only Kev's magic."

"Now, wait –" the boy said.

"I mean no offense, Kevan, truly I don't. Your seeker-spells are a great boon to us. Still and all, that won't do us much good in a battle, and you told me that you've only just begun your training at arms."

He subsided. "Yes, that's so."

"Talopea grants Mischa some formidable abilities," Ariana said, going red as she recalled precisely how he'd distracted the guards to let them out of their cell. "He is a healer, and progressing not too poorly as a swordsman."

"A thousand thanks, Ari," Mischa said, grinning.

"As for myself," she went on, "I am also adept at swordplay, and while I'll never be anyone's expert archer, I know one end of an arrow from another. My real strength is in my magic, and that misbegotten soulless whoreson took it from me." She rubbed again at the cold truesteel and frowned. "You, Wyndrel, said to me that you were of the Order of the Gryphon. If that's true –"

"I do not lie."

"Very well. As I understand it, the Order of the Gryphon is for those who've proven themselves in the Orders of the Lion and the Eagle both. Swordsmen, and warmages."

"Yes, that is so. And I know what you will next say. That the *gilthanat* embedded in my bone –" he slapped his upper arm where a circular knot of scar marked the wound, "– has deprived me of half my strength. That may be true, but I do not need magic to deal with Tiercel."

"But we *will* need magic to deal with the *Rhunvala*," Ariana said. "She has . . . for want of a better word, *powers*. While she claims she's sworn to take no elven life and I believe she would hold to that vow even if it meant losing her own, there are other and worse things she might be able to do to us. My father witnessed a *Rhunvala* in battle before and I know of what I speak."

"Not to mention," Mischa said, "that her vow about elven lives leaves little in the pot for me."

"I am aware of the situation, and the odds against us," Wyndrel said. "That changes nothing."

"What good will it do us, you, or the kingdom if we get ourselves killed?" She was losing her temper now, feeling it hiss and burn through her mental grasp just as the reins of the horses had done to Wyndrel's hands, but was helpless to stop.

"I don't plan to die."

"No one *plans* to die, you infuriating man!"

His breath blew out between his teeth with a sound like a disgruntled dog. "Eight years with no one else to speak to, you'd think I wouldn't tire of talk so quickly, but I am tired of yours. Either come along or go back, I care not, but *I* am going. You've had your say."

Kev threw her a look of pure distress. Ariana stalked to Wyndrel and jabbed him in the chest with her forefinger.

"If not for us, you'd still be down in the dark. I think you owe us the courtesy of hearing us out."

Wyndrel's hand flashed and seized her wrist. "The only one I hear going on about this is you. I've given you your choice. Make it, and let the others do as they will. As for what I owe you . . ." He raised his other hand and tinked a fingernail against her chest. It rang on the truesteel.

She stared at him and he returned it, sapphire eyes to gold. The moment spun out like a thread.

Kev broke the tense silence, clearing his throat. "We . . . um . . . we might be able to get more horses. If we change course. That might be for the best anyway, I thought."

"Speak on," Wyndrel said without taking his eyes from Ari's.

"Well, I thought perhaps we might do better not to try and follow Sir Tiercel directly," Kev said. "If he somehow found out, he could ambush us. We know where he's going. We could try instead to get there first, be waiting for him."

"At the dragon's lair, you mean," Mischa said. "While normally I'm all for adventure and challenge, that seems a bit much."

"Hush, Mischa, let him speak. Go on, Kev," Ariana said.

"He's headed on a more southerly course. It makes sense, I suppose, if he really is *Morvalan*." This most of all distressed Kevan, who was still young enough to shiver at cradle-tales of evil elves stealing children away in the night and sacrificing them to their bloodthirsty god. "If we stay further north, and make for Lake Eltar, we could acquire horses there."

"What's to stop them from being summoned out from under us again?" Mischa asked. "Mine is stabled comfortably in the city and had I known this was going to be such a fuss I'd have gone to get it."

"I'm not saying we should *steal* more," Kev said. "We could buy them. Eltarrin may be a small town, but it's no mere village. It prospers."

"Eltarrin," Wyndrel said. "Is that not the home of the Floating Gardens? My father promised to take me there one day, but we never had the chance."

"I thought the big city was all it was?" Mischa turned quizzically to Ariana.

She massaged the wrist that Wyndrel had released. "Perras Peliani is where most of the Emerin's people live, but there are a few other towns. Feyna Rel, for instance. Or one that I heard was leveled by dwarves during the war."

"If we are careful," Kev said, "no one will know who we are. We could arrange for horses and what supplies we still need. Mayhap we might find a physician to see about the *gilthanat*. If you could regain your magic . . ."

"That would be well worth a side trip," Ariana said. "Well, Wyndrel?"

"By that, I take it you still plan to accompany me."

"With a sensible plan, yes. Kev's put forth a sensible plan. Are you going to follow it?"

His answer was to gather up as many of the fallen packs and bags as he could carry. For one of his strength, that was several. He looked at Kev. "Seeker-mage, lead us there."

"Yes, Your Majesty."

Ariana rolled her eyes at Mischa, and slung her own pack over her shoulder.

They set off at the briskest pace they could manage. The palace's old storerooms had provided armor, weapons, magically-preserved foodstuffs. They lacked certain key essentials such as spare clothes that would actually fit Wyndrel's powerful build – he couldn't even get Mischa's spare tunic over his chest – and basic items such as plain soap, flint and steel. Not to mention the little taken-for-granted things that Ariana knew her mother would have packed. Lockpicks, for instance.

She blamed Emerinian society and its love of magical conveniences. Who needed soap when there were spells of cleaning? Who struck fire with flint and steel the old-fashioned way when every schoolchild's first spells included the making of fire and magical light? In that, at least, they should be fine with Kevan.

Their trip out of the city had been a hair-raisingly uneventful one. At every step along the palace's escape tunnel, Ariana was sure that guards were going to spring out, perhaps shooting them full of arrows before even finding out who they were. Or that some ancestor of Wyndrel's might have decided the tunnel should be closed off, or protected by some sort of trap, enchantment, or watch-dog. She'd already seen the sorts of monstrosities shaper-mages could devise. What better place to put such an abominable creature than to guard a secret passage?

But there had been none, and they had reached the end without incident. Wyndrel had torn through a thick screen of bushes like a man possessed, not fully seeming to accept and appreciate his freedom until he was out of the castle and the city.

The horses had been "borrowed," as he put it, from one of the outlying inns. It was true, as she'd told Mischa, that Perras Peliani was all one vast city, but each of the counts had estates located in the countryside around it, and the roads leading off to those estates were lined with taverns, homes, and businesses. Just their luck that none of them had paused to think what might happen when the missing horses were discovered.

They had left all the trappings of civilization behind. Out here in the midst of the deep woodlands, it was a simple matter to forget that there had ever been a city. To forget that there were other places in the world where people lived, worked, made love, argued, committed crimes. They could have been all alone in the world.

Light and shadow chased each other as the wind stirred the boughs. Ariana breathed deeply of the fragrant air and smiled. Her aggravations with Wyndrel aside, her worries about Tiercel and Tilanne aside, she was almost enjoying this outing.

She might not be of the same mind when many days had gone by and she was footsore and aching, but for now it was most pleasant to stride along, even at Wyndrel's hard pace.

This was the Emerin. So much of it; so many different moods. Had she really been fool enough to say, standing there in Perras Peliani, that she was home? She flushed to recall that yes, she had. Not that the city wasn't fine. It was fine and grand and magnificent, everything that she'd imagined. But, the wonders of Perras Peliani aside, the rest of the Emerin thus far hadn't shown the best of faces to her. She'd had a brief stay in the spectacular Waterfall Terrace in the palace, and a longer stay in the chilly dungeons beneath. She'd left the city before having much time at all to experience elven life in its purest form, and instead gone traipsing off on a quest that had pitted her against shaper-mages and all manner of their bizarre creations.

They made good time that day despite the loss of their horses, and camped on a hilltop partly ringed by a ridge of stone to provide a serviceable windbreak. The furs and blankets they'd gotten from the storerooms were musty and old, but adequate for the warmth of a mild night. Dinner was eaten in the companionable silence of weary but content travelers.

"We'll draw straws for watches," Wyndrel announced when twilight had settled over the land. He picked four twigs and snapped them into varying lengths, hiding them in his fist so that only the ends stuck out.

Mischa groaned. "Must we? When Ariana and I were on our own –"

"I had my magic," she reminded him. "Without it, there are no spells of warning to rely upon."

"I'd gotten quite used to a full night's sleep," he grumbled, drawing a straw.

"Which I'd wager you never had in Thanis," Ariana said. "Not with so many ladies about."

"For *that*," he retorted, "I'd gladly give up sleep. But to sit staring into the darkness, jumping out of my skin at every rustle and cracking branch? That sort of tension is bad for the nerves, Ari, and worse for the complexion. I'll have worry-lines and grey hairs 'ere long."

"At least you're first," she said, comparing the straws they now each held. "Middle watches are worse than end ones."

"Have either of you ever stood watch before?" Wyndrel asked in a scathing tone. "Do you even know of which you speak?"

"Not personally, no." Ari bristled. "But our parents –"

"Good for them. Let's see how *you* do." He piled more wood by the fire, enough to keep it burning through the night, and went to his bedroll.

"Tell me again why I'm doing this," Ariana muttered.

"For the scenery?" Mischa's eyes were fixed appreciatively on Wyndrel, who had stripped off the tatters of his shirt.

"Very funny."

"Wasn't trying to be. He's a fine one, Ari, that you must admit."

"Until he opens his arrogant mouth."

"Are you saying you don't fancy him?"

"Brilliantly deduced, Mischa."

"Mind if I have a try, then?"

She chuckled sourly. "Best of luck. I doubt you're his type."

"Ah, right, we short-eared, unattractive humans." He surveyed Wyndrel a moment longer as the other man stretched out on the ground, wrapped in blankets. "You told me, though, that one reason elves didn't find us so appealing was that we weren't as willow-slim as your kind. What of him, then? He's better built than a dwarven fortification. Is he unattractive?"

"Some might find him so," she said.

His hazel eyes twinkled at her. "Some, but not you."

"Oh, go stand your watch."

Chuckling, he went to a log that afforded a vantage point and sat down. Ariana glanced at Kevan, who'd been listening silently with a quirk of a grin. When her gaze fell upon him, he quickly busied himself unrolling his own furs.

"Good night, Lady Ariana."

"It's just Ariana, or even Ari," she said. "And good night to you, Kev."

* * *

CHAPTER TWO

For in that town there walked a thing unspeakable, and their hearts were filled with dread.
– Elwyndas, The Shaper's Fate (ballad)

Rantiel Herann was debating whether or not to have another cup of tea before bed when he heard an eerie cry on the night wind. It sent chills racing along his spine. The wooden cup slipped from his grasp. It struck the table and rolled to the floor, and splashed his slippered feet and bare ankles with the cold dregs of tea.

Sleekfur had been dozing on the hearth, as close to the fire as she could get without her silver-white belly fur at risk of being ignited by a stray spark. At the sound of that strange cry, she shot up. Her ears twitched, her tail puffed, and a low, wavering yowl issued from her throat.

"Shh, girl," Rantiel said. His heart was galloping, galloping.

What in the name of the gods had that noise been?

His first thought was to call for Illan and Dharra, asleep in their small rooms off the kitchen. But as he opened his mouth, he changed his mind. If the cry hadn't disturbed the apprentices, he wasn't about to. Not until he knew for a surety that there was some good reason.

He was closing on his millennial birthday, an age at which he ought to be attended by devoted children and grandchildren, respected by all, vaunted for the wisdom that his ten centuries had brought. But young people today had lost all respect for their elders. His neighbors either bored or irritated him when he was forced to go into town. He lived apart from his family and that was the way they all liked it.

The apprentices were a necessary evil, now that he wasn't as spry as once he'd been. It galled him to admit he needed younger backs to do the work around the place. They'd learned, though, right quickly and well, that he wasn't about to tolerate backtalk from the likes of them. They knew to keep their opinions to themselves and mind their manners, or they'd be sent away so fast it would dizzy their heads.

That didn't stop them from thinking him a doddering old fool. He didn't care much what they thought, so long as they behaved. But he wasn't about to give them one more reason to roll their eyes at each other when they didn't think he could see, or one more tale to carry into town.

No, he'd see for himself first.

There *was* something out there. He knew it; Sleekfur knew it.

Probably youngsters from town, out on a lark. He'd been the butt of their pranks before. They came in the night and stole fruit from his orchard, used his barn for their romantic assignations, left wine bottles in his field. Only a few days ago, he'd gone into town and complained to the constable, naming the ones he suspected. This must be their spiteful revenge.

Trespass on his land, would they? Bother him with animal calls? They'd see about that. He wasn't too old to defend what was his.

A bow hung over the mantle with a quiver of arrows beside it. Rantiel took these down and slung the quiver's strap across his body from shoulder to hip. He strung the bow, grunting as he did so – it had been twenty years or more since he'd fired it, and it was a tougher pull than he remembered.

Sleekfur rubbed around his legs. Her back came to above his knees, and when she pushed hard she could nearly knock him over. Her fur still stood on end and she made the chittering sounds he associated with her hunting.

"We'll find them, won't we, girl? Give them a bit of a scare." Rantiel bent down and took the spotted pantera's heavy, triangular head between his hands. "No killing, now. Scratch them up a bit if that's what it takes to teach them their lesson, but no killing."

Her serious, lambent eyes met his. She made her chittering sound again. *Eh-eh-eh-eh.*

Rantiel was in loose trousers and a patched tunic gone colorless from age. He threw a light cape around himself and went out, still in his slippers.

The porch of the farmhouse faced across a dooryard of short grass to the large barn. To his left was a fenced garden patch, to his right an arched wooden footbridge over the creek that bisected his property. The night was clear, the silver moon overhead and the black moon rising in the east like a slitted eye. The wind gossiped among the *alkarra* orchard's leafy boughs. The ripening fruit's sweet, syrupy scent hung thick on the air.

Again, the cry. It drifted out of the night.

Sleekfur hissed.

"Let's go find them, girl," Rantiel said.

Bow in hand, he descended the porch steps. The pantera stayed close by his side as they crossed the yard. His soft footfalls on the bridge were swallowed up by the burbling of the creek. It took a moment for his eyes to adjust to the diminished moonlight beneath the trees, but soon he was able to see clearly.

He should have been able to hear them by now. Giggling. Plotting their next bit of mischief. Referring to him by terms they hadn't learned at school.

But there was none of that. Only a third utterance of that uncanny cry. And a rending, splintering sound he identified all too readily.

"Wretches!" He broke into a shambling run.

Sleekfur paced him, then streaked past him. He had a momentary blurred impression of her feline form darting ahead. He saw her crouch-gather-leap, and bright terror spiked through him.

"No kill, Sleekfur, no kill!" Ah, he could just imagine the trouble if she tore the face from one of those insufferable infants. He would never hear the end of it.

The pantera screeched. Not in hunting. Not in victory. In agony.

"Sleekfur!" His terror was instantly replaced by rage. Harm his pantera, would they? Well, mayhap they'd be sent running for home with arrows in their backsides, and let them explain *that* to their families. In his day, the young had known to show proper respect!

He plunged ahead, though the shadows here were so thick as to defeat even elven sight. Sleekfur was screaming, screaming, her voice like that of a woman being tortured.

And then, even worse than the screams, came a wet ripping. Then silence.

Rantiel thought his heart might burst, whether from grief or exertion or anger he didn't know. He grabbed for an arrow, nocked it, and charged on.

A looming shape rose up. Up and up. Hunched and awful. At the end of one long arm, it held Sleekfur's dangling corpse. At the end of the other, which was shorter, stunted, and bulging, it held the fruit-laden branch that had been wrenched from one of the trees.

The cry came again, all challenge and fury now as the creature towered over the old man. He could not see clearly and was *glad* he could not see clearly, for what little he could see told him that this was no natural beast but something hideous and wrong.

He loosed the arrow without fully realizing he did so. The strength ran from his limbs like water. The arrow struck and buried itself harmlessly in the ground between the thing's splay-toed, taloned feet.

"Sleekfur," Rantiel said, in a weak croak that was barely a word at all.

The creature advanced. He could smell it, through the fragrance of the *alkarra* fruit and the hot reek of his pet's blood. Its scent was bitter and earthy, acrid, a nose-wrinkling, sneeze-bringing scent that made him think of worms after a hard rain, drowned worms on the cobblestones.

The pantera's torn body and the broken branch dropped, cast aside by the creature. Its mismatched arms reached out for Rantiel. He could only see that they were thorned with claws, an impossible number of claws. They ran and dripped with blood.

Rantiel closed his eyes. He knew he was going to die. His frail old form was braced for it in grim anticipation. He would die, but no one could make him *look* at the beast.

Its breath, sweet with fruit juice, washed over him and blew his thinning hair back from his face. It would be right in front of him now, its jaw surely as crowded with teeth as its hands were with claws. Teeth jutting off in all directions, pointed and vicious.

But then, as his life dangled on a thread, shouts and running feet disturbed the stillness. Rantiel heard his name being called, recognized the panicked voice of Dharra Felthris.

Air buffeted him. He felt something brush by him, something scaly and hairy and damp. Cold. There was no heat to the beast. Even its breath had been cold as a tomb. It whirled away from him, bumping him hard enough to send him sprawling.

His eyes flew open. The creature was fleeing into the deeper reaches of the orchard. It did not run upright like a man nor on all fours like an animal, but went hunched over in a clumsy yet swift lope.

Light, blindingly white and pure, spilled over him. His apprentices were there with magelights shining from their hands. Both talked at once, was he all right, what happened, where was Sleekfur – this last question bitten off in a strangled sob as the light reached the remains of the spotted pantera.

Rantiel did not answer. He groaned and pushed himself up, the scene revealed in uncompromising brightness. The blood. The broken branch. Sleekfur. The tracks. Pressed deep into the soil. The tracks.

* * *

"You asked for my conclusion, Constable," Selara Viska said. "There you have it."

She picked up a pristine white square of cloth and cleaned her hands with it, although as far as Ainvar Lynellen could see, not the slightest stain or smudge marred them. They were ivory-pale, exquisitely shaped and perfect. The sort of hands that a man might happily spend an entire evening lavishing kisses upon. The sort of hands that promised to know every detail and every secret of a man's body.

Which, he thought, they did. Just not to bring pleasure. Hers were a physician's hands, and not in the gentle manner of most healers. Her touch was brisk and efficient, cold and businesslike.

The rest of her, while equally lovely, was equally forbidding. Straight jet-black hair was gathered into a bun at the nape of her swanlike neck. Her face was severe in its beauty, her eyes as cool and sharp as obsidian.

"An hallucination," Ainvar said. "You're certain that's all it was?"

"He is close to a thousand years old and has been breathing *alkarra* pollen for at least eight hundred of those years," she said.

"What of the pantera?"

She sniffed. "Dead."

"Yes, Doctor . . . I saw that much for myself when I brought it in. What slew it?"

"Its neck was wrung and its chest torn open. Either of those would have done. I cannot confidently tell you which was the cause of death."

"Could *Tars* Herann have done it himself?"

"Hardly."

He raised his eyebrows expectantly at her. She exhaled through pursed lips.

"Oh," she said. "So therefore, this monster must have done it. Is that what you're thinking, Constable? You were out there. Did you see any monsters? Any tracks?"

"The old man said there were some, but in all the confusion, his apprentices running to and fro, they trampled the ground thoroughly."

"Have you considered *them?*" She took the cloth to her hands again, fastidious to the point of obsession. The pale skin was reddened from the rubbing. "Rantiel Herann is not well-liked. To his apprentices, he's doubtless a tyrant. Far easier for me to believe that someone, some *person*, did this. If not the apprentices, surely there are others who've voiced grievances about him."

"Many," Ainvar said. "But none who'd do something like this. Slaughter a pantera? Pull it apart like a roast fowl? Who among us has that kind of strength?"

She looked at him then, long and speculatively. Had she been any other woman, he might have dared to hope that she was evaluating with a lover's eye his lean archer's build, firm jaw, and the upswept tips of his ears just visible through his chestnut hair. Not so Selara Viska.

"You are a strong man, Constable. And you're the one to hear all these many complaints. Such a man could grow tired of them, and desire to throw a scare into an old nuisance."

"Flattered as I am by your opinion of my strength, Doctor, you're far afield. I am entrusted to keep the peace."

"If not you, someone else," she said with a shrug. "My purpose is to treat my patient. That I shall do. He is physically unharmed but for some bruises, and his heart is weak. I expect him to be on the mend very shortly. It is, however, his mental state that concerns me. He's not fit to be left to his own recognizance."

"That is for him and his family to decide," Ainvar said.

She nodded and turned to the shelves that lined one wall of the room. They were covered with glass vials and ceramic pots, all neatly labeled and free of dust, as scrupulously clean as the rest of her office. She set to rearranging them, and turned to speak to him over her shoulder. He couldn't help admiring the way her slender body twisted, and the way her functional snow-white overtunic molded to her hips.

"Excuse me?" He grinned abashedly as he realized he hadn't paid attention to what she said.

"A bear could have killed the pantera," she said. "They still roam the woods, and one might have crossed over to our island. Entirely possible that he saw a bear, and his mind did the rest."

"Ah. Yes. Thank you, Doctor."

"Was there anything else, Constable?" she asked when a few moments had gone by and he hadn't yet left.

"I was . . . no. Nothing. I'll let myself out."

He did just that, knocking himself in the brow with one curled fist when he reached the outer office and opened the door. Golden sunlight fell on him and made him aware just how cool, almost icy, that room had been. Did she utilize some magic to keep it that way? Or was it nothing more than the chill Selara Viska gave off?

Chiding himself – to think, he'd been on the verge of asking the woman if she'd like to go out for a glass of wine sometime, the more fool he – Constable Lynellen went out into the street. The physician's building, which consisted of her office downstairs and living quarters above, was a ways removed from the main market street. Still, a respectable crowd managed to linger in the area, ostensibly on their way to see to various errands but really waiting for him. This was the talk of the town, the most excitement to rouse Eltarrin in years.

He had been sleeping in the small apartment above the guard station when a frantic Illan Norr had come pounding at his door. The reflexes he'd honed in the war had remained keen despite the town's peacefulness, and he was out of bed with sword drawn before his eyes were all the way open. Shortly thereafter, he'd been thundering along the road in the moonlight with the youthful apprentice clinging in a death-grip to his waist.

At the orchard farmhouse, the other apprentice had been waiting. The two young plant-mages had shaped a stretcher from lengths of wood and carried the half-conscious Rantiel Herann back to the house. There, Dharra Felthis had forced an herbal sedative on him while Illan ran for help.

All the shocked man could do was mumble fitful, unnerving half-heard words. *Scales . . . claws . . . tracks . . . cold.* The apprentices had also brought back the body of the pantera – neither of them said as much but Ainvar was left with the clear impression that they cared far more for the cat than for their master – and, presumably thinking he'd want it as evidence, the stripped branch that had been broken from one of the *alkarra* trees.

Herann kept no horses, preferring to hire them at harvest time. He did keep his own wagons, though, and into one of these Ainvar and the apprentices loaded the sleeping man and the oilcloth-wrapped body of the pantera.

The apprentices hadn't been willing to return to the farmhouse in the dark, spending what little remained of the night at the town's only inn. They were among those waiting for Ainvar as he emerged from Physician Viska's office. He went to them.

"The doctor says that he'll be well soon," he said, raising his voice enough to be sure the onlookers could hear. "She theorizes that a bear might have been responsible. I'll need some woods-wise hunters to search the orchard. Dogs, too."

A perceptible wave of relief went through the assembled crowd. A bear, of course, why had no one suggested it already? A bear, they could handle. Far better than rumors of some shaper-mage monstrosity.

"Dharra . . . *Tarsti* Felthis," Ainvar said to the young woman. "As senior apprentice, you'll come with us."

She looked both pleased and distressed by his words. She took a deep breath, steeled herself, and nodded. "Very well, Constable. What about Illan?"

"He'll stay here, should the doctor or her patient need anything." Ainvar turned to the youth with a grim smile because he knew this was the one whose careless feet had obliterated the tracks. "You, *Tars* Norr, will inform the physician of my wishes in this matter."

The youth's puzzled but hurt frown indicated that he did not know why he was being singled out, but he clearly knew a punishment when he heard one. He hung his head and trudged toward the physician's door with steps that might have been approaching the gallows.

"The rest of you leave this to us," Ainvar said, sweeping them with his gaze. "We'll have all well in hand by dusk, I assure you. Nothing to concern yourselves over."

As he mounted his horse and waved his arm to lead his small group of searchers, he fully believed what he told them and had as of yet no reason not to.

* * *

His father didn't emerge from the workshop, but shouted some instructions as Nerevian left the house.

"Tepwood, if you can find it, Nerevian. And pearl-shells, but only the whole ones, mind."

"I know, *Vala*, I know." His bag swung at his side, empty except for a few tools and the parcel that held his lunch. He opened the door, smiled expectantly into the sunlight, and skipped down the street.

He stopped at the corner to turn and wave and his mother returned it from the stoop. She blew him a kiss and mouthed her usual farewell: "Be careful!"

Be careful. As if he wasn't always. Sometimes he thought she would never realize he wasn't a baby anymore. She still bathed him, laid out his clothes, cut his meat . . . once when he'd witnessed a mother bird spitting up regurgitated food for her babies, had counted himself lucky she didn't do *that* too.

They lived on a narrow, winding street that climbed toward a hill. The shrine to Valannin – the spring visitors called it quaint – at the top was a marble pedestal in the middle of a round lawn, ringed with bowers and open to the sky. On special occasions, the townsfolk came and left little tokens here, offerings of thanks to a god that Nerevian hardly knew anything about.

The few times he'd asked, his parents and teachers had given him vague answers: Valannin the Wise Lord, god of thought and scholarly pursuits. As far as Nerevian had been able to determine for himself, Valannin and the other gods were like the ancestors. No longer around, but good to pay remembrance to all the same.

He passed the shrine with barely a glance, headed for the bower on the far side. It gave onto a path that went crookedly off into the forest, down the hillside that sloped steeply to the beach.

What he liked best about this path was the way it ended so suddenly. He'd go through the woods, seeing nothing around him but trees and bushes, and all of a sudden he'd go up one final rise and the lake would be there.

The lake was like a piece of the sky fallen to earth, reflecting the mood of the weather above it. Today, it was clear and pale blue, and along the shore the water mirrored the trees and rising mountains as well as any lookingglass. Little lapping waves rose and fell against the coast. Those wavelets provided his family's livelihood. The water-sculpted wood and stones and shells that washed ashore were what his father needed.

Someday, Nerevian would be a craftsman too. If his mother ever trusted him with a carving knife. She seemed convinced that the very instant she allowed him to even try, he'd lop off half his fingers and be maimed for life.

In the meantime, he was developing an eye for pieces that his father could use. This rounded section of log was already almost a bowl, that smooth-worn rock could easily be chipped and polished into the likeness of a horse, these shells were just right for a necklace.

He unlimbered his bag and wandered the beach in a weaving course. His gaze scanned the ground, not looking for anything but taking it all in, and that way he was better able to single out the best pieces to add to his bag.

After a while of this, his stomach spoke to him. He found a comfortable rock and sat down, the bag between his feet, while he rooted through it and came up with a sealed jug.

Turning the jug over and over, Nerevian scowled. There was a lake in front of him, a lake as fresh and clean as anybody could want. He could have just brought a cup and dipped it full. But no. The lake was full of fish scales and fisher-bird droppings and gods-knew what else. His mother would let him drink nothing but pure water on his outings, *created* water, made by magic so she'd know it was good for him.

Sighing, he reached into his bag again for his lunch. He might disagree with his mother's stance on beverages, but no one could make a better almond-butter and *alkarra* jelly breadroll than she could.

A shadow fell on the sandy, rocky beach beside him. This beach, harder to get to and arguably less scenic than the ones closer to town, was not frequented by many besides himself. Surprised but not afraid, he turned.

A greeting froze on his lips. The strap of his bag fell from nerveless hands.

He was given a sudden violent shove. Nerevian tumbled off the rock, skinning his knees and elbows. Stones dug into his back as he scrabbled like a freshwater crab.

His bag was snatched up.

"That's mine, give it to me!"

Indignation overpowered his fear. He launched himself from the ground, grabbing for the bag. It was lifted beyond his reach, the way one of the bigger boys from school might laughingly hold his books while teasing him. Except the figure wasn't laughing, wasn't teasing.

At the furious glare of its eyes, the boy forgot his indignation, his lunch, the driftwood and shells he'd spent the morning collecting for his father. Terror replaced all thought.

The hideous face leered at him, snarled at him. He screamed and turned to flee but his feet tangled in themselves and sent him crashing back down. His flailing hands scraped trenches in the rocky sand and then he was up, up and running. Not into the woods, no, he'd heard enough scary stories to know that fleeing into the woods was sure doom. He'd be chased, caught, savaged, and killed.

He ran down the beach instead, shrieking for all he was worth.

Ahead was a spur of high wet-backed stones like a natural breakwater. He scaled them as fast as he could, slipping and banging his shins, rubbing his palms raw. At any moment, he just knew he'd feel that horrible hand closing around his ankle. It would yank him backward while his fingernails etched furrows in the stone.

The hand never touched him. He was up, he was over, he was rolling down the far side sure that he was about to break all his bones or pitch into the lake . . . or both, where he would drown as his shattered limbs floundered madly.

He hit a heap of rotting lake-grass. A damply fetid stink rose around him but he barely cared, so grateful for the soft, if slimy, landing.

Nerevian risked a look up, expecting to see his pursuer coming over the top. Nothing was there, nothing to see except the sky.

Not at all reassured, crying now instead of screaming, he got unsteadily to his feet. The lake-grass squelched with every step, threatening to dump him on his face. He made it to dry land without further falls, every part of him in pain, blood seeping from his hands, knees, elbows, and chin.

His chest hitching, tears turning the world into a watery waver, Nerevian was just beginning to calm down, just beginning to realize he had escaped, when he heard movement behind him.

* * *

CHAPTER THREE

Mirror blue, mirror true, and by flowers all surrounded.
– Elwyndas, The Song of Shannia, Part Three, Verse Eleven

"All this land," Mischa Narrin panted as he struggled up a rise and paused at the top to wipe his brow. "All this empty land. It's uncanny. In the Northlands, you can't go a day or two in any given direction without a village, or a farm, or a shepherd's house, or something. Why aren't there more settlements?"

"The human lands must grow all their food," Ariana said. "Thus they must spread out, and make the best use of the land. To us, magic provides. Food is grown, but by mages who excel in the sorcery of the living earth, plants, or animals."

"No peasants, in other words?"

"Precisely."

"It goes far deeper than that," Wyndrel said. "There is a lack of a . . . frontier spirit, shall we say, in the Emerinian people. No urge to explore, no urge to claim a plot of land for one's own. With all that we most value readily at hand in the cities, why go anywhere else?"

Kevan, who had been scouting ahead and making use of his seeker-magics to assure they were still going in the right direction, came bounding back to them with the youthful exuberance of his fourteen years. Although Ariana was only twice his age, barely out of girlhood by Emerinian standards and a dozen years away from legal maturity, she felt more tired from just watching him.

"The lake, I saw the lake! If we press on, we could be there by nightfall."

"And sleep in real beds?" Mischa asked hopefully.

"And buy horses," Ariana said, rubbing at her legs. "You haven't exactly brought us the flattest, easiest route, Kev."

He grinned. "But the shortest one."

"One matter above all," Wyndrel said in a cautionary voice that demanded attention. "When we reach Eltarrin, let no mention be made of my real name or status. It's best that I go by Rell again. To do otherwise would raise too many questions."

"Fair enough." Ariana settled the straps of her pack into the familiar grooves they'd worn into her shoulders. "If you'll be mindful not to order the townspeople around, Your Majesty."

"Are you saying I put on airs?"

"Not at all. Only that you've a tendency to be a tad heavy-handed when it comes to giving orders."

"Oh, please, in Talopea's name, let's not start this again," Mischa said. "If you two want to spend the afternoon arguing, Kev and I will go on without you."

"I am accustomed," Wyndrel said, eyes smoldering, "to commanding soldiers. Not, as you'd imply, to ordering my subjects about."

"We're not soldiers. And of us all, in truth, only Kev could be called your subject. Mischa is a citizen of Thanis, and I of Gamelin."

Wyndrel went from smolder to flare. "Why must you needle me at every turn, woman?"

"I'm not needling." Which was an untruth and she knew it, yet was somehow helpless to stop. "You're the one expecting us to do exactly as you say and only as you say without debate."

"Perchance because I know what I'm doing."

"I know what I'm doing too! Mischa and I did well enough before you came along."

"Mmm-hmm," Mischa said. "Right up until we actually *had* the Emerald, and then it all went to pieces. I nearly starved in the woods, you were dragged off to the dungeon –"

"Mischa," she warned.

"So that's it, is it?" Wyndrel asked, lip curling in an amused grin only a step removed from a smirk. "You got rather used to being in command and can't bear to see another take it from you."

"It wasn't like that at all. When Mischa and I traveled together, we both made the decisions."

Mischa looked about to say something beginning with "Well . . ." but she silenced him with a look. Alas for her, Wyndrel missed neither. His sardonic chuckle burned into her like acid.

"And when my parents went on their adventures," Ariana said, plunging on, "they and their friends listened to each other, decided together, recognized that each one of them had his or her own insights and talents that could be put to the benefit of all. That's a lesson I think you need to learn."

"One which you think you can teach me? *You?*"

"I'll tell you one thing. If you don't learn it now you'll have a time of it when you *do* become king. The Emerin is not about to welcome some domineering bully who runs roughshod over the opinions of others. The Council won't accept a king who acts without heeding their advice."

"The Emerin *needs* just such a king," Wyndrel said. "The complacency we've lived in for centuries must come to an end. My father, gods rest and keep him, was a good king who cherished the Emerinian way of life and never wanted to see it change. Yet all around us, the world has changed while we've stayed the same. It moves on without us. If we are to survive, we must adapt."

"They don't desire to change," she said. "Why should they? There is no want, no deprivation in the Emerin. No peasants, as we said. No poor. No crime. No hunger. No fear. They like it fine just as it is, just as it's been for hundreds, or thousands of years. They will resist, and vehemently, anything that threatens their comfortable, safe way of life."

"What they want, and what they need, are not always the same."

"I know that. My father was raised in the Emerin. It wasn't until he left it that he saw how narrow and blind his life had been. Accepting what he was told because that was the way it had always been done, risking nothing, challenging nothing."

"Then we are in agreement here. Why do you persist in arguing?"

"Because you're a madman or a fool if you think you can stroll into the Council chamber and take the bit in your teeth."

"Run roughshod . . . take the bit in my teeth . . . I must be some belligerent warhorse to you, all snort and steam and crushing my foes underfoot."

"Aren't you?"

"As we have the same foes just now, I wouldn't think you'd mind."

"I want nothing more than to see Tiercel crushed, yes. But if that's how you mean to rule . . ."

"Until Tiercel is crushed, I shan't have the chance to rule."

"Not all your adversaries will be like him. Not every problem can be solved by cold steel."

"I am well aware of that."

"Stop!" Kevan cried. "Please, my liege, my lady, listen to yourselves."

Ariana did stop. Her head was drumming with pain and she just wanted to seize Wyndrel and *shake* him like a nut tree until some sense rattled down into his brain. Yet Kev was right – they were on the same side in this, and somehow she'd gotten trapped in the mire of an argument that didn't exist.

"This is pointless," she said. "Let us press on."

"If no one has further objections?" Wyndrel asked with exaggerated politeness.

"I wasn't objecting . . . ooh!" Reduced to wordless, fuming exasperation, she shoved past him and continued on.

He passed her after a few paces, not looking her way but with his gaze fixed straight ahead and his longer legs moving in longer strides. She hastened her steps, then slowed. No. She was through getting into ridiculous contests with him. If he wanted to run all the way to Eltarrin, let him.

"If it weren't for the Emerald, I'd let you see how well you fared against those two on your own, *Your Majesty*."

No one was close enough to hear her spiteful mutter, and she was glad because she was ashamed of it the moment it reached her own ears. She thought of the catty, bitter women of the duke's court and her face grew warm. What had gotten into her that she, daughter of the ever calm and collected Arien Mirida, would act and speak so?

It was him. It was something about him that got under her skin. That made her palm itch to slap that smug and superior look off his face. He was the greenlion from the Temple of Karria all over again, his easy insolence and arrogance, so sure that he could do whatever he wished because he was stronger, faster, a mighty warrior, *king*.

Well, she may have not done all that splendidly against Tiercel, but she hadn't been locked away from sunlight for eight years like Wyndrel had.

Mischa and Kev trailed along behind her. Ariana heard Mischa's bemused laugh.

"You know," he said to Kev, "the first time they couple, they'll have to do it standing."

Ariana's jaw dropped.

By his tone, so did Kevan's. "The first time they *what?*"

"Couple," said Mischa. "By Talopea, you're fourteen . . . even in the Emerin, you're old enough to at least know what that means, aren't you?"

"I know what it means," Kev stammered. "But I just . . . I cannot fathom why you'd think they . . . you cannot mean it. They don't even like each other."

So affronted she could hardly breathe, Ariana made her feet keep moving. Her ears flamed.

"Trust me, Kevan, I know whereof I speak. Flint and steel make the best sparks, and the best heat comes from friction."

"Whatever that means," the page floundered. "Why would they . . . standing? Why standing?"

Again, the bemused laugh. "Can you see either of them going back-down for the other?"

Ariana wanted to whirl on Mischa, but knew that in her current state, if she started cutting with her tongue she'd end up cutting with her sword. Because he'd smirk. She would protest, he would smirk in that knowing Talopean way, and that would be the end of him.

Instead, she quickened her pace until she could see Wyndrel ahead, and beyond him, the sunlit sparkle of a large body of water.

* * *

Wyndrel had never been to Eltarrin, but when he was a boy his father had oftentimes described the island town to him. That description had stayed so well in his memory that that Wyndrel saw it with familiar eyes.

Shaelan had spoken of it so often and so fondly because he and his last wife, Wyndrel's mother, had come here after their wedding. They'd spent the entire Season of the Fair Dancer here, at an inn overlooking the Floating Gardens.

Whenever his father had told of it, his old eyes had brightened and the decades fell away until he was that man again. Not young, no, not by any means; he had been well over a thousand when he'd married for the third time. But love had restored him, and bittersweet memory – how much he'd loved her, how he'd grieved for her when she died – showed on his face.

Memory, too, was bittersweet for Wyndrel. He had never known his mother except from portraits and tapestries. He had lost his father, and while he'd always known that day would probably come long before he, Wyndrel, reached adulthood, he'd never dreamed it would have been by violence and treachery.

It hurt to think of his father. Yet here, gazing down on Eltarrin, somehow it hurt less. Here, his father had only been happy and loved. It was not like the palace, the halls and chambers of which had witnessed Shaelan's sorrow and declining health. Here, Wyndrel could remember him and be glad.

The others came up behind him, Ariana in the lead. She stopped, and the look of wonder that widened her glorious sapphire eyes was almost enough to make him forget how irksome she could be.

The lake was a nearly perfect oval, fed by waterfalls cascading over the cliffs that hemmed it in on the south. All was grey stone, blue water, and the lush fall colors of the forest. Small islands dotted the lake's expanse and smaller fishing boats sailed or rowed between them.

Eltarrin itself was located on the largest island, which was closest to the lake's western shore. So close, in fact, that a covered bridge connected it to the mainland. Along the west, south, and southeastern shores, the island was colorfully skirted by what seemed to be beds of flowers in all varieties, floating upon the water.

"The Floating Gardens," Ariana said.

Wyndrel nodded, his momentary annoyance with her pushed aside. "They grow on mats of *lheifa* vine, which weave together solidly enough to support layers of soil, the abundance of plant life we see before us, and the weight of those who would walk upon them. The bridge, too, is of *lheifa*."

Most of the island was forested, but the southwestern section to which the bridge led was the site of the town. Cobblestoned streets wandered whimsically, sometimes branching to go around trees that grew in their center, then rejoining. The buildings were not much like the high graceful spires of Perras Peliani, but more like cottages, more like things that had grown rather than been made.

"It's lovely," Mischa said. "When I saw the city, I thought how it looked exactly as a place of elves should look. This is nothing like it, yet it, too, looks exactly as a place of elves should."

"The Gardens are a marvel," Ariana said.

"In the spring, everything blooms," Wyndrel said. "We've come too late in the year to see it at its height, but I do not find it lacking."

He led them down to the edge of the lake, where they found a road. This road was not paved, but well-packed earth, broad and showing signs of frequent use. It led from the bridge north, following the curve of the shore and then vanishing into the woods. Wyndrel consulted an inner map and concluded that the road must go to Feyna Rel.

The bridge, up close, did indeed turn out to be made of the vines. They had been coaxed into that shape, no doubt by the application of plant-magics, firmly anchored on either end and arching above the water. The underside of the roof was thick with a pale-green moss, from which finespun clusters of tiny, bell-shaped, white flowers hung.

Not only bell-shaped; they tinkled a crystalline music as the travelers crossed. The vines were sturdy, but their footfalls set off enough of a shaking to jostle the bell-flowers into making their sweet sound. Ariana laughed aloud, delighted, and raised her hand to skim the bells. Melody answered, and white petals drifted down to powder her silver hair.

"It seems they like you," Wyndrel said.

She looked at him guilelessly for a moment, then away, faint color touching her cheeks. "They're very pretty."

The end of the bridge was the beginning of the cobblestoned streets. Long wooden docks extended out over the *lheifa* mats to clear water, and a few sailing craft were tethered there, rising and falling with the gentle waves. The docks were not bustling with activity, no fishermen unloading their catch. In fact, the streets were empty, the town hushed.

Sunset light slanted red-gold and turned leaded glass windows to rubies, topaz, rich amber. The roofs of the cottages – some buildings were three stories high, yet cottages was the best word to fit – were made of *lheifa* as well, so closely entwined as to be waterproof. The walls were mostly brick, some plastered over and set with mosaics of stone chips in rainbow colors. Most of these mosaics depicted floral scenes, giving all of Eltarrin an effect of the gardens that surrounded it. This effect was intensified by the presence of windowboxes, and a thousand small details such as door handles crafted to resemble fern fronds and curtains embroidered with flowers.

Lamp posts were situated at intervals along the streets, and these too lent themselves to the floral design of the town. Each post was a sculpted stalk, topped with a closed bud of some translucent substance similar to stained glass. As dusky shadows lengthened, the buds lit up from within – a soft glow that grew stronger until the glass petals unfolded and let the light shine out.

"That is very nicely done," Ariana murmured.

"But where is everyone?" Mischa asked.

Wyndrel frowned. Surely the arrival of four strangers – all of them armed and one of them human – would be something that would draw attention. Yet they had seen no one. Neither did he have the sense of eyes marking their progress, perhaps from curtained upstairs windows.

"Would they go to bed so early?" Kev asked, perhaps thinking of Perras Peliani and the wine shops that were lively all night, the theaters, the concerts, the dances.

"Let us make for the center of town," he said. "The market should be there, and the taverns."

No one hailed them. No one appeared.

"They're all gone," Ariana said.

"They're here. They must be."

"Then where?"

"My eyes see only so well as yours."

"It's not entirely deserted," Mischa said, pointing to an indigo silk-cat basking in the last rays of the setting sun. The cat blinked at them in disinterest.

"If I had my magic I could speak to it," Ariana said bitterly.

"Magic, yes. Kevan, find the nearest elf, barring us."

"*Arala Valan*," the boy said. His brow furrowed as if he were working out some complex riddle, then cleared. "This way."

They proceeded on, leaving the cat to its fading sunshine. The street turned and branched, and soon they passed more shops. The traditional signs were on or above the doors – a clothier, a spice shop, a book shop, a bakery. Judging by the goods on display in the front window of the last, they'd been made fresh just that day. Wyndrel's mouth watered at the prospect of warm bread, sugared cake, pies. But the placard propped beside the door proclaimed the shop closed.

"If they are all gone, I'm getting into that bakery," Mischa said. "If I have to gnaw down the door with my teeth."

"I think betwixt the two of us we can break the door down," Wyndrel said.

The town square was not a square but an oblong, angled sort of plaza that was open in the center. A few trees, protected by fences of stiffened *lheifa* vine, sprouted from gaps in the brick-work. Benches, more like swinging hammocks supported by posts, took advantage of the shade the trees provided.

Roughly at the center of the plaza was a fountain, made of the same glasslike substance as the tops of the lampposts. It was multicolored, shaped like flowers of all kinds – not roses, of course, roses had no place here – and the water filled the basins of their cupped petals, overflowed, and finally fetched up in a pool with a shaped-stone rim. The top of the rim was wide enough to sit upon.

Several streets led off from the plaza. At the end of one, Wyndrel saw a building that he would have recognized anywhere, the inn where his parents had stayed.

"No, sire, this way," Kev said.

"Rell," he prompted, smiling.

"Rell, yes, my apologies." Kev returned the smile awkwardly, it clearly not suiting a page of the royal palace to call the rightful king not only by name, but by such a short nickname at that. "My spell . . . it tells me they're this way."

Turning away from the inn, Wyndrel let Kevan lead the way. A short, wide street ended at one of the largest buildings in town. Lights, magelights that lacked the irregular flicker of torch or candle, shone from the windows on the bottom floor. The windows above were dark. A low but steady rustle, the sound of many people whispering or shifting or just breathing, reached his keen ears.

"Must be the night of the school recital," Ariana said.

"Or a town meeting," Wyndrel suggested, indicating with a gesture of his head the sign posted on the wall. *Town Meeting*, it announced. It had been hurriedly but neatly made, and was signed, *Ainvar Lynellen, Constable.*

"What should we do?" Mischa asked. "It isn't our town, and outsiders might not be welcome. Should we find an inn and wait? Although I must warn you, if we have to wait long my stomach will launch a rebellion."

Before they could discuss – or argue, as was more likely – the sharp crack of a gavel sounded from inside and someone declared the meeting adjourned. Moments later, the double doors opened and a host of elves, most pensive and some alarmed, bustled out.

At once, Wyndrel knew that much was amiss in Eltarrin. These people had a look he'd sometimes seen in the war, a look of helpless terror and perplexity that said they didn't know how they'd gotten into this situation and had no idea how to get out.

They froze at the sight of the strangers, and one, a frail-looking woman with a nervous face, let out a short scream.

"Hands away from weapons," Wyndrel said, voice low. "Let's not give them any more reason to be afraid."

He did as he said, holding his hands out away from his sides. Ariana followed suit. The Eltarrin elves stared at them as if slowly realizing these strangers weren't who they'd initially thought they were. Then a tall man in grey, a pattern of scarlet birds sewn along the collar and cuffs of his tunic, came to the forefront. Wyndrel was hardly surprised to see that he held a bow with unerring skill, or that the arrowhead aimed at them had the deadly shine of truesteel.

* * *

CHAPTER FOUR

He who keeps the peace among others must keep the peace within himself.
– Elwyndas, Vaithric, Act V

Ainvar Lynellen had to suppress a shudder every time he thought of how close they'd come to having what had been called, during the war, a "regrettable error."

The meeting had done that to him, wound his nerves tight as his bowstring, and when Fiella Elgraine had screamed from the front steps, he knew in a flash that this was it. The very subject of the meeting had chosen to attend uninvited, and would leave a bloody swath in its wake.

So he rushed out, sheer will parting the crowd like water before him, nocking his bow as he went. Not that it would do much good, oh, no, painful experience had taught him that. If he needed reminding, he had but to flex his right arm and feel the taut pull of the still-mending flesh where Physician Viska had put him back together like a cloth doll.

Injured or not, he was going to defend his town. If it meant doing so at the cost of his life, so be it. Why not? He'd been prepared to lay down his life for the Emerin, had come back from ravaged Keyda whole and sound when others had been sent back in rosecloth or disfigured or driven mad by the experience. All that had been for a lie, for the malicious lie of a minotaur. This at least would be clean, honest. In defense of his town. In defense of the people who'd named him to this post.

But when he got there, sighting past the razor-edged truesteel arrowhead that he might line it up with the head or heart of his target in hopes that this time it would work, he had an eyeblink to realize that he was aiming at a man.

His right hand loosened the barest perceptible amount. The string came close to slipping from his fingers. These arrows had been made with dwarven armor in mind. At this range, his shot would go through the man's bare flesh. Through and into the silver-haired woman he had instinctively thrust behind him for her protection. She, with a look of indignant fury directed not at

Ainvar but at her companion, stepped around so that she was in front of him again.

That moment lived forever in Ainvar's mind. He was going to shoot, going to shoot, couldn't be stopped . . . and then, with a quaking breath, lowered his bow.

A horrible silence followed. The people of Eltarrin stared, either at their constable or at the strangers. The strangers stared only at Ainvar, and his bow.

He closed his eyes to block out those accusatory gazes. He could see his pulse, dull red beating on the inside of his eyelids. Could hear the rushing thunder of it in his ears.

When it slowed to a tolerable level, he opened his eyes again. No one had moved in that brief interval, and now it seemed they were all looking at him. Waiting for him to do something, say something, make the first move.

Someone had better, and soon. Eltarrin was a town that relied on visitors. If word got around that the greeting such visitors now got was a truesteel arrow in the heart, it would doom them.

His throat made a dry click and only then did he realize his mouth was parched as a desert. A dusty croak was all that emerged on his first attempt at speech. He coughed, and tried again. "Yes?"

The strangers watched him warily, although the bow was now at his side and the arrow safely returned to its quiver. He studied them in return, noting that in addition to the bare-chested man – *look at the size of him!* he thought in amazement – and the woman, the third was a stripling whose eyes and mouth were round as saucers, and the fourth was of all the incredible things, a human.

Others were realizing this too, with varying degrees of shock. Ainvar had seen humans before, primarily Keydan refugees and the Highlord's troops that had been sent in supposedly to arbitrate but ended up pulled into the fray. Most of the rest of the townsfolk had not been in the war, or seen the Northlands Embassy in Perras Peliani, and what they knew of humans was taken mostly from stories.

Despite being the object of the intense scrutiny of the townsfolk, the elven man and the woman were engaged in a heated whispered argument. Ainvar caught but one word in three, yet the gist of it was plain. She was armored, he was not, and he could keep his silly manly ideas of chivalry to himself. He, in return, responded something to the effect of scathingly asking apology for his gentlemanly upbringing.

The woman seemed on the verge of saying something fiery, but the human gave her a sharp nudge. He was dark-haired and scruffy, though not as plain-featured as most of his race, and smiled tentatively at the gaping Eltarrin elves.

In the Thanian speech, he hissed, "Now might be a good time for someone to say something."

"Leave it to me."

Ainvar's attention was drawn back to the bare-chested man, whose voice was of an uncommonly deep and rolling timbre, though still harmonious and undeniably of a noble accent. Once he got past his astonishment at the man's imposing physical presence, he had the fleeting impression of recognition. He'd seen that face somewhere before, but just when, and under what circumstances, eluded him.

"Good evening," the man said, with a curt nod, one soldier to another. "We are travelers in search of lodging. Is the inn open?"

One man forgot his hesitation at the prospect of a few off-season *valn kairis* and pushed to the front of the crowd. "It most assuredly is. I am Kelardin Sarra, the proprietor."

A slew of unasked and possibly unanswerable questions filled the air with the turbulent pressure of a gathering storm. All it would take was one, Ainvar suspected, and the clouds would burst in a full torrent. But nobody, either Eltarrin-born or stranger, asked that one.

"Sorry to have disturbed you," the woman said. "We first thought the town was empty."

She was all in silver-grey, from the truesteel helm and corselet to the mist-colored trousers and high iron-grey boots that sheathed her long and shapely legs. In the uncertain light, only her eyes had color, but what color it was! A vivid and brilliant blue, the color of an autumn sky just before the first stars appeared.

Her remark tiptoed up to the edge of the unanswerable but did not quite cross it. Ainvar inclined his head deferentially – she had to be someone of renown, attired as she was and carrying herself like a queen, and in the company of such a bodyguard.

"And we are sorry to have given such an impression," he said. "A town meeting, concluded now. We were all about to return to our homes and business. Were we not?"

"Yes, quite so, Constable," Sarra said. "If you, lady and gentlemen, would accompany me, I'll see to it that rooms are made ready at once."

The assembly slowly dispersed. Haltharan Tannel, Lairis Ciratan, and their respective families hovered near, their expressions ranging from silently beseeching to fearfully scowling. They had not been at all satisfied with the outcome. The very implication that their children would be so rude and irresponsible as the rest of their neighbors had concluded rested poorly on their consciences. They wouldn't rest until he *did* something, would give *him* no rest until then either.

Ainvar assuaged their worries the best he could, promising them that if nothing changed in the next few days, he would reverse the meeting's decision and do as they wished. "But for now, for tonight, go home and get some rest. All will look better in the morning."

They didn't want to, would have rather stayed and pressed the point, but he was implacable and they finally went.

By then, the strangers had vanished around the corner with Sarra, bound for the inn. Ainvar waited until the last of the crowd had headed off, and Eranic, his second, had finished shutting away the lights and locking up the town hall. A wasted effort, he often thought. What was there to take but meeting records and property deeds and all the other papers that a town couldn't get along without?

His little apartment above the constabulary would be waiting for him. Old General would be watching from the front window already, eager for his walk and his supper and a quiet evening at his master's feet. But the prospect of re-heated stew and a good book didn't appeal to Ainvar. He wanted company, more company than a dog could provide. He wanted more pieces to the puzzle that clamored in his head.

Selara Viska was just visible, her white overtunic seeming to hold its own serene glow in the dusk. But that was an idle fancy if ever there was one.

He turned instead toward the inn, thinking that a glass of wine and some of Kelaya Sarra's baked whitefish would be exactly what he needed. And maybe a little conversation. Maybe some news of elsewhere in the Emerin.

Quite a few people had apparently had the same idea. By the time the constable entered the warm common room, with a small fire cheerily ablaze beneath the ornately-carved mantle and the terrace doors propped open so that guests could enjoy their wine at one of the many small tables overlooking the Gardens, the place was half full. An expectancy filled the room, and many a glance was thrown toward the stairs that ascended to the upper floors where the rooms were.

The strangers were nowhere to be seen. Ainvar asked for a glass, reconsidered, and got a bottle. He reasoned that his arm was well enough now that he need not heed Physician Viska's prohibition against too much blood-thinning alcohol. He'd lost enough, she had said, and would do himself no good by trying to replace the rest with wine.

* * *

"We don't see many guests this time of year, oh, no," Kelardin Sarra said, a ring of keys clinking and jingling in his hand. "In the spring, mind you, we're full up, oh, yes, with a list of hopefuls should we have a cancellation. They tip very well, very well indeed, and I've had not a single complaint in all the years I've owned the Bough and Vine. This inn has been in the family for four generations. We were written up once in the Perras Peliani seasonal journal, what a proud and glorious day that was! I still have a copy under glass in the main room downstairs . . ."

He trailed off as he realized that the words were running from his mouth like water and none of his unexpected guests seemed to be paying him any attention. They were looking around at the hallway, with its waist-high tepwood paneling, lovely green and gold silk wallcover above that, and the magelit lamps shedding their comforting glow.

Kelardin took advantage of their distraction to gawk at them anew. Curiosity burned in him but manners kept him silent. His gaze was pulled again and again to the human, and each time he saw that fleshy face and those pathetic rounded nubs of ears, a mixture of pity and revulsion welled in his heart. He'd never seen one before except in drawings, and if offered a wager he'd be showing one to a room in his inn, he would have laughed.

Yes, he burned with questions, but the only one he allowed out was, "And how many rooms will my lords and lady require, or would a suite be preferable?"

"A suite will be fine," the silver-haired woman replied.

"How much?" her bare-chested companion cut in.

Kelardin laughed edgily as it occurred to him that these strange travelers who did not arrive in a coach or on a sailing vessel or even on horseback, but who had come on foot bearing battered old packs and looking as if they'd been lost in the woods for ages, might have no money at all.

Looking again at the abnormally powerful build of the man, and imagining the scene if he were to turn them away, the innkeeper took several quick breaths.

"As it's the off-season," his voice sounding high and fainting, "the usual price is fifty *valn kairis* for a single, seventy-five for a double, and one hundred and fifty for a suite to sleep four."

"Fine," the man said. He dug into a purse tied to his belt and came up not with a sheaf of paper currency but with old-fashioned silver coins and loose gems.

"For how many nights?" Kelardin said by rote, gaping anew.

"At least two," the human pleaded in thickly-accented Emerinian.

"It may take at least that to make our arrangements," the woman said.

"Two, then." The man's long, unkempt golden hair fell in his face as he bent his head to study the coins.

Kelardin thought fleetingly of raising some objection or at least mentioning the oddity – who used metal coin anymore? That handful of treasure looked like something that could have been scooped from some dwarven jewel chest or dragon's hoard. If it were Thanian money, it would be of little use to him here. "Very good, sir. That will be three hundred *valn kairis*."

The coins, he saw on closer inspection as the man counted them out into his palm, were of elven make. Silver *kaimas*, unless he was mistaken. Not in flawless condition, but far from worn. A numbing thrill swept Kelardin at the idea that a collector in Perras Peliani or Feyna Rel might pay quite a bit for these antiquities. They had to be two thousand years old at least, pre-dating the reign of King Shaelan.

He wisely said nothing about any of this as the large man calmly deposited a fortune into his keeping. Neither did the other three, who acted as if this was perfectly in order.

"This is our best suite," he said when he trusted himself to speak again. He led them to the end of the hall, unlocked the door, and threw it wide with a flourish.

It would have been far more impressive by daylight, when the sitting room's many windows would have been bright with the view of the lake and the Gardens, but a pale, cool moonlight and the rippling dark water beyond made for a scene of different, but no less enchanting, beauty.

They passed him, first the woman and then the human and then the youth and lastly the man. The human, poor lesser thing that he was and lacking the keen vision that was only one of many things to make the elven race so superior, promptly barked his shins on a table.

The youth touched one of the many lamps, this one having a stained-glass shade like a rainbow. A kaleidoscope of light spilled out, and Kelardin stood straighter with pride as they exclaimed over the room.

"Comfort at last!" The human shrugged out of his pack, letting it fall heedlessly to the rug, and threw himself into a velvet-cushioned couch that all but swallowed him up in its softness.

Kelardin smiled, almost preened. He bustled in and cast a quick spell to ignite the fire that was laid and ready in the marble-fronted fireplace. As his guests unlimbered themselves of their loads, he went about the room touching more lamps, then indicated the two doors.

"Each of these leads to a short hall, with two small bedrooms and a bath," he announced.

"A bath!" the human and the woman groaned in unison.

"Dinner?" the man asked.

"We will be serving tonight, yes, of course. Would sir prefer to have something brought up, or dine downstairs?"

The four of them exchanged a weighted, wary look that brushed away Kelardin's pride in the room and reminded him that these were peculiar folk. All at once, he regretted his words. Not only because of them, but because of what was going on in the town right now. The last thing Eltarrin needed was to have outsiders getting wind of its troubles.

"We've had a long day, *Tars* Sarra," the man said. "Something brought up will be fine." He fished more *kaimas* from his purse and gave them to Kelardin. "Be generous with the wine and the meat."

"You needn't worry about that!" the innkeeper said, a bit offended that they might imply he wouldn't.

When they had no more requests – demands, really; there hadn't been so much as a please or a thank-you forthcoming – Kelardin Sarra let himself out and promised them that a tray would be brought up very shortly. He closed the door behind him, wrestled with the temptation to listen, and reminded himself that this was a quality inn, not some way-house.

He went downstairs, stuffing the coins into his own purse as he did so. A good thing too, because in the short while he'd been up with the guests, the common room had filled up considerably. *Main room, main room,* he scolded himself. *Hardly common.*

Most of the tables were full. Kelardin was pleased to see the constable among them. If the strangers did decide to become troublesome, no better man in all of the lake region was there to deal with them. After all, it was what Ainvar Lynellen was paid to do.

Kelaya was behind the bar, looking harried. When the Floating Gardens were in full bloom and the inn was full every night, they hired on a full staff to tend to the increased business. But the recent odd events and the appearance of strangers in town had combined to make half of Eltarrin drop in for a glass or a bottle and mayhap a dinner as well.

"My word, Kelardin, have you ever seen the like?" his sister said as he approached. "Tharani is in the kitchen, but I cannot keep up with the calls for wine."

"I'm here now, and among the three of us all should be well."

"For tonight, but if it keeps on, we'll need to have Frynne and Jalla come in. And don't you begrudge me the cost, either. We work ourselves to death keeping this place up." To illustrate her point, she took a deep, weary breath, and scrubbed her hands up the sides of her face.

"Send for Frynne and Jalla if you think they're needed," he said. "We can afford it."

She withdrew a bit from him and eyed him as if to ask who he was and what he'd done with her real brother.

He leaned close. "Look on these, sister!"

Holding his hand below the level of the bar, he showed her the glitter of silver. At first, she was unimpressed, but when she realized what she was seeing, she gasped and looked, for a brief moment, girlishly excited and almost pretty.

"They paid in that? Who *are* they?"

"I know not."

"You didn't think to ask? Who they are, from whence they come? Why they're here at this time of year? What's come over you, Kelardin?"

"They're not our usual breed of guests," he said. "Something about them . . . I had the feeling, and rather strong, that they'd not welcome any meddling questions. They've been long on the road, and I'll warrant they've seen some trouble."

"Well, so too have we," she said. "You didn't tell them . . . ?"

"Great moon and stars, sister, do you think I want that getting out? Weren't you listening at the meeting? 'Twas I who argued strongest of all that we keep this to ourselves and not seek aid from outside! You know as well as I what that sort of story would do to us. We need the spring visitors to keep body and soul together. If they stopped coming to Eltarrin, we'd starve. We'd lose the inn."

"I know, I know . . . I was there, and I did listen. But I also know *you*, Kelardin, and as much as your ears want to hear, your mouth likes to chatter."

"You make me sound like some gossipy noblewoman," he said. He put the coins away and busied himself filling goblets.

Kelaya poured several small bowls full of almonds that had been rolled in honey and crushed cinnamon-sugar, and deftly slipped one bowl onto each tray as he finished arranging the goblets. Even as they argued, they worked with the smooth skill of much practice.

"Having been privy to overhear their talk for most of my life," she said, "I can safely say you're not nearly as bad as a noblewoman."

"My thanks, sister," he said sourly. "I'll take these around. Tell Tharani that our guests would like a meal sent up. Much meat, and wine. Once that's done, you can return to the kitchen and she can mind the tables and I'll look after the bar."

"Good," she said, swiping at a lock of hair that simply would not stay in the clip that held the rest of the wild chestnut mass out of her face. "The constable's asking for baked whitefish."

"He does admire your cooking, Kelaya . . . a very good sign."

Her eyes narrowed. "Leave off, Kelardin. Hasn't your matchmaking caused enough trouble?"

"That is hardly my –" He caught himself and raised his hands in supplication. "You know I would never wish harm on anyone. I only wish to see you happy."

"I am, and would be more so if you'd quit seeking me a husband." She thrust a tray into his outstretched hands and turned him toward the waiting room.

He carried goblets from table to table, resisting those who wanted to hear more about the strangers, claiming – legitimately – that he lacked the time now to stop and talk. But when he came to the corner where Constable Lynellen sat, he did let himself linger.

Once again, he had to assure someone that no, he hadn't gone and told the strangers everything that was going on in Eltarrin. Once again, he had to endure the implication that if there was anything he loved better than money, it was talk.

"Honestly, now, Constable," he said, feeling most peevish. "Between you and my sister . . . rest assured, I'm not about to spill our secrets. But I still think something's got to be done."

"Something does, and something will," Ainvar Lynellen said. "You have my word on that. But I can do little if I'm weak from hunger, now, can I?"

"I'll have Kelaya bring your whitefish out," Kelardin said. He could already hear her objections, but it couldn't hurt to try.

* * *

CHAPTER FIVE

When my duty to my people presents itself, I shall not shirk.
– Elwyndas, Joraic the Third, Act II

Ariana had to smile at the sight of Kevan Brindani. He had made it as far as getting his boots off before falling so soundly asleep on one of the sitting room couches that not even the arrival of their dinner had roused him.

She covered the boy with a blanket and doused the nearest lamps so that he no longer squinted in his sleep. His face smoothed. Ari tucked the edges around his shoulders and straightened up, shaking her head.

"Poor lad," she murmured.

"Good lad," Wyndrel said. "Not many grown men could have kept up with the pace we set."

"And he did it without a word of complaint," Ari said, turning to him.

Wyndrel sat in shadows of his own, the remains of the repast spread on the table before him. The moonlight through the wide windows turned his hair silver-gilt.

"A fine page, who'll make a fine squire," he said, holding a glass of wine aloft and twirling it to watch the ripple and play of light on liquid.

She crossed and perched on the arm of a chair near him. "He wouldn't say or do anything to make you think he's weak."

"A valued quality."

"But, Rell, he is still only a boy."

He regarded her from beneath one cocked eyebrow. "Spoken by the girl who's not yet thirty."

"You're not that much older yourself. But we neither of us are children. The lives we've led have seen to that. I was brought up by a more human standard, and for you, the war made you a man before your time. We have seen and done things that have aged our minds and spirits beyond our bodies."

Wyndrel made a wordless noise of agreement and sipped the wine. Distantly, muffled by the doors and hall between them, came the low and pleasant sound of Mischa singing in his bath.

"Kevan has not gone through such trials," Ariana continued. "He did seek and find Mischa, and did aid in our rescue. In the Northlands, he'd be considered nearly of the age of adulthood, but he was raised Emerinian."

"I am aware of that."

"What you seem not to be aware of is that he will push himself to the breaking point for you."

"No, I am aware of that as well. I admire it. He'll be a knight one day, and do his family proud."

"If he lives through this. That's what I'm trying to say. You admire his determination, and so do I, but look what it's done. He would not speak up if he were in pain, or sick, or frightened. He would go on until he collapsed rather than have you think less of him. And as strong as his spirit is, you must remember his lack of years."

"I should not expect so much of him, then?"

"You're hard to keep up with," she said frankly. "Your long strides and your endurance have all but walked mine and Mischa's legs off getting this far, let alone Kev's. It will do you no good to have allies if you leave them behind, or drive them until they cannot go on. Without Kev, how would you find Tiercel? Kev is our lodestone."

He exhaled in a sigh that came close to being a growl. "I understand your concern. Can you fault me for hurrying?"

"No, of course not. I want to stop them as badly as you do –"

"I doubt that."

She was on the verge of a retort, but relented. "Perhaps so. The wrongs done you are far worse than those I've suffered."

"We'll see about obtaining horses tomorrow," Wyndrel said. "At the very least, one to carry our provisions and ease our burden. Kev is light enough that he could ride if need be."

Ari blew out a long, slow breath and tipped back her head. Her hair whispered over her shoulders like a silvery shawl as she rocked her neck side to side. "I hope we can purchase more than one. We need more supplies. Clothes – you most of all, if they can make anything to fit you on short notice. Waterskins, perhaps, though Kev is a wonder at leading us to streams, if there are streams near enough. To think I should be able to spin water from the air! A curse on Tiercel and his dwarf-metal!"

"Agreed," Wyndrel said, but he sounded as if his mind were on other things. "Though in truth, it's been so long since I cast a spell that I'm not sure I'd even remember how."

She opened her eyes to see him watching her intently. The inn's silken robe she'd donned after her bath – and what a welcome bath it had been after washing in creeks and the icy water of the prison cell spring – had fallen away from her legs, revealing them to the mid-thigh. She was suddenly very conscious of the fact that she wore nothing else, as nightclothes had not been a priority in packing after their escape.

Sliding into the chair, Ari draped the robe more demurely. Wyndrel said nothing except to clear his throat and take another sip of wine.

A tense silence had come from nowhere. No, Ari supposed, that wasn't entirely true. It came from the prison, and what had happened in the moments before their rescue. An inadvertent result of Mischa's god-given power, that was all it was. He had called upon Talopea to enthrall their guards with lust for each other, and because it was divine and not magic, the effect had reached even into the cell. That rush of heat and sensation had thrown them into each other's arms, both going from anger to passion in a mere heartbeat's time.

Mischa protested that Talopea, through him, could only encourage and inflame desire that was already present, not create it from nothing. Ariana refused to believe that . . . or wished she could refuse.

"Did you find our greeting by the townsfolk a touch on the odd side?" she asked, uncomfortably warm under his smoldering gold gaze.

"Odd?" He looked out the window again, at once relieving and disappointing her. "Being held at arrowpoint by a Knight of the Hawk? Having a hundred elves or more staring at us as if we'd sprouted horns? When I have hardly spoken to a living soul in the past eight years? Whatever could be odd about any of that?"

"A Knight of the Hawk, truly?"

"I recognized the insignia on his tunic. He was likely in the war. He has the look of one who'd seen great evil."

"Admittedly, I haven't spent all that much time in the Emerin myself, but leveling a truesteel arrow at someone hardly seems a welcoming reception. This from a town that earns its keep from visitors."

"They're frightened of something and I doubt it's us."

"We do appear imposingly threatening," she said with a grin. "You most of all. They could hardly take their eyes from you."

"You earned a fair measure of their attention too."

"But initially, they jumped at the sight of us as if expecting something far worse. Our host, I noticed, was most glad when we elected to dine up here rather than go downstairs."

"They're hiding something, you think."

"I do so think," he said, finishing his wine and refilling his glass from the bottle. He tipped it inquiringly her way and when she nodded, filled one for her.

"What could they be afraid of? It was something so urgent as to demand a town meeting, and you're right, they all did seem jumpy as rabbits."

"We should be alert tomorrow, and see what we can learn."

"You don't think that Tiercel and Tilanne came here before us, do you? If they spied us following somehow, they might have arranged some trap here."

He contemplated this with a frown that somehow suited him far better than any smile. When he frowned, he looked both noble and brooding. Serious. Pensive. All the more handsome.

"Tiercel would not terrorize a town of innocents into doing his work," he finally said. "If he knew I were free, he'd confront me directly."

"Still, we should have given it thought before," Ari said, disgusted with herself. "They could have poisoned us. They could creep in tonight with murderous intent. Should we take watches?"

"If they wanted us dead, the archer could have dealt with it far more efficiently."

"My mother would have my hide for this. She was always testing me, asking me what I'd do if danger threatened, how I'd escape if cornered. It annoyed her that my answers were so often a simple matter of magic. I miss my warning spells, my shielding spells. I never knew how much I'd come to depend on them. Tal would be leaps ahead of me by now."

Wyndrel laughed. "Your *mother* did such things?"

"Ah . . ." Ariana said, her mind racing. "She . . . it's quite a long story. And too late to go into it.

I should be off to bed."

He rose from his chair as she rose from hers. "Who are you, Ariana Mirida? I vaguely recall the name. Some old scandal to do with Count Elyvorrin. His daughter, wasn't it? She was to have married a man named Mirida, but died untimely. For that, the count blames your father and by extension, you."

"Yes, that's right."

"But who are *you?* Not Elyvorrin's granddaughter, surely."

"Perish the thought! That man is no kin of mine, I promise you." She shook her head. "More than that, you need not know."

"I think I do." He took the glass from her hand and grasped her by the upper arms, not hard but not so lightly that she could easily twist away. "If we're to be allies, I should know. What's kept your father away from the Emerin all this time? Fear of Elyvorrin? And if so, why did he allow you to come when you're still so young?"

"Not fear of Elyvorrin. He chose an exile on his own terms, when the Emerin became too tragic a place for him. He, his family, our bloodline, carried a curse that he'd known nothing of until it claimed Alinora Elyvorrin practically on the eve of their wedding. He spent a century seeking a way to end that curse, hoping also to find some way to bring his lost love back to life. During that time, he met my mother. She . . . is not of the Emerin."

"What are you hiding?"

"Nothing."

"Why, then, do you try to pull away? Why do you bow your head, hide your face?"

"You're . . . bothering me."

"Am I too close?"

"Yes."

"Too close to the truth," he asked, "or too close to you?"

She looked up through a shimmering veil of her own hair into those truegold eyes. His hand came up like something in a dream and brushed her hair away, fingertips lingering on the satiny skin of her brow. She could read a hunger in every line of his countenance. Eight years in a dungeon . . . a war before that . . . a youth gone off to war . . . how long since he'd been with a woman? A better question – had he ever? Or had the responsibilities come before the pleasures?

And oh, but he was so powerfully attractive. Another elfmaid might not have thought so, might have looked on his muscular chest, broad shoulders and bulging arms with disfavor. He was far indeed from the blade-slender elven ideal. Yet she, brought up more among humans, whose first lover had been Gavin Chastain . . .

With monumental effort, Ariana wrested her thoughts under control. Her voice was hoarse, almost husky, but firm as she said, "Do not flatter yourself, Your Majesty. You and I could never be close."

His grip tightened to the very beginning edge of pain. "Why do you do this?"

"I don't know what you mean."

"If I had my magic, a truthsay would prove that a lie."

"So you say." She tore free of him, the slippery silk aiding her though she would feel the imprint of his grasp for some time.

"Are you trying to make me look a fool?" He spoke as if he were restraining himself from shouting only by the greatest of will.

"Not at all," Ariana said contritely.

"Well, then." He relaxed the barest amount.

"The gods beat me to it," she added through clenched teeth.

His eyes flashed, but before he could speak, a lazy drawl from the hallway interrupted.

"Mayhap it's me," Mischa said, slinging a towel around his neck and combing his damp hair with his fingers, "but personally, I've never seen the point of these violent, tempestuous love affairs. Some say the resulting passion's fire burns all the hotter, but I prefer a gentler, more playful, more pleasant encounter."

Ariana and Wyndrel both glared at him with such smoke that he chuckled self-consciously.

"I only thought I'd toss in my two marks," he said. "You'd be surprised how many couples seek the advice of us Talopeans."

"We are not a couple," Ariana said at the same moment Wyndrel said, "We are not seeking your advice."

Mischa nodded sagely. "Of course."

"Don't view everything through Talopean eyes," Ariana added.

"I can hardly help that. I was born and raised in the church."

"Then keep your marks to yourself," Wyndrel suggested, clenching one fist ominously. "And your opinions."

"Consider it done." He paused as he was about to turn. "So, then . . . I take it you two won't be sharing a room?"

"Certainly not!" Ari snapped.

"Because there's one with a wonderful, large bed."

"Go on and take it," Wyndrel said.

"Thank you. What I was going to add was that *I'm* not adverse to sharing." He looked from one to the other of them, a crooked little smile telling them that the offer was open to either. Or both, knowing Mischa.

Wyndrel blanched visibly, which almost made Ariana laugh. She set her hand on his arm to forestall him stalking across the room and pummeling Mischa senseless – the heat of his skin was like a physical shock, making her tingle – and lifted it quickly away.

"We've no shortage of beds," she said. "I think we can each find our own."

Mischa rolled his eyes skyward and shook his head in a sublime gesture of disappointment. "You don't know what you're missing."

"I've a fair idea." Wyndrel grimaced, perhaps remembering, as Ariana was, the image that had greeted them when they escaped their cell. He pulled away from her and went to the other door, turning once to look back at Mischa with astonished amazement. The door closed behind him and Ariana suspected that the only reason it did not decisively slam on them was out of kindness to the sleeping Kevan.

"Think he likes me?" Mischa asked rakishly.

"I think he came quite close to damaging your good looks," Ariana said. "Your mother would never forgive us if we brought you back with a broken nose."

"Don't say such things, Ari, even in jest!" Looking alarmed, he covered his nose with one hand.

"Good night, Mischa," she said, and went in search of her own private bed.

* * *

The day dawned clear and lovely, and it was with an air of renewed hope and optimism that the four of them set out to explore the rest of the town. A bath and a bed – or in Kevan's case, a couch – did wonders for their morale.

They dined downstairs that morning. Fluffy rolls, fresh fruit, and a light breakfast wine were far better than the hurried fare they'd grown accustomed to on the road.

Despite the distractions of the food and the scenery, Ariana remained very aware of the edginess of the townspeople. Their reaction to Mischa only confirmed it. Even in a city such as Perras Peliani, which boasted frequent travelers from Thanis and had its own Northlands Embassy, the average elf rarely encountered a human. Out here, in a more isolated setting, they might never have seen one at all. Yet while they did stare at Mischa, and murmur as he passed, it was almost as if in afterthought. As if something far greater troubled them.

Be that as it may, the town was quite charming when seen by daylight and with people out and about. Its eerie emptiness of the evening before faded quickly into memory.

Wyndrel doled out a small sum of coins to each of them. He'd found them in one of the storage chambers, a few doors down from the one in which Ariana had obtained her truesteel corselet. He nearly hadn't bothered, for they had not expected to be anyplace to need money, but it turned out good that he had.

Their only concern had been whether any in this enlightened day and age would accept such dated coinage. The innkeeper's lack of hesitation proved it to be unfounded and they set about filling in the gaps of their supplies, wardrobes, and provisions with good will.

The need was greatest for Wyndrel himself. He would continue to lack armor, for anything he could wear would have to be made to order and they could not spare the time it would take. That bothered Ariana. Their quarry, as she well knew, was well armed and well armored indeed. The thought of Wyndrel trying to take on Tiercel in battle, when the best protection he could come up with was a leather vest, chilled her blood.

If it chilled his, he gave no sign. Emerging from the leatherworker's shop with his new acquisition fitted snugly to his chest over a new shirt of sturdy cloth, he smiled in satisfaction.

Ariana saw to the purchases of their other odds and ends – soap, waterskins, some spices to add flavor to their preserved food, a map of the area that was probably inaccurate but better than nothing. She also bought a few changes of clothes for herself, and paused to look wistfully in the window of a small shop that specialized in powerstones and other minor tools of the mage's trade.

It caught her in a thousand nagging little ways, this *gilthanat*. Some of the shops had sensing spells in lieu of bells, to alert the owner when a customer came in. To those spells, though, Ariana was invisible. She startled more than one shopkeeper that way. When she was fitted for clothing, the seamstress could not use magic to determine her measure. All of the magical conveniences that characterized the Emerin, that the elves took for granted, now became stumbling blocks.

She supposed it had its bright side – hostile magic would be less effective against her as well. Not all of it, though. Fire or lightning created by a spell became a real thing once the spell was complete, and she'd not be immune to an attack such as that.

"Horses," Wyndrel said, coming up behind her as she gazed at the window display of opals, scrying crystals, and the like. "We still need horses."

"I've not seen a stable."

"I asked. We must go to the edge of town, and speak to a man named Ciratan." He called to

Kevan and Mischa, who were just then coming out of a craftsman's shop, each carrying a wrapped parcel. Mischa wore a bemused look, and Kev was shaking his head.

"What is it?" Ariana asked.

"The artisan," Mischa said. "I fear I frightened him."

"I thought he'd spring straight to the rafters and cling there like a silk-cat," Kev said. "But with his nerves so shaken, he gave us a good bargain."

"Or did it to hasten us out the door," Mischa added wryly. He tucked his parcel into his pack.

"Find something interesting?"

"A few gifts for my family," he said. "You whisked us out of Perras Peliani so fast that I didn't have time to look around, let alone shop."

"You did so look around," she said. "You ogled your eyes full of the passers-by, particularly the elfmaids."

"Either way, I felt I should bring back something as a token of my travels. To prove to Rayle and Josef that I actually went, and haven't been hiding away at some inn all this while."

Behind and above them, a frantic voice cut into their conversation. "That cannot be all, Doctor. He's very delicate, you know, a very delicate child, and he's been through a terrible fright."

Like most of the shops, the artisan's had living quarters on the upper floor. An exterior stair led from a door to the street, and the frantic voice belonged to an elfwoman of middle years. She had been the one, Ariana remembered, who'd screamed at the sight of them the night before. At the moment, she stood on the landing with her hands wringing in her apron, and the object of her plea was another woman in a severe white overtunic and even more severe expression. A satchel was in one hand, and the sun glinted on the silver badge of the Emerinian physician's guild.

"Your son is in fine health," the doctor said. "There is nothing physically wrong with him."

"And thank the gods for that!" the distraught mother cried. "He could have been hurt. He could have been . . ." she faltered as if unable to bring herself to speak the unspeakable.

"He wasn't," came the cold reply. "Only a few bruises and scrapes, which I've already healed. You do him no favors, *Tarsi* Elgraine, by treating him as if he were spun of glass."

"I'm only looking out for my son. Is that so wrong? Is that a crime? All this time I've hated letting him go off alone like that, and the only reason I agreed to it was because my husband and everyone else in this town assured me that there was no possible way my Nerevian could come to harm. Now look. Look at what's happened. If I'd had my way and kept him at home, he would have been perfectly safe."

"You asked for my professional opinion," the doctor said, turning to look back up at the other woman as she reached the bottom of the stairs. "If you were expecting some physician's order to lend credence to your desire to keep him bedridden and helpless, you'd do well to consult some other doctor."

"Well!" *Tarsi* Elgraine gasped, hands fluttering to the base of her throat.

"Now, if you'll excuse me?" Without waiting for an answer, she turned again. This brought her face to face with Ariana and the others, who had been watching the interplay. Her eyes were dark as jet and no less hard. Metal clinked in her satchel as she diverted her steps around them and passed without a second glance.

"We'll see about you, Selara Viska!" the Elgraine woman shouted after her. "You may think that being the only doctor in this region gives you power, but we'll see about that. People need to be *cared* for, the ills of mind and soul as well as the body. A doctor who only cares about cutting up and stitching up won't find the world beating a path to her door."

With that, she retreated behind her own door and slammed it resoundingly. The doctor did not so much as flinch. Spine rigid and ruler-straight, she continued on her way.

Wyndrel, his eyes suddenly alight, strode purposefully after her.

"What are you doing?" Ariana called.

He ignored her. "Pardon me, Doctor? A moment, if you will?"

"Yes?" That one word spoke much – *this had better be good, whoever you are,* it said.

"What about the horses?" Mischa asked as Ariana hastened to catch up with Wyndrel.

"You are, I take it, a surgeon?" Wyndrel asked.

"That is one of my areas of proficiency, yes," Selara Viska said without thawing.

"I'd like," he said, "to schedule an appointment."

* * *

The land where Lairis Ciratan kept his stables was set apart from the town, in a long sloping meadow fenced by rambling rock walls. Rising trees on all sides made it impossible to see the lake from the meadow, contributing to an illusion that they were not on an island at all. In the early-morning light, the meadow still steamed and fogged as the sun warmed the chill from the ground.

At the center of that expanse of green-gold grass was the house, a white-painted villa with arched columns supporting the roof of the porch that ran the entire length of the building. One tree, an ancient oak, spread its mighty boughs to shade the house. The stables, two rows of them facing each other across a fenced corral, were long and low.

Ariana, Wyndrel, Mischa, and Kevan paused at the edge of the forest, gazing out on this placid scene. Horses grazed, not many but of such fine quality that even from a distance Ariana's hopes were buoyed. A few people were in sight, attending to various chores. They peered attentively as the foursome set out across the meadow.

By the time they reached the house, a young man clad all in brown had come out to meet them. His smile was strained and perfunctory as he introduced himself as Bellar Dreise.

Wyndrel sensed that Dreise was in no mood for pleasantries – which suited him fine, as he had long since lost whatever patience he'd had for the leisurely Emerinian way of doing things. He had wanted to come out here last night, when they'd finished their shopping, but his companions had dissuaded him, pleading that dinner and an early bedtime would leave them fresher to negotiate for horses.

Now he succinctly stated his request. Four horses, with tack and gear if possible. What price?

But rather than conclude the deal swiftly and painlessly, Bellar Dreise chewed unsurely at his lower lip. Throwing repeated glances over his shoulder at the house, he said, "I am most terribly sorry, but Lord Ciratan is not conducting business today. Other matters occupy him. I'd suggest you come back another day."

"We wish to continue our journey," Wyndrel said. "On horseback rather than on foot. I was told in the town that your lord has horses to sell."

"I'm sure that he will be delighted to speak with you," Dreise said. "Just not today."

At that moment, the front door flew open and an older man emerged. He was dressed for the hunt, belting on a sword while a frightened-seeming youngster trotted alongside him with a bow and quiver.

"Bellar, what is this? Why are the horses not ready?" the older man demanded.

"We've just finished saddling them," Dreise said. "I was seeing to these visitors."

Wyndrel studied the older man, vaguely remembering him from the night before. Ciratan had looked no less stormy then, and he now had the resolute and misguided air of someone setting off on a task that was pointless and certain to fail, but determined to do it anyway.

"We wish to purchase some horses," Wyndrel said, addressing the man directly.

"That's not possible at the moment. I have need of them all." Ciratan broke off, looked at Wyndrel and his companions as if seeing them for the first time, and a crafty, calculating gleam came into his eyes. "You're a competent-looking lot. Are those weapons for show, or can you use them?"

Mischa scuffed his foot in the dirt, but Wyndrel met Ciratan's odd-gleaming gaze squarely. "We're adept enough. Why?"

"My lord," Dreise cut in, "are you sure this is wise?"

"I told you last night. If the constable will do nothing, then matters must be taken into my own hands. What would you have me do? Leave it to Tannel? Pah! He thinks they've run off. I know better. I know my own son better."

"Your son is missing?" Ariana asked. "Is that what this is all about, why the entire town is so skittish and out of sorts?"

Guardedness dropped over Ciratan, Dreise, and even the youngster carrying the bow and quiver, just as a knight might drop the visor of his helm.

"And if he's just missing," Kev added boldly, "why would you need weapons to find a lost boy? Something else has happened, hasn't it?"

Ciratan came to an abrupt decision, slapping a palm on the sheath of his sword. "They," he said with a sneering gesture in the direction of the town, "think that my Lairis and Haltha Tannel have run off together, eloped, or some such rubbish. But believe you me, Lairis is a good and responsible youth. He would never do such a thing without informing me. Something's happened to them."

"My lord!" Dreise said sharply. "You shouldn't –"

"*It* has taken them," Ciratan finished.

"*It?*" Ariana asked dubiously.

Dreise was in agonies. "My lord, it was agreed, all the town agreed that no word of this would leave the island!"

"All the town also agreed that there was no reason to link the absence of Lairis and Haltha with what happened to old Rantiel Herann, or the Elgraine boy, or the thefts, or what the constable saw. Am I to sit by and do nothing when my son could be in mortal peril? I think *not!*"

He thundered this last, making Dreise quail before him. More men had gathered around, all of them pensive and unhappy. Most were armed, and leading horses by the reins.

"Stop!" Wyndrel could voice thunder of his own when he chose, and his easily overtopped Ciratan. The word burst from him like dwarven cannonfire and echoed around the meadowed valley. He looked sternly from face to face. "I will hear all of this, sensibly and in order."

"Rell . . ." Ariana began.

"If there is some mischief afoot here, we must investigate," he said. "We'll have little other aid or cooperation from the townsfolk while they're in this state."

She subsided, but the spark in her blue eyes told him she would have more to say later, and at length.

He brushed aside her glare and turned to Ciratan. "If you'd have our aid, we must know what this is all about."

* * *

CHAPTER SIX

Courage conquers fear.
– Elwyndas, Shoral's Return, Act II

Ainvar Lynellen spent the morning in the constabulary, writing down his instructions for the people, animals, and items that he wanted assembled should it prove necessary to mount a search for their pair of missing lovers.

Was it really so unreasonable to believe that Lairis and Haltha had gone off for some time alone, away from their overbearing kin? Since the moment they'd first shown interest in each other, both sides had been after them to announce the formal courtship. Weddings happened so seldom on the island, and were always a cause for great celebration and festivities. No one could blame the two for wishing to get away from all the fuss for a while.

That was all fine and well to say at a town meeting. In the small hours of the night, though, his conscience worked on him. His memories worked on him. Much as he would have liked to believe it had been nothing more than a trick of light and shadow, he couldn't forget the arrows.

If he was wrong, if they all were wrong, and the lovers had indeed been harmed by whatever stalked the woods near Rantiel Herann's *alkarra* orchard, he would never forgive himself.

His night's sleep had been populated by dreams in which he drew and fired and saw the silvery streak of his arrows speeding true toward their target, heard the meaty thunks of them striking home . . . and dashed up to find nothing, not even a drop of blood . . . and something rose up behind him with a horrible growl.

He shuddered.

"Constable?"

Ainvar jumped, heart slamming. Lost in the recollection of the dream, he hadn't heard Eranic come in. The younger constable grinned apologetically.

"I'm sorry, sir."

"Not your fault, lad. Thinking."

It hadn't been that way in reality. Not entirely. Nothing had risen behind him in a cold cloud. But he'd heard the arrows strike. After all his decades as an archer, he knew the sound of a solid hit, a killing hit. Yet there'd been nothing. No blood. And he didn't even know what it was he'd fired on.

"About . . . about *it?*" Eranic asked.

"I fired on it without being fully sure of my target, without clear sight of it," he said, hating the admission even as it left his lips. "I don't even know what it looked like. A man-sized shape, but that was all. It could have been one of our neighbors, one of our friends . . . and the rest I thought I saw, no more than imaginings and shadows."

"But you said it didn't bleed. You hit it, and it didn't bleed." Eranic nodded toward the quiver handing on its peg. "Nor was there a body, sir, and two truesteel war arrows would drop nigh anyone."

"True. But it preys on my mind. Rantiel Herann couldn't describe it, and I'm not even permitted to speak to our only other witness."

Eranic made a sour face. "Lest you 'upset' him, such a 'delicate and high-strung child.' Surely, as important as this is . . ."

"Tell that to a worried mother," Ainvar said, sighing. "Never mind that now. Here's the list. If you could see to arranging it, I'll dash to the inn. I haven't yet eaten."

"And no wonder." The younger constable snorted. "What with half the town coming around to pester you about the strangers. What do they want you to do? Arrest them? Hasten them on their way?"

"They worry, and rightly so, that if news of our troubles reach the cities, it will damage Eltarrin's idyllic reputation. Never mind that the reception these travelers already received was hardly the politest."

"No one blames you for that. How were any of us to know? At least you didn't shoot."

"At least," he said. Just the thought of it still made his skin prickle with dread.

"I'll tend to this," Eranic said, picking up the list and scanning it closely. "We could have a search party gathered by morning."

"Fine. I'll be back directly." He threw a light cape around his shoulders and fastened it with brass clasps, each boasting the raised and red-enameled emblem of a hawk. Although he usually didn't carry them in the course of his day, he also took his bow and quiver.

The town bustled with noontime activity. He passed the kofa shop without pausing, wanting something heartier and more substantial than the warm, sweetened brew and a pastry or two. The Bough and Vine served lunch on the terrace, a buffet of sliced meats, cheeses, fruit, and bread.

As he entered, Kelardin Sarra hailed him excitedly. Ainvar could see the long table set up on the terrace, covered dishes shining in the sun. A few others were out there, nibbling at their meals and watching a brisk breeze skim sailing boats along the lake. He thought of simply raising a hand in a wave to the innkeeper, but knew that would never do.

"Good day, Kelardin," he said, detouring to the bar.

The other man was polishing goblets with a fine white cloth, doubtless in preparation for what he hoped would be just as busy an evening as the previous. "A good day indeed, Constable. Have you come for lunch? Kelaya's in the midst of stuffing fowls for dinner, but I'm sure that if there's something special you'd like, she would be happy to oblige."

"I'd hate to disturb her. Cooking is an art, and she is an artist. I'll partake of the buffet. But save me a place for dinner."

"She wouldn't mind at all," Kelardin insisted.

"I do not want to be any trouble," Ainvar said as firmly as he could without sounding stern.

"For you, Constable –"

"Kelardin, I'm pale with hunger. I need nothing fancy." He looked out on the terrace again, from here being able to see all of it. "Have your guests already eaten?"

"They had breakfast early," Kelardin said. "And then went out. More shopping to do, they said." A peculiar, petulant, almost sulky, look crossed his face.

"Is something the matter?" he asked, denying his ravening stomach a while longer in favor of indulging his curiosity.

"Well . . ."

He could see the innkeeper wrestling with the decision of whether to speak or not. Finally, with a resigned flap of the hands – *might as well, it'll all be known soon enough anyway* – he did. "They're an odd bunch, those four. Not just in the way that they look, mind you, though that's odd enough. Have you ever seen the likes of that man? Enormous, he is. As tall as Lairian Ciratan, and wide as any three other men put together."

Ainvar nodded. "I saw one or two during the war who were put together like that. Always did wonder how the quartermasters kept them in uniforms."

"But what struck me oddest of all," Kelardin said, "was that they paid for their lodgings with these." He rolled coins onto the richly gleaming wood of the bar, and Ainvar picked one up.

"I haven't seen one of these in years," he said. "My father had a coin collection from all over the world. I'd imagine it's worth a pretty *kairis*."

"Except that they're out there now, spending them all over town," Kelardin said bitterly.

The constable laughed, understanding now the cause of his pique. "Afraid you won't get full value if everyone's got them?"

"I wouldn't mind so much if I had the most. But I hear they mean to buy horses next, and everyone knows Lairis Ciratan is as avaricious as they come."

"Make a trip to Feyna Rel, then," Ainvar suggested. "Sell yours first to collectors there."

The innkeeper brightened. "I may at that! Thank you, Constable. For that, I think you need a glass of wine."

"I'm working," he said. "Just lunch."

"You're certain you don't want Kelaya to –"

"Quite. I can manage." He smacked Kelardin companionably on the arm and headed for the terrace, where he came very close to colliding with Physician Viska. "Pardon me, Doctor. I wasn't heeding my path."

Her ebony eyes regarded him with what in someone else, he might have believed to be amusement. In her, it was more likely contempt. "Quick to evade Sarra, 'ere he trots out his spinster sister for your inspection once more?"

"Is it that apparent?"

"Not to all. I, however, am practiced at viewing such interactions with a degree of detachment and scientific observation." She had a plate in her elegant hands, and moved past him toward the table where she began filling it with food.

He joined her. "Does he attempt this matchmaking with everyone, or am I the sole recipient?"

"More the current prospect, I'd say." She held up a roll in a pair of serving tongs and tilted her dark eyebrow at him in a query.

"Yes, please." As she put it on his plate, he risked a glance back into the common room. No, pardon, *main* room, as Kelardin preferred it to be called. The innkeeper had gone back to polishing goblets. "I wonder that she doesn't tell him to stop, that she's not interested."

"Perhaps she is."

He scoffed and selected a slice of melon to complete his repast. "I doubt it."

"Why haven't you told him that *you're* not interested?"

"That would be rather rude, wouldn't it? Imply that I don't think his sister is good enough?"

"Don't you?"

Ainvar felt as though he'd been innocently walking along and blundered into a pricker bush. No matter which way he turned, he found more thorns. "I never said that."

"Well, she is quite plain," the doctor remarked dispassionately as she sat and speared a slice of meat on her eating tong.

"I don't mind that," Ainvar said, surprising himself by speaking so openly about such a subject to Selara Viska of all people. "It's the fact that she thinks she's so uncomely that any kind words directed at her, she takes for a veiled insult, or a lying attempt to be kind."

"Ah, yes. All flattery viewed with suspicion, each comment dissected seeking the hidden meaning."

"She's quite a worthy young lady in all other ways," he said, still hardly able to credit that he was saying these things to her. "A splendid cook, compassionate, and kind."

"I see." She said it as though he had just explained why he preferred iron grey for his uniform tunic over slate grey. "Inner beauty."

"And then there are those who, while outwardly beautiful, hide their inner beauty behind a cool ivory mask," he said, feeling undone and thinking that if she could fire these verbal volleys at him, he could at least return it.

Selara only eyed him over the rim of her glass, and again he saw that glitter of amusement or contempt. Ainvar gave up.

"Have you seen our visitors?" he asked as a change of subject.

"Yes, as a matter of fact I have," she replied. "Two of them have appointments with me on the morrow."

"Are they ill?" Here was a new worry . . . the strangers had clearly been on the road for some time, and if they brought sickness . . .

"No. A . . . a surgical challenge," she said. This time, her eyes sparkled in anticipation. Her lips curved into a slight smile.

This, Ainvar realized with something akin to amazement, was what Selara Viska looked like when she was happy. And only the prospect of cutting into someone could make her look that way.

* * *

Dharra Felthis poked her head into Illan's room. "Well?"

He was sprawled on the narrow cot that served as his bed, a bottle of *alkarra* cordial resting slantways against his hip as he peered owlishly at the pages of a book. Another bottle, empty, was on the floor in the corner. The syrupy-sweet odor filled the room.

"Well, what?" Illan asked, rolling his head to the edge of the cot. It dangled over, and he regarded Dharra from this upside-down vantage.

"Do you mean to loaf the day away in here? Drinking?"

"Thought I might."

"There's work to be done," she said.

"Pfff!" He blew out a chuckling breath. "You can't think to go out there."

"I can and I do. It's our job, Illan. With *Tars* Herann away, we're responsible."

"With *Tars* Herann away, who'll know? Or care?"

"*We* will," Dharra said pointedly, though she could see that she might as well be addressing the air, or a stone wall. He had no intention of . . . "Illan? Is your window . . . is it nailed shut?"

She stepped closer and examined the long nails that had been haphazardly driven through the window frame and into the sill. A discarded hammer sat on the sill amid a scatter of unused nails.

"Mmm-hmm," Illan said, turning a page. "I'll do the door tonight. Be sure you're back by sundown."

"Have you taken leave of your senses? You're not barricading us into the house."

"You'd rather be savaged in your bed? Ah, wait . . . no matter; you're going out there. You'll be savaged in the orchard."

"I'm not going to be savaged either way. This must end, Illan. Get hold of yourself. Put the cordial away, wash your face, and put in a day's honest work. That will clear your head and you'll stop this jumping at shadows."

"Shadows? Was it a shadow that killed Sleekfur?"

"It was a bear, or a bigger pantera, or some other beast that did it," she said. "And probably over the hills and far away by now. It's broad daylight, too, not the dead of night. Come on. We've chores to do."

"If you think I'm going out there, day or night, you've lost your wits. I'm staying right here, safe and sound, until the constable brings the bleeding, dripping head of that thing to hang on the town gates."

Dharra wrinkled her nose. "Wouldn't *that* just do wonders for drawing visitors to Eltarrin."

He rolled over, looking at her right-side-up. Sobriety tried to surface through the alcohol-addled haze of his eyes. "Dharra, don't go out there. The trees can fend for themselves."

"We made a promise," she said. "Mayhap that means little to you, but it means much to me. I plan to become a renowned plant-mage one day. Shirking my duties as an apprentice is hardly the way to do it."

"I warned you," Illan mumbled, flopping onto his back again and raising the bottle to his lips. "Never say I didn't."

"Fine! But when *Tars* Herann, or whoever he chooses to take over in his stead, arrives, we'll see who's thanked for looking after the place, and who's dismissed to earn his keep elsewhere."

She spun and left him to his drinking and bleary-eyed reading. In her own small room, barely more than a closet, she tied a kerchief over her sunshine-blond hair and checked her garb. Sensible trousers, low boots, a many-pocketed tunic, and tough but soft leather gloves. Satisfied, she picked up the basket on her cot and took a quick glance through to see that her shears and other tools were all in place.

As she walked back through the house, she debated trying one last time to persuade Illan, and decided against it. The state he was in, he'd be more of a hindrance than a help anyway.

The old farmhouse felt much bigger and emptier, as if it, too, knew that Rantiel Herann was gone and not likely to come back. The woven mat by the fire, and the wide-brimmed bowls in the kitchen, seemed to mourn Sleekfur. Dharra told herself to put those away someplace, so she'd no longer have to look at them and their silent, grim message.

The day was bright and perfect. Dharra collected a small barrow and a ladder from the shed, and trundled her way out into the orchard.

Alkarra fruit were best harvested when the first frost had added sweetness to them, but there was work to be done all the year 'round. The barrow rolled steadily ahead of her as she made her way deeper into the orchard. Methodical by nature, Dharra knew precisely where she'd left off and came unerringly to the next tree.

She touched the wavy roughness of the bark, breathing words of magic. At once, a tingling warmth spread from the tree into her hand and she was aware of its condition, from root to leaf. Where it was infested with insects. Where a windstorm had weakened one branch. Where a borer-bird had drilled into the trunk.

She propped the ladder against the tree and climbed up into the foliage. Yellow-orange fruit surrounded her like a multitude of small suns. She found the hole left by the borer-bird, so recent it was still tacky with sap, and covered it with her palm.

"*Ninshan*," she said, and energy flowed out of her. The wood softened, shifted, melded smoothly together to close up the hole and heal the slight injury.

The damaged branch was almost higher than the ladder would reach. Dharra stepped carefully onto a limb with one foot, the other balanced on the top rung on tiptoe. She stretched, her foot leaving the rung, just able to graze the branch with her fingertips. The wood crackled as it straightened and strengthened. The rustle of the leaves sounded like a whispered thanks.

A thudding, resonating through the earth and into the tree, brought her head up in alertness. Something large was coming her way, shaking the ground with its tread.

Panic filled her mouth with a taste as bitter as the oil of an *alkarra* pit. She groped with her toe for the ladder, found it, and set her weight upon it. But the ladder twisted, wobbled, and fell away.

A startled scream erupted from her throat as she plunged. The limb she'd been standing on slammed painfully into her hip. She grabbed at it, hands flailing for purchase.

And then there she was, dangling half in and half out of the tree, her legs waving in futility below. Winded, she gasped for air.

The thudding rushed closer, hideously eager.

She screamed again, knowing even as she did so that the only one close enough to hear was Illan and he had likely drunk himself into a stupor by now. Even were he sober, he'd never come to her aid. His terror would see to that.

Her hands, sweaty with fright, slipped out of her gloves. She fell, hearing the snorting exhale of hot breath below her, some enormous creature poised to catch her like some gift from the gods.

* * *

CHAPTER SEVEN

Death is the cruel stealer of grace.
– Elwyndas, Gilliana, Verse 21

"It began with Rantiel Herann," Lainiar Ciratan said as he led his string of mounted searchers away from the house. He spoke with an emotional stoniness that Wyndrel Perras took to mean the man was clinging to the last vestiges of his self-control. "Something had been at his orchard, and when he went to investigate, it attacked him."

He reined in and instructed half of the searchers to bear west, with Bellar Dreise as their leader. The other group, of which Wyndrel, Ariana, Mischa, and Kevan were a part, would go east.

"It slew a spotted pantera the size of a grown wolf," Ciratan went on. "Herann escaped unharmed, but suffered a shock to his nerves that nearly did him in. He is no young man. His apprentices fetched the constable, who took the barest of looks around before concluding it was nothing. A bear or a boar, at the most. Physician Viska opined that it was naught but hallucination. Either way, it was no great cause for alarm."

Ariana, riding beside Wyndrel, kept looking at him as if to ask him what he thought he was doing. She was right – they needed to be on their way soon if they stood any hope of stopping Tiercel before he reached the dragon's lair. But they would never make it without horses, the only way to get horses was from this man, and the only way to win his help was by helping him. Further, though this was only a nebulous feeling at the back of his mind, he knew that this town was in dire danger and he could not turn his back on them. They were, or would be once matters were settled, his people.

"The next day, however," Ciratan said, "a crafter boy on an errand for his father was frightened on the beach. He saw something so horrible that it struck him dumb, and later could only describe it as awful. Whatever it was stole his bag from him, but luckily for the boy left him unharmed."

"Couldn't he give a bit better description than that?" Ariana asked. "It's not much to go on, one word."

"It frightened him so badly that he's been abed ever since," Ciratan told her. "No one's been able to see him, or get anything more from him."

"If it's the boy I'm thinking of," Mischa said in a low voice to Kevan – forgetting, as he usually did, that he didn't *have* a low voice – "it's his mother, not his fright, that's kept him abed and silent."

Ciratan spared him a dour frown. His knuckles were white from the tightness of his grip on the reins. "That evening, my son, Lairis, went out. He'd planned to meet Haltha Tannel, and have a moonlight supper on the beach. He never came home."

Wyndrel eyed Mischa with a warning, to forestall the lusty priest from making some observation. Ariana, too, was silently cautioning him.

"They've been courting for some years now," Ciratan said. He swiped at his eyes and swallowed, and went on a touch unsteadily. "We expected them to announce an engagement very soon. Lairis had taken a brooch with him, a jade brooch, to give to Haltha. It had been his mother's."

Ariana bit the fullness of her lower lip and looked as if she would have liked to place a comforting hand on the tall man. His pose, stiff and taut, said that he wanted no comfort.

"At first we thought – the Tannels and I – that they'd decided to spend the night alone. There are cottages all along Nimias Beach, you see. They're rented out in the spring, but at this time of year, they're empty. But when they still hadn't returned by suppertime the following day, I knew something was wrong. *Tars* Tannel tried to suggest to me that they'd eloped, that they'd run away together to Feyna Rel or someplace to be secretly married. I knew that was nonsense."

"Why?" Wyndrel asked.

"Why? For one, Lairis would never have done such a thing. He and I have only each other since his mother died. We're more brothers than father and son. Haltha, too, is quite close to her family. Neither of them would have deprived us of the joy of such an occasion."

"There's no telling what people in love might do," Ariana said gently. "Sometimes they do what seems right to them, even if it's incomprehensible to others. They might have wanted to spare you the expense of a wedding."

"You do not know them. And even if that were it, they did not go to Feyna Rel."

"How can you be so sure?" she pressed.

"I own the only stable," he said, looking at her as if she were daft. "None of the horses were missing. Nor were any of the island's boats. They would have had to walk, and it is much too far a journey for that."

"I'll say," Kevan muttered.

"But to conclude that they . . ." Ariana groped for the right words. "That they ran afoul of this mysterious creature . . . a creature which has only been seen by two people, neither of whom sound like the most reliable of witnesses . . ."

"If it were only that, I'd not leap to such a conclusion," Ciratan said. "But the constable himself, with his own eyes, saw this creature. Those cottages of which I spoke may be empty, but there is a caretaker who makes sure they remain in good condition. He was doing this, when he found that several of the cottages had been broken into, their kitchens ransacked."

"Looking for food," Wyndrel said. "The kitchens, the farmer's orchard . . . tell me, the bag the boy lost, did it contain any food?"

Ciratan nodded crossly at the interruption. "His lunch. If I may go on?"

Wyndrel gestured in affirmation.

"The caretaker sent for the constable that very evening. As the constable was checking each cottage, he heard something, and then saw the creature. He claims he failed to get a good look at it, and that is all he says. I suspect there's more to the tale. But he's loath to cause an uproar and so does nothing, while two of our children are missing. The coward."

"Coward? The man is a Knight of the Hawk," Wyndrel said, his honor stung. He had earned the Orders of the Lion and the Eagle both during the war, and knew full well how difficult such rank was to attain.

"We may have made a mistake choosing him for the post," Ciratan said. "Not all who came back from the war came back brave."

Ariana jabbed Wyndrel in the ribs and shook her head. He fumed, but forced his temper to cool. It would do them no good to further aggravate the only horse-owner in town by dragging him from the saddle and giving him a personal lesson in how brave a man came back from the war.

They had entered the woods by then, a narrow strip of them that rose to a ridge. On the other side of the ridge, Ciratan told them, was the orchard belonging to Rantiel Herann. Beyond that, another strip of woods separated the orchard from the beach.

"The land out this way is largely untamed and untenanted," he said. "Though the constable does not believe it so, a large beast could easily dwell here undetected. There are ravines, caves, and copses that could hide it."

"What do you expect to find?" Mischa asked. "Tracks? On an island as large as this, that might be impossible."

"Jade," Kevan spoke up abruptly. "Jade's quite rare, isn't it?"

"Not in Tradersport," Ariana said. "It comes from the Southern Isles. But it isn't often found in the Emerin."

"Well, then," the boy said. "That's what we do!"

"What do you go on about, lad?" Ciratan asked.

"Our young friend is a seeker-mage," Wyndrel said. "If the brooch you mentioned is on Eltarrin, Kevan will find it."

Kev concentrated, murmuring, "Jade, jade," under his breath as though to familiarize himself with it. Then he raised his head, and said, "*Ara Nak*," in a clear voice.

Ciratan watched with cautious hope. "Can he truly –"

"Shh," Ariana said.

The boy thrust out his arm. "That way! And not far, either. If we're quick, my spell will lead me right to it."

"Pavaire's brooch? Are you sure?" The hope gained strength, but Ciratan clearly did not want to trust it fully, lest he be disappointed.

"How much other jade is there on this island?" Kev asked.

That was sufficient. They let Kevan take the lead, and Wyndrel noted that the youth rode skillfully and well. He would make a fine squire and a fine knight, if he were this adept so young. Some commendation should go to Count Brindani for raising such a fine son.

The only problem with seeker-spells, as they'd found before, was that the shortest way was not always the easiest, or the quickest. The horses struggled up a steep, wooded hill, the riders having to duck repeatedly else be slapped by boughs. They reached the top and descended toward the orchard, which was bordered by a split-log fence.

"The jade is not moving," Kevan reported a few moments later. His face clouded as he said it, perhaps imagining reasons why that might be so.

"Shall we make for the orchard gate, my lord?" one of the other riders asked.

Evidently, the same bleak thoughts Kev had been having had also been plagued Lainiar Ciratan. He shook his head. "We go straight on. Over the fence."

It was low enough to allow them to jump the horses. The tame ground of the orchard made for a far easier ride. No more brambles and drop-offs, only flat and well-kept land with *alkarra* trees growing in even rows. Wyndrel's mouth cramped with the desire to pluck one of those half-ripe round fruits and bite deep.

But as he surrendered to that helpless desire, it was shattered by the scream that exploded from just ahead.

He reacted without pause, kicking his steed into a gallop and plunging past the startled Ciratan. He drew his sword as he charged.

A barrow rested to one side of a tree, and a ladder lay flat on the ground. Above it, dangling from the branches, were a pair of trousered legs and flailing feet.

His sharp gaze darted about, seeking the creature, this mysterious and ill-described beast. Nothing. Only the person in the tree, struggling . . . and slipping.

Wyndrel kicked the horse again. It leaped forward and his arm shot out just in time to catch the falling body. She – for it was a she, slightly built and slender – screamed once more on the way down and stopped jarringly as he arrested her fall.

"Oh," she said, blinking at him. Her eyes were a light misty-green, and tendrils of bright yellow hair peeked from beneath the kerchief she wore on her head. "I thought . . . a horse, it was a horse I heard." She tittered a nervous laugh.

The rest of the group reached them. Wyndrel wheeled his horse about. He still had his sword out, the girl curled in his strong left arm. By her plain attire and the gear in the barrow, he knew she wasn't, but had to make sure.

"Is this your son's lady?"

"No," Ciratan said.

"I'm Dharra Felthis," she said. "Senior plant-mage apprentice. And . . . sir . . . thank you. That could have been a nasty fall. The ladder fell, you see, and . . ." She trailed off, looking up at him with a dazzled smile.

And was that a flash of jealousy in the sapphire eyes of the tempestuous Ariana Mirida? It was there and gone too quick to be confirmed, like distant lightning on a summer's day, but Wyndrel rather thought it was. Indeed, hoped it was.

He lowered Dharra until her feet found the earth. She brought her hands up in an instinctively feminine motion to smooth her hair, tucking the wayward strands beneath the kerchief.

"I was only glad to be able to help," he told her.

"The spell," Kev said. "It's waning, but we're close. Very close. It should be just over here." He pointed toward a place where the *alkarra* trees lost the evenness of their rows due to the contours of the land, a small rill bisecting the orchard.

Dharra looked from one face to the next in confusion. "What is all this?"

Mischa gave her his most charming smile, which faded as she recoiled against the side of

Wyndrel's horse. "We're searching for the missing lovers. Have you seen them?"

"Lairis and Haltha? No."

"This way," Kev said urgently, and kneed his horse in the direction he'd pointed.

Ciratan followed. Wyndrel glanced from Ariana to Dharra, and extended his hand. "You'd best come with us, just for safety's sake. If there is something out there . . ."

"I told Illan there wasn't," she protested, but took his hand and let him swing her up on the steed behind him. Her arms went readily around his waist.

"Look out for wild beasts, girl," Ariana said, though Dharra was probably her senior by ten years or more. "You might get devoured." With that, she was off in pursuit of the others.

"What did she mean?" Dharra asked anxiously.

"Nothing," Wyndrel said. Inwardly, he was both amused and pleased. So Ariana *was* jealous, was she? That was well worth considering.

A horrible cry split the air. It spiraled high into a howl, and in the howl there were words. Or one word, but filled with such tearing anguish that one word sufficed.

"No! Nooooo!" Lairian Ciratan shrieked.

Wyndrel urged his horse into a gallop again, and moments later was shouldering his way through the stunned crowd gathered on the creek bank. Most of them were immobile, leaving Mischa and Ariana to restrain the struggling Ciratan. Kevan, ashen-hued, sat on his horse with the reins held slack.

The rill widened here into a shallow pool, partially dammed on one end by a natural jumble of stones. Water burbled over and through these, and flowed off downhill.

Two bodies were crumpled in the pool. The woman's hair mercifully hid her face, but her lover was flat on his back with his arms and legs splayed, and his eyes bulging from a mask of raw horror. Even in that distorted state, there was no mistaking the resemblance to Ciratan.

Pinned to the collar of the woman's tunic was a brooch of milky jade in a swirled setting of gold.

* * *

Ariana stood grim and silent as the bodies were lifted from their watery tomb. She felt absurdly like an honor guard to the dead, and wasn't entirely sure what she was supposed to do here. But it had been their gruesome discovery, courtesy of Kevan, and at least one of them ought to stay to see it through to the bitter end.

Her friends were still nearby, but not among the group gathered on the shores of the creek. Wyndrel was off with those of Ciratan's men who were still fit and able to go on, searching in an expanding spiral for tracks or some other sign of the killer. Mischa had offered his assistance to the stern doctor, but Physician Viska frostily ignored him and Mischa had decided instead to escort Dharra back to the farmhouse. The girl had gone into a fit of screaming hysterics at the sight of the corpses and had to be physically pried from a death-grip on Wyndrel. Kevan had been with those who'd ridden to fetch the constable and the doctor and was currently explaining to the former how his seeker-spell had guided him hither.

That left Ariana, sentinel to the dead lovers. She kept one hand to the hilt of the thousand-year-old sword at her waist, all of her senses honed and alert. Not that she believed the killer was still nearby. This murder was not fresh, the bodies blue-white and wrinkled from the water. They had lain there broken for a day or more.

Selara Viska, who had waded unconcernedly into the creek when others could not bring themselves to do so, confirmed Ariana's guess and learned more besides with a few quick spells. "Their necks were snapped," she said, her tone factual and untouched by emotion. "Their other injuries – fractured bones and some cuts, gouges – would not have been fatal."

At her direction, a trio of Ciratan's men and the deputy constable had joined her in the pool. They brought the bodies to the shore and laid them out on the earthen back. All four men had gone pale when the task was done, and one retreated rapidly to be sick.

The doctor took no notice of this, and Ariana took little. Their attention was fixed on the young couple, their long lives cut tragically short. Water streamed from their sodden clothing, running downhill to rejoin the pool.

Ariana moved closer. "His knife. The sheath is empty."

"You," the doctor said, jerking her head at one of the remaining men without looking away from the bodies.

Despite the shortness of her message, he understood, and after swallowing hard several times, he waded into the creek again and scanned the stony bottom. "Nothing."

"He must have drawn it to defend himself," Ariana said. "But no battle took place here."

"There are no tracks," the deputy constable said. "Not even theirs. If they'd come to picnic by the creek, where are their tracks? And why would they come here, when we've all the beaches and far better spots than this? Rantiel Herann was never one to welcome anyone trespassing in his orchard even if they took no fruit."

"Ciratan said they'd gone to the beach for a moonlight supper." Ariana looked about again, though she already knew what she wouldn't see. "Where is the meal they brought?"

The doctor interrupted, though she sounded more as if she were speaking to herself. "This suggests to me an assault. Look at their arms."

Ariana did, and saw right away what Physician Viska meant. The youth, Lairis Ciratan, had a ladder of gashes on one forearm, bloodless wounds whose edges had been blanched white by the immersion. Such wounds would have been earned when he raised his arm to ward off an attack. There were no such gashes on the girl.

"Yet not only an assault," the doctor mused. "A beating would not have done this, not broken them like this. It seems more like a . . . a fall."

"A fall?" Ariana moved to the edge of the creek for another look. The ground at the edges of the pool was littered with leaves and splintered twigs, and many of the boughs above had cracked, or split, or dangled with the lighter wood showing through the bark. "Fell . . . through the branches? From above?"

Something caught her eye, an irregular snarl in the upper limbs of one of the trees. Her first impulse was to reach out for it with her magic, and she even went so far as to form the essence word of the spell on her lips before remembering the hateful dwarf-metal that stole her power.

She turned to the deputy constable instead and pointed to what she'd seen. He, much more lightly armored than she was, swung into the tree with ease and climbed until the object was within his reach. He pulled it loose – a strap of some sort, she saw, had gotten entangled – and dropped it into her waiting hands.

It was a satchel of finely tooled leather, the strap skillfully worked into a design of flowing knotwork, the clasp made from some sort of iridescent shell.

"I recognize the workmanship," the deputy, whose name was Eranic, said as he jumped lithely down. "It's of Nerevar Elgraine's craft. I'd wager anything that's the one his boy was carrying the day he was attacked on the beach."

"He was hardly attacked," Selara Viska said absently. "Given a fright, yes, but there wasn't a mark on him except a few bumps and bruises." She had examined both bodies with clinical detachment, and now straightened up to push her hair back from her temples with the backs of her hands. "It is early to say, but I conclude that they were confronted, Lairis attempted to defend the both of them, and was overpowered. Their necks, both of them, were then broken and the bodies borne away. These rips in their clothing and corresponding punctures beneath lead me to believe that they were lifted roughly by something with claws."

This pronouncement brought stunned silence to the small group. Finally, hesitantly, Eranic spoke. "A bear?"

The doctor's dark head moved solemnly side to side. "No bear would do this."

"Lord Ciratan said that the constable saw something," Ariana said, turning to the deputy.

Eranic stared at his feet. "That's not for me to say."

"You help no one by withholding," she pressed.

"We are none too eager in this little town of ours," Physician Viska said, "to share our troubles with outsiders."

"There's no harm in accepting help when it's offered," Ariana countered. She may have initially disagreed with Wyndrel's desire to involve himself – and by extension the rest of them – in Eltarrin's problem, but the pitiful sight of those two young lovers cast aside like so much garbage had lanced deep to her heart.

"You are strangers here," the doctor said. "And one of you, pardon me but it is true, is a human."

"Yes, one of us is," Ariana said. Her pride and temper bubbled up. At times like this she was perilously close to saying something about her own ancestry, as if to somehow hammer it into the elven consciousness that not all that came from humankind was bad.

"Never mind any of that," Eranic said. "What seems most important to me is finding who, or what, has done this and putting an end to it. Haltha and Lairis deserve justice. If not a bear, what could it have been?"

"They were dropped," Ariana said, raising her gaze again to the trees and seeing the way the branches bent downward. "Whatever had them was high. Flying. Are there dragons in these parts?"

One of the watching men, he who had gone into the pool again in search of the missing knife, moaned. "If a dragon's come to Eltarrin, we're done for. Once word of it gets out, no one will come here. We'll be finished."

"This is about more than springtime visitors," Ariana said. "This is about your homes, your families, your very lives." She took a breath, telling herself she shouldn't be doing this but also ruefully aware that if she didn't, Wyndrel would. Or already had, as far as she knew. "We can help you."

"Against a dragon?" the man asked, shaking his head. "Impossible."

"Better than doing nothing," she said sharply. "But if we are to help, we must know everything, that we might better be armed and prepared."

"The constable . . ." Eranic began.

"Is not a fool," the doctor said, silencing the deputy. "Nor more worried about his purse than his duty to the people of Eltarrin, as are some. Either tell her, or find him that he might do it himself. As for the rest of you, bring a cart. We'll take them to town. I'll be able to better examine them there, as well as make them more presentable for their families."

"It's too late for Lord Ciratan," another of the men said. "He'll never forget –"

"Even so, he would hardly want his son left here," she cut in. "See to it."

They all but fled from her, leaving Eranic uneasy in the face of Ariana's even, expectant gaze.

"I'll . . . I'll tell the constable of your offer," he said.

Ariana nodded.

He left, and the two women were momentarily alone with the dead. They regarded each other, measuringly. It occurred to Ariana that if she'd ever sat down to think about what a real *Morvalan* might be like, the image that would have formed in her mind could well have had a resemblance to the doctor. Cold, bordering on cruel, with icy eyes that knew nothing of compassion or caring.

Yet Selara Viska was *Alvalan* through and through . . . and the one *Morvalan* that Ariana to date had met was far removed from her. Kai Tilanne had been kind in her way, at least when it came to dealing with her fellow elves.

"Could it have been a dragon?" Ariana asked.

"It is not beyond possibility, but I think not. A dragon would have bitten, or clawed, or burnt its victims. Unless a mere hatchling, a dragon would be too large to roam Rantiel Herann's orchard without leaving clear tracks and signs of its passage. And what Nerevian Elgraine saw on the beach was no dragon."

"What did he see?"

"That, I cannot tell you. I made a pledge to his parents, as their doctor, that I would not." She sighed and looked at the satchel, which Ariana still held. "Were it not for that bag having been found here, I would say his experience had nothing to do with these others. Yet now, I am unsure."

"You agreed with me when I argued that we needed to know everything if we were going to do anything," Ariana said.

"Yes."

"Then tell me what the boy saw. It may be vital. If lives might be saved or lost depending on whether or not you speak . . ."

"I am aware of that. Yet I made a pledge."

"I see," Ariana said. "I'll go to the family myself, then, and ask them."

"That would be unwise," the doctor said. "The Elgraines are more leery than most of strangers, particularly ones so . . . well, strange."

"Will you tell me, Doctor?"

Physician Viska spent long moments studying the faces of the two dead elves. They could hear the creak and rumble of a cart being pulled toward them, and the distant voices of men calling back and forth in their search.

Without looking up, she whispered, "Very well. I'll tell you this much. What the boy saw, what he described to me, was not a dragon, not a bear, not any other beast of the woods. What he described to me . . . sounded human."

* * *

CHAPTER EIGHT

Blades and poisons . . . a physician and a murderer differ only in intent.
– Elwyndas, The Raimerrian War, Act XII

"Human?" Ainvar Lynellen repeated when the words of Selara Viska were reported to him. His eyes darted reflexively to the only human in the room, unable to help himself. Mischa wore a resigned and faintly chagrined smile. "No. What I saw was anything but human."

The tiny chamber at the rear of the constabulary had never seen such a gathering. Eranic had been hard-pressed to find enough chairs for them all. As it was, the youthful seeker-mage opted for the floor instead, where he sat beside Old General with the dog's head in his lap.

The rest of them sat around an oval table, Ainvar at one narrowing end and Rell at the other. Physician Viska was to Ainvar's left, and with so many chairs pushed in around so small a table, every time either he or she moved, their knees brushed. Under other circumstances, he might have found it delightfully diverting.

Eranic was on his right, the deputy's expression intense. Opposite them, Ariana and Mischa flanked Rell in much the same position.

Night had fallen over Eltarrin. Ainvar did not need to look out to know that the cobblestone streets were empty, and doors that had perhaps never been locked were now barricaded with sideboards or other large pieces of furniture.

A low terror held sway in most homes, excepting those of the Ciratan and Tannel families. There, grief reigned. The bodies of Haltha and Lairis had been brought to town, and soon would be returned to their kin that they might be decently wrapped in rosecloth and interred. Eltarrin was small enough that it boasted but a single communal crypt, a catacomb hidden beneath the town so as not to disturb the paying guests with a reminder of mortality.

"If not human," Rell said, leaning forward, "what?"

Ainvar paused. The large man, no longer bare-chested but no less impressive for it, had introduced himself as a knight in the Order of the Gryphon. Ever since he had done so, something had been tugging faintly at Ainvar's recollection. There weren't many of that order, which required demonstrated mastery of both swordplay and war magics. It was an accomplishment indeed, and almost unthinkable for a man so young.

"It stood half again your height," Ainvar said at last. He shivered as the memory swept over him like a chill wind. "Broad, too. Upright like a man, but hunched. Crouched over. Its arms seemed abnormally long, and I glimpsed, or thought I did, a tail. It had also the suggestion of wings."

They pondered this. Eranic was pensive, for this description was far more concise than the one Ainvar had given him before. He felt badly for not being fully honest with his second-in-command, but just saying it was madness. He stared at his clasped, clenched hands rather than watch their faces and see the disbelief he knew would be there.

"I shot it," Ainvar added, dragging the words out as if they were barbed and painful. "I nocked my bow and fired on it twice. Truesteel war arrows. I heard them hit home. I know they hit home."

"Of course," Rell said. "You are of the Order of the Hawk."

"Yet there was no blood. By the time I got there, whatever I'd shot at was gone. As were my arrows." He faltered, glancing sidelong at the doctor. She nodded almost imperceptibly. "Then came a sound from behind. I know not how, but it had gotten around me. It lashed out at me and I saw the shine of claws."

He pushed his sleeve clear to the shoulder, exhibiting an arm that was blotched with the pink-white of new skin. Darker striations, the very rose-color of mourning, latticed him from the elbow on up.

Eranic gasped, and blanched milk-pale. "You were hurt? You were wounded by it? And did not tell me?"

"I told only the doctor," Ainvar said, inclining his head toward Physician Viska. "She was good enough to mend my arm, although it is not yet up to full strength. We agreed that it was best to keep it to ourselves, so as not to cause panic."

"I am your deputy," Eranic protested. "I should have been told at least!"

"Yes, you should have been," Ainvar said. "And I did mean to, and would have in time."

Eranic did not look mollified. Hurt was etched plainly on his features.

"That thing, whatever it might have been," Mischa said in his harsh accent, "nearly had the arm off of you, if I'm any judge."

Selara Viska sniffed her opinion of his judgement. "Had he not received immediate healing, he might have lost the use of it, but the arm itself was far from severed."

Ainvar did not disagree, but he remembered pushing himself up with his other arm, his bow on the ground beneath him and arrows strewn all about from his spilled quiver. The flow of his blood looked black, a river of it. His arm had been a mangled ruin with the dull gleam of bone visible through the mauled flesh. Somehow, he'd stumbled back to town unseen by anyone, and made his way to the physician's door.

He hadn't even felt the pain until she opened it and stood there outlined in light like some benevolent spirit stepped straight from the pages of an Elwyndas play. Only then had white-hot agony ripped through him, consuming him like fire.

Now, as he pulled his sleeve back down to hide the still-tender scars, he looked around at this unlikely assemblage.

"That is what I saw," he said.

Ariana and Rell shared a glance. "Shaper-mages?" she asked.

He scowled. "What else could it have been?"

"Not again," Mischa said. "Not after the wasp-men, those bird-people, and Shedra. Don't those people have anything better to do?"

"Shaper-mages?" Physician Viska scowled as well. "But their Enclave is far from here, far to the north."

"Yes, so we learned," Mischa said, making a bitter face. "The hard way, at that."

"Their Enclave may be to the north," Rell said, "but their mischief stretches far beyond that. They seem to like nothing better than turning one thing into another."

"Or combining the both," Ariana said. "Could this creature, Constable, have been some combination of dragon and man?"

"It may have. All I know is that it must be found, and stopped."

"We must speak with the boy who encountered a human," Rell said. "There must be a connection."

"Nothing can be done tonight," Eranic said. "Even if the Elgraines will see you."

"They'll see me," Rell said.

Ariana elbowed him and gave him a hard, warning look.

"But," he continued, shifting his focus, "if we are to find this creature, and presumably fight it, we shall need to impose upon you earlier than anticipated, Doctor Viska."

"Have we time for that?" Ariana asked, and her hand strayed to her collar.

"Time for what?" Ainvar turned quizzically to the physician. "Just what is it they'd have of you?"

"A matter of surgery," she said. Although it had been a long day for all of them, and a longer night, that eager light came into her eyes again. "I can begin at once, if you wish."

"My offer of aid still stands," Mischa said. "Talopea's gifts are not affected by that metal."

The doctor rolled her eyes in elaborate skepticism.

"We may not have the time," Rell said in answer to Ariana. "But I would sooner go into this at our full strength. Is it not you who constantly harps at me the folly of taking on some stronger foe when hampered? I am merely heeding your advice."

Ainvar decided he did not need to know. Not yet. He rose, which signaled all the others to do likewise. "I shall go to the Elgraines now, tonight. I've let Fiera bend me to her will too long already. For the sake of the town, she'll have to accommodate me. Eranic, stay here lest anything should happen. We'll plan to meet again with first light, and devise a plan of action."

* * *

Selara Viska opened the case in which she kept her instruments. The bright magelights with which she illuminated her surgery glinted on metal. All in here was order, as she liked it. Clean. Crisp.

"You keep a very tidy workplace," her patient observed. Ariana had shed her truesteel corselet and was in a loose shift. She was a bit more full in the breast and wide in the hip than was fashionable, not that it detracted from her natural suppleness. Her silver hair had been bound back to keep it out of the way.

"Why wouldn't I?"

"I didn't mean to give offense. It's just that the other hospitals I've seen have been nothing like this."

"Where was that?"

"Tradersport." At a gesture from Selara, Ariana boosted herself gracefully onto the sturdy marble-topped table. She yelped, then grinned. "Cold."

"Tradersport," Selara said scornfully. "Human excuses for hospitals? Long wards of wooden beds, where the linens aren't changed for days and the so-called physicians do not even bother to wash their hands between patients? They kill more than they save in those places. If not outright, by amputations and cautery and other barbaric practices, then by infection. Anyone needing such treatment would do well to kill himself straightaway and spare himself the pain."

"But the temples are much better," Ariana said, sounding defensive.

"Oh, so they say. I wouldn't know and don't care to find out. Lie back."

Ariana did so. Her gaze followed each of the doctor's movements as Selara wet a cloth with a cleansing ointment, and bathed her hands in the same.

Selara took her customary place beside the table. "I am usually wont to offer a spell to relieve pain, but obviously that won't be effective yet. Would you prefer some herbal concoction?"

"Please," Ariana said. "Why test myself being stoic when there are other means available? Though . . . now, I'm sure that if your mind is made up, your mind is made up –"

"You'd be correct in that."

"But it might help to have Mischa in here. I have experienced his abilities."

Selara raised an eyebrow, and the other woman chuckled.

"That did not sound exactly as I meant it to," Ariana said. "His *healing* abilities."

"I am a trained surgeon and physician of the Emerin," Selara said. "I need no priest in here chanting homage to some human god. If you would rather seek his care, we can be done now."

"No, that's all right. I'm sorry."

"Accepted." Selara mixed herbs into wine and gave the cup to Ariana, and as she waited for the medicine to take effect, she busied herself examining the area she'd be cutting.

An ugly scabbed wound marred Ariana's creamy skin, just above her left collarbone. The flesh there had gone a puffed and angry red.

"You've scratched at this?" she asked with an undertone of accusation that was not lost on her patient.

"Not much," Ariana said. "The scratching always turned out to hurt worse than the itching."

"How did this happen?"

Ariana told her, as Selara laid out her instruments and draped more clean white cloths around the wound, of an enemy who had inflicted the *gilthanat* upon her. She was slurring toward the end, and her eyes had gone cloudy, a sure sign that the medicine had taken hold.

"I'm beginning now," Selara said.

She touched the tip of a surgical knife to the wound, pierced it, and muttered imprecations against the man who'd done this clumsy job as thick pus welled up. She heard her patient hiss, saw that she had tightly closed her eyes.

Once begun, she worked swiftly and well. From time to time Ariana twitched or moaned, but for the most part lay still as Selara cut away the infected tissue and opened the flesh around the wound. She'd never done anything like this before, not without her spells to rely upon. She had to go by feel and instinct to find the thorn-shaped wedge of metal, and move with delicate care to free its barbed edges.

Blood ran freely, a fair amount of it, staining the clean white cloth, pooling in the hollow of Ariana's throat, and trickling down to make a scarlet necklace. Selara reached into the cut she'd made with forceps and seized hold of the *gilthanat.* She spoke no encouragement or comfort, concentrating only on getting it out without making more work for herself.

It came free, a vicious-looking blue-black thing that was a fang, a blade, a thorn, and a bristle of fishhooks all in one. Selara dropped it into a jar, and set the jar well away so that the metal's effects would not interfere. She held her hand suspended, palm down, over the hole in Ariana.

"*Sala Rhun,*" she said, to stop the bleeding. If any slivers remained . . .

But no. The spell worked. The flow of blood stopped.

Ariana was shuddering, gasping. Selara cast another spell to ease pain, and her breathing smoothed, the lines that furrowed her face relaxed.

From there, it was easy as could be. She dusted the hole liberally with powdered herbs to fight the infection, ran a truesteel needle threaded with silk to draw the edges of the incision closed, and then spread both hands over the spot.

"*Salahin Roas,*" she said. Healing magic spun out of her, knitting up the damaged flesh.

Ariana had opened her eyes. She reached, but Selara caught her wrist.

"Let it mend. It is not a perfect recovery, not at once – magic is strong, but you'll still feel some ache and tenderness, and a few days might be needed before the scar fades."

"It's gone, though? Truly gone?"

"See for yourself." She pointed to the jar and showed Ariana the wicked thorn that was clotted with her own blood.

"*Tentalin.*" Ariana held up one cupped hand. A wondrous expression of joy lit her face even more than the radiance of the magelight that bloomed in her palm. "You've done it. Thank you, Physician. You may have saved my life."

* * *

Ainvar had been right. Fiera Elgraine did not even want to open the door to him, citing the lateness of the hour and the need her family had for a good night's sleep. But when he insisted, and would not leave without having the chance to speak with her son, she finally relented and let him in.

His next challenge came when he tried to enter the boy's room alone. The mother planted herself in the doorway and refused to let him close it.

"I won't have you badgering him, Ainvar Lynellen," she said. "My poor babe needs his rest. I won't have you in here interrogating him, do you understand me? I'm staying right here to be sure that you don't. A few questions, you said, only a few questions."

"I don't mean to interrogate Nerevian," he said.

The boy was sitting up in bed with the covers bunched protectively at the level of his neck, eyes wide and fearful. If anything was distressing him, Ainvar thought, it was more his mother's histrionics than the presence of the constable, even on such a late and unexpected visit.

Nerevar Elgraine tried to put a hand on his wife's shoulder, tried to steer her away. "Let's give them a moment, Fiera. I'm sure the constable has no intention of –"

"You'd do it, wouldn't you?" she demanded, whirling on him. "Turn your own son over to be accused and pounded at. He's a fragile child, much too fragile for all of this. He can't take any more shocks, any more of this upsetting business. Oh, it was a mistake to even let you in!" This last was delivered as she spun back around to Ainvar.

"*Vali*, I'm all right –"

"No, no, *tashta*, you're not, you've had a dreadful ordeal and you must stay quietly in bed and rest. No disturbances. No excitement. We mustn't endanger your health."

"Physician Viska assures me that Nerevian is in good condition," Ainvar said.

"*Her!*" Fiera went livid. "That's the last time we trust her with the care of our son, let me tell you. But of course you'd take her side, wouldn't you? She just waggles her fingers and you're at her beck and call. It's disgraceful, Constable, simply disgraceful. You might as well trot around at her heel with your tongue hanging out."

Ainvar rocked back, as much from her vehemence as what she said. "I'm not at all sure what you mean, *Tarsi* Elgraine, but it has nothing to do with why I'm here tonight. I need to speak to Nerevian, and I will. Alone."

"If you think for one moment that we're leaving you alone with him –"

"Fiera, please!" her husband begged.

"*Vali* . . ." Nerevian was on the verge of tears, and Ainvar knew that once the boy started to cry, that would be it. Any chance he'd have would be gone like a snowflake in a fireball.

"All is well, Nerevian," he said. "Your father is just going to take your mother downstairs for a bit and we're to have a talk. Is that all right?"

The boy bobbed his head. His mother opened her mouth to protest further, but Nerevar Elgraine showed spine for once and guided her forcibly to the door. It closed behind them, and both constable and boy exhaled wearily.

"Please don't be cross with her, Constable," the boy said. "She's only looking out for me."

"I know that, lad." He went to a chair at the side of the bed, knowing without needing to be told that Fiera spent many a night perched here, "looking out for" her son. "But you're growing up, you know, and every bird must learn to fly sooner or later."

"*Vala* says it's because of my brother," Nerevian said with unsettling candor. "They've been married three hundred years, and my brother died when he was a little boy. They told her she'd never have another one, but then I came, and she's afraid something will happen to me, too."

"It's kind of you to understand her so," Ainvar said. "Nerevian, can you tell me what happened on the beach?"

The boy haltingly relayed his story. How he'd gone out, as he usually did, looking for wood and shells and stone for his father to craft and sell in their shop. How something had appeared, frightened him, and stolen his satchel.

"And *Vala* made it for me, too," he added, downcast.

"We've found your satchel," Ainvar said. "You'll have it back soon, I promise you. But I must know what you saw. It's very important."

"It . . . it . . ."

"Was it like a bear? Or a dragon?"

"No, Constable. It was a . . . well, it was my size, and looked almost like one of us, except it was round-faced and ugly and had fuzz on its cheeks like an unripe *alkarra* fruit, and its ears were stubs. It was all red, too, around the nose, and breathed through its mouth like it was snoring. It snatched my satchel away and ran."

"On two legs?"

"Yes, sir, and it wore clothes, shabby rags but they were clothes."

"Could it have been a human?" he asked.

Nerevian gulped. "It might've been, I suppose. I've never seen one before."

"Not even when the town meeting got out?"

The boy looked at him. "*Vali* wouldn't let me go to the meeting."

"Of course. So it took your satchel, and then what?"

"It pushed me, and I ran. I could only think of getting away. I got over a rise onto the next stretch of beach, and was sure it was following me, but it wasn't."

"I'm told you gave *Tars* Welas quite a fright," Ainvar said.

"Yes, sir. I didn't mean to. I was standing there, looking back the way I'd come, thinking I'd escaped, when all at once I heard someone behind me. I thought it was the . . . the one I'd seen. So I screamed."

Ainvar nodded. Jrynne Welas, one of the town fishermen, had been the one to lead Nerevian back to town. He'd said that the boy shrieked so as to nearly peel fifty years off his life, and would have run blindly if Jrynne hadn't caught him.

"But you saw no large creature," he prompted.

"No. It was as tall as me or a little taller, and thin."

"Thank you, Nerevian. That's the end of my questions. I'll see that your satchel is returned as soon as possible. How are you feeling? Honestly?"

"Fine, sir. I was scared at first, and I scraped up my hands and knees –" These, he exhibited with a young boy's pride, although Selara Viska had healed them fully. "I had nightmares that night, though, and *Vali* says I was fevered. She wants me to stay in bed."

"What do *you* want?"

"I don't want to disobey her," Nerevian said, shrinking against his pillow. "But I do feel fine and well, I do. I'm tired of being caged up here. How is *Vala* going to get the things he needs for the shop without me to go out and find them? I want to be a help to him."

"I'm sure you are a great help. I'll speak to the doctor and your parents, and you'll be up and around again very soon, I promise."

He rose, smiled at the boy, and headed for the door. As his hand closed on the handle, Nerevian spoke again.

"It was sick, I think. Maybe it was looking for help. Do you think it might have been, Constable?"

"I don't know, Nerevian. But I tell you this, I mean to find out."

* * *

CHAPTER NINE

There are magics of which even we do not know.
– Elwyndas, The Mages Royal, Act II

Ariana flexed her arm. Healing skin pulled with a stretch that felt at once painful and good. She massaged the slight sunken spot where the wound had been. The horrid, invasive solidity was gone. She could once more detect the ever-present *aether*, life's blood of magic.

"She did well," Mischa admitted. "Yet another reason why the Emerin needs no gods."

"What do you mean?" Ariana asked.

They were in the outer chamber, she and Mischa and Kevan. The latter two were engrossed in a game of cards – Ariana saw with amusement that Mischa was introducing a popular Thanian gambling game to the youth. Wyndrel was taking his turn under the capable but cold blade of Physician Viska, behind a closed door.

"Well, she's right about human hospitals. They're abominable. Why? Because anyone with even a touch of faith can pay a visit to a temple, be it of Talopea, Galatine, or Helia, and be cured. The alchemists brew potions more potent than any medicine. Thus, our poor Lesser Race has never much needed anything more."

"But not all priests can heal," Ariana said. "Those of Steel, for instance. Or Haarkon, I'm told."

Mischa suppressed a shudder. "Please, Ari. Would you want me going around with the name of that *Morvalan* god on my tongue? We Talopeans in particular, whose province is life and all the pleasures thereof, would just as soon not be reminded of the god of the dead."

"I'm sorry, Mischa."

"As I was saying," he went on, shuffling the deck of waxed parchment cards, "because you elves have no priests, and snub alchemy, you've needed to make these achievements in medicine through magic. Otherwise, you'd die out."

"We have gods," Kevan said. "My family has a shrine to Valannin on the estate, and there's one here in town, too."

"Shrines, yes," Mischa said. "No temples, no priests, no books teaching the lore and will of the gods. No way to call upon divine aid."

"There is Karria's temple," Ariana said. "And clearly, the *Rhunvala* had priestly powers."

From the rear of the building came a heavy thump, followed by a terrible rending crash. Ariana was on her feet like lightning, racing to the door. She could hear Wyndrel's voice raised in a shout, and the startled cry of the doctor. Mischa and Kev were close on her heels as she tore the door open and plunged through.

A wide, shuttered window had been smashed in. Slats of wood were everywhere, panes of leaded glass littered the floor. The magelit spheres that hung suspended in silver wire cages swung wildly, sending light and shadow spinning and leaping. It dazzled Ari so that she had to stop, one hand half-shielding her eyes.

The marble-topped table was overturned, pinning Selara Viska's legs to the floor. The doctor sprawled in a strew of her tools and vials, black hair loose from its bun and fanning out around her head like a drape.

"Wyndrel!" Ariana cried out.

Two large figures were struggling in the crazed flicker of light. One, dark and lumpy and horrific, threw the other across the room with uncanny strength. Wyndrel, tossed headlong, collided with the shelves and brought most of them down with him. A melange of scents – bitter, spicy, acrid – filled the room as jars broke and powders spilled. Wyndrel grunted and fell to the floor.

Ariana grabbed for her sword, only to find that she hadn't belted it back on. Nor had she bothered with her armor.

The creature reared up. Light danced across a grotesque face dominated by a forethrust, wedge-shaped muzzle filled with teeth and a pair of lambent yellow eyes. It spied Ariana, who stood as if thunderstruck in the doorway with Mischa and Kev jostling behind her, and roared.

The roar, at once deep and screeching, drove into her head like a steel spike. The creature unfurled lopsided wings that flapped like leather. It was smooth and scaly, not shaggy-furred as the beasts that had once stalked her parents had been, but the same vast and terrible dread overwhelmed her. Born of some nightmare, given unnatural life, and ready to kill.

It sprang, bunched legs propelling it with strange agility. As its full weight landed on the table, the doctor screamed in agony. But the crushing was short-lived as the creature launched itself from there to the fallen shelves, and Wyndrel, coughing and groaning in the debris.

Ariana gathered her energies, flung out her hands, and cried, "*Nia'des!*" An arid wind issued from her palms, sucking the moisture from the air. Her mouth went dry. Her lips split in tiny, stinging cracks.

The full brunt of it struck the creature. It howled with pain, its skin turning flaky and white. The clawed hands that the constable had described swept up a shelf-board and swung it. Ariana ducked, not quickly enough, and was knocked backward off her feet. A spatter of something granular and crusty pelted her face. She fell against Mischa, the breath blown from her lungs.

The creature stooped to the wreckage and raked through it, ignoring Wyndrel as the battered man slowly staggered to his feet. It came away with several unbroken jars. Studying them, it made a whining and uncertain sound.

"Shaper-mage monstrosity," Wyndrel said. "I have you now!"

He had picked up a shelf-board of his own and brought it down hard on the creature's shoulder. A piece of its arm came off but there was no blood.

It turned away from Wyndrel, striking him with its flailing tail as it made for the ragged gap in the wall where the window had been. A bound and it was through and into the night with its burdens cradled against its chest and its wings beating clumsily at the air.

Ariana recovered her balance and dashed in again. Wyndrel hurled the board aside with a vicious battlefield oath. They went to the trapped doctor together. Selara Viska was barely conscious, her dark eyes swimming with pain, blood seeping out from under the massive weight of the table.

"Kev," Ari called. "The constable, quickly. Mischa, help us."

"But watch out, Kev," Wyndrel added. He was breathing in harsh gasps, and only now did Ariana notice that his arm was laid open along the line of the old scar. His blood trickled to add to the mess on the floor. He did not seem to care as he bent over the table and grasped its underside.

"When he lifts it," Ariana said to the doctor, "Mischa and I will pull you out."

"My legs," she said in a foggy voice. "They're shattered."

"We're going to get you out."

Wyndrel lifted, straining with exertion. The edge of the table rose. He shook with the effort, his jaw and eyes squeezed tight. Through gritted teeth, he said, "Be quick, Ari."

"Now, Mischa."

Together, they slid the woman from under the table. One look at her legs was enough to make Ariana wince. Shattered was as good a word as any, better than most. Shards of bone jutted through torn flesh and cloth.

"Got her," Mischa said.

The table slammed down and Wyndrel leaned against it, panting hoarsely.

"Your arm," Ariana said. "You're bleeding."

"Never mind that now. How is she?"

Mischa knelt beside her, one hand curled around the artful and suggestive golden symbol he wore on a chain around his neck. His other hand hovered above the doctor's alabaster face, then moved slowly down, tracing the contours of her body without quite touching her.

"I don't know if Talopea can help her," he said. "The gifts of my goddess can only be bestowed on those who appreciate Her. And pleasure, it seems, is not something with which the good doctor is overly familiar."

"You have to try," Wyndrel said.

"I will, fear not. I'm only saying I have my doubts."

His eyes went half-lidded and sultry as he sank into prayer. But before he could lay his hands upon the injuries, Selara Viska revived enough to push him rudely away.

"No . . . chanting," she said. "No priests. Let me see how it is."

"He knows what he's doing," Ariana said.

"I'll be the judge of my own condition."

"If she won't accept it, I can't force healing on her," Mischa said, looking up at Ariana with a helpless shrug of surrender.

Ariana blew out a frustrated breath. "I hardly know anything of the healing magics, but I suppose I could try –"

The doctor's expression was anything but welcoming. "An untrained healer can do as much harm as good. Leave me be, would you?"

She got into a sitting position, and swayed as she saw the damage that had been done to her legs. For a few moments she did nothing but look, then inhaled calmly, closed her eyes, opened them, and reached for the nearest of her instruments.

* * *

Kevan and the constable arrived on the run. Wyndrel met them at the door.

"It was here," he said. "The creature."

"Selara?" Ainvar Lynellen asked with a desperation that revealed more of his feelings than he perhaps would have been comfortable to show.

"She's been badly hurt." Wyndrel paused, then added, "She is a truly brave woman. I've never seen the like. It is as if they are not her legs at all but belong to another, so that she cannot be distracted by the pain as she does what must be done."

"And what is that?" The constable's tone was full of dread, fearing the worst.

Wyndrel shook his head, not to convey bad news but merely to say that he did not know. "She would have neither help nor advice from us. Ariana is keeping lookout and Mischa lingers nearby, lest the doctor change her mind and accept his offer of healing."

"Why won't . . . no, of course she wouldn't." Lynellen held his bow at his side, and rubbed his brow as if he could ease away the lines of tension there. "The creature came here. For medicine?"

"How did you know that?" Wyndrel asked sharply.

"There are two, that must be it," Lynellen said, almost as if speaking to himself. "Two, and they are in league. Or the creature serves the human, perhaps."

"Constable, explain."

"Nerevian Elgraine saw a human on the beach. A young male one, I'm surmising – he said it was near his size, and thin, and had no beard but down on its cheeks. He also told me that it seemed ill, this human. If the creature is under his control, it may well have been sent to find medicines to aid its master."

Ariana emerged from the back room, pale but resolute. "Wyn . . ." Seeing the constable, she caught herself and bit at her lower lip. "Rell, you should see this."

"I set you to watch the back," he said.

"Mischa is. She won't have him even nearby, and unless she faints from blood loss or shock, there's not much else either of us can do."

"Blood loss? How is she?" Lynellen asked in renewed desperation.

"Her legs are broken, both of them," Ariana said. "Quite badly from the knees down, as well as her ankles and most of the bones of her feet. She wants me to send for Nerevar Elgraine, though why a village craftsman could be of immediate use is beyond me."

"He's a shaper-mage," Kev said. "That's what he had in his shop. Things shaped from wood, and stone, and shell. And ivory. If he can shape ivory, he can shape bone. I'll go for him, if you'd like, my lady."

"Kev, you are a wonder," Ariana said, favoring the young seeker-mage with a smile that, while weary, was of such brilliance it stirred Wyndrel's heart and lifted some of the despair from the face of Ainvar Lynellen. "If you would, please, though it seems we should make better use of you than as a messenger."

"I was a page," he said, grinning. "I'm well accustomed to it."

When he was gone, Ariana turned to Wyndrel again. "You should see this. It's . . . it's peculiar."

"Stand watch, constable," Wyndrel said. "I'll be back momentarily."

"I am coming with you," Lynellen said.

"This is hardly the time for debate –"

"Rell," Ariana said. "He should see it too. I think it has bearing."

Lynellen looked narrowly at Wyndrel. "Order of the Gryphon? Yes . . . but I wonder . . . you seem oddly familiar to me . . ."

Ariana beckoned swiftly, distracting him before he could tip to the truth. "It's in here. I didn't want to move it."

Wyndrel followed, with Lynellen at his side. She led them into the back room, the surgery. The constable's attention was seized at once by the sight of Selara Viska on the floor, grimly tending to her ruined legs. Ariana was right. It was as if they belonged to some other, for all the emotion that she showed.

Mischa sat on a stool, keeping one eye on the hole where the window had been and another on the doctor. Ariana skirted the overturned table and went to the heap of shelves and jars. She stooped, and pointed to something amid the spilled medicines.

"There," she said. "Do you see it?"

At first, Wyndrel mistook it for a piece of broken crockery. It was a curve like the side of a bowl, thick and rough where it had been chipped off from a larger object. But the outside of it was scaled, and the shape of it was wrong.

"I cast a spell on that creature," Ariana said. "To leach the moisture from its tissues. It's very painful, very debilitating. Much of its skin flaked away. Then you struck it with a board, and this entire piece broke off from its arm."

"It has the look of clay," Wyndrel said.

"I think that's just what it is. That was no living being, but some sort of construct, or golem, made of clay."

* * *

Kevan Brindani could hardly keep still. Every throb of his pulse sent more exhilaration coursing through his veins.

His boyhood dreams had been filled with things such as this. Secret missions, noble quests, providing invaluable service to his king. He had been born too late to ever meet the old king, aged Shaelan. As a page at the palace, he'd served the Council, under the auspices of the Royal Stewards, and hoped only to distinguish himself enough to win the notice of a knight and be taken on as a squire.

Now he was the king's own, treated not as a child but as a young man and integral part of their force.

"You can find more of it?" Wyndrel asked of him, indicating the crumbled bits of clay on a cloth in Kev's hands.

"Yes, sir."

He'd been about to say "sire," but the constable was there, and the doctor, and the craftsman from the town. True, the three of them were paying little mind to anything else, but Kev did not want to be the one to give up the secret. Much as he might have liked to, because the looks on their faces when the realized they were in the presence of their own true king would be amazing.

The craftsman, Elgraine, had been astonished and frightened by the sudden summons. Kev wasn't sure just what he would do if the man had refused to accompany him. He did not intend for anything to fail in the tasks set him. But Elgraine had agreed.

The sounds were the worst. The grisly shift and pop and creak of bone softening under the shaper-mage's wizardry, being molded like wax into their proper shape. He could hardly bear to listen to it, thinking how awful it must feel and wondering how the doctor could manage without screaming. Her mouth was firmly set, her own hands busy with healing magics, as the two of them worked in concert to put her legs back the way the gods had intended.

Ariana, arrayed once more in truesteel, slim waist girded with a swordbelt, was likewise ready to set out but refused to budge until Mischa had seen to Wyndrel's wounds.

"It's nothing," the king protested, despite a steady if sluggish stream of blood flowing down his arm.

"She wasn't able to finish," Ariana said. "Is the *gilthanat* still embedded?"

"Yes, but a bandage –"

"And you were sent flying into the wall, the shelves," she persisted. "You're hurt."

"Not so hurt that I cannot go on."

"If no one will allow me to heal them, and no one will share my bed," Mischa said, "remind me why I even came on this journey? And please do not tell me it was for the life experience. My preferred life experience can be better found elsewhere."

Ariana, fists on her hips, addressed Wyndrel as if he were no king but a schoolboy, and an uppity one at that. "Stoicism has its place, but so too does good sense. For pity's sake, Wyndrel, it isn't as if you have to make love with Mischa for him to heal you."

"It'd help –" Mischa fell silent as they both glared at him.

"We're wasting time, but we'll waste more if we get halfway to our goal and you collapse," she said. "You're impressing no one with this act."

As it happened, he was impressing Kev, but Kev hardly thought it would be appropriate to speak up. He concentrated on the chunks of clay, and extended his seeker-magic to find more just like it. The clay was odd stuff, a bluish-grey in color except where it had been bleached white by Ariana's spell.

With ill grace, Wyndrel submitted to being attended by the priest. Mischa grasped his upper arm, and appeared to be resisting with great strength the urge to caress.

"So that's it," Mischa said, amused. "I'd never have guessed."

"What?" Ariana asked.

"Nothing!" Wyndrel made to pull away, but Mischa held tight. And already, as healing power welled up in the priest, the cut on Wyndrel's arm and the scrapes and bruises on his body melted away like frost on a windowpane.

Mischa was flushed by the time it was done. "Must we do this tonight? It's so late . . . we could return to the inn and sleep until dawn."

"Somehow I doubt it's sleep you crave," Ariana said. "And yes, we must go. The creature, or its creator, may know it's been seen and might try to flee the island. If we don't stop them now, we might never have another chance."

"If they leave the island, then all's well, isn't it?" Mischa asked.

"No," Wyndrel said, donning his shirt and vest. "Because they may return. We finish this tonight."

"Go with them, Constable," the doctor said. She was very pale, and her forehead was beaded with sweat, the only outward signs of the torture she must be enduring as her bones moved and altered and resumed their original positions.

"I don't wish to leave you," Ainvar Lynellen said. Of the three, he was by far the most distraught, and it was plain even to Kevan that the constable would have liked nothing better than to hold and comfort her. But it was also plain that there had never been a woman seeming less in need or desire of comfort.

"Don't be a sentimental fool, Lynellen," she said. "Your duty is to Eltarrin, first and foremost."

"We can see to this ourselves," Wyndrel said, making an offer of it.

Lynellen raised his head and studied him. "She called you Wyndrel."

"Yes," he replied, with a sideways, baleful look at Ariana. "So she did."

"Yet you cannot be . . . if you are who I suspect you are, then you should be dead."

"We go to find and defeat this creature, Constable. That is what matters now. Come with us if you wish, for we would be glad of your bow. Or stay if your heart bids you more strongly."

"Go," the doctor commanded. "You do no good here but get in the way."

He got up, moving a bit like one who could not quite credit what his eyes and ears were telling him. His gaze was fixed on Wyndrel.

Wyndrel looked to Kev. "Lead us."

"I shall." Kev gave himself over to the spell. When the object he sought was far, he would have a sense, an inner sense, of approximately how far and which way it was. When it was nearer, he felt it like a tug in his mind, like an unraveling thread that only he could perceive.

They left the doctor and the craftsman to their work, and went out into the night. Kev moved unerringly, in as straight a line as possible. Soon they were headed out into the dark, wilder regions of the island. Untamed, untenanted, as Lairian Ciratan had said. The lush tangle of forest woven through with trails.

Onward, onward. Kev scrambled over fallen logs and around boulders, as keen on the trail as any hunting hound might have been. He was aware of the others behind him, Mischa tripping and bumping into things and complaining how elves might be able to make their way with only the light of a few stars to guide them but he was a lowly human and could certainly use a torch. Ariana, still reveling in her regained magic, cast a magelight to glow upon Mischa's Talopean pendant, imbuing it with clear white light that pierced the dark forest like a beacon.

They crossed a trail and left it behind, and soon were in a section of woods where the trees had grown old and gnarled, and the ground was lost beneath generations of fallen, rotting leaves. The land was rough, rising and falling in steep hills and sudden ravines.

Kev saw a light, not the shining beacon from behind him but a spark ahead. He hissed for Mischa to hide the other, and darkness ruled again as the pendant was thrust out of sight.

There, flickering in a gully ahead, was the unmistakable orange of firelight. It cast shapes onto a wall of natural rock. Kev crept closer. He came to a large old tree that leaned out at an angle over the gully. A small creek was at the bottom. It must have once been a bigger creek, carving out this watercourse and undercutting the roots of the very tree whose trunk Kev held onto as he peered down.

Beneath him was a shallow cave, walled and framed in the tree's web of roots. The fire was built at the mouth of it, and a small, huddled figure was as close to the flames as it was possible to get without catching alight.

The seeker-spell still tugged at Kev, wanting to lead him across and into the forest on the far side. He looked that way and his body froze in place.

The creature was on the other side of the gully from him, standing motionless atop a boulder. Its eyes were amber and flame as it saw him.

It leaped, jaws gaping wide, wings spreading. Ungainly as it was, the thing was quick.

Kev reeled back with a cry, yanking at the short sword sheathed at his side. He could not get it free, pull as he might – he had peace-bonded it, obeying his father's rule without even thinking, and now that obedience was going to cost him dearly.

The creature landed in front of Kevan with an earth-shaking thump. His mind floundered for a word, and the closest he could come up with was "dragon-kin," for just as an elfkin was bred of human and elf, and orckin of human and orc, so too did this resemble nothing more than some twisted child of humanity and dragonkind.

A substantial chunk was missing from one arm, and patches of its skin were gone as if molted off, shed the way a snake's skin did. But it still looked fearsomely capable of tearing his head from his neck with claws as long and sharp as any blade.

He flipped the strap that secured his sword in its hilt and drew it, steel singing as it left the scabbard. He got the weapon in front of him just as the claws scythed down. Sparks flew, slivers of blue-grey claw were sheared off, but the blade snapped clean in half and left Kev with a jagged end no longer than an eating knife. His arms were wrenched painfully by the impact and he sprawled on the ground, wet leaves soaking through his clothes, as the dragon-kin monstrosity loomed over him.

* * *

Chapter Ten

The only truth and safety is in the castle of one's mind.
– Elwyndas, Astarra Alone (poem)

For Ainvar Lynellen, the world seemed to slow. The creature was there, right *there*, towering over the fallen seeker-mage with its wings outspread and its teeth bared.

His fingers found an arrow, set it to the string, drew back. The razored edges of the truesteel arrowhead struck glints in the magelight that Mischa held high. Rell charged, a broadsword that looked like a toy in his large hands driving forward in a thrust. Ariana was a pace behind him with her own blade shining.

Ainvar loosed his arrow. It skimmed over Ariana's helm, past Rell's head, and struck the creature at the base of its throat. At such close range, the arrow tore completely through and out the other side. A fatal wound in any living thing . . . but it left only a bloodless hole.

The battle was joined. Rell interposed himself between Kevan and the creature, beating it back with a fusillade of skillful blows, but in so doing set himself squarely between Ainvar and his target. Ariana, too, darted in to slash and danced back to dodge when the deadly claws came at her.

The creature stood its ground, screeching defiantly. It barely bothered to evade the attacks, lashing out with tireless fury. Kevan had severed the claws of one hand, they had all seen it, yet even as the fighting progressed they seemed to grow anew. Extruding themselves from the strange blue-grey substance of the thing.

So, too, did the hole in its throat fill in, closing seamlessly. And there was no sign of the wound on its arm, from whence had come the clay they'd examined in Selara Viska's office.

"It's healing," Ainvar said, arrow trained and waiting for a chance to fire when he wouldn't risk hitting Rell or Ariana.

"Repairing," Mischa said. "It isn't *alive*."

"Then how do we bloody-well kill it?" Kev hacked at its tail with the stub of his broken sword, cutting off the end. He ducked as the renewed claws carved deep gashes in the tree next to him.

Ariana sank her blade to the crosspiece in the creature's abdomen. The tip emerged, coated in wet-looking clay, from its back. "Damage it enough and –"

It slapped a wing at her, the bony strut catching her across the face. Her head snapped back. She landed heavily, unarmed, her sword still wedged through the creature's midsection like a skewer.

"Ari!" Rell cleaved at the offending wing. It parted with a sound like torn canvas. Part flopped to the ground, the rest dangled at an askew angle from the creature's back.

Mischa moved in, handling his sword as though he'd had some training but little actual practice. A raking blow from the creature scored across his breastplate. With more luck than deftness, he chopped at its arm and half-amputated it at the elbow.

An opening, and Ainvar fired. The arrow plunged into one gold-burning eye and snuffed it.

Ariana sat up, dazed, and pulled off her dented helm. Blood dripped from her forehead. "– and it will lose the magic that animates it," she said groggily. "It'll fall apart."

Rell went to work with a will, fighting like a man possessed. Ainvar had never seen such strength in an elf, coupled with well-honed ability. The cuts made by Mischa and Kevan seemed paltry by comparison, and even his own arrows couldn't measure up to the shearing strikes from that broadsword.

Clay fell off the creature in softening clumps, smacking the damp earth. It was still trying to repair itself, the arm that Mischa had nearly cut off pulling back together and shortening as it did so because the golem was cannibalizing its own substance. It was already smaller, shrinking in on itself as it sought to retain its form.

Movement from beyond the creature caught Ainvar's eye. A small shape, clambering up the far side of the gully with halting, crippled clumsiness.

He had been holding an arrow ready, and now pivoted to bring it to bear on the figure. As it reached the top, and turned to throw a horror-stricken look at the golem, Ainvar let fly.

The arrow flew straight and true, embedding itself in the small figure's thigh. With an agonized shriek, his target toppled down into the gully again.

Rell rose to his full height, broadsword raised overhead, and brought it down in a single whistling stroke that split the creature in half. It collapsed, heaved once as if trying to hunch its pieces close enough to rejoin, and fell still.

"*Nia'des*," said Ariana, and the clay turned dry and riddled with cracks like a drought-beset riverbed. Kevan trod on the larger bits, breaking them apart.

"The other," Ainvar said. "The human. Over here."

He led the way at a run, jumping easily into the gully. And there, sobbing and wailing at the edge of the creek, hands clamped about the shaft jutting from his leg, was a human. It was a boy, surely not yet a man, thin and reedy with a scruff of down for a beard and the awkward limbs of youth. Blood darkened his crude woolen trousers.

When he saw them coming, he bleated in fright that overcame his pain and tried to roll and crawl. Ainvar aimed another arrow at him. "Do not move."

Either the words, or more likely the arrow, made his meaning clear. The boy resumed wailing and holding onto his leg, and babbled a string of nonsense in a language that meant nothing to the constable.

"That is not Thanian," Rell said.

"Nor Hachlanian nor Southern," Ariana added, walking a trifle unsteadily with one hand held to her brow.

"Do you speak Emerinian?" Ainvar asked.

The boy looked at him blankly. His face was tear-streaked and blotched and with bubbles and streams coming from his nostrils. He said something broken and pleading.

"He's sick," Mischa said softly. "And hurt."

"He is a thief, and a murderer," Rell said.

"He's only a child," Kevan objected in a whisper.

"And a mage," Ariana said. "I can see it in the aura that surrounds him."

The four of them looked then to Ainvar, and he sensed a deference in them. This was his town, and for him to decide.

"We must know more," he said. "Where this boy came from, what he's done, and whether there are more of his kind about. But he must be bound and gagged, and not given the opportunity to cast any spells. His magic . . ."

Ariana nodded sagely. "Is not like ours. We don't know what he might be capable of. We don't even know if gagging him will help. I've heard that the Darkwood wizards use spells without essence words."

"If you gag him," Mischa said, "he'll die. Look at him. He's sick, as I said. Hear how he breathes through his mouth? Stifle that, and he will suffocate. He's scorching with fever, too, and just listen to the damp rattle of his lungs. If you wish him dead, it'd be kinder to lop off his head."

"We make it very plain to him, then," Rell said. He dropped to one knee, forcing the boy to meet his gaze. Slowly and deliberately, Rell showed him the edge of his sword. "Any spells, any tricks, and you've thrown your life away. You may not understand what I say, but you understand my *meaning*, don't you, boy?"

The human cringed, more tears pouring from his eyes. A pitiful bleating noise came from his throat. As consumed with pain and fright as he was, Ainvar doubted he'd dare try anything.

"Good enough," he said to Rell. "I think he does understand."

As the others tied the boy, and wrapped bandages around the leg and arrow to hold the impaling shaft in place until it could better be removed, he stooped to enter the dank, undercut root-cave. He found a basket that must surely have been the one Lairis and Haltha had taken on their moonlight stroll, and anger built up in him.

Here, too, were some pieces of wood and shell that must have come from Nerevian's satchel. A heap of *alkarra* rinds. Empty crocks that had been taken from the ransacked cottages. A knife, no doubt the very one that had belonged to Lairis. And jars from the doctor's shelves, their contents mixed randomly into a tea that smelled more as if it would kill than cure.

"He sent the beast to find medicine," he said, stirring the dregs with a twig. "Any medicine at all, hoping something would help."

"Here's something interesting," Ariana said, lifting – very gingerly and by one corner pinched between her thumb and forefinger – a blanket that reeked of sick-sweats and filth. "There's a pack here, of a design I've never seen."

"Bring it," Ainvar said. "And some of the clay, too, if you would. I think we'd do well to find out how this happened."

"How did he get to the island?" Mischa was staying near the boy, something that must have been a chore given the state he was in and the vile stenches that clung to him. He did this, Ainvar saw, because the boy regarded the elves with abject terror and kept reaching out to his fellow human as well as he was able, as if begging for aid or sanctuary. "Not across the bridge, surely."

"That creature could fly," Ariana said. "We know that from how the young lovers were found. They'd been dropped from a height. It must have been bringing them here, or looking to hide them, but they proved too great a weight, perhaps. So it could have flown here, carrying the boy."

"But from where?" Mischa asked. "It's obvious why . . . he was sick and hungry and made for the nearest signs of civilization, but couldn't come openly and expect any sort of a warm welcome."

Rell shook out the blanket, folded it into a sling, and wrapped the boy so that he could be lugged like a bundle of wood. This unwieldy arrangement, he slung on his back. Ainvar brought the basket and other stolen items, while Ariana scooped an amount of the clay into an empty crock.

They set off at a more reasonable pace, taking the easier route rather than the straightest possible line. As they went, tiredness set in. Ainvar realized how late it was, and what an eventful few days it had been. So much, so fast . . . it made his mind ache. During the war, he'd gotten used to things happening far more quickly than the norm, though even then it had seemed to the few humans with whom the army had associated that it took the elves forever to make a decision or get anything done.

Eltarrin still slept beneath the darkest curtain of the night by the time they had reached Selara Viska's home. She lived on the edge of the town, a bit removed, a bit remote, much like the doctor herself. That was how the creature had been able to approach unobserved, and how the five of them and their prisoner were able to do the same.

The window was a gaping maw in the rear wall, revealing only darkness within. A single magelight glowed in the front room. Circling around to the door, Ainvar opened it to find Selara slumped in a chair, her splinted and thoroughly-bandaged legs extended before her on a high, padded hassock.

She was chalk-white, with dusky shadows under her eyes, and was so still that his heartstrings plucked a panicked series of notes. So pale . . . the strips of cloth wrapping her legs . . . as if someone had come along and interrupted the undertaker halfway through the process of preparing her for the tomb. If he had breathed the scent of roses just then, he might have screamed.

"Selara?" he asked.

Her lips parted, but she did not speak. Instead, she sipped at the air and rolled her head slightly, letting it loll against her shoulder.

Relief like a wave washed over him. He entered, the others coming in behind him.

Nerevar Elgraine was nowhere to be seen. Of course, the doctor would have shooed him off once he had performed all the help she required, or would accept. Ainvar could almost hear her stating that she had matters well in hand, and for the craftsman to go home and keep his mouth closed about any of this. The last thing she'd want would be every well-meaning busybody in town poking their noses in and disturbing her privacy.

Rell deposited the boy, who had evidently lapsed into unconsciousness, on a table. He went from there straight to Ariana, who had sagged into a chair with a groan. Kneeling before her, the large man rested his hands at the sides of her face and peered intently into her eyes.

"I'm fine," she said.

"You're hurt."

"Only a little dizzy."

"Mischa," Rell called.

"Rell, it's all right, only a bump."

He touched her brow and showed her the red tips of his fingers.

"It's nothing," she insisted.

"I shouldn't have let that thing near you."

"Pardon me, Your *Majesty*," she said heatedly, "but *I* went to *it*, if you remember. Quit coddling me and treating me like one of your frail and useless Emerinian girls. It took a swordmaid to retrieve the Emerald of Karria, after all!"

Ainvar gaped, not sure which element in her outburst shocked him more. Kev made a warning hiss, waving his hands in negation. Mischa rolled his eyes.

"Indeed," Rell said. "No Emerinian girl would talk like that."

"Yet another problem with this kingdom."

"One that I, at least, should like to see changed." He went so far as to wink at her before looking around, sensing that Ainvar was staring at him. "Yes, Constable?"

"You . . . you *are*, aren't you? Who I think you to be."

"We had for reasons of our own intended to keep it secret, but yes."

Ariana had the good graces to look abashed. She withdrew into the chair and passed her hand over her forehead.

"Does no one know? In all the Emerin?"

"Only some other few, and they are my enemies," Rell – *Wyndrel*, Ainvar thought, *Wyndrel Perras* – replied. A dire edge hardened his golden eyes as he spoke. "But we haven't time for all that now. Suffice that I am who you believe me to be, and am on a quest to regain what is rightfully mine and stop my chief betrayer from committing an act of grave damage. We came to your town seeking horses and supplies, and must soon depart."

"Whatever aid we can offer . . . gladly . . ." Ainvar was so overcome he barely knew what he was saying.

"Spare us the bowing and oaths of fealty for now," Mischa said. He had removed his breastplate and was apparently more concerned with the rips in the shirt beneath. His skin was untouched, but he hardly noticed that. "Another shirt torn. Whatever happened to that enchanted mending needle, Ari?"

"It went to the same place as the cloth-of-cleaning," she said. "And my Silversilk, and all else that Tiercel took from me."

"Tiercel?" gasped Ainvar. "Tiercel Reyes, the knight-general?"

Such a dark and ferocious look crossed Wyndrel's face that the constable took an involuntary step back. "We have no time for that, either," he said in a clipped tone.

"Do we have time for sleep?" said Kevan. "Or supper? Or anything?"

"We must learn what we can about this human boy," Ariana said. "I have an idea, but . . . none of you may much care for it."

"You can't mean to torture the poor thing," Mischa said. "He's already half-dead, and what good would it do if none of us can understand him?"

Glancing apprehensively at the others, Ariana said, "There are magics that are forbidden in the Emerin. They are not taught, they are not tolerated, and are not even widely believed to exist. My father, however, was a self-tutored wizard and hence picked up a few tricks that Feyna Rel would frown on. Strenuously. He taught some of them to me."

"Forbidden magic?" Ainvar was beginning to wonder if he had really fallen into some restless, troubled sleep and was dreaming all of this. "What next?"

"What manner of magic?" Wyndrel asked.

"I can look into the boy's mind," Ariana said. "I can read through his memories as though they were books shelved in a library. It's difficult, it will exhaust me, and he's bound to resist such an intrusion. But, since I haven't yet learned any language-magics, it's the only choice I can think of."

"I'll not tell Archmage Feyna if you'll not," Wyndrel said with a wry smile. "Your father sounds like quite the intriguing fellow."

"I only wish I'd been a better student," she said. "My decision to leave home came suddenly, and there are gaps in my knowledge that I am already regretting. But there's never any knowing just which spells will come in handy."

Wyndrel looked at Ainvar. "Well, Constable . . . do you mean to arrest this woman if she practices a little forbidden magic in a good cause?"

"If you have no objection, my lord king, neither do I."

"There you have it, Ariana. Whenever you're ready."

"Shouldn't we get that arrow out of his leg first and heal him?" asked Mischa. "Not that I expect Talopea's powers to do much for the likes of him – he looks to have had scarce little pleasure in his life."

"We'd need Physician Viska for that," Ariana said. "Unless you planned to yank out the arrow by brute force. It's clear through his leg."

"Does he need to be awake?" Wyndrel asked.

"I think it's better if he isn't," she said. "He'll be less able to fight me that way."

* * *

When no one had any further objections, or at least ones they were willing to voice, Ariana summoned all of her concentration. She was seated at the end of the table upon which the unconscious human boy had been laid out, her hands cupped around his head without touching it.

The room was deathly still. None of the others seemed to want to make a sound, fearing they'd distract her. She had to admit that they probably would. It was one thing to go over such spells in theory, quite another thing to actually put them into use. But she wasn't about to admit to them, least of all to Wyndrel, that she'd never done this before.

Her thoughts flashed for a brief moment to her father, and his patient tutelage. How far away that sun-dappled schoolroom seemed, with its high, arched windows looking out on the inlet where the tall-masted ships of Tradersport bobbed in the harbor.

She could remember sitting there as a young girl, feet not able to reach the floor but swinging beneath her desk as he taught her to read elven letters, or quizzed her on the *lhilatin*, the essence words of each type of magic. A quick smile flitted across her lips as she thought of Darkfire, dozing on a windowsill and rousing occasionally to add mental comments that she couldn't hear but that often made her father laugh in his soft, pleasant way.

That had been their time, father and daughter. She'd had similar times with her mother as well, learning swordplay and knife-throwing, but most of what Cat had been willing to teach, Ariana hadn't been interested in learning. She'd known from an early age that she didn't have it in her to be a Nightsider, or a Black Dragon, shadowing the city streets by night, relieving merchants of their purses or settling disputes with a quick dagger. The heritage of her grandfather, and her mother, was meant for Tal.

Thinking of her parents and younger brother brought her a pang of homesickness. Tal could be, and often was, a horrid pest, always prying into her secrets . . . but she missed him. Was he getting on well in Thanis? He'd be safer there than Tradersport, until their mother found some way of dealing with the noble who'd threatened him. But it was also entirely possible that, free from the scrutiny of his mother, he'd get into mischief the likes of which he'd never done before.

Pushing all of that aside with an effort, she cleared her head of all but her concentration. She called up the mental words and difficult gestures, different for each spell, and basked in the steady presence of the *aether.*

"*Seyalar,*" she whispered, hands cupped around the boy's head.

The connection was instantaneous and jolting. She spun, tumbling through a hodgepodge of images and sensations, all seen through the eyes of a child. Exerting her will, she tried to restore order to the hectic turbulence of his thoughts.

Back, back . . . calendar pages turning day by day . . . and here was the boy, huddled by his meager campfire, wracked with sickness and misery and loneliness and fear. Eating because he knew he had to, half-certain that the "elf-food" would destroy him. Elves, a groundless and superstitious hatred for elves, burning like fire in his mind. Evil, cruel, lordly, deadly.

Here he was being borne aloft in the misshapen arms of the golem, gliding over the deep waters of the lake toward the lights, toward the buildings, dreading it but so hungry, so sick. Before that, the woods. Wandering lost and afraid, the creature plodding beside him as his silent protector, his guardian, his only weapon and only defense.

And earlier still . . . the making of the beast. A crate, fallen and burst apart, and a huge brick of blue-grey clay, slowly being worked by small hands into a draconian shape. A body shaking with sobs, a face hot and wet with tears. The elves hadn't found him, he had hidden too well, but now he wished they had.

Elves had slaughtered his family.

Ariana jerked as a familiar face filled her inner eye. Ice-blue eyes, short-cropped black hair, handsome features twisted into a malicious sneer.

"Tiercel," she said aloud without knowing she did.

A pair of wagons, towed by shaggy ponies. Crates, boxes, bundles. All their life's possessions. People. Humans. A mother, a father, a host of relations and children. Bringing valuable supplies and provisions, the life-clay not least among them. Promises of work, lodging, wages. Promises of apprenticeships for some of the children, Prakah among them.

Yes . . . Prakah . . . that was his name.

All of those promises worthless now as the elves attacked. Ariana saw, through Prakah's memory, the ambush and butchery that had taken place. Some of the humans struck back with magic that she could not even begin to understand. They hammered at their foes with unseen fists made of raw magical force. Others quickly worked the clay into snakes, into spiders, into hideous monsters of their own imagination. Breathing life into them, they turned them loose.

A noise, the terrible shrieking bone-quavering noise . . . it sundered the clay creatures into mush, felled the humans one by one. It was Tiercel's sword, howling and wailing and screeching like rusted nails being drawn out of thick oak.

Prakah ran from it, ran wildly without looking, without caring, wanting only to get away from the noise before it flattened him to the ground too. He spied a hole, a burrow, at the base of a tree and squirmed into it feet-first, writhing over onto his belly and poking his head out just as Tiercel and the *Rhunvala*, her face not sneering but tight-lipped and somber, slew every last man, woman, and child.

The ponies they cut loose and drove galloping off by slapping their haunches with the flats of their blades. They ignored the wagons and their contents. Prakah slid deeper into the burrow, hiding, hoping only to stay small and unseen.

When he'd emerged at last, the evil elves were gone and his family had been left where they'd fallen. Mad with grief and terror, Prakah stumbled around begging them to wake up although he knew they were dead, all dead.

They would come back. Any time now. The elves would come back to see if they had left any alive, and they would find him.

Weeping, Prakah came to the crate of life-clay. It had been for Canah, a gift for Canah brought by ship all the way, a gift for the great wizard. But there was no way to get it to Canah now, even if Prakah had known where his castle was. Or where *he* was.

No apprenticeship. No family. No one to help him, and no one to come looking. He had only himself, and alone he would die.

So he took the clay, all of it, and just like he and his brothers and sisters had done with ordinary clay, worked it with his hands and made it into the biggest, strongest, most ferocious monster he could think of. When it was done, it stood far taller than Prakah himself, and he had to climb onto the overturned crate to breathe life into its mouth.

The amber eyes had come alive then, and he had his protector.

Ariana heard, as if from a tremendous distance, her mumbling voice. She was speaking snatches of what she was witnessing, and it probably made no sense to anyone who could hear. But she was helpless to stop.

Back, and back more. The people alive again, the wagons restored. Hope and merriment, tinged with undercurrents of fear. They trespassed in the hated elf-lands, but if they could reach the castle . . .

She pressed deeper. Prakah was stirring now, aware of her. She could feel his presence, buzzing and stinging in her mind like a hive of bees.

A ship. Wagons disembarking from a ship. A village, small and muddy and composed of wooden shacks with thatched roofs. A village on the sea, the sun sinking behind the trees . . . the eastern coast?

The images, the memories, fragmented. Ariana pursued them determinedly, catching glimpses and perceptions of a sea voyage, rollicking and tossing on the waves, and an island.

"Hramad," she heard herself say, like one talking in her sleep.

Prakah struggled in her mental grip. But what she had seen was so startling that she had to know more. She seized him relentlessly. Hramad . . . an island nation . . . wizards . . . human wizards waging war on one another . . . he knew little of it, only what he'd overheard listening to the adults. But war, there was war, and some wizards had fled or been exiled . . . and hidden in the elf-lands . . . Canah . . . mighty Canah, who could bring substance from nothing . . .

Canah was *here* . . . in the elf-lands. He had taken his most faithful followers and sent for more, apprentices, a land ripe for the taking and never mind the squabbles on Hramad. He would have the elf-lands, depose them as his ancestors had done of old . . .

Pain burst all around Ariana. She was at the center of it, at the center of something that was all knives and fire and iron-fisted crushing. A scream tore from her throat, more felt than heard, lost as she was in this consuming and soul-shredding agony. It was followed by a sensation of speeding away, through blackness so total it encompassed everything, speeding faster than dragonflight across impossible distances.

The next thing she knew, she was curled up and trembling, eyes squeezed shut, afraid to look or feel for fear that her body had been torn to pieces. A steady, shaky series of cries issued from her, and she was powerless to stop them.

Warm arms were around her, holding her close to a broad chest. She could hear a solid, thumping heartbeat counterpointing her own racing pulse.

"Ari? Ariana, say something."

"Wyndrel?"

"I have you. You're all right. Nothing is going to harm you."

He was cradling her against him, stroking her hair. She opened her eyes and saw that she had somehow ended up on the floor, her chair overturned. The others were gathered around the table, and the moment her gaze fell on the boy, she knew.

"He's dead, isn't he? He died while I was in his mind." Her throat was dry and raspy as she tried to swallow. "I killed him. He fought me, he resisted me, and it killed him." She convulsed, her stomach heaving.

"Yes, he's dead," Wyndrel said, outwardly calm but she could feel the tension in him. "I thought . . . he could have taken you with him. Maybe there's a reason why some spells are forbidden."

"It almost did. Oh, my head. Did I speak?"

"Yes, but we couldn't follow most of it. Wizards, an island, something about Tiercel?"

"I'll tell you all of it, but not now. I can't right now." She looked again at the body of the boy. She had killed wasp-men, and been partly responsible for the death of the shaper-mage Quisfahr, she would gladly run Tiercel through given the chance . . . but this? A bound and helpless human boy with no possible way of defending himself?

Wyndrel held her tighter. "We had to know, Ariana. It had to be done."

"That makes it no easier."

"I know. Can you stand?"

She realized that she was pressing close to him, seeking comfort from his strength and nearness, and would have blushed if it hadn't felt like every drop of blood had drained out of her. "Yes. I can stand."

He rose, lifting her with him and setting her onto her feet, ready to catch her if she faltered. "We can do no more tonight. We must have rest, all of us. There will be much to do on the morrow."

The others were looking at her, awed or afraid or sympathetic, or a mix of all three. She could see her own exhaustion mirrored in their eyes. The constable most of all was pale and unnerved.

"Yes, all right," she said. "Rest. That would be welcome."

"I'll stay here," the constable said, with a glance at the doctor that was much tenderer than he probably thought it was. "I wouldn't want her to waken alone to find a dead human on her table. Someone should be here to explain."

"A good idea," Wyndrel said. "We'll return to the inn, but tomorrow we will have to decide what to tell the townsfolk."

"The truth?" Kevan suggested.

"Certainly . . . but how much of the truth?" Wyndrel managed half a grin. "Send for us, Constable, if you have need of us."

He agreed, and the four of them went out into the night that was slowly becoming the dawn. The eastern sky was fading from indigo to blue, and the stars in it were losing their brightness, being swallowed up by the encroaching day.

The streets of Eltarrin were still silent and unoccupied. The inn's main door was kept unlocked, and no one was up to ask them difficult questions as they made their way as quietly as possible up the stairs and to their suite of rooms at the end of the hall. Kev and Mischa barely even said goodnight, already almost asleep on their feet.

Ariana felt the same way. She fumbled at the straps of her armor with fingers that felt all thumbs, couldn't manage it, dredged up the energy to cast one last little spell – "*Lisik!*" – and they came unfastened of their own accord. The heavy truesteel fell away and only then did she realize she'd left her helm somewhere out in the woods. At the moment, it hardly mattered.

"Ariana," Wyndrel said.

"Hmm?" Her eyelids were rusty portcullises; she could almost hear them creaking as she raised them.

"You did well tonight. I'm sorry for what I said."

She managed the ghost of a smile. "Which time?"

He kissed her brow. "Pick whichever you like, or all. I'll not underestimate you again. Sleep well."

"Thank you," she said, and did just that.

* * *

CHAPTER ELEVEN

All the woodlands to the sea, to the mountains north and south.
– Elwyndas, Nightfall in the Emerin, Verse Six

By the time some days later when they left Eltarrin, Ariana had grown more withdrawn and silent than Wyndrel cared to see. Had he wished for her acid tongue to be stilled, her willful nature to subside? He had, and now that those had come to pass, he wished it otherwise.

It was the boy, the death of the boy. Bad enough she'd been with him, feeling what he felt, as it happened. Worse, in her eyes, was that she'd caused it. Not in the heat of battle but by prying into his soul. And using forbidden magics at that.

He did not know how to comfort her, or even if he should. Death was something each warrior had to come to terms with himself . . . or herself. Not every foe would be an armored and equal match. Not everyone slain would be a foe. He had learned those lessons, those painful lessons, during the war.

Ainvar Lynellen had elected to keep his knowledge of Wyndrel's identity to himself. He went to great pains to assure him of that, but Wyndrel shrugged it off.

"The day will come, and hopefully not long now, when all the Emerin will know," he said. "Do not go out of your way to spread the news, but do not curse yourself if you speak of it. Though I should think that for a while, at least, you and the fair doctor will have many other things to speak of before you have need of such a topic of conversation as myself."

He spoke lightly, but inwardly he was troubled. What Ariana had seen in that boy's memories tore at him. An island of wizards, human wizards whose magic was of a sort so different as to be nearly incomprehensible? Establishing settlements in the Emerin, too . . . and with a burning hatred for the elves. These things preyed on him.

The gratitude of the town had seen them provided with horses – Lairian Ciratan was devastated over the loss of his son, but thankful to have the body to inter and to know that the ones responsible had paid in the most final way – and what other clothes and supplies they'd yet lacked. They also had an offer from one of the boatmen to ferry themselves and their steeds to the lake's far shore.

Wyndrel did not hesitate in accepting. To go around, even riding, would be to add time to their journey and they already knew that Tiercel and the *Rhunvala* were well ahead of them.

So it was that on a gloriously golden afternoon, they made their farewells. Selara Viska, stoically holding herself upright on crutches, permitted the constable to stand at her side. While nothing in her expression showed it, something in her demeanor seemed to have thawed.

She had insisted that she finish her work on Wyndrel, removing the embedded *gilthanat* from his bone and putting his own stoicism to the test. He had been so long without magic that it was a physical shock to feel the *aether* all around him again. Spells he hadn't thought of in years were his to command once more, if he could recall all the words and gestures.

That, then, would be his main concern. To reacquaint himself with his magic, to find and revive the warmage he had been.

But a lake-going vessel was not the place to be doing such. He would not have been so foolhardy as to practice fire or lightning – his aim, he was sure, had deteriorated markedly – and neither did he think it was for the best to work other war magics in the view of the crew.

It was a quiet crossing, each of them lost in their own thoughts. Even Mischa had little to say. Kevan, who had never experienced battle before, had to come to terms with the difference between his imaginings, and reality.

The serenity of the lake seemed to help, the beautiful views of hills and trees mirrored in the water. Once, a flock of pure white birds had taken off in a storm, soaring high, and such a sight could not but lift any heart.

They reached the far side, docking at a fishing village peopled by no more than half a dozen small families, and by the silences that fell and the looks that followed, they were none too accustomed to seeing strangers. Not wishing to upset them, and eager to be on his way, Wyndrel urged the others to set off at once. Their horses, prancing and frisky, were pleased to have solid earth beneath their hooves again.

The forest closed around them like a green curtain. There was no road east from here, only game trails, but the undergrowth was light and they made good time on that first day's ride. They camped that night in a clearing, and at last Wyndrel felt that they could speak freely.

"You should not dwell on it so," he said to Ariana as they settled around the fire to eat.

Mischa nodded in support, but Ariana shook her head.

"How can I not dwell on it?"

"You didn't mean to kill him, Ari," Mischa said. "No one blames you."

"Except myself."

"They would have killed him anyway," Kevan said, his eyes bereft of much of their usual merriness. "Wouldn't they have? For what he did?"

"The laws of the Emerin frown on executions," Wyndrel said.

"Even for humans?" Mischa asked dourly.

"Even for humans," he said. "I cannot say, though, whether the families of the murdered young couple might not have attempted to take matters into their own hands. Such anguish can easily cloud one's judgement."

"He was executed all the same," Ariana said. "And while we're speaking of the laws of the Emerin, it was with forbidden magics that I did it. What is the sentence for that?"

"It does not matter," Wyndrel said. "You're not on trial for doing what had to be done. These are exceptional circumstances, Ariana."

"So, as king, you're willing to overlook the law if it is to your best interest?"

His grin was hard, more of a baring of the teeth than any actual pleasure. "I mean to kill Tiercel. I do not plan to bring him back to the city and put him before the Council and let him be judged for his crimes. He is to die for what he has done. Either it is an execution, or it is a murder, and either way, I care not. It will be so."

"And from what you told us," Kevan said, "Sir Tiercel was responsible for the deaths of all of those other humans."

"Yes," Ariana said. "He and Kai Tilanne. They never stood a chance. It was a bloodbath, a slaughter."

"Of those who had come into this land uninvited and with hostile intent," Wyndrel said. "In a way, a strange way, we are in Tiercel's debt for dealing with them."

"That's a horrible thing to say! Thank him, for hewing down those helpless people?"

"Those enemy wizards," he said. "An entire land of wizards whose magic is foreign to us and who hate us? What have we ever done to them? They come in secrecy, meaning no good . . . perhaps killing them was an extremity of response, but it might well have been for the best."

Her silver head was bowed, hiding her lovely face from him. "Did they attack for the good of the Emerin? Or because the *Morvalan* cannot abide anything human?"

"And what have we ever done to deserve that?" Mischa asked. "I've been disapproved of for my religion – the Galatinites in particular go into foaming fits at the very mention of Talopea, theirs being one of those faiths that thinks strength is in self-deprivation – but my religion is, in a way, something I chose. Most here in the Emerin want nothing to do with me because they find me unappealing . . ." He looked deeply wounded and baffled at this, and Wyndrel had to chuckle despite himself. ". . . but they have their reasons, and clearly not all elves feel that way."

Here, Wyndrel shot Ariana a startled look, but she still sat with her head down, her hair spilling around her shoulders like a moonlit waterfall, and did not react. In their travels together, she had done nothing to encourage Mischa . . . had even, in an exasperated way, been regularly called upon to discourage him . . . but she had been raised outside of the Emerin, and who knew what manner of tastes and habits she might have?

He was disturbed to find himself more than a little worried by this. And, truth be told, awash in a sudden and vague jealousy. He supposed it was his due after that little bit of business with Dharra Felthis, the plant-mage apprentice. The shoe was well and properly on the other foot now.

"But to be hated purely because of my race?" Mischa shook his head, "That's new, and most uncomfortable for me. In Thanis, we have folk of all races living in . . . well, I'll not go so far as to say harmony, for that would be a lie. But making do. While there are conflicts, as often as not it's between rich and poor or by virtue of one's temple or some other, more individual, factor."

"As I understand it, and I must foremost point out that my knowledge of it is by no means complete," Wyndrel said, "the *Morvalan* want all humans . . . and by extension all the younger –"

"Lesser," Ariana said. "They call them Lesser Races."

"Yes. They would see them killed off or enslaved. It is my belief that Tiercel, especially once he had become a high general in the wake of my father's death and my disappearance, made every effort to extend the war."

"No," Kev said, dismayed. "No . . . why? He couldn't have!"

"Because far more humans were dying than elves or dwarves. We met to do battle not on dwarven land or our own, but on that of the poor humans who had the misfortune to be in the middle. They sent troops to try and protect their settlements, emissaries to plead for truce, and still we fought."

Kevan hunched back against his pack, picking fretfully at the crust of his bread. His face was stormy, and Wyndrel did not blame him. He'd felt much the same when that rude awakening had come to him.

"These others, though," Ariana said, raising her head. "These Hramadans. They hate us as surely as the *Morvalan* hate humanity. It seethed in that boy. He'd never even laid eyes on an elf until Tiercel, but he'd been taught to fear and despise us at his mother's knee. And I don't know why. No one ever, that I could determine, told him *why*."

"I'd known," Wyndrel said, "that I would face many challenges just in the reclaiming of my throne. Or claiming of it, I should say . . . I've never sat upon it as king. This new threat is a most unpleasant surprise, which I could have done without. Yet I will not turn a blind eye to it."

"One thing at a time," Mischa said. "Let's get you that throne first. I'm still not sure how we're going to do that. Tell me honestly. With your magic back, the both of you, can we win this?"

Ariana smiled bleakly. "We have to."

"I know that, Ari, and I'm sure everyone's going to put forth their best effort and all. I'm just wondering what our chances are. I'd like to survive to tell my brothers about this. Not that they'll believe it."

"It is a fair question," Wyndrel said. "Would that I had an equally fair answer. In honesty, Mischa, I do not know. I lack armor, true, but I have spells to armor myself in magic. Tiercel was no warmage. He may be the better swordsman, but I have the greater strength. Were it a matter only of myself against Tiercel, I believe I'd be the victor. It is the other that changes the chances."

"The *Rhunvala*," Kev said, and shivered and drew his cloak closer about himself despite the warmth of the evening.

"She is the enigma, she is the difficulty. I have witnessed Ariana's quickness and skill, and would consider her the match of nearly any man –"

"Thank you ever so much," she said, but he was glad to see spirit rather than that morose silence from her.

"– we outnumber them, as well, and both you and Kevan are not lacking in swordsmanship. It is her faith that concerns me. We do not know what she can do, what powers her god grants. And, forgive me," he added with a look at the priest, "but I somehow doubt that she'll be susceptible to *yours*."

"I wouldn't even try," Mischa said. "Unless she and Tiercel . . . ?"

Wyndrel blanched a little, and once again could not look at Ariana. But she was just as studiously not looking at him as she answered. "I think not. From what she said to me, Tiercel lacks any romantic interest in her and she returns the sentiment."

Mischa's smile widened into something approaching lasciviousness, and Ariana blushed. Wyndrel felt his own face grow warm. Her mistake – acknowledging that Mischa's Talopea-inspired power could only work where an attraction existed – cut the legs from under their repeated protests.

Kev cleared his throat into the awkward hush. "We'll have to find them first. My liege –"

"Could you, Kevan, do you think, bring yourself to call me Wyndrel?" he interrupted. "There's no need to stand on formality out here. When we return to the palace and you're my royal squire, then you may make use of such titles. Until then, Wyndrel."

"Wyndrel." It was a struggle, but he did it. "I know we'll spend as much of the day in traveling as is feasible, but in what little other time we have to spare, would you . . . would you teach me? I should like to be better with a sword, and warmagics if you're willing."

"Gladly," he said. "It is too late to begin tonight, so I suggest we retire. The morning will be soon enough, before you've put in a heavy breakfast. I'll take last watch and wake you before dawn."

Looking as though he was regretting it already, Kev nodded.

Mischa stretched. "Does that mean more sleep for the rest of us while you're at that?"

Ariana extended one long leg and kicked his ankle. "You could do with some training yourself. I think we should make a habit of it."

"Oh, so be it," Mischa said as he got up and unrolled his fur-trimmed bedroll. "It's unfair, though. I don't see anyone going out of their way to help me practice *my* skills. If I miss too many more of my nightly devotions, Talopea's going to start viewing me with disfavor. I'd hate to suddenly be unable to call upon Her healing gift."

"Why, Mischa, that's the most devious and unkind attempt I've seen yet," Ariana said. "To threaten us like that is beneath you. If I didn't know better, I'd go so far as to say it's an affront to your goddess. Holding us hostage like that."

"It's hardly a threat, Ari. It's difficult enough to heal the lot of you anyway."

"What's that supposed to mean?" she shot back.

"I think we can leave this discussion for another time," Wyndrel said sternly. "To bed."

"Which is what I've been saying!" Mischa said.

"To our *own* beds," Ariana said. "And I'll take first watch."

* * *

The morning exercises, whether they were at swordplay or magic, proved to do more than hone their skills.

Ariana found the pearly pre-dawn to be a time of enchantment and unreality in which all things seemed possible and the cares of the rest of the world felt far distant. The shared effort, the encouragement, fostered a friendship among the four of them. Even when the elves practiced their magic, Mischa listened and ventured the occasional question, until he had more than a layman's understanding of the art.

"If there are so few mages among humans," he said one day as they saddled their horses in readiness for the journey ahead, "if that talent is so rare in us, how can there be an entire nation of them?"

None of them had an explanation, though the theories occupied some of the long hours as the horses went single-file between the gnarled oak trunks and over the multitude of tiny streams that made up the midsection of the Emerin.

Even Wyndrel, Ariana thought, had become less of a pain in the hindquarters since Eltarrin. Maybe the fact that there were no decisions needing to be made was the reason: when there was nothing to clash over, they didn't clash.

Whatever his other flaws, she could not deny that he was the best swordsman she'd ever seen. Her own mother might have been faster, might have been better able to land a precisely-aimed blow into a vulnerable spot, but his sheer strength and size made it unlikely that a single blow would stop him. He had, too, legitimately earned his warmage rank, and under his guidance she swiftly became more adept with her ice-magic attacks.

He, in turn, had only praise for her ability. "How and where did you learn to handle a blade with such grace and deftness?" he asked after one particularly exhausting session. He had stripped off his shirt – she was more accustomed to seeing him without it than with it, really, and was not about to complain – and wiped his glistening skin with a cloth.

She, after dunking her head into a convenient creek and trembling deliciously as cold water trickled from her soaked hair down the back of her neck, laughed. "From my mother."

"The style's so unusual," he said. "Not at all Emerinian. When you chose such a light sword, I nearly spoke up, but you've shown me that I would have been wrong to do so. You could skewer a grape without splitting it."

"I'll show you a lesson I had from my grandfather," she said, wringing out her hair. "Kevan, bring me those sweetfruits."

"These are for our breakfast," he said, but proffered her the bowl anyway. The sweetfruits, just ripening, were firm with shiny purple-blue skins.

"Not grapes," Ari said to Wyndrel as she set four of them in a row on a branch that was just at arm's height, "but they'll do."

"Now, Ariana," he said, amused. "As good as you are, that's setting yourself an impossible task."

"Care to place a wager?"

He spread his hands. "What have I to wager with? And have I not already provided for most of our needs?"

"I know what –"

"Be still, Mischa," Ariana said without looking around. "Here's my wager, oh king . . . I will spit each of those fruits without losing a one, and you'll stand my watch in addition to your own tonight. If I fail, I'll take your watch."

"I'd sooner hear Mischa's suggestion," he said with a quirk of one golden brow, "but those terms will do. I look forward to my night's rest."

"If you heard my suggestion, neither of you would get much sleep."

"Be *still*, Mischa."

Ariana drew her sword, wondering if she had gotten herself in for more than she could deliver. This was not the weapon she'd grown up with, being longer and of a different shape than the saber-style her mother and grandfather had favored. The morning practices had helped her to familiarize herself with it, yet pride had led her into making a boast she wasn't all that sure she could fulfill.

The others gathered around to watch. She positioned herself, weight forward on the balls of her feet, sword gripped casually, the other arm held slightly out to the side. She lunged and the tip of the blade pierced purple-blue skin.

She turned triumphantly and offered the speared fruit to Wyndrel.

"You nearly split it in twain," he observed, as he took it and bit in.

"Nearly isn't did," she replied, and faced the branch again.

But he had been right and she approached the next thrust more cautiously, almost too cautiously. The fruit wobbled on the point, but she tilted the sword and it stayed where it was until she tipped it into Mischa's hands. The third was close to perfect, and Kev's shining eyes as she gave it to him was almost as rewarding as Wyndrel's exclamation of disbelief.

Pride was almost her downfall. Her final strike, which she tried to make look carefree and easy, knocked the sweetfruit off the branch. Gasping, she stabbed at it as it fell, and the luck of her mother was with her because she impaled it mid-air.

She brought that one to her own hand, which shook a bit from the near-miss. The males applauded, Wyndrel with a sardonic slant to his smile that told her he knew just how close that had been.

"My mother is much better," she said. "She could snatch arrows from flight and run along a taut rope as if it were a bridge. My grandfather taught her all that he knew, lore of the Southern Plains and tricks of his own besides."

Mischa hissed at her, eyes darting in warning. Ari stopped, and heard her words clanging in her mind. A sinking sensation replaced her stomach and her mouth, which had been poised to taste sweetfruit, went dry.

"The Southern Plains?" Wyndrel asked, head cocked. "Your . . . your grandfather? But that . . ."

Kevan looked back and forth, puzzled, his face sticky from juice. "What?"

"Are you saying your grandfather is Plainsfolk?"

Ariana lowered the sword, letting it hang at her side. She drew her chin up. "Yes. He was of the Bharosyuhn, the People of the Horse. He left home as a lad and traveled the Northlands, and was a lord of Gamelin 'ere he died."

"But that cannot be." He absently wiped his fingers on his trousers and moved toward her, searching her intently with his gaze. "Plainsfolk are human. You are no elfkin, Ari. I'd stake my life on it."

"My grandmother is from Lenais. Their child, my mother, is elfkin. She passed her elven blood in full measure to me, and my father was born in the Emerin."

Birds twittered unconcernedly in the branches and one of the horses snorted as if to remind them that they were usually mounting up and riding by this time. Wyndrel wore a look of furrowed concentration, perhaps reading her aura or determining her race by a spell, perhaps just trying to come to terms with what she'd said.

Kev's jaw hung from its hinge. She saw his expression from the corner of her eye and could have laughed had she not been so tense with expectation and self-recrimination. Her father had warned her of this very thing, and she had blithely promised him that she could hold her tongue. Except Tiercel had known, and told Kai Tilanne, and the repugnance in the *Rhunvala's* amethyst eyes had been like a blow.

She waited for the same reaction in Wyndrel. True, Kai Tilanne had eventually seemed satisfied that, misbegotten or not, Ariana was elven-pure. Her parentage had then ceased to matter, except in Tilanne's deep but unspoken disgust about the perversity of Ariana's father . . . and worse, grandmother.

Wyndrel looked away from her and she winced. He seemed to be grappling with it, and she could imagine the debate that must be running through his mind. He needed her help and thus couldn't afford to send her away . . . and yet . . .

"I see why you were so unwilling to tell me your secrets when I asked in Eltarrin," he said at long last. "Not Elyvorrin's kin at all, then."

"Gods, no," she said. "Thankfully. I'd want no kinship with him."

Another long moment spun out, the wind sighing in the leaves. The four of them were so still that a doe stepped lightly into the clearing before realizing they were there, then bounded away with great leaps of fright.

"Well," Ariana said. "You wished to know and now you do. What comes next?"

He shook himself all over as a dog does when shedding water. His eyes cleared and he came back to himself from a seeming long way. "We have our breakfast and ride, what else? And then I suppose it'll be my turn to share some secret of myself, to keep accounts in order."

Relief spread through her like a balm. She smiled, and nodded. But catching Kev's still-frozen expression as she turned, she paused.

"Kevan?"

The boy, too, shook himself. He did his best to look brave and unconcerned. "Yes?"

"Are you . . . are you well with this?"

"Not yet, Lady Ariana," he said honestly. "It needs some . . . getting used to."

"Thank you, Kev."

They ate, sweetfruit and bread and porridge that had been flavored with honey. Mischa rhapsodized bemoaningly about the bakeries that he missed so dearly. But it was good-natured enough complaining, and when they finished they swung astride their horses and turned their heads east, toward the unseen and distant mountain that housed their destination.

A lengthy journey lay ahead of them. Ariana had studied the Lenaisian-made map that they'd gotten in Eltarrin, and was amazed anew at the sheer size of the Emerin. They had not even come halfway, and still had to pass between the rising peaks of the Stepstone Mountains and enter into what the Lenaisians had discouragingly named "The Forest of the Great Unknown."

* * *

Part Two:

The Village and the Lair

CHAPTER TWELVE

I will see them burn for their temerity.
– Elwyndas, The Two Brothers, Act IV, Scene 2

Tiercel Reyes, his helm set squarely on his head and his eyes narrowed into deadly arrow slits, did not move as he stared down at the town on the shore. Did not move, but for the fisting and unfisting of his hands.

"They dare," he said at last, nearly spitting the words.

"Dare they do," his companion, Kai Tilanne, replied with an only slightly better veneer of control. "Confirmed are our suspicions."

"We should have kept one of the wretched vermin alive to question," he said. "Where were they going, I wonder?"

"Had they a southerly course been taking," Tilanne said, "venture would I to guess that 'twas the Mountain Kingdom they sought. Known to us has it been that alliances with foreign wizards he's had, humans from across the sea, whose magics strange to us are. Magics such as we with our own eyes did behold."

"I remember quite vividly, thank you." Tiercel rubbed at his ribs.

He and Tilanne had kept to the south near the River Farelin, in territory that was neither strictly Emerinian nor *Morvalan*, but a borderland between them where few ever went. Their journey had not been uneventful, by far the worst experience being a run-in with a bear and a nest of basilisks. He had spent some days in terrible pain, medicine against venom in a war that raged throughout his bloodstream, until the medicine and his own hardy constitution won out.

Following that encounter, all had been fairly peaceable . . . until the humans. A wagoncade of them. In the very elven lands! Interlopers, trespassers.

There had been no discussion. None was needed.

Not even when the humans had revealed themselves to be something other than the useless livestock of the Northlands or the Mountain Kingdom, not even when the humans had unleashed those bewildering spells upon them, had he and Tilanne given ground in retreat.

They were two, their opponents were many. But Tiercel's sword Discordant, chosen for him by Kaledhol Himself, dropped his foes before him with its keening magical shriek. And Tilanne was a warrior the likes of which even he had never seen, relentless and undaunted in combat. Even in the war, even in the ultimate extremities of battle, he had known no soldier to fight with her fervor. With her faith.

Tiercel's aching ribs had been cracked by blow after blow from some powerful and unseen force like a great hammer of air. Their foes had some control over the lowly life, insects and reptiles, but Discordant had made short work of such small perils. Taken by surprise, the outcome for the humans had been bleak indeed.

In the end, they had been cut down, their beasts scattered, and their bodies and belongings left to rot.

The wagons had left a crushed trail through the forest, which made the riding easier for Tiercel and Tilanne. Now, many days later, they had reached the trail's beginning, and the Emerin's eastern shore.

"They must be of Hramad," Tiercel said now, berating himself for not seeing it sooner. "The island to the east."

The sea, visible at last, stretched toward the horizon. If there was an island out there, Tiercel could not discern it through the piling clouds that foretold a storm.

He saw only the village. A human village on elven land! The buildings were hovels, wooden walls plastered with mud, thatched roofs. Most looked to have no more than a single room inside, and as humans led their animals in and out, he was convinced that the beasts shared the living quarters with the families.

"Into our very realm they come," Tilanne said bitterly. "Alliances with our most dire foe they seek, and our people destroy they would. For this outrage I'll stand not." She went toward her horse, tethered with his out of sight at the bottom of the hill.

"Tilanne, wait. What are you doing? Do you mean to attack the town?"

"Dost thou not mean to? Dost thou mean these humans to leave unchallenged in thy own Emerin?"

"We did well enough against one small traveling band of them, I grant you, taking them by ambush. A townful might be more than we can manage when our force numbers but we two."

Her amethyst eyes met his and he knew then and there he might as well have been talking to a statue. As far as Tilanne cared, they were humans and they were here, and that, by the gods, was enough. She would do her duty as a *Morvalan*, as a *Rhunvala*, even if it meant her death.

It galled him to admit it, but she was right. They could not allow these humans to remain here, polluting the very Emerin with their filth and stench. If they were in alliance with the Mountain King, bringing magic to augment his already formidable armies of fierce hill-men and orcs, something had to be done.

"Let us at least wait until nightfall and not charge in now with blades slashing," he said. "The moon will be kind to us, but mask their sight."

She nodded brusquely and came back to where he was hidden by a screen of brush looking down on the ugly, vile canker of the human settlement.

The coast here was sandy and wide, with rolling dunes marked by tufts of wiry grey-green grass. The humans had not been brave enough to build within the forest, but they had chopped down its trees and hauled them and constructed a long dock extending out into the deeper waters. A wall of heaped branches encircled the landward side. Tiercel counted no more than two dozen buildings, and four small boats.

The humans went about their business, herding pigs, haggling over chickens, grubbing in the earth like ants. Their fields consisted mainly of the same grey-green grass that grew wild on the dunes, and they were harvesting it with long sweeps of scythes. Wagons, identical to the ones that the elves had met on the way, hauled bundled sheaves of the grass through a gate in the barricade.

To the north, rearing like the crest of a towering wave, was the extinct volcano that was home to Racandros the Sixth. They had to go there, but neither of them could leave without doing something about these humans. Left to their own devices, who knew what they might do? Who knew what they might be up to?

These ones had no love for elves – that much had been clear from the moment the wagon drovers had spotted Tiercel and Tilanne. Even had the two not been disposed to attack anyway, they would have soon found themselves fighting for their lives in defense.

"Is it worth the delay and the risk to take them now?" he asked.

She spared him a look at once evaluating and grim. Not scornful, but evaluating. As if she was asking herself – asking Kaledhol in the inner chambers of her mind – whether her people were right to have put their trust in Tiercel. Whether he was truly worthy, truly *Morvalan*. His question sounded far more cowardly aloud than it had before he asked it, as if he were putting his own safety and comfort above the Cause. He could not hold her gaze for long.

"If fight them now we do not, fight them later we inevitably shall," she said. "And maybe on their terms rather than ours must such a fight occur. If by surprise we strike them, overpower them we shall."

"We are close to the dragon's mountain," he said. "Once we've traded the Emerald for the Phial, we could bring the Phial here. Test it. Assure ourselves that it is the plague-poison it is said to be."

Tilanne touched the pouch she wore on her belt, the one that contained the Emerald of Karria. A slight frown creased her brow. Tiercel knew that she still had misgivings. He was too, if fairness demanded he admit it. There was something improper in turning over a relic of the elven gods to a dragon's hoard, even if only for safekeeping.

But what else could be done with it? No one in the Emerin except a swordmaiden or a king could even touch the jewel without being struck down with terrible, green-fire pain. He had felt it himself, seen what it did to Elyvorrin. While a cruel part of Tiercel would have enjoyed presenting it to the Starleaf Council and watching them try their luck with it, to be driven across the room screaming one by one, he knew it was too risky. Suppose the Emerald deemed one acceptable? That would be the ruination of all his plans.

If it were in the keeping of Racandros, it would be safe. And what he sought in exchange might be worth any number of godly artifacts, if it truly was what he so deeply hoped it to be. The Phial of Sevarre. Human-bane. A contagion, a disease, a lethal poison strong enough to cleanse the lands of the entire miserable race.

He had learned of it from his uncle, Tanneivan, who had forsaken the Emerin to travel, and set about earning his living as a killer-for-hire. Tanneivan knew poisons, he knew the artful thrust of a knife in the dark, he knew the slim strangle-wire and the countless ways of making a murder seem an accident of misadventure. It had been Tanneivan whose blade stilled the heart of the last

Thanian king, casting the Northlands into civil war that had lasted until the coming of the Four Heroes, and the rise of the Highlord.

As a restless youth, curious as to some of the hidden secrets no one in his family seemed willing to discuss – where had the Reyes line come from, if their roots were not to be found in the Emerin? What had become of his father's two younger brothers, both of whom had gone away? – Tiercel had eventually come to Thanis and met Tanneivan there.

In the course of a brief spate of lessons that couldn't properly be called an apprenticeship, the last of his Emerinian self had been scoured away and replaced with a painted veneer beneath which beat the heart of a *Morvalan.* The heart, but as Tilanne was even now wont to point out, not the mind. Not quite the soul. Their ways were still strange to him. He had lived too long as an *Alvalan* to fully comprehend what it was that made the *Morvalan* as they were. While he felt Kaledhol's presence in him and around him, he had not been raised with it, steeped in it, the way she had been. He was still too Emerinian.

But he liked to think it was the very division in him, the balance between his outward and inward selves, a division and balance best characterized by the swords he wore, that put him in a position to do the greatest good for both peoples. For the side of him that wore Lionheart, the golden and jewel-studded sword given him by a grateful Council, he wanted to see the Emerin united and prosperous under the strong hand of a king. For the side of him that wore Discordant, the crystal-hilted blade he'd been drawn to in a *Morvalan* ritual, he wanted to eradicate the humans and end that threat to the southern elves once and for all.

The Phial of Sevarre could be the answer to his prayers. Tanneivan only knew that it had been made by an elf who bore a deep and abiding grudge against humanity, but Sevarre had been caught, stopped, before he could unleash the fury of the Phial onto the world. Those who'd stopped him quickly realized what they had. They were afraid to destroy it, lest that somehow release its power. They were afraid to keep it accessible, lest someone of clearer sight find it, and use it.

So they had done what Tiercel now intended to do with the Emerald of Karria. They'd given it into the care of the dragon, that no one might retrieve it.

Would Racandros be willing to part with the Phial? Would he be willing to trade? The Emerald was by far the more valuable. What was a crystal container filled with liquid compared to that? Surely the dragon could have no great love for humans. The moniker of Ostran Dragonslayer aside, most elves lived in respect, even awe, of dragonkind. Humans were the ones with their legends and their heroic quests and mighty deeds, all of which were probably false.

Dusk could not come swiftly enough. As they waited, Tiercel and Tilanne assessed the village and its inhabitants and planned for their assault.

Night arrived, rolling in from the sea with the storm. Soon the sky and sea and rain blended into a seething darkness. Even keen elven eyes would be hard-pressed to see in such weather.

Tiercel and Tilanne waited, waited. These human beasts woke and slept by the pattern of the sun and soon only a few shutters showed thin lines of firelight through their slats. No guards patrolled the negligible walls. The dogs, ostensibly set to roam, would be huddled in whatever shelter they could find against the inhospitable weather.

"It's time," he said when he could wait no longer.

Together, they descended the hill from their hiding place and struck out across the field. It was a stubble of cut stalks and muddy earth. The rain could not touch the elves, shielded from it as they were, but the nearer they drew to the town, the more Tiercel was aware of a stinging in his eyes.

"The salt-spray, is it?" Tilanne asked, blinking and rubbing at her face with her black-gloved hands.

"I smell the sea, yes, but why should that bother us?" He pressed on, approaching chest-high uncut stands of grass that were unbending in the rain.

But the further they went, the more viciously their eyes burned, and flooded with tears that could not quench that fire. They had to stop to swab at their reddened, leaking eyes with cloths. Tiercel saw that Tilanne's were puffed, and her normally fair face was blotched.

"Barely breathe can I," she said.

Tiercel's nose tickled with an incipient sneeze. His face itched, itched like multitudes of ants were burrowing into his skin. A throbbing pain filled his head and dry soreness lined the passage of his throat.

All he could think of was dwarven weapons-of-war. Strange ores dug from far beneath the earth. Metals that gave off deadly gases. Smoke of acidic lethality.

But it wasn't the same, this smell, this feeling.

The sneeze burst from him, flinging his head forward and dislodging his helm so that the metal brim with its design of golden lions slid to the bridge of his nose. Thank Kaledhol for the noise of the storm; no one was alerted.

"*Salahin Roas*," he invoked, trying a spell of healing that did no good whatsoever. This was no wound but a hateful sickness that could not be so easily mended.

"No illness is this that before have I seen," Tilanne said, gasping for air and rubbing – rather than clawing – at her skin.

Scratching only temporarily relieved the itch, Tiercel, to his dismay, quickly found, before it came back tenfold. He forced his hands to remain at his sides, fingers held stiffly out. "It must be some sort of poison."

Through her misery, Tilanne found the humor for a hard smile. "Ironic indeed would that be, thy errand considering."

"If it is smoke or fumes, the rain should wash it from the air . . ." He was struck by a revelation of his own foolishness, and undid the spell that protected him from the weather.

At once, icy rain doused him. He tore off his helm and lifted his face to it, hot tears streaming along with the cold rivulets. Freezing courses ran under his collar. But the itching diminished.

Tilanne was quick to mimic him, going further to cup rain in her hands and dash it against her skin. When she turned to him, he recoiled from a visage gone so puffed and red that she might have been beset by a hive of bees. Livid white marks showed where she had dug at the itching skin with her fingertips.

He touched his face, finding that he was in an equal state. The rain relieved much of the suffering, but the need to sneeze, the feeling of suffocation, and the thick fluid clogging their heads and lungs was not so easily remedied.

"The grass it is," she gasped. "The very grass, a bane to us must be."

"We've not even touched it," Tiercel said.

It was all around them, the long blades scraping together in the wind with a sound that rasped on the nerves like a file. The tall stalks bore no shaggy heads of kernels as did grain. They resembled no crop-plant he'd ever seen, not even in Keyda before the blight.

Tilanne touched the nearest stalk. It bent, but not with the ease of a leaf. The ease of a wire, maybe. Rigid but pliable. She yanked her hand back with a hiss.

"My fingers," she said. "Even through the leather of my glove, my fingers it burns."

Not doubting her, he still had to try it for himself. The mere contact made his hand tingle and itch. An indignant anger made him strip off his glove and reach out again over her protest.

The stalk felt like thin metal, and on his bare skin was a molten agony. He snatched his hand away and cradled it, staring at the blisters already bubbling on his skin. A spell of healing smoothed those away but could do little else.

"Back to the woods," he said through his pain.

Concealed, they dared remove their armor and rinse themselves thoroughly to wash away every trace of the hated grass. Shredded flecks of it that had been left by the scythes clung to their boots, their clothes. Their magic had kept the rain but not the wind from them and the wind could have thrown miniscule specks into their faces. They had breathed of it.

"A weapon it is," Tilanne said. "Now their purpose here we know. This grass they cultivate and grow, for clearly no adverse effects on them it has. While we, laid low by its mere presence are."

"It is strong, too," Tiercel said when he could speak again. His hand, though no longer blistered, seemed puffed to half again its normal size and beating in time with his heart. "Not strong enough to use as a sword, perhaps, but if they layered it or wove it into armor . . ."

"This must the first such harvest be, else surely those we fought before so armored would have been."

They watched through the slanting sheets of rain for signs of activity and saw none. Their aborted approach had indeed gone undetected, which Tiercel took as some small comfort.

"Now we have more reason than ever to destroy them," he said. "But how, when we cannot even come to their wall?"

For that, neither of them had an immediate answer. They kept scrubbing at their clothing, hoping to rid it of every trace of the grass.

"If the mere scent of it as poison to us is, and the touch like fire-nettles burns," Tilanne said after a while, "what might happen if ate of it we did?"

That was too horrible to contemplate, and Tiercel knew by her expression that she wished she hadn't even said it. But once raised, there it was, that awful specter.

"It would be agony. It would be death."

"Kaledhol our souls preserve."

He flexed his hand. The swelling had gone down, his fingers no longer feeling like stuffed and nerveless sausages. "We cannot allow them to persist in this. I'd give much for a squadron of archers or warmages, as swords are no good from here. I don't suppose Kaledhol can aid us?"

"Of Him I can His might on myself beseech," Tilanne said. "My arm to give strength, or my body to shield. No bolts of divine wrath does Kaledhol provide. With us, He surely is, but even *Rhunvala* can to overpowering numbers or deadly weapons fall."

Thunder growled in the sky as if voicing the god's agreement. Lightning flashed behind the clouds, giving their contours the aspect of a monstrous form. The rain was a torrent, the wind a living thing bent on torture.

"We'll have to burn them out," Tiercel said.

She looked askance at him. "In rain such as this?"

"I may not be a warmage, but every soldier picks up a few useful spells. Magefire will burn even in this downpour. I must only get near enough to cast it." He soaked a clean cloth in water, and wrapped it around the lower half of his face. A second, veil-thin cloth covered his eyes without blindfolding him. "Be ready for them if they flee."

Tilanne nodded, slipping her shield onto her arm and resting her other hand on the hilt of Baleful Gaze. "Ready shall I be."

Tiercel drew up his hood and crept forth. He circled to come at the fields from upwind, crossing a muddy area where vines crawled through the mud and bulging gourds lay among them like severed heads. The rain was a cold, drenching wretchedness, but as it helped keep him clean of the malevolent effect of the steely grass, he loved it like a brother. Not like *his* brother, perhaps, but a brother nonetheless.

The high, swaying grass was ahead. Scraping together, blade against blade, as if each honed the sharpness of the other. He reached a place where it had been harvested and hurried across toward the very thickest portion of it. His eyes stung, but the wet cloth protected them and he was unhampered as he extended his hand with palm out and fingers forming a funnel-shape.

"*Flammehar*," he said in a low, fierce whisper.

A fever surged in him, sweat breaking out on his brow and back and beneath his arms despite the wintry chill of the storm. The heat roared through his body and down his arm, gathering, narrowing, intensifying. A hot haze, as of embers, surrounded his glove.

The spell shot from him in a cyclone of fire. Orange and white and searing red, it spiraled and whirled. As it hit the nearest stalks, they glowed with a forge's dull heat and then burst into flame. An ordinary fire would never have withstood such rain but this was magefire, needing no fuel and bending the natural law.

And the grass . . . the grass, strange and unknown . . . seemed to exude an oily substance from its oddly metallic stalks. This caught, this ignited, and Tiercel staggered back as a bellowing wall of fire leaped up in front of him. He squinted against the blast, covered his face with his arm.

The flames raced through the fields. Before Tiercel had withdrawn to even reasonable safety, a sweeping wave was hurrying, blazing, spreading. Smoke billowed up in noxious plumes, blacker than the clouds and rising to twice a man's height before being tattered by the wind.

Tiercel retreated at a run, sparks showering around him, on him. Had he not been soaked to the skin, his clothes surely would have caught and gone up. The fumes filtered through the wrappings over his face and his skin erupted in a furious rash. His eyes sealed shut, tears flooding from them.

He ran blindly through the field of gourds. Vines tangled at his legs, his boots came down on the bulbous rinds and punched into them, making him slip in slews of seed-filled entrails.

Then, crazily, as he'd heard happened to other soldiers but had never experienced for himself, he was on the battleground again, hearing the inexorable rumble of the advancing war machines and feeling them shake the earth, the screams of the injured ringing in his ears. His mind's eye saw what his living eyes could not, the lines of dwarven warriors in their gleaming iron mail, the shine of firelight on the curved edges of their axes and the barbed points of their crossbow bolts.

Not real! he told himself.

His foot hooked under a gnarled and ropy vine and he fell headlong with a jarring, mud-splattering finality. Weapons rose and fell, the dwarves relentlessly hewing their way onward over the bodies of the fallen, the maimed and dying. Cries ended as the dwarves reached them. If the victim was an elf, a cruel slash of an axe did the deed, or a mace flashing down to crush an elven skull. If dwarven, if one of their own but beyond hope – he had seen this once and only once, but it haunted him – death was accomplished by means of a long steel spike placed against the temple and hammered into the brain with one sure blow. Dwarven mercy.

"Tiercel!" Hands were on him and he fought them in a panic before realizing they were elven hands, Tilanne's. She was coughing, the smoke blowing briskly this way and that at the fickle spite of the wind.

She helped him up, nothing to his blurred sight but a dark figure all black and red. Leaning on her, having wrenched both ankles badly in his flight, he hobbled toward the trees. The very elements had gone mad, all the world a maelstrom of leaping fire, pouring water, raw earth, and howling air.

By the time they reached the shelter of the trees, his sight had begun to return. He unwound the cloths from his face and turned to look at what he'd wrought.

The fields were engulfed. The wall around the village was catching, and some wind-borne sparks were busily consuming thatched roofs that had been treated with tar to repel the wet and the vermin, but now served only to fuel the raging fire. Shrieks, human and animal alike, could be heard over the storm and the crackling, hungry flames.

"Flee, they shall," Tilanne said. Her cheeks and brow were soot-smeared, but her eyes were violet and alight.

Tiercel nodded and drew his sword. They positioned themselves uphill and upwind of the conflagration. "Let them come."

*   *   *

CHAPTER THIRTEEN

We have brought this enemy upon ourselves. Their very creation is our doing, and our undoing.
– Elwyndas, The Shaper's Fate (ballad)

The victory torches were bright and ablaze, waved in the hands of the throngs that lined the Rebel's Way. They were cheering, cheering for Desah as his chariot rolled over the paving stones that had been mortared with bone powder and elf-blood.

The horses pranced their hooves high, tossed their mighty heads. Ribbons of gold adorned their braided manes and tails. The *druhj* holding the reins, and the two who held the poles of the canopy that shaded Desah from the brilliant sunlight, sweated in their ceremonial garb of gold-cloth.

He stood erect and magnificent in flowing robes, a high collar stiff with jewels framing his head. The staff gripped in his brown, strong hand was dazzlingly gem-studded, each diamond throwing off tiny fires. The cries of the adoring crowd filled the world.

"Desah!" Greatest of them all. Wizard-Lord.

"Desah!" Conqueror of armies. Slayer of elves.

"Desah!"

The chariot shook, as if the road over which it rolled was beset by an earthquake. Dropped torches flared clothing into gowns of flame. The joyous adulation became a cacophony of terrified screams.

Shaking. Shaking. The walls of the city crumbled and went up in smoke . . .

The walls of sleep crumbled. The shaking went on.

"Desah!"

He tore through the final barrier dividing sleep and wakefulness to find Saiye bent over him, her hands on his shoulders, her voice frightened and imploring.

"How dare you touch me?" He struck her, cuffed her from him with his beringed knuckles.

The girl spun away and fell, face bleeding. Desah lunged from his bed, the sheets fluttering around him.

"This room is my sanctuary," he said, looming over her. "You know it is not your place to –"

The tirade broke off as he realized that the fire and the screams that had ended his dream had somehow followed him through into reality. The room was alive with dancing orange light, hazed with smoke that came in through the shutters.

His house was the largest in the village, which still was not much to boast of. It had three rooms downstairs and two above, and the upper floor was his private refuge. His study, and his bedroom. Saiye had intruded, but his flash of anger at the young *druhj* was forgotten as he strode past her sobbing form to throw the shutters wide.

Hral was burning.

The fields . . . the steelgrass . . .

People ran everywhere, men shouting to each other, women crying out for their children. A baby wailed. Goats and shaggy ponies plunged past, bleating and trampling, as Desah looked on in astonishment. Before his very eyes, Kres the drover was borne beneath their hooves. His arms flew up as if in surprise and when the animals passed, all that was left looked more like a flattened sack than anything that had ever been human.

Shock rooted Desah to the spot. He could not comprehend what he was seeing. The night raged with storms and fire, wind and rain, screams and death. Could this be Hral? Could the village that he'd been set to oversee be coming apart so suddenly?

He hated this place, the mud and squalor of it, hated the betrayals and assassinations that had made his family flee their island home with its sprawling villa and rich green fields. He had hated the sea crossing and the pitiful refugees who'd survived it and then looked to his father for leadership. He hated his father for going away, accepting great Canah's offer and leaving him, Desah, here to look after things in his stead when he could have taken Desah with him to the castle and the more suitable life it offered.

The rest of the family had gone, yet he, the eldest, had been made to stay. As if it was some honor to be chosen.

Not even the appeasement of having the pick of the *druhjes* was enough to make up for it, because of them all, only Saiye was pretty enough to interest him.

Still, he had been left in command of Hral and now it was burning. It was in shambles. The people, *his* people, were clamoring in the streets for help. Some were pinned and roasting alive beneath the rubble of their homes.

And the steelgrass! Their priceless, invaluable crop!

The thought of what his father and Canah would say when they learned that the crop had been turned to ashes got Desah moving. He whirled from the window to his trunk, flung open the lid, and dug through the garments within. Trousers, boots, and a tunic . . . where was his swordbelt? He found it at the bottom, the leaf-shaped bronze short-blade secured into its leather sheath.

Saiye, hair dragging as she crawled to him with head humbly bent, babbled apologies. She knew how he loathed to be disturbed, but the fire . . . the fire . . .

Desah stooped and grasped her shoulders, and drew her up. "No, Saiye, you were right to wake me. What's happened? What's done this? Are we attacked? Have the Fiendish Ones found us?"

The mention of them made her totter on unsteady legs. The color bled from her face. "I know only the fire. The storm . . . Jehef said a skybolt from the storm must have struck the fields."

"Vecah grant it be only that and nothing more." He tugged his tunic into place and tied it. "Fetch me my armor."

The *druhj* hastened to do so, bringing him the woven garment of steelgrass from where it hung on a post with a crossbar to lend it the shape of a man. He slipped it over his head and the edge of it fell to his knees, split at the sides to allow him freedom of movement. He cinched his belt around it.

The roof of his chamber smoldered. Even as he noticed it, a chunk of thatch fell in and broke open on the floorboards, disgorging winking embers like merciless elven eyes.

Saiye pranced back from the fire on bare feet, her anklet's beads jingling. "What shall we do?"

"Have the *druhjes*, if any are left that haven't fled, gather all that can be carried. Make for the shore. Be wary. I will find you."

She hurried to obey. Desah lingered only long enough to retrieve his mother's amulet from a carved box on his bedside table. The milky gem at the heart of the ornate gold swirl glowed from deep within. Seeing that glow, he cursed in fear and fury.

"Elves! They *are* here!"

Saiye had gone and did not hear him, which was for the best. If they knew . . . the hatred his people harbored for the race they called the Fiendish Ones was deep and bitter, but among those of Hramad whose magical gifts were judged not worth developing, the elves inspired more terror than rage. They would be paralyzed if they knew, and then all would be lost.

"You had to take the rest of the wizards with you, didn't you?" Desah ranted, as if his absent father could hear him. "Because the danger would be greater for those who ventured deeper into the forest, to join Canah. Those who remained would be safe, you said. And now look, look what's befallen us! I only hope the reason they're here is that they already found you, old fool, and cut you down like a frothing dog."

He slipped the amulet's chain around his neck and dropped the pendant beneath his armor. No sense letting the others see it, flashing like the moon, getting brighter and brighter the nearer the Fiendish Ones came.

Desah strode from his house, ignoring the frantic activity as Saiye and the rest of his personal *druhjes* scrambled to load whatever they could into a cart. The rain fell heavily, but not heavily enough to douse the crowns of flame that many of the buildings wore.

"To me!" he bellowed. "To me, people of Hral!"

The response left something to be desired. Yell to rally them though he might, only half a dozen men and one old woman came to him. The rest had scattered with their families into the fields or toward the sea or even along the trail that led into the dark heart of the forest. Others struggled to bring the animals under control, or hurled buckets of water at the flames. Just as he attracted the attention of many of them, the long low barn went up in a sudden inferno as the oily sheaves of steelgrass stored within it succumbed to the heat.

"We have to stop this or we're all dead," Ythri, the old woman, said.

Desah was gladdened to see her. She had survived the intrigues of Hramad and the sea voyage, but upon reaching land had announced she was through traveling. When his father and the rest had set out with their wagoncade of gifts, supplies, and apprentices for great Canah, she had elected to remain behind. Now she might help him save them all.

"The fire, Ythri. I thought an earth-walker, but I cannot do it alone."

"That's the spirit!" She cackled. "We'll bring up an earth-walker to stomp out the fires."

They parted to let her through, respect in their eyes as she moved with one bunched hand clamped on the knob of her cane. Her grey hair streamed wildly around her lined face, her toothless mouth grinning broadly.

"You." Desah pointed to one of the men, Fenoh, a big and burly farmer with limbs like treetrunks. "Stand forward. The rest of you, move back."

The men did as he directed, Fenoh not happily. Desah and Ythri stood side by side in front of him, the tall young lordling and the old but hale crone. They were going to attempt something Desah had never done and only seen done once, something he never would have attempted without the help of another wizard.

They spoke no words of magic, made no elaborate gestures. Ythri leaned heavily on her cane, her age-yellowed eyes fixed intently on the ground at Fenoh's feet. Desah fixed his gaze and his will on the same spot. The other men backed away, murmuring to each other, throwing nervous glances at the sullen red walls of fire that surrounded them.

The mud bubbled. It flowed up from the ground over Fenoh's feet and legs. The farmer swallowed and looked as though he wanted to run, but he could not with his lower extremities coated in an upwelling cone of damp earth. The magic left no hole or sunken spot in the ground but the substance kept coming as if from nowhere.

It piled on itself, higher and higher. Now it was at his hips, his waist, his chest. Fenoh's pleading eyes, brown and afraid, met Desah's.

"Put your arms at your sides," he said.

Fenoh, who had been holding them up, away from the mud and dirt, lowered them. At once the earth swallowed them up. He was buried to the neck, more and more heaping soil rising up around him. It was a wide conical shape, an anthill the size of a man with a man's head perched at the apex.

Then even his head was gone as the earth piled over it. There was only a tall mound, growing and growing. And growing still, until the top of it towered over the hovels.

Ythri scooped up a handful of mud and, leaning her cane against her knees, worked it in her wizened hands. The muddy mass she held took on a shape, manlike but with squat, broad legs and a short, wide body.

When the miniature was completed, she breathed into its rudimentary mouth. It stirred in her grasp. She pushed it into the mound that stood where Fenoh had been. At once, the mound shifted and took on the same shape. Manlike. A golem of earth standing as high as any building in Hral. Slits opened on the small knob of its head, opened into empty sockets like holes in an embankment.

"The fire," Desah said. "Extinguish it."

The earth-walker trudged toward the densest, hottest part of the blaze. The ground shook at its tread, and it shed bits and clods of itself with every step.

Desah turned to the watching men. On every face, he saw each man's relief that he hadn't been chosen, coupled with a secret envy for Fenoh. To be striding out across the fields like that, a behemoth, unstoppable, invulnerable, crushing out flames with each jarring impact of a massive foot . . . such power, such strength! Who wouldn't wish to know what that was like, if only for a moment?

"The village is lost," he told them. "Save what you can."

"It's long until the next ship is due," Ythri said as the men ran to join the rest. "What will we do?"

"We'll go west and join my father," he said. "And Canah."

"I was afraid you'd say something like that."

"What else can we do? We cannot stay here. I still don't know why you didn't go before. Surely life at Canah's castle is better than living like this."

"I've had my fill of wizards who think they know everything," she said. "You forget, Desah, I'm much older than you. I've seen countless ones like Canah come and go. They're all the same, wanting to establish their strongholds and their armies and make dominions for themselves. It's been that way ever since our people rose up in rebellion, and look what it's gotten us. We spend more time bickering and backstabbing among ourselves than we've ever spent fighting our enemies."

"We only lack a strong leader! We –"

"That is exactly why Hramad is in the state it's in," she said. "Everyone wants to be that strong leader no matter who has to be killed to do it. Canah nearly died because of that brand of thinking, and he should have learned better. Even you, Desah . . . I know your dreams. You would become mighty and powerful and go back to Hramad as an overlord."

He flushed. "Who wouldn't dream such a dream?"

"Anyone with wisdom. How long does an overlord live on Hramad? How long before the assassins come, or the challenges are made? We are so busy killing ourselves off that we've lost sight of what our forefathers wanted."

"That isn't true!" Out in the fields, the earth-walker methodically stamped out the fire, and Desah turned his attention from it to the old woman. "We will destroy the elves. We but need a strong leader –"

"You see? You see? Just as I was saying. It has been that way for hundreds – nay, thousands! – of years, Desah. I have seen them come and go. Leham, Selbon, Canah . . . all the same."

"You never knew Leham or Selbon. Their time was the time of my great-great-grandfather, two centuries ago."

"I told you I was old."

He started to retort, but just then a terrible noise overpowered the sounds of storm and fire. The earth-walker, a dark hulk in the dying glare of the flames, stopped in its tracks. Its huge arms came up as if to cover or claw at its ears. The entire mammoth body quivered.

"Desah," Ythri said sharply, her gaze on his chest.

Looking down, he saw a pale glow even through the woven steelgrass of his armor. He pulled out the amulet and it was bright as the moon.

"Elves!" The very word spat from him like an oath that tasted foul.

Ythri's face folded into a hideous mask of hate. She clutched her cane like a weapon.

The earth-walker shuddered itself apart under the terrible onslaught of magical sound. As it fell apart in a heap, Desah caught the briefest of glimpses of Fenoh, reeling and stumbling through mounds of shattered earth.

Seeing this, many of the villagers ran for the road. They had their belongings strapped to their backs, carried in their arms, or pushed before them on carts. A man, trying to lead a line of tethered ponies, was knocked through the charred wall of a house and the burning mass of thatch fell on him, pinning him with his thrashing legs sticking out and his agonized screams muffled.

"No!" Desah cried, his voice lost in the greater din. He ran after them, calling to them, ordering them to turn back. "That way is death, death!"

They did not hear, did not heed. All that they knew was that the forest was ahead, dark and concealing, away from the ear-splitting noise that had brought the earth-walker to pieces. So they ran, pushing each other, bulling blindly along.

A figure, wreathed in a rose-red light, stepped onto the road in front of them. Desah's mind went numb with horror at the sight of an elfwoman, dark hair blowing like a war-banner, black-bladed sword raised not in salute or in warning but poised for a killing blow.

She swung, and a man's head parted company with his neck. His body continued on a few paces unawares, blood jetting from his neck-stump, then toppled.

The fleeing people tried to reverse their course as one, but bumped and stumbled and tripped and slipped. Goats made indignant blatting sounds and butted with their short, curled horns at their owners. A woman, driven into berserk impulse, rushed at the elf with a stick. The elf turned it with a shield, and a heartbeat later the two pieces of the woman landed in the mud.

Desah had been chasing after them begging them to turn about. Now they had, and plunged toward him. He formed his will into a wedge of invisible force extending in front of him. It shunted them aside, sending some sprawling, but prevented them from reaching him and trampling over him just as the beasts had trampled over Kres.

The elfwoman, in black armor and with eyes like death, advanced on him. Desah let the wedge collapse and made a hammer of force, driving it at her.

She sensed it somehow, unable to see it, and interposed her shield. For all the good that did – she was hurled, shield and all, backward to land hard at the base of a tree. Before she could regain her feet, Desah drew his blade and ran at her.

From behind, he heard his people erupt in renewed screams. Steel sheared through flesh and bone. Helpless not to, Desah glanced back and saw a second elf, this one a male, cleaving through them like a scythe through the harvest.

Scythes! He thought of the scythes, neatly packed away in the barn. Weapons, they would be weapons . . . but no, no one could get to them. The barn had collapsed, was a smoking ruin.

A voice like dark honey and warm starlight, speaking words he could not understand, brought him whipping about again. The elfwoman stood, regarding him as though he were the lowest of worms and it would not even be her pleasure to kill him, only some distasteful task that she must perform.

She took a step toward him and stopped, eyes widening as she saw and realized what he wore. Emboldened, Desah brandished his blade and moved closer. "Come on, then. Brave the steelgrass, Fiendish One. See what it does to you."

His words might not have made sense to her, but she could hardly mistake his tone. It was her turn to feel fear, and he relished it. She knew what the touch of steelgrass would do. Her reddened eyes and swollen face showed that she'd already come close enough to suffer from it. She would not get closer.

He would.

Desah thumped himself in the chest. "Come on . . . afraid?"

She stepped back.

He stepped forward, grinning. His village was ashes, his people dead or scattered, and those who survived this mad night would probably starve or freeze before they could find help. But he would have this one. He would slay an elf and prove that it could be done.

As he prepared to charge, she leveled her sword at him. Desah laughed derisively.

A stifling fist clutched him tight. He froze in place, unable to move. His arms and legs stiffened, his skin going grey. Air locked in his lungs. He saw the world swivel around him as he fell, and landed awkwardly on his side with his rigid limbs propping him at strange angles against the ground.

In the last instant before everything went dark, he knew that she had worked some magic of her own on him, and that he was going to die.

*   *   *

CHAPTER FOURTEEN

I am plagued by doubts and possibilities.
– Elwyndas, The Wizard Geheric, Act VII

This is not war, thought Tiercel Reyes. *This . . . this is hunting.*

Yet it was not even hunting. He did not have to seek them out as they hid and evaded, not at first. They ran directly at him, away from Tilanne and into the lethal arc of his blades. He wielded one in each hand, Discordant in the right and Lionheart on the left. He was not so adept at this as some he'd known, but the magical keenness and balance of the blades as well as his natural skill compensated nicely.

Not even hunting, really. It was . . . harvesting.

He laughed aloud as that thought came to him. Harvesting, yes, cutting them down like wheat. Like their own accursed crop, now burned and gone.

A few, in their frenzied terror, struck out at him with whatever tools and burdens they held. Their blows were clumsy and ill-aimed. The only wound he sustained came more by accident than design when a shrieking woman missed Tiercel's head altogether with a wildly-waved meat cleaver and hit a stony outcrop in a sputter of blue sparks. The blade of the cleaver snapped from the haft, rebounded, and gashed him along the side of the thigh.

Not a single one of them utilized the foreign magic that their wagoncade counterparts had. No fists of force, no summoned crawling or stinging swarms. He did not stop to ponder it, except to be grateful.

Tilanne approached from the other direction. The remnants humans were now trapped between them. Some flung down their burdens and sought safety in the woods. Others thought their sheer numbers would let them overwhelm him. A few even tried to surrender and plead for mercy. They were all most grievously in error.

He and Tilanne came face to face amid the groaning or silent bodies. She met his gaze with detached dispassion. He jerked his head by way of acknowledgement.

"A wizard of theirs I saw," she said. "In armor of this witch-grass woven, as thou surmised, he was arrayed."

"Did you deal with him?"

"To stone I turned him." She nodded in the direction of her dripping sword and he recalled its power, akin to the stony gaze that lore attributed to the basilisk. "Once transformed, no longer did the grass my eyes cause to sting."

"Excellent. Some have escaped, but their village is no more."

"Do we the others find, and finish?"

"No." He wiped his eyes. The wind was rising, coming from the sea and carrying smoke and ash from the scorched fields. "Let us put this place behind us. If any of them survive, they can tell their fellows what just two of our kind did to many times that number. They'll think twice before invading our land again."

"And the fire?"

"The rain is mastering the rest of it," he said. "We need not worry that we've set fire to the Emerin."

She cleaned her blade, and he did the same with both of his. Not staying to search, they hastened back to the faraway spot where they'd left their horses and packs. The storm, fire, and sounds of battle had stirred both steeds to nervousness, and they were glad to be away.

They rode the rest of the night and well into the morning, putting the remains of the village well behind them. The storm settled into a steady rain as the sky lightened. At last, Tiercel signaled for a halt and they made their camp, both exhausted and neither in much of a mood for talk.

Tiercel woke first, every part of him aching from the night's exertions. His eyes felt sore and abused but the rash on his skin had faded and he no longer breathed through a raw and rasping throat. Drops beat against the walls of his tent. He donned fresh clothing and sat cross-legged by a small fire shielded from the rain by a stretched oilcloth, examining his armor and tending to it with a rag of cleaning. When that was done, he moved on to pay careful attention to his swords, and the remainder of his gear.

He heard stirring in the other tent and moments later, Kai Tilanne's dark head appeared. The rest of her, in a loose, sleeveless shift that fell to her knees, emerged and she stood as straight as their shelter would allow, stretching.

How different she looked out of armor. It never failed to surprise him. The black corselet with its design of roses and basilisks lent her an imposing aura, made her stature seem great. Without it, she could have been any elfmaid, provided one did not look too closely and note the strong lines of her arms and legs. She seemed younger, less severe, her heart-shaped face not quite so stern. Pretty . . . yes, she was pretty, and that was a term he never would have thought he'd ascribe to a *Rhunvala*.

Not that he was overly affected by her prettiness. He had seen too many good men ruined by women's beauty. They would pine for an unrequited love, or be trapped into a marriage they'd later come to regret, or be misled and tormented by feminine wiles. More than once, he'd known two men, dear friends, closer than brothers, come to deadly rivalry by a woman's whim. Oh, they well knew the use of their fair weapon, women did. They excelled at it.

It was, perhaps, much more an Emerinian than *Morvalan* view. Tiercel knew that things were different indeed in the southern lands. None of the artful games of Emerinian courtship were played there. Men were men, women were women, each elf knew his or her place and role, and they had no patience for, and little understanding of, the societal manipulations of their northern kin.

Even if he had been interested in a *Morvalan* female, he was not at all sure Tilanne would be that one. She was no typical example of her breed. She was *Rhunvala.* Chosen of Kaledhol. Hardly the sort that he'd feel at ease dallying with. She had that air about her, that air of knowing. As if she could see into him and knew more about him than he did himself.

So he settled for admiring her legs on an aesthetic level, and did not let any other desire stir his blood. There would be time enough for all that when he was ready to wed. In another century or two . . .

Or sooner, if Elyvorrin has his way.

This thought came into his head as if spoken from afar, and he groaned aloud. He had tried not to dwell on it, on the count's insistence that Tiercel take his widowed daughter-in-law to wife and become stepfather and guardian to Elyvorrin's grandson.

Faessia. What to do about Faessia? She feared him, and he did not trust what the strain of a forced match might do to her brittle mind. He had told her that theirs would be a union in name only. He would be free as any Emerinian would to seek other lovers – discreet affairs were to be expected; it was the having of illegitimate children that was strictly frowned upon. But someday, far in the future, he might wish for a genuine wife and family of his own. Carry on the Reyes name and all that.

It was a worthy name of a long and glorious tradition. He could not trust his elder brother to live up to it. Trevorn's wife had died birthing a daughter, and if Treilla were left to be the only heir, the family name would die out.

"My uncle had no sons, did he?" Tiercel asked.

Tilanne, in the act of heating water for a morning tea, turned to him with a raised eyebrow at the sudden question. "Kai Terindor a wife and children had, but his grandchildren daughters were."

"So there are no more by the Reyes name in the southlands."

"To my knowledge, no."

He sighed and set down his swords, the blades of which crossed. "My other uncle, Tanneivan, was married. But when his wife learned of his . . . well, occupation, shall we say? . . . she took the children and left him and resumed her family's name."

"Thou, then, the last of thy line art?" She smiled, seeming to read his thoughts in that way she had. "But fear not, Tiercel, for soon enough wed shalt thou be."

He made a sour face. "I have no wish to get sons on Faessia Elyvorrin, as you well know. But neither can I let the Reyes name die out. What would come of my family if I did not return from this journey? If the basilisks had slain me? I have no heir."

"A problem indeed." She sat opposite him and worked her hair into a plait.

"You do not seem greatly concerned."

"Oh, thy people little true awareness of death have," she said. "Complacent they are, in their longevity secure. Centuries they have, or so they believe, and unprepared are when violence or illness their lives cut short. We *Morvalan* no such illusions of immortality have. We full well know how fragile, and precious, is life. Yet also do we know that a life well lived in Kaledhol's service a reward shall earn, that not wasted shall our time in this world be. Thy people, whose backs to the gods they've turned, lack even this."

"Thy people, thy people," he mocked, irritated. "I am as much of the south as of the north."

"When still so accustomed to the Emerin's comforts thou art, to the Emerin's ways? Thy own needs and wishes before that of others dost thou put."

"The entire reason I've come all this way is for the good of elvenkind," he said.

Her amethyst eyes were direct and deep. "Thou hast long of the Phial known."

"It isn't as if I could very easily come and fetch it before. I had to have something to trade. You yourself told me of the interactions the *Morvalan* have had with Racandros in the past. He trades, he barters. For goods or for lore or for items of treasure."

"But only when the Emerald into thy hands did fall didst thou this plan devise. Why hadst thou not by some other means tried?"

Tiercel shot her a glare. "I haven't had the time, have I? In case you weren't aware, there was a war on."

"Which five years ago did end."

"Five years is nothing. I've been busy. And I don't think I care for your tone. Of what, Kai Tilanne, are you accusing me?"

"Accuse thee do I not. Wonder, only, do I if the timing of thy mission more for thy own benefit is."

"Were you anyone else, I'd answer that with a duel," he said coldly. "I have done much for the elven race. I kept us at war when others would have brought peace, and the war ran a far costlier toll in human lives than it did elves or dwarves. Further, and perhaps you overlooked this in assuming that I've arranged all this solely for my own benefit, those additional years of war saw to the utter destruction of Keyda. Do you know what that means, Tilanne?"

"That all the land from the edge of the Emerin to the mountains near Thanis as a wasteland is," she said. "That untamed magic and dwarven devices a taint upon the land have put. That no one there can live, that nothing there will grow, except that which twisted and strange and dangerous is."

"Exactly. And where, do you know, does the Northlands get the bulk of its food? All of Keyda was grainfields and pasturelands, orchards and crops. They raised most of the Northlands' food there, you see. What the Highlord has in his granaries and storehouses will last them a while, but Gamelin and Goldenfields cannot possibly hope to grow enough to make up for it. They'll starve. In ten years or less, there will be famine among the human realms. They'll starve."

She looked at him, startled.

"I saw to it. They will starve. And with Keyda, damaged Keyda, between us and them, they can hardly seek to raid us. They'll turn west to Hachland, and within a generation there will be war again. War among the humans. Montennor will not intervene. Nor will we. All we'll have to do is sit back and let them slay each other."

"I confess, Tiercel, I had not this extent of the war foreseen," Tilanne said.

"Of course, that doesn't affect the rest of them much. Not the Mountain King or the Plainsfolk or the Islanders, or Hramad. But that's where the Phial comes in. One thing at a time, you see. I am using my wits. This is not just so that I, Tiercel, can have fortune and power."

Silently, almost contritely, she inclined her head.

"They'll be gone," he said, gazing at the rain-drenched trees as if seeing beyond them to a better place. "The greatest threat to us will be gone. Oh, there will still be other matters to deal with . . . the orcs might run rampant with the humans out of their way, and we'll still have the minotaurs and other shaper-spawned abominations to contend with . . . but in the end, and hopefully within our lifetimes, we shall see elvenkind be as we were meant to be. As we once *were*. The rightful rulers of this entire world."

* * *

The rain continued as they made their way toward the mountain. It snowed at times, wet slush that turned the going slippery as it melted into the earth. They spoke little.

As they came ever closer to their destination, Kai Tilanne grew more troubled. The Emerald of Karria, snug in its pouch secured to her belt, felt heavier and heavier.

Had it been Kaledhol's, she knew she could not have gone through with this. Bad enough that so many items of great elven enchantment had ended up in the dragon's hoard over the millennia. The oldest would have been taken as plunder by Racandros' forefathers, as they razed the golden city of Govannisan to the ground and drove the elves and dwarves from it in terror. More would have come from smaller raids, young dragons eager to prove themselves by snatching what treasure they could. But in recent memory, that which had gone unto Racandros' lair had been given deliberately.

Sometimes, it was for safekeeping. Every elf had heard tell of some item of great power that was also of too great a danger to possess. Curses or mishaps happened in the casting of such potent spells. Or occasionally, ambition would get the better of sense and wizards would make that which was too powerful to be safely used.

She remembered asking Alarice, a childhood friend whose talent for sorcery had been strong, why such items weren't simply broken or undone. Fair Alarice had given her a sad smile, a rueful laugh. "Thou little of the high magics know, Tilanne," she had said. "And of the High Mages, less. When so much of one's thought and energies and even one's very life into the crafting of an item is put, one might as one's own child come to see it."

"And they would as soon their own child harm," Tilanne had said, understanding, "as they would their greatest work. Even if deadly it turned out to be."

"Tales there are of wizards from the north whose children deadly turned out to be," Alarice said. "Who their own parents usurped and betrayed. A child may on a parent turn, an item may on its creator misfortune bring . . . but when such love and effort into the making of it has gone, who could such a grim thing undertake as to destroy it?"

"Wasteful it seems," Tilanne said. "So much time spent in the doing of something that useless, or worse, turns out to be."

"Wasteful? Thou'st not the half of it heard when of wastefulness and northern wizards speaking," Alarice said scornfully. "When useful spells and items they could be creating, instead their time on frivolous luxuries they squander. Spells they have their very hair to cut or grow at whim, the color of their clothing to change, the hour of the day to know. When a scissors, a dye vat, or an hour-candle would the same result have. As we our very lives struggle to defend, they are harps crafting that by unseen fingers melodies can play. To ease and pleasure are they devoted, and for our cares, care they nothing."

Now, as the mountain of the dragon rose high before them, Tilanne thought of that conversation. At the time, she'd wondered how Alarice could know so much, for they had been young and neither of them had ever left the southern lands, or met any *Alvalan*. Yet Alarice had been right.

She had spent the past few years living in secret in the Emerin, hidden away in chambers beneath Elyvorrin's estate or in unused parts of the palace that Tiercel knew. Her role was to be his counsel, his guide to the ways of the *Morvalan* and Kaledhol, but also to learn what she could of the Emerin and its people.

There had been much talk at the *Odan Rhunvale* about that. Proud as they were, the *Morvalan* did not like to admit to failure. They did not like to admit that they were on the brink of disaster. The Mountain King was gaining in strength so rapidly, and their numbers increased so slowly, that it was only a matter of time – a short matter at that – until his armies overran their defenses. They could not hold out much longer.

It had been decided that their best hope was to see if some measure of support could be found from the Emerin. But centuries of separation and damaging rumors had left both sides unsure. How much of what was told was true? Just what did the *Alvalan* think of the *Morvalan*? Would an alliance even be possible?

So it was that when Tiercel came to the southlands, Tilanne was compelled to return with him. She had long known that her place in the south was out of it. Her mission was twofold – to educate Tiercel, and also to learn of the Emerin. What she had seen and heard, going among them in secret, had dismayed her. They were even more selfish than she'd feared, concerned more with their social standing than with issues of life and death. They passed sleepless nights fretting over perceived insults, lapses in fashion, and what others might or might not think of them. They made crises out of things so inconsequential that it was all she could do to keep from shaking them.

At the core of it, their priorities seemed directly opposite of everything she had been raised to believe. They put themselves and their comforts first, and then their families. The greater good of their people ranked a distant third if it was considered at all. They knew no real hardship or adversity.

They paid the barest acknowledgement to the gods, depicting them more as figures of mythology in their art than as actual deities. And when it came to Kaledhol . . . to them, His name was feared and never uttered, and if they thought of Him at all it was as some dark villain, some god of wrath. This, she knew, was a holdover from the flight from Govannisan, when the followers of the other gods had blamed the followers of Kaledhol, and by extension Kaledhol Himself, for failing to protect them from the dragons' attack.

Had it been her place to question, she would have wondered at Valannin for allowing the elves of the Emerin to have grown so lax and disrespectful. It was Valannin, lord of knowledge and wisdom, that they mostly claimed to follow.

Tiercel seemed less perturbed by the whole matter. In his eyes, Denethel and the Lenaisians alike were rustic, uncivilized. Barbaric, even. He qualified it in his mind that yes, the Emerald was a divine object, but it wasn't as if it were Valannin's own.

Still, it felt wrong. This was not something that had been made by mages. This was, if the stories were true, something that had been formed by the very hand of a god.

She wondered, too, about Tiercel. She did not doubt that his motives were, ultimately, for the good of the elves. It was his methods that gave her pause. He had, rashly perhaps but well-intended, sworn to convert the young prince Wyndrel to the *Morvalan* way. This, Tiercel claimed, would eventually give the *Morvalan* the ally they so desperately needed. A king sympathetic to their cause would be of incalculable help.

Yet it had not gone so smoothly. Wyndrel had seen too much of Tiercel's other methods, perhaps even knew of Tiercel's role in the death of the old king. That was something else she found upsetting when she let herself think of it. He had been so old, of an age that even few elves could hope to attain. Surely he would have died soon anyway, without hastening him along.

Which was Tiercel's very argument. Surely he would have died soon anyway; better that he do it when some good might come of it.

The prince, though, had not proved easy to sway. Tiercel, irked by Wyndrel's resistance, would have arranged a similar fate for him had not Tilanne so stridently intervened. They could not hope to serve their people by slaying them. No more. No longer. In the end, Tiercel had agreed.

"We should reach the base of the mountain tomorrow," Tiercel said, cutting into her thoughts. He had his head craned far back, peering up at the peak that vanished into the low masses of clouds. "It may take us a day or more just to scale it. We'll find a campsite where we can leave the horses, and go on foot."

The ancient volcano, its fire long since dormant, stood impassive and huge in their path. Its sides were sheer cliffs and deep crevasses and slants where rocks looked poised to slide and tumble in a deadly hail. Trees grew partway up its slopes, thinner and sparser as the land climbed.

"A trail should there be," Tilanne said. "By my people made long ago, and still infrequently used. If find it we can, easier might the way be."

"I'm pleased that he's not unaccustomed to callers. Surprised, though, that he'd share his lore with elves. Doesn't he fear it will be used against him?"

"Asked that once I did," she said. "And laughed did my teachers. The size of him, the might of him, any such considerations renders moot. The lore that he shares not of his own kind is, either. Many breeds of dragons are there, fallen in stature and intelligence since Govannisan. Only contempt has he for the lesser breeds."

"Well, then," said Tiercel with a smile. "We ought to get on just fine, Racandros and I."

* * *

CHAPTER FIFTEEN

Who shall put paid to this insult, this injury? I will have satisfaction. I will have blood!
– Elwyndas, The Madness of Anomed (ballad)

The rays of the sun, when they finally penetrated the smoke and clouds, revealed a scene of such devastation that the survivors of Hral broke down and wept.

Ythri's eyes remained dry and hard as she surveyed the remains of the village. The tightening of her gnarled fist on the knob of her cane was her only outward sign of emotion.

With a swiftness that belied her age, she whirled and struck Saiye sharply across the face. The girl's sobbing broke off suddenly and she cringed. The others tapered off, keeping their wary distance as if they feared Ythri's wrath might lash out at them next.

She held her temper with an effort. They were only *druhjes*, for the most part, a scant few that Saiye had taken at Desah's order to gather and save what could be carried to safety. That meager pile of bundles and goods lay nearby, and not far beyond, the three ponies that had escaped the barn grazed fitfully with the singed patches showing vividly on their hides in the sullen light.

One wagon, too, had come through the burning unscathed. It could bear the wounded and infirm, or it could bear the supplies, or it could bear some of each.

Her attention turned to the wounded. One had been all but incinerated and clung to life by his fingertips. A woman had had both legs broken when she'd leapt from her window with her baby in her arms; the child was unhurt but the mother had only ceased her screams when Ythri had touched her brow and put her into a magical slumber.

Those two were the worst, but many others sported arms in makeshift slings, and crude bandages made from torn strips of clothing. Their eyes were shocked and hollow, and all looked to her because she was the only one left with any real magic. They wanted her to lead. Except that they also wanted nothing more than to slink off and nurse their pains and mourn their dead.

"We cannot stay here," she said. "The Fiendish Ones may have gone, but they'll return to be sure they finished their grim task. If we wait, they'll find us."

"Where will we go?" Waron asked.

He alone had the courage to meet her gaze. Though his parents had both been strong with magic, in him the gift was mild, erratic and limited. He could weave some potent spells, but only when he was alone and made use of much ceremony. In fleeing his house he'd had the presence of mind to grab up the satchel that held the chalks and powders and other tools of his trade, and clutched it as though it were an infant.

"You say that as if we had some choice," Ythri said. "With no ships here and none due, we cannot return to Hramad even if we'd find welcome there. The Mountain King might take us in but we could never reach his kingdom alive. We must follow Keshad's route, west through the woods to the castle of Canah."

The group murmured unhappily as she spoke. By the time she uttered the names of Desah's father, and great Canah, a resignation settled over them and they bowed their heads in reluctant acceptance.

Ythri set Waron to organizing them, and hobbled away, lost in her own fuming thoughts. Canah. She had no wish to go to him, because Canah was too sharp-sighted, too wise. Given the chance, he'd suspect, he'd know.

Two of the ponies were harnessed, the third left for Ythri to ride because she could never walk such a distance on her old legs. She had to conjure a hand of force to lift herself to its back. With no saddle to hold her in place, she knew that she'd have to trust to the grip of her knees and fingers, the parts of her body that troubled her the most. There was little else to be done for it, and she supposed others had worse to complain about.

Waron was clever, winnowing out and leaving those things that would be useless to them, taking only that which would keep them alive. Saiye, both sides of her face bruised from the blows she'd been dealt, helped two other *druhjes* splint and bind the legs of the injured woman and load her into the wagon with her baby nestled in a basket at her side. The burnt man, feeling no pain because his nerves had been seared away, was conscious and aware when Waron came for him with a knife. His wail of protest was brief. Ythri nodded. He could not have been helped, and would only have been a burden. Such was the way of the cruel world. No one argued, even the dead man's brother. They left him and packed the bundles of food and clothing around the woman. What wouldn't fit was slung on the backs of the strongest.

"What if there are Fiendish Ones?" Saiye asked. "We cannot fight them. They'll kill us."

Ythri scowled at her. "Yes, I'm sure they will."

The girl was pretty enough beneath the bruises, so it was easy to see why Desah had chosen her as a bedmate, but she was a fluttering and useless thing. She would have been better suited to posing at the foot of a throne, bedecked in finery and jewels. Ythri waited to see if there was more, but Saiye only scurried away, crying again. She had more water in her than a wellspring, it sometimes seemed.

They set out, no one eager to linger in this awful place. Ythri was deeply worried about elves, and the single sheaf of steelgrass that had been saved did little to assuage her fears. They'd be a fine sight, each waving a stalk at their attackers. Some good it would do them against arrows.

Waron took the lead, a sturdy walking-stick in one hand and the leash of Hral's only remaining dog in the other. He had not gone far when he stopped and cried out. "Ythri! Ythri, come!"

She had been riding a few paces behind him, already hating the plod and jounce of her steed, and brought it up to where Waron stood staring into the underbrush. Something large and grey was there, like a rock . . . a rock shaped like . . .

"Is it Desah?" Waron asked.

"Help me down." Ythri leaned over the statue. "Elf-magic! It *is* Desah. They've petrified him."

Desah had been caught in a stance that suggested he'd been running at the moment his body had been cast in stone. He lay awkwardly on one side, limbs jutting at angles, his sword not far from his hand as if he'd dropped it in the final moment of his mobility. Everything was captured in detail, down to the woven strands of steelgrass that made up his armor, and the astonished expression on his face. Ythri could even see the chain of his amulet.

The *druhjes* gathered around, moaning and muttering in their horror. Saiye burst into tears again and Ythri shoved her ruthlessly aside.

"Do you have quicksilver?" she asked Waron.

He had been gaping down at Desah, lost in his own frightened thoughts, and for a moment turned his gape on her, not comprehending. Then understanding came and he scrambled at his satchel. "I do . . . I think I do."

"You'd better. Everyone else, away. You heard me, away!"

They did as she bade, but only to a distance that would still let them see as Waron brought out a pot and anointed Desah's stiff form with the thick, silvery stuff. He chanted as he did so, a spell of reversal, the words glottal and strange. The old magic, its roots in the days long past when Hramadans had met in secret to conduct their sorceries. Every so often, one like Waron would spring up who was a reminder of those nearly forgotten times.

Ythri, watching, thought dourly that she, too, was such a reminder. Or would have been if not for the truth she and her family had been so careful to conceal, generation after generation. An old, unwelcome memory sought to intrude on her, a phantom pain dating back to childhood, and she steadfastly refused to let herself think of it.

Waron, meanwhile, chanted and sketched symbols in the earth all around Desah, pouring a fine spill of colored powders from his fist to fill in each mark. The quicksilver, entirely coating Desah's body, bubbled. It gave off a quick, acrid smell that made Ythri's nose wrinkle. Then it appeared to sink into the stone, and each symbol full of powder ignited with sizzling noises and wisps of colored smoke.

The watching *druhjes* all uttered a simultaneous, breathy exhalation, "ahh," both in awe and unease. Even Saiye stopped her weeping.

The grey faded from Desah's flesh. He softened, sagged, collapsed. He sucked at the air, then suddenly thrashed his way to his feet, eyes blazing, snatching for his sword. He nearly beheaded Waron before recognizing him, only Waron's swift duck saving his life, and looked startled at the small group around him.

With neither pleasantries, explanation, nor preamble, Ythri yanked the chain at his neck and pulled the amulet into view. The milky gem was dark. Relief seeped through her.

"They've gone," she said. "The elves. They are not near."

Desah was weakened by his ordeal, and in no mood to argue as they coaxed him to sit beside the wagon drover. Saiye trotted at his knee, dashing to fulfill his every request for food or drink.

They journeyed the rest of the day and made a small camp. By then, Desah had regained his wits and they exchanged news. He was none too delighted with their destination, worried about how this would all reflect on his leadership. Keshad had barely put Hral into his care before Desah had let it burn flat. But he acknowledged that Ythri was right. They had no other choice.

The going was slow, and the deeper they got into the hostile woods that the elves called Emerin, the less inclined anyone was to talk. Soon they were proceeding in a dreadful hush, everyone stealing frequent glances at the amulet that Desah wore. The fact that it remained dark did little to comfort them, and more than once Ythri saw someone scanning the trees, expecting a sudden deadly hail of elf-arrows.

On the second day, three of their number took sick from eating toadstools, and even after Ythri had brewed up a potion to purge their stomachs of it, half of the *druhjes* were convinced that the elves had deliberately set poison upon them. Saiye became hysterical and refused to eat anything but that food which they'd brought with them.

"You must do something about that useless girl," Ythri said to Desah as they sat at the fire while the rest set up camp. "Her yammering foolishness is more trouble than we need."

He turned to her, aggravation on every line of his features, but before he could speak she hissed and pointed at his chest. A ghost of a flicker played over the milky gem.

Desah went pale but he passed it off with a show of bravery. "They're still far."

"Not far enough. If we're found –"

"You don't need to tell me what will happen if we're found."

"I will set a ward," she said, and rose grimacing to her feet.

She paced off a wide circle around their camp, envisioning a rippling fence of light unwinding behind her. Anyone crossing it, anything not animal, would be struck down with debilitating nausea and illness, which would render even an elf-mage unable to case a spell or wield a weapon. Too, she would know the moment the line had been crossed, and where.

Nothing disturbed them that night. They pressed on with the morning, through a dark and primeval glade where the leaves were decades deep underfoot, and the air was sour with the smell of windfallen, rotted fruit. Some still clung to the trees but nobody, not even Ythri, was tempted to take any. Not here.

The *druhjes* had noticed the amulet's more pronounced glow. As it brightened, their spirits – already weak – dimmed. They dragged their feet, and talked in low voices among themselves that they were going to die, and die horribly. That it might have been better to wait for a ship, and seek passage home. After all, they told one another, they were only *druhjes*, not responsible for what their masters made them do, and surely they could find new contracts of servitude on Hramad.

When Desah overheard this, he flew into a fury. "If you think you'll suffer at the hands of the Fiendish Ones, it's nothing compared to what you'll suffer at *my* hands if there's so much as a breath of betrayal! They defeated us before because we were unready. They will not be able to do the same again. I will not allow it." As if seeking to quell the fears that ran rampant through the *druhjes*, he tucked the amulet out of sight.

Ythri held her tongue. Somehow, in his mind, Desah had turned things around and decided that if he could lead them all safely to the castle of Canah, he would have redeemed himself. Here, she thought, was a young man blindly readying himself for dire disappointment.

* * *

At midday, Desah brought them to an urgent stop. He had foregone riding on the wagon's hard seat in favor of walking, and had taken the lead. Now he turned to the others, and silently drew the amulet from his armor. It was bright as a star, and Ythri was not the only one to stifle a noise of dread.

They heard it next, unmistakable, the high clear laugh of an elf. And musical words, merry and light. Ythri sought the dusty archives of her memory and translated them.

"It's only water, Mischa. What are you afraid of?"

Another voice answered, speaking the speech of the elves but with a coarseness that was unmistakably human. "Freezing solid. I'll heat mine over the fire, if it's all the same to you."

The rest of the refugees from Hral cowered like sheep, not comprehending and on the very edge of panic.

Desah beckoned to Ythri and Waron. "I wish a closer look."

"We can avoid them," Ythri said. "Our path bears north."

"But if they are unprepared, we can avenge our home and our dead." He touched the hilt of his sword, and his grin was feral.

There would be no disputing him. Waron looked pleadingly at Ythri but she shook her head, gripped her cane, and followed Desah through the forest as quietly as she could. After a moment's hesitation, Waron did the same.

They came to a place where the land fell steeply away, a rock face bordering a glade where a spring-fed pool glimmered like the heart of a diamond. Though snow powdered the higher branches, it did not coat the ground, or rime the pool with ice. Still, Ythri harbored no illusions as to the chill of the water.

A boy was wading into it, an elven youth with hair the shade of a fox's pelt. His fair skin pebbled with gooseflesh and he wore only smallclothes, already shivering as the water climbed to his thighs. Discarded garments lay on the bank, near a human man who was busying himself with pans and waterskins.

The sight of the human took Ythri's breath away. His was a handsomeness that she had never seen on Hramad, where the constant intrigues and threat of assassination made most men pinched and wary.

Had she been two hundred years younger . . .

While she permitted herself such wayward thoughts, Desah crept to the left, where the descent was easiest. She clutched at his tunic and gave him a look, but he only made a throat-slitting gesture and continued.

"On second thought," the boy in the pool said through chattering teeth, "you may be right."

"Aren't I usually? But you've gone that far, Kev. May as well finish."

"I'm turning blue. And we should make haste to help with the camp."

The human, who spoke the language of the elves but not familiarly, smiled. "I think our absence would be appreciated more than our help. Didn't you notice how they urged us on this errand?"

"You're imagining things."

"Am I? When both of them can create all the water we'd ever need by a wiggle of their fingers?"

That gave the boy pause. As he seemed to search for the right retort, he crouched and liberally splashed himself, then clambered out of the pool. "Surely they aren't . . ."

"Shall we sneak back and watch?"

"No! Have you no manners, no morals?"

"Certainly. Which is why I'd wait to be invited before joining in." The human dunked waterskins and watched the bubbles rise as they filled.

The boy regarded him as if this was not the first time he'd been astonished, and was telling himself he should be used to it by now. He dried off and reached for his clothing.

He halted mid-motion, staring at the surface of the pool. Ythri saw his reflection in it, and realization burst over her. If she could see his reflection . . . then he could see . . .

She opened her mouth to call a warning to Desah, but Desah chose that moment to act.

An unseen hand of force slapped the young elf, knocking him headlong back into the water with his leggings tangled around his feet. A terrific splash went up, dousing the human. He shied back, sputtering.

"Gracefully done, Kevan," he said. "This is the much-vaunted elven agility one hears so much about."

Kevan lunged to the surface, spraying fans of droplets. His eyes and mouth were wide circles in the pale mask of his face. As he sucked in a breath to speak, Desah's spell struck again, this time from above. The boy was driven under, and the roiling water was contained, pressed down, as an invisible barrier like the world's clearest sheet of ice covered the entire pool.

The human, Mischa, backed away with his jaw dropping. He recovered almost immediately and rushed to the edge, hammering with his fists and shouting the boy's name. Desah forgot about stealth and plunged down the slope, sword out. Ythri cursed, tried to pursue, felt her knee give way with a brittle pop. She bit back a wail and fell. Waron caught her as easily as if she weighed no more than a bundle of dry twigs in his arm.

Mischa gaped at Desah, stunned. He spoke. Not in the elven tongue, not in Hramadan, but they didn't need to know the words to recognize the surprise, the interrogative.

"Elf-loving traitor to your breed!" Desah raced at him.

Ythri, though half-blinded by the pain lancing from her knee, heard madness in his voice. First Hral, then petrification, and now this. He had gone mad.

Mischa yanked a sword of his own from a sheath at his hip, just in time to parry a wild lunge from Desah. Steel and bronze clashed, and Desah's blade was deeply nicked.

Ythri, all but carried by Waron, reached level ground. She could see the boy submerged in the pool, beating desperately on the underside of the magical barrier, his image distorted by the water. She half-fell onto a convenient rock and gasped for Waron to help Desah before he got himself killed.

The amulet swinging around Desah's chest flared white. He backed Mischa across the glade, sustaining several more nicks to his sword and a shallow cut to his arm. Waron, holding his stout walking stick, faltered as if unsure whether or not to enter the battle.

It was decided for him a bare heartbeat later, when two more elves appeared. Ythri, who could do little more than watch as she cradled the hot ball of pain that had replaced her knee, made a strangled cry of horror. These two were adults, in their powerful prime. The one in the lead, a male whose build was like that of no other elf she'd ever seen or heard of, punched Waron in the belly so hard that Waron bent double and his feet left the ground. His breath was expelled in a cough.

The other, a female, raced past the struggling men to the pool. She ran right out onto its surface and threw herself prone, hands splayed on what seemed to be nothing. "Kevan! Oh, gods, Kev!"

Desah shrieked. His fury at seeing more elves gave him a surge of strength, and he batted the weapon from Mischa's grasp. A return swing, nearly a blur of speed, tore through Mischa's tunic and opened a diagonal gash from shoulder to hip. Even as Mischa clapped his hands to his bleeding body, Desah spun away from him.

The male elf, who had pummeled Waron senseless and dropped his body in a heap, turned to meet Desah. He had a sword at his side but had not drawn it, nor did he now. He merely flexed his fingers as if anticipating Desah's neck being crushed in them.

But as he stepped up to meet Desah's charge, stepped close to the steelgrass that girded him, the elf was beset by a fit of sneezing. His eyes gushed copious tears and his tawny skin went scarlet.

"*Tah'hassa*," the female at the pool cried out. Beneath the barrier, a wavering pocket of air appeared. The boy floundered into it, coughing mutely, but his movements were losing strength.

"Wretched elf! This is for Hral!" Desah slashed

The elf, even through his sneezes, dodged and grabbed. Desah's wrist was caught in that fierce grip. Ythri saw the play of muscle and tendon as the big elf squeezed. The sword fell. Desah tried to yank free, clawing furiously at the fingers that held him, crushed him.

The din had alerted the *druhjes* and, unwisely but loyally, they came rushing to the aid of their lordling. Some of them, at least. Once they glimpsed the strange battle awaiting them below, a few – Saiye among them – stopped short at the top of the rock face.

The female elf screamed incantations at the barrier, trying to dispel it, and despite everything else Ythri experienced a gleeful thrill of pride. *That* for elf-magic . . . they thought they were so brilliant, that they could do everything. Well, here was something they couldn't counter, couldn't deal with. *Consider it repayment*, Ythri thought, *for all that the Hramadans have suffered.*

Her heart pounded, pounded. At first she mistook it for vindication and excitement, but then it spasmed in her breast and an oily nausea churned in her stomach. A pang shot down her arm, another encircled her torso.

Desah was about to be picked up and hurled like a cloth-stuffed doll. Ythri concentrated past her pain and jabbed a forefinger at the elf. His arms went as limp as if the bones had been removed, flopping to his sides where they dangled, so much meat, from his shoulders.

Two *druhjes* caught the elf-woman's feet and dragged her toward shore. She writhed and spun and drew and struck all in one smooth motion, and one *druhj* fell back with blood spouting from his neck. The other lost all pretense at valor and ran.

"Take them, finish them," Desah ordered. He did not bother with his battered sword, but made a clutching sweep with his hand and the male elf was yanked into the air, his arms still flailing in their boneless paralysis. Desah flung him toward the rock face.

He hit with cracking force, left a smear of blood, and bounced down to the pool. The elf-woman shot a lethal spray of icicles at the *druhjes*, impaling them with freezing daggers. Ginrie took one in the hollow of the throat and fell, scrabbling at the ice even as she died.

Saiye shrieked a warning. "Desah! Behind you!"

Mischa, the torn front of his tunic sodden and crimson to the hem, held his sword overhead in both hands with the point angled down. Desah turned just as Mischa drove it at him.

The tip plunged through the woven steelgrass with a metallic screech, and deep into Desah's chest. Mischa leaned, threw his weight on it, and pushed the blade in. Farther. Farther. To the hilt.

Desah's back arched as the point emerged, ripping through his armor. He bent his neck and gaped his jaws as if he might bellow to the sky but all that came out was a glut of dark blood. He dropped, Mischa letting go the sword, and his heels drummed the earth. His bowels loosed in the extremity of his death throes.

Then he was still.

The barrier over the pool vanished. The male elf, who had been lying dazed upon it, fell into the water. The female had taken a step off to threaten the *druhjes*, but the violent losses were too much and, as one, the *druhjes* fled.

Mischa turned from Desah's body and was wrackingly sick.

A clammy sweat ran down Ythri's face. Three dead – no, four. She had thought Waron simply unconscious but had missed seeing the way his neck had been brutally wrenched. The others were gone. Only she was left. And something was grievously wrong with her.

At the pool, the female had cast some other spell, causing the water to well up in a great wave that carried the male and the youth to shore, depositing them there and then receding in streams and rivulets.

Ythri slipped from the rock and leaned against it, almost reclining. Her throat was tight, her breath whistling through a pinhole. She rubbed her frail chest. Her heart was skittering, falling slack, skittering.

The elves ignored her. From what seemed a great distance, she heard them talking to the boy, begging him, ordering him to breathe, to live.

Someone stood over Ythri. The human. Mischa. His tunic hung in flaps, but the wound across his body had faded to a pinkish, healing scar. A glint of gold . . . an amulet shaped like . . . like . . . surely it wasn't shaped like what she thought she was seeing.

He knelt, reached out.

"Mischa!" It was the elf-female. "We need you. Now."

As he began to rise, Ythri clamped down on his hand with the hard birdlike claw of her own. "Hramad," she croaked, and found elven speech in the recesses of her mind, the secret speech passed down through her family whenever the unfortunate trait, the hideous corruption, surfaced. "Hramad will destroy them. They think . . . they are gods. But we . . . remember. Even . . . gods . . . can . . . die."

Mischa recoiled and touched the amulet around his neck. He said something, spoke a name, but none of it mattered to Ythri. She was fading, fading into darkness, and after almost four hundred years of life, she went without protest.

* * *

CHAPTER SIXTEEN

It is thee and I who must go on, for all our land is in need.
– Elwyndas, Sir Blaine's Last Battle (ballad)

Wet, wounded, and bedraggled, the four of them returned to the spot they'd chosen for their midday meal. The spot that would likely be the night's camp . . . and possibly Kevan's resting place.

Gods, no. Ariana shuddered and made a sign she hadn't thought of since childhood, one taught to her by old Bess. A warding-off sign against Haarkon, god of the human dead.

As Wyndrel, in pain but stoically refusing to admit to it, stretched Kev out on a bedroll, Ariana glimpsed the boy's face and wondered if her half-formed prayer had been too late. If Kev had, despite Mischa's best healing efforts, died as Wyndrel carried him from the pool . . .

But no. Kev was breathing. His lips and eyelids and the flesh beneath his fingernails were tinged with blue, he was shivering until his teeth clattered, but he was alive.

She had used her magic to dry him, and draw the water from his lungs. Now she hastened to make a fire and they all huddled close around it.

"Tell me he'll be all right," she said to Mischa.

"I've done what I can, Ari. You know how Talopea's gifts work. When the patient is one who, like Kev himself confessed to me, has only kissed a girl once or twice . . ." He trailed off and shrugged with his hands spread.

Wyndrel grumbled.

"Speaking of which," Mischa said, turning to him, "I'd best see to you."

"I'll mend."

"Now's no time for manly stubbornness," Ariana said. "We're not safe here, if those people decide to come after us."

"They'll be running until moonrise," Wyndrel said. "They weren't soldiers, this bunch. Servants for the most part, that's my guess. And sorcerers."

"Prakah's folk," she said, embracing herself as the memory of the boy in Eltarrin drove what little warmth she'd regained from her body. "Their spells are foreign to me. I don't like that. How can it be? The talent for magic is so rare among humans, yet so many of these ones had it."

"If the others had, they would have used spells against us," Wyndrel said. "We must have slain their wizards. What I don't like is the stuff that one's armor was made of. I thought my eyes would melt from my head. And the old woman . . . the way she pointed at me and took away the use of my arms . . ."

"There was something funny about her, did you notice?" Mischa asked.

"She died 'ere any of us laid a hand on her," Ariana said.

"That's easily explained. Her heart gave out, no wonder given her age. I took a moment to examine her and it's mad, but I'd swear to it . . . she had elven blood, Ari."

"Elven blood? You mean she was elfkin?"

"Impossible," Wyndrel said. "It surely would have shown, would it not?"

"If you'd taken a look at her ears you'd have seen why. Someone snipped them. Long ago, possibly when she was no more than a baby. Snipped the points." Mischa stopped, and made an apologetic noise when he saw how she and Wyndrel both blanched with horror. "Sorry. It's true, though. Talopea sometimes grants us the power to see within someone, to determine what ails them and learn the ways of their body, which can be used for both pleasure and healing. When I touched her, even though her life had fled, I was able to read the years of her life like rings of a tree. She was centuries old."

"Elfkin," Wyndrel said. "Elfkin among a people who hold such a hate for our race. If it's so, I suppose it makes sense that she would have been mutilated in that way."

"It's horrible," Ariana said, lightly touching the tips of her ears. "But no less so than what they do to elfkin born in the Emerin."

"Oh, please, not that drowning-at-birth legend again," Wyndrel said. "Even if that ever was done, it hasn't been for half a millennium or more. Times have changed."

"You mean they're welcome now?"

He stretched and groaned. "Don't prod me, Ariana. The sun's not even at its zenith and the day's already been too long. No more bickering."

"Fair enough. I won't bicker, but I will insist you let Mischa tend to you. That was an awful blow you sustained, hitting the rocks that way. It's a wonder your bones aren't broken."

"I'm not so sure they aren't," he admitted, feeling at his ribs. "But they will mend."

"Faster with Mischa's help." Seeing his reticence, and the strange glance that passed between them, Ariana was suddenly sure of something she'd only guessed at before. It stole the rest of her words and she could only look at him in amazement.

Wyndrel flushed belligerently and averted his eyes. "And what of it?" he said as if she had voiced her realization aloud. "I was too young when I lived in the palace, and there was hardly opportunity once I'd gone off to war. Oh, there were women in the armies, warmages especially, but I had other things to think of. And then Tiercel's intervention put a pause to any other plans I may have had."

She raised her hands. "I said not a word."

"See that you don't."

"I'm still willing to try," Mischa said. He hastily added, "The healing, I mean, since I already know your answer to any other offer."

"We are nearly to the mountain," Ariana said, pointing to the peak that reared above the trees and dominated the horizon. "If luck is with us – or against us – we'll be catching up to Tiercel soon. The humans might be long gone but they might also come after us and attempt ambush. We'll have to stand watch. I think we'd all feel more secure with you at full strength, Wyndrel."

Grumbling anew, he nonetheless sat down and permitted Mischa to lay hands upon him. Ariana withdrew to a discreet distance. She couldn't help thinking about him. Oddly, the revelation about his history was something of a temptation.

I could teach him, she thought, and blushed with a tingling heat. *No, he'd never trust me enough to be vulnerable with me. He'd think that I would criticize and argue, and it isn't as if I want him anyway.*

Except that was a lie. She watched him, eyes closed and fists clenched as he tolerated Mischa's healing touch, and did want him. He was arrogant and brooding and impossible, and she wanted him.

* * *

"He shouldn't be moved," Mischa said the next morning. "He's still too weak. We very nearly lost him."

The night had passed uneventfully, if damply as a new storm had moved in on wings of rain and wind. The mountain glistened with a new layer of snow, and lacy ice had formed on the highest branches of the tall trees. A biting cold was in the air.

Wyndrel looked from the mountain to Kevan, who lay pale in a sleep so deep it was almost a living death. He had roused a few times, long enough to sip at a hot broth, but never for long.

Ariana was worried about his mind. She'd heard stories from the sailors of Tradersport of men who were plucked from the sea when they should have been let go, men who were forever diminished. As if they'd lost something vital to the water, and could never regain it. Her own father had almost drowned once, brought back at the point of last hope, but he had eventually recovered.

"We cannot afford to lose more time," Wyndrel said. "For all we know, Tiercel is there already, delivering the Emerald into the dragon's keeping."

"I agree, we mustn't dally," Ariana said, "but what of Kevan? He cannot travel, and we need him to show us the way."

"Well, I hardly think that," Mischa said. "There's yonder mountain. Probably just a day or two's walk from here. I'd think the dragon's lair wouldn't be too hard to miss. Just search for the cave with a big pile of charred bones outside."

"You're ever so helpful, Mischa."

"He's right, Ariana. We could go on without Kev, leave him here with Mischa to look after him. The destination of our quest is in sight."

"You'd have us take on Tiercel and the *Rhunvala*, just the two of us?"

"He makes sense, Ari," Mischa said. "You know I'm never much good in a battle."

"You were yesterday. The way you slew that man –"

He twisted away from her. "I'd rather not dwell on that. Shaper-mage monstrosities, that's one thing. Him . . . he was of my own kind."

"Your own race, mayhap, but not your own kind," Wyndrel said.

"I'd never killed a person before," Mischa said, stubbornly clinging to his tone of self-recrimination. "I haven't the nerve or the stomach for it. The only use I'd be against those two elves is to enrage the *Morvalan* woman to the point that she attacks me to the exclusion of all others, gaining you a few precious moments."

"You undervalue yourself, Mischa," Ariana said.

"I can be more help to you and to this quest by caring for Kevan. Without him, we'd have a hard journey home, assuming any of us live. I say Wyndrel's plan is best. You two go on ahead, while we stay here. If you can, come back and we'll be waiting."

"Dividing our forces? Splitting up? That's never a good idea," Ariana said.

"Sometimes, it's the only way." Wyndrel clapped Mischa on the shoulder, then knelt and patted Kevan's hand. The boy's eyes were open, hazy but seeming to follow their conversation. "We shall return, I promise you."

"You shouldn't –"

"Do you think we're going to fail?" Wyndrel cut in, looking at her.

"Realistically? The two of us against the two of them?"

He rose in a smooth flexion of his body and came to her, and grasped her upper arms in a gentle but firm hold. His eyes were gold, gold as a dragon's, and serious. His hair was a tumbled mane around his high, proud ears. "We are in the *right*, Ariana Mirida. If there is justice at all in this world, if the gods reward those who do good, then we shall triumph. I swear it."

"Kai Tilanne's god might see it differently," she said weakly, lost in that golden gaze.

"Sometimes things are meant to be done a certain way because that is the way things *must* be done. I must confront Tiercel. And I do not plan to lose."

"No one ever plans to."

"I mean to do this whether you are with me or not, Ariana. But I'd rather have you at my side, and have you believe in me."

"I'm not going to let you do this alone. It's my fault Tiercel has the Emerald in the first place, and I've a score to settle with him as well. There's no way I'd sit back and do nothing. I'm willing to risk my life in this cause, Wyndrel. I'm just not all that optimistic about our chances."

"I have confidence enough for us both."

"You," she said, "have confidence enough for all the Emerin."

"As is only fitting. I am the Emerin."

* * *

Ariana and Wyndrel elected to leave the steeds at the camp with Mischa and Kevan, as the horses would be no good ascending the mountain. They took only what they needed – weapons, food. They wanted to be able to travel quick, and light.

The first part of their trek was in silence but for the sweet trills of birds and once, the cry of a pantera. Ariana wasn't sure how she felt about being alone with Wyndrel. Mischa might not be the best guardian of anyone's virtue – far from it! – but having him there, and Kev, made it seem different somehow. Safer, somehow.

Without Mischa's presence, the air between Ariana and Wyndrel felt charged with energy, an erotic counterpart to the intense *aether* she'd experienced at the palace. She could barely stand to look at him, let alone allow her gaze to linger.

They stopped that night in a glen, where moss-covered rocks reared from the forest floor and the crowded branches above provided shelter from the rain. Ariana was nervous and clumsy, dropping things as she made the fire, spilling a cup of wine as they sat down to their simple meal.

"We'll be there tomorrow," he said, sitting on a rock with his cloak around him but the hood thrown back. "How are you at climbing?"

"Not very good, I'm afraid. Life in Gamelin didn't lend itself to that, and my mother was always disappointed in me that I lacked her skill."

"This mother of yours sounds more and more intriguing with every mention."

"You don't know the half of it, and would probably think less of me if you did."

"Oh?" At this, he arched a brow. "You've already confessed to me that she's elfkin. What else could there be?"

"Do you know aught of Thanis?"

"Some, that I learned in the war. Why?"

"Have you ever heard of the Nightsiders?"

The other brow joined the first. "The guild of criminals?"

"The very same. My grandfather was one, and my mother too. She leads the Black Dragons now, Gamelin's order of thieves and spies."

"And your father is an Archmage?"

"What can I say?" She lifted a shoulder in a half-shrug and laughed. "I come from an odd family."

"Easy to see why you're not betrothed, though."

"What?" Her laughter cut off. "Why . . . I . . . for your information, I'm well under the traditional age for such things, even if my parents believed in betrothals. What makes you say that, anyway?"

"I only meant that there must not be many men who'd dare marry you. Such indomitable will in an elfmaid is, well, daunting to many an Emerinian."

"That's the fault of the Emerin, not mine."

"I fully agree, and I meant no offense. Truce?"

"Truce. What of you, then? No betrothals? I'd have thought they arranged those things for princes when you were still in the cradle."

He shrugged. "For all I know, once I assume my crown, some highborn lord will turn up with an agreement signed by my father."

"Or you'll have every noble maiden in the Emerin beating at your door."

"Am I meant to be comforted by that?"

"I don't know how you could be. Myself, I'd be horrified. Mischa thinks I'm afraid of letting any man get too close, but –"

"You're afraid of us? Afraid of men?"

"No! Nothing like that. I . . . I just . . . cherish my freedom. I'm in no hurry to pledge myself to someone who will expect me to . . . well . . ."

"Behave properly?"

"Yes! To behave like a . . . like a *wife*. My parents are exceptional, you see, and I don't want to settle for anything less."

"Nor should you. Good night, Ariana." Within moments, he was asleep in the uncanny way that soldiers learned, ready to wake at the first sign of danger.

Against her will, Ariana smiled. "Sometimes," she whispered, "you're really not such a pain after all, Wyndrel Perras."

His eyes did not open but his lips moved in a whisper of his own. "I could say the same of you."

* * *

Even if Ariana had been as expert a climber as her mother was, it wouldn't have served her well against the mountain.

There was only one path, a little-used series of switchbacks and carved out handholds and ledges in the sheer stone, but they did not dare use that way. On the very morning that they were ready to begin their ascent, they saw two dark-cloaked figures moving, slowly and carefully, up it.

"Tiercel," Wyndrel said. "How fortuitous."

"Not fortuitious if they reach the top before us," Ariana said. "If we follow them they'll see us, and all they'd have to do would be drop boulders down on our heads. We'll have to find another way up, a more direct way."

She regretted those words, because Wyndrel took her at them. His idea of a more direct ascent was to scale the mountain by pure strength and tenacity. When she couldn't match his pace, he bound them together with ropes and hauled her from perch to perch.

"Oh, how I wish I'd learned to levitate," she panted at one point. "It was next on my list of spells to have my father teach me."

"I never learned it either," he said. "Quite a few warmages did, that they could float above the battlefield and unleash their spells, but I preferred to stay on the ground to meet with sword what I couldn't stop with magic."

"But you can slow your fall, can't you?"

"Since I was a child. That's one of the first they teach in Emerinian schools."

"Good." She looked down at the dizzying drop, chasms and cliffs and sheets of ice. "Good. But let's hope we don't put it to the test."

Soon they came to a place where a waterfall plunged down a smooth-sided vertical chute, cascading seemingly thousands of feet to a turbulent pool. A few stunted trees grew from the sides, their bark glistening with spray. If they fell too near that cataract, not even a spell of fall-slowing would do anything but delay the inevitable. In the end, they'd still land in the water and its force would batter them to pieces.

The precarious climb proved easier than it looked . . . which Ariana thought was good, because it had looked impossible. She crept from handhold to handhold, the rope swaying in a curve from her to Wyndrel, and tried not to look down at the seething, rushing water. Her world narrowed to the cliff face, the next hold, the next careful sliding of her foot.

Then she was above a wide, safe ledge without fully knowing how she'd gotten there. Wyndrel lifted her down, and it may have been only her imagination but it seemed he held her a moment longer than was needed to steady her balance.

"On the way back, assuming we live," she said, "may we use the path?"

"I think that's reasonable. Ready to go on?"

The next stage was at an easier angle, but the footing was more treacherous, a slope of all lava shards and sharp rock that cut through gloves and left their hands raw with tiny scratches. More than once, runnels of loose rock slid out from under their feet, tumbling over the edge toward the river. A single misstep, a slip, and they could follow suit.

They reached the top without incident and found themselves on a broad, shallow slope leading up to the mouth of an immense cave. Above their heads, the mountain soared toward its peak, where the snow seemed poised to come rumbling down in a cascade of white death.

Mischa had been right; there *was* a pile of bones. They were more picked-clean than charred. As the wind shifted, she smelled sulfur and leather and spice, and thought of Darkfire with a sudden stab of homesickness. This was similar to Darkfire's scent, but on a much greater scale, and this one was also redolent with blood.

"This must be it," Wyndrel said. "The lair of Racandros."

He untied the rope from their waists, stuffed it into his pack, and set his pack aside. Ariana did the same with hers, working her neck and shoulders to relieve them of the stiffness.

Only then did she pause to admire the land laid out around them. To the west, the whole of the Emerin spread like a green carpet. The afternoon sun sent amber rays through rents in the clouds. The tops of other mountains, none so high as this, rose here and there above the trees. To the south was the jagged range of the Dragonheights, and the dark forest of the *Morvalan*. To the east, above the sea, clouds piled upon one another and portended more rain and snow.

"Now what?" she asked.

"Now we wait."

As it turned out, they did not have to wait long. Before the sun touched the treetops, a figure, and then a second, appeared at the far side of the ledge. They proceeded toward the opening and had gotten halfway across the expanse when Wyndrel stepped forth, the brisk wind off the sea streaming his golden hair back from his temples.

"Tiercel."

He did not shout it, did not make the name an oath, but his voice was judgement and deadly promise, punctuated by the silvery noise of his sword leaving its sheath.

* * *

CHAPTER SEVENTEEN

The time is now, my rival, my foe.
– Elwyndas, *On the Field of the Fallen, Verse 11*

At last, Wyndrel stood face to face with his hated enemy.

The thought of this moment had sustained him through eight long years in his lonely prison, and Tiercel's expression of utter shock and disbelief, turning instantly to fury, was everything he could have wished.

Behind him was the *Rhunvala*, a tall slim figure in black. Having only heard of her from Ariana and Mischa, Wyndrel was briefly startled by her youth and prettiness, and the proud manner in which she held herself. She, too, was shocked at the sight of them.

Ariana came to Wyndrel's side, her sword out and her jaw set. He waved her back.

"No, Ari. This is my battle."

"What? You . . . no, oh no you don't!"

"It's how it's done." He pointed to Tiercel and cocked his thumb at himself. *You, and I,* that gesture said. *This is between us.*

Tiercel jerked his head in a curt nod.

"It's foolishness!" Ariana said stridently. "Men boasting and strutting like gamecocks . . . foolishness! You cannot approach this like a fair duel, Wyndrel. Not against a scheming, lying traitor such as Tiercel."

Ice-blue eyes became daggers at her, Tiercel's lip curling. "And I suppose the daughter of a thief and a murderer knows all there is to know of fairness."

"You," Wyndrel called to the black-armored woman. "*Rhunvala.* If you have honor, you will stand back and let us conduct this between ourselves."

Her nod was much more eloquent than Tiercel's.

"*She* might keep to it," Ariana said, "but he never will! Don't be a fool, Wyndrel!"

"You know nothing of me, and nothing of *proper* elves, you blood-tainted slut!" Tiercel said. "As for you, Wyndrel, I cannot begin to guess how you escaped and followed me here, but I see now that you'll never be the sort of king the Emerin needs. I'd hoped that captivity might give you time to think on what's best for this land and its people. Clearly, I was mistaken. Eight years didn't, eighty wouldn't. So I will do what I should have done before, and be rid of you."

"You are welcome to try," Wyndrel said. "But I am no longer the boy you imprisoned. I've learned much thanks to you, Sir Tiercel, though I doubt you'll find the lessons to your liking."

As if some unseen marshal had given a signal, they started toward one another. Tiercel bore two blades, one that Wyndrel recognized as Lionheart, a treasured weapon that must have been granted him by the Council. The other, the one Tiercel drew, was dark with a hilt of some rough crystal.

Wyndrel closed with him and a sudden and deafening sound – part screech, part wail, part ill-tuned instrument – filled the air. It rang in Wyndrel's ears, shook the very bones of his body, and sent rational thought flying into pieces.

Tiercel, seeing him flinch from the terrible sound, leaped and slashed. Wyndrel turned the blow and could not hear the clashing of metal, but saw his greater strength nearly jar the hilt from Tiercel's hand.

He thrust. Tiercel twisted. The tip of Wyndrel's sword sheared through chainmesh but did not bloody his foe. A return attack by Tiercel went one better, parting the leather of Wyndrel's vest and slicing his shoulder.

The sound, the unbearable, apocalyptic sound!

It was all he could do to keep his balance. Tiercel pressed the advantage, backing Wyndrel across the ledge. He grinned in cruel anticipation.

A ball of ice flew past Wyndrel and shattered on Tiercel's chest. He was thrown from his feet by the force of it, hailstones and freezing water exploding around him. The sword bounced across the stone, stilling its awful cry.

"Ariana, no!" Wyndrel roared, spinning to her in rage. She was at once defiant and contrite. He gave her a look that would have made a dwarven warrior step back.

Tiercel, sopping, rose up on his elbow. He had the bright sword Lionheart in his hand. He cocked back his arm and hurled it, point-first, like an unwieldy javelin. It sped uncannily straight and true.

Lionheart struck Ariana, scoring her truesteel corselet without piercing the metal but returning the favor she had done to Tiercel by flinging her off her feet. Except Tiercel's back had been toward the rising wall of the mountainside, and Ariana's was toward the edge.

A wordless, horrified cry burst from Wyndrel as she stumbled over the pile of their heedlessly-dropped belongings. Her feet tangled in his pack, the straps snaring her leg. She placed a foot for purchase on a stone that gave way, and fell, dragging the pack with her.

He had one last glimpse of her wide sapphire eyes. Then she was gone, gone without a single scream. Gone off the ledge, toward the swift and violent waterfall below. Lionheart clattered to the ground where she had been.

"I told you," Tiercel said, standing and retrieving his sword. "And she accused *me* of fighting unfairly. Shall we settle this now?"

Seething, Wyndrel turned to him. He wanted to rush in, swinging blindly and furiously, until there was nothing left of Tiercel but bloodstains and unidentifiable scraps littering the stone escarpment. But attacking in a rage would only be a quick way to get himself killed, and he did not intend to die. Not quite yet.

"You've wronged the Emerin, Tiercel Reyes," he said. "You've betrayed your people and your king. That can never be forgiven."

"I do not seek forgiveness for being the savior of my people," Tiercel said. "You still do not understand. Nor do they. But someday, some will. They'll thank me for what I've done. It might have seemed harsh, but it was necessary."

"Never seek to justify yourself to me." Wyndrel went at him.

Tiercel was caught off-guard by the sudden onslaught. He gave ground, parrying, his arms and shoulders jarred by the greater strength of Wyndrel's blows. Then he rallied with a speed and skill unrivaled by any in the Emerin.

The *Rhunvala* stood motionless, watching with a burning intensity as Wyndrel and Tiercel went back and forth before the dragon's lair exchanging slashes, thrusts, parries.

There was no more need for talk. No banter, no threats. Steel spoke for them now.

* * *

When Ariana fell, she instinctively called out. "*Shalis!*"

Pitiless gravity relented and she slowed in mid-air, still falling but at half her previous rate. For all the good it would do . . . she was directly over the waterfall, and all she did was delay the moment that the torrent would crush the life from her.

Wyndrel's pack, which had been caught on her leg, came loose. It was no longer affected by the spell once it ceased contact with her, and plunged away into the mist and shadow.

A stubby, twisted tree, gnarled and glistening black, leaned at a crazed angle from the underside of the ledge. Its very presence there told of the tenacity of living things to persevere in even the least likely of places. Ariana lunged for it, felt bark slick with spray, lost her hold, found it, and got an arm over it so that she hung by the crook of her elbow with her hands locked over her wrists.

She dangled there, feet swinging perilously close to the thundering falls. She could no longer anything from above, the noise of the water drowning out all else. Her arms already ached. The edge wasn't far above her head. A body-length, maybe a little more. Might as well have been ten times that. She couldn't climb up there, couldn't reach any sort of a hold. Only the tree prevented her from the deadly drop . . .

And the tree was bending. Slowly, almost imperceptibly, but bending under her weight. She could see granules of earth crumbling away where its roots sank into the cliff wall.

* * *

An appalling, maddening noise woke Racandros from his slumber. He opened his eyes and thought of a time, thousands of years before, when one of his clutch-mates had gotten her wing entangled in an iron-thorn bush. Her cries had been like that, burrowing and stabbing into him until he would have done anything, up to and including biting her throat out, to silence her.

He heaved himself up, coins and gems pattering from his scales. He heard voices as well, elven ones, and the clamor of combat. He smelled fresh-spilled blood.

Racandros lumbered to the entrance. He poked out his head on his long supple neck, and peered down. Two elves, both injured, neither surrendering. A third looked on. They were unaware of him.

Racandros thought of inhaling deeply through his fire-pouch and blasting the lot of them in cinders over the edge. He thought of snatching one up, the watcher perhaps, in a taloned forepaw and crunching through armor to the raw and juicy meat beneath.

But he'd only just roused and was logy from sleep, so he blinked his large eyes and ran his tongue over his dozens of teeth and observed the battle from the dark upper corner of the cave's mouth.

It went on and on, the two seeming evenly matched. The strikes they landed were insignificant, painful but not fatal.

And then it was over in an instant. One of the elves, cut with many wounds, feinted a thrust but delivered a deftly-aimed swing. The other took it across the thigh, the leg nearly severed, bone glinting through in the moment before a pumping flood of bright red concealed all.

The crippled elf fell sprawling, clutching at his leg, jaw clenched against the pain. His opponent stepped up, paused as if contemplating mercy. The fallen one snarled a hateful curse up into his face, and that decided it.

The bloodied sword flashed down. The elf thrashed. Racandros had seen deer thrash so when he toyed with them by impaling them on a single claw.

And then stillness. A last shuddering exhalation from the loser, and stillness.

* * *

Wyndrel Perras stood looking at Tiercel's body. He waited for the exultation, and felt only emptiness. There was no joy in this victory, none of the vindication he'd expected. He felt wretched and sick at heart.

This death had not brought his father back. It had not returned to him the eight years of freedom he'd lost. If it had saved the Emerin, he found it hard to care just then, for the Emerin seemed very far away.

He hurt. Every part of him hurt. He was cut in several places, bleeding. But worst of all was the terrible bitter grief, like bile in his throat.

Tiercel had, in his last breath, found some sort of peace. Wyndrel could see it in his face, which was serene, not anguished, not suffering. That look had come to him in the moment that Wyndrel's sword sank through his torso.

"In Thy might, in Thy mercy," came a murmur from his left.

He turned, raising his sword.

The *Rhunvala* was there, but she was not attacking him, not even looking at him. She knelt, touching her knuckles to her brow in a curious gesture of prayer over Tiercel. When she raised her head to Wyndrel, her amethyst eyes were filled with a sort of wary resignation.

"With Kaledhol is his spirit now," she said.

Wyndrel gritted his teeth. This wasn't at all how things were meant to end. Hot anger brimmed in him and he wanted to lash out at this woman who took her companion's death in such stride. He stalked to the edge of the stone outcrop, chewing his lip, fists curled so tight that they hurt. Below him, the waterfall churned and roared.

"Ariana! Ah, no . . . no . . . Ariana!"

"Wyndrel?"

A lancing chill, a prickling sensation, went through him when he heard the faint call, almost lost in the watery, rushing thunder. He threw himself flat and stuck his head over the edge.

She was there, dangling beneath him, clinging to a bent tree that poked like a crone's finger from the cliffside. Bare handspans from her feet, the river plummeted. She was soaked, silver hair pasted to her head and body.

He shot up again, whirled. The rope . . . the rope was . . .

The rope was in his pack and it had gone over with her. It was gone.

The tree jolted, tilted. Ariana bit back a scream and grappled with it. But she was sliding along the water-polished length, and the tree itself was tearing free of its rooted moorings.

"Hold on," he said, and swung his legs over.

"Wyndrel, no, don't, you'll fall."

"Hold on! I can reach you."

"It's too far."

He braced his toes against the sheer stone wall, supporting himself by one hand clamped on a laughably tiny ledge. He stretched, bent, extended his arm.

"Take my hand, Ariana."

"You cannot hold us both." She hadn't been near tears before but he saw that she was now, more afraid that she'd get both of them killed than she'd been of losing just her life. "Please, Wyndrel, climb back up."

"Not without you." He strained, so close. "Ari, reach for me."

"I won't take you down with me." She held fast to the tree, despite the creak and lean of it. "You can't die now. Not after you've won. The Emerin needs you. The Emerin needs its king."

He saw with sharp and fevered horror that she was about to let go. She would let herself fall rather than risk pulling him after her.

"But that king, Ari . . ." His voice broke. "That king needs a queen."

She stared at him, stunned.

"Take my hand, Ariana. Please, take my hand."

The tree tore loose. Ariana's arm thrust up. Their hands clasped. He pulled her up until her arms went around his neck. He encircled her waist and held her to him, their bodies pressed close.

"You unbelievable, magnificent, foolish man," she said. "And I must be just as foolish!"

"And just as magnificent." The fingers of his other hand were abraded and bleeding on the stone, and he knew she was right, he could not hold them here long. He could not get them back to safety.

"The both of thee, the Emerin needs," Kai Tilanne said from above them.

Wyndrel looked up. Kai Tilanne leaned over the edge, her hair framing her face in dark wings. She reached down with one black-gloved hand.

"You're a madwoman if you think –" he began.

"Trust her, Wyndrel," Ariana said. "She won't let us fall."

"Kaledhol, to Thy servant, Thy strength grant . . . *ha-nahia!*"

Light wreathed her arm and hand. Rose-light, wine-light, blood-light. She grasped Wyndrel's wrist, and he inhaled in shock at the power he felt humming through her. Then, she lifted. Lifted them straight up, drawing them up to the edge and then back over it and onto hard, bare stone.

Wyndrel closed his eyes, wrapping both arms tight around Ariana as they lay on the rocky slope. He could feel her shaking, or perhaps it was him shaking, perhaps both of them. It didn't matter. They were alive. He held her and did not want to let go, but at last he reluctantly did so.

They drew apart, got to their feet. Together, they looked at the *Rhunvala.*

Kai Tilanne faced them squarely, her back straight, her head high. She extended one hand. In it was a sparkle of green, the Emerald of Karria catching the last remnants of the daylight. It rested in her gloved palm, a jewel the size of an apple and as pure and beautiful as the soul of the Emerin itself.

Wyndrel took a step and reached out. He hesitated with his fingertips just over the gem, steeled himself, and touched it.

A warm verdant light blossomed in it and in him. He sighed and laughed and nearly wept at the same time. Taking the Emerald, he raised it before his eyes. He heard Ariana's joyful cry.

"The true king, thou art," Kai Tilanne said. "And thine by right the Emerald is."

"I used to hear tales in the palace when I was a boy," he said, hardly aware of what he was saying. "Rumors. Of how much my mother had loved my father, and how she wanted more than anything to give him that which he most desired. A child. Even if it was not of his blood. Even if it meant that she had to . . . look elsewhere. I never doubted his love for me, his pride in me. I was his son in all ways that mattered to him. Now I know . . . with no room for doubt . . ."

It came to him then that he was telling these things that he'd never thought he would reveal to anyone. He closed his hand around the Emerald.

"You took it from me," Ariana said to Tilanne. "Why do you give it up without a fight now?"

"Never my prize was it to keep," she said. "Far rather in the care of a king I'd see the Emerald than have it to the dragon go. An artifact of the gods it is, perhaps the only one that ever the Emerin shall see, and to the Emerin it belongs."

"Aren't you supposed to be an enemy of the Emerin?" Wyndrel asked.

"Grieve do I that the Emerin would think it so. Tiercel's friend, yes, that I was, but thy enemy, I am not. If of punishment thou dost deem my actions deserving, such punishment shall I with no quarrel accept."

"It seems that much of what we know of your people is untrue," he said. "If you're willing, Kai Tilanne, return to Perras Peliani with us. Come openly, as a friend. I would learn more of the southern forests, and our kinsfolk there."

"Such gladly shall I do," she said. "But first wouldst I Sir Tiercel an honorable burial give."

"Of course."

Tilanne walked away from them. His gaze following her, Wyndrel caught a shine of something high in the opening of the cave. Ariana, beside him, stiffened at the same instant as she saw it too. An enormous dragon peered down at them from the entrance to its lair. Yet surely if Racandros wished them ill, they would have known it by now. He offered a respectful half-bow, then turned away.

They stood in silence for a time, watching the *Rhunvala* as she knelt by Tiercel's body. Because it felt like an intrusion, they moved away, gave Kai Tilanne her privacy. Wyndrel felt no vindictive urge now that Tiercel was dead. He did not need to impale the body on a spike as a warning to anyone who would defy him, did not want to take some token or memento of their duel. He had satisfaction. He had the Emerald. He had, strange as it was to contemplate, a potential ally.

And then there was the matter of the woman next to him. The stubborn, headstrong, willful, outspoken, infuriating, breathtaking woman next to him.

"Ariana . . . what I said to you . . ."

"It was the desperation of the moment, Wyndrel. I won't hold it over you. I'm sure you were not serious."

"Never more so." He caught her by the shoulders and made her face him. "I meant what I said. If you'd have me, I would share my throne and my life with you. Be my queen, Ariana."

She ceased her initial effort to pull away. "Shouldn't your queen be a proper Emerinian lady, who'll flutter and coo, obey and agree?"

"I'll have the Council and a court of fawning nobles to agree with me," he said. "I need someone who won't be afraid to stand up to me, criticize and question my decisions, argue with me, and kick me in the backside when it's needed."

"Well, that much, I can do," she said, a smile forming.

"I cannot promise you complete freedom. Queens are bound by certain expectations, just as kings are. But I can give you my word that I'll never press you to act the proper Emerinian anything. I love you as you are, Ariana Mirida."

"This is madness, you know. We'll drive each other to drink, throw crockery, probably kill each other before the wedding day –"

"I take it that's an acceptance, then?"

She answered him with a kiss that said more than any words ever could.

* * *

Part Three:

The Council and the King

CHAPTER EIGHTEEN

We who craft what is to be are greatest above all.
– Elwyndas, Veriandor, Act V

Kysander Feyna, Archmage of the Emerin, lifted his glass and studied the swirling wine with a cool half-smile. "All is, at last, in readiness. When next the Council meets, they shall name you king."

Seated across from him, the firelight casting shadows on the planes and sunken valleys of his face, Alinor Elyvorrin was not so calm. "How can you be so sure of it? I am not well-loved by my fellow counts. The Fistrels most of all would like to bring an end to my plans."

"Most of the advisory members, including myself, obviously, give our firm support to you."

Elyvorrin brushed distractedly at a lock of his hair. It had thinned noticeably, its once-silky texture gone brittle and fine. Its hue had lightened toward white as well. His eyes had a look that the Archmage did not much care for. "The advisory members have no votes. They do just that, *advise*, and that only."

"How well I know it," Feyna said. "But that is what we have done. We have tendered our advice to the counts, and I am assured that enough of them will favor you to let you win the crown. And when you have, I do hope you'll remember all we've discussed."

"Yes, yes, I haven't forgotten." He drank of his wine without seeming to taste or savor it. "When this is done, will I have my daughter back?"

"Lionnen? That must be between you and her. I'd not stand in the way of such a reconciliation, if that is what you're wondering."

"And I must do something about my daughter-in-law as well. She has become overly close to Idelhar Fistrel. He knows she is promised to Sir Tiercel, he *knows* this! He would turn her against me for no other reason than spite. I should not have sent Tiercel away. Not now when I need him the most. You are sure I've enough of the other advisory members? Sure of it?"

"Even in his absence, Sir Tiercel is a great help in that," Feyna said. "The other knights admire him so that they are bound to follow his lead, whether he is here or not. They are fighting men, veterans of the war. Men who lost friends and brothers and sons . . . as you lost your son. Were any Fistrels risking their lives on the battlefield? I think not."

"No, they are *ambassadors*," Elyvorrin said with a sneer. "Slinking cowards of diplomacy rather than conflict. But that still leaves it closer than I'd like."

"You have Riachlain's full support as well. His loyalty to you is well known."

"Yessss." He drew out the word, savoring it as he hadn't bothered to savor the wine. "Riachlain. My first little vengeance."

"I beg your pardon?"

"I could not reach *him*, you see. So I struck at his foster-parents, the ones who'd been unwise enough to take in that orphaned Mirida brat. I struck subtly, of course. I gave no outward indication that we were any the less friends! Oh, no! And they were eager to believe that I held them blameless for Alinora's death."

"Are you speaking of Riachlain's precursor on the Council? Karadan, wasn't that the name? He died of a brain illness some decades back, as I recall."

"Brain illness, indeed!" Elyvorrin laughed. "It was despair, believe me. Brought on by his many misfortunes . . . misfortunes in which I had a hand. Elmilias Karadan was on the brink of impoverishment, heavily indebted, nearly destitute. I was so very concerned. So solicitous to his widow . . . we even had her to Celin's wedding!"

"It was on your counsel that Vessala Karadan sold her properties to Lian Riachlain," Feyna said, "and went to live with her kin in Thorise. I have friends there, and have seen her on occasion. She has aged beyond her years. Her spirit is broken with grief."

"Good." He said it savagely, his eyes a flash of emerald fire. "I would have them all suffer as I have suffered. Mirida most of all. My letter should arrive any day now. Would that I could see his face as he reads it . . ."

"Well." Feyna rose, setting aside his empty glass. "Be that as it may, we must first attend to matters here. As confident as I am of your chances, I plan to speak further with the other counts. If you will excuse me?"

Elyvorrin, those green eyes glittering, had been staring into the fire again with an unfocused and faraway look, as if seeing something else in the dying flames. As if, perhaps, seeing his rivals being slowly and agonizingly consumed to ash. He came back to himself with a start. "Yes, Archmage, of course. Good evening."

"Good evening, Count Elyvorrin."

A domestic appeared to show him out. Feyna turned up the collar of his robe against the chill as he left the house. In the fans of magelight from the streetlamps, flakes swirled like moths. He let the snow powder his dark hair and felt it flick against his cheeks and brow in a series of soft, cold kisses.

His carriage waited patiently, the hooded figure within not quite so patiently. She leaned over to open the door as he approached.

"I think you are making a mistake," she said before he had even settled himself into the cushioned seat. Beneath the hood, little of her face was visible but for a pointed chin and the glint of a golden lightning-bolt pendant on a chain around her neck.

"Just one, Zanyssa? I must be improving in your regard."

"Just one, but a great one. Elyvorrin is tottering on the very edge of insanity. You mean to see a man like that on the throne?"

"But, my dear niece, his madness fits neatly into my plans. He need only last long enough to put those new laws into effect. Should he then fall apart under the strain of the kingship? Well, what of it? With him unfit, and Celinar too young, there's none to rule as regent but our own sweet Lionnen. Who is beholden to me."

"And who is none too sane either." Zanyssa pushed back her hood from a cap of white-blond hair that did nothing to soften the sharpness of her features. "She is more a child than Celinar, afraid of her own shadow when it comes to anything other than high magics."

"I am well aware of her faults and her strengths. Do you know, my original intention was to wed her to your brother?"

Sparks snapped, an outward sign of her quite literal shock. "What? Zanderian destroyed the Gate at Cecres Keep and very nearly killed me! He's turned against us!"

"I said it was my original intention, before I knew any of that. Think of it. With Zanderian as her consort, our reluctant little queen could have handed over all the tedious matters of rulership to him, and kept on with her magic. I'd have the best of both worlds." He sighed. "Alas."

"So am I to kill Zanderian or not?"

"I'd prefer to have him alive, to bring him to the mind-mages and have them do it right this time. He is still my nephew. Still your brother. His current addled condition is not his fault. But if killing him is the only way, then no matter how we might regret it, it must be done."

Her pale eyes seemed heavy with the charge of the air before a storm. "And what of Lionnen? Since your plan is all fallen to pieces? You cannot still wed her to Zanderian. I suppose you could always marry her yourself."

Feyna laughed. "Oh, no. I have relations and political connections enough to find her some other suitable husband. Besides, I've had my share of wives."

"And your share of other men's wives if what I've heard is true," she added in a muttered undertone. Louder, she said, "So you don't wish to be king yourself?"

His smile felt as predatory as a wolf's. "Kings come and kings go. They are so very much in the public sight. No, Zanyssa. The kingship is not for me. It does not offer quite enough power, you see."

* * *

Idelhar Fistrel leaned across the table and took the hand of Faessia Elyvorrin. "You need not be so quiet. We can speak freely here."

She let his touch linger for a moment before pulling her hand away. "Should we meet in public like this? Mightn't we be seen? Mightn't we be overheard?"

The tavern was small, cozy, quaint and not bustling with customers. Still, it was a tavern, and people came and went. They passed beneath the leaded-glass window in the gentle snow, and there was nothing to prevent any of them from glancing up and seeing her. Several of them did glance up. Though Faessia recognized none of them, all it would take was one to carry word back to her father-in-law.

"In this place," Idelhar said, "we needn't worry. Can you not feel it, Faessia? Can you not feel how different it is here?"

"It feels . . . strange." She frowned. "And I know this will sound most peculiar indeed, Idelhar, but . . . I'm not even certain I know where we are. I've lived in Perras Peliani all my life and have never been here before. Never even seen this . . . what did you call it?"

"It's called the Crimson Court," he said, gesturing out the window. "For the brickwork, you see. Isn't it lovely?"

"I do not think I care for it," she said, not meaning to hurt his feelings but unable to keep from voicing the disquiet she'd felt ever since he brought her into this little neighborhood of close-crowded buildings that leaned together at odd angles around an irregularly-shaped brick courtyard. "It . . . it hardly seems Emerinian at all. As if we're *in* the city, but no longer truly *of* the city."

Idelhar did not give any sign of being hurt by her words. Rather, it was as if they pleased him in some obscure way. "So it does."

Wherever she looked, she saw secretive nooks and tilting gables and crooked lines. Much of it was red, that deep brick-red almost the shade of mourning, adding to her discomfiture. The rest was all slate-dark shingles, and white wooden trim done in knotwork designs rather than the softly flowing style to which she was accustomed.

She toyed with the utensils laid out before her and wondered what her father-in-law would say when she returned to the Elyvorrin mansion. He had already chastised her for her visits to the Fistrels, and although he'd not outright forbidden her from having anything further to do with Idelhar, she suspected it was only because he believed his disapproval should be warning enough and had thus not felt the need to state it baldly. Yet here she was.

Celinar, her son, had not been shy of his opinions. "His family and ours are rivals, Mother! By associating with a Fistrel, you show a lack of faith in Grandfather. He's to be king, you know."

The very thought – Alinor Elyvorrin as king – was enough to make her shudder.

"Are you cold?" Idelhar asked. He slipped the cape from his shoulders and made as if to offer it to her.

"No." She looked at him, and this time when he reached for her hand she did not pull away from his comforting touch. "I am frightened. Frightened of so many things, Idelhar. Of the count, and what he'll do. What would happen to the Emerin if he becomes king? Do the other counts not know what manner of man he is?"

"Not all of them trust Elyvorrin. Some say he has not been entirely right in the head since your mother-in-law's death."

"Since long before that," Faessia said. "Since Alinora."

"Well, yes. Perhaps so."

"First he was closeted away with Tiercel all the time," she said, twisting her napkin. "Plotting. Taking advantage of my son's affections . . . using Celinar and myself like pieces in a Towers game. Lately he's been closeted away with the Archmage as well."

"Yes, I know. And that troubles me most of all. Feyna is a man of ferocious ambitions and even more ferocious intelligence. That makes him as dangerous as a dozen Tiercels."

"I wish sometimes that I could take Celinar and flee far from here. But he would never go. He adores his grandfather now, strutting and preening in his squire's array, bragging to all who'll listen that the mighty Tiercel is to be his stepfather. I have lost my only son."

"If Elyvorrin becomes king, your son Celinar will be his heir.

"And love him though I do, Idelhar, I cannot in good conscience say that Celinar would make any better a king than would his grandfather. Least of all with Tiercel's guidance."

"Faessia, I do not like to frighten you even more –"

"Oh, please, Idelhar, do not!"

"But I must. I have known Tiercel long years. There was a time when he and my sister were sweethearts, and he and I were closer than brothers. But there is a darkness in him, a corruption in his soul."

"You cannot frighten me by telling me that which I already know," she said. Then she suddenly understood where Idelhar's thoughts were leading, and gasped, feeling the blood drain from her face. "Are you saying that Tiercel might . . . that he could . . . that if something happened to my son, that would leave Tiercel able to seize power?"

"It may. I'd not like to believe it could go so far, but I dare not underestimate him."

"I will not let it be so! I will never marry him. Without that, he has no claim over Celinar, whatever else might happen."

"And you still have had no word of Tiercel? Where he's gone? What he's doing?"

"Nothing," she said. "Not, mind you, that I object to his absence. May he never return! May his shrew of a sister spend her days planning his funeral rather than his wedding!"

"Would that I could be of more direct help," Idelhar said. "I could arrange for you and Celinar to go away, to start a new life in a new place . . . but I dare not move openly without knowing what the Archmage is up to. He is already, and with good reason, suspicious of my family. I wonder at his part in all of this. He and Elyvorrin were at odds before. Why now are they the closest of compatriots?"

"It's something to do with poor Lionnen, I think," Faessia said. "She and I, we are caught in this. Helpless. Trapped."

"You will not always be."

"If only I had your surety." She took a quavering breath, glanced out at the shadowed Crimson Court, and saw a woman whose skin and hair were white as snow and whose eyes glimmered like garnets. Beautiful, but in an uncanny and unearthly way. Beautiful and terrible. She looked away quickly.

She concentrated instead on Idelhar, his wise but youthful face, his ash-blond hair caught back in a loose ponytail, his eyes dark and steady as he watched her.

"What of Jennica?" Faessia asked.

"Jennica recovers nicely, but her memory is still dark in places. I think her time as a page-in-disguise has come to an end, since she is nearly a young lady now and not so readily garbed as a boy, but her usefulness is by no means over."

"And her friend, the Brindani boy? Has there been any news of him? Has he been found?"

"He is still missing. As is someone else. Does the name Ariana Mirida mean anything to you?"

"Of course it does," she said. "If there is one man in all the world that the count hates above all others, it is Arien Mirida. But I did not know he had a sister."

"A daughter. I have reason to believe that she came to the Emerin, and has not been seen since. Jennica thought she remembered hearing Elyvorrin and Tiercel discussing a captive, but cannot be sure."

"Woe to her if she's fallen into the count's hands," Faessia said. "I cannot begin to imagine what revenge he might wreak."

* * *

CHAPTER NINETEEN

I am content in what I do, for I am beholden only to my love.
– Elwyndas, The Swordmaid's Tale, Act I

As the sky darkened over Tradersport, a gong signaled the beginning of the evening's events at the Sand-Pits.

A swarm of youngsters, mostly boys but with a few scrappy girls among them, scurried along the tiers and walkways with tapers, lighting torches. Many unseen hands pulled in unison on a system of ropes, causing the canvas panels that had shaded the rows of seats to ripple on their pulleys as they retracted, rolled, and left the arena open to the cool dusk.

Sometimes, it seemed to Cat Sabledrake that half the populace of Gamelin could and did crush themselves into the ranks of benches, platforms, and private boxes. Few of the cheering multitudes realized how much careful work and preparation went into these events, how many thousands of people were needed to put on these blood-soaked, deadly shows night after night after night.

Cat knew. Not *all* of it, but as leader of the Black Dragons, she had to keep up on all of those things which had to do with gambling, violence, and information. The Sand-Pits was a thriving source of all three.

It put the dog races and dice-dens of the Lower Rings of Thanis to shame, she often thought with a wry, hidden smile. Then again, Thanis did not build its profits on the sweaty and whip-wealed backs of slaves.

The events were varied, most often pitting warriors against each other but sometimes turning wild animals loose on the sands, or flooding the arena to stage mock sea battles, or raising the dome of a wire net to create a sort of aviary in which deadly birds or wyverns provided the challenge. Sometimes trenches would be dug and filled with flaming oil, or snakes, or sharpened spears, to add an extra element of danger.

The scents of spices, meat, fruit juices, pastries, and potent brews wafted tantalizingly from every direction, overpowering the perfume and perspiration of the crowd. Vendors in colorful costumes squeezed through the press of people, hawking drinks and stuffed rolls and sugared nuts.

On summer days, the heat rose from the sand in visible waves, and the warriors could barely manage to walk across it despite heavy-soled sandals. Even now, in the milder winter, the evenings were balmy and pleasant. There was just enough coolness in the air to remind Cat that back in Thanis, the Bannerian Mountains would be laden with snow and the wind sweeping down from them could turn alleyways and rooftops slick with ice.

Tonight, anticipation and betting ran very high. The mightiest of the warriors – Great-Horn the Minotaur – was going to fight. Every seat was filled and the aisles were crammed.

Cat did not want to be here. She had grown up believing that combat should be a matter of life and death, something conducted as quickly and quitely as possible, attracting no attention. In dark alleyways, perhaps. Without a crowd of spectators screaming lethal encouragement.

But someone wanted to make sure that one way or another, this was Great-Horn's last fight. Her Black Dragons had gotten wind of the rumor only that afternoon. They did not know who was behind the plot. A rival slave owner? A disgruntled wagerer who wanted back in blood what he'd lost in silver?

So here was Cat, wearing a long, loose, concealing garment over her more customary attire of black leggings, close-fitting vest, low boots, swordbelt. Her people were spaced throughout the crowd, alert for trouble.

Great-Horn, when she had spoken to him before the match in hopes of getting him to postpone it, was unconcerned. "Let them try," he'd said in a rumbling chuckle. "Men try to kill me every day. At least this is variety."

He was nothing but corded muscle and leathery hide topped with brass-tipped horns. His hooves were shod in sharpened iron, and his teeth were filed to predator's points. He fought in a loincloth and brass greaves and vambraces, his only nods to armor.

Had he so desired, he could have won his freedom thrice over by now, but the Sand-Pits were his life. He had palatial quarters beneath the arena, where underground tunnels and chambers very nearly made up a city of their own. He had the finest of food, and anything else he might request.

Cat had even heard, though she tried not to think of such things, that he was often visited by wealthy Gamelinian women with a taste for the unusual.

A hundred trumpets voiced a fanfare. The crowd that had finally begun to settle into their seats came to their feet, roaring. Cat had to stand on a bench to see over the many heads.

Torches blazed on the walls of the arena, turning the sand to gold. A single spire, looking thin and spindly but in reality as thick through the middle as a grown man was tall, rose from the center of the oval arena. Spokes went around it in an ascending spiral to a round platform. An official in a tunic of red, black, and gold stripes stood atop this platform and raised a wooden cone to his mouth. Despite it, his voice was all but drowned out by the stamping feet and cheering din of the crowd.

Cat did not watch the arena floor, only catching the entrance of the trio of dwarves slated to be Great-Horn's opponents out of the corner of her eye as she scanned the sea of heads and waving arms. She noted several industrious pickpockets at work, not all of whom answered to her, and vowed to deal with that later.

There!

A vendor had ducked behind a group of large men, dock-workers by the look of them, who had choice spots near the rail. It was a woman, in a skirt and halter outfit so tiny it could have been a trick of the light. She unslung the strap of her tray from her neck, lifted out a thin wooden sheet of oilcloth packets, and withdrew something from a hollow space beneath. Too slim to be a crossbow, too short to be even a Plainsfolk hunting bow . . .

A wand? A mage's wand?

Biting back a curse, Cat threw off her overgarment and dashed for the aisle. A wand! Despite the tremendous pride most of the folk of Gamelin took in having an Archmage of their very own, hardly any of them had any real experience with magic. Or experience defending against it.

She saw other dark-clad figures converging on the same spot. No one else in the crowd seemed aware of the vendor, except for a few men who tore their attention away from the battle below long enough to admire her generous figure and overlook completely the fact that she had a wand in her hand and death in her eyes.

Cat slid past and through and around people, thinking that she should just scramble atop them and spring from one to the next like the animal for which she'd been named.

One of her best marksman had climbed a post for vantage, aiming a handheld crossbow at the woman. Even from a distance, Cat could see Aland's frustrated scowl and knew that he wasn't sure enough of his shot.

Cat weaved in and out, almost getting elbowed in the face by a plump, sweet-looking youth who was jumping up and down and yelling for blood. She dodged him. A knife flickered into her hand as if drawn by magic of her own.

The woman with the wand had pressed between two of the men, and they only too gladly made room for her. She leaned out over the rail, extended the wand toward Great-Horn.

"Cathlin! Cathlin!"

That urgent call pierced its way through to Cat just as she reached the rail. She identified the high, pure voice at once but couldn't credit what she heard. She looked back.

"Mother?"

Miralina Sabledrake had one slender white arm raised high, her golden hair and silken cloak billowing around her as she gestured. "Cathlin! You must come! At once!"

Startled – her mother *never* went to the Sand-Pits! – Cat almost forgot herself and her place and her purpose.

But the would-be killer was taking aim, none of the other Black Dragons were close enough, and if Aland fired, he risked hitting an innocent spectator. The Bastard Duke was willing to overlook much, but he could not turn a blind eye to an accidental murder.

So Cat turned away from her mother. She threw a leg over the rail, quested for a toehold on the lip of stone that supported the torch sconces, felt fire lick at her ankle, and then was balanced by toes and fingertips. Her left hand was cocked back to her ear, the knife glittering, glittering in the periphery of her vision.

The wand's tip was bright with white-blue energy. Below, oblivious on the sands, Great-Horn bellowed his battle cry.

Cat threw.

Her knife sped end over end and sheared through the supple length of wood. There was a blinding burst of white light. The woman shrieked and fell back, out of Cat's sight, with her hands clapped to her face. Chaos instantly erupted.

The men, the dockworkers who'd been standing at the rail, drew batons of ironwood that had been strapped to their lower legs. Cat belatedly realized they were accomplices of the woman and could have kicked herself for not seeing it sooner.

One of them stormed toward her, pushing people out of his way and flipping some over the rail. They fell, arms wheeling, crying out. Another man scooped up the woman and shoved toward the nearest exit. The third saw the Black Dragons all around and snarled in challenge, not about to go down peaceably.

"Cathlin!" Miralina called.

With the panicked people in the stands surging in all directions, Cat could not get back over the rail. She glanced down, dropped, landed on her feet with a puff of sand. The man who had been pursuing her paused. For a moment she thought he was coming after her, but he settled for hurling the baton – she leaped aside easily – and vanishing into the throng.

A hot gust of steamy breath hit the back of her neck. Cat whirled. A minotaur loomed over her. *Solarrin!* she thought.

But it was Great-Horn, of course, only Great-Horn, the groaning bodies of his opponents lying behind him and the spectators who'd gone over the rail gaping to see the champion right up close.

"So, you were right." His horns bobbed, winking flashes of torchlight, as he nodded. "My thanks, Dragonleader."

"My duty," she said, trying to quiet her galloping heart.

"Cathlin!" Miralina floated gracefully down. "You're needed at home."

"Mother, this isn't the best time."

"It's your Arien. Something's the matter with him. Please come, Cathlin. Please hurry."

* * *

Windclyffe Manor was one of many estates along the river, set back behind high iron fences and surrounded by gardens that flourished under Miralina's adept magical touch. It had been a place of light and love, but now, with Cat's father gone to his grave and the children away, it seemed hollow and empty and staffed by too many servants, who outnumbered the remaining family members five to one.

"It's nothing to do with Tal, is it?" Cat asked as she sprang down from her mother's coach and rushed toward the house. Her throat was tight with dread. "We sent him to Thanis for his safety, blast it, and if something's happened to him . . ."

"I do not know." Miralina kept pace with Cat, having grown up in the untamed forests of Lenais, where fleetness of foot was a skill to be prized. "A letter came. Bess took it, and told me that the messenger had gone first to the Tower, but finding Arien gone, brought it to the house. He was not here either."

"No, he was to meet with Duke Larind today," Cat said. "What was the letter?"

"I *never* pried into your father's secrets, nor will I pry into those of you or your husband," she replied with a sort of lofty propriety that would have sounded more at home on an Emerinian lady. "Bess left it for him on the entry-hall table. When he came in, I saw him gather it up among his other papers. He got only so far as the door to his study when he uttered a terrible cry, and dropped everything. I begged him to tell me what the matter was, but he only crushed and crumpled this letter in his hand and could not speak. I've never seen him look so stricken, Cathlin, not even when you lost the babe."

A pain almost twenty years old and not yet healed stung Cat's memory. She and Arien had returned triumphant from Thanis after a long and desperate quest to restore Talus Yor to his rightful place as Archmage and free the Northlands from the cruel grip of Solarrin. They had come to Tradersport that Arien might finally get to know the daughter whose existence had been a secret from him, and the three of them with Cat's approving parents had set about forming a true family of their own.

When Cat had discovered that she was with child again, their joy knew no bounds. But Ariana's birth eight years before had nearly been too much for her. She had miscarried, and knew that the midwives had been right. She was not made for childbearing. It was for the best, they told her, if she never became pregnant again.

Those tidings had hurt Arien far more than Cat herself. She had been raised with a father's devoted love and the extended clan of all the Nightsiders as well as Osnard and her mother's friends from the Golden Lion. But to Arien, who had been orphaned young and never knew his kin, the prospect of a large family had made up for the early years of loneliness. He might have wished for many children, but never at risk to Cat. There were spells to prevent conception, spells common to elven women that her mother taught her. They had their precious, precocious Ariana, and for the most part, it was enough. Yet every now and again, one or the other of them would turn wistful, imagining the sons or daughters that might have been.

Cat well remembered the night she believed to have been Tal's beginning. It had been one of the occasions when not one but both of them had given in to melancholy ponderings. Arien, holding her so warmly in his arms, had murmured into her hair what a joy it would be to have a son as like her as Ariana was like him, bringing a completion to their circle, a balance to their family.

Touched by emotions that were more tenderness than passion, they had made gentle love for long hours. And the next morning, somehow, she had just *known.*

Miralina's magic had confirmed it. While she did not know how her spell could have failed, she cautioned Cat that it might be best to take steps, not put herself in such danger. Cat had refused. Although the next year and a half were fraught with worry for them all, at the end along had come Tal. Small, but perfectly healthy, and a little bundle of mischief nigh from the day he was born.

If something had happened to him . . .

Just the thought of it made her pale and afraid. She could face down gangs of ruffians with nary a qualm. She routinely walked fearlessly into places where brave men hesitated to tread. She had taken on ancient curses, fought orcs and undead and evil elves beyond counting. But those risks were her own, to herself. Not to her children.

Bess was in the front hall, wringing the hem of her apron in her hands as she nervously watched the closed study door. She had collected and stacked Arien's papers back on the table. Her relief upon Cat's entrance was palpable.

"Oh, miss," Beth said. "He's locked himself in and will not answer me."

Cat brushed past her and rapped at the door. "Arien?"

No reply. She reached out with her mind along a link that had been accidentally formed long ago. *Darkfire?*

The drake's reply was muddled. *Cat? Cat, oh good, oh scales and fire, good, you've come. He's . . . Cat, he's drinking.*

Heady waves of blurriness played havoc with her senses, even as her eyes widened in shock. "Drinking?" she said aloud. "But he doesn't . . . Arien hardly ever . . . only wine, and then only rarely."

He is, I'm telling you, Darkfire said. Then, inside her mind, the drake broke into drunken song. It was a bawdy soldier's ballad that he must have picked up from Alphonse or Rayke in the days gone by.

Darkfire! She cut sharply through his singing before he reached the lewd chorus. *What's done this? Do you know?*

But the bond between mage and familiar was such that each experienced what the other felt, whether hunger or anger or the oblivion of drink. Darkfire's response was so slurred and senseless that Cat could make nothing of it. Which meant that Arien . . .

She could not believe it. This was not Arien.

He abhorred drunkenness, a reminder of days more than a century before when he had sought forgetfulness in the bottom of a wine bottle. Before the library, before he knew the truth of the curse that had killed Alinora. He'd vowed never to let himself return to that state, and in all the years she'd known him, she had never seen him take more than two glasses of wine at an occasion.

"I went through the keys, miss," Bess said, "but he keeps the only one to this door, doesn't want anyone in there tidying and disarranging his things."

"I'll see to it, Bess." Cat went to one knee, slipping a leather packet from her sleeve.

If anyone had ever told her she'd be picking the locks in her own home . . .

Her hands shook. She saw her mother looking at this unheard-of phenomenon with amazement, and even greater anxiety. Cat folded the offending hands together and took a deep breath, calming herself. When she felt she could, she went to work again.

As it clicked open, she made a little noise of disgust. "We need better locks in this house."

The door swung into the study and the strong smell of gnomish brandy came to her. It was his habit to keep a well-stocked supply for their guests but she had never seen him touch the more potent spirits. Never.

Her mouth was dry and her nerves were bowstring-tight. She could have done with a drop of something herself. But her primary concern was her husband.

He slouched in a chair by the fireplace, his head tipped against the wingback and his silver hair glinting with the red glow of the embers. His cloak was pooled around on the floor, for he hadn't even bothered to remove it.

"Arien?"

He stirred, and made a desolate sound. Cat closed the door and went to him.

Darkfire was splayed across Arien's lap on his back, feet curled close to his body, wings draped over Arien's legs, the supple lengths of his neck and tail making a cursive design. A square, faceted, brown glass bottle leaned against Arien's thigh, the stopper gone. No goblet . . . had he taken it straight from the bottle? Another first, for she'd never known him to do that in his life.

Cat knelt before him. His head was down, hair concealing his face. One hand clutched the arm of the chair as if he feared it might fly away from him, and the other was fisted around a letter of creamy parchment. She reached for it and he clenched his fist tighter.

"Arien, what is it?" She brought her hands to his face, brushing the hair away and lifting his chin so that he had to look at her. It took all Cat's fortitude not to recoil. His truesilver eyes were shadowed and red, and his color was ashen.

"Oh, Cat," he groaned.

"It isn't Tal," she said, willing it to be true. "We had a letter from Sybil only a little while ago and she said all was well. They were having a grand time, Tal and their little Jessa, making all sorts of trouble. He didn't even want to come home until after Wintersfest, even though everything is fine here now with George and his mother gone. Please tell me he's fine."

"Not Tal," he said, and exhaled. The fumes of brandy were enough to make her eyes water. "Isn't Tal . . . isn't him."

Arien opened his fist. The letter fell, landing on Darkfire. He turned over his hand to show her what else was contained therein.

The opal *ilgilean* caught the color of the fire in flecks and swirls. The ring, an onyx signet in the shape of a dragon, gleamed in the light. The sight struck her harder than any blow.

"Ariana?" Cat whispered, picking up the signet that she had received from her father and passed in turn to her daughter. "I told her to send it if she needed us."

"She did not send it." He swallowed, and a single hard but silent sob made him lurch in the chair. "*He* did. He has her, Cat. He has our daughter, our *tashti*. He means to make her pay for my crimes."

"Who? Who has her?" She was already filled with thoughts of knives and poison and rescue, a seething craving for action welling up in her.

He rolled his head until he was regarding the vaulted ceiling with those awful, haunted eyes. "The count. Alinora's father, Cat. Count Elyvorrin has our Ariana, and he wants his revenge."

* * *

CHAPTER TWENTY

So the warming fire burns, so the roasting chestnuts turn, so the songs from hearth and hall, so the gifts for one and all.
– Elwyndas, Wintersfest Eve (poem)

His grandfather was going to be king. That meant that someday *he* was going to be king. King of all the Emerin! The most important and most influential ruler in all the lands.

And he still didn't have anyone to talk to.

Celinar Elyvorrin roamed the empty house, sulking and ignoring the domestics.

Life had been so splendid there for a brief while. Oh, yes, well, Grandmother Donystria had died and that was terribly sad and all, but he had gotten over it the moment his grandfather announced that he, Celinar, would have a privilege that every youth in the Emerin dreamed of. He was to be squire to Sir Tiercel, hero of the war and the Emerin's greatest knight.

How he had enjoyed being fitted for his armor and new, adult clothing! He had even gotten his long hair shorn in the swordsman's style, the better to fit under a helmet. He had been so eagerly looking forward to the advent of his lessons that he could hardly sleep at night.

The lessons, when they began, were harder than he'd anticipated, leaving him sore and aching. But it was worth it, every bit of the pain, to win the slightest nod of approval from his idolized mentor. Best of all, Tiercel was not only to be his teacher, but his stepfather as well, and that would surely make him the envy of all the other youths in the Emerin.

His mother certainly failed to appreciate *her* good fortune, though. Weeping and wailing and carrying on as if to be the noble Tiercel's wife were some punishment instead of a great honor. It made Celinar quiver with awe to think that his younger siblings would be of the heroic Reyes blood.

But then Sir Tiercel had gone away, called off abruptly on some business of such importance that he didn't confide it even to his own squire. He had returned on the night of Celinar's belated birthday party, brought some grim news that led to the count flinging a brandy glass down among the revelers, and then was gone again.

Hah, but Celinar had laughed at that. The way they had run squeaking in all directions, like mice, as the glass came whirling down to shatter in their midst. It wasn't as if they'd been here for him anyway. All they wanted was to feast at Elyvorrin expense, and put in appearances. None of them liked him, and now they were all jealous into the bargain.

But to think that Sir Tiercel had been here, and left again without even pausing to greet him . . . that hurt. Celinar knew that Tiercel had many important things to attend to, and sometimes they were of such import that he couldn't spare the time for pleasantries. He knew that. But it failed to make him feel better.

Now here he was, with Wintersfest approaching. The house should have been filled with activity, family, visitors. Instead it stood silent but for the discreet footfalls of domestics. The decorations of gold ribbon, evergreen, red velvet, and silver bells went unappreciated.

During this season, they were usually out on the estate, enjoying County Shanlen's white-blanketed beauty. It was different being in the city for Wintersfest, strange. But he understood why they had to be. The Council would be making its decision any time now and all the key figures needed to be present.

His grandfather was ever shut away behind closed doors, sometimes with the Archmage or another of the Council members, more often alone, plotting and planning. His treacherous mother preferred the company of Idelhar Fistrel, nephew of their chief rival, to even that of her own son. His aunt had paid brief calls, but Aunt Lionnen was so bland and quiet as to be nearly invisible.

The household's most frequent guest lately was Tavalara Ilhedrion, sister of Sir Tiercel. Celinar did not see much commonality between them, except for the black hair and ice-blue eyes of the Reyes family. She was always turning up with new ideas for the wedding, and when Faessia was nowhere to be found and the count was busy, it fell to Celinar to entertain her and listen to her excited plans.

Tavalara had a son, but he was older than Celinar and had just completed his physician's training and celebrated his engagement to Liana Riachlain. There was a niece, too, but she was barely more than a baby. No kin of fit age to be Celinar's friend.

He thought bitterly of the birthday party and all the young nobles who'd attended. Pages and squires, maidens-in-waiting, mage apprentices. All of them well-born, raised in the same style as he had been. They should have been his friends but they resented him. Even if they didn't act like it, Celinar knew that they did. And acted as though they were his betters.

Kevan Brindani, for instance. He was only the third son of a count, not even close to any meaningful inheritance and laboring as a page to the palace stewards. What cause did he have to be boastful? Yet it was Kevan who'd caught the eye of a girl who Celinar had admired from afar, Meliara.

Celinar laughed spitefully, remembering how the rest of the night had gone. He'd been the one to find Meliara waiting for Kevan, who had promised to walk her home. She had been impatient, cross, and her feelings were hurt by him not turning up. Never one to waste an opportunity, Celinar had gallantly offered to take his place and strolled with her through the gardens and tree-lined streets. At the gate of her family's house, he had stolen a kiss and she had dimpled so prettily and blushed so demurely that he had, emboldened, stolen another before she, giggling, broke away and fled into the house.

He had gone home as if his feet walked on clouds rather than cobblestones, arriving to find some of the revelers still there – they had not even noticed the absence of the guest of honor, but he felt too fine to be irked. He had disdained them and gone to his room, and had been there when the violent noises came from his grandfather's study and he, along with half the Household, rushed to see what was the matter.

Such an embarrassment, Sir Tiercel blundering a spell. True, he was a swordsman first and no professional mage, but it pained Celinar to think of Tiercel being less than perfect in anything.

Even so, he had gotten many fabulous gifts and two kisses from the girl Kevan liked, so Celinar had been quite, quite pleased by his birthday celebration. Best of all was the rumor that something had happened to Kevan that night. He had returned to the Brindani house only briefly and then disappeared, claiming some errand, and had not been seen nor heard from since.

He decided then and there to pay a call on Meliara. Surely no one would object to an unannounced visit, not from the one who would someday be king of all the Emerin. They'd be glad to have him, glad. He didn't have to sit about and wait for them to come to him. That would happen in due course, once they finally, fully realized who they were dealing with.

Donning a fur-lined cloak, he chose a suitable bottle of wine from the cellars and set off on foot, through the snow, whistling a tune that made his breath frost in white wreaths around his head.

* * *

The Fistrel house was filled with music and light. Various cousins and kin had come from all over the city to join in the festivities, and all in attendance seemed to be having a delightful evening. Most truly were, but the more perceptive of them detected a forced merriment, a strain, on the part of their host and his immediate family.

Idelhar Fistrel waited until his guest, Faessia Elyvorrin, was engaged in a spirited song-game before surreptitiously absenting himself from the gathering. Her laughter was pleasing to hear as he took his leave by way of a door concealed behind a tapestry. Laughter and Faessia had been infrequent companions as of late.

He ascended a spiral flight of stairs to a hall lit at regular intervals by ever-burning candles that shed a cool blue light by which only mages' eyes could see. Many doors opened off of the hall, the last a sliding panel that gave onto a small, oddly-shaped nook of a room with a cupola roof of stained glass.

The room was almost bare of furnishings except for a round rug and a high curved bench with a cushioned seat. The bench sat facing a large and ornate mirror in a silver frame, worked into designs of shells and flowers. It reflected the room, but diffusely, so that Idelhar's image was a specter as he sat upon the bench.

His fingers brushed the glass. He breathed words of magic. From deep within the mirror a pale and shifting radiance appeared, and grew. It became briefly, dazzlingly bright and then subsided to reveal a woman's face.

"I have been waiting, Idelhar," she said. "You're late."

"You spend too much time among the humans, dear sister," he said. "You've become accustomed to their hasty habits."

Virine Fistrel, daughter of one of the oldest and noblest of Emerinian families, esteemed ambassador to the Northlands, wrinkled her nose at her brother. They had been born within only five years of each other and shared the same ash-blond hair, and were often mistaken for twins even by those who should have known better. Their father and uncle actually being twins lent itself to the perpetual misconception.

"When you are supposed to contact me at a specific hour and that hour is half gone, what else am I to think but that you're tardy? I expect you have some excuse."

"We've a houseful of guests, in case you'd forgotten."

"Ah," Virine said, nodding. "How goes it?"

"Not well," Idelhar said. "Matters are troublesome to say the least. Our uncle is fraught with tension, as is our father, and try though they may to hide it . . ."

She sighed. "Is it beyond all hope?"

"Barring some unforeseen boon, it may well be. I never thought this would happen. That Elyvorrin and the Archmage should ally against us . . . it's unnatural."

"Elyvorrin cannot abide the Archmage. That's what you always told me."

"It is what I always believed. The count made no secret of his enmity toward the High Mages when Lionnen joined their ranks. Yet now he and Feyna are seemingly the best of friends, and between them they've turned the opinions of most of the Council to support Elyvorrin's claim. We are in dire straits, Virine."

"Did Feyna . . ." She paused and licked her lips pensively. "You've oft suspected him of . . ."

"Can you not even bring yourself to say it? Forbidden magics. Oh, I can suspect until the moons collide and it doesn't amount to anything."

"Well, what ever is the good of this secret society of yours?" She bristled. "Wasn't your purpose to oppose Feyna, and find proof of his illegal goings-on?"

"Proof, that's the thorn of it. I know it's happening, just as I know that Father was manipulated by the Archmage Solarrin. But knowing something, and being able to prove it, are such very different things. As for our 'secret society,' as you put it . . ." He spread his hands in a gesture of futility. "The very secrecy that was to keep us safe, so that no one group should know enough about the others to endanger them in the event that some of us be found out, has worked against us. Most of the inner circle have died and those of us who remain do not know who we dare approach, or if there are traitors among us."

"So it has all been for nothing?"

"I would never say that. If nothing else, we still have the Crimson Court."

Virine shuddered. "That horrid place, Idelhar, honestly. I don't know what you see in it. Whenever I'm there I feel that nothing is as it seems, and that our world is but a thin barrier between us and some unfathomable reality. I prefer to know what's what, thank you."

"Faessia did not care for it either."

"You took *her* to the Crimson Court? Idelhar!"

"It would be of great benefit to us to have one of Elyvorrin's own on our side. The man is going to become king unless some miracle occurs, and since it seems we cannot stop him, the best we can hope for is to know something of his plans."

"So, to that end, you'll seduce Faessia."

"I've done no such thing," he replied indignantly. "And I'm surprised you'd think me capable of –"

"Pff, I know you too well, brother. Have you?"

"No. She yet mourns her husband, and let us not forget that she is betrothed."

Virine scowled. "I do not like this, Idelhar. Tiercel . . . he has changed so much since we were children. He cannot be trusted anymore. What happened to him? Was it the war? Did he have that taste of power and find it to his liking?"

"It began before that, I believe," Idelhar said. "You know he was never satisfied with the Emerin. He always wanted more, yet did not have any ideas as to what more there might be. That's why he would make so many journeys. Searching for his destiny."

"His destiny." She sneered. "I may not have the talent for spying that you do, dear brother, but I've found out a thing or two about our childhood playmate. Did you know he had a kinsman here in Thanis? A man of character so vile that he was even expelled from the Nightsiders?"

Idelhar chuckled sourly. "How bad must one be before the thieves cast you out?"

"If I'm correct, he assassinated the last Thanian king and sparked the fires of civil war that ended with the coming of the Four Heroes," Virine said. "Murdered a king for coin, Idelhar."

"That's ancient history as far as the humans are concerned."

"But not so long ago for us. His family has *Morvalan* ties and he has assassins for kin, and somehow he becomes the Emerin's most favored knight and general?" She shook her head. "It bodes ill. And when you tell me that he is sworn to the next king, a man none too rational himself, I fear for our land."

"You need not convince me. I am well aware, and share your foreboding. But there is little we can do. I have told Faessia she is not bound to obey the count's wishes but she is afraid to defy him. At least with Tiercel gone, I have the chance to meet with her."

"Where has he gone? That is another question that keeps me wakeful by nights. Where and why? What could be so important that he be absent at this pivotal moment?"

"I don't know," Idelhar said, hating the admission. "I'm certain that Brindani's son and Mirida's daughter are caught up in it somehow, but the pattern of it eludes me."

Virine sighed again and brushed hair from her temples with the backs of her hands. "All will come clear in the end, I'm sure."

"Yes, but by then it might be too late for the Emerin." He echoed her sigh. "How is Thanis?"

"Wet and dreary. The Highlord's palace is not a comfortable place in the winter. The wind comes in at every crack and crevice, and the stones seep with moisture. I would not leave my chambers until spring if it were possible, but my duties won't allow it."

"At least you have the Lord's Retreat. How is lovely Kyra?"

"She thrives. You must come and hear her sing soon. She is a marvel, and she has made the Lord's Retreat nearly as fair and welcoming a place as Perras Peliani itself. What of your young ward, Jen?"

"Jennica has given up dressing as a boy," Idelhar reported with a grin. "Her encroaching womanhood was making the costuming a challenge, and after her injury I felt it was safest to forego involving her. You should see her, Virine. It both gladdens me and fills me with sorrow to see Jennar and Danica so clearly in her."

"Wish her well for me, and give my love to our father and uncle."

"I shall. When will you come home?"

"If nothing else, I suppose I must come for the coronation."

"The coronation . . . ancestors help us," Idelhar said.

"The deed's not done yet. There might still be hope." She pressed her fingertips to her lips and then brought them to the glass, a thrown kiss flying over all the distance between Thanis and the

Emerin. "Be well, brother."

"And you, Virine. Merry Wintersfest."

The glass clouded and she was gone, leaving Idelhar alone in the small room. He sat for a while with his head down and his hands folded between his knees, lost in thought. At last, the faint sounds of the music penetrated his reverie and he rose, putting on a well-practiced smile as he returned to the guests.

* * *

The cottage was at the end of a winding lane, tucked in amid snow-covered trees with warm light shining in welcome from its windows. It could have been lifted complete from the pages of a children's storybook, the home of some benign and wise sorceress.

Vangier had no children of his own but many nieces and nephews, and was quite familiar with such stories. They hearkened back to older days when tales of the gods were still popular, and that wise sorceress of fable was always Livana Silvermoon, goddess of magic, taking elfly mortal guise to lend aid to those in need.

He went up the curving brick walk, which had been scrupulously cleared of slippery ice. The yard behind the tidy waist-high fence was dotted with white humps where flowerbushes slept, and bare trellises for climbing vines stood against the sides of the house.

On the stoop, ringing the bell, he smelled spices and sweet-butter. Wintersfest treats in the process of creation, scents that brought back strong memories of his own childhood.

The door opened, and the woman before him peered quizzically out as she wiped her hands on her apron. She could have passed for Livana, Vangier thought, at the end of the goddess' phase before she was reborn as a maiden. The thick cable of plaited white hair falling to the hem of her robe, the kindly silver eyes in a lined but still beautiful face . . . even the beaded circlet around her brow was a pattern of crescents and disks.

She looked at him as if she knew she'd seen him before but could not quite place him. Vangier inclined his head and introduced himself.

"The High Steward, yes, of course," she said. "I remember you now. Will you come in?"

"I apologize for disturbing you so late," he said.

Talian Maevarra's laugh was soft, musical. "The young have far more reason to seek their beds early than do the aged. Those of us who have such little time left prefer not to squander it in sleep."

Vangier followed her into the entry hall, shaking snow from his cloak and hanging it on a peg. "I shan't bother you long –"

But nothing would do and she would hear none of what he'd come to say until she had ushered him into the sitting room, provided him with a cup of hot kofa and a dish of jam-filled pastries, and gone off into the back rooms of the house to inform her husband that they had a visitor. Moments later, the former High Physician Folistran came in, moving with assurance despite his blind eyes through the familiar arrangement of furniture.

Until meeting Folistran, Vangier had believed King Shaelan to be the oldest elf he had ever or would ever meet. A full twelve centuries had marked the span of Shaelan's life. Yet the man now settling into a chair across from him was even older than that. He had been a contemporary of Shaelan's father Traehormic, and healer to the king, his queen, and their infant son.

Talian returned with kofa for her husband and herself. "Do you take sugar, High Steward?"

"No, thank you." He sipped, and chewed at a pastry despite the fact that his appetite had been scant as of late. "These are quite good."

"You're generous to say so. I've never been much of a cook," Talian said.

"My wife judges herself too harshly," Folistran said.

They chatted for a while of inconsequential things – the first snowfall, the holiday season, the anniversary festival of Elwyndas that would be taking place in a few short years. At last, putting down his empty cup, Vangier cleared his throat.

"Lady Talian, I have a few questions for you, if you'll indulge me."

She paused with her cup halfway to her lips, surprised. "Oh? I thought you'd come to speak with my husband. How could I be of help to you, High Steward?"

"It concerns a young woman who paid a visit to the palace recently. I heard, through one of the pages, that she was known to you. Is that so?"

"Ariana Mirida. My great-great-niece, give or take a generation. You graciously installed her in the Waterfall Terrace, and I met with her there. Has she returned?"

"You knew that she'd left?"

"Why, yes . . . didn't you?"

"No," Vangier said. "She'd told me that she wished to speak with the Council, but had gone before that could be arranged. I did not inquire as to her purpose."

"She wished to petition to have her father's name cleared of unjust charges, and regain control of the family lands," Talian said. "But I fear she lacked the patience for any sort of delay, and meant to find some more immediate way of capturing the Council's attention that they might hear her out."

"And her father, your nephew –"

"Arien, yes. Grandson of my brother, or something to that effect."

"He is the Archmage of Gamelin?"

"So Ariana tells me. I'm pleased he has done so well for himself, and overjoyed that he has finally found love and happiness and family." She touched Folistran's hand and smiled. "And made it possible that I might do the same."

"Lady Talian, I am troubled," Vangier said. "I delivered her request to an advisory member of the Council, and was assured that he would bring it to the attention of the others. Yet, having made discreet inquiries, I now know that he never did bring it to their attention at all. Indeed, he absented himself shortly thereafter and has not been seen since. Now, the page your niece befriended has gone missing as well. Anything you know of this, anything that would ease my mind, would be of great help."

"I would gladly ease your mind if I could, High Steward," Talian said, her brows knitted with worry. "Yet I fear that this news has only served to upset the serenity of my own. Ariana's quest should not have taken her this long. I would have expected her back by now and causing an uproar among the Council. I hadn't realized it's been so long."

"What did she mean to do?"

"We Miridas never do anything the simple way. Her intent was to bring the very Emerald of Karria and present it to the Council, that it might choose them a king and put an end to all the debates and arguments. Then, with that out of the way, she hoped to put her petition before them."

Vangier would have fallen had he not been seated. "The Emerald of Karria? But . . ." The words *only a swordmaid* made it to the tip of his tongue and he swallowed them back, remembering the tall and graceful woman who'd been clad in Silversilk with a sword at her hip.

"She should have been back by now if she was successful," Talian said. "Who was this member of the Council? Would he have gone with her to aid her, or gone after her to stop her?"

"It was Tiercel Reyes," Vangier said absently, picking up his cup and finding it empty. "Of the Order of the Lion."

"Ah, his nephew is a physician, you know," Folistran said in a casual, society-chatter tone of voice. "I spoke at his class's graduation. Apt surgeon, I've heard. Talented lad. He'll go far, I think."

"Tiercel Reyes is sworn to Count Elyvorrin, is he not?" Talian asked.

"He is, but why . . . ?" Vangier gasped, rumors swimming through his mind. "Ah . . . Mirida . . . Elyvorrin's daughter . . . but surely all that is unfounded suspicion. Sir Tiercel is the finest young knight in all the Emerin. He would do no harm to her. Surely not."

"Can you be certain, High Steward?"

"I . . . I should like to say so."

But he remembered how Tiercel had looked when Vangier told him about Ariana Mirida. A strange, cold light had come into the knight's eyes, and there had been something in his smile that Lishalla had later commented on. *He hardly looks handsome at all when he's like that*, the domestic had said. *If he ever smiled at me that way, I believe I'd faint from fear.*

"I see now why you're troubled, High Steward," Talian said quietly. "For I share that feeling. Something has gone amiss with my niece's quest, and I cannot help but think that this knight of yours had some hand in it. You say the boy is missing as well?"

"Kevan, third son of Count Brindani, yes. He informed me that he was needed at home, told his family his duties would keep him at the palace, and promptly vanished. By the time his father and I realized that neither knew where he was, he could not be found. Not even by seeker-spells. He may be too far from the city, or shielded somehow, or –"

"Are there places where seeker-spells cannot reach?" she asked, avoiding that final "or" with its dire implications. "I've heard that the palace dungeons are impermeable to magic."

"Some of them are, yes," Vangier said, startled. "I hadn't thought of that."

"Your page seemed smitten with my niece," Talian said. "If she made enemies, he might have been willing to risk all to help her, and ended up sharing her peril. Perhaps there are those on the Council who would not want the Emerald to be found, and if they learned of her quest, might wish to stop her."

"They could have been sealed away in the dungeons all this while?" Vangier shook his head. "Hideous as it is, that would explain much. I will investigate at once, Lady Talian. Thank you."

"Thank *you*, High Steward, for taking an interest. If you learn anything of my niece, please inform me."

He rose and bowed to them both. "I shall, I swear it."

* * *

Chapter Twenty-One

Let nothing stand between us when my child is in need.
– Elwyndas, The Queen's Lament, Act VII

Arien Mirida woke wondering how in the world he'd gotten out to sea, and in such terrible weather. The cabin rocked from side to side, and rose and fell on enormous swells, and he could hear the echoing rhythmic boom of waves beating against the hull.

He opened his eyes and saw his own familiar bedroom ceiling. The posts of the bed he shared with Cat were hung with swaths of forest-green cloth, the matching drapes were drawn over the windows, and the room was all cool verdant shadow.

Not rocking. Not rising and falling. Not a ship at all, and the booming that he heard was the sound of his own pulse. It was his head that put him in such misery. A feeling all too familiar, though one he'd thought was long forgotten and never to be endured again. His mouth was caked with sourness, his stomach churned.

A tentative mental query brought no response except for a sickening swoop of his consciousness. Darkfire was there, but not there. In a place deeper than sleep. Arien had put him there. Had put them both there, with the help of gnomish brandy.

It had been wine in the old days, not the fine elven stuff to which he'd once been accustomed but whatever sour pressings and fermentings he could afford. After enough of it, he'd no longer known, nor cared, what he was drinking.

On those occasions, though, he had most often wakened to find himself on some tavern floor, or in a cramped Thanian alleyway. Very rarely, he'd have managed to stagger back to the dismal room he'd let at a Sixth Ring boardinghouse. He had never, in those days, revived in a setting such as this.

And he'd been cared for, too, he realized. He had been undressed and put to bed, and there was a tray on the side table holding a silver spoon, a glass of water and a folded paper packet tied with twine.

He sat up – this made his head dip and weave again – and plucked at the string with a child's intent concentration and finally undid it. The packet contained one of Miralina's herbal remedies, some Lenaisian medicine that smelled of white flowers picked in high mountain meadows.

Arien dumped the powdered herbs into the water and stirred, then drained the glass. His body woke up and cried out, parched and hungry. He summoned his wits and cast a spell, re-filling the glass with water more pure than anything that could be drawn from even the freshest of wells.

Miralina's handiwork began to take effect. It occurred to him that he didn't know whether she had learned that remedy as part of her healing magics, or whether it had been something she'd acquired during her years as a barmaid. Either way, it steadied him and made him feel less like he was about to collapse or be ill.

As he drank more water, feeling the liquid spread through him as if being absorbed into his every fiber, he wondered what had driven him to break a century-old vow. The fact that he had done this boggled Arien's mind. After all that he'd been through, to have fallen so hard and without warning was unthinkable. He had come through other trials and never resorted to this. When he had lost his magic, he had contemplated suicide but never once yearned for a drink. When he believed that his beloved Cat despised him, it had been agony and yet he had remained untempted.

He had been under great strain lately, yes, with the duke of Gamelin wasting away from an incurable disease before his very eyes, his suffering unable to be eased by sorcery or by the gifts of the priests. And then there had been that vile business with George, and the death of the duke, and the ascension of Larind . . . Larind the Bastard, whose manners were rough and who needed constant instruction in all that was to be expected of him for all his heart and his intentions were the best.

But surely all those things, while difficult, were not nearly enough to send him to . . .

The answer came to him like a slap. The glass fell from his nerveless fingers.

Ariana!

The full horror of it broke on him in a wave. Had he been standing, he would have been sent reeling back down.

Ariana. Count Elyvorrin. The letter.

That letter . . . recognizing the seal upon it had sent an icy blade slipping deep into him, and reading the words so carefully inscribed had turned the core of him to a howling frozen wasteland. He had given no thought or debate to his next actions, just went for the brandy as if it were the only possible decision in all the world.

He could hear voices from beyond the door that connected the bedroom to the private sitting room where he and Cat often spent pleasant evenings. Although the thick door prevented him from making out the words, he knew the speakers. Cat and her mother. Arguing? Could they be arguing?

Arien went to the wardrobe and dressed in the first clothes that came to hand. Loose trousers, a silken shirt, slippers, a robe. He opened the door and stopped short at what he saw. Cat was stuffing items into a pack. For one wild, appalling moment he feared that his drunken lapse had led her to leave him, and the bottom fell out of his soul. Then he saw more clearly, saw the Silversilk she wore beneath her dark and functional garb, saw the hilts of knives peeking from her boots, saw the swordbelt cinching her slim waist.

The letter, the hateful and smug letter with its so-obvious threat, which he dimly rememberd crumpling into his fist, had been smoothed. It was on the table. Miralina stood near it, and was in the midst of telling Cat that it was folly to go, folly, when the door opened and they both looked around at Arien.

So much needed to be said, and he did not know where to begin.

"Arien." Cat spoke first, and set down her pack and came to him. Not angrily, and with gentle understanding in her nightblue eyes. Worry lived there too, and the line of determination he had seen so many times before made a little crease between her brows.

She put her arms around him and he held her, buried his face in the warm tousle of her dark hair.

"Cat, oh my dearest Cat, what have I done? This is my fault, all of it."

"Stop, Arien, don't blame yourself."

"How can I not? All this time, I've known that my deeds cannot have gone unnoticed. I should have gone back myself, and seen to these things years ago. I did not. Instead, I let Ariana go, and now look what's happened."

"You warned her."

"I did, but she . . ." He set her apart from him and shook his head. "Cat, you know how she is. She listened but did not *hear*, did not believe. My saying how things are in the Emerin can never prepare someone for the actuality of it. She has only seen the petty conniving of Gamelin's court. Those of the Emerin have had hundreds of years to perfect the art."

"He will not have harmed her yet," Miralina said. "By the tone of that letter, Arien, he expects you to come to him. It is upon you he truly wishes to visit his revenge. It is you he wants to see dead."

"Yes," Arien said. "He will kill me if he can. But he will kill Ariana first, that I might watch her die."

"No," Cat said. "I'm going to go bring her back."

"Cat, no, you cannot go to the Emerin," Arien said, horrified anew.

"That is what I have been telling her," Miralina said. "That land, for all its marvels, is nothing like Lenais. They will not welcome her there."

"I don't care if they welcome me. I'm not going openly. I've been there before, Arien, if you recall, and no one was the wiser."

"If I recall? I shall never forget." He shivered as he also remembered Count Elyvorrin. That had been the last time Arien had seen him. Seen him twice, through old and young pairs of eyes, thanks to the peculiarities of time. It had been in the chamber where Alinora lay wrapped in rosecloth.

Thinking of that spell now made him blanch. He had considered himself so learned, so sure that all magic was useful and helpful and safe. Now he knew better. Now he knew that time-magic was so rare as to be unheard of, all but impossible. Only one mage had ever perfected it, and died leaving behind only a few spell-scrolls.

"How long has he had her?" Cat asked. "The letter says something about a season of the hunter, what does that mean, Arien?"

Releasing a trembling breath, glad to have a question he could answer, Arien combed his fingers through the snarls of his hair. "The Emerinian calendar is reckoned differently from that of the Northlands, although some terms – months, weeks – have made their way into the vernacular. In fact, the Northlands calendar itself bears little resemblance to the way it was originally. It began as a true lunar calendar, Lestran reckoning, they called it. But when the faith of Lestra was overthrown, the Galatinites established the seven-day weeks and four-week months that went into common usage. It's really quite odd, the matter of Lestra. If you go to the Plaza of the Gods –"

"Arien!" Cat nearly shouted. "Now is not the time for a lecture on comparative reckoning!

How long?"

"In the Emerin, the year is marked four major constellations, each corresponding to one of the four elven gods. Astronomers, in the service of the crown, watch the skies to determine when each new season begins, and each is approximately eighty-four days long, until the next constellation takes prominence."

"The Hunter is Denethel," Miralina said.

Cat frowned. "Aren't there supposed to be five elven gods?"

"No one but the *Morvalan* take heed of the last," Arien said. "The Season of the Hunter is autumn, followed by the Season of the Sorceress – Livana. The count's letter is dated . . . what?"

Miralina read from it. "The thirty-sixth day in the Season of the Hunter, 7904 . . . S.F.E. ?"

"Since the Founding of the Emerin." Distracted, he ran his hands through his hair again. "Which means he wrote it not quite mid-autumn, and it is well into winter now."

Cat looked stricken. "So long!"

"I suspect that was his very purpose," Arien said. "There are far quicker ways to send a message, but he chose this one. Knowing that we would tally the days and think with dread of how she must have fared in his keeping."

"What are you saying?" Miralina asked, her fair face distraught. "What would this man, this madman, do to her? Does the Emerin not pride itself on being the most civilized of realms? Surely there would not be torture!"

"It is no good to dwell on such things," Cat said. Her knuckles were pressed hard to her forehead as if to push out the thoughts. "What matters is how quickly I can get there. I'll ride to Unity, then Treaty Rock, and skirt the edges of Keyda until I reach the forest –"

"Cathlin, please be sensible," her mother begged. "I have heard of the elven city. It is vast and great. Its dungeons and prisons will be defended by magic that you will not be able to pass. You won't even know where they're keeping her, and this count hardly sounds the sort you can threaten at sword's point."

"Magic or not, there's no dungeon made that can defeat a Sabledrake," Cat said.

"No, Cat," Arien said, settling his hand on her shoulder. His head had fully cleared now, the brandy something that might have been in a dream. "I will go. The Emerin is my birthplace and I know its ways although I've been away for most of my life. The charges against Ariana are ones that I'm meant to answer. I'll not allow her to be punished for what I've done. It is long past time that I settle the matter of Alinora, in the eyes of the Council and the law. I should have done it long before. I hid from my responsibility. That is over now."

"What do you plan to do?" she asked. "Go forthrightly to Count Elyvorrin and expect him to treat fairly with you? He blames you for Alinora's death but you did not murder her, Arien."

"If surrendering myself to Elyvorrin will save our daughter, then so be it."

"I refuse to surrender either of you." Cat's eyes flashed like lightning. "Not my husband, and not my daughter."

"Stop!" Miralina's voice was a whipcrack of command unlike her usual temperate tone, startling them both into silence. "Now you've come around to fighting over which of you should go? There are other means, by Denethel's bow. You have friends in Thanis and the Highlord owes you much. Go to him! Speak to the ambassador from the elvenwood. This does not have to be settled by subterfuge or sacrifice or violence."

"We can't wait on diplomacy," Cat said.

"I do not intend to sacrifice myself," Arien said. "But neither do I intend to simply whisk Ariana from under the count's nose. I want this entire matter over between us, so that he may never again strike out at our family."

"And if he tries to kill you himself?" Cat asked. "Or have you killed?"

"I'm able to take care of myself, my love. And I can be to the Emerin in the blink of an eye."

She hissed in breath between her teeth. "You can, can't you? Even though it's so far, and you've been away so long?"

"Things change slowly in Perras Peliani. I'm confident that I can find my way to someplace familiar enough to me."

"All right, then. When do we leave?"

"Cat . . ."

"I am going with you. I don't care what they think of the likes of me in the Emerin. I don't care if they throw daggers or rotten fruit or vile names; I've heard them all. You will not leave me behind."

"I could," he said.

"I would not be able to forgive that."

He had never heard such coolness in her voice, not directed at him, and he wished he could have taken back those ill-considered words. Looking at her, he saw that she truly did mean to go to the Emerin, one way or another.

"I cannot believe this," Miralina broke in. "Here you stand, bickering over which of you goes when neither of you should! You have a son to think of as well, need I remind you? What will become of Tal, whom you've already sent away, if you both go off to the Emerin and never return?"

"Then we'd ask only that you look after him," Cat said. "Mother, *Vali*, we have to do this. Tal would want us to." She touched Miralina's hand. "When I was little and you were stolen away, Da wanted to go after you then and there, but he couldn't leave me alone. When I was older and able to fend for myself, he went and I was left behind. This time, it's my daughter who's gone, and I will not be left behind again."

"No, you won't," Arien said. "Cat, I am sorry. Of course we will do this together. You and I. We will go, and we will find her, and we will bring her safely home."

"And what am I to do?" Miralina cried. "Sit and wait and hope for some word?"

"Write to Sybil –" Cat gasped. "Sybil! Her oldest boy went with Ari . . . what's become of him? There was no mention of Mischa in the count's letter. We'll have to find him, too. But as I was saying, Mother, write to Sybil. Tell her what has happened. Maybe she'll want to send Tal back, or invite you to join them. But we won't be gone long. One way or another, this will be over soon."

She only looked at the both of them for a bleak, endless moment. It occurred to Arien that his mother-in-law was younger than himself, yet somehow he had never thought of her as an elfmaid of his own generation. She was already widowed, already a grandmother.

Thinking of that made him think of the Chastain lad, Gavin, the elder twin. Who loved Ariana and would have wed her, if she had accepted his suit. Arien knew he had but to ask and both twins would be armored and ready to ride.

If need be, he supposed he could have amassed quite a force, drawing on the favor of the new duke and the friendship Ariana had with the wife of Lord Falconhurst – the lord in a most generous and expansive mood since he now had a fine sturdy son in addition to his many daughters.

But they could not start a war. The Northlands could not bear it. Keyda was in ruins. Relations between the races were shaky at best. It would hardly do to break the Treaty of Jeline or take advantage of Larind's good will. Or the Highlord's. Or even that of Talus Yor. This was a private matter, a personal matter.

Miralina, clearly still doubtful, left the sitting room and closed the door so that Cat and Arien were alone. His wife, so small but so vibrant, regarded him steadily. She had lived half a century and still seemed so very much to be the selfsame girl who'd saved his life one Thanian night, forever shattering his comfortable routine and wakening him to a world so much the better because it included her.

"I should know better than to attempt to dictate what you will and will not do," he said. "One would think that after so many years I would have learned."

"One would," she said, with a smile that soon faded. "We must find her, Arien."

"We shall."

"How soon can we leave?"

He sighed and looked around at the mess she'd made of weapons and other belongings. "I'll need to gather my things. We cannot take much, for we'll have no horses to bear the burdens. But do, Cat, in addition to your . . . working garb, include some finery fit to wear before the Council."

She gaped at him. "I can't go before the Council, not me, an elfkin."

"It may be necessary." He cupped her face in his hands and ran his thumbs over her high cheekbones. "I am done with the lies, Cat. All of them, those spoken and those left unspoken. I am not ashamed of you, lovely and vital wife of mine. Let all the Emerin see you and know how very wrong they've been."

"If you're certain . . ." she said.

"Never more so." He kissed her. "Now, let us see to the packing."

* * *

Chapter Twenty-Two

I was lost in the darkness and I called to you, but you did not hear.
– Elwyndas, The Tragedy of Cessaria, Act II

The deep red magelights turned the palace walls to blood. Vangier swallowed through a throat gone dry as he paused before the gates.

Absurdity. Why should he feel hesitant? This was his home. He and his family had served the royal Household for generations, and their quarters in the Stewards' Wing were as much their own as any manor or cottage in the city. He had passed through these gates countless times on business both his own and the crown's, since his long-ago youth when he had begun service as a page.

Yet somehow, now, in the night and lit by that sanguineous glow, the palace had an air of foreboding and danger.

Nonsense. It was his errand that gave him these qualms, nothing more.

Reminding himself that as Lord High Steward, he had permission to tread anywhere he liked, he squared his shoulders and made for the gates.

The sentries stirred at his approach, surprised to see him so late. Vangier knew them both, had known them since they were boys. There was no reason to be apprehensive of them, no reason to think that their eyes could see into him, could see down to where dark suspicions now dwelt in his heart.

"Good evening, Lord High Steward," one said, stepping from the shadow of a stone ledge overhang.

Vangier nodded, not trusting himself to speak for fear of a guilty quaver in his voice.

"Winter is surely upon us," the guard remarked, huddling into his cloak and peering up at the whirling snowflakes.

The conversation – though such a one-sided thing could not properly be called by that name – seemed to Vangier some tactic of delay. He knew better. He knew it was nothing more than the habitual boredom of the night-watch. They had only each other's company most nights, and a different face was a welcome distraction. There was nothing sinister in the young elf's overtures.

In fact . . . it was the other one who more disturbed Vangier. He had said nothing, the second guard, only looked on with gleaming eyes from beneath the fur-trimmed edge of his hood. A white line of scar marked one cheekbone, and Vangier suddenly remembered that many of those who had chosen to keep such mementos of the war had been under the command of Tiercel Reyes. They had somehow come to consider such scars badges of honor, and disdained the help of shaper-mages.

Ilarion, the talkative one, faltered as he became aware than he was the only one speaking. He offered an abashed grin. "Far too cold a night to stand about when you've places to be, Lord High Steward. My apologies."

"Think nothing of it," Vangier said, his skin wanting to creep from the way the other guard – Denilar, his name was – watched him so avidly, so silently.

"I shouldn't keep you." Ilarion went to the gate and it swung obediently open. He stood aside to let the steward pass.

Feeling oddly relieved, as if he'd made some narrow escape, Vangier entered the palace grounds. The gardens were hushed and still in the snow. A faint twinkle illuminated the crystal dome over the Chamber of the Skies, shed by the sparkling leaves of the *valn* tree that grew within the meeting-place of the Council.

Very few windows were lit but he wondered how many slept in the palace tonight. How many were wakeful in the dark? Everyone knew that they were close to having a new king, and that prospect was not as much of a relief as it was meant to be.

Something had changed. Unnatural alliances had been made. The stewards, the maids, the cooks, the grooms, the pages, even the lowliest of cleaning-domestics and apporters knew it.

The guest quarters, which housed the counts and advisory members of the Starleaf Council during times they were in session, were full too. And many of the other rooms were occupied by highborn lords and ladies from leading Households. All wanted to be on hand, all knew that great change was on the verge.

Vangier knew it too, and nervous acid bubbled in his stomach. Like all the palace staff, he had been accustomed to the stability of King Shaelan's long reign. They had known it couldn't last forever, that change was coming, but no one had expected it to be like this. They craved a return to stability, the Emerin needed a king . . . but some of them, Vangier included, were secretly beginning to think that a bad king might be worse than no king at all.

It might all be settled, for better or for worse, tomorrow. The Starleaf Council would meet once more, and the counts would vote. The rumors that Vangier had been hearing indicated only one possible outcome.

"At once," he had promised Talian Maevarra, and he had fully intended to do so, within a day or two at the latest.

But what with all the arrangements that needed to be made, the emergencies demanding his attention, and the fine details that he could trust to no one save himself, it had taken half a score of days before he was able to set aside a night to pursue his whims and suspicions.

He crossed to the kitchen entrance, where the air emanating from that warm room met the outside chill and the result was a slippery morass of slush and dripping icicles.

The cavernous kitchen rooms were empty, a sight that disoriented him because he had never before seen them when they were not bustling with activity. Well before dawn, the kitchens would come to life, but for now everything merely waited in readiness.

The corridors were empty as well. Vangier had never noticed before how loud his footfalls were, how they echoed. He cringed at each sound, fancying that he would wake everyone and have to explain what he was doing here in the dead of the night.

"The dungeons," he whispered, and even that sounded loud as a shout. He actually covered his mouth like a schoolboy caught in class, and threw a quick, furtive glance behind him.

The dungeons. Startling to think that most in the palace wouldn't even know they existed, let alone where to look. Would Sir Tiercel have known? Of course he would have . . . he'd been a page, and the pages poked their noses into every corner.

But pages eventually grew up, and Vangier's boyhood had been a few centuries before. He descended several staircases until he was well below the wine cellars, pointing out to himself how very embarrassing it would be to become lost. He, the Lord High Steward, who held keys to every room – though that was a formality, really, a symbolic token of his office. Most of the doors were left unlocked. Those that weren't boasted magelocks and spells of warding and other such defenses as to render keys useless.

He reached passageways so disused that they no longer had magelights, or even the life-sensing torches that flared into warm flame when someone drew near. No cobwebs; he could not have tolerated that and would have rousted a squadron of domestics from their beds if he'd seen a single one. But the air was stale. Not dank, not musty . . . but rather . . . less than fresh.

A final flight of steps brought him to the iron-barred cells that lined the walls of a dungeon corridor. Holding up his magelight, he peered into each and found them utterly bare. Not so much as a wisp of straw or shred of cloth. No rats, certainly not. And absolutely no skeletal remains hanging from manacles, or other such barbarities.

The dungeons were antiquities more than anything else, reminders of an age long past when the Emerin had need of such dismal punishments. Vangier thanked his ancestors and all the gods that he lived in more civilized, enlightened times.

He was on the verge of giving up and seeking his own bed when he thought of the deep cells. The ones hewn from the bedrock far below the palace, and then drained of their *aether* to make prisons capable of holding even the most powerful wizard. All the spells in the world would do no good without the *aether* through which the magical energy flowed.

It would also, he realized, be a perfect place to hide someone. No seeker-spells or scrying could reach.

Vangier went back the way he'd come, his magelight bobbing in his wake. He knew where the entrance to the lowest level was, knew of the stair that went down so steeply that it was very nearly a ladder of stone. The pages in his day had sometimes dared one another, all in boyish bravery and challenge, to descend that seemingly-endless shaft, unaided by light or magic.

He recalled it so vividly that a shudder worked outward from the core of his body. Blind and practically deaf, feeling his way one careful step at a time with fearful, questing toes. Counting as he went. Hands searching for purchase on the walls, which were clammy with moisture and cold no matter what the time of year. A piece of chalk in his belt to mark the point when he could not bear to go any further.

Who had it been? Nethiar who'd gone the furthest, a hundred and five steps into the fathomless black.

Except that Halleah had gone further. Halleah had gone all the way to the bottom. Screaming. At least, for part of the way he had screamed . . . until there came a horrible wet snap and then the muffled thump and tumble, receding away into silence. Leaving behind a terrified circle of boys, unable to believe that the very peril they'd courted had actually come to pass.

That had been the end of the game. It would have been the end even if they hadn't been found out, because who among them would have been foolhardy enough to try again? Not after hearing those sounds, those awful sounds. But the stewards of the time had known that sooner or later, boys would come along who thought it no more than legend, and the dares would begin anew.

The door at the top of the stairs had been sealed and then forgotten. Vangier hoped to find it that way still, but when he came to it he saw that the bars had been removed, the spells undone. It opened at a touch on hinges that rasped only slightly.

An icy exhalation blew his hair back from his brow and froze a sheen of sweat he hadn't even known was there. His magelight threw a strong glow but it looked weak, swallowed up by the dizzying jagged slant of the stairway.

They'd been haunted by nightmares after Halleah's death, all of them. For years thereafter, until time eventually brought surcease. Now those nightmares came back to Vangier as if he'd wakened from one, crying out for his mother, only moments before.

Try those steps? It would be insane. He was far less spry than he'd been as a page, that was beyond doubt. Having a light did nothing to inspire his confidence.

It isn't as if there's anyone down there, he told himself.

If that's so, who unsealed the door?

He had come this far. There was nothing else to do but continue.

The thought came to him as he gingerly set his weight on the tenth step down that he had told no one where he was going. The aged healer and his wife knew of Vangier's promise to investigate the dungeons, but would they even know of these deeper cells? Folistran might; he had been a young man in a time when the *aether*-deprived prisons were still in use. But would he remember?

Fall, a grim voice spoke up in his mind, *and it won't matter much to you because you'll be as dead as Halleah. When they do find you . . . if they ever do . . . you'll look like he did. Older, but just as broken.*

The faded smudges of old chalk marks were still on the walls. He never would have seen them if he hadn't been looking. Pale marks or initials, so faint that anyone else might have mistaken them for discolorations in the stone.

"Fifty-six, fifty-seven," he heard, and was startled to find that he had been counting under his breath.

The magelight bobbed over his right shoulder, since he could not even contemplate freeing a hand from the banister. He didn't fool himself into thinking his hands would do anything to arrest a fall, but that changed nothing. His grip was almost a clamp.

"Seventy-two, seventy-three."

The air down here was fresher, but colder. He saw narrow fissures in the rock and when he pressed an ear to one could hear rushing water.

"One hundred and four, one hundred and five, one hundred and six."

A completely unexpected thrill of vindication went through him as he beat Nethiar's best, and he was immediately ashamed of himself. He was far too grown for such foolishness. If Nethiar, who had gone on to become a bank manager of solid and eminently respectable reputation, could see him now . . .

Ashamed, yes . . . he was ashamed of himself . . . but he couldn't help wishing he'd brought a piece of chalk.

Down and down and down some more. "One hundred and eighty, one hundred and eighty-one."

He saw a flat square of flagstone. The end of the stairs. He eased his halting, ginger descent and almost laughed with relief as he reached the bottom.

Two things occurred to him simultaneously.

This was not the bottom, but only a landing, and even steeper flights of steps vanished down to the left and the right.

And this . . . this must have been where they'd found Halleah. He was standing on the very spot where one of his own childhood playmates had lain, skull cracked into crockery shards, limbs twisted, mouth gaping in that final scream.

Vangier sucked in a shaky breath. He was thinking of Halleah's parents and how they had wailed and wept when he was brought up, wrapped in a blanket that would soon be replaced by rosecloth. Caught up in that bleak memory, he neglected his spell and his magelight whiffed out, casting him into absolute darkness.

He thought for the barest of instants that he saw another light, high above him on the stairs, but when he blinked, it was gone and he attributed it to the eye-dazzle of his own light.

The black, like cold damp wool, pressed in on all sides. He held that shaky breath and now his chest burned. Superstitiously, he was afraid to let it out because when he inhaled, he would be taking that utter dark into his lungs.

Blind and deaf, for he could hear nothing but the distant water and a grating scrape from above that convinced him the millennia-old stones were shifting, that they would choose now of all possible times to cave in. He would have survived what Halleah could not, only to end up buried alive and starving slowly.

He let out his breath in a whoop and took another, steeling himself in the very real expectation that he would drown. As if it was not air around him at all but water, a subterranean lake of inky, uncharted depths.

It was only air, and brought him to his senses. He raised his shivering hands to his face, rubbed his arms, assured himself of his reality. As panic slowly bled away from him, he was able to calm his mind enough to re-cast his spell. Soft light blossomed in his palm. He clutched at it eagerly, fingers passing through the misty sphere.

As he looked down, his heart took a violent jolt. Somehow, although he was not aware of having moved, he must have sidled sideways. His foot was almost to the edge of the landing.

Gasping, Vangier moved the other way, until he was at the center. He pressed his back to the landing's one blank wall, deriving reassurance from its solid strength. He leaned against it.

He sprang away from it, suddenly sure that it would swivel or tip or open in some concealed way and drop him shrieking into a bottomless pit.

The wall did nothing of the sort, but he was no longer in a state of mind to trust it. He looked down both new flights of stairs and they were equally precipitous, the steps barely wide enough for a bird to stand upon with any confidence. But from the leftmost one, the air smelled different. Hints of other scents mixed with those of water and stone. Wine, and slow decay.

It was as good a reason as any. Still not over his fright, he ended up lowering himself to a sitting position and creeping down the stairs like a child, on his backside. A mortifying pose to be sure, but who was there to see?

At last, when he was beginning to wish he'd paid better attention to his geography lessons because he felt as though he might emerge on the far side of the world and couldn't remember what was there, the stairs opened out into a spacious room. It would have been comfortable enough had there been windows, for by the flicker of his magelight he saw furnishings and many crates of supplies.

He saw, also, signs of a battle. Tables were upended, a bottle had smashed on the floor amid spoiled food, boxes and trunks had been opened and their contents strewn about. A truesteel arrowhead caught the light from where it lay near a pile of blankets that seemed to have been stripped from the beds.

A guard chamber. And recently inhabited, if he was any judge. The remains of the food could tell him that much.

Where were the guards? Who had been stationed in this deep chamber? And why?

He looked toward the only door leading from this room, a door that doubtless gave onto the cell. The old-fashioned system of locks and gates was proof of that, and he suspected that if he got too close, his magelight would go out as it entered a region where there was no *aether* to sustain it.

That was something he had no great urge to do. Being bereft of magic would be worse than being bereft of air. And yet . . .

Was someone imprisoned beyond that door? Might he have found Ariana Mirida, and possibly even the Brindani youth?

The air was moving, stirring. He sensed it in a prickling of the fine hairs of his neck and knew even before he heard the rustle of cloth that he wasn't alone.

Vangier turned, raising his magelight high.

Denilar was there, hood thrown back so that the scar on his cheekbone was clearly visible. His breath puffed around his head in a cloud. He had one hand resting on the hilt of his sword and the other hidden in the folds of his cloak.

The look in his eyes was one of murder.

Too stunned by that cold, flat expression, Vangier could only stand where he was with his mouth agape.

"What are you doing here, Steward?" Denilar asked, in a sorrowful tone that sounded genuine. "Why did you have to come here? This is none of your concern."

Then the condition of the room dawned on Denilar. He looked around, brow furrowed. His gaze finally came to rest on Vangier again, and by then the steward had found his voice.

"You're away from your post, guardsman," he said, striving for brisk disapproval and almost succeeding. "I hope you have a very good explanation for this lapse in duty."

"Where are they?" Denilar demanded as if he hadn't heard, demanded more of the room at large than of the steward. "Where are the guards?"

"I'm speaking to you," Vangier said. "There is no one else present. Explain yourself." He curled his fingers. "*Lartei*."

It wasn't strictly within his authority to do that, to cast a spell of truth-compulsion on Denilar. In fact, it wasn't strictly legal for him to even know such a spell of forbidden magic. The High

Steward before him had passed it on as a final legacy before retiring, saying that it was sometimes a necessary evil. He could get in trouble for it, but Vangier would be more than happy to have the chance to justify his actions before court and Council. It would mean living to see the upper chambers again.

"I followed you," Denilar said, the words jerking out of him. "I knew you were up to something and I meant to find out what."

"Tell me what you know about this place."

But Denilar clenched his jaw and stayed resolutely silent. Vangier cursed inwardly. The spell was only a mild *geas;* he could not force Denilar to speak but only make him unable to lie when he did speak. He could still choose to say nothing. The guard's eyes darted anxiously, searching the room as if looking for help.

A most unsettling sensation had taken up residence in Vangier. He felt as though he were treading a taut wire over a chasm. The light he thought he'd seen as his went out made sense now, for Denilar had been behind him. That meant the guard had made it all the rest of the way in the dark, but Vangier was not in the mood to be impressed by his mastery of that boyhood dare.

"Then stand aside and let me pass," Vangier said.

"I'm sorry, Steward. I cannot do that."

The unsettling sensation was worse and now Vangier knew it for what it was. Fear.

"How do you intend to stop me?" It was not a question he wanted to hear answered, but it had to be asked.

Denilar's reply was eloquent in its way. He drew his sword, and brought his other hand out of hiding, shimmering with red magefire.

"This is an outrage," Vangier said, shocked. "You would threaten a steward of the palace? You, a guard? Where is your loyalty, Denilar?"

"To my commander," he said. "Sir Tiercel Reyes."

Vangier backed away but he had nearly run out of space. He cast about for a weapon, for all the good it would have done him even if one had been within reach. His training at arms and archery had never seemed so distant, and he'd never been all that good at it. Not enough, assuredly, to stand any chance against a veteran soldier and palace guard.

"I will not just let you kill me," he said, dispensing with the idea of weapons and preparing to counter with magic. It had been decades since he'd been called upon to cast anything dangerous, such spells not being often necessary in his position.

"I do not wish to," Denilar said, and as the compulsion was still in effect, Vangier believed him. Remorse was written on every line of his face. Yet so was determination.

"You do not wish to, but you will. Why? What have I seen that is deserving of death?"

"This." He gestured encompassingly. "But first, tell me where they are. The other guards. What have you done with them?"

"There was no one here, and even if there had been, what could I have done against them in so short a time before you arrived?"

Denilar looked again at the disturbed contents. "Someone fought here." His eyes widened. "He couldn't have escaped! There is no way!"

"Who? Who escaped?"

"The pr–" Denilar bit off his words but he had said enough. He howled a hoarse, guttural cry, and lunged.

Vangier scrambled away from him, hoping to dart around and make for the stairs. He got four paces before sharp steel slashed into his side. Enormous pain, the likes of which he'd never known, burst through the steward. He fell over the upended table and hit the floor.

His forearm fit neatly into the deep gash below his ribs. Blood poured forth. Someone was screaming, screaming like a slaughtered animal, and he dimly realized it was himself.

The guard, his eyes gone so large that the pupils were ringed with the white of pure madness, kicked the table away and chopped at Vangier's head.

He rolled, still screaming. Sparks leapt where the blade scored stone, missing his flesh.

"Burn you!" Denilar swore, and fitted deed to word by flicking his hand at the sprawled, struggling steward.

A snapping, turbulent cloud of embers leapt from his fingers and struck Vangier. His clothes ignited in several places, greedy flames leaping up. Wherever a spark touched skin, it burrowed in and left a charred hole.

"Denilar!" came a sudden shout.

Vangier saw the blade coming down, knew he couldn't evade it a second time, not with his flesh scorching and his life's blood running along the mortared seams of the floor. But Ilarion was there in time, parrying the blow meant to cleave Vangier in half.

Denilar reeled back, his expression a mask of torment and a spurting wound in his chest. "Ilarion –"

"What in the name of the gods is this?" The younger guard put himself between his partner and Vangier, staring in horror at the red streaks on his sword. "What have you done? What have *I* done?"

Shaking his head, Denilar kept retreating. He dropped his weapon. His body shook with anguish and agony. Ilarion stepped toward him with his hand outstretched.

"Denilar, forgive me!"

Vangier could only lie where he'd fallen and watch as Denilar came to the wall. He wore the hunted and trapped look of an animal who knows there is nowhere left to run. As Ilarion, shocked and white, went toward him intending to help, Denilar shook his head again and produced a short but wickedly-pointed dagger. He placed the tip under the shelf of his jaw.

"No!" Ilarion cried. "It isn't too late. A healer, a physician –"

"And then a court-martial," Denilar cut in, weakly but harsh enough to override Ilarion. "It'd be execution or exile, you know that. I've failed."

With that, he drove the knife up. His body stiffened, every muscle quivering, and he stood rigid for what seemed an eternity before collapsing. Ilarion stared, tears pouring down his face.

Vangier, with an effort that made it feel as if he were tearing himself in two, hitched over enough to clutch at Ilarion's ankle.

"Please . . . help me," he said. And whether it was because he had forgotten his magelight again or because he was dying, everything went dark.

* * *

Chapter Twenty-Three

That is that. Our hope is lost.
– Elwyndas, The King's Brother, Act XI

"It ends tonight," Idelhar Fistrel said. "They shall meet, they shall each speak, and then they shall vote. Barring a miracle, by this time tomorrow the announcement will have gone out across the Emerin, that Alinor Elyvorrin is to be king."

Faessia did not reply. She had lifted a corner of the curtain aside and peered out at the avenues as the carriage rumbled over cobblestones. The homes they passed were done up in Wintersfest decorations, and heavily-cloaked callers went from door to door bearing baskets of treats to their neighbors and friends.

"I should be there," Idelhar muttered, cursing the restriction of his rank that forbade him entrance into the Council chamber.

His father officiated in Virine's place, and as the heirs of the various counts were allowed to join their fathers, his cousin Bethel would be there. The Fistrel family would be well-represented. The Elyvorrins not so much so, although Celinar, puffed with pride and arrogance, had gone to be with his grandfather. All Idelhar could do was wait.

He had tried to take his mind off matters, and to distract Faessia as well, by suggesting this carriage-ride through the snowy, tree-lined streets. Perras Peliani had its own ever-changing beauty with each season and under normal circumstances, such a ride would have lifted his spirits.

These circumstances, though, were hardly normal. He looked off in the direction of the palace, unable to see it but envisioning in his mind's eye the *valn* tree, its leaves reflected in the glossy black of the long table, and the thronelike chairs drawn up to it while the tiers of seats where the advisory members and other onlookers rose against the walls.

Each of the members would be given the chance to have his say, and thanks to his habit of keeping open ears everywhere, Idelhar already feared he knew how each speech would go. It was too late for opinions to shift no matter what was said. They could not be swayed now.

Even so, he yearned to be there and see for himself, hear for himself.

"I fear I must beg your pardon, Faessia," he said. "As pleasant as this is, I cannot bear to be away from the palace. Allow me to see you home."

"Home?" Her laugh was brittle.

"You know of which I speak."

"Yes. A manor empty of all save the staff, none of whom like me and all of whom think me ungrateful. I should be honored above all, they say. Betrothed to the valiant Sir Tiercel, mother to the next king, what more could any lady desire? Yet I, the undeserving, complaining wretch, fail to appreciate the generosity of my father-in-law."

Idelhar patted her hand and found it like ice. He was not often at a loss for words but there seemed little he could say to her now.

"My son, my own son, feels the same way," she said. "He'll return tonight bearing tidings that he thinks should have me overcome with joy, and will be cross with me when I weep instead."

"Remember this, Faessia," he said, holding both her cold hands in his. "You are the only one who can agree to wed with Tiercel. The count cannot compel you to do it. Resist him, refuse him. You have the strength."

"Have I?" Tears glimmered and she swiftly blinked them away.

He gave her his handkerchief and leaned out to instruct the driver. The carriage swung away from the main avenues and entered the district where the mansions were set well back behind high hedges or decorative fences. They reached that of the Elyvorrins and turned into the long sweeping curve of the drive.

Faessia glanced out the window again and was about to let the curtain fall when she frowned. "Someone is here. Who would come calling on such a night, knowing that the Council meets and no one is here?"

Idelhar moved to a spot where he could see what had captured her interest. He saw a man on the front terrace, a man in a white cloak trimmed in silver foxfur. His hair was a truesilver shade, shoulder-length and straight, held back from his brow by a simple circlet. He was speaking to the Elyvorrin's housekeeper, but broke off and half-turned as the carriage rolled closer. At the foot of the steps, swathed in a black mantle, was a small, slim figure whose features were concealed by a deep hood.

"I do not know him," Faessia said.

"I do," Idelhar replied, excitement building in him. "What his presence here and now might mean, I cannot say . . . but this is no coincidence."

The black-cloaked figure slid unobtrusively deeper into the shadows as Arien Mirida brought an intent silver gaze to bear expectantly on the carriage. A small dark shape on his arm, a drake, stretched a long neck quizzically in their direction, eyes sparkling like gems.

The driver came to a halt and hopped down to open the door. Idelhar stepped out first, offering his arm to Faessia, and saw several expressions flit quickly over Mirida's face. He had clearly been braced for some confrontation, and upon seeing that they were not who he expected, was both relieved and disappointed.

Faessia addressed the housekeeper. "Chaia, is anything amiss?"

She inclined her head. "Milady, this gentleman just arrived and wished an audience with the count." Her tone was puzzled, and she kept darting looks at the driveway. There were no horses, no coach, and the expanse of snowy lawn was unmarred by footsteps except for a tramped-down trail that came from around the corner of the house. "I was just telling him that the count is not presently in."

"It is a matter of the utmost urgency," Mirida said.

Idelhar climbed the steps. "My lord Archmage, what a pleasure," he said, reaching out a hand and offering his most winning smile.

Mirida's eyes narrowed, but his manners were impeccable. He touched his gloved fingers briefly to Idelhar's. "It seems you have the advantage."

"I am Idelhar Fistrel. This is Faessia Elyvorrin."

"Celin's wife, of course." He bowed.

"Celin's widow, I grieve to correct you," she said. "But forgive me . . . you are . . . ?"

"Arien Mirida." He gestured toward the black-cloaked figure, still hanging back out of the reach of the light. "And my wife, Cathlin."

"You are Arien? Why . . . my husband spoke of you often!" Faessia said. "You were boyhood companions. And you . . ."

"Yes," Arien said, understanding. "I was Alinora's betrothed. But that is far behind me now. It is on other business that I am come here tonight. I must speak with the count."

"Does this concern your daughter?" Idelhar asked.

"You *do* have the advantage."

"Or do you?" came a low whisper. "Tell us where she is."

Faessia gasped. Idelhar did not move, except to let his winning smile widen into an appreciative grin.

"Is that a dagger I feel pressing into my back, Cat Sabledrake?" Yes, it was . . . he could feel the point jab harder.

"If you know who I am, then –"

"Please," Idelhar said. "Count Elyvorrin is not here, but if you will share our coach, I will take you to him. On the way, perhaps, we might exchange information. I think we're all on the same side in this."

"Idelhar, no, she tried to . . ." Faessia looked ready to faint dead away.

The coachman and the housekeeper were thunderstruck. Mirida gave his wife a glance both stern and imploring. She relented, sliding the dagger back into its sheath as she moved to his side.

"You do know he only wanted to bring you back to the Emerin to kill you," Idelhar said.

Silver brows arched. "The thought did cross my mind."

"Take us to the palace with all haste." Idelhar assisted Faessia back into the carriage. As soon as all four of them were in and underway, he settled back and looked them over, shaking his head in quiet amazement. "How did he do it? How did he convince you to return now, of all possible times? I know that your daughter came here, that she unsuccessfully sought audience with the Council, and that she disappeared shortly thereafter. That is all I *know*, but I suspect much more. Now you."

Arien gave him a crumpled and smoothed sheet of parchment. Faessia put her head close to Idelhar's as they read the count's letter.

"These were sent with them," he added, showing them a signet ring and opal pendant.

"Arien's magic read the past of the items," Cat said. She spoke the elven tongue fluently, but with an accent that was curiously exotic. With her hood still up, Idelhar could just see large dark eyes and a determined chin, and a few curls of dark brown hair resting against her cheeks. "She was frightened, and in pain."

Arien's hand closed reassuringly over hers, which was curled into a knotted fist. "I received many impressions, images that made little sense, but enough to let me know that I must take Elyvorrin's threat most seriously indeed. Now, where is he?"

"In the Chamber of the Skies," Idelhar said. "Where even now, they might be naming him the next king of all the Emerin."

"What?" Cat's head jerked up. Her hood fell back, fully revealing her features. "King? *Him?*"

Idelhar was prepared for it, if not quite prepared for the exotic quality of her beauty. Faessia, less traveled and much more sheltered, uttered a cry and then stifled it by putting a hand to her mouth. Cat blanched, but held her ground and raised her chin as if daring either of them to say something.

"It is a long and difficult thing to explain," Idelhar said. "But meeting you now gives me a hope that I thought had died. If Elyvorrin is holding your daughter against her will, and by every indication he must be, then no vote can be made until the matter is fully investigated. Your timely arrival may have saved us all."

"I am not interested in the fate of the Emerin a tenth so much as I am the fate of my daughter," Arien said. "Tell me all that you know. Or . . . suspect . . . as you put it."

Idelhar did so, relaying all that he'd heard from Vangier about Ariana Mirida's appearance at the palace with her human friend in tow, how she had requested an audience, and how they had vanished soon after, leaving only a short, apologetic note. He added that it had been Tiercel Reyes who instructed Vangier to say nothing of it to the Council, and further that Tiercel was the sworn man of Alinor Elyvorrin.

"There is one thing more," Idelhar added. "Many years ago, when Tiercel and I were friends, we were sent to Thanis to see what we could find out about you, Archmage. Tiercel was prepared to kill you at that time, believing you to be a threat. I dissuaded him. Our friendship withered from that day forth."

"Tiercel," Cat said. "I ran afoul of an elf by that name once. He was some kinsman or apprentice to Tanneivan, who had been turned out of the Nightsiders."

Faessia, stunned into silence, only sat gazing at each of them in turn. Her posture suggested that she would have liked to have been anywhere else but knew there was no way to leave politely, trapped as she was in the coach with them.

"So this Tiercel Reyes may be involved in our daughter's capture," Arien said.

"I'm not entirely sure who's involved with what," Idelhar said. "Whether Tiercel is twisting Elyvorrin for his own purposes, or the opposite . . . how Feyna fits into it . . . I don't know. But it seems we may finally find out. Tonight."

* * *

The poet Salwyndas, whose ancestor had been the great and famed Elwyndas, was best known for his tiresome habit of speaking primarily in quotes and verses. He was also known for his ongoing life's work, which was to research and set to epic poetry the circumstances under which each king of the Emerin had gained his crown. On a momentous occasion such as this, he deemed it only fitting to open the meeting with a recitation of the work-thus-far.

His distinguished forebear might have crafted poems and plays that withstood the test of time, but Alinor Elyvorrin decided that when he became king, the first order of business would be to find some other master of the arts to take Salwyndas' place. The thought cheered him immensely.

Celinar, in a stiffly-embroidered doublet that made him look every bit the young prince-to-be, sighed and rolled his eyes as the poet droned on and on. The only difference between him and the rest of the Council was that the others had far more experience concealing their boredom.

Elyvorrin amused himself instead by watching the Fistrels. Both looked as though they had bitten deep into some sour, wormy fruit and wished desperately to spit it out. He liked seeing them look that way. He liked it very much. He looked forward, in fact, to seeing them like that for centuries to come.

The only pall on the evening was Tiercel's continued absence. It shouldn't have been this long, should it? How far away was the eastern shore? The Emerin was not that vast, was it? He hated to admit even to himself that he was beginning to wonder, with sinking dread, if perhaps Tiercel wasn't coming back at all. The wild woods were dangerous even for a knight of his merit. And the quest itself was by no means without risk. Dragons could be savage, after all.

Salwyndas ended with the coronation of King Shaelan, perhaps deeming it impolitic to mention the unfortunate Prince Wyndrel. It wasn't as if the boy had even been of age, and a battlefield crowning followed by almost immediate death hardly made for a reign worthy of song.

Feyna, who had appointed himself the master of ceremonies, stood up with a rustle of his elaborate robes of office. The pained looks of the Fistrels grew more so. Feyna, on the other hand, gave every impression of confidence and pleasure.

"My fellow members of the Council, and honored guests, welcome" he said, bowing to the counts and their various heirs. "We are well-met tonight, for at last we turn our faces forward and begin a new age for our fair land. As the esteemed Salwyndas has just so lengthily reminded us, the House of Perras ruled the Emerin for nearly eight millennia and made this kingdom a place of marvels. Now the time has come to trust in a new House to lead us. I put forth to you that we are overdue in naming a new king from the honorable assembly here gathered. Let us do so, that our people might put the sorrows of war and loss behind us and move on into that new age."

Denryl Marrion rose, clearing his throat. "I, Denryl, Count of Marrion, propose that we of the Starleaf Council name and accept Alinor Elyvorrin, Count of Shanlen, as our king."

"Seconded," Gariel Aistrian said.

Revandir Brindani stood up, and his tone made it seem he was ready to make his words an invitation to a duel. "I propose that we name and accept Bethelyn Fistrel, Count of Fistrel, as our king."

All attention turned to Kelnor Valnnatis, the only one left who could choose to second Brindani's motion. Under the combined stare of so many eyes, the Count of Valnna quailed and looked as though he would have liked to sink through the floor.

Brindani prompted him with a glare. "Kelnor!" he said in a low, urgent mutter. "Now's the time . . . speak up!"

"Count Valnnatis, had you something to say?" the Archmage asked.

"I . . . no," Valnnatis said, dropping his head in shame. His hands trembled, and perspiration glistened on his face.

The shock, rage and betrayal evident on the Fistrels and their supporters made Elyvorrin want to throw back his head and laugh.

"I see," said Feyna. "My lords, there is a proposal set before us that –"

The doors flew open. Idelhar Fistrel rushed in. "Members of the Council, I beg your apologies, but I must interrupt."

Elyvorrin shot to his feet. "What is the meaning of this, Fistrel?" he barked at Bethelyn. "Your nephew presumes to intrude on a private meeting of the Council? I –"

As the other counts raised their voices in bewilderment and annoyance, another man stalked in after Idelhar. His white cloak flared, silver hair streamed back from a circlet on his brow, and his eyes were steel glazed in frost.

"You." Elyvorrin felt something twist deep inside him.

Other people came in after Mirida, but Elyvorrin paid them scant notice even though one of them was his own cowardly and treacherous daughter-in-law. He was too consumed with wrath at the man who went to the center of the room, walking as boldly as if he had committed no crimes. As if he had every right to be here! As if he were *blameless!* How dare he!

"I am very aware of the inappropriate nature of this intrusion," Idelhar Fistrel said, "but I bring with me one who has a concern that must be addressed before this Council can go further. May I present Arien Mirida, the Archmage of Gamelin?"

Feyna, whose face was stormy and disdainful, flicked a slight gesture of magic at Mirida. All at once, his expression changed. He went white with shock, repeated the gesture, and recoiled into himself. His eyes were sharp with speculation, evaluation.

A terrible feeling of things flying madly out of control swelled all around Elyvorrin. He had never expected Mirida to come *here*, openly, to the very innermost seat of the Emerin! He had planned on their encounter being private, personal, and secret. Above all, secret.

"This man," he said, leveling an accusing finger, "is a criminal of the worst nature, an exile, a liar, a grave-robber, a thief of hopes, and a murderer! I insist that he be arrested this very instant, and held until he can be made to answer for his deeds."

"I have come here to answer for them," Mirida said. "Are you prepared to answer for *yours?*"

Gone was the polite but diffident young man who had always behaved as though he knew in his heart he wasn't truly good enough for a priceless maiden such as Alinora. It was an assessment that Elyvorrin had always shared, but then, what man in the Emerin would have been good enough? That Arien would have been a better match for Lionnen, the both of them thin, tepid, scholarly and meek.

This commanding figure was an Arien Mirida he did not know, an Arien Mirida who did not seem about to give way. The first crawling threads of fear colored Elyvorrin's anger.

"This is most irregular." Feyna, for once, sounded unsure and badly rattled. He was still staring at Mirida as if he could see something that shook the very foundations of all that he believed.

"I am the acting head of this Council," Bethelyn Fistrel said. He threw a puzzled look at his nephew but Idelhar nodded and motioned him on. "I declare a brief pause while we hear what all of this is about."

"This has nothing to do with the Council," Elyvorrin said. "He and I have business of our own."

"You made it the business of the Council years ago," Brindani said, "when you arranged to have his name stricken from the Book of Lists and his property taken away. Under other circumstances, this man would be sitting there, in Riachlain's seat. I say whatever's brought him here is needing of all our attention."

Lian Riachlain, made a wide-eyed gesture of innocence, as if proclaiming that he had no knowledge and nothing to do with any of this.

"I do not deny that I left the Emerin, though my exile was self-imposed," Mirida said.

The daughter had had the temerity to speak insolently to Alinor Elyvorrin . . . the father had the even greater temerity to *ignore* him, and address his remarks to Fistrel!

"I do not deny that I have lied, robbed a grave, or stolen hope," he went on. "I am, however, no murderer. I present myself to be questioned and truthsaid by any or all of you at your convenience."

"If it is at our convenience, why interrupt this Council?" Denryl Marrion asked. "In case you'd not been told, we've some rather important –"

"What brings me here is this letter, which came to me from Count Elyvorrin. He holds my daughter prisoner, and would exact upon her the fate he feels his daughter suffered at my hands."

"Lies!" Elyvorrin knocked over his heavy chair and it hit the marble floor with a noise like a thunderclap. He rounded the table and would have snatched the incriminating letter from Mirida, torn it and burnt it until there was nothing left, no proof, but his way was blocked when a slight figure in a heavy cloak stepped in front of him, with a shining sword held level at his throat.

Outcries and indignation filled the chamber. Weapons? The threat of violence? In the very Chamber of the Skies?

Elyvorrin came to a halt.

One slim hand came up and unclasped the cloak. It fell away. And there she stood. The scrawny, half-blooded whore who'd usurped Alinora's rightful place. She met his gaze with large, deep, sapphire eyes set.

"My husband is willing to settle this dispute in accordance with Emerinian law," she said in a firm, sure voice. "But give me a reason, Elyvorrin, just one, and I'll show you how we settle things where *I* come from."

"Order and silence, I will have order and silence!" Bethelyn Fistrel cried, hammering on the table in an effort to quell the uproar.

"Do we understand each other, my lord count?"

Elyvorrin eyed the blade, and her deadly-serious gaze. He wanted to strike her down where she stood, this impudent monstrosity, this creature that never should have been born, but he could not with all the Council watching. He nodded curtly.

"Count Elyvorrin, please take your seat," Fistrel said.

"Do not order me about, Fistrel. You haven't the right."

"I am still head of this Council, as I reminded you only moments ago. Be seated. Idelhar, if you'd be so kind as to find a steward, that we might have more chairs brought in? Thank you."

Idelhar sketched a quick bow and hurried off to find whoever was in charge now that the Lord High Steward had neglected his duties. Despite Fistrel's call for silence, everyone kept talking at once, the noise filling the room until the leaves of the *valn* trembled. Mirida waited at the center of it, head held high.

It was Gariel Aistrian, the young hothead, who finally summoned the courage, or lost sufficient tact, to ask, "What is the meaning of it to bring an *elfkin* here, Mirida? Husband, she said? She's not your wife, surely!"

"She most certainly is," Mirida said, setting a hand on her shoulder. "My wife, and the mother of my children."

A flurry of horrified gapes and gasps greeted this. The elfkin looked around at them, eyes all but blazing, not showing even the least bit of decent shame or fear.

Elyvorrin could not bear it anymore. "You, Mirida, are as much an abomination as she is! Moreso, even! You, who were once of a noble House, you . . . this is the utmost vileness . . ."

"Enough, Elyvorrin," Bethelyn Fistrel ordered. "You will have your say."

"Oh, you cherish this, Fistrel, don't you? Yes, this is just what you've been wishing for, but it will not help you. I am in the right. I have been grievously wronged by this man. He killed my daughter!"

"No," Mirida said. "I will tell you how Alinora died . . . both times. While it may be the judgement of the Council that I hold the blame, I did *not* kill her."

* * *

CHAPTER TWENTY-FOUR

Even the mightiest tree will fall when the earth beneath it weakens.
– Elwyndas, Song of Lenais

"You'll not believe all that has happened, sister," Idelhar Fistrel said into the smooth, glassy surface of the mirror. "I scarcely know where to begin. Elyvorrin is not king. Elyvorrin has been sent, under guard, to his house."

Virine cried out in disbelief tinged with joy. "His claim is done, then? How?"

He told her of Arien Mirida's arrival and what had gone on in the Chamber of the Skies. She would hear it soon enough, anyway . . . as soon as word reached Thanis. It was already the only topic of conversation throughout Perras Peliani. In the wineshops, the marketplaces, the theaters, the universities, anywhere one went, all that one heard was the story of the two deaths of Alinora Elyvorrin.

"Yes, I knew much of this," Virine said impatiently. "I have been present at the Highlord's court long enough to hear of it. What more? There must be more."

"Feyna . . . Virine, you should have seen Feyna! When Mirida came in and I introduced him as an Archmage, naturally Feyna was quick to read his aura. He must have nigh been blinded by the talent Mirida possesses! It's far greater than any I've ever seen. Rocked Feyna back on his heels, let me tell you."

"What a delight that must have been." Virine laughed. "I wish I had seen it, yes, I do. Is Mirida to be punished?"

He waved that off. "I've not told you the rest."

Two days after Mirida's startling appearance, a guard named Ilarion emerged from the dungeons with the wounded and barely conscious Lord High Steward strapped to his back, and a shocking story of his own. A man dead by his own hand, two others locked into the deepest *aether*-deprived cell when they had purportedly been assigned to a far-ranging border patrol. All three of them with links to, and orders signed by, Tiercel Reyes.

"I knew it," Virine said. "I knew he was up to no good. Has he been found?"

"Not yet. A search is underway, but the guards refuse to speak about what they were doing there, who they were guarding, and how their prisoner got the best of them and escaped. There's no sign of Tiercel, or the Mirida girl, or Brindani's boy."

"What of Elyvorrin? And the Council? How are they taking all of this upheaval?"

"As you might expect," Idelhar said, making a wry face. "It's turned all Perras Peliani on end. Mirida flaunting his wife, making everyone reevaluate the tales we were all told as children of the deformed and pathetic wretches the elfkin are . . . she is, up close, actually quite comely, once you get used to her."

She gave him a look of sisterly annoyance. "Just as the Lenaisians have been claiming for ages. But it is one thing to hear about far-off, and barbaric Lenais. It is something else to have one there in the very palace. They don't plan to stay, do they?"

"They will not leave until they've found their daughter, but I do not expect they intend to make the Emerin their home. Would you, if you were her?"

"Well, brother, that is all considerable news indeed! Would that I were there to see Feyna and Elyvorrin put in such a pinch."

"It's stirred the pot with far more agitatation than ever I dared to dream. And there's yet more."

"More? Can the Emerin withstand much more?"

"A kinswoman of Mirida's, Talian Maevarra suggests that Ariana went north to the Temple of Karria to retrieve the Emerald. She meant to use it to get the Council's attention and make them hear her request."

"The Emerald of Karria! That could settle the kingship, if the legends are true," Virine said. "I've heard more than enough, Idelhar. I'll be on my way home as soon as I can, tomorrow if possible. I'd not miss the rest of this for anything!"

* * *

His world was falling apart. Alinor Elyvorrin could feel it unraveling, strand by strand, as if the tapestry of his life were but some cheaply woven cloth.

He had gone from triumph to despair with such dizzying speed that his mind could hardly comprehend the change. At one moment, he had been poised to be king with all obstacles removed from his path. At the next, he was a prisoner in his own home and beset by questions as relentless and deadly as any flight of arrows.

If he told . . .

No. All would be lost. Even a single word would doom him. If he confessed to the keeping of Mirida's elfkin-born whelp, they would want to know how he had come by her in the first place. That would lead to Tiercel, and the Emerald. If it were known that he'd had the Emerald in his possession, but sent it away, that would be a blatant admission of his unworthiness to be king.

Everyone had turned against him. His allies were silent now. Even Feyna had distanced himself.

What would happen if he told of his alliance with the Archmage?

He pondered it briefly, then shook his head. Feyna had committed no crime. He had made a bargain, to be sure, but there was no law against that. It might be viewed as scheming, this plan of his to reverse the old laws barring High Mages from holding property, but it was hardly illegal.

Theft of an ancient artifact and abduction of a girl . . . even the daughter of an elfkin and a murderer . . . that was a touch more extreme.

Elyvorrin stared unseeingly at the walls of his darkened study. The house was quiet. The domestics were too cowed by the presence of the Council-appointed guards to stir from their quarters, and his family had abandoned him. Thankless Faessia had taken her son to an inn, over Celinar's protests.

The boy, at least, would believe none of what was being said about his grandfather. His loyalty pleased Elyvorrin, but he could take little comfort in it. In the end, Celinar would see that the accusations were true. His disappointment would be all the greater for his belief.

Mirida had done this. Once again, Arien Mirida had ruined everything that Alinor Elyvorrin held dear. Nothing had gone as it was meant to.

How had he come to the Emerin so quickly? The courier should have only just reached Gamelin. It should have been the better part of a season at the earliest before Mirida could have arrived, and then he would have turned up only to find that the man he sought was the new king.

He could not even rid himself of Mirida by releasing the girl. Had she been kept in that dungeon cell? How had she escaped? Why would the guards not say? What did they know that made them keep their silence?

One had already gone to the extent of taking his own life.

"Perhaps he was the wisest," Elyvorrin said, unaware that he spoke aloud.

In death, the guard would be spared the shame of being put before a court. He was free from the humiliation, free from whatever sentence might be handed down. Imprisonment? Death? Something worse?

Exile? Would it be exile?

Elyvorrin shuddered. There *were* fates worse than death, and exile was chief among them. To lose everything . . . his lands, his fortunes, his station, his family . . . to lose the treasured gift of living in the Emerin . . . it was unthinkable.

Where, after all, was there to go? No right-minded elf could live among the humans unless it was to eke out a grueling existence in Thanis. A man such as Alinor Elyvorrin could never go there and keep any sort of status, not with Virine Fistrel was ambassador. There was Lenais, but no properly bred nobleman belonged among the barbarians, wearing furs and sleeping in caves or huts. The southern lands? What little he knew of the *Morvalan* was not enough to inspire confidence in his ability to live among them, either.

Exile. It might as well be a death sentence, for it was only a death by slower and more miserable means than any execution.

Yes, the guard might have been the wisest after all.

* * *

Celinar Elyvorrin could not sleep. In an inn, in a strange bed . . . try as he might, he could not get comfortable. The bed was far below his standards, for one thing. Was this dismal place the best his mother could afford? Was this the sort of accommodations befitting the heir of a count? A future king?

She had scolded him fiercely when he'd said as much. Scolded him! His own mother! He was still shocked. She had even told him that his destiny was by no means graven in stone. With the current mood of the Council, the likelihood that Grandfather would be chosen king was crumbling away.

He refused to believe it. "Grandfather and Sir Tiercel will settle this, you'll see," he had said. "It's all jealous lies spun by our enemies. I don't blame Grandfather for refusing to dignify any of it with a response. When Sir Tiercel returns –"

She had slapped him then. Celinar had never been struck in his entire life, and had never seen his mother raise a hand in anger to anyone. What was the world coming to?

Neither had she come crawling around to weep and beg his forgiveness. Very well, then. Let her be that way.

It wasn't right that she should be keeping him away from home in the Elyvorrin family's time of need. His place was at his grandfather's side. They were the only ones left, he and the count.

"I'll prove to him that we have not all turned our backs on him," Celinar said, and felt better the moment the vow left his lips.

He dressed in the dark, and went into the sitting room that divided their bedrooms. His mother's door was closed. The soft sounds of her sobs had given way to the hush of sleep. The hall was lit only by a few candles, and no one else was about as he made his way to the stairs, to the bottom floor, to the street.

No coaches were out either, and he resigned himself to a walk. Part of him wished that someone would accost him, and give him a chance to release his pent-up fury. But such things did not happen in Perras Peliani. The scattering of other people on errands so late hardly bothered to look at him.

By the time he reached the gates, his legs were weary from trudging through the snow. It was deep, and wet. Wintersfest was done. A new year was coming. A new year that should mark the beginning of the Elyvorrin reign. Not one that should be weighed down by disgrace and scandal.

As he approached the house, he was ready – almost eager! – for a guard to dare stop and challenge him. Let them. He had every right to be here. Yet he came closer and closer and no one stepped forth. Not even when he opened the front door and hesitated in the grand entryway with its soaring curved stairs and crystal chandelier.

Something was wrong. A large heaped mound partially blocked the entrance to the hall leading to his grandfather's study.

Celinar went to the heap and recoiled, gasping, as he saw the slack faces of men. Guards. Dead. Palace guards. The ones posted here by the Council.

No, not dead after all. They were breathing. Sleeping the deep sleep of magic. They had been enspelled.

His heart slowed from the rapid pace brought on by his fright. He looked over them, down the hall, to the door of the study. It stood ajar and no light burned within. No sound came, either.

"Grandfather?" he called, knowing from his lessons that he could not wake the three men unless he pinched or kicked them. They would be oblivious to all else until the spell wore off. "Grandfather, it is Celinar."

He heard no reply and had no sense of his grandfather's presence. He was not there, and why would he have put the guards to sleep unless he meant to go somewhere? But he had not come out by way of the drive and the gate, else Celinar would have seen him. That meant he had to be on the grounds.

Where would he have gone?

No sooner did he think the question than he knew the answer. Where else? Where he always went to brood over troublesome tidings. Were these not by far the most troublesome of all?

Celinar went out on the back terrace. He saw recent tracks in the wet snow, leading where he knew they would lead. Off toward the wooded copse that surrounded and concealed the family crypt.

It wasn't right. His poor grandfather, so bereft and alone, seeking solace in the company of the dead because he felt that none of his living kin cared a bent twig for him.

He hurried, already anticipating the warm welcome that would light his grandfather's eyes when he realized that he was not so alone. That Celinar, at least, loved him and cared for him and would stand by him no matter what.

The marble walls of the crypt peeked through the thorny vines of rosebushes, heavy with dark-red blooms despite the season. Plant magic, all for show, and to fill the air with the subtle perfume of death. Celinar's nerve faltered. He never liked this place, hadn't liked it when he'd been brought to say his last farewells to his father, hadn't liked it when Grandmother Donystria had died, didn't like it now.

The door was half-open and although there was only darkness within, he thought he detected movement. A shadow, going back and forth, back and forth, as if pacing. He could hear a peculiar scraping noise.

"*Tentalin*," Celinar said, summoning up a green-gold magelight. He stepped into the crypt. "Grand –"

His throat clicked, instantly dry with horror.

The shadow. Back and forth, back and forth.

Not pacing.

Swinging.

The magelight gave a ghastly color to Alinor Elyvorrin's face and shone in his wide-open, empty eyes. His head was bent cruelly to the side, a length of rope knotted tight about his neck. Its other end was tied to a rafter, and his dangling feet scraped the lid of his firstborn daughter's pale casket.

Celinar screamed, snuffed his magelight, and ran for the house.

* * *

CHAPTER TWENTY-FIVE

The moment of your destiny is at hand, my lord.
– Elwyndas, Nalnarennian the Vindicated, Act IV

Vangier laboriously swung his legs over the edge of his bed and set his feet upon the floor. His head swam and his vision blurred, and he felt a pulling stretch all along his side. But it was not as bad as he had feared, nowhere near as bad as he had feared.

He leaned forward, preparing to rise.

"And what in Valannin's name do you think you're doing?"

Lishalla descended on him with righteous ire, herding him back into bed before he could voice a word of protest. She had the blankets drawn up to his chin in a trice.

"But, Lishalla –" He caught himself, for his tone was weak and petulant, a child's sickroom whine.

"You were told to rest, and rest you shall." Her curls bounced as she thrust her fists against her hips and gave him a stern look.

"Unless I've forgotten who I am, I am yet the Lord High Steward."

"So you are, and when you're well again I will gladly let you order me about," she said with a sort of saucy firmness that made him smile despite his irritation. "But even the highest is bound in obedience to the commands of the physicians."

"I wanted only to see the Great Hall," he said. "Today of all days, Lishalla, all must be in readiness."

"For pity's sake, what have you been training Vangissan for if not for an occasion such as this? He is to succeed you someday, and take over your duties in case an emergency keeps you from them. This most certainly qualifies."

"Vangissan is not ready for such a responsibility."

"Have you so little faith in your own son?"

"It is not that I lack faith in him." Vangier made to sit up again but she glared him down. "It is that today is of such import . . . and the Great Hall . . ."

"He handled it perfectly well when it fell to him to ready the Chamber of the Skies on the last meeting of the Council. Why should this be any different? If anything, it must be less so, for at least today he knew in advance that you would be absent. You gave us quite a scare, I'll have you know."

"I hardly planned to be absent that day either. But today, Lishalla, is far more than the Council. All of the nobles and notables of the Emerin are to be in attendance –"

"Hmf!" Lishalla straightened the covers with such brisk tugs and tucks that Vangier was soon bound in place. "That's not the half of it. They're making it into a carnival. Everyone who can talk, buy, or threaten a way in will be there, all of them starved for scandal."

"All the more reason why I should at least make sure –"

"Vangissan has it well in hand."

"Lishalla, I insist that you allow me to complete my sentences."

She had the good grace to blush. "It's just that you had us all so worried, Lord High Steward. We wouldn't have known what to do without you."

"On the contrary, it seems you all are perfectly well able to get along without me."

"I did not mean that. You could have been killed!"

He closed his eyes, not wanting to think about those endless hours lost in the dark, with poor Ilarion fighting to get them out while at the same time keeping him from bleeding to death. They had been so hungry, so thirsty. Under other circumstances, it would have been a word and a gesture and Vangier could have provided for their needs with a few simple spells. Wounded, barely able to think, he had not been fit to summon so much as a grape.

The physicians had been able to mend the hideous slash to his side, but the flesh there was abominably sore and whenever he moved, he half-expected his skin to rip open again.

"The Great Hall has not been used in twenty years," he said, guiding the conversation back to the points that he felt mattered. "Not since the assemblage King Shaelan gathered together to announce that we were at war with Montennor. When I think of the state it must have been in . . ."

"It was not so bad," Lishalla assured him. "We domestics gave it a thorough cleaning, and Vangissan has been overseeing things all morning."

"He has never managed such a large affair before." Vangier fretted just thinking of it. "The food and drink alone will overwhelm him. I should be there to offer my advice."

"Well, you cannot. None of us want to see you do yourself more injury."

"What of my testimony?"

"That heroic young guardsman who saved your life is due to speak." Her eyes sparkled, and even in his present sour mood he was glad to see it.

"Ilarion knows of the dungeons, but not of my conversation with the healer's wife."

"That dear elderly lady? She is to be in attendance as well."

Vangier slumped against the cushions. "You have a ready answer to everything, don't you? So much is at stake here . . . the future of our kingdom will be affected by what goes on in that room today. The guards that Ilarion found in the dungeon cell must be made to talk. This conspiracy must be exposed."

Lishalla grew somber. "I cannot believe that Count Elyvorrin hanged himself. What could have made him do such a thing? It's awful, Vangier. Awful."

"He must have been afraid that the truth would be worse than death," Vangier said. "Such a terrible, tragic waste."

At that moment, someone tapped at his door.

Lishalla frowned. "I told them," she said huffily on her way to answer it, "that you were not to be disturbed. Whoever it is, I'll have his –" The rest was lost in a startled gasp.

Vangier craned his neck and his jaw dropped at the sight of Kevan Brindani. The boy looked decades older and wildly unkempt, the neat haircut of a page grown shaggy, his skin weathered yet drawn. He wore ill-fitting clothes hard-worn from travel, and was in such a disreputable state that his own kin might not have recognized him.

"Kevan?" Vangier struggled against the tight-tucked blankets, trying to sit up.

"Lord High Steward, I have returned!" Kevan's grinning salute of greeting turned to a gape as he took in the bedridden Vangier. "Are you ill, sir? Hurt? What's the matter?"

"Never mind that. Where in the world have you been, young man?"

Lishalla grasped him and gave him a little shake. "And look at you, my word! You're a mess!"

"Unhand him, Lishalla, and send him here," Vangier said. "But you'd best be ready to explain yourself, young man. Have you any idea how worried your family has been? That note you left . . ."

"I swear on my honor I never expected to be away so long," Kevan said. He did not look at all repentant. "But once you've heard why, I'm sure that you and my father both will understand."

* * *

"And I thought that the Sand-Pits were impressive." Cat sat very close beside Arien, her skin acrawl as though every elven eye in the Great Hall was fixed mercilessly upon her.

"This room hardly holds a fraction so many as the arena," Arien said.

His composure was outwardly unruffled as he turned his head to take it all in. She knew the strict effort of control required for him to give that appearance. Inwardly, just as hers did, his soul boiled with the anguished need to *do* something. Darkfire, perched on his shoulder, had the snapping tail and wild eyes to display Arien's actual state of mind.

Yet here they were, obliged to go along with all this Emerinian pomp and foolishness. Days had gone by already with nothing to show for it. Did these oh-so-proper elves fail to realize that Ariana's life might depend on swift action? If it was not already too late.

Cat refused to let herself think such thoughts. It was not too late. She would know, she was certain of it. Her heart insisted that Ariana was alive.

Had it been up to her, everything would be different. She would have gotten the information she wanted from Count Elyvorrin or those guards if she had to coax it from them at knifepoint. There would have been none of this ludicrous delay, none of this confinement under guard. See how well that had worked! They hadn't seriously believed, these sheltered Emerinians, that the count would do anything but comply. They never could have foreseen that he would enspell the guards, and then hang himself.

Such things simply were not done in the Emerin.

It showed on every face. They were not accustomed to dealing with death, not when their lives spanned centuries. They did not live cheek and jowl with it as the humans did. They never pondered what might wait beyond that final veil. Death was abstract to them, distant.

The war had brought it closer to home. Many fair elves had died in Keyda, young and healthy ones whose ends came in violence and pain. Five years had passed since the Treaty of Jeline and they were still reeling from it. But suicide . . . that was even more foreign to their way of thinking. What Count Elyvorrin had done was incomprehensible to them. To Cat, just from what she'd known of the man, it seemed fitting. Inevitable. He had died on the inside when Alinora did, and this was no more than completing the process that had begun a hundred and fifty years before.

"A fine vengeance, too," she said in a harsh whisper.

Arien leaned close. "What was that?"

"He went to his grave and took his knowledge with him. How it must have pleased him, in that last moment, to think that we would be left wondering what had become of Ariana. He must have gloated about it." Her fists were so tight that her nails caused her pain. "There are times, Arien, when I wish your magic extended to necromancy as Solarrin's did."

"Cat," he said, looking shocked.

"We'll have the truth from these guards, won't we? Promise me, Arien."

"We shall have the truth." He touched her hand, exerting gentle pressure in an attempt to make her relax. "I only hope they do know something worth telling."

"This is rubbish," Cat said. "Lawyers. Didn't Elwyndas himself write that they should all be killed? Look at them down there. Arguing for the rights of those two. What of our rights? What of Ari's? Why should they be allowed to keep silent when it's plain that they know the truth?"

"The laws of justice must be observed," Arien said. "Without an orderly system, without wisdom and rational thought, there is no civilization."

"Let me have them for an hour, or less, and I'd find out all they had to tell."

"I know you would."

"Or you, Arien. You could drag the truth from their lips. But you won't, until and unless the entire Council gives permission?"

He turned her head so that she looked into his eyes. "Cat, trust in me. I am going along with this for now, but nothing is going to keep us from Ariana. Not the laws of the Emerin, not the lawyers, nothing."

On the other side of Arien, his kinswoman Talian Maevarra had been listening quietly. She reached around to grasp their hands. "Hush, now, children. The Council wants to see to the truth of this matter as well, believe me. They'll do what must be done."

Cat sighed and nodded. She felt uncomfortable in so many ways, the object of scrutiny and talk. She wondered if she might have done better to dress more like the Emerinians, but all that would have done was draw more attention to her – behold, the elfkin trying to pass for an elf. They would stare at her either way, and she was not about to give them the satisfaction of trying to please them.

Of all the pairs of eyes that cut her with sharp looks, the sharpest of all came from the boy seated with the counts. Celinar Elyvorrin, clad head to foot in the dark red of mourning, could not seem to decide whether she or Arien was more deserving of his hatred. His mother, similarly attired, was beside him. As Celinar was still many years from adulthood, she was to serve as his count-regent. But Faessia had no glares for anyone. She wore a dazed, adrift expression like one who could not be entirely convinced she was not dreaming.

"I'm glad he's dead, though," Cat said. Let the nearby elves scowl; it wasn't as if they weren't already.

Arien regarded her from beneath one raised silver eyebrow and Darkfire turned sparking eyes upon her.

"He did us a favor, really," Cat continued in a lower voice. "Had he not taken his own life, either you or I would have had to take it from him, before he tried to do the same to us. To you. He would have killed you, Arien, without a second thought."

"They are beginning," Lady Karadan said.

Arien's foster-mother sat with them, though clearly she retained many misgivings. She was a lady of some five centuries and looked half again that old, worn and weary. Her clothes were fine, but a hundred years out of fashion. She wore only a few pieces of jewelry, heirlooms too precious to have been sold. Although she was glad to have the old scandal at last set straight, and although she was clearly proud of what Arien had accomplished – an Archmage, a man of wealth and influence even if only in the human realms – she was just as clearly dubious as to his choice of a bride.

Lian Riachlain, himself ill at ease and put on unsteady footing thanks to his close ties to Count Elyvorrin, called the assembly to order.

An eager silence fell. The Great Hall, as Arien had noted, could not rival the main arena of the Sand-Pits in size, but it far exceeded them in terms of splendor. The vast space soared to a vaulted five-paneled ceiling, covered with intricate golden molding. At the center was a spire of twilight-colored crystal. Along the walls were dozens of recessed boxes fronted with waist-high lattice-work railings. Silver braids of cord held back draperies that could be drawn across each to give privacy, but at the moment all were open. The floor was white marble inlaid with sinuous patterns of semiprecious gemstone. Rank after rank of chairs had been set up in long rows, not a one of them unoccupied.

The speaker's platform was a raised stage of wood that gleamed with the rich color of brandy, whorled through with darker grain. A tapestry behind it depicted the crowning of the first Emerinian king, Aelfwyn of the Crown.

The members of the Starleaf Council sat in front of the tapestry. Cat read the same mix of emotions on most of their faces. They were rigid with apprehension, but seeking to mask it, desperate to convey the impression that the Council was well capable of handling these disturbing, turbulent matters.

The prisoners were brought in, wearing the green and silver of the Emerinian army. Medals glittered on their chests. One was a lean, dark, foxlike man with a hard edge to his sharp features. The other could have stepped from a painting illustrating the tall and fair elven ideal, were it not for the gnarled lump of scar tissue where one of his ears had been.

A sympathetic stirring went through the crowd. Decorated veterans, these, and one of them had suffered a terrible and deeply personal maiming while protecting the Emerin. They had been among the brave and valiant soldiers who served under Sir Tiercel, the hero, the general. No one wanted to believe that they, or by extension, he, could be involved in any sinister plot.

Elyvorrin's death had given credence to those who felt Tiercel was blameless. Perhaps, they argued, Sir Tiercel had been unaware of the count's deception. Perhaps he had been misled. Men of great honor, after all, expected everyone else to behave honorably. It was those who were untrustworthy who distrusted others.

The mages appointed by Kysander Feyna stood by self-importantly in their fine, elaborate robes. It would be their task to truthsay the words of the guards.

Cat's eyes narrowed as she studied the guards. They stayed close together while Riachlain made his opening statements. It was as if they were drawing courage from each other, and the bond between them would only be strengthened by this adversity.

"They'll not talk," she said. "They have a pact, a pact between them. They'll die sooner than break it. I can tell by the way they stand."

"You have been brought here," Riachlain said, "to prove yourselves innocent of any wrong doing. Will you answer, truthfully and honestly, the questions put to you?"

The pair exchanged a glance, and then the fair one – Retharn – stepped forward. Cat nodded to herself, lips curled wryly. She had expected this. Retharn, with his mangled stump of an ear, made all of the elves cringe and want to turn away. They could hardly look on him without feeling sympathy and pity.

"We have done only as obedient soldiers should, following our orders. We will say no more until given leave to do so by our commander."

"You cannot expect that to be acceptable." The harsh growl belonged to Doijyn Armsmaster. "After the king, *I* command all the armies of the Emerin. That makes *me* your commander, lads. You will answer."

Retharn shook his head, slowly and deliberately, letting everyone have a good view of his ear.

"Do you speak of Sir Tiercel Reyes?" Riachlain asked.

Neither of them answered. Riachlain opened his mouth to go on, and was interrupted by a deep, resonant voice.

"If you wait for Sir Tiercel, don't bother." One end of the tapestry flapped, and the most powerfully-built elf Cat had ever seen strode onto the platform. "Tiercel Reyes is dead. I slew him myself."

* * *

CHAPTER TWENTY-SIX

At last, I am come into my own!
– Elwyndas, Lyflar's Inheritance, Act VIII

Wyndrel Perras could not have hoped for a better reaction to his announcement.

The assembled roomful was first thunderstruck, and then everyone began shouting at once in a swelling roar.

Even muffled by the tapestry, behind which his companions waited in the secret passage, Wyndrel could hear Ariana's half-amused, half-disgusted snort. She knew he had been planning this for the duration of their return, all the way from the Emerin's untamed eastern coast. All the way from the foothills of Racandros' lair.

Or so she thought, but she underestimated him. This moment had existed in one form or another in his mind for years. Now that it had come, he intended to savor it to the fullest.

The Lord High Steward, after overcoming his shock, had wanted to attire Wyndrel in appropriately majestic garb. But Wyndrel had refused. He wanted to appear to them as he was. Travel-worn clothes, a sword of much more function than finery at his belt, his hair a long full mane that looked wild by contrast to the impeccable grooming of the Council. He basked in it, very conscious of the image he presented. Head held high, legs braced in a strong stance, fists on his hips as he drew a full breath.

Lian Riachlain waved futilely for order. Half the onlookers were on their feet. The counts demanded to know the meaning of this, who did this intruder think he was, what was going on here? Each strove to make himself heard above the others, with the result that the entire chamber seemed to shake from the din.

Of all the room, the only ones to immediately recognize him were the two guards, Pahelin and Retharn, who had been his captors for eight years. He could see it in their eyes, the knowledge that they were doomed. All would come out, all would be revealed, and their fates were already, and unpleasantly, decided.

Kysander Feyna flung wide his arms, the full sleeves of his ornate brown robe flaring. Lightning leapt from his hands, splitting the air in crackling lines of yellow-white. When the display faded, he had achieved what Riachlain had tried in vain for, a tense and expectant silence.

Wyndrel saw that the Archmage was about to speak, and beat him to it.

"Who am I to intrude here, you ask?" He had never fully appreciated the power of his voice until now, hearing how it resounded against the marble. "What business have I here? What do I mean, that I have slain the beloved and renowned Sir Tiercel? Are these the answers that you wish?"

"Yes," Feyna said, sounding put out and irritable and peevish. "If you'd be so kind."

This time, Celinar Elyvorrin broke in as Wyndrel was about to speak. The boy was standing despite his mother's best efforts to urge him back into his seat, and his face was pallid but for twin splashes of scarlet on his cheeks. "Sir Tiercel cannot be dead! Murderer!"

The contradiction was lost on no one but many murmurs echoed Celinar's sentiment all the same. Among them was Sir Rylian Marrion of the Order of the Lion, a brother knight to Tiercel.

"Tiercel Reyes was a traitor of the worst kind," Wyndrel said. "He, and a number of men loyal to him, were responsible for the death of the king, and the loss of the prince. Tiercel sought to continue the war when there would have been peace. For his own power and glory, perhaps, or perhaps merely to exact a higher toll in lives. Tiercel Reyes conspired with Count Elyvorrin to commit acts of abduction and imprisonment. He arranged to take, by force, a holy artifact from one who had rightfully obtained it."

As he said this, Wyndrel became aware of two among the stunned crowd whose faces were taut with fierce emotion. Their hands were locked together tightly. He knew at once that he was looking upon Ariana's parents. There could be no mistaking them, not with her father's hair shining the same shade of truesilver and her elfkin mother's sapphire eyes so wide.

"When this artifact proved unsuitable for their purposes," he went on, "when it rejected Elyvorrin as an unfit king – and Sir Tiercel likewise – they decided that it was best removed far from the hands of any others who might seek to claim the throne. They would see it delivered into the keeping of the dragon Racandros, to be left there in his hoard."

Anger and outrage flavored the increasing stir of conversation. It was only added to by the mages who had been waiting to truthsay the guards. Both kept signaling, with increasingly frantic gestures, that yes, this man spoke the truth. Or, at the very least, believed that he did.

"This artifact of which I speak? The Emerald of Karria." Wyndrel beckoned.

Giving him a look that said she thought he was being too great a show-off for words, Ariana and the others emerged from behind the tapestry. Mischa wore a vaguely uneasy smile as he came out into the sight of so many elves, doubtless feeling keenly out of place.

A cry came from the direction of Count Brindani when he saw his son. Hot, exultant joy blazed in the eyes of Ariana's parents. A sleek black drake let out a shrill warble.

Tilanne came last, and in her black armor with its embossing of roses and basilisks, with her scarlet-lined cloak and her ruby earrings, she should have instantly seized the attention of every last person in the room. Amid so many striking figures, including Wyndrel himself, she was far and away the most noticeable, and yet somehow, no one paid her much mind. She had that way about her, he had come to realize over their journey. That quiet, devout way of subtle strength, of not drawing the eye.

"The Emerald of Karria, as legend tells us, can only be safely handled by a swordmaid or a king," Wyndrel said. "I present to you the swordmaid, Ariana Mirida, who brought it from the Temple."

Ariana produced the pure green gem. It caught the light and threw forth fans of color, drawing gasps and exclamations of awe.

"On the slope of the dragon's lair," Wyndrel said, "those of us who had gone after Sir Tiercel to stop his treachery met him. We fought, he and I, a duel to the death. Thus were we able to bring back the jewel."

"We . . . we did say . . ." Gariel of Aistrian cleared his throat and stammered as everyone looked at him. "Ah . . . ahem . . . in a meeting of the Council . . . that it was unlikely for the Emerald to be brought to us, but if it should . . . well . . . that we'd abide by it. Do we . . . shall we . . . the counts . . . each touch it and see if it accepts us?"

"That won't be necessary," Aethelyn Fistrel said, beaming.

He, at last, had figured it out, Wyndrel saw. The former ambassador had been perhaps the most frequent of guests to the palace when Shaelan had been alive, and had known both king and prince well.

"Explain yourself," Kysander Feyna snapped.

"Who am I, you asked?" Wyndrel reached out and plucked the cool, polished sphere from Ariana's hand. It glowed, it hummed, it pulsed with the beat of his heart as he held it aloft. "I am Wyndrel Perras, son of Shaelan. I am your king."

* * *

"I must admit," Ariana said to Mischa in the tumult following Wyndrel's announcement, "it does make a much bigger ado, coming back with the true king, than it would have with just the Emerald."

Darkfire launched himself from Arien's shoulder and arrowed across the room. She raised her arm. The drake latched onto it and promptly burrowed his head under her chin. She could not hear his thoughts, that being a gift reserved only for her father and mother, but she could feel delight coming from him.

She petted the drake. "I'm all right, tell them I'm fine, never better, and so very glad they're here. Though so sorry that they had to find out the way they did. It *was* Elyvorrin, wasn't it?"

Darkfire chirped.

"It was frightening, but I'm unhurt. Tell them that." She rubbed her cheek against Darkfire's scales, breathing in the leathery, spicy scent of him, then shook her arm and sent him winging his way back to her father. Her eyes met Cat's, and they shared a smile.

"One at a time, if you please!" Wyndrel bellowed, raising both hands with their palms out to quell the din.

He had put on the Ring of Twilight and it twinkled on his finger. The Emerald was on the table before the Council, placed there casually as if inviting any of them to try their luck. None had made so much as a token gesture in that direction, though each of them devoured it longingly with his eyes.

"I will tell you all of it," he said. "But first, there are some matters to which I must attend. Count Brindani?"

The count, tall and straight and coppery-haired, with a rugged cast to his features, stood. "Sire?"

"My lord count, I thank you with all my heart for the loan of your son. Our quest could not have succeeded without Kevan. He has demonstrated courage, cunning, and unwavering loyalty to me. Although I know he is by custom a bit young for it, I would, with your permission, have him as my own squire."

Brindani blinked. Ariana hid a grin, knowing how hard it was for Emerinians to come to a sudden decision, but she doubted that this one required much debate. Kev's father did not disappoint her. "If Kevan is willing, I fully grant permission."

Kev was blushing but grinning so that his head seemed about to split. It was more than answer enough as to his willingness.

Wyndrel clapped him on the shoulder. "So be it. Kevan, as you were first to swear yourself to me, so shall you be first in my service."

A cheer, confused but heartfelt, arose. Only Celinar Elyvorrin, whose lips were pinched in a sour scowl, did not join in.

Wyndrel turned to Mischa next. "Mischa Narrin, we all owe our escape and our health to your abilities. There are no churches here in the Emerin and I know you wish to return to your own people, but I hope that you will return, often, as an honored friend."

They shook hands, Mischa's eyes twinkling. "I'll be sure to do that. But you're right. My home is in Thanis and I think I've had more than enough adventure to keep me for many, many years."

Tilanne had remained still and somber throughout, and only Ariana noted a slight tightening of her jaw as Wyndrel addressed Mischa. The *Rhunvala* had not so much as threatened Mischa over the course of their journey. She had ignored him as best she could, putting up with his presence, but it had clearly gone against her grain. She had grudgingly allowed when asked that the *Morvalan* could sometimes tolerate humans when they performed some useful function. Like dogs, she'd said. Some could be trained.

When Wyndrel approached the *Rhunvala*, where she stood by the tapestry having gone largely unnoticed, it made the rest of the room suddenly aware of her. Once they saw her, it was obvious what she was. A new ripple of astonishment and more than a little dread went through the room.

"This is Kai Tilanne Murres," Wyndrel said. "She has agreed to join my court and advise me on matters concerning her people, the *Morvalan*. It is my desire to establish relations with our southern kinsmen, and allay the rumors that have driven a wedge between our lands. We have much to learn from each other, and with Kai Tilanne's help, we shall take those first steps. She is a friend, an ally, and has my trust."

Ariana heard a spate of quickly muffled protesting outcries, but no one dared make a blatant case of it, not yet, at any rate. She wondered at Wyndrel's decision to do this. Not that she disagreed with it; quite the contrary. She liked Tilanne, had from the beginning despite their differences, and knew that Wyndrel could have no better advisor. But so much change, so fast . . . how much would these hidebound Emerinians take before they rebelled?

She swallowed and stood straighter as Wyndrel moved to her. He inclined his head, and offered his hand. When hers closed over it, she was swept with a shiver.

They'd not had much occasion for privacy, but there had been that night . . . that first night as Tilanne kept watch over the camp and Mischa tended to Kev, and she and Wyndrel had gone off into the forest together.

The memory sent a warm flush coursing along her veins.

It was the first time she'd seen him hesitant, the first and probably only time he would follow her lead without argument. The passion they'd first sampled in the dungeon, kindled by Mischa's inadvertent intervention, had been replaced by something stronger and sweeter, perfectly matched.

With her hand held tight in his, Wyndrel walked past rows of onlookers and stopped in front of the raised box where her parents and Talian sat. The pride that radiated from them filled Ariana's heart to bursting.

"Archmage Mirida," Wyndrel said, bowing. "Lady Mirida. I have committed a breach in manners by asking your daughter to be my bride before seeking your permission and blessing. I hope that you'll forgive me."

The elves had taken the news of Kai Tilanne fairly well, all things considered, but this was too much for them. Objections came from every corner, protestations that it was too soon, much too soon, that the king of the Emerin needed a fittingly highborn bride. This last elicited a cold tilt of the eyebrow from Arien and indignant retorts from both Talian and the woman seated with them – Lady Karadan, Ariana realized.

Cat, paying no attention to all that, leaned forward. "Ari? Is it true? Do you love him?"

"Yes, Mother."

Through it all, Wyndrel retained perfect equanimity, his gaze set levelly on her father. By the rapid flicker of Darkfire's eyes, Ariana knew that the drake and her parents were sharing a hasty mental conversation.

"You wish to marry our daughter," Arien said at last. "This is rather abrupt."

"We are prepared for as lengthy an engagement as is deemed suitable by my advisors," Wyndrel said, with a significant glance at the Council. "I would not place the simultaneous burdens of both a coronation and a royal wedding on my court."

"Ariana? Is this your will?"

"It is, *Valanor*."

He smiled at Cat and they linked hands. "As my family well knows, I have never been able to deny my daughter anything. My wife agrees. Ariana, Wyndrel, you have our permission, and our most heartfelt blessing."

* * *

It would take a good deal of time and a good deal more wine and willowbark tea for so many surprises to rest well in the minds of the Emerin. Those who'd come to the Great Hall expecting a trial had gotten far more than any of them could have anticipated.

Retharn and Pahelin were, at Wyndrel's decree, returned to their cell until a proper court-martial could be assembled. They, and others of Tiercel's sworn men, would be called upon to answer for their crimes both during and after the war.

Someone called for a feast, and as if this were what he'd been waiting breathlessly for, Vangier sprang into action as best he could. The Lord High Steward was in no condition for it, of course, but would not be dissuaded. He issued orders like any general, and while the resulting meal was not up to what he felt were proper royal standards, no one found cause to complain.

Ariana found Kai Tilanne at a corner table, alone, wrapped once more in that odd serenity that characterized her. A goblet of wine sat before her, and she was regarding the chattering, colorfully-dressed elves with interested amusement in her amethyst eyes.

"How do you fare?" Ariana asked.

Tilanne shrugged and uttered a soft laugh. "A thing of blood and darkness to them am I. Long will it be until accustomed to me they are, and still strange do I find their ways. Far different it is from hiding to observe, than to in the midst of them be."

"They're going to have to get accustomed to us both," Ariana said. "And to Wyndrel, as well. I don't think they know what to make of him."

"Odd it is," Tilanne said, "but feel do I that . . . please no offense at this take . . . in some way, perhaps, Tiercel's goal might yet through Wyndrel be reached. His hope it was that he might the young prince to more of a *Morvalan* way of thinking turn. Resisted and rejected this did Wyndrel, and so was he by Tiercel's order jailed. Yet might it not be that somehow, by that very process, effected was such a change?"

"He's less Emerinian than most, if that's what you mean. But I doubt I know enough of your people yet to say for certain. Come with me a moment, Tilanne, will you? There's someone I want you to meet."

Ariana wended her way through the crowd, a space opening around her as those nearby realized the dark shape of the *Rhunvala* moved among them. Many a scandalized look was directed in particular at Tilanne's earlobes, where the ruby roses were visible through strands of her hair.

She came to her parents, her father engaged in conversation with Lady Karadan while her mother and Mischa stood off to one side, talking about Thanis, about Sybil, about what troubles Tal and Mischa's sister Jessa were likely getting into.

"*Valanor?* You might not remember . . . no, that's silly, I know you remember, you remember everything. But you might not realize . . . you've met Kai Tilanne before."

Curiously, yet courteously, Arien regarded the *Rhunvala*. "Why . . . you were the brave young woman at the fortress that night. Of course."

Tilanne nodded. "Many of my people by thy hand and thy magic, and by the hands and weapons of thy friends, that night did die."

"Oh, but . . ." Cat, having come over to listen, trailed off.

"I suppose that's true," Arien said evenly.

"Most pained and distraught we were, those losses to have suffered." Tilanne did not look at Cat, perhaps could not quite bear to look at Cat. "Yet now, come have I to believe that for the best it was. Donnell and Solarrin no friends of ours were. Used us they did, and never did they our Way embrace. Far worse for us would it have been if successful was their plan. And so, for that, I thee thank."

* * *

So much had happened, a dizzying too-much for elven minds to assimilate. Despite the feast and the many questions still clamoring for answers, the night ended early. The crowd thinned, and a domestic named Lishalla appeared to report that she had been assigned by Vangier as Lady Ariana's maidservant until such time as the queen-to-be was able to review the staff and choose one for herself.

Ariana caught Cat's wry grin, a grin that said *I don't envy you any of this in the slightest, tashti*, and returned it. She let herself be taken away to the rooms that had been assigned her – again, according to Lishalla, only until something more appropriate could be made ready.

Looking around at the luxurious splendor that put the guest quarters of the Waterfall Terrace to shame, Ariana could not even begin to imagine what a more appropriate set of rooms might be.

She was exhausted from traveling and the excitement of the day, and couldn't find the strength to object when Lishalla and a pair of other young women insisted on helping her undress and bathe. They found her from gods-knew-where a silken nightgown and a cloudwool wrapper, combed out her hair, turned down her blankets, and finally left her in solitude and peace.

A knock came at the door just as she was about to go to bed. She went to it, opened it, and a moment later was in Wyndrel's arms. He kicked the door closed behind them.

His kiss drove thoughts of sleep far from her mind. When it broke, she looked up at him, smiling, her arms about his neck and their bodies pressed close.

"What happened to that lengthy engagement?" she asked.

"Have you any idea how long an Emerinian engagement can be?"

"Well . . . when you put it like that . . ."

They kissed again and then he pulled her tight against him, his breath warm and tickling against the sensitive curves of her ear.

"We're going to change many things in this kingdom, you and I, Ariana," he said. "I can think of no better place to begin."

* * *

EPILOGUE

A thin beam of sunlight shot through a hole in the wall and landed unerringly upon his eyelid.

Racandros turned his head, but as the sun continued to rise over the sea, the beam followed him with almost deliberate persistence. Finally, it shifted and moved and twinkled across his hoard. By then, though, it was no use. He was awake.

He yawned jaw-crackingly and heaved himself to all fours, shaking off a litter of jewels.

A freshening spring breeze met him as he emerged from the cave. The roar of the cataract was tumultuous from the snowmelt. The cobalt sea was whipped into whitecaps and glassy, curved swells. He detected the strong scent of roses, and, faintly, the corruption of rotting flesh.

Oh, yes.

The elf.

He had watched as they interred him, the dark female scooping out a shallow hole and then arranging the dead male in it with his arms folded across his chest. They'd piled stones upon him, making a cairn that no scavenger could have dug into even if any scavengers were allowed on the dragon's mountain.

Racandros himself could have dashed it apart with a single flick of his tail, but he had no interest in eating elf-flesh. Especially elf-flesh that had been spoiling in the earth.

They had taken his swords. Racandros found that interesting. He thought that most warriors liked to be entombed with their weapons, and wizards with their staves. This one had gone into the ground unarmed.

Peering downslope, he could see the budding green rosebush rising from the cairn where the dark female had spoken words, and sprinkled oil, and cast petals over the stones.

The dragon grumbled. He wasn't sure that he liked having his home become a makeshift graveyard, or anybody's garden. But done was done, and as the others had left promptly thereafter, it wasn't as though they meant to stay about and make a habit of it.

A strange business, that. To come so far, only to fight on his very doorstep and then go home without speaking so much as a single word to him. He wished he'd woken a trifle earlier, enough to hear what had brought them in the first place.

Well, it did not matter. Curiosity was for cats and pantera. The elves were gone, spring was come, and a stirring in his blood he hadn't felt in a long time made Racandros stretch his wings and think of flying north to see if Melandros still made her lair in the same place.

Perhaps he wasn't too old to think about another brood of hatchlings after all.

* * *

The End

About the Author

Christine Morgan lives in the Pacific Northwest with her husband, daughter, and trio of cats. She is a graduate of California's Humboldt State University, with a B. A. in Psychology. Her overnight-shift job as a residential counselor in a psychiatric facility allows her ample time to write as well as the occasional flash of inspiration.

She divides her writing time among a variety of genres – horror, fantasy, childrens' fiction, and erotica among them. In addition to the *MageLore* and *ElfLore* fantasy trilogies, she is the author of the Silver Doorway series of children's books, and the Trinity Bay horror novels, *Black Roses*, *Gifted Children* and *Changeling Moon*. She was nominated for an Origins Award for her zombie short story "Dawn of the Living-Impaired," and various others of her works have appeared in anthologies, magazines, and several online forums.

A longtime gamer, Christine can often be found at regional conventions, running games as well as promoting books. She has a fond relationship with the folks at Steve Jackson Games and other names in the gaming industry, all of whom have been incredibly supportive and helpful. In 2003, Christine and her husband Tim released their first role-playing game supplement, the controversial *Naughty and Dice: An Adult Gamer's Guide to Sexual Situations.*

Christine's other interests span a wide gamut – robotic combat, British comedy, documentaries, pirates, superheroes, and reality game shows make up the majority of her television viewing habits; horror, mysteries, and thrillers dominate her bookshelves; and she enjoys cooking and crafts.

Christine welcomes and appreciates feedback from readers. She can be reached by e-mail at christine@sabledrake.com and invites visitors to her websites, www.sabledrake.com and www.christine-morgan.com.

The adventures of Cat Sabledrake and Arien Mirida can be found in:

The MageLore Trilogy

Curse of the Shadow Beasts
MageLore Book One

Arien Mirida, elven wizard in exile, hopes to find an end to the curse that has plagued his family for generations. His only hope is a young thief, and a forbidden love that will either save, or destroy him.

Dark of the Elvenwood
MageLore Book Two

A sinister plot is taking shape in the mysterious southern reaches of the Emerin, in the home of elves who serve a bloodthirsty god. To combat this menace, Arien Mirida must abandon his peaceful life and be reunited with the one woman he cannot forget.

Archmage of the Universe
MageLore Book Three

With the city of Thanis and the impressionable young Highlord under the control of the evil minotaur mage, Solarrin, Arien and his friends embark on a dangerous mission. Their objective is to find Talus Yor, the only wizard whose powers rival Solarrin's. But they face one great obstacle: Talus Yor is dead.

The Silver Doorway series is also set in the world of the MageLore and ElfLore trilogies

by C. M. Morgan

Life is complicated for the Broderick kids. They've just moved to a new neighborhood. Their parents are having problems. Mom is always busy with work, Dad is always busy on his computer. Half the time, it seems like they forget they even have children.

The kids are having problems too. Twelve-year-old Katie doesn't like having to take care of little brother Sam. Katie's twin Kevin is only interested in sports, and is mad at Mom and Dad. Eight-year-old Sam can't stand being bossed around by Katie.

The rest of the family thinks Dad's sister, Aunt Ellie, is weird. But when the kids discover a secret room in Aunt Ellie's basement, and a glowing silver doorway that leads to another world, the realize how weird their aunt really is.

Other kids sometimes come through that door. Kids from a world where magic is real, and so are gnomes, elves, goblins, and dragons. They come through the door looking for help from a good sorceress. Instead, they get Katie, Kevin and Sam.

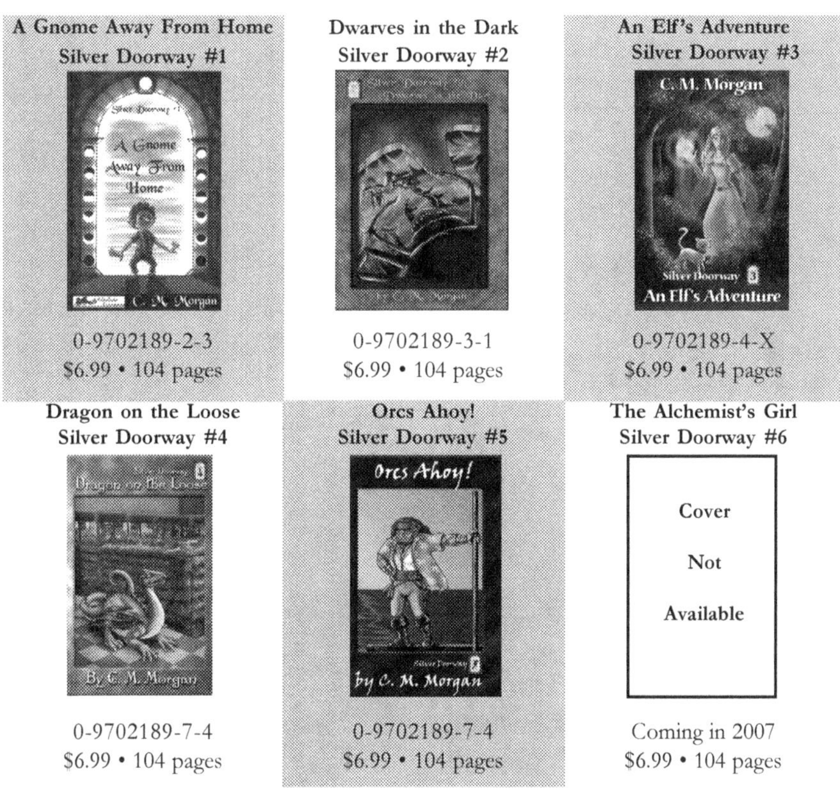

Silver Doorway books are written for younger readers, ages 7-12.

Order these and any of Christine Morgan's books or short stories at http://www.sabledrake.com

$14.95 • 0-9702189-5-8 • 300 pages

With her marriage over and her career on hold, children's writer Theresa Zane returns to her childhood home of Trinity Bay, California to live with her father. There, in the lush green of the coastal redwood forest, Theresa meets the man of her dreams. Literally.

He is an incubus, able to infiltrate the sleeping minds of women and take on whatever form fulfills their darkest, most hidden fantasies. The strength of Theresa's spirit draws him like moth to flame. He decides that he will not rest until she is his.

The women of Trinity Bay fall prey, one after another, to the power of their dreams. The incubus, draining their life energy, inspires them to acts of violence and suicide, and leaves his victims troubled by the lingering image of a black rose. The same black rose that appears in an heirloom necklace that Theresa Zane finds in her home. The same necklace with a past linked to Seacliff, the mansion on the hill overlooking the town.

A series of brutal, horrific murders all across the country are connected only by one clue – a single black rose left at the scene of each crime. Further investigation into the backgrounds of the men reveal one other thing they have in common, one person they all knew. This lets a Trinity Bay chief of police and two New York City detectives guess who the next targets might be, but how can they be protected against a force that can reach out from beyond the walls of nightmare?

Only Theresa can combat this menace, and she'll need a necklace with a haunted past and the help of three dead girls to do it.

$16.95 • 0-9702189-9-0 • 372 pages

The children of Trinity Bay are like any ordinary American kids. Lora Blake has a way with animals. Toby Edwards is the school brain. Jenny Forrester can talk her parents and friends into going along with anything.

But in the innocent-seeming gifts of these children and others like them, someone has discovered a power of terrifying potential.

A new force inhabits Seacliff, the house on the hill. From the outside, it appears benign – part school, part home, part hospital. Dedicated to healing, helping. But the true work going on at Seacliff is much, much darker.

As the project progresses, it will draw first the children, then their families, and finally an entire town into its shadow.

Gifted Children is Christine Morgan's second Trinity Bay novel. It is set three years after the events in *Black Roses.*

$14.95 • 0-9771005-0-2 • 284 pages

For thousands of years, they have lived among us. Their abilities have given rise to our oldest legends and our deepest fears.

They are changelings. Shape-shifters. Hunters. Creatures of the night. Ruled by the moon, and by their own savage hungers.

Some wish only to survive unnoticed in our world, to be left alone and have as little to do with us as possible. They keep to their laws and traditions. They keep to themselves. Their first and only loyalty is to the pack.

But there are those who are outcasts from their own kind. Outcasts, like the beautiful and ruthless Simone Drachen and her perversely devoted son.

They have broken the ancient laws, tasted of the forbidden, and gained greater power from it. To them, humans are not something to be avoided and tolerated.

To them, we are prey.

And now they have come to Trinity Bay, where one troubled young woman will be caught in the midst of their deadly conflict.

Aiden Ferguson has lost everyone she ever cared about. Orphaned, alone, reclusive and shy, she leads a quiet existence in her little house on the beach, until a chance meeting with a handsome stranger begins to draw her out of her shell. An unexpected friendship with a flamboyant actress draws her out even more.

For the first time in years, Aiden is learning to love life again . . . just as her life, her soul and her very humanity are threatened by the cold white light of the . . . Changeling Moon.

$19.95 • 0-9702189-6-6 • 108 pages

Naughty & Dice: An Adult Gamer's Guide to Sexual Situations

Written by Origins Award nominated author Christine Morgan and 20+ year gaming veteran and game store manager Tim Morgan, ***Naughty & Dice*** takes a light-hearted yet serious look at the topic of sex in RPGs. The tone of the book is centered around themes of tolerance and respect. It is recommended for mature readers, and is easily adaptable to any roleplaying game system.

Naughty & Dice includes chapters on:

- instructions for factoring a character's "Sexuality" statistic.
- rules for sexual gifts, drawbacks and abilities.
- character types and adventure ideas.
- pregnancy, contraception and sexually transmitted diseases.
- enchanted items, spells, potions, and types of sex-related magic.
- an overview of sex in history, mythology and folklore.
- genre-specific looks at horror, aliens and fantasy races.
- OGL conversions, feats and classes.
- and much more!

In addition to the works presented here, Christine Morgan's writing has appeared in many magazines and story anthologies.

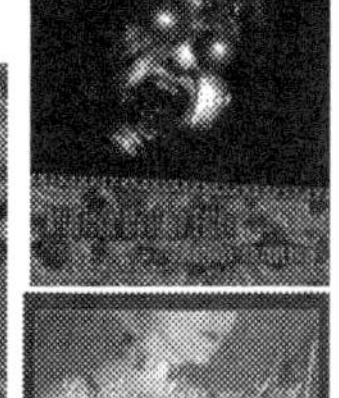

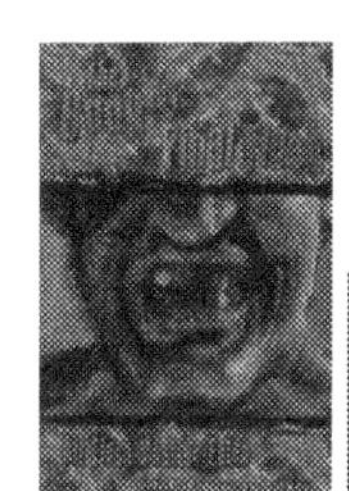

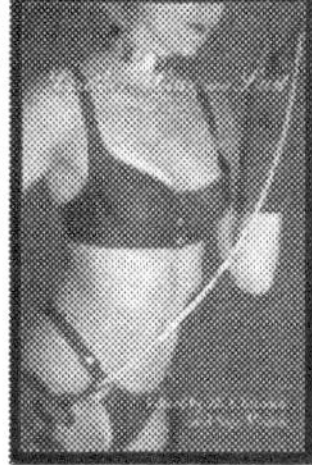

"Coppers, the Alchemist" in *Pyramid Magazine #17.*
"The Reaching Wall" in *Cthulhu Sex Magazine #14, Vol 2*
and in *Horror Between the Sheets.*
Several entries in *GURPS Villians.*
"The Dawn of the Living Impaired" in *The Book of All Flesh.*
"Seven Brains, Ten Minutes" in *The Book of Final Flesh.*
"I Am . . ." in *Leather, Lace & Lust.*
"Safe Sucks" in *Closet Desires IV.*
"Monsters" in *Path of the Bold.*
"Don't Look Back" in *Fear of the Unknown.*
"Death and the Scream Queen" in *Hell Hath No Fury.*

She is a regular contributor to *The Horror Fiction Review*, an old-school 'zine by Novello Press.

Sabledrake Enterprises keeps a few copies of most of these in stock and we can fill orders on a first come, first served basis for anyone interested.

Visit **http://www.christine-morgan.com** for the latest information.

www.ingramcontent.com/pod-product-compliance
Lightning Source LLC
Chambersburg PA
CBHW081131300726
48982CB00005B/921

* 9 7 8 0 9 7 7 1 0 0 5 1 4 *